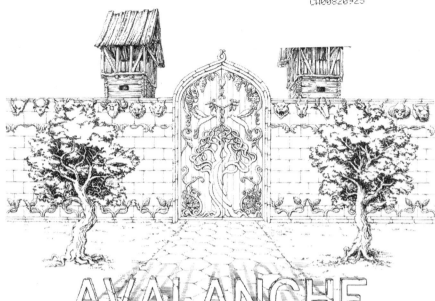

AVALANCHE

STREET RATS OF ARAMOOR
BOOK 6

written by
MICHAEL
WISEHART

Copyright

STREET RATS OF ARAMOOR: BOOK 6
AVALANCHE

Books

STREET RATS OF ARAMOOR

(First book takes place 20 years prior to The Aldoran Chronicles)

Book 1 | Banished

Book 2 | Hurricane

Book 3 | Rockslide

Book 4 | Sandstorm

Book 5 | Wildfire

Book 6 | Avalanche

THE ALDORAN CHRONICLES

Prequel | Shackled

Book 1 | The White Tower

Book 2 | Plague of Shadows

Book 3 | The Four-Part Key

Book 4 | The Tunnels Beneath

Map of Aldor - West

Hi-Resolution maps in the Shop:
« *www.michaelwisehart.com/aramoormarket* »

Map of Aldor - East

Hi-Resolution maps in the Shop:

« *www.michaelwisehart.com/aramoormarket* »

Map of Aramoor

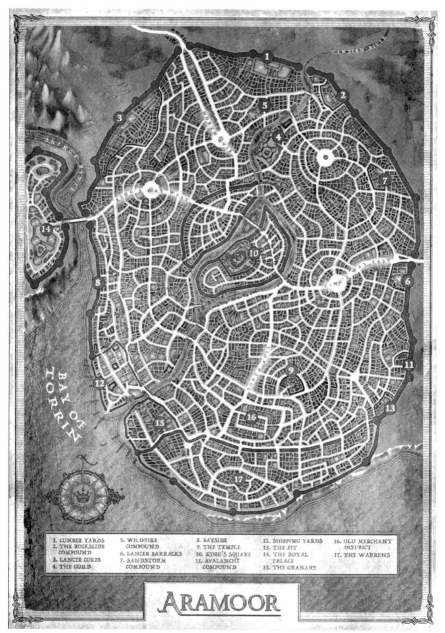

1. LUMBER YARDS	5. WILDFIRE COMPOUND	8. BAYSIDE	12. SHIPPING YARDS	16. OLD MERCHANT DISTRICT
2. THE ROCKSLIDE COMPOUND	6. LANCER BARRACKS	9. THE TEMPLE	13. THE PIT	17. THE WARRENS
3. LANCER CORPS	7. SANDSTORM COMPOUND	10. KING'S SQUARE	14. THE ROYAL PALACE	
4. THE GUILD		11. AVALANCHE COMPOUND	15. THE GRANARY	

ARAMOOR

Hi-Resolution maps in the Shop:

« *www.michaelwisehart.com/aramoormarket* »

Foreword

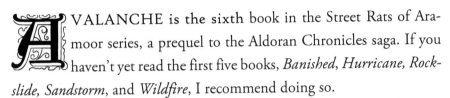

AVALANCHE is the sixth book in the Street Rats of Aramoor series, a prequel to the Aldoran Chronicles saga. If you haven't yet read the first five books, *Banished, Hurricane, Rockslide, Sandstorm*, and *Wildfire*, I recommend doing so.

This series ties directly into the Aldoran Chronicles saga, thirteen years prior to the first book: *The White Tower*.

As with my other books, there is a Character Glossary at the back if you need it.

Street Tribes of Aramoor Logos

Hurricane · Avalanche · Rockslide · Wildfire · Sandstorm

AVALANCHE

Chapter 1

WHAT DO WE DO with him?" Red asked in a panic as she and Po stared down at the prince's bleeding body.

"Help me get him into the light," I said. I was panicking as well, but I tried not to let it show as I lifted Dakaran's limp frame by his arms and dragged him out of the alley. I stopped under the closest street-lamp to inspect the wound, pulling up his shirt. Blood poured from a hole on the left side of his abdomen. My palms started to sweat. It was bad. I'd seen men die from wounds like this. "How could you let this happen?"

"Why are you asking me?" Red hissed. "I didn't do this."

I ripped off one of the sleeves of my shirt and re-packed the hole from where either Red or Po had attempted to stop the bleeding before, then unhooked the prince's belt to try tying the bandaging off. "You're the one who dragged me out of bed in the middle of the night to tell me that the crown prince has been stabbed. I naturally assumed—"

"Why were you in bed this early in the evening?"

"I've been on patrol at the Cylmaran border for the last two weeks. I was tired."

"What in the flaming Pits were you doing in Cylmar? Don't you have enough to worry about here?"

My jaw tightened. "We're on the brink of war, or have you been so long underground now that you don't have a clue as to what is happening in the world?"

Red flushed, but Po just stood there watching, her silent shadow.

"Here," I said, lifting Dakaran by the arms, "help me get him to his horse."

Red grabbed one of the prince's feet, and Po grabbed the other, and we carried him over to the hitching rail that was in front of the Fishnet tavern, a place Dakaran often frequented when he wanted to get out of the palace. *Best lamb and mint sauce in the city*, he would say. Dakaran had first introduced me to the tavern over four years ago. We had been too young at the time to patronize such a place, but the prince's willingness to spend coins had earned him the proprietor's silence, along with the nickname Master Silvercoin. Dakaran enjoyed being there because no one knew who he was—and didn't care.

With their help, I managed to heft Dakaran's limp body up over a horse whose brand marked it as belonging to the palace stables. I was going to have to have another talk with Bozz, the royal ostler, about looking the other way whenever Dakaran wanted to sneak out. At the very least, he should send me word.

Dakaran groaned in his delirium as he was dropped over the saddle.

I looked down at the blood on my hands and spun on Red. "And what in flaming gut rot was he doing with you?"

She sneered. "He wasn't with me, if it's any of your business, which it isn't." Her eyes narrowed. "Unless, of course, the thought of me and Dakaran has brought on a bout of passionate jealousy, then he was certainly with me."

Po frowned as Red grabbed a random horse and swung up on the saddle. She leaned over and helped her quiet companion up behind her. "Lucky for him, I happened to be passing by."

"What do you think you're doing?" I asked as I swung up behind Dakaran to hold him in place.

"What does it look like? I'm coming with you, of course."

I glanced over my shoulder and back toward the darkened alley at the side of the tavern. "And where's his protection detail?"

"How should I know? I told you. He wasn't with me." She hmphed. "You know Dakaran. He dodges them every chance he gets. He probably took the hidden passages out of the palace."

I ground my teeth. "I wish he hadn't showed you those."

She smirked. "You were there."

"Don't remind me."

After my rescue of Red from the Warrens, in which Dakaran and Room Eleven had been involved, the prince had asked me to introduce him to some of my friends, especially Red and Sapphire. Sapphire had shown enough sense to realize that with the kind of business Sandstorm regularly facilitated, she should keep her distance. Red, on the other hand, was more than happy to show her interest, so he had invited her back to the palace. Dakaran was ridiculous enough to believe that impressing her with his wealth was going to earn him her favor. He certainly didn't know Red. No telling how many times she'd been back over the last couple of years without Dakaran's knowledge, just to pilfer.

I grabbed the reins with one hand and Dakaran's belt with the other. "Lucky for you, he hasn't bled to death already." The prince's face was pale, and his forehead was slick with sweat. "We need to hurry."

"Where are you taking him?"

"To the one place he might stand a chance of surviving: Sandstorm."

Red cocked her brow. "How long has it been since you've been back?"

I sighed. "About as long as you." I spun the horse around and kicked it into a full gallop, and we rode east along the riverfront, heading for King's Way East.

Despite her bravado, Red did not have the experience with horses I had, and it showed as she tried to keep up. Po clung to her for dear life as she did her best to keep from falling out of the saddle.

"Why not take him back to the palace?" Red asked as soon as we turned off King's Way East onto Circle Drive. "They've got excellent physickers there, don't they?"

"Because I need the best."

She smirked. "You know he's not going to be happy seeing you."

"A risk I'm willing to take."

We rode north to Bailey Street, then east again, passing Master Fentin and Mistress Orilla's orphanage on the way. There were a couple of lights on inside, and I caught a glimpse through the front window of the old couple sitting by the fire as we passed. They had a tendency to read for an hour or two after putting the children to bed, as it was the only quiet time they had.

They were up later than usual tonight.

I turned off Bailey, and we rode a couple of streets north, taking the next avenue to the right. We crossed over a small rise and spotted the Sandstorm gate ahead. My heart started to pound, and I took a couple of deep breaths, releasing slowly to calm the excitement. It had been over a year and a half since I'd left. I wondered how much had changed. I hadn't seen Reevie or Sapphire in all that time, not since that final day. I didn't like dwelling on it. The last time we'd spoken, Reevie had told me that if I wanted to throw everything we'd been through away for a bunch of lancers, then I was no longer welcome at Sandstorm.

Quite the ironic twist, I thought, as I ran my thumb over the branded X on my wrist. I had been banished once again.

There were torches out front, and I caught movement through the bars as we rode up to the front of the drive and stopped.

I pulled back my hood. "Toots, are you out there?"

A head popped over the wall. "Protector, is that you?"

I hadn't heard that name in a while, and it brought with it a momentary smile.

Toots, who had clearly hit his growth spurt and was old enough to have a bit of fuzz on his upper lip, stared at me from over the manor wall.

"What's you doing here?" he asked. "And who's that with you?"

"It's me, you imbecile," Red said, pulling her own hood back. Po leaned out so they could see he was there as well. "Now open the gate," she hissed. "We have an emergency."

Toots disappeared behind the wall, and moments later several bodies rushed around to unlock the gate and pull it open. Several runners shot up the lane toward the manor house, no doubt to warn the others of our arrival.

I didn't have time to stop and chat, so I kicked the horse just as soon as the gate was wide enough to pass, and we rode up the drive to the manor house, with Toots calling out after us. I felt bad not stopping, but there were more important things to worry about this night. I stopped just outside the courtyard, hopped off, pulled Dakaran down from the saddle, and draped him over my shoulder. Pausing only a moment to check my balance, I rushed across the courtyard. I could hear Red's and

Po's boots on the cobbles behind me as we raced for the front of the manor.

The doors swung open just before I arrived, and a young man with dirty-blond hair stepped out. When he saw me, he sheathed his sword.

"You're about the last person I'd have expected to show up like this," Bull said with a smile, then looked at the body over my shoulder. "Who's that?"

"It's the prince."

Bull's eyes widened. "And you brought him *here?*"

"Is Reevie here tonight?" The last I'd heard, he and Physicker Saban traded evenings at Saban's infirmary near the Rose and Crown. I hoped this wasn't his night in town.

"He's here," a woman's voice from inside the manor said. "Why?"

I looked up to see Sapphire walking up behind Bull in an elegant black-and-purple dress with a long slit down either leg. Her hair was back in a single braid, and she had a sword in one hand, which she also sheathed once she saw me.

"Who have you got there?"

"It's Dakaran." I pushed my way past Bull and headed through the doors. Red and Po trailed a step or two behind.

Sapphire growled when she spotted Red. "I should have known you'd be with *her.*"

"I'm not with her," I shot back. "She and Po found him. Now please get Reevie. Dakaran's been stabbed. He's lost a lot of blood." I walked through the doors and started left down the gallery. "Is the infirmary still down here?"

"Yes," Sapphire said, glaring at Red as she and Bull rushed to catch up.

"What's going on?" a familiar high-pitched voice asked, followed by a noted vibration in the floor as Mouse and Tubby came bounding around the corner and down the hall in our direction. Mouse was sitting on one of Tubby's enormous shoulders. "Protector? Is that you?"

Mouse had grown, though not as much as he would have probably liked. Tubby, on the other hand, had enjoyed a very noticeable growth spurt. His head now reached almost halfway up the vaulted windows.

Not having time to answer, I headed for the third door on the right.

Bull ran ahead of me and opened the door, grabbing a lantern off one of the nearby tables before heading inside to start lighting the rest of the room. I carried Dakaran in and deposited him on an exam table to the left, then put my ear to his chest.

"Is he still alive?" Sapphire asked, pushing past Red to get a better look.

"He's breathing, but barely."

"What happened?"

"I wish I knew." I drew my belt knife and started cutting away the shirt. "Here, help me get this off."

Sapphire moved to the other side and helped me remove his belt and blood-soaked clothing. I looked at the wound. It was seeping. I pressed my hand over it. "Get me some clean bandages," I said to Bull, who'd just finished lighting the rest of the lanterns. I looked at Sapphire. "Has anyone sent for—"

"What's going on in here?"

I tensed at the voice but didn't turn.

"He's been stabbed," Sapphire said.

"Who's been stabbed? What's happening?" Reevie pushed his way through the room, shooing those between him and the tables out of the way. "Woken out of my sleep," he grumbled, "not told a thing. Move aside so I can—" Reevie's eyes met mine, and he froze. Reevie looked much the same, though perhaps a little taller. His face had filled out, and he looked like he might have put on a little more muscle.

We stared at each other a moment in silence before I finally spoke. "I need your help. It's Dakaran. He's been stabbed."

Reevie stood with his mouth agape, as if trying to decide if I was really there or if he was dreaming. He then looked down at the bloody prince and set his jaw. "Move, everyone!" Red turned to get out of his way, and Reevie gasped again. "What is this, some sort of reunion, or did I just wake up and miss the last two years of my life?" He snatched the clean bandages from Bull and pushed my hands aside. "Let me see the damage."

I moved to let him get a closer look, and he scooted one of the table lamps closer. "Yep, he's been stabbed alright." He checked Dakaran's pulse and breathing and even his eyes. "Lucky you found him when you did." Reevie placed the clean bandages over the wound and motioned Bull over. He grabbed one of his co-chief's large hands and held it over the wound. "Press here and keep it tight."

"Why did you bring him here?" Reevie asked, purposefully not looking at me. "You've got physickers at the garrison, or the palace for that matter."

"Because you're the best."

Reevie stared at the prince a moment, then turned and limped over to the fully stocked shelves on the other side of the room and began pulling bottles and jars off each and carrying them back to a table next to Dakaran.

"What can I do?" I asked.

"Stay out of my way."

I moved back, joining Red and Po to watch Reevie go about his work.

A quick glance over my shoulder showed the gallery just outside the door quickly filling with kids of all ages, trying to get a peek inside. I was surprised by how many faces I didn't recognize. Had Sandstorm grown that much over the last year and a half?

There were still plenty I did know. Petal and Squeaks had joined Mouse on Tubby's shoulders. I saw Collen's head rising above the others, his darker skin standing out. I was surprised to see Toothless next to Forehead. I would have thought Toothless had gone with Red when she left a year ago. It was strange to see Red's former guard and Forehead still around, considering they were older than I was, perhaps even older than Sapphire, who would have celebrated her twenty-first birthday not all that long ago.

We were all getting older. A couple weeks back, Master Fentin and Mistress Orilla had thought to throw me a small party for my twentieth. Unfortunately, I had been called away on assignment before we got the chance to have it. I had finally left my teen years and reached manhood, though if age was based on experience, I'd wager I'd be nearing my forties by now.

A cork popped as Reevie opened a bottle, and I turned back from the door.

"Where's Muriel?" Reevie snapped.

Sapphire called out the door, "Someone go get Muriel."

"I'm here," a soft voice replied, followed by a loud screech that could have only been Redwing. The others in the hall parted, and a girl with tangled brown hair stepped through the door. A large hawk balanced on her gloved arm. Muriel was taller and more filled out than the last time I'd seen her, but her appearance was just as unruly as I remembered. She had always been in charge of the birds, mainly the pigeon cages, and liked them better than most of her peers.

Muriel had taken to helping Reevie in the infirmary during our first year at Sandstorm. She placed Redwing on the back of a cushioned chair in the corner and handed Bull her glove.

"Get that bird off there," Reevie groused. "I sit on that to read. I don't want my hair plastered with bird droppings."

Muriel gave Forehead the glove and then helped nudge the hawk onto the Sandstorm guard's arm.

Reevie looked at Muriel. "Send someone to tell Cook to heat up some water and grab some of that Bristonian wine from the pantry."

She nodded and took off out the door, grabbing a child I didn't recognize on the way.

Dakaran groaned and tried to turn over, but Bull held him down.

"How's he doing?" I asked nervously, inching forward.

"He's doing terrible," Reevie said. "He's got a hole in his gut. How would you be doing?"

"Do you think you can save him?"

Reevie looked at Dakaran. "Possibly. I've been reading some journals from an apothecary in Easthaven who seems to have found some new uses for herbs like cholaris that those in my field are very skeptical about. I've tried them, and the results have been promising." He started measuring out ingredients from several jars into his mixing bowl, adding in some clear liquid from a stoppered bottle.

"So what does that mean?" I asked.

"It means I'm going to do my best. But I'd do a lot better if people would quit hassling me." He finally turned. "Alright, everyone out! I have work to do, and I can't do it with all of you standing around gawking over my shoulder."

I pointed to Dakaran. "I want to—"

"No!" He pointed to the door. "Out!"

"But the prince is my respons—"

"Not right now he isn't. He's on *my* table, and I want *you* gone."

A hand squeezed my shoulder, and I turned.

Sapphire nodded toward the door. "Probably for the best," she said softly. "Having you here isn't making things easier on him. Besides, he's why you brought the prince to us. Best do as he says."

I sighed. She was right, but it still didn't change the fact that I felt I needed to be there. The prince was my responsibility. More so, he was my friend, and I needed to make sure he came through this. I wasn't one to sit around and wait on things to happen, especially when I wasn't the one doing it. I took one last look at the prince and then joined the others in the long hallway outside. Bull shut the door.

The gallery was packed.

"Well, bless my soul. For once, the rumors are true."

I turned to find Gustory pushing through the throng of kids. The middle-aged bard was looking much the same with his dark feathery hair and slightly weathered face. Perhaps a little greyer around the temples, but he still held that warm smile he always had while offering one of his wondrous tales. He started to offer me his hand, then switched to a full hug. As soon as he released me, he took a step back and gave me a once-over.

"You're looking well, Ayrion," he said, glancing toward the infirmary door. "I hear we have a member of the royal family, though, that's not."

"I only hope I got him here in time."

The bard nodded. "I will pray for the prince's recovery." He turned, and his eyes widened. "Miracle of miracles. If it isn't our Lady Red and Master Po. This is proving quite the exciting evening." He frowned. "Last I heard, you'd taken up residence with some very unsavory characters." He leaned in a little closer. "Have you seen the light and decided to return to us?"

"Afraid not, storyteller," Red said, then smiled. "Though, I must admit to missing your evening tales."

Gustory placed his hand over his chest. "High praise indeed." The bard looked back at me. "Is that the same coat from when you rescued that ambassador in Ecrin?"

"It is."

"Yes," Red said, "it does seem familiar." She looked down at her own coat, and I realized how similar it was to mine, the only difference being hers had been dyed red and fastened with buttons instead of buckles. Years ago, when I had first started wearing a black leather jacket, she had immediately gone out and commissioned a similar red one to be made. She must have done the same again now that I had switched from a jacket to a full coat.

I wanted to roll my eyes, but imitation was the surest form of flattery. I guess looking at the two of us standing side by side, I could see why Sapphire had thought we were together.

"Hi, Protector."

I turned around.

"Up here."

I looked up to see Petal sitting on Tubby's left arm. Squeaks was on the right, with Mouse still on his shoulder. She had a bright purple ribbon in her sun-kissed hair. She and Squeaks both had to be pushing sixteen now. I couldn't believe how fast time had flown. I remembered them when they were still small children, barely waist high. Squeaks had once fallen through the trap step back at the Granary and gotten stuck, forcing Reevie and me to fish him out. Now he was nearly as tall as me, though rather lanky.

I smiled. "Hello, Petal. You are looking well."

"We've missed you," Petal said. "Are you moving back in?"

I smiled. "Afraid not. I had to bring someone for Reevie to take a look at."

She frowned, as did many of the others.

"Tubby miss too," Tubby said in his booming childlike voice.

"And I missed you as well. I've missed all of you."

"Then why did you leave?" Mouse asked, holding on to the top of Tubby's head as he tried to find a more comfortable spot on the giant boy's shoulder.

I took a deep breath. How to answer something like that? "I had to leave because the king wanted me to join the lancers and train his son."

"Not doing too good a job of it, I take it," Mouse said, looking over at the door.

I might have laughed if it hadn't been so true. "I wasn't with him when he was injured. Don't know what happened. I'm sure we'll find out more when he comes to after Reevie's had a chance to work on him." I looked at Mouse. "The prince isn't the only one I'm responsible for. The garrison commander has ordered me to begin training a special unit of lancers. And now that we are on the cusp of war, I'm barely able to find time to sleep."

"What war's that?" Toots asked, pushing his way through the crowd.

"Hey," Collen said, "why aren't you on duty?"

"I came to see the Protector."

"Then who's guarding the gate?"

"Stringbean's there. He'll be fine."

Collen didn't look too happy, but he didn't send Toots away either.

"I take it negotiations with Cylmar haven't gone well?" Gustory asked. "I hear things in town when I perform. Last I heard was that the king had sent a team to the front to negotiate a truce."

I shook my head. "Yes, I'm afraid that initial negotiation didn't go so well. I just returned from the border yesterday. Skirmishes are happening almost weekly now. We could have used someone like you during these negotiations. That gift of yours could have been quite useful."

Gustory frowned. "From what I've heard, it sounds like the problem isn't with the negotiator, but with who you're negotiating with."

I grunted. "I can't argue with you there. Kind of hard to work out a peace with someone who doesn't want it."

I turned and looked at the mass of kids standing around and realized this was hardly the kind of topic that needed discussing on my first day back at Sandstorm. Still, I needed to talk about something, anything to keep my mind off what was happening on the other side of that infirmary door. If something were to happen to Dakaran, I didn't know what I would do. The thought of having to approach the king and queen and inform them that their son was dead was something I didn't even want to consider.

With each year that had passed, and all the time spent in the palace with the Black Guild and with Dakaran, I had grown quite fond of the king and queen, almost at times looked to them as family. No one could ever replace my mother and father, but there were moments when I had viewed Dakaran's parents as something akin to my own.

Gustory must have sensed my hesitance and turned to those gathered. "Story time!" he shouted. "And then it's off to bed."

Groans filtered through the crowd, as the kids clearly didn't want to leave, but they slowly began to work their way down the hall toward the library. Gustory would no doubt send them off to their rooms with a harrowing adventure that would leave them anxiously wanting more. I remembered how much the bard's tales had moved me. Gustory's gift of magic was truly unique. He could imbue his audience with whatever emotion he wished, depending on the story he was telling.

"I don't know what we'd do without him," Sapphire said. She, Bull, and Collen remained behind, along with Red and Po, who were standing next to me. "Bringing him to Sandstorm has been one of the best decisions you've made, and that says a lot, considering Sandstorm likely wouldn't be here if not for you."

I watched the crowd of children follow the bard into the library and shut the door.

"Let's sit in the study," Sapphire said. "It'll be more comfortable than standing out here in the hall."

I looked at the infirmary door.

"Reevie will let us know if something changes." She turned to Collen, who was standing on the other side of the gallery near the window. "Are you on watch tonight?"

He nodded.

"Wait by the door, and if something happens, come get us. We'll be in the study." She started to turn but then stopped. "Oh, and see if you can get Cook to whip up a fresh batch of sticky buns. I have a feeling it's going to be a long night."

AVALANCHE

Chapter 2

APPHIRE AND BULL ESCORTED Red, Po, and me back to Noph's old study in the west wing. A small fire crackled in the fireplace on the right.

"The room looks unchanged," I said, noting the arrangement of furniture near the fireplace. The sofa and loveseat shared the same dark ebony wood, padded with soft purple cushions, the same rich ebony that lined the desk and chair at the back, along with the standing shelves on the right. The same dark purple curtains hung on either side of the windows, and even some of Noph's old paintings decorated the walls. "I thought you were going to turn my old bedroom into the new chief's study?"

"We did, sort of," Bull said. "Reevie spends most of his time in the counting room working on ledgers."

"We use this study down here for entertaining guests," Sapphire said.

"So, I've been relegated to a mere guest. My, how things have changed." I smirked and took a seat on the right side of the sofa, closest to the fire. The days had grown warm enough now that wearing my coat was becoming a burden, but nights like tonight were still cold enough to need it. Red and Po joined me.

"So how is Sandstorm doing?" I asked, turning to the two chiefs, who were seated on a second smaller sofa across from the three of us. "I would have come to visit, but after Reevie's ultimatum, I figured it best to keep my distance. I do hear things from Master Fentin and Mistress Orilla from time to time, and they tell me Reevie hasn't been around as much as he used to."

Sapphire frowned. "He's about as busy as you nowadays, what with the infirmary in town and his work with Physicker Saban."

"He's still working there?" Red asked. "I thought by now he would have opened his own infirmary."

"I think he feels an obligation to Saban, since he was the one to take Reevie on as an apprentice, and he seems to enjoy the work. Besides, not everything is about gold," Sapphire said, not quite glaring at Red, but enough to demonstrate the unspoken dislike.

Red bristled. "I didn't say it was. But there is something to be said for working for yourself and not someone else."

Like Red, I was surprised that Reevie hadn't at least thought about starting his own practice. That had been his dream predating our days living under the Granary. His father had encouraged the idea before his father had been wrongly accused of killing Lord Ackelman's daughter.

"We hardly see Reevie ourselves," Bull admitted. "When he does show, he hides himself away inside his counting room. We were surprised to see him at supper this evening. Normally, he grabs a bite from one of the food stands in town before heading home, since he's usually too late to eat with us."

"How are you two doing, then?" I asked. It had been hard enough to keep things running when there were three chiefs, but with Reevie being gone so much, Sapphire and Bull would be forced to cover his duties.

"We're managing," Sapphire said, her head high. I should have known she would be too proud to let us know if they were struggling. "Business has been a little slow of late, forcing us to increase our picking."

I cringed. I had never liked the picking and had been happy to see Sandstorm take over some of Noph's ventures, which had been lucrative enough to keep them from having to resort to it.

"This war you mentioned is affecting our livelihood," she said. "Most of our usual clients have suspended or deferred our services for now. You can almost feel the tension in the air. They're concerned about supply lines being interrupted if this war spills over into Elondria. They're also uneasy about rising costs and the possibility of a new war tax."

"People are worried," Bull said.

I nodded. I knew exactly what she meant about tension being so high it was palpable. "Yes, I've felt it. Not in the city, but things are tense at the garrison."

"I can imagine," Bull said. "It must be hard being a lancer, especially during times like these."

"It's not a picnic, that's for sure. While the rest of Aramoor goes about their lives with minimal inconvenience, we lancers wake up every morning wondering if this is the day we march to war. The day we leave and possibly never return."

No one spoke for a while. The only sound was the fire crackling merrily in the hearth, as if ignorant of the uncomfortable silence, which was thankfully interrupted by a knock at the door.

"Come in," Sapphire said a little too eagerly.

Collen stuck his head in.

"How's Dakaran?" I asked, jumping to my feet. "Has Reevie finished?"

Collen shook his head. "I'm just here with the sticky buns. Cook threw a fresh batch together as soon as he heard the Protector was here." Collen stepped in, followed by two servers carrying trays of dessert and drink.

"So, no word yet?" I asked.

Collen shook his head. "Afraid not. No one has been out since Muriel returned."

I sighed and retook my seat. The two servers set the trays down on the table between the sofas, along with a stack of plates, cups, and cloth napkins, then promptly departed. Collen shut the door behind them, after assuring us that he would let us know just as soon as he heard anything.

"So, you think the war is inevitable?" Red asked, helping herself to a sticky bun and a cup of fresh cream.

"I think it's been inevitable for some time," I said, wiping glaze from my mouth with a napkin. Sapphire quirked a puzzled eyebrow at me. Not that long ago, I would have licked the frosting off, not wanting to waste a drop. It seemed working in and around the palace had improved my manners. "As long as Overlord Saryn has his eyes set on the Black Hills and their mines, I don't see this going away anytime soon."

My first run-in with Cylmarans had been with a band of slavers in the Black Hills, and that had left a rather sour taste in my mouth for the place. My second visit into Cylmaran territory hadn't improved things. I had been tasked with breaking into the overlord's castle and rescuing our Elondrian ambassador and his wife. However, that rescue wouldn't have been possible if not for some brave Cylmarans who had put their lives on the line to smuggle us out on their boats. Even now, one of my Room Eleven squadmates was a Cylmaran who I considered one of my closest friends, though Fipple would probably deny his heritage if asked.

Even though I cared little for Cylmaran politics, I couldn't deny there were still very good people that lived there, as anywhere.

Sapphire looked at me and Red a moment, as though trying to decide something before finally speaking. "So, who wants to tell me what happened to the prince? I have my suspicions," she said, casting a wary eye in Red's direction.

"For once, it wasn't me," Red said. "Po and I just happened to be passing by when we spotted several men leaving the alley beside the Fishnet tavern, and one was wiping blood off his knife. No need to guess as to what they were doing, and as soon as they left, Po and I went to have a look."

"No doubt to see if the others had missed searching his pockets," Sapphire shot back.

Red smiled. "We went to see if we could be of . . . any assistance."

I looked at Red and cocked a brow. Even I didn't believe that excuse.

"Lucky for you that we did," she said. "As soon as I saw who it was, I sent Po running for the garrison to get Ayrion."

"And you want us to believe that Po actually knocked on the garrison door and spoke with a lancer?" Sapphire asked. "You lived with us for the better part of a year, and I barely heard Po string five words together."

"I talk when I need to," Po said.

"That part I can attest to," I said. His showing up at the garrison had been a shock. "One of the sergeants woke me to tell me I had a visitor at the gatehouse. As soon as I heard what happened, I grabbed a horse, and we rode across town to the tavern. Dakaran and Red were there just like Po said, and you pretty much know the rest."

"So, no one has any idea why Dakaran was lying in an alleyway in the middle of the night with a hole in his gut?" Sapphire asked.

"Oh, I can venture a guess," I said. "The Fishnet is one of his favorite places to go when he sneaks out of the palace, and he has a bad tendency to pass coins out to the staff, especially the servers. In fact, he's so known for his generosity that it's earned him the name Master Silvercoin."

Bull rolled his eyes. "Well, that's just stupid. So these men might not have been trying to kill him because they knew who he was but because he was flaunting his purse?"

"Sounds like your kind of men," Sapphire said to Red. "Slit your throat for a couple of coppers."

Red balled her fists but kept her faux smile plastered to her face. "If my people had known who he was, they certainly wouldn't have dragged him into a blind alley and stuck a knife in him. Killing the crown prince is a great way to start a war right here in Aramoor. Besides, he'd be worth a lot more alive than dead. Not saying they wouldn't do such a thing—there are plenty that would."

Which brought up another point of contention with me. "And what in the flaming Pits of Aran'gal possessed you to leave a comfortable place like this to take up with the very cutthroats that kidnapped you and tied you naked to a bed? I mean, I know you missed me when I left, but you couldn't have been that forlorn about it. After everything Sapphire and I did to rescue you from the Warrens, to have you just up and join them a year later? Pretty insensitive, don't you think?"

"It wasn't as simple as that," she said. "You know I was miserable here. It was nice of you to take us in and all, but ever since I lost my tribe, I lost my purpose. There was nothing to challenge me. And you know I need a challenge," she said, winking at me.

I hmphed. "You are the challenge, you mean."

She smiled. "There was nothing for me here, and there wasn't really much for me out there either. But Kerson found me in the market one day and offered me a place in his clan."

"Are you crazy? You do realize he tried to kill us, right? Kerson holds me responsible for Spats's disappearance."

"Well, from what I've heard, you *are* responsible for his disappearance."

"Regardless, how could you take up with the Warrens?"

"Because I had nowhere else to go. Sure, you tolerated me here, but I was never really welcome, and after all our history, I just couldn't stomach living under these two's leadership." She looked at Bull and Sapphire. "No offense."

"Offense taken," Sapphire said.

Red looked at me. "The point is, I needed to make my own way, and the Warrens offered me a chance to do that. Being there, I don't have to carry the stigma of who I was, a street chief who'd lost her tribe. Down there, I'm just Kira, and even though I'm not exactly high on the spear pole at the moment," she said, a dark smile spreading across her face, "I will be."

Knowing her, I didn't doubt it. I just hated to think what she would have to become in order to make that happen.

"How have you been?" Bull asked me. "I see dark circles around those eyes."

I smiled. "I won't lie. Chances to sleep have been few and far between, and what I do manage is restless. I'm a little irritable."

Red snorted. "More than a little."

A knock on the door had us all turning once again.

Collen stuck his head in without waiting for Sapphire or Bull to tell him. "Reevie's done if you—"

He didn't finish before I was racing out the door. I ran down the hall to the long gallery, noting the library was empty when I passed. Gustory must have finished his tales, and the children had all been sent to their beds. The infirmary door was open, and Muriel waited just outside, drying her hands on a clean cloth.

"How is he?" I asked.

"He's alive," Muriel began as I shot past her and into the infirmary.

Reevie stood in front of a table on the left, cleaning blood from his hands, but Dakaran wasn't there. I turned and found him on one of the cots on the right, and quickly made my way to his side. I knelt. His chest was still rising, and he seemed to be breathing more freely. I released a heavy sigh of relief.

"How bad is it?" I asked. "Will he make it?"

The others caught up as Reevie turned. He looked at me for a brief moment, then turned and addressed the others as though I wasn't even in the room.

"The wound was deep, but astonishingly enough, it hadn't punctured anything vital. I've cleaned it, dressed it, and sewn it up. I've given him some medicine for the pain and to aid in healing, but the rest will be up to him. He's not out of the woods, and depending on how he does tonight, we should know more by the morning." He dropped the bloody cloth he'd been wiping his hands on in a hamper beside the table. "I've done what I can. Muriel can look after the rest. Cold compresses to help keep the fever down and sleep is what he needs."

Reevie placed a couple of bottles still lying on the table back on their respective shelves and then started for the door.

"That's it?" I asked. "You aren't even going to speak to me?"

Reevie didn't even turn to look. "I did what was asked. Now I'm going to bed. Hopefully, you won't be here when I wake up." With that, he left the room and disappeared down the hall.

Red whistled. "When he holds a grudge, he really clings to it. I've seen newly bonded lovers that don't embrace as tightly."

I shook my head, tempted to go after him, but then thought better of it. It wouldn't have done either of us any good to have an argument in the middle of the gallery. I stared at the open doorway a moment longer before finally turning back around. I hoped I would be able to find time to talk with him at some point, but I doubted I would be able to during this trip.

Reevie was clearly still too upset to want to see me, and I had other responsibilities that hindered me from waiting around for my former friend to acknowledge me. In fact, I realized in the rush to come save Dakaran, I hadn't had the chance to tell Overcaptain Tolin I might not be there in the morning. I did tell Gellar I would be out but didn't tell him why or for how long. He had been the only one still awake in our room when the gate guard came to get me.

Hopefully, Gellar would relay the message to Tolin.

The overcaptain had given Room Eleven tomorrow off to rest after our return journey from the front, but we were supposed to report to him as soon as we woke. I had no idea how I was going to make it back for that. I also needed to set up the schedule for the Black Guild, the special lancer unit I had been tasked with developing after Room Eleven's successful mission into Cylmar to rescue the ambassador and his wife.

That one mission had changed our lives within the lancer corps. We were no longer looked down on as the rejects from Room Eleven. We were now the respected members of the Black Guild, a guild that many of our fellow armsmen were eager to join. Training the new men wasn't the difficult part, especially after the king had opened up the rooms in the palace for our use. The most difficult part was managing the sched-uling.

I had a newfound respect for Overcaptain Tolin and Captain Asa and the hours they spent in their offices. In my early years as a lancer, I thought they simply used them to get away from the men, but there was a whole lot more to training than simply directing others in how to fight.

I stared out the doorway where Collen was chatting quietly with Muriel. Their conversation looked personal by the deep way they were staring into each other's eyes, and there was a brief moment when he placed a hand on her arm that had me wondering if the two had formed some sort of attachment. I'd never seen it before, but then again, it had been over a year since I'd been around.

I smiled. It was a welcome surprise amidst all the other chaos in my life. Muriel had always been the quiet one, keeping to her birds, while Collen was always at the front of everything with his duties as captain of the beaters, along with being the chiefs' right-hand man. It seemed a strange sort of pairing, and yet at the same time, I could see it working. I wondered if anyone else knew, or if they were keeping it to themselves.

The prince groaned softly, and I was pulled from my mind wander-ing. His blanket was up, so I couldn't see the bandaged wound, and he had a wet cloth draped over his forehead with a bucket of fresh water nearby. I sat on the side of the cot next to his and dipped my fingers in the bucket. It was still cold. They must have brought up some of the winter ice from the cellar. Most of it was probably gone by now. The ice rarely lasted till the end of spring and required daily checking to remove the melted water to make it last as long as possible.

I stared at Dakaran's chest as it slowly rose and fell, wondering how all of this had happened. From what Red and Po had described, it seemed like the prince hadn't even put up a fight. None of the other men she and Po had seen appeared to have been wounded or killed, which was quite strange given the prince's skill. Dakaran had been under my tutelage now for the last five years, though after his year of lancer service ended, and my working with the Black Guild increased, our time spent together in training had slowed. Still, he should have at least been able to draw a sword.

I leaned over, pried opened Dakaran's mouth, and took a sniff. Well, that explained it.

"What are you doing?" Bull asked, walking over with the others. "Why were you looking in his mouth?"

"I was smelling his breath."

"And?" Sapphire asked.

"And I wouldn't hold a candle too close to his face."

"That bad?" Sapphire said.

"I was trying to determine how Dakaran could have been ambushed so badly without fighting back, but he's as drunk as a sailor on a three-day leave."

Muriel pushed her way through the group to the other side of the cot and removed Dakaran's compress. She dipped it in the water and wrung it out before placing it back on his forehead. Dakaran didn't stir. Whatever Reevie had given him had left him in a very deep sleep. Knowing Reevie, he'd probably doused him with some of his ether.

One of my first experiences with Reevie and his ether had been during a street battle we had fought outside the old Avalanche compound. I had just arrived at Hurricane when Spats decided to go to war with Cutter. Our fearless leader had kept shouting "Cut their feet!" like an imbecile. Reevie had hidden behind some crates on the side of the street, tossing out jars of ether. Come to think of it, he'd done the same during the tribal war that we started at the Pit.

I couldn't help but smile as I remembered those earlier days.

Muriel checked the cold cloth once more to make sure it was on securely, then left the infirmary and shut the door behind her, giving us some privacy.

"Isn't someone going to notice that the prince is missing?" Sapphire asked. "What are you going to do about that? Last thing we need is the city going on high alert because that drunken idiot didn't show up for breakfast tomorrow."

"We can't try to move him," I said. "You heard Reevie, he's not out of the woods. We risk doing even more damage if we were to take him back to the palace now."

"Then what do you suggest?" she asked. "I have a feeling they're going to notice his bed wasn't slept in."

"If they bother checking," I said. "You know how Dakaran can be. Look at him now. Do you think if he had made it back to the palace tonight, that he would be up in the morning all bright eyed and ready for the day, or do you think he'd probably sleep most of it away? You remember what it was like when I first started training him."

Bull groaned. "I remember. Half the time you went to the palace, you were forced to wait on him. The other half, he just didn't show."

"Exactly. He's not as bad about it as he used to be, but judging by the way we just found him tonight, I don't think anyone will be knocking on his door at first light."

"But doesn't he have guards watching his room?" Sapphire asked. "I would have to assume they'd notice him not returning tonight."

I shook my head. "No, but he does have a couple at the end of his hall."

"And they won't know that he left," Red said with a smile, "because he would have taken the hidden passageway out."

Sapphire looked confused. "What hidden passageway?"

I glared at Red, but the cat was already out of the bag. "There's a secret way in and out of the palace that Dakaran showed me years ago. It's how he sneaks out at night and goes into town."

Sapphire's face tightened, and she pointed at Red. "And how would you know about that?" She looked at me, just as angry. "You told her about Dakaran's secret palace entrance? Are you insane? She's about as trustworthy as a cutpurse. And if it hasn't escaped your memory, she's now one of the Warren Underground."

"I resent that. I'm much better than a cutpurse." Red smiled wickedly. "I can get men to turn over their coin without even lifting a finger. Besides, it wasn't Ayrion who showed me the passage. It was the prince himself."

Sapphire looked at me again, stunned.

I nodded. "He did. But then again, he's never been very smart."

"I wasn't the only one." Red hmphed. "Po and Reevie were there as well."

I rolled my eyes. Red needed to keep her mouth shut.

Sapphire gaped. "Reevie was in the palace?"

Bull looked just as shocked.

"You had your chance," Red said. "If I remember correctly, Dakaran invited both of us, but I was the only one gracious enough to accept his offer."

Sapphire's face reddened. "Hah! You probably thought you'd seduce him like you tried to do with Ayrion and snag yourself a prince. What? Did you think you'd become queen one day?"

This time it was Red's turn to sneer, but I noted she didn't respond. I had a feeling Sapphire wasn't far off the mark. Say this for Red: she was ever the opportunist. But Dakaran's fancies tended to flit from one flower to the next, and Red had been left behind.

"So how did Reevie end up in the palace?" Bull asked. "And why wasn't I invited?"

I groaned. This was getting out of hand. "Dakaran showed me the hidden entrance and passageway through the palace back when we first started training."

"That was like four years ago," Bull said.

"Yes, so I was what, sixteen? Dakaran was the one who first showed me the Fishnet. He was also there with the lancers when Sapphire and I rescued Red. He—"

"I go by Kira now," Red corrected. "Red was my street name. I'm no longer a street rat."

"Fine. When Sapphire and I rescued *Kira*. He had asked me to introduce him to the both of you," I said, looking from Sapphire to Red and back. "In fact, he kept pestering me until I finally obliged. Kira was the only one to say yes."

Bull looked at Sapphire incredulously. "You turned down an invitation from the prince?"

Sapphire hmphed. "It was pretty obvious why he invited us. I wasn't about to be some snot-nosed boy's latest fancy."

"Regardless," I said, "Kira accepted the prince's invitation to go eat with us, and she doesn't go anywhere without Po, so we all had lunch one afternoon at the tavern."

"And Dakaran wasn't kidding when he said they have the best lamb and mint sauce in town," Kira said. "It's to die for." She licked her lips and glanced sidelong at Sapphire.

I squeezed the edge of the cot, pretending it was her neck. "Anyway," I continued, "Dakaran invited them back to the palace afterward to show them around, and we ran into Reevie on the way there. He was returning from a house call for Saban, and Dakaran invited him as well."

"So all of you just hung out at the palace with the prince?" Bull asked, sounding quite envious.

"We even met the queen," Kira said, rubbing it in.

"Will you shut it?" I said, having had enough of Kira's gloating. "I think they get the picture." I looked back down at Dakaran. "The question now is how do we get him back?"

"Quickly," Sapphire said, then turned and stormed out of the room.

I glared at Red, or Kira, or whatever she was calling herself these days, but she simply ignored it. She and Sapphire had never gotten along, even when Kira was living at Sandstorm, and usually I was the one caught in the middle. But I didn't want Sapphire to leave the same way Reevie had, so, taking one last look down at the prince, who seemed to be sleeping soundly, I stood and went after her.

AVALANCHE

Chapter 3

I CAUGHT UP WITH SAPPHIRE in the gallery near the library, and she stopped. The others remained in the infirmary, which was surprising, given how much Kira enjoyed getting under Sapphire's skin.

"You're not mad at me, are you?" I asked.

Sapphire sighed as she turned. "No. I just can't take another minute with her. I'd almost forgotten how annoying she can be. Her leaving was one of the best things that could have happened to Sandstorm."

"Knowing where she ended up, I'm not so sure about that."

Sapphire shrugged. "I guess that depends on how you look at it."

I cocked my brow.

"Fine. Perhaps not."

The library door was open beside us and still had several lanterns lit inside, along with a fire in the hearth, so I led her in, closing the door behind us. We sat in a couple of seats by the fireplace. The library always had plenty of seating. It was where the kids sat and listened to Gustory's nightly adventures.

"It's been a long time since we've talked," I said, my chest tightening as I stared into her bright blue eyes. I had always thought she was beautiful, but she had grown even more so during my absence. It wasn't just her figure, or how well her elegant new clothes suited her. There was something in the way she carried herself, a silent grace that pulled at me. Her long, wavy blonde hair glistened in the firelight, for once not pulled back into its usual braid. "I've missed our conversations."

She smiled. "I've missed them as well."

"There's times that I wish . . ." I bit my tongue. I was letting my emotions get the better of me. I was twenty years old, and Sapphire had been the only girl I'd ever cared for, the only girl I'd ever kissed. Seeing her again, even after all this time, had some of those same sentiments creeping back in. The same ache that I'd felt the day we decided to end our relationship outside the Warren's wall was just as alive today as it was back then.

"I know," she said, trying not to look at me, focusing instead on the golden flames dancing across the half-eaten wood inside the hearth. "I wish the same at times." She turned. "But I still believe we made the right choice."

I stared at the side of her face for a moment, then nodded, though it felt forced, probably because it was. Seeing her so close, sitting across from me, had me wishing to recant everything we had previously decided, wishing to tell her that I'd been a fool for leaving. My mouth moved of its own accord.

"Has there been anyone else?"

I don't know why I asked. I certainly didn't want to know if there had been.

"No," she said matter-of-factly, and I breathed a small sigh of relief. "My time is solely devoted to Sandstorm, like yours is to the lancers."

I shook my head. "Don't we make a sad pair. Too busy with our lives to actually live them, surrounded by people yet completely alone."

She looked at me, then back at the fire. "Fate has an unpleasant sense of humor."

"But that doesn't mean that perhaps one day . . ."

She smiled. "Perhaps."

"Do you believe in destiny? That our lives are already mapped out for us?"

She sat quietly, thinking. "I don't know. I believe we make choices and then have to live with the consequences."

"But can we make other choices to alter those consequences, or are we destined to live them out no matter what we do?"

She turned and looked at me. "I'm not sure what you're asking."

To be honest I wasn't all that sure either, except being this close to her again, I found myself questioning the choices I'd made, whether leaving her and Reevie had been the best option. At the time, it had felt like the *only* option, what with the king breathing down my neck, but now, looking back, I wondered how things might have been if I'd chosen to stay. "I just wonder if—"

The door to the library opened behind us, and Muriel stuck her head in partway. "I think he's beginning to wake. I figured you'd want to know."

I balled my fist, and for a split second I found myself enraged at the unintended interruption. It couldn't have come at a worse time. But the more I thought about it, the more I realized that perhaps it had been the perfect time. Perhaps it had stopped me from saying too much, from digging myself in a hole that I wouldn't be able to get out of.

Offering Sapphire an apologetic smile, I stood. She followed me up, and we left the library and our somewhat awkward conversation and headed back to the infirmary. Kira and Po were nowhere to be seen.

"Where are the others?" I asked Muriel as I made my way over to Dakaran's bedside.

"I think they left," Muriel said.

I turned. "Without saying anything?"

Sapphire clicked her tongue. "That's Red for you. Thinking only of herself."

I sat down on the stool next to Dakaran, watching helplessly as he shifted back and forth, occasionally groaning in pain, but he still had yet to open his eyes.

"Most of Reevie's patients act like this when coming out of a deeper sleep," Muriel said. "Nothing to worry about." Once again, she took the prince's compress from his forehead, dipped it in the bucket of cool water beside the cot, and then placed it back over his forehead. "His fever seems to be breaking. He's not quite as warm as he was."

"Where did Bull go?" Sapphire asked, standing at the foot of the cot.

"I think he went to get a bite of something from the kitchen."

"You look like you need to do the same," Sapphire said to Muriel. "Go take a break. We'll sit with the prince."

Muriel looked at Dakaran but finally nodded and left the room. Sapphire and I were alone to enjoy another round of awkward silence.

"So how are things going with the lancers?" she asked. "Apart from not getting any sleep and being too busy to have a life and a possible war looming in the not-so-distant future . . . Are you happy?"

I thought a moment, then smiled. "Surprisingly, yes. You wouldn't think it, especially with what's going on, but . . . yes, I think I'm where

I need to be. At least for now."

She looked both happy and sad for me at the same time, and given the surprising ease of my answer, I was glad I hadn't pushed us further inside the library, chalking it up to a moment of weakness at seeing her once again. Regardless of how I felt, one thing was for certain: the situation was most confusing.

She nodded. "As long as you're happy." She grabbed the stool beside the next cot over, carried it back, and sat down across from me on the other side of Dakaran.

"Do you think Reevie will ever forgive me for leaving?" I asked.

She stared at the prince, then pursed her lips. "I don't know. I would have said yes a year ago, but clearly I would have been wrong. He took it hard, you know. Buried himself in his work. Your leaving affected him more than he let on."

"It wasn't like I left him specifically. If I had another choice . . ."

"You would have made the same one all over again," she said with a knowing smile. "It's who you are, Ayrion. You're a protector. I guess in a way, I always knew you'd end up in the military. You're a warrior, and one of the best. I can see why the king would choose you to train his son."

I looked at Dakaran. "I suppose you're right." It was in my blood. Perhaps not the protector part, but the fighting aspect, given my heritage. I was just glad to be able to use my gifts for something other than renting myself for hire as an assassin or mercenary. It was one of the only aspects to leaving the Lost City that I found agreeable.

Thinking about it had me wondering how my family was doing. It had been such an unexpected gift to have run into my father and brother in Ecrin two years ago. I had almost been tempted to leave with them, if for no other reason than to see my mother and sister once more. Sadly, I doubted I would ever see any of them again.

Dakaran groaned once again, shifting far enough that his arm flopped off the side of the cot. I leaned forward and placed it back on the bed beside him. "Come on, Dakaran," I said softly. "You've got to pull through this. Don't make me show up at the palace with your corpse."

"You wouldn't actually do that, would you?" Sapphire said. "They'd lay the blame on you. If he doesn't make it, we can find a way to hide him. Plenty of places in this city that no one visits. We could even take him down to the old shipyards and dump his body in the bay."

I shook my head. "I wouldn't do that to Rhydan and Ellise." It felt a little awkward calling them by their names and not their titles. "Their son disappears and they're forced to spend the rest of their lives never knowing, always wondering if he might somehow return. That would be far worse."

"Worse than them taking their son's death out on you?"

"I don't plan on dying anytime soon," Dakaran rasped, causing Sapphire to jerk. His eyes fluttered open. "Though, I'm glad to hear you wouldn't just toss me in the bay." He coughed and winced at the pain.

I smiled at him, releasing a heavy sigh of relief at seeing him conscious. "You had me worried half to death. You keep sneaking out of the palace like that and I'll kill you myself."

Dakaran coughed again and looked around the room, stopping on Sapphire. "Hello. I'm Prince Dakaran. Who are you?"

"We've met before," Sapphire said with a grunt.

"I highly doubt that. I would have recognized someone as beautiful as you."

She rolled her eyes.

Dakaran tried sitting up and then grabbed his stomach. "What happened?" He looked up at me. "Where am I?"

"You don't remember?"

Dakaran shook his head, still looking half-dazed.

"You were stabbed in an alleyway behind the Fishnet. Ring any bells?"

Dakaran paused, his mouth tightening against the pain. "I remember an argument with some men at a table next to mine." He shook his head. "But . . . other than that, I don't remember anything else. I was stabbed?" He grabbed his blanket and pulled it down. His shirt was missing, and he had several layers of bandaging around his midsection. "Why would someone stab me?"

"Because you were probably tossing silvers to the waitresses again like an imbecile. If you ask me, you got what you deserved. How many times do I have to tell you not to do that?"

Dakaran frowned, then looked around the room once more. "How did I get here? Wherever here is."

"Red and Po happened to be passing by the tavern and found you."

"Kira's here?" Dakaran attempted to lift his head and look around.

"She was. But she left a while ago. Anyway, she sent Po to fetch me from the garrison, and—"

"When did you get back?"

"What?"

"When did you get back from the front? I didn't know you were here, or I would have invited you to come eat last night."

"I just returned today. In fact, I was just crawling into bed when they came and got me. As soon as I saw you, I loaded you on a horse and brought you to Sandstorm."

"Your old street tribe? Why didn't you take me to the palace physickers?" he asked angrily. "It would have been closer."

"I brought you to the one person I thought could give you the best chance at life."

Dakaran sighed. "Let me guess, your little cripple friend. Ree . . . whatever."

"Reevie."

"And from the looks of it," Sapphire said, "it was the right choice."

Dakaran stared at her. "You do look familiar now that you mention it. Where did we meet before?"

"We met the night Ayrion and I rescued Red and Po from the Warren Underground."

Dakaran's eyes brightened. "That's right. Now I remember. We rode in with the lancers." He then frowned. "I also remember you turning down my invitation."

"Yes," she said as she stood from her stool. "I'm sure Your Royal Smugness is not used to hearing *no* very often." She looked at Ayrion. "I've got things to do before bed. Will you be here in the morning, or do you plan on disappearing like Red?"

Ayrion smiled. "I'll be here."

"We'll both be here," Dakaran said, offering her one of his more dashing smiles, which was thoroughly ruined by his sickly complexion, sweat-soaked face, and bloodshot eyes. He looked like death warmed over.

She cocked her brow. "I swoon with anticipation." With that, she turned and left.

"I like her," Dakaran said.

"Yeah, well, stop. She's no more interested now than she was back then."

"I think I'm bleeding."

"What?" I turned and looked at his wrapping. Sure enough, there was a small red splotch forming over the wound. "You probably opened it while trying to get up. Stay here while I find someone to take a look."

I left the room and headed down the hall to the kitchens. Muriel was sitting at one of the prep tables, eating a bowl of something that smelled like a heavily spiced tomato soup, while Bull was busy scrubbing off his plate.

"The prince is awake," I said, "but he's bleeding through the bandage. I think he might have torn a stitch when he tried sitting up."

Muriel huffed. "Why was he trying to sit up?" She dropped her spoon back in her bowl and stood. With a sigh, she got up to follow me back to the infirmary.

"I don't think he knew he was injured when he tried to sit up. He was still groggy from the med—"

The infirmary was empty.

"Flaming idiot! I told him to stay here." I rushed out of the room and back into the long gallery. It, too, was empty. No sign of Dakaran anywhere. "Search the rooms that way," I told Muriel, pointing back toward the kitchens, "and I'll go this way." I turned to head down the hall, stopping long enough to glance out one of the side windows overlooking the courtyard, just in case the prince had decided to go outside in his delirium.

The courtyard was empty, so I made my way to the next room down. It was empty as well, so I headed to the library. The door was half-open, and I peeked inside and found the oaf lying on the ground.

"He's in here," I shouted down the hall to Muriel. "Go get Bull to help me move him back to the infirmary." I opened the door and headed inside. The prince was writhing on the floor and looked up when I knelt beside him.

"I think I fell."

"I think you're trying to make my life a living misery. If you want to kill yourself, I'm sure I can find some very creative ways to manage it that won't leave stains on the carpet."

"I was looking for Sapphire."

"I'm sure you were. I ought to just leave you here to bleed out."

Sweat beaded his forehead, and his breathing was growing more labored.

"If you don't stay in bed and let the medicine do its job, then I just might be tossing you in the bay after all."

The door squeaked behind me, and Bull and Muriel rushed in.

"What happened?" Bull asked, seeing the prince lying on the floor.

"His Royal Stupidness thought he'd take a nightly stroll," I said. "Grab his feet."

With Bull's help, I carried Dakaran back to his cot in the infirmary. I turned to ask Muriel if we should remove the bandages, but she was nowhere to be seen.

"Now where did *she* go?" This was getting frustrating. I looked at Bull. "Help me get these bandages off." At least we could see if he'd torn the stitches. I looked at Dakaran. "And if you try moving again. I'll tie you to the bed."

He started to look up at me and smiled, but it quickly turned into a painful moan as we began to unwrap the bindings.

"What's going on in here? What are you doing to my patient?"

I turned to see Reevie hobbling into the room with Muriel just behind him.

"I thought it best if he had another look," Muriel said apologetically.

I stood, holding the half-undone wrapping in my hand. "He might have torn a stitch when he tried sitting up earlier, and then when I went to get Muriel, the prince, in his delusion, decided to go for a walk. I found him on the floor in the library."

Reevie pushed Bull aside and unwrapped the rest of the dressing. "Yep, he's torn a couple of the stitches." He looked at Muriel, who was

standing at the foot of the bed. "Grab the black bottle off the shelf and mix a fingerful with a half cup of brandy, the strong stuff."

"The stronger the better," Dakaran said.

Reevie ignored him.

Muriel was only gone a minute or two before she was returning with a small cup, which she handed to Reevie.

Reevie took it and then looked at Bull. "Help me lift him up enough to drink."

Bull was standing beside Muriel at the foot of the bed and nowhere near Dakaran's head, but apparently Reevie wasn't about to ask me to help, even though I was the one standing there. I waved Bull off and lifted Dakaran myself.

Reevie didn't acknowledge it, but he did manage to get the cup to Dakaran's lips. "Now, drink it all," he said, and the prince gulped it down.

"What is it?" I asked.

Reevie didn't reply.

"It's something to help him sleep," Muriel said from the foot of the bed.

Reevie stood there a moment, staring at Dakaran. I wasn't sure what he was waiting for, but I watched as well. Within moments, Dakaran's eyes began to flutter and then droop. Pretty soon, he was unconscious once again. Reevie turned to Muriel. "Bring the needle and thread, and whatever of the poultice I have left from earlier."

I moved back alongside Bull to give Muriel room and to keep from making Reevie nervous as he began to re-dress the prince's injury. It wasn't long before they were finished, and the prince was wrapped once more in new bandaging.

"How long will he be out for this time?"

Muriel turned. "As much as we gave him, the entire night, hopefully."

I nodded. "Probably for the best."

"Now," Reevie said to no one in particular, "if you think you can manage to keep an unconscious man in his bed, I'm going back to mine. If he tries climbing out again, let him bleed." He turned and left the room, shutting the door behind him.

"He is not very happy with you, is he?" Bull said, running his big hand back through his dirty-blond hair. "Most worked up I've seen him in months."

"I'm going back to my supper," Muriel said, and headed for the door. "Do you think you can keep him from opening his bandages again?"

I looked at Dakaran, who released a loud snore. "I don't think he's going anywhere for the time being. And if he tries, I'll have Bull sit on him."

She nodded and left the infirmary.

I looked at Bull. "You don't actually have to stay. I'm sure you have a busy day tomorrow. Go get some sleep while you can."

"Are you sure?"

I nodded. "I'll stay with him."

He looked at the prince, then back at me, and shrugged. "Okay, but if you need anything, my room's the one beside your old room."

I smiled. "I have a feeling that whatever he just drank is going to keep him out the rest of the night. I probably should have asked Muriel to make a little extra for me."

Bull smiled and headed to the door, then stopped and took one last glance back over his shoulder at me and Dakaran before heading out and shutting it behind him.

I looked down at the prince and shook my head. Even with a hole in his gut, he nearly killed himself chasing after a woman. Dakaran's dalliances were going to be the death of us both.

I sat on the stool for about an hour, watching the prince breathe. My eyes began to slip shut, so I stood and walked around the room, slapping my face every so often to try keeping awake. I wanted to walk to the kitchen and see if there were any leftovers or a glass of spiced cider, but I was afraid if I left the room, I'd return to find it empty once more, so I remained where I was.

I did grab Reevie's chair from his desk against the back wall and carry it over. It at least had a back on it. Pretty soon, my eyelids were beginning to droop, and I was back to shaking my head and slapping my cheeks. The prince hadn't moved since Reevie had fed him his tonic. Whatever it was, it had done its job. I wished I had a bottle of that for myself to use at the garrison. At the very least it would keep me from having to lie awake listening to my roommates' snoring. Thoughts of my bed at the garrison had my mind wandering and my eyes slowly shutting.

A hand grabbed my shoulder, and I jumped in my chair, reaching for my weapon as I startled awake.

"It's just me," Sapphire said. "You fell asleep."

There was light coming through the door from the windows out in the gallery. Dakaran was still asleep, an arm dangling over the side. I placed it back on his cot and yawned.

"I tried staying awake," I said as I stood and stretched. "But I feel half-drugged myself."

"You look like you need two or three days of straight sleep."

"That bad, huh?" I grabbed my coat from the back of my chair and put it on. The room felt a little cooler than it had been last evening. "Any chance of getting some breakfast?"

"I'll have Collen and a couple of his beaters stand watch if you want to go get some. Reevie will probably be down shortly himself, so now would be the best time to grab something if you're hungry."

My stomach growled my answer, and we both laughed.

"Lead the way," I said, and started for the door. About the time I reached it, Dakaran groaned, and I stopped.

Sapphire looked at me and sighed. "Fine. I'll bring you a plate."

"Thank you."

She left, and I walked back over and retook my seat next to the prince's cot. My head was swimming, and I was having a difficult time focusing. I really needed sleep. For a moment, I almost wished Red hadn't found the fool. But like it or not, he was my friend, and the eventual heir to the throne. I just hoped that I was able to find a way to get him back to the palace without anyone knowing. Aramoor was a large city, and it was a long way to take someone with a hole in their gut.

Of course, thinking about it, was it really all that necessary to sneak him back in? I ought to march the prince straight through the front doors and tell the king and queen exactly where he was and what he'd been up to. Maybe they could talk some sense into him.

Of course, if I did that, Dakaran would probably never forgive me. I paused a moment. Would that really be such a bad thing? I started to laugh when Dakaran turned over in his bed, this time flinging both arms off the side. A line of drool dripped from his mouth like it would from a nervous dog. I groaned and lifted his arms and placed them back on the bed, then retook my seat as I waited for him to come fully out of whatever Reevie had given him.

I hoped the sleep and the medicine had worked a miracle, because one way or another, I was going to need to get him back to the palace and out of my hair. I had duties of my own that needed attending to. I couldn't sit around playing nursemaid to a nitwit, even a royal one.

AVALANCHE

Chapter 4

AFTER A QUICK BREAKFAST of sausage, eggs, and cheese, I sat quietly watching as Dakaran slowly made his way out of his medicinal stupor. He tossed back and forth before his eyes began to open. He looked just as confused as he had been last evening when he'd first woken to find himself in Sandstorm's infirmary.

Dakaran looked up at me and blinked. "What are you . . ." He looked around the room, and his eyes widened as recognition sank in. "I thought perhaps I'd been dreaming." He glanced over at the door. "Where's the pretty girl that was here last night?"

I rolled my eyes. Of course that was the first thing he'd ask. "Sapphire's got more important things to do than to watch over your scrawny backside."

Dakaran frowned, then looked at me. "Apparently, you don't. Every time I wake, I find your ugly face staring back at me."

"Oh, trust me, I've got more important things to do as well. For one, sleep."

"Yes, I wasn't going to say it, but you are looking a little worse for wear."

"And it's your fault. If you weren't sneaking out to the tavern every night, attracting cutthroats with your flashy smiles and heavy-laden purse, I might actually get some much-needed rest. How are you feeling?"

Dakaran pulled the blanket to his waist and felt around the newly wrapped bandaging. There were no bloodstains seeping through this time. "Better than last night, I think."

"Feeling good enough to eat?"

Dakaran licked his lips. "Always."

"If I go fetch you a plate, will you promise me you'll still be here when I get back? Or do I need to call a couple of my beaters to come make sure of it?" I was glad Reevie wasn't there to hear me slip and call them *my* beaters.

"You get that blonde girl from last night, and I'll promise never to leave my bed again."

I narrowed my eyes. "Another comment like that, and you'll be wearing your breakfast."

Dakaran smiled. "Oh, alright. I promise not to leave."

I stared at him a moment before finally nodding and stepping out of the room. I was surprised to find Collen standing guard outside the door. "How long have you been here?"

"Since dawn."

"You should have woken me."

"You looked like you needed it. Besides, His Highness was snoring loud enough I could hear him all the way down the hall."

I smiled. "Thanks." I left the room and headed down to the kitchen. I grabbed a plate of sausage, eggs, and cheese, along with two tankards of fresh cider, since Sapphire had forgotten to bring a drink with my breakfast and the strong sausage had my mouth tingling. On the way back, I had to weave my way through the growing number of Sandstorm kids heading down the gallery for the dining room. Many slowed when they saw me, while others waved and smiled as though I'd never left.

"Protector."

I turned to find Mouse running up the hall behind me from the direction of the kitchen. I handed Dakaran's plate and mug to Collen, who was still standing outside the infirmary. "Can you see the prince gets these?"

Collen took the food and headed inside, and I turned to see what Mouse wanted.

"I was afraid I'd dreamed it all last night," Mouse said. "But you're really here." He rushed up and hugged me, then stepped back with a big smile. He was still wearing his pig sticker on his hip.

"Nope," I said with a smile. "It wasn't a dream. I'm really here."

"It's about time you wised up and moved back in. Things have been awful boring around here since you left."

"That's probably a good thing. But I'm afraid I'm only here for a visit this time. I still have my responsibilities to the lancers and the king."

Mouse's jovial demeanor slipped. "I was hoping . . . never mind."

"So, how have you and Squeaks and Petal been doing?" I asked. "Keeping Tubby in line, I hope?"

He nodded, but then pursed his lips. "If I keep growing, I'll be too big for him to carry."

I looked down. "I have a feeling you'll never be too big for Tubby."

He shrugged. "Suppose not."

"How are the pickers doing?" When I'd left, Mouse had been head picker, in charge of training the rest.

"Been doing alright, I guess," he said, scratching the back of his head. "Not much need for me around here since you've been gone." His smile broadened. "But things are getting a little harder nowadays, so we've been getting in a little more practice." He sounded quite thrilled about that fact, but I guess when his sole identity and worth was based on his ability to pick, it stood to reason. Despite my aversion to that particular source of income, I had to admit, Mouse was a phenomenal sneakthief.

"I better get to work," he said. "Will you be around later?"

I looked at the infirmary door. "I don't know. I've got to get the prince back to the palace, so it will depend on how well he's doing this morning."

"Well, no offense, but I hope he catches the drips, if that's what it'll take to keep you here."

I grimaced at the thought. "Let's hope it doesn't come to that."

Mouse offered me a sinister smile and tapped his pig sticker. "I could always give him a matching hole in the other side."

I cocked my brow. "I'll make sure to let His Highness know."

His eyes widened. "I was just joking. You wouldn't tell him I said that, would you?"

"I suppose I can be persuaded not to if you were to run and see if there are any sticky buns left over from last night."

Mouse smiled and then turned and shot back down the hall.

I chuckled as I watched him go, then turned and headed into the infirmary to find Dakaran sitting up while finishing off his breakfast. Collen was standing next to his cot, holding Dakaran's tankard. I took a swig from my own. It was mildly spiced, just enough to add a little something extra to the fruit, a hint of tang behind the sweetness.

"How are you feeling?" I asked now that he was sitting up.

"Like I've been stabbed."

"You think you can make it back to the palace without keeling over on me?" I asked sarcastically.

He put his hand over his wound and groaned. "Probably not. I think I need a couple more days here with Sapphire."

I ground my teeth. "You're well enough to be moved." I looked at Collen. "Does Sandstorm still keep a coach?"

Collen nodded. "Haven't used them in a couple of weeks, but they're still in the carriage house."

If a coach was still there, then that at least would afford us an easier way to get across the city—and assure us some privacy. The difficult part would be having Dakaran sit up long enough at the bridge's gate house to make it look like nothing was wrong. The last thing I needed was to get blamed for this debacle. Hopefully, Yorig was on duty today. I could use a friendly face. I normally stopped to chat whenever he was there.

Yorig had been on duty the day I'd met with the king and accepted his offer to join the lancers. He'd also been there on more than one occasion when I had to help sneak Dakaran back in from one of his nightly forays in town. I only hoped today was such a day. It would certainly make things easier.

Collen collected Dakaran's plate, then handed him his tankard to finish off.

"Can I get another one of those?" Dakaran asked Collen as he handed him back his empty tankard and licked what remained from his lips. "That was rather good."

"I can see what's left," Collen said, taking the tankard and plate and turning for the door.

I walked him out and then stopped him in the hall. "Be sure to tell Sapphire to stay clear of the infirmary if she can. I don't want the prince changing his mind and trying to extend his stay."

Collen smiled a wide toothy grin. "I'll let her know." He then headed down the gallery toward the kitchen.

Unfortunately, I needed to head back inside the infirmary with the royal pain in my rump, but instead of going in, I waited by the door, just enough in to keep an eye on Dakaran, but enough out to see what was happening in the main gallery beyond. I had planned on seeing whether Dakaran was strong enough to stand on his own but was afraid of having him do too much without Reevie getting a look at him first. Sadly, I had no idea how long it would be before the healer graced us with his presence. I didn't even know if he'd eaten breakfast yet or not. For that matter, I didn't know if he'd gotten out of bed yet.

If he was still in his room, I was tempted to walk up there and sit on the edge of his bed and force him to talk to me. I really did want to tell him I was sorry, and that I missed him. I missed all of them. Being back had stirred feelings I had kept buried since leaving. I'd spent the majority of my teen years with this lot of rapscallions. We'd been through more than I cared to remember.

I ran my thumb along the branded flesh on my wrist, a daily reminder of where I had come from, of the people I'd left behind.

Dakaran stared at me from his cot across the room. "What are you looking at?"

I pulled my gaze away from the scars. "Nothing." My heart ached at times, but I did my best to tamp it down, filling the void with work. Room Eleven helped with that. They were as close to me as brothers. We'd fought side by side, each willing to give their life for the others. Yet, no matter how busy I kept myself or how many substitutes I brought into my life, no one could ever replace those here at Sandstorm.

"It's hard to let go, isn't it?"

I looked up to see Gustory standing on the other side of the door. I hadn't even heard him approach.

He nodded to my wrist and the X. "Once you let them in," he said, "it's impossible to let them go." The bard stared down the hall in thought. I wasn't sure if he was referring to the street rats or his lost family.

"Does the ache ever leave?" I asked.

"I hope not." He finally smiled. "But that doesn't mean it won't lessen." He took a deep breath and slowly exhaled. "There are times, though, when I find myself forgetting their faces." He cringed. "Those are the worst days. But they aren't every day."

I could feel his sadness. Spotting the crystal ring on his finger, I realized he was infusing his words with magic. He looked up at me. "Thankfully for you, yours are still here to come see." He started to leave but then laid a hand on my arm. "Perhaps next time, don't wait so long."

I nodded, and he turned and headed down the long gallery hall, leaving me to stare after him. The man certainly knew how to make a point.

"I found one, Protector," Mouse said, running down the hall from the direction of the kitchen. He held out a plate with a single sticky bun on top. "Here," he said, licking some glaze from his lips. "It was the last one."

I stepped out of the doorway and into the gallery. "Thank you, Mouse." I wondered how many buns had been on the plate before he'd left the kitchen.

He smiled and took off down the hall in the opposite direction. I took a moment to eat the sticky bun, and then licked my fingers clean before returning to the infirmary. I didn't want Dakaran seeing it and demanding we make him a fresh batch. By the time I stepped back in the infirmary, Collen had returned with a fresh tankard. He handed it to the prince, then returned to his post outside the door.

I stuck my head out the door. "See if you can find Reevie and ask him to come take a look at the prince's wound, so we know if it's safe to transport him or not."

Collen nodded and headed down the gallery toward the west wing.

I walked back inside to find Dakaran propped up with his pillow against the wall, gulping down another swallow and exhaling with a loud sigh. "This stuff really is good. Some of the best cider I've had."

"I'm glad you're enjoying it. How's the wound? Any pain?"

He looked down and pressed gently around the bandaging. "Some. I think it's worse now than when I woke. And I'm feeling really dizzy."

"And you will for a while," someone behind us said.

Reevie walked in and around to the opposite side of Dakaran's cot.

"The medicinal tonic I gave you should take the rest of the day to wear off. I strongly suggest bedrest for the next several days." He paused. "And by bedrest, I mean your own bed, which I know for a fact is much more comfortable than this cot." He then proceeded to unwrap Dakaran's bandaging.

The wound didn't look quite so red as it had last night, and the blood on the inside of the wrapping was minimal. Reevie was known for his poultices, but even this was amazing work. Whoever it was in Easthaven that he had been reading certainly knew their stuff.

Reevie smeared another layer of green salve over the wound, then redressed it. He handed the prince a small jar of the salve. "Use this twice a day for the rest of this week. It should have healed enough to move about by then without fear of re-tearing." Reevie turned and immediately started for the door without so much as looking in my direction.

"Thank you, Reevie," I said.

He paused in the doorway. He didn't look back, but he did at least acknowledge me with a nod before hobbling his way out and down the hall.

I guessed that was as good as I was going to get. I needed to find a way to break through that hardened shell of his, but I wasn't sure how. Regrettably, I had more important things to worry about at the moment. Namely, getting Dakaran back to his own bed.

"I suggest you rest. You'll need all the strength you can muster if we plan on transporting you across the city. And I doubt you'll want to take the main palace entrance and attempt climbing all those stairs with the palace attendants and staff watching."

"No," Dakaran said. "We'll take the hidden passageways up."

"I thought as much." I helped him back down into the cot and placed the blanket over him. "Try to get some sleep. Perhaps the dizziness will lessen if you do."

Dakaran handed me his tankard and the jar of balm Reevie had given him, and then closed his eyes. I barely had time to grab my swords and make it to the door before I heard heavy breathing behind me.

That was quick, I thought. I closed the door so he wouldn't be disturbed by those passing in the hall and began to put on my weapons— one on my back, one at my waist. "Don't let anyone in," I said to Collen on my way to the front entrance.

"What about Reevie?" he asked.

I turned. "Don't let anyone in except the chiefs," I corrected, then headed outside to the outer courtyard to get some fresh air. There was a slight nip to the early morning breeze I found refreshing, and I breathed it in to clear my head. I started to sit on one of the benches until I realized it was covered in dew. The last thing I needed was a wet backside.

I heard Redwing screeching somewhere behind the manor house. Muriel must have been feeding him. It was a strange feat, watching over both a hawk and a coop of pigeons. I didn't know how she kept the one from eating the others, but she clearly had her ways.

Not being able to get my run in this morning, I decided to stretch my legs and take a walk. My meandering led me around the side of the manor, where I followed the brick pavers over to the carriage house. It was a two-story building with enough room up top to house the coachman and his family, but since the carriages hadn't been used in some time, and it sounded like Sandstorm was having financial difficulties, I wondered if the coach staff was even still here. I turned the handle on the door at the side of the house and found it unlocked, so I opened it and stepped in.

Sure enough, both the coach and the carriage were sitting in their places. Light shone in from the windows on either side, allowing me a better look at their state of readiness. I walked around to the front of the carriage to get to the covered coach on the other side and opened its door. It didn't squeak, which was a good sign. I reached in to run my hands across the seat but stopped when I heard footsteps behind me.

"Can I help you?"

I turned to find a middle-aged man about my height with brown hair combed to the side and some dark smudges on his cheek, possibly grease. He carried a large wrench like he was ready to wield it.

"Is Norell about?" I asked. "I'm Ayrion. I was a former chief of Sandstorm."

The man lowered the wrench. "Ah, the people here speak highly of you. I'm afraid Norell left Aramoor several months back. Had some family in Raine that died and left him a piece of land, so he and his family moved there." The man scratched the back of his head. "Wish I had such luck." He walked over and held out his hand. "Sorry, my name is Gittrick."

I looked down at his grease-stained palm and fingers.

"Oh, sorry about that," he said, and attempted to wipe it on his already-dirty trousers, then held it out again.

I shook it, then turned and pointed at the coach behind me. "Are they in working order?"

"Tip-top shape. I take my job very seriously."

"That's good to hear, because you'll be escorting His Highness back to the palace today."

Gittrick's eyes widened, and he noticeably gulped. "I heard rumors that the prince was here. Didn't believe them, though."

"More than rumors, I'm afraid. How soon do you think you can have the covered one ready?"

"I can have her hitched within the hour. Will that be soon enough?"

"Plenty. But better make it two. I'd rather wait to make the crossing until after the morning rush, give people a chance to get to work."

"Good thinking. So, Ninth Bell?"

"That will be fine." I headed for the door at the side but stopped before making it all the way out. "It was nice to meet you, Gittrick."

He smiled. "You as well, Master Ayrion."

I left and headed back to the main house, meeting Bull on the way.

"I was wondering where you'd gotten off to," Bull said. "Doubted you would just up and leave with the prince still here."

"I was checking on the coaches to see if they were in working order. I met Gittrick. Norell and his family moved to Raine?" I had liked Norell. He had always been willing to listen when I needed someone to talk to and didn't want to bother Reevie or Sapphire.

Bull chuckled. "Yes. Kind of funny if you think about it."

I looked at him curiously.

"Raine's a fishing and farming community," he said. "Don't think Norell has ever done either. But to own my own piece of land, can't say I wouldn't consider doing the same."

"You'd leave Sandstorm?"

"Well, maybe not. But I'd at least consider it."

I smiled, and we headed back through the courtyard for the front of the house, where I found Sapphire waiting with crossed arms. I grimaced. What had I done this time?

"When are you leaving?" she asked.

"Why, you want me gone that badly?"

"No, but I want him gone," she said, nodding back toward the infirmary. "I'm sick of warding off his advances."

I grinned. "I would have thought that being wooed by a prince was every girl's dream."

She huffed. "Not that one."

"I was just talking with Gittrick. He said he can have the coach ready in a couple of hours. Is that soon enough?"

"Yesterday wouldn't be soon enough."

I tried not to smile. "I told Collen to let you know to keep out of the infirmary. Didn't he tell you?"

Her lips tightened, but she didn't admit to anything.

"The less he sees of you the better," I said. "The last thing I need is Dakaran demanding to stay longer."

"He can demand all he wants," she shot back. "But come noon, if he hasn't left, I'll toss him over the gate myself." A flash of a grin crossed her lips as she headed back inside. "Just keep him out of my hair," she called back over her shoulder as she marched down the open gallery toward the back.

I looked at Bull, and he shrugged.

"How is she doing?" I asked. "I figure I stand a better chance of getting an honest answer out of you than her."

Bull glanced down the way to make sure she wasn't still there. "To be honest, she's wearing herself thin. She's always taken on more than she can handle, and with Reevie now gone most days, working at the infirmary in town, and this looming war . . ." He sighed. "I'm afraid she's going to crash eventually. I'm doing everything I can to pick up the slack here at Sandstorm, but she prefers to keep all of Sandstorm's business endeavors close to the hip. I still don't know half of what she does."

I shook my head. "Sounds like Sapphire."

I completely understood. I was the same way, preferring to do things myself than to hand the tasks to others and risk it not getting done quickly enough, correctly, or at all. It was a shortcoming that I was still trying to overcome myself. Having Room Eleven there helped. I could depend on them to get things done. It might not be exactly how I would have done it, but I could trust it would get done, nonetheless.

I placed my hand on Bull's shoulder, which was above mine by a couple of inches. "Just focus on ways where you can help. Can't do more than that. If you need anything, you know where to find me."

"Where's that? The Cylmaran border?"

I groaned. "Fair point."

"We'll be fine," Bull said. "I'm sure we'll pull through like always. We haven't failed yet."

I patted his arm and started for the infirmary.

"Chief! Help!"

I turned back around. Bull was still at the door, and he looked outside to see who had called him, then turned to me. "I might need your help right now," he said and rushed out into the courtyard.

I ran after him, spotting a group of kids walking up the drive from the gate below. They looked to be carrying several of their own. We ran across the courtyard and met them at the edge of the drive. Three of the kids were being toted by the rest of the group, unable to walk on their own. Their faces were bruised and blood-streaked, with cuts and swollen eyes.

"What happened?" Bull demanded.

"We were attacked by Avalanche beaters."

I lifted one boy from the grip of those attempting to cart him back to the manor, and Bull grabbed another. There was still one more, and those toting him didn't look in the best shape themselves.

I looked around until I spotted Stringbean, who must have been on gate duty this morning. "Run ahead and tell Reevie to meet us in the infirmary."

The lanky teenager took off running for the house, and we headed after him, but at a slower pace to keep from jostling the injured kids. I remembered the time Stringbean had shown up at the Granary half-beaten himself to tell us that our pickers had been attacked.

"What happened?" Sapphire asked, rushing across the courtyard to meet us. "Jostlin? Triss?" The boys in question didn't respond, and she looked at Bull.

"They said they were attacked by Avalanche beaters."

Her face hardened, but she didn't say anything, simply grabbed the third injured child and marched alongside us as we made our way into the house and to the infirmary. Reevie was just rounding the far corner of the gallery when we stepped inside.

"Why is it whenever he shows up people need a physicker?" Reevie asked.

"Poor timing," I said and placed my kid down on one of the cots, while Bull placed his on the other. Unfortunately, the third bed was being taken up by Dakaran, who watched curiously.

"What's all this?" he asked.

"Sleep time's over," I said, and then started to lift the prince up to his feet to give his cot to the third child. I'd only managed to get him about halfway when his face paled and he suddenly spewed his breakfast.

I leaped out of the way, but not quickly enough to keep my boots from getting caught in the deluge, grumbling inwardly about the fact that my magic didn't warn me about things that weren't going to cause me physical harm.

"Get him back down," Reevie said. "He clearly still has too much tonic in him."

"Yeah," Dakaran said woozily. "I told you I was feeling dizzy. Are you trying to kill me?"

Collen helped Sapphire place the third child on the table on the other side of the room, then after speaking with Bull to the side, he rushed out of the infirmary.

"What happened?" Reevie asked.

"They were attacked by Avalanche beaters," Bull said.

"Again?"

I turned. "What do you mean again?"

Reevie looked at Sapphire. "We can't keep doing this. This is getting out of hand."

"What's getting out of hand?" I asked. "What's going on?"

Sapphire looked at the kids and then at me. "We might be facing a war of our own."

AVALANCHE

Chapter 5

EVERYONE OUT!" Reevie shouted. Behind us, the infirmary was filled with Sandstorm members, all wanting to see what had happened and to whom.

Bull shuffled everyone out to give Reevie room to work while Muriel began pulling bottles and canisters from the shelves as fast as Reevie called for them.

"The outside wounds aren't so severe," Reevie said. "But I'm worried about what might be going on inside. One of them has a broken arm for sure, the other possibly a leg." He looked over at the boy who was lying unconscious on the table. "And I don't know what's wrong with him yet."

The two boys who were still conscious groaned as Reevie went from one to the next, examining the damage.

I looked at Sapphire. "What's going on? Is this Cutter's doing?"

"He's pushing us," she said, "testing to see how far he can go before we respond. After he killed Kore and took over what was left of Rockslide and their compound, he managed to pen us in. We haven't been relying on picking for our daily bread, so we've been able to keep out of his way. But now he's sending raiding parties into our territory to see how close he can get to Sandstorm before we respond."

I balled my fists, my tribal chief instinct kicking in. "How long has this been going on?"

She paused, then looked at Bull as though not really wanting to say.

"Since you left," Reevie shot back, not bothering to turn as he plastered some of his pale green salve on a cut over one of the kid's eyes.

Sapphire affirmed his allegation with a nod. "I think having you here might have been one of the factors holding him off. Knowing your relationship to the lancers, let alone the royal family." She glanced over at Dakaran. "It might have swayed his decision to keep to his own territory, but once news of your leaving had spread and it became apparent that you weren't returning, things began to change."

"Avalanche has the entire southern half of the city in addition to Rockslide's territory. What more does he want?"

"He wants it all," Reevie said, his back still to me as Muriel swapped Reevie's poultice for clean bandages.

"Cutter's had his eyes on Sandstorm since Noph made it such a lucrative place to be," Sapphire said, "but he'd never be able to handle the business ventures it takes to keep a place like this running. He seems to think that just being in Sandstorm Manor will somehow make him wealthy. He has no idea all I do around here to keep this place afloat."

"Like Reevie said," Bull added, "Cutter wants the entire city. Even back when I was in Avalanche, he has always schemed of ways to take over the tribes. If something isn't done about him, the lancers won't be the only ones marching to battle." He looked at the young boy lying unconscious on the table. "Melon isn't even a picker. He's a watcher. All three are watchers."

"How close were they posted?" I asked, my stomach knotting.

"Only a few streets north of here. I've already sent Collen to assemble the Guard and take a look."

I nodded. That must have been what they were talking about earlier, before Collen shot out of the room. I was starting to feel backed into a corner. It wasn't like I didn't already have enough on my plate.

Not only did I have the crown prince lying on a cot with a stab wound, and the larger possibility of getting a call at any time that the lancers were shipping out to war, but now I had to worry that my friends' lives could be in jeopardy, and it was partly my fault.

"I was planning on taking the prince back before Ninth Bell, but I think we'll wait and see what Collen has to say first. Besides," I said, looking down at my soiled boots, "it might be best not to move him for a little while."

I walked over to the injured boy on the left while Reevie worked on the other. "How many of them were there?"

The boy Bull had called Triss looked up at me with one eye, the other covered in gauze. "At least a dozen of them, I reckon. They snuck up behind us. Must have taken one of the alleys near Trunkin Lane. Didn't see them till they had us cornered."

"What happened afterward? Did you see which way they went?"

The boy shook his head.

"They're just kids," Dakaran said, sounding puzzled. He stared at Triss from the next cot over.

"Welcome to the life of a street rat," I said.

Was the prince so far removed that he didn't understand how things worked out here? Perhaps spending some time in Sandstorm would be good for him. Maybe it could help him see the struggles of those living on the streets. Perhaps he could help make a difference. His mother had done so. Her work raising funds for the orphanage and for the children's apprenticeships had been invaluable over the last few years, but there was more to be done.

For me, I had always wanted to find a way to put an end to the tribes, replace them with a few more orphanages that would give the kids a chance to get into good homes, or at the very least into stable work so they could provide for themselves. It was certainly more favorable than living in a tribe until they were too old, when they were eventually forced back onto the streets with no knowledge or capability to survive.

Most ended up in the Warrens.

I left Reevie to his work and headed outside, since there wasn't much more I could do but get in the way. I walked down to the front gate to wait for Collen. If there had only been a dozen from Avalanche, the Sandstorm Guard should be enough to chase them back to where they had come from.

"Protector, did you see what happened?" Toots asked, walking out to meet me.

"I did. Reevie is seeing to the injured now." I looked at the gate's bars ahead and the decoratively shaped S in the middle. "No sign of the Guard's return?"

"Nothing yet."

We walked down to the gate and stared through the bars to the empty lane beyond. The sun was rising, and its light shone through the trees behind us on either side of the lane, forcing me to squint until my eyes adjusted.

"Are you here to help?" Toots asked.

I took a deep breath, not sure how to answer. "I'll do what I can, but I can't stay long. I have other people that need me."

He looked up, disappointment in his eyes.

"Let's wait and see what Collen says when he gets back." I stared out at the empty road in front of Sandstorm, wondering if I should go take a look for myself.

"Any word?"

I turned. Bull and Sapphire were walking down to meet us.

"Not a peep," Toots said. "Good thing the Protector's here. If Avalanche tries something, they'll soon wish they hadn't."

I sighed inwardly. That wasn't exactly the kind of reputation I wanted, but I guess that's why they called me what they did. If it made them feel a little safer, that was fine with me. However, with me there or not, if Cutter was gearing up for some kind of full-on offensive, I wasn't going to be enough to stop it. Reevie and Sapphire were right. Cutter and Kore had always craved Noph's territory, and now that Kore had been dispatched and my focus turned solely to the lancers, there was nothing really standing in his way.

"I could hear your mind fumbling about from over there," Sapphire said as she stopped beside me, Bull to her left.

I smiled. "I was wondering if there was a way to warn Cutter off somehow, make him think we are more fortified or more dangerous than he believes."

"We?"

"I mean you."

"We can double our watches," Bull suggested. "Send beaters out with each patrol, but that will weaken our defenses here by thinning out our fighters."

"Which direction does Avalanche usually come from?" I asked.

"North," Sapphire said. "It's too far for Cutter to send beaters up from the Temple and across some of the more trafficked areas like King's

Way East. Easier to come at us with those he has inside Rockslide's old compound. Why? What are you thinking?"

"I might have an idea. Not saying it's a good one, but it might be enough to get Cutter off your back for a little while." I frowned. "Or it could potentially force his hand and make things even worse."

"Sounds risky," Bull said, not looking particularly thrilled.

"What in life isn't?" Sapphire said, then looked at me. "What do you have in mind?"

"I don't want to say just yet, but it might require getting the king involved."

"The king?" Both Sapphire and Bull stared at me with gaping mouths.

"They're back!" someone on the wall beside us shouted.

I looked through the gate to see Collen and a group of Sandstorm guards making their way up the street in perfect formation. With their purple-lined black capes and sure, disciplined movements, they looked as resplendent as any Elondrian Lancer. I smiled. It appeared my training hadn't gone to waste.

Toots opened the gates, and Sapphire, Bull, and I walked down to meet them.

Collen dismissed the Guard and joined us at the side of the gate. "We didn't see anyone," he said. "They must have already headed back to the compound. We did see where the fighting took place, and managed to talk to one man who saw the whole thing from his window. It sounds like our kids were cornered and beaten. The man was too scared to come down and try stopping them on his own."

"Can't blame him for that," Bull said.

"No," Sapphire added sadly, "but what will happen is that the locals will start complaining, which will bring an even stronger patroller presence."

"Would that be all that bad?" I asked. "Don't you have an understanding with them?"

"A limited one. That understanding, as you call it, takes a good bit of our capital each month. However, if the local residents begin feeling unsafe, our tentative agreement might go away."

"It may be better to simply talk with the locals yourself," I suggested. "Reach out, perhaps offer help when needed. Best to get them on your side before things get any worse."

She turned to Collen. "Do you think you could show me where the gentlemen who witnessed the ordeal lives?"

Collen nodded. "Take you right to his doorstep."

She released a sharp exhale. "Guess it couldn't hurt to try." She turned to Bull. "Grab my purse from the study, will you? Best way I've found to smooth ruffled feathers is with a coin in the hand."

"I'll be right back," Bull said and headed up the drive. Bull might be one of the chiefs, but Sapphire was clearly the one in charge.

Sapphire dismissed Collen back to his duties, then turned and looked at me. "Will you still be here when I get back?"

"Not if I can get Dakaran off his bed without emptying his gut. I really do need to get him back to the palace before people start asking questions."

She fiddled with her braid. It was the first time I'd seen her hair braided since arriving. "It's been nice having you here," she said, "even under the circumstances. Next time, don't wait so long."

I smiled. "I'll do my best to get by more often. I guess I'll just have to suffer Reevie's wrath."

"He does miss you. He just has a terrible way of showing it."

"I hope one day we can find a way to mend what's been broken. It will never be as it once was, but I certainly don't want to leave things as they are now."

"I think if you can find a way to help keep Cutter and Avalanche off our backs, that will go a long way. What you do speaks louder than what you say."

I turned and looked back up the drive, staring at the roof of the manor house, which was just visible between the trees. "As soon as I get Dakaran back into his own bed and out of your hair, I promise I'll see what I can do about Cutter."

"If whatever you are planning falls through, please send word. We need to know if we should be preparing for a battle."

"It wouldn't hurt to be ready either way. Get Collen and Bull working with the Guard and the beaters. And make sure to set up more active patrollers with the watchers, including beater protection."

She smiled. "I miss this. It almost seems as though you never left." She reached up and ran her fingers across my jawline, where my beard had grown in. It was currently longer than I liked, but still short and not quite unruly yet.

"Sorry," I said, feeling at the whiskers myself. "I haven't had a chance to trim it since coming back from the front."

"Don't," she said. "I like it." She stared at my face a moment, then finally stepped forward and hugged me. "We do miss you."

"Me too."

She kissed me on the cheek and stepped back about the time Bull arrived with her coin purse. Sapphire tied it to her waist, opposite her sword, then took one last look at me and headed down the road. Part of the Sandstorm Guard accompanied her.

I'd forgotten how good it felt to be on the receiving end of one of her kisses. I watched proudly, and with a fair amount of longing, as she headed off to deal with Sandstorm business. I wished I was around more to help, but I knew the kids were in good hands with her. I watched until her head disappeared behind the hill, then walked back to the house with Bull to see if Dakaran was stable enough to make the trip across the city.

Inside, I found Muriel looking after the newly bandaged Sandstorm members. They had managed to find another cot for the third boy, who appeared to still be unconscious, though I wasn't sure if it was due to his injuries or the strength of Reevie's tonics. He did have bandaging around his head, which led me to believe someone had taken a bludgeon to it. Those sorts of injuries could oftentimes be worse than a blade.

I walked over to Dakaran's cot. He was awake but not yet sitting up. "How are you feeling? Good enough to take a ride?"

He kept glancing over at the injured kids. "I think I can make it." He looked like he wanted to be anywhere else.

"Then I'll have them bring the coach around, and we'll see if we can get you in it."

The coachman was nearly ready. He already had the team half harnessed by the time I reached him. He even had the palace horse Dakaran had ridden tied off at the back. *Good man*, I mused. Thought of everything.

Now for the fun part: getting the prince out of bed and into the covered carriage without retching. Perhaps those extra tankards of spiced cider he had this morning might not have been the best idea.

With Bull's help, we slowly half-walked, half-toted Dakaran out of the infirmary and across the open gallery, out through the front courtyard and into the coach, where he immediately lay down on one of the seats, his face quite pale.

I hopped up on the opposite seat.

"Do you have everything?" Bull asked. Behind him, a rather large crowd was gathering to see us off.

I checked my blades—one on my back and the other at my waist—and I nodded. My chest tightened as I stared out the side window at all the kids. Most I had known since they were barely waist high. I didn't know what to say, so I simply waved as Gittrick slapped the reins and the coach jerked forward. We headed slowly down the drive, and I waved again as we reached the gate.

"Come back and see us!" Toots shouted, running beside the carriage as it passed. He stopped a little way down the road but continued to wave.

A slight burning at the corners of my eyes had me turning to look out the window so Dakaran wouldn't see my rise of emotions. Not that he was looking. By the time I looked back, his eyes were closed, and he appeared to be focusing all his energy on holding back another round of spewing. I wished I had thought to bring a pail.

We reached the end of the street, and the coach turned right. Dakaran started to roll, and I stood to catch him. About the time that I did, the coach door opened and two people quickly hopped inside. My hand went for my sword, but the space was too confined, and by the time I realized who it was, Kira and Po were already inside, seated on the bench behind me, staring.

"What?" she asked. "You didn't think we'd let you just leave without saying a proper goodbye, did you?"

"What's going on?" Dakaran peered through his lids. "Oh, it's just you."

"What do you mean *just me*?" Kira asked. "I remember a time when you were happy to see me. Very happy." She winked.

Realizing that I was still gripping my sword, I released it and sat on the end of the bench next to Red. "What happened to you two? Last I heard, you were heading to the kitchen for something to eat, and then you disappeared."

"Had some business in town that needed to be taken care of," she said, gently rubbing the knuckles on her right hand, which looked red and a little swollen.

"Should I ask?"

"Not unless you want me to tell you."

I sighed and looked out the window. "You might want to get out while you still can. We're heading all the way across town, in the opposite direction of the Warrens."

Kira smiled. "Suits me. We haven't seen the palace in some time. Master Stuck-up over there hasn't seen fit to invite us. Besides, I figure you might need help carting him up those dark passageways. He's looking rather peaked."

Dakaran groaned, too sick to complain, and I hated to admit it, but she had a point. I might need Po's help if Dakaran couldn't keep his legs under him.

"Fine," I said, "but stay in the coach until I tell you. And for the love of Aldor, try to behave."

She offered me one of her more alluring smiles, and I shook my head.

I had a feeling I was going to regret this.

We bounced along through mostly residential streets until we reached Circle Drive. I had told Gittrick to stay away from the more populated King's Way East and West, and instead take one of the bridges north of the Island. Circle Drive was the perfect course, except for the fact that it ran through Avalanche territory. I kept an eye on the streets as we passed, feeling a little safer once we crossed the Tansian River and started southwest for Avis. Circle Drive would eventually arc back around to King's Way West, but not until after we had skirted the busier Merchant District.

Dakaran groaned and complained each time the wheel hit a rough patch of cobble, jostling him and his nervous stomach.

"Whose idea was this?" he whined. "Whoever it was, they need to be tossed off the palace bridge."

"Keep up your complaining," I said, "and *you'll* be the one getting tossed off."

Dakaran moaned. "Where's your pity? I've been stabbed, remember?"

"How could I forget with you reminding me every couple of minutes? And I'd have a lot more pity if you weren't sneaking out in the middle of the night, waving your purse in everyone's face."

I did finally stick my head out the window and ask Gittrick to slow the team a bit more. Problem was, it seemed the slower we went, the more dramatic the uneven cobbles were on the coach, making it bounce even more. Ultimately, there just was no pleasing the prince, but it wasn't like I couldn't empathize. Someone had shoved a piece of metal inside him and left him for dead.

We reached the roundabout on King's Way West and headed right. I could see the gatehouse to the palace bridge looming in the distance.

"Do you think you'll be able to sit up?" I asked him, noticing the sweat beaded on his forehead.

Clearly, Reevie's medicines were wearing off and the pain was worsening. I hoped the palace physickers had something available. Dakaran was still carrying the small jar of pale green salve that Reevie had been covering his wound with, though I doubted the palace healers would be willing to use it, not knowing what it was or where it had come from.

The coach began to slow, and then pulled over to the side of the road as we neared Lancer Avenue. I looked out the window to see what was happening. I didn't see anything blocking the way ahead, so I stuck my head out.

"What's going on?" I shouted up to Gittrick.

As soon as the coach came to a complete stop, Gittrick turned. "Do I drive straight up to the bridge? What do I say when I get there? I've never had to take anyone across before. I don't know what to do."

I leaned far enough out to see the gatehouse. "You see that line in front of the bridge towers?" I asked, pointing to where the road ended at the foot of the long bridge. He nodded. "Just get in that line. You shouldn't have to say anything. I'll get out and do the talking. Coaches are hired to bring people to the palace every day. You've got nothing to be worried about." I offered him a comforting smile, hoping to soothe his nerves, and he finally turned back around and popped the reins.

As soon as we were within spitting range of the bridge towers, I moved across to the other seat to help Dakaran up to a sitting position. "We need you looking at least alive," I said.

Dakaran's face paled, and I quickly lowered him back down. "You know, maybe this will work too." I opened the door as soon as the coach stopped and hopped out. Behind me, Kira started to do the same, and I quickly put my hand out to stop her. "What do you think you're doing?"

"Coming with you."

"No, you're not."

Her face hardened.

"Or I'll tell them the prince is being held hostage by a couple of Warrens cutthroats."

She ran her hands down the front of her shirt seductively. "Like anyone would believe that."

I shut the door behind me before she could say anything else. We were about five back from inspection. Looking around, I didn't see Yorig anywhere.

Drat. I was hoping that—

Wait, there he is.

A tall, fair-skinned man stepped out of the gatehouse on the left, and I walked around the coach and waved him over, willing Kira not to follow me out. Yorig was even fairer skinned than me, and often on the receiving end of jokes from the other bridge guards about how quick he was to burn and yet never darken.

"Haven't seen you in weeks," Yorig said, his wide-brimmed hat keeping the sun out of his face. He smiled and shook my hand. "I was getting worried something had happened."

"I've been at the front for the last couple of weeks. Just made it back yesterday."

He looked behind me. "And you're out escorting coaches? I'd be at home curled up with my pillow if it were me."

"Oh, trust me, that's where I would be if it weren't for this one," I said, nodding back toward the carriage.

"Who you got in there?"

"You wouldn't believe me if I . . ." I laughed. "Sometimes I forget who I'm talking to." I motioned him over to the side of the coach and cracked the door open.

Yorig stiffened when he saw Dakaran lying there, and I shut the door again.

"Who are the other two?" he asked.

"Friends of mine who happened upon the prince last night and sent for me. I tried letting him sleep it off, but it seems he had a little more than I thought."

"I was wondering what happened to him," Yorig said.

"What do you mean?" I could feel my muscles tensing. Were they already looking for him?

"I was here when he rode out last night but never saw him return. Figured he was sleeping it off in one of the inns." He shrugged. "Been known to happen."

I nodded. "Yes, well, I've been tasked with getting him back to his own bed, and preferably without the king and queen knowing."

Yorig frowned and patted my shoulder. "Don't envy you none."

I sighed.

By this time, most of those in line ahead of us had already gone through. I waved Gittrick forward, walking beside the coach with Yorig.

"They're fine," Yorig said to the other guards who were walking over.

The palace sentries saw me and waved us on. I was at the palace almost as much as the garrison these days, when I wasn't being called to the front. Between my time training with Dakaran and my work with the Black Guild, I took at least half my meals here.

I hopped inside and tapped the roof for Gittrick to take us across. As soon as we got halfway over, I stuck my head out the window. "You don't need to stop at the gatehouse on the other side, just follow the road on around to the right, and we'll park over by the stables."

Gittrick nodded and kept the horses moving at a very slow pace. It was clear the man was nervous, having never been this close to the palace before. I remembered how nervous I'd been on my first visit. Of course, my first visit had consisted of breaking into the king's study and stealing the royal seal. Still, I was surprised the coachman was handling it as well as he was. I was also glad to see that he had thought ahead and changed into his official black-and-purple coachman uniform and hadn't stuck with his earlier work clothes. We might have drawn a few more curious eyes.

The coach pulled up alongside the stables, and I opened the door and stepped partway out. "Go ahead and pull all the way around the side. I'm going to get him out there."

Gittrick nodded and directed the team to the other side of the large two-story stone building, which had a long row of hitching rails down the side and enough space to turn the carriage around. As soon as he stopped, I stepped the rest of the way out. Kira and Po clambered out behind me. Bozz was standing at the front, and I waved him over. His head had been hanging out the front to see who'd just driven in. As soon as he saw me, he stepped the rest of the way out.

"Whose coach is that?" he asked. "Too fine for the garrison."

"Never mind whose it is. I need your help."

"With what?" he asked, slowing on approach, looking at Kira and Po suspiciously.

I opened the door. "With that."

Bozz looked inside, then grimaced. "Where's he been? I waited up half the night for him to return." He spotted the palace horse at the back of the coach and walked over and untied it. "I bet you're good and hungry," he said, patting the horse's neck. "Did they leave your saddle on all night?" He shook his head and walked the horse around to the side of the coach and looked in once more.

A loud bang and squeal, followed by men shouting, came from inside the stables.

"What was that?" I asked, spinning toward the front of the building where the noise was coming from.

Bozz huffed. "One of the new horses." He looked back inside the coach at the prince. "Will he be alright?" What he was really asking was: Would he—Bozz—somehow get blamed for all of this?

"He will be if we can get him up to his rooms without people knowing about it."

"My lips are shut," Bozz said, giving Kira and Po another scrutinizing glare, no doubt wondering if they would keep their mouths shut about the incident as well. "If there isn't anything more, I'm going to give this poor animal a rubdown."

I nodded, and Bozz walked the palace horse around to the front and into the stables. I looked up at Gittrick. "You can go. Just follow the road you came in on. No one will stop you on the way out. And thank the chiefs for loaning us the coach. You're an excellent driver." I fished out a silver from my purse, which I had in my pocket, and tossed it up to him. I figured the prince owed him at least that.

Gittrick smiled and tipped his hat. "Thank you, sir." He tucked the coin in his vest pocket and waited for us to drag Dakaran's limp body out of the carriage. As soon as he was out and the door shut, Gittrick tipped his hat once more, then, looking around, snapped the reins and slowly began to turn the coach in the paved lot beside the stables.

I tucked Reevie's jar of paste into my coat and scanned the road leading back to the bridge, along the open bailey between the bridge towers and the palace walls. There were several groupings of palace guards and staff moving about, which had me wondering how we were going to drag Dakaran across the road and over to the crevice in the palace wall without looking suspicious. Gittrick had just finished turning the coach and was starting to pass us.

"Go slowly," I called up to him. "And stay to the right of the road."

Gittrick pulled back on the reins and slowed the team, and I hefted Dakaran's arm up around my neck. Po did the same. "Come on. Help me get him in back of the carriage."

"What?" Kira asked. "We just took him out of it."

"No, I mean behind the carriage," I said, already dragging the prince's unwilling legs out from the stables. "We can use it to hide our approach." Behind us, the shrieks of a very unhappy horse echoed out of the stone building as we used the Sandstorm coach to hide our approach for as far as we could.

"I'm not feeling too good," Dakaran said, stumbling along.

"Hold it in," I countered. "We're almost there." The nook in the palace wall was just ahead to our right, hidden behind a row of thick bushes.

"Hurry," I told Po. "The carriage is getting away from us." By the time we reached the wall of shrubs, the coach had begun to pull away.

We left the road, and I guided Dakaran and Po to the edge of the ten-foot-tall hedge, Kira right beside us. I spared a quick glance over my shoulder. It appeared the guards in the bailey were focused on the approaching coach and not us. We reached the far edge of the bushes, and I peeked out.

My jaw tightened. There was a small patrol of guards heading our way. "Hurry," I said to Kira, nodding toward the shrubs. "The guards are coming."

She quickly pressed herself against the stone and slipped behind the bushes. "Come on," I told Po and started through myself, dragging Dakaran along with us. I heard the guards' boots on the cobbles, and Po barely tumbled through before the patrol started past.

Dakaran moaned, and I covered his mouth. Had they heard him? We waited. The footsteps on the other side of the bushes slowed but didn't stop. I waited until the rhythmic thumping of boots had faded entirely, then breathed a small sigh of relief and motioned to Po.

We carried Dakaran into the crevice between the two towers until we reached the side where the creepers grew across the stone, though they were little more than bare vines this time of year. Sprouts were just beginning to form, but the vines were still thick enough to keep the doorway and wall hidden from sight.

"He's not looking so good," Kira said.

"I know. We need to get him into his bed before he hurls again." I fished the key Dakaran had given me out of my pocket and handed it to Kira. She took it and pushed through the vines to the other side. I waited for the sound of the latch being released, then started through as well.

By the time we worked our way past the hanging wall of creepers, Kira had the door open and waiting on us. We had reached the entrance and started in when I heard Dakaran make a familiar noise from his throat, and I quickly turned him around and aimed his head out the doorway.

Dakaran retched, this time missing me and my boots.

"Gross," Kira said, holding her nose, looking quite pale herself.

As soon as Dakaran finished, I had Po help me get him back inside. "Here, hold him up." I quickly dug around in my coat for my flint and tinderbox and lit the lantern hanging on a peg to the left of the door.

With the lantern's aid, I took the key from Kira and shut and locked the door. Turning, we all stared up at the long circular climb of steps in front of us. This wasn't going to be easy.

"Let's get him up the stairs before he spews again," I said. Po was quick to agree and nearly yanked the prince's arm off as he headed for the first landing.

We climbed the stairs, one slow step after another, Kira toting the lantern while Po and I hauled the prince. We passed several landings, each with its own secret passageway that led deeper into the palace compound. I'd never tried exploring the other corridors to see where they all went and had often wondered what they had been originally intended for. Unfortunately, the distraction didn't help ease the pain in my legs or back from dragging Dakaran's body up half the palace.

We finally managed to get Dakaran up to the correct floor and down the corridor to the door that would take us to his bedchamber. Po and I were sweating quite profusely by the time we reached it. Kira hung the lantern on the peg beside the door and stuck her ear to the wood.

"Do you hear anything?" I whispered.

She shook her head, and before I could say anything more, she turned the latch and opened the door. She stuck her head out and looked both ways. "I don't see anyone."

"Then open it," I said, and I started us forward, stopped momentarily at the door to blow out the lantern she had hung on the wall.

"Everything's spinning," Dakaran mumbled.

I looked at Po. "Hurry." We maneuvered the prince out of the secret entrance—which was masked with a small built-in bookshelf—and Kira shut it behind us. We headed left down the hall toward Dakaran's chambers. I stopped just before rounding the final bend to make sure there were no guards posted outside. It looked clear, so we kept going.

"Open the door," I told Kira as Po and I maneuvered Dakaran in front. Kira reached for the handle, but the door swung open without her. Kira gasped and took a step back.

Queen Ellise stood in the doorway glaring at the four of us.

AVALANCHE

Chapter 6

HE QUEEN GOT ONE LOOK at her son's limp, pale form, and her face hardened. "What is going on here?"

I had hoped that once the palace physickers had seen to Dakaran that he could have kept them from telling the king and queen, but there was no hiding the truth now. Best to get it out and over with.

"We need to get him into his bed, Your Majesty," I said.

She moved aside, and Po and I hauled Dakaran in through his sitting room, heading for his bedchamber, which was on the right. Kira followed us in, trailing just behind.

"Did he sneak out again last night?" the queen asked. I could almost hear her jaw tightening.

"You know about that?"

"I'm the queen, of course I know."

Kira opened the door, and we carried him in and placed him down on the rather decadent four-poster bed. I steeled myself, then turned to face the queen. "You might want to send for the palace physicker, Your Majesty."

She crossed her arms and looked down at her son. "Let him stew in his own drunkenness. Perhaps, then," she said, raising her voice in case Dakaran was lucid, "he'll think twice about doing it again."

"He's not drunk, Your Majesty," I said. "He's been stabbed."

Her face went slack. "He's been *what*?" She rushed back through the sitting room and out the door. I could hear her shouting orders all the way down the hall to the guards stationed at the other end. After a few minutes, she returned. "Now, tell me what happened."

I relayed all the events I knew, starting with Kira and Po finding Dakaran in the alley, then fetching me, and us taking him back to Sandstorm for Reevie to tend to.

"I know the palace physickers would have been closer," I said, "but he needed the best help I could give him, so I took him to the one person who I believed could save his life. Reevie has healed wounds many physickers would have declared impossible. He was doing better earlier this morning, but the tonics Reevie gave him to ease the pain are beginning to wear off."

I pulled out the jar of green paste that Reevie had been using on the wound and placed it on the stand beside his bed. "I strongly suggest you continue to use whatever's in that jar. I believe it's what kept him alive."

Behind us, I heard footsteps hustling across the sitting room. We turned as a couple of the white-robed physickers rushed in. They bowed to the queen and immediately proceeded to Dakaran's bedside, shooing the rest of us out of the way.

I told them what I had told her as they began to unwrap the bandaging and inspect the wound.

"When did you say that he received the injury?" the oldest of the three men asked as he carefully examined the wound, wiping away the green paste to get a better look.

"He was assaulted last night."

Two of the men chuckled.

"You find this funny?" the queen asked heatedly.

All three men quickly bowed. "No, of course not, Your Majesty," the older physicker said, "but this wound was not inflicted last night. You see here? The skin closure is too extensive. I estimate four, maybe five days ago."

"I had dinner with my son last evening, and I assure you, he was in perfect health."

The three men looked confused and then started mumbling to themselves. "I don't know what to tell you, Your Majesty," the head physicker said, tugging nervously on his white beard. "I can't account for the regrowth of skin around the wound. I've been a healer for over forty years, and I can say assuredly no wound has ever closed so quickly." He picked up the jar of green paste next to the bed and looked inside, adjusting his spectacles, then took a whiff and handed it down to the next.

Queen Ellise looked at me. "It seems your precautions were warranted." She looked at the healers and pointed at the jar. "Make sure my son is given that as needed."

"Yes, Your Majesty."

"Also," I added, "the herbs the prince was taking for the pain are wearing off."

The old physicker stared at me over his spectacles. "Where did you acquire this . . ." He held up the jar. "This healing balm?"

I smiled. "From a street rat."

The man gaped at me.

I looked at Dakaran once more and the three physickers standing over him, then turned to Kira and motioned for her and Po to join me in the sitting room, which was larger than Dakaran's actual bedchamber. "Let's leave them to it."

The queen stepped out as well, shutting the door behind her. She studied Kira for a moment, then smiled. "Well, you have certainly blossomed into quite the young woman," she said. "Last time I saw you, you were just a gangly little thing."

Kira stiffened. "I have never been gangly."

"I see you also still have a penchant for speaking your mind." The queen looked at Po. "And you," she said, raising her hand about level with Po's shoulder, "were much shorter."

Po smiled awkwardly.

"I'm thankful the two of you were there," the queen said. "My son owes you his life, and I owe you a debt."

Kira's eyes brightened, and I could see the wheels already turning.

"I'm sure it was done out of honest concern," I said, giving Kira a harsh look, "and not for personal gain or the hopes of collecting on any future debts."

Kira smiled. "Of course, but one should not lightly pass over a favor from the queen."

The queen smiled. "She's one to watch out for, Ayrion."

I hmphed. "Don't I know it."

The queen reached into her handbag and pulled out a small purse and tossed it to Kira. "A token for your troubles. And I meant what I said. We owe you a debt."

Kira bounced the small pouch in her hand and smiled. "Perhaps one day I'll collect on it."

The queen turned to the front door. "Guards."

The door opened, and two men stepped inside. "Yes, Your Majesty?"

"Please escort our guests out by way of the kitchen. Tell the staff to make sure they are well fed."

Po licked his lips hungrily.

"Yes, Your Majesty." The two men bowed and stepped back into the hall, waiting on Kira and Po.

Kira glanced back over her shoulder at me. "Well, are you coming?"

"I've got business here."

"So this is goodbye again?" She walked over and surprised me with a full kiss on the mouth. I was too stunned to push her away. "I'll be seeing you," she said with a wink, then sauntered into the hall with Po trailing right behind.

The guards shut the door behind them.

"That girl's going to be a handful," the queen said, looking over at me with a smirk. "I hope you can manage her."

"I have no intention of managing her. She's not my problem."

The queen chuckled. "I don't think you'll have much of a choice with her."

I grimaced.

"Was there something else concerning my son that you needed to speak with me about?"

"No, Your Majesty. But if your favor would happen to fall in my direction, I do have a request. It concerns the street kids who took your son in last night and nursed him back to health."

"Oh?" She selected a chair near the hearth and directed me to one just opposite.

I sat. "As Your Majesty is aware, I grew up with the street tribes of Aramoor, and with Your Majesty's help, we have been able to find good homes for countless children. We've even been able to secure local apprenticeships due, in large part, to your patronage of the Bailey Street Orphanage."

The queen looked concerned. "Has something happened to the orphanage?"

"No, Your Majesty. However, my former tribe is in trouble."

She leaned back in her seat. "Sandstorm, wasn't it?"

I nodded. "Over the last several years, we have seen one tribe after another fall. Of the original five, there's now only two. My goal has always been to put an end to the tribes and funnel the children in them through the orphanage."

The queen folded her hands. "I don't see how your Master Fentin and Mistress Orilla could handle such numbers."

"Your Majesty is correct. We would need one or two more orphanages established for that to happen. But that's a problem for another day. My concern right now is that the other tribe, Avalanche, and its leader, will stop at nothing to hurt my former tribe and those living there.

"While I was there last night with your son, several of the children were carried in, beaten nearly to death. I have since learned that Cutter, the chief of Avalanche, has been moving toward an all-out war against Sandstorm. Apart from children dying needlessly, this is a battle that would take place inside an established community. The local residents could get caught up in it and hurt for something as simple as trying to aid a child who was being attacked. I certainly wouldn't want to see this happen."

"That is concerning," she said, staring at me a moment. "I take it you have something specific in mind to prevent this?"

"I do, but it would require the king's approval."

"Then why come to me?"

"Because of your personal connection to these children through the orphanage. I would imagine that the suggestion would carry more weight coming from you than from me."

The queen chuckled. "How very diplomatic of you, Ayrion. And here I thought your greatest strength was your swords."

I smiled sheepishly.

"What exactly is it that you wish my husband to do?"

I leaned forward. "Avalanche has expanded their territory by taking over parts of the fallen tribes. This has allowed them to box Sandstorm in from the south as well as the north. After one of the tribes known as Rockslide was dismantled a couple of years ago, Cutter sent part of his tribe there to pressure us from the north."

The queen pursed her lips. "You have chosen some rather interesting names for your tribes. All natural disasters."

"I'm not sure where the names came from," I admitted. "They were chosen long before my arrival in Aramoor."

She nodded. "Please continue."

"Part of Avalanche's tribe currently resides in an abandoned garrison on the northeast side of the city, not that far from Sandstorm Manor."

The queen looked thoughtful. "I remember when we consolidated those barracks with the main garrison. We thought it easier than rebuilding. I didn't realize there were kids living there now." She maintained her composure, but I could already see her mind at work as she stared into the distance. "What did you have in mind?"

"I would like the king to send the patrollers into the old compound and clear them out for good."

She thought a moment. "You do realize that will mean most of them will end up in the workhouses, don't you?"

I stared at the fire a moment before answering. "I wouldn't have asked if I didn't think there was any other way to try to prevent further bloodshed. Those in Avalanche have been given every opportunity to leave. Sandstorm was built on taking in rejects from the other tribes, which means those that chose to stay with Cutter have done so for their own gain, knowing who he is." I paused. "Perhaps we could send some of the older boys into the lancers and maybe give them a chance to turn their lives around through structured discipline. And if any of the younger ones are willing, we could give them the opportunity to go to the Bailey Orphanage."

The queen remained reclined in her seat, staring at the flames in the marble hearth.

"Whatever you decide, Your Majesty, I fear we don't have much time."

The queen took a deep breath and then stood, and I quickly followed her up.

"I will speak with my husband about your concerns, but I want you there as well to better explain the situation. I can only relay to him these facts, but you are the one whose passion has brought them to us. The king needs to see that."

"If you think it will help, Your Majesty, I'd be more than willing."

"Good. Then I suggest—"

The bedchamber door opened, and the two younger physickers stepped out.

"How is my son?" the queen asked.

They bowed. "He is resting, Your Majesty," the shorter man on the right said. "We have given him a potion for the pain, which will help him sleep. We have also reapplied the"—he glanced my way—"green paste to the wound. Senior Physicker Elriss is staying with him for now while we gather more supplies."

"Very good," she said, and they bowed once more and hurried out the front door.

The queen watched as they left, then turned. She studied my face. "It doesn't look like you have had much sleep yourself lately."

"No, Your Majesty. I just returned back from the front yesterday. I had been hoping to catch up on some last night and this morning."

"I hope you can keep from yawning while we speak with the king."

I smiled. "I will do my best."

With that, she headed out the door and into the corridor beyond. I remained just a few steps behind. From there we headed around to the adjoining hall. To the right, the outer hall ended at the king and queen's chambers, while on the left, it snaked its way down to the king's study.

She headed for the study.

We passed several doors before reaching one with two guards stationed out front, both carrying halberds. As soon as they realized she was coming their way, one of the guards turned and knocked.

"What is it?" the king called out from the other side.

The man stuck his head in. "The queen is here to see you, Your Majesty."

"Then why are you not opening the door?"

The guard quickly opened it and stepped back to allow us to enter. I followed the queen in, stopping partway to bow to the king. "Your Majesty."

The king stood from his desk. "Ah, Ayrion, just the man I wanted to see."

The queen cleared her throat.

"And, of course, I always want to see you, my dear," he said as he walked over and kissed her cheek. "That goes without saying."

She gave him a scrutinizing glare, and he smiled, then turned and looked at me. "I hear you have just arrived from the front. I'm supposed to be meeting with Commander Goring and Overcaptain Tolin this morning. Anything I should be made aware of beforehand?"

"Before you dive into politics and battle readiness," the queen said, "you might be interested to know that our son is lying in his bed at

present with a knife wound to his gut."

The king looked as though he hadn't quite heard her correctly. "What?"

"I said our son has been stabbed and might have died last night if not for a couple of Ayrion's friends finding him."

The king immediately started for the door, but she waved him off. "You might as well stop there," she said. "The healers are with him, and it appears that he will make a full recovery, thanks again to another one of Ayrion's friends. They have given him a tonic that should let him sleep for now, and he'll be out for several hours, I'm sure."

The king turned to me. "What happened?"

I once again went through the events that had transpired the previous night and today, not leaving anything out, not even Red and Po helping me carry him up to his room, though I did leave out us taking the hidden passageways to do it.

The king thumped the top of a nearby table with his fist. "That foolish boy. I wish I had kept him in the lancers. He was much better behaved there, little time for him to spend on his own vices."

"Not everyone is cut out for military service," the queen said.

"Unfortunately," he said, then looked at me. "It appears we owe you and your friends a debt."

"Funny you should mention that," the queen said. "Ayrion has spoken with me about a concern he has right here at home with the street tribes, namely the one that just saved our son yesterday evening."

I could only admire how well the queen guided the conversation. She had him right where she wanted him.

"Oh?" King Rhydan motioned us to some prearranged seats in front of the fire on the other side of the room, probably set for his upcoming meeting with Commander Goring and Overcaptain Tolin. Thankfully, the hearth was only partially stoked and the heat coming from it minimal. My back was already sticky under my coat.

"And what is this concern?" the king asked as he took a seat and nodded for me to do the same. "Not enough gold in the coffers to maintain the orphanage?"

"For once, our coin is not the concern," the queen said, though I wanted to correct her. Gold was always a problem. "It seems there is another war brewing right here in Aramoor. Ayrion's friends are coming under attack by a rival tribe that is seeking to take over the streets. Apparently, these attacks have not gone unnoticed and are escalating to the point that local citizens are beginning to fear leaving their homes."

The king's face hardened.

Queen Ellise looked at me. "It might be best if he hears the rest from you."

I nodded. "Thank you, Your Majesty." She had done what I needed her to do, which was to gain the king's ear. I only hoped my arguments would be enough to persuade him. I began with my desire to see an end to the tribes and to move the children into stable living conditions via the orphanage. "We can't just keep leaving these kids on the streets. Most end up in the Warrens. As soon as they become too old for the tribes, they are kicked out with nowhere to go and no hope of fending for themselves."

"Lessening the supply of bodies for the Warrens' use sounds like a worthy goal to me," the king said, waving for me to continue.

I explained how the tribes had begun to fall over the last couple of years, leaving only two, and how Avalanche and its chief, Cutter, wished to go to war with my former tribe. I told of the children who had been attacked that very morning. "Avalanche has always been relegated to the southern half of the city; however, with the other tribes having fallen,

Cutter has sent part of his tribe to live in the abandoned northeast garrison, which isn't that far from Sandstorm's place of residence."

The king looked a little perplexed. "What is it you want from me?"

"I want to find a way to prevent this war and keep the bloodshed off our streets."

"And how do you propose we do that?"

I looked at the queen, and she nodded for me to continue.

"I'd like to set up a patroller raid to go into the garrison and weed out those living there. I think that will send a strong enough message to Cutter, to keep him at bay for the time being, and away from the kids in my former tribe."

"The very kids who saved our son last night," the queen made sure to add.

The king looked at the queen, then over at the hearth. Had I said enough? Should I have said more? Explained it better? The silence had me leaning forward in my seat, my back sweating even more.

"And what exactly would happen to these kids if we were to do this?" he asked.

I breathed a partial sigh of relief. At least he was considering it. "I told Her Majesty that perhaps we could fill some of the lancer ranks with the older ones. Creator knows, they could use the discipline, and perhaps those of the younger who are willing, we could send them to the orphanage."

"And those who refuse either?" he asked.

"If they are too stubborn to accept our offer, then I guess there's always the workhouses." I shrugged. "Better that than the Warrens. At least there, they will be fed and sheltered. We don't want them running back to Cutter and starting the cycle all over again."

The king sat back in his seat. "Give me a couple days to consider it."

I gritted my teeth. "We might not have that much time, Your Majesty."

The king stared at me a moment, and I wondered if I'd pushed too hard. "I have meetings most of the day concerning Cylmar," he said, "but I promise to have you an answer no later than tomorrow."

"Thank you, Your Majesty." There wasn't much I could do about it now except wait and keep an eye on Sandstorm, somehow.

"Now," he said, "tell me about the front."

The queen stood. "I'll leave you to your discussions."

"As soon as our son wakes," the king said, "come and get me. I wish to be there."

She smiled and headed across the room and out the door. The king watched her until the door shut, then turned to me.

"Where were we?"

I leaned forward far enough to rest my elbows on my knees. "The Cylmaran forces are swelling in number every few days. More and more tents are popping up along the front, and the river patrols are increasing. It looks like Overlord Saryn is expecting a confrontation, perhaps even hoping for it."

The king looked down and shook his head. "I was hoping for a way out of this that didn't require bloodshed. War is never a solution I wish to pursue. I would much prefer honest communication over the threat of violence, but . . ." He looked up, his face hardening. "If I'm left with no other option, then I will defend Elondrian rights to the end."

I knew he meant it. "Whatever happens, I hope it happens sooner rather than later. The whole city is feeling it. Merchants are raising prices, and people are stocking up as if they believe the war is on their very doorsteps. There's fear in the air."

The king exhaled slowly as he sat back in his seat. "I'm afraid conflict is a way of life. I just prefer not to seek it out."

"Unfortunately," I said, "it has the nose of a bloodhound and tends to find us no matter where we are." I looked up. "I don't wish to preempt Commander Goring's upcoming briefing, but I believe there's talk of Overlord Saryn himself coming to the battlefront. If you wish to pursue talks, now might be the best time before this conflict ignites into something too large to pull back from."

The king nodded. "I will speak with Goring and Tolin about it. Is there any other news?"

I thought a moment, but then shook my head. "I can't think of anything that they won't already relay."

The king stood. "Then I'll let you get back to your bed. I'll be sure to tell Overcaptain Tolin to give you the rest of the day."

I smiled. "I wish I had the time, but I must see to the Black Guild's progress. After being away for several weeks, I need to make sure they are still keeping up with their drills."

"Yes, how are they coming along? It's been a while since I've been through that part of the palace for a visit."

"It's been going well, Your Majesty, especially over this last year. I've even had to start turning away new candidates."

"That speaks well to your leadership."

I smiled. "Or to how many of the men wish to be invited to the palace to train. Or possibly are simply trying to get out of latrine duty."

The king laughed. "Fair enough. I guess if I had had the choice, I would have done the same. Still," he said, placing one hand on my shoulder, "your work hasn't gone unnoticed. I want you to know that."

His touch sent a slight chill down my arm, reminding me of my father's hand on my shoulder after winning the Tri'Nephrin, how proud he had been of me. "I'll do my best, Your Majesty."

I stood and started to bow.

"Oh," the king said, "I almost forgot. If you are around later this afternoon, I have something I wish to show you."

My curiosity was piqued. "I will be down in the training room with the Black Guild. Do you have a specific time you would like me to be here?"

"I'm not sure how long the meeting with the commander and over-captain will run," he said, thumbing his chin. "I'll send someone down to fetch you as soon as it's over."

"I await your word, Your Majesty." I bowed again and headed for the door. I grabbed the handle, then stopped and turned. "Is there anything else you require?"

The king had already made it back around to his writing desk, which sat directly in front of the large chifforobe that I had hidden in with Dakaran the day I snuck into the palace. "No," the king said, "other than to say thank you once more for my son. And be sure to thank your friends as well."

"I will, Your Majesty." I bowed and stepped out of the office.

AVALANCHE

Chapter 7

OW WHAT? I STOOD outside the king's study, trying to decide what I needed to do first. I had to meet with the Black Guild, but that wasn't until after lunch. I started walking down the wide hall, away from the royal family's chambers, toward the stairs down to the next floor. I had no idea what time it was, or how long it had taken to get Dakaran up to his room, let alone the amount of time I'd spent talking with the king and queen. I did know my stomach was rumbling.

Staring down the hall, I couldn't help but remember my first time in the palace. I chuckled as I stopped at one of the doors on the right, which was cracked slightly, and peeked inside. It was empty, so I pushed it open and walked in. Nothing much had changed over the last seven years. Three tables sat side by side in the middle of the room, left that way for larger meetings that the king didn't wish to hold in his study. I walked to the farthest window on the right and pushed it open.

The cool breeze was inviting, and I unbuttoned my coat to let some of it in. I stuck my head out the window and stared down at the narrow decorative ledge a few feet below and shook my head. How in the world had I ever made it all the way around to the king's study on that? It was a long drop to the cobbled courtyard below.

I had certainly come a long way since that fateful day. How many people were afforded the opportunity and privilege to simply walk into the king's study and sit down for a meeting, or have him clap them on the back and tell them they were doing a good job? At this point, I knew more about the palace than most of its attendants—me, a humble street rat and outcast Upakan.

I stared out across the courtyard below for a few minutes, enjoying the morning breeze before finally closing the window and leaving the room. My stomach growled once again, and my first thought was following the queen's earlier mention of stopping by the kitchen on the way out, but as I turned something else came to mind.

I needed a horse.

I took the grand stairs down to the main floor. I always felt somewhat regal as I descended, pretending I was someone important. I used to enjoy running my hand down the gold-inlay railing, but today there were several palace cleaners attending to each of the balusters, so I kept to the middle. Last thing I wanted was to earn their ire by leaving fingerprints on the freshly polished rails.

At the bottom, I crossed the checkered marble floors of the enormous foyer, listening to the echo of my boots on the polished stone, along with the dozen or so others passing by. I held my head high as I moved through the lobby, an Upakan street rat that had been granted admittance to the royal palace, one who the king had taken notice of.

The sentries opened the large doors on the far side when they saw me coming, and I nodded in their direction and headed through. I stopped on the steps out front and glanced up at the enormous stone sentinels standing on either side of the doors and those standing down at the front entrance, warriors seemingly guarding the palace from all intruders.

Taking a deep breath of fresh air, I started down the steps and around the giant fountain at the center of the enclosed courtyard, following the cobbled walkway through the open tunnel leading out into the bailey beyond. The bridge and gatehouse were just ahead on the right, but I needed a horse, so I headed left and around to the stables. Looking up at the sky, I was surprised to see how close to noon it already was. No wonder my stomach was doing so much talking.

Bozz saddled me up a fresh mount, and I left the palace, waving at Yorig as I passed the guard towers on the far side of the bridge. He was busy inspecting what appeared to be a cart of fresh vegetables and wasn't able to stop and chat, so I kept going. I held the horse to a slow trot as I made my way down King's Way West, stopping before reaching the bridge that crossed over onto the Island. Instead, I took a road to the right that ran alongside the river, following it all the way down to the Rose and Crown Inn.

There were only a couple of spots open on the hitching rails, so I quickly dismounted and took one to keep from having to pay for stabling.

I wondered how many of Room Eleven I might find inside. I spotted a couple of lancer horses, but there was no telling who they belonged to. The men from the corps who frequented the Rose and Crown were predominantly officers. But this was Room Eleven's day off, and having lived off rations for the last couple of weeks, I was sure they were eager to spend their hard-earned coin on a proper meal. I knew I was. I had been dreaming of Nippin's stuffed pheasant and creamy potatoes for weeks.

The elderly innkeeper greeted me at the door just as soon as I opened it and stepped inside. "Master Ayrion, it's been far too long." The skinny man was looking even more gaunt than usual, his cheekbones protruding unhealthily at the sides.

"It *has* been too long," I said, "and I plan on making up for it right now."

Nippin smiled as he stared at me over his spectacles. "That is exactly what I was hoping to hear you say."

"Please tell me they are serving my favorite today."

"For you, Master Ayrion, I will make sure of it. And while you wait, I'll send over some of our finest ale. Finest in the city, you know."

It was something he said every time I visited. He also happened to be right.

"Better make mine cider. I still have a full day ahead of me. Can't afford to be foggy-headed."

Nippin smiled. "Very good, sir." He turned and looked across the foyer into the common room, which was at least two-thirds full. "I believe you have a table already waiting on you near the front."

I nodded my thanks and headed inside. It wasn't difficult to see which table was for me. I spotted Barthol's head over the crowd, and by the time I was halfway across the room, could see that the rest of Room Eleven was there as well, drinking and laughing and looking ready to eat.

Barthol was the first to see me coming and waved me over. "What happened to you last night?"

The others stopped their conversation to turn.

"I told them you'd left," Gellar said, smoothing his deep-red beard, which today he was wearing in a single braid, "but I thought you'd be back."

"I thought I would as well," I said, taking one of the empty chairs at the back of the two tables that had been pushed together for the group.

"Tolin wasn't too happy with you not showing up for debriefing this morning," Waylen said, shifting his weight on his chair to find a more comfortable position.

"Especially after having just arrived from the front," Fipple added.

Stumpy sat quietly with his arms crossed and a smile on his face that made him look like he knew a secret but wasn't inclined to tell.

"So, who was at the gate for you?" Waylen asked, brushing peanut shells from the long, thin braid that he called a beard hanging from his chin. "Was it one of your street friends?"

"Sort of," I said, eyeing the nearest tables to see if any were close enough to be listening in. The table behind me was filled with several well-dressed gentlemen, seemingly too preoccupied with whatever business they were discussing to care about our conversation, so I turned back around. "A former acquaintance of mine found Dakaran last night in an alley outside the Fishnet."

Stumpy shook his head with a heavy sigh. "His drinking is getting worse."

"Should have left him there," Fipple groused, his topknot hanging loosely down his back. He'd finally overcome his fear of being seen with it, and now refused to cover it with his hood.

"I'm sure his proclivity for wine played a part," I said, "but that wasn't why they rode across half the city to come get me." I leaned in. "He'd been stabbed and left for dead."

"Stabbed?" Gellar and the others leaned in as well. After Dakaran's year with us in the lancer corps, and after joining us on our precarious mission into Cylmar, my roommates had grown rather attached to him. Experiences like that tended to build lasting relationships, which was the only reason I was telling them.

"How is he?" Barthol asked.

Gellar's mouth twisted. "He's not . . ."

"No. He's not dead. Though, if Red hadn't found him when she had, he would have been."

"Red?" Waylen tossed a couple more nuts in his mouth. "Isn't that the girl you went down into the Warrens after?"

I nodded.

"And she just happened to be passing by at that exact moment?" Fipple asked, one brow cocked in cynical fashion.

I grunted. "Trust me, I thought the same at first. But knowing Dakaran, I have a feeling he was probably waving his coin purse around a little too liberally."

"And a few of the seedier patrons thought they'd relieve him of it," Stumpy said.

Fipple grunted. "And then make sure he didn't talk by sticking a knife in him."

"Where is he now?" Barthol asked.

I filled them in on the events of the previous night, including the troubles Sandstorm was experiencing with Avalanche, and finished with my meeting with the king.

"If you need any help with this Cutter fellow," Barthol said, "just let us know."

I smiled. One thing I could say about Room Eleven, we stuck together. If one person had a problem, we all had a problem. "I'll wait and see what the king is willing to do first. I'm hoping the patrollers will be able to handle it without lancer involvement."

"Still," Stumpy said, "your friends have done right by us on more than one occasion. If they are in need of assistance, we'll be there to

help."

"Thank you," I said, bolstered by their support. I was quite proud to be a part of such a group. "If the need should arise, believe me, you'll be the first to know." I looked down at the empty table. "Has anyone ordered yet?"

It took a while, but our food was eventually served. I had a feeling the stuffed pheasant hadn't actually been on today's menu, which meant the kitchen staff had gone out of their way just for us. It helped when you were friends with the proprietor. Regardless, one thing was for certain: it was worth the wait.

Entertainment for the lunch crowd came by way of two instrumentalists, a gentleman and his wife who had been quite popular with the early afternoon patrons whenever I and my roommates had been here over the last two years. The gentleman played a lute, and his wife accompanied him with a fipple flute, which, strangely enough, was an instrument that Fipple disliked to hear. I wasn't sure if it was from being teased about the name or the sound of the instrument.

I personally found it rather soothing.

After the meal, we headed back to the garrison. I was hoping to catch Overcaptain Tolin before he left for his meeting with the king and let him know I had returned. I dropped off my horse at the stable and asked that they leave him saddled. I wasn't planning on being long. I could already see some of the Black Guild assembling in front of Barracks One, getting ready to head over to the palace for the day's training.

Working out the logistics of special training hadn't been easy, but with Overcaptain Tolin's help, we had managed to maintain a regular routine without too much interference with the everyday duties in the garrison. Those lucky enough to gain entry were excused from one exercise duty and one cleaning duty per day, which, as I'd mentioned to the king, likely explained the swollen ranks.

"I'm going to see if Tolin's in his office," I said to the others and started across the open yard toward the main building. A quick glance over my shoulder showed confused looks on their faces, as though they weren't quite sure if I wanted them to accompany me. In the end, they remained where they were in front of the stables.

I headed up the steps and into the main foyer of the office building. It was a large open room with hallways leading to the lower offices and a grand staircase leading up to the second floor, which was where Over-captain Tolin's office was located. I made my way across the room, many of the lancers nodding in my direction as I passed. It still felt strange to be recognized by them, especially when most were older than me. I was barely out of my teens, and I was already known by name within the garrison walls.

Then again, there was hardly a time when my name hadn't been spoken—though that hadn't always been in my favor. I remembered forcing a knife to Captain Henzlow's neck my first day in the garrison. I was only fifteen. As justice would have it, Henzlow hadn't made an-other promotion in the last five years and was eventually transferred to the east garrison.

I took the stairs two at a time. The sword at my waist bounced against my leg annoyingly, and I placed my hand against it to hold it in place. My other sword was still strapped to my back. At the top landing, I headed right, then took a corridor on the left that headed away from the balcony and back toward the overcaptain's office. I passed Captain Asa's new office on my way. The door was ajar, and he appeared to be pacing. In all the time I'd known the short but stout redheaded man, I'd never known him to sit longer than it took to finish a plate of food, and even then, he fidgeted the entire time.

If Asa was still here, there was a good chance the overcaptain was as well. I stopped outside Tolin's door and listened, but I didn't hear anything on the other side, so I knocked and held my breath. I waited for a few moments, and just when I was about to walk back down to Captain Asa's, someone spoke.

"Come in."

I exhaled and opened the door.

Tolin was seated behind his desk, poring over some papers, pausing only long enough to look up and see who it was. "Ayrion. Just the man I wanted to see."

I seemed to be hearing that a lot lately. I stepped in and shut the door behind me.

"I missed you at the debriefing this morning," the overcaptain said. "I hope everything is alright."

"In a way." I guessed I should probably tell him why I'd missed it. I figured he'd probably hear it anyway during his meeting with the king, as Tolin had been something of a mentor to Dakaran during the prince's brief stint in the lancers. "I was called away urgently on the prince's behalf."

Tolin groaned lightly. "What sort of mischief has he gotten himself into this time?"

"The kind that left him alone in an alley with a hole in his gut."

The overcaptain's head shot up. "The prince was attacked?"

"And left for dead. Though I doubt the perpetrators knew who they were robbing at the time." I expounded on the events of last evening and this morning. I was getting a little tired of the repetition, but I didn't leave much of anything out, except for how we got the prince into the palace. I even told the overcaptain about the situation with Sandstorm and Avalanche.

"Dakaran was extremely lucky to have been spotted the way he was, and that your street friends knew enough to come get you."

"Yes, the prince owes his life to quite a few people. Perhaps he'll have learned a valuable lesson from the experience."

One of Tolin's brows arched. "One can only hope." He stood and began to gather half the papers from his desk. "What all did you discuss with the king? I'm on my way to the palace now for a meeting with him myself."

I stood. "We talked mostly about my former street tribe, though I did tell him about the growing number of Cylmarans at the border. I also told him that there were rumors of Overlord Saryn coming to the front himself, which can only mean—"

"He's looking for war," Tolin said.

I nodded. "Perhaps. The king hopes to find a route toward mediation."

Tolin grunted. "Afraid he might be too late for that."

"Can't hurt to try if it means keeping us out of war."

Tolin snatched a few items off one of the shelves behind him and stuffed them in his satchel. "I'm sure the king will address it." He turned and headed for the door. "Walk with me."

We left his office, and I shut the door since his hands were full.

"How is the Black Guild's training coming along?" he asked as we started down the corridor. "If things escalate, we might need to field them, and I want to make sure they're ready."

Captain Asa's door opened, and he stuck his head out. "Is it time?"

"On my way down now," Tolin said.

Asa stroked his ducktail beard. "I'll be right behind you. Gotta find my good cloak." He disappeared back inside, and we continued down the hall.

"The Black Guild will be ready," I said. "Though I'm not sure what we are supposed to be ready for. It's not like we are an army unto our-selves. There's only about thirty or so in the guild."

Tolin nodded. "If the king decides he wants to attempt mediation, he will need a strong group protecting him on the front. Sounds like an ideal mission for the Black Guild. Were they able to continue their train-ing while you were away?"

"Yes. In fact, I was about to ride back over to the palace myself and see how they are progressing."

"Good," Tolin said, taking the balcony around to the main staircase. I followed him down, and we crossed the lobby and headed outside. A young lancer stood at the bottom, holding the overcaptain's horse. He saluted when he saw the overcaptain coming. Tolin would have saluted back, but his hands were too full, so he managed a head bob instead.

"Here," Tolin said, "help me with the saddlebag."

I opened the flap, and he dumped the items inside.

"Thank you, Nemeth," Tolin said to the lancer as he accepted the horse's reins. "I can take it from here."

The lancer saluted and headed for Barracks Three.

"They seem to be getting younger every year," Tolin said with a sigh.

"Either that or we're getting older," Captain Asa added as he de-scended the stairs behind us and walked around to where his horse was tied to the rail next to the overcaptain's. "I notice there was no one here holding *my* horse," he grumbled.

Tolin smiled. "I think you scare them."

Asa laughed. "Good!" He looked at me. "So, where were you during this morning's debriefings?"

I looked at Tolin, and he nodded as he swung up into his saddle. "I'll tell him on the way over."

"Thank you, sir." Leaving the two officers, I headed across the yard, noticing the Black Guild standing beside their horses in front of the stables, with Room Eleven in front. They turned and straightened when they saw me coming.

"Mount up," I said, still half a stone's throw away. The stable hand looking after my horse walked it out to me, meeting me just in front of the group.

"I made sure he was fed and watered, sir."

"Thank you . . . ?"

"Tudwell, sir."

I smiled. "Thank you, Tudwell." I really did need to try to get to know the stable's staff better. The man was taller and looked familiar, but I couldn't be sure. For all I knew, he was a new hire since I'd been away.

I swung up in the saddle, and behind me, the Black Guild mounted. They were quite the mismatched lot, all wearing some form of dark clothing, whether black or charcoal grey, or dark blue or green. One was even wearing a dusky red waistcoat. Without any formal uniforms, the men attempted as best they could to copy my look, though none had a long black leather coat such as the one I wore. There were a couple of longer coats in the bunch, though they were mostly made of wool. Some wore jackets and jerkins. There were even a few vests, worn over dark tunics.

Most simply wore a dark cloak.

Along with the clothing, they had taken to wearing two swords, some even attempting to get one strapped to their back. I would have been flattered if they weren't so clumsily attached. I could have sworn I saw one tied with rope. We were quite the sight, and no doubt, if ever called into battle, would be the laughingstock of our side.

I needed to talk with Commander Goring about the situation. The

Guild was new, and I hadn't wished to rock the boat by suggesting they pay for us to have new uniforms made. I also didn't wish to cause any animosity between us and our fellow lancers, but with the king personally requesting our presence, I didn't think it could hurt.

With a wave of my hand, we headed single file across the yard toward the gate. There was no need to stop and sign out or tell those on watch where we were going. A single nod and the sergeant was marking down our departure on his board. We rode up Lancer Avenue to King's Way West, and from there over the bridge to the palace. I didn't see Yorig this time. His shift must have ended for the day. He was generally assigned the early shift at the bridge.

Once across, we took the road to the right, through the bailey, and down to the royal stables. Instead of stopping out front to turn our mounts over to the stable hands, we rode around the left side of the building to the hitching rails.

Bozz looked frazzled, leaning against one of the open doors with his arms crossed. He had deep circles under his eyes, as though he hadn't gotten the best night's sleep, or any at all. He waved me over, and I dismounted and handed him the reins.

"I just wanted to make sure to keep this horse separate from the rest," he said, then led the horse inside without saying more. He was a palace horse, after all, and not one belonging to the lancers.

I turned to find my men gathered at the side of the building, chatting quietly amongst themselves. They looked eager to get inside and begin practice.

Another set of loud squeals followed by the thunderous clap of a hoof against a wooden stall had all the men looking toward the front of the stables.

"Sounds like Bozz has his hands full," Fipple said.

Some of the men chuckled.

"Fall in line," I called out, and we started up the walk toward the palace entrance.

Several of the palace guards rode by and snickered at our haphazard appearance. I turned and gave my men a look to make sure they remained where they were.

"I'm getting sick of their attitude," Gellar whispered just behind me.

"Love to put them in their place," Fipple added, earning a couple more grunts from some of the others.

More than once over the last couple of years, I had been forced to step in before an actual fight broke out between the two groups. It was always worse with newcomers, those not used to being jeered at for their makeshift attire. And apparently, it was still quite annoying for those who'd been here since the beginning.

Admittedly, I wasn't all that keen on it myself, but I had learned to put up with it, starting all the way back to my time in the Lost City, when the older trainees would make fun of me when I tried, and many times succeeded, to keep up with them. Even in the street tribes, I was the outcast, drawing all other rejects to me in turn. And then, on entering the lancers, I was the youngest recruit to ever step through those gates. This fact didn't land very well, especially when Overcaptain Tolin placed me inside Room Eleven.

One thing was for sure, I was going to need to talk to someone about uniforms. At the very least some sort of designated patch that could set us apart. I'd mentioned the patch idea to the commander before, but he always shot it down. He didn't want to break unit cohesiveness by separating us out any more than we already were. Those duties we were getting out of were being placed on the others.

I deliberated on when the best time to broach the subject would be as we headed into the enclosed courtyard, around the fountain, and up the stone steps to the great doors leading inside. Somehow, asking for more favors right before heading off to war didn't seem the best idea.

The sentries at the top of the steps opened just before we reached the landing, some notedly wagging their heads as we passed. I wasn't sure if it was out of jealousy for our special treatment or simply just out of the belief that because of the way we looked, we were somehow inferior. Either way, I tried not to let it get to me, taking extra care not to let it get to the others as well as I marched them quickly into the main atrium. The echo of our steps followed us across the reflective checkered tiles as we made our way to the right of the grand staircase and headed deeper into the palace compound.

I remembered getting lost a time or two inside these winding hallways when first setting up the practice room with Dakaran, but now, I didn't even have to think about where I was going, my feet directing me on instinct. The corridors widened and narrowed, depending on which direction we took, and the palace staff were quick to move aside when they saw us coming, quite used to seeing groups of armed men moving about the palace at all hours of the day.

Near the back, we headed down a final corridor and stopped at the third door on the right. It had been a while since I'd been inside the practice room. Weeks, actually, though it felt more like months.

"What are we waiting on?" Gellar asked impatiently, the men lined up behind us as I stared quietly at the door.

"Just wondering how many more chances we'll have to step into these rooms before we're ordered to the front."

"With any luck, more than we expect," Waylen said, shifting his sword a little higher on his bulging waist.

"I hope you're right," I said, then leaned forward and turned the handle.

AVALANCHE

Chapter 8

HE PRACTICE ROOM WAS set and ready for our arrival, as it usually was—a fire crackling in both hearths, several tables lining the right wall with trays of pitchers and empty mugs waiting to be used. Along the front were racks of practice weapons and benches for sitting and placing the men's gear during training. There were also several rows of shields stacked in the corner, of a different design from the typical lancer shield. These were about a third smaller, which provided more mobility but left the legs less protected.

It didn't take the men long to stow their gear and line up in three rows to begin warmups. The training space had been two individual rooms at one time, but after a well-placed word from me to the king, the royal architects managed to take down the center wall, giving us ample space to practice.

The men looked eager, some too eager, as they fidgeted from one foot to the other, peeking around others to see me. Room Eleven remained at the front. Most of the faces were familiar, but there were a couple that were not, which had me curious. I had Fipple begin running them through their warmups, taking only a minute or two to watch before pulling a couple of my roommates aside.

"Is it just me, or are there additions to the group I haven't seen before?"

I wondered if they had recruited more cadets without us knowing, or were they faces I simply didn't remember? It was hard enough keeping up with my roommates, let alone an entire guild of trainees I only saw a couple times a week.

Barthol leaned in. "Apparently, we lost a couple members while we were gone. Transferred to the east garrison."

"Transferred? Who'd we lose?" I tried looking through the faces to see who might be missing.

"Gilford and Elwin," Waylen said, playing with his long, thinly braided chin beard.

I gritted my teeth. "I need to have a talk with Tolin. I can't afford to spend this much time and effort training men just to have them up and transferred on a whim. What's the point in having a guild if there's no guarantee its members will be here from one month to the next?"

"From what I heard," Gellar said, "the men decided to fill the ranks while we were gone, thought they'd impress us by finding new members and having them ready for training by the time we returned."

"You seem to have heard a lot."

He shrugged. "Just keeping my ears open is all."

"And how exactly did they choose these new members?" Stumpy asked.

Gellar swallowed and lowered his eyes sheepishly. "By placing names in a bucket."

I groaned loud enough that Fipple turned from his drills to look, but I waved for him to keep going.

"Any of you know who the new recruits are?" I asked. "Their capabilities? Whether they can work with others?"

They all shook their heads.

"Great. Well, not much we can do now but keep an eye on them."

My roommates nodded, then jumped in line with the rest.

I took over from Fipple and spent the next quarter hour running the men through warmup exercises and stretching, something the lancers didn't do enough. Upakans were taught early in their training that it was the best way to prevent injury.

The two newer recruits, who were in the second row in the middle, were doing their best to keep up with the others, watching what those around them were doing and copying. The man on the right was about average height, perhaps late twenties, with dark brown hair. He had a strong chin and eyes that looked ready to learn as he studied those around him and tried to mimic their movements. The other, on the left, was a few inches taller, and quite thick in the chest and arms. He looked to be in his early thirties with brown hair that hung to his shoulders, though it was tied back with a single cord. He wore a dark scowl with teeth gritted hard enough to crack nuts.

After we were good and warm, I had Barthol run them through some basic drills with their practice swords as I walked around and provided further instruction. I didn't want to jump into the more advanced drills quite yet, what with us having been gone for the last several weeks and returning to find new faces in the group.

"Lower your elbow a little more," I said to one of the new men. He was the shorter, less gruff-looking man on the right. "You want to keep your ribs protected."

I watched the taller man beside him as he swung his practice blade back and forth with enough power to lop off an arm or two. He was putting so much effort into it, he practically spun in place with each swing. I wasn't sure if it was for my benefit or if that was the way he typically handled his weapon.

"Try not to spin so far," I said. "With a single-handed weapon, you don't want to pivot quite so much. Power is a good thing with two-handed weapons like the battle-axe and longsword, but for this, we want fast, clean strikes."

The recruit grunted, obviously not happy with me correcting his stance and execution.

I took a step back and watched the two execute their next set of blocks and strikes. The first raised his elbow again during his, leaving part of his chest exposed. The second spun so hard during his swing that he nearly hit the person next to him.

"What's your name?" I asked the shorter man.

"Tilson, sir."

"Nice to meet you, Tilson." I reached for his practice sword. "Do you mind?" He handed it to me, and I demonstrated the proper technique, keeping my elbow tucked in when I did. "When you raise that elbow, it leaves you vulnerable here," I said, tapping my ribs.

Tilson nodded, and I handed the sword back. Some people, like myself, did better when they could see it for themselves. The next time, he managed to keep the elbow down and smiled when he realized he'd gotten it.

The scowl on the second recruit's face said he wasn't going to be so easy to convince.

"Like this," I said to the taller man, pivoting my own waist, but only partway, as I replicated a strike to the midsection with nothing in my hands.

This time, the man exhaled loudly and actually rolled his eyes.

I groaned inwardly. This was going to be a tough one. It seemed there was always one or two who felt they knew better when they first joined. For all I knew, he was a fine swordsman, but *fine* wasn't going to keep him alive on the battlefield. I wasn't in the habit of training *fine* warriors. I was training these men to be elite.

I stepped back and watched the taller man block and strike once more, and again he nearly spun halfway around from putting too much power into the swing.

"We don't need to cut our opponents in half," I said. "You're over-working your arms, putting too much into it. It's going to leave you vulnerable when you spin too far and find your back open, or at the least bent over gasping for breath." I stepped forward. "Here, let me show you." I reached for his sword, and he pulled back.

"I think I know how to swing a sword," he said defensively.

"Swinging the sword isn't your problem. It's the fact that you're swinging everything else as well. You nearly hit the man beside you twice. I doubt he thanks you for that."

"No, he does not," the man to his left said, earning a sharp look from the new recruit.

"What's your name?" I asked the new recruit.

"Howell."

I noticed he didn't add *sir*.

"Well, Howell, the point is, when training with a single-armed weapon, you don't have to chop your opponent's head off to kill him. A single flick of your wrist will do it just as well, and doesn't require as much of your strength. You open the front of his throat and he'll die just the same. The goal here is to slice and cut, not chop and maul. You'll get plenty of that when working with the longsword and axe."

I stepped away to let Fipple continue the exercise. As frustrated as I might have been at the recruit, I knew me standing there wasn't going to be helpful, because no matter what I said, the man was stubborn enough to keep doing it his way as long as I was singling him out, so I headed back to the front and watched the group as a whole. I did my best not to appear to be staring at anyone in particular, but kept an eye on the new trainees in my periphery.

From what I could see, no one was having any real difficulty keeping up with the basic drills, including Tilson and Howell, so I had them pair up in teams and face off to begin working on their live striking and blocking. I had Waylen work with Tilson and put Fipple with Howell, knowing the former Southern Watcher would have no problem keeping Howell in line.

Again, I walked the room, giving simple instruction as it was needed, though there wasn't much required. It seemed they had retained our lessons well. Even Howell was doing his best not to swing quite as hard as before, but just enough to let me know he wasn't going to give in completely. I wanted to roll my own eyes.

After drills, we opened the room to sparring sessions. The men strapped on their protective guards, and everyone gathered in a large circle with their practice swords in hand. Everyone waited for Barthol to call out the first two names. As soon as he did, those he called stepped out and met each other in the middle to see who could claim the first three points.

Live sparring was the best way to apply the principles being taught. It gave me the opportunity to see where each of the men were in their training, their scale of progress. It also allowed me to jump in when I saw a specific problem and work to correct it.

Tilson was the first of the newcomers to be called into the ring, and he stood off against Shelmik, who was a two-year veteran of the guild.

Shelmik had a long face with a hooked nose and dark brown eyes. He was average height, a little skinnier than most, but quite agile with his blade. The two bowed as they faced off, and Barthol called the start.

Tilson was nervous, his movements stiff, as the two men circled. I could almost see him running through his drills in his head as he tried to determine what to do first. Shelmik was patient, letting the recruit find his balance before forcing the advance. He didn't push too hard too fast, testing the newcomer's abilities and resolve. Tilson seemed to be more focused on keeping his arm down than the placement of his feet, and soon enough he stumbled slightly, giving Shelmik the opening for a quick point with a swift jab to the front of Tilson's chest guard.

Tilson's footing had improved by the end of the third round. Though he still had not garnered any points himself, his movements had smoothed, providing him a better defense of his position. Shelmik had to work a little harder for that final point.

Several more matches were called, the men performing very well. There were a few that stood out as being better than others, but overall, it seemed the matchups were fairly even.

Barthol called out two more names. "Howell. Bulsby."

Bulsby was similar in height and weight to Howell, which no doubt was why Barthol had paired them. He had a round face with thick brows that shelved a set of bright green eyes. I was curious to see if Howell's claims could be backed up by his ability. The only way to put something like that to the test was in the ring.

Howell faced off against Bulsby, his sword up, a serious look in his eyes. Bulsby, on the other hand, kept his guard loose, his face blank, not showing how he felt one way or the other, which had Howell scowling all the more. Bulsby was an aggressive fighter, much like Howell, but one who I had helped early on to see the advantage of using speed and precision over strength.

Barthol called for the fight to commence, and Bulsby barely had time to take a single step before Howell rushed him. The new recruit shouted as he swung left, then right, then left again, putting as much power into the strikes as he could, clearly hoping to overwhelm his opponent from the beginning. I sighed in frustration. He hadn't listened to a word I'd said.

Bulsby deflected Howell's wooden blade each time, causing Howell to spin even farther as he swung all the harder. Howell chased Bulsby all over the ring, but Bulsby continued to repel the heavy-handed attempts, waiting for Howell to overextend himself. Just as soon as he pivoted a little too far, Bulsby took advantage of the easy point by tapping Howell on his exposed back.

"Point!" Barthol shouted.

Howell grunted angrily as he and Bulsby returned to their respective positions to start again.

Barthol barely got the word out of his mouth before Howell was once again lunging forward. Bulsby seemed to be a little more prepared this time and blocked Howell's attempted thrust to his midsection, elbowing him on the way by. The strike knocked Howell sideways, doubling him over for just a moment, but then he had his sword up and deflected Bulsby's quick attempt at a second point.

Howell immediately went on the offensive, not waiting to even recover his breath from where Bulsby had elbowed him. He was once again depending solely on strength and drive alone to gain the upper hand. Bulsby circled, blocking and moving, not letting Howell muscle through. Soon enough, Howell opened himself up, and Bulsby landed another point, this time to the chest with a swift thrust.

Howell struck the floor with his sword in anger, and before I could step in, Barthol called him out.

"We'll have none of that here, unless you want me to step into the ring." Barthol was by far the biggest man there by nearly a head, and even Howell didn't look like he wanted that to happen. "This is a place of learning," Barthol said. "Take advantage of it, or we'll find someone else who will."

Howell gritted his teeth but wisely kept his mouth shut as he tightened his grip on his sword. I could see this wasn't going to work. He needed a different sort of demonstration.

"Wait," I said, stepping in. "I want to replace Bulsby." Bulsby's head shot up. I could see by the way his thick brows hung over his eyes that he was wondering if he'd done something wrong. I shook my head. "I can see you've clearly been practicing in your off time."

"I have," he said, lowering his weapon.

"Barthol will make sure to give you another opponent to finish your round just after this one."

Bulsby nodded and walked out of the ring, finding a place within the surrounding circle.

Howell looked nervous but tried to hide it with his scowl. "Should I feel honored that the head of the guild wants to stand against me himself?"

I didn't know if I wanted to laugh or punch the man in the face. He was as defiant as they came, a clear candidate for the former Room Eleven, back before it had made a positive name for itself. Still, I remained where I was, not bothering to reach for a weapon.

"On the contrary, I have someone else in mind." Howell needed someone that he didn't perceive as being a threat, someone who could clearly teach him that you didn't have to be strong, or even have all your limbs, to be an excellent swordsman. I turned and looked at Stumpy and smiled.

He nodded and stepped into the ring.

"I can't fight him," Howell said, sounding almost offended. "He's . . . he's crippled. Wouldn't be a fair fight."

"I could beat you with one hand tied behind my back," Stumpy said. "Oh wait." He held up his left arm.

The men around the ring laughed, which had Howell's scowl turning into a snarl. "Fine. But I won't go easy on you."

Stumpy laughed. "Funny, I was going to say the same thing." He moved into place across from Howell, his smile still plastered on his face.

Barthol looked at me, as though wanting to make sure I really wanted to do this. I nodded, and he looked at the two in the ring. "Weapons at the ready."

The two men poised.

"Fight!"

Howell didn't rush Stumpy like he had Bulsby. Instead, he circled. He looked hesitant. I wasn't sure if it was because he didn't feel comfortable attacking someone who he perceived as being lame, or because Stumpy had gotten into his head and he wasn't so sure he could win. Perhaps he was afraid he might lose to someone with such a clear disadvantage.

Stumpy moved in time with Howell, circling like a cat, his feet crossing smoothly, his sword up and loose. He looked comfortable, which was clearly making Howell even more tense. The circling started to grow a little awkward as both men waited on the other to make the first move.

"I promise I won't bite," Stumpy finally said with a smile.

It was just enough to elicit Howell's response. His mouth tightened, along with the grip on his sword, as he lunged. His sword swung in a swift downward arc, and Stumpy didn't even raise his own to block. Instead, he ducked and sidestepped with a clear open strike to Howell's midsection—which he didn't take, enraging Howell even more, who then unleashed a volley of strikes, each powerful enough that if they had made contact, would have probably broken Stumpy's arm, even through the protective guards.

I was about to step in and call a stop to it, but one look from Stumpy and I held my place. Stumpy swatted and ducked, sidestepped and deflected, letting Howell get a little closer with each advance, waiting for him to slip up. The longer Howell continued his barrage, the lower his guard fell. His swings slowed as he expended everything he had to claim that point. The men standing around whispered amongst themselves, wondering if they should stop it before someone was seriously injured.

But I let it go for now.

Multiple times, Stumpy could have claimed a point, but he never did, giving Howell the opportunity to get it all out of his system, while demonstrating that he was the better fighter. The recruit was red-faced as he continued to hammer away at Stumpy's defense, completely unable to land a single solid strike against the man, no matter how hard he swung. Each time, Stumpy was able to deflect and parry with what appeared to be little effort.

At this point, Howell was growing desperate to save face. He started using diverting tactics, trying to fool Stumpy into believing he was going to strike one place and instead attacking another, but nothing worked. He was clearly standing against a far more skilled opponent. Finally, with nothing left to lose, he forgot his sword altogether and charged Stumpy straight on, shoulder first, looking to tackle him before he could get his sword up and around.

Stumpy spun at the last second and grabbed Howell's tunic. He kicked the big man's legs out from under him and sent him flying out of the ring, scattering several of the men as they dove to get out of the way. Howell landed on his face, and some of the men cheered Stumpy's success, though most watched to see Howell's reaction.

Howell rolled over, his face red, and reached for his weapon, which he had lost in the fall, but before he could grab it, Stumpy was there with the tip of his wooden blade at Howell's throat. He leaned over and looked down at the man.

"Just because I'm missing a hand doesn't make me less dangerous. Nor will your strength make you more so. If you want to become one of the Black Guild, you will need to be willing to listen. The only way that will happen is by losing the attitude. Trust me," he said, looking around at some of the others, "we've all been there at one time or another. The difference is that we realized it before it was too late."

I smiled. I couldn't have put that better myself.

Stumpy removed his sword from Howell's neck and reached down with his left arm, the one ending in a stump. "If you're willing to learn, then we are willing to teach. Sound reasonable to you?"

Howell looked up at the others, and the room grew quiet. He finally nodded and grabbed Stumpy's forearm and pulled himself up.

Oddly enough, the rest of practice went fairly smoothly. In fact, Howell seemed to stick close to Stumpy during the training, even to the point of asking for help on a few of his techniques. Stumpy had clearly won the man's respect, which would probably be good for both of them.

Tilson, too, wasn't shy about asking for help and feedback on his performance. Neither man was overly skilled, and if given the choice, they wouldn't have been my first pick for the guild, but what was done was done. I was willing to at least give them a chance to prove themselves. Still, I was going to need to talk with Tolin. I couldn't afford to lose any of my men. Hopefully he'd be willing to transfer the other two back, even if it meant me having to increase the Black Guild's ranks.

After practice was over, I dismissed the men, and they headed straight for the tables of drink waiting for them at the side. Barthol brought over an extra mug for me, as I was busy stacking the shields in the far corner.

"Smart choice," Barthol said, "pairing Stumpy with Howell." He handed me the cup. "Thought I was going to have to step in there for a moment with him and Bulsby."

"Yes, it did seem to work out, didn't it?" I took a drink of the heavily watered ale and glanced back over my shoulder to where Howell was chatting quietly with Stumpy at the side.

"What are your plans for this evening?" Barthol asked. "Today is supposed to be our day off, after all."

"My plans at this point are eating and becoming very well-acquainted with my pillow."

Barthol chuckled. "That's right. I keep forgetting you didn't get any sleep last night."

"Yes," I said sadly. "But before I go, I probably need to check in on His Royal Annoyingness. Then I need to have a word with Overcaptain Tolin about these transfers. Also . . ." I looked back at the door. "I've been waiting on a runner from the king. He mentioned earlier about having something he wanted to show me, but his meeting with Commander Goring must be running long."

Barthol frowned. "I was going to suggest we get some of that lamb and mint sauce over at the Fishnet, but after what happened to Dakaran, perhaps that's not the best idea."

"Eat where you want," I said. "I have a couple of friends I need to pay a visit to first."

Barthol scratched the back of his head. "And when exactly is it that you are planning on getting all this sleep? You've already suggested three different meetings for this evening, and that's not including supper or your visit with the prince."

I blew out my lips. "There's just not enough hours in the day."

"Not if you keep trying to fill them all. Would it hurt you to attempt to take some time for yourself?"

"If I can't get our guild members back, it might."

Barthol raised his mug in salute. "Good luck with that."

Once the ale was finished, the members gathered their belongings, and we made our way back through the palace toward the front entryway. In the grand foyer, I pulled them to a stop and told them I still had some business at the palace and would have to see them later. The guild left, all except for Room Eleven.

I looked at them curiously. "I thought you were going to get something to eat?"

"We will," Barthol said. "But first we have a sick friend to go see."

AVALANCHE

Chapter 9

I COULD HEAR RAISED voices on the other side of the king's study door as we walked down the hall toward the royal chambers. Apparently, their meeting was still going. I wondered what all they were discussing. Would Commander Goring attempt to talk the king out of going to the front to mediate a truce? If I were in his position, I might be tempted to do the same, especially knowing how untrustworthy Overlord Saryn was.

We continued down the hall, stopping shy of the king and queen's chambers, and took the last corridor on the right, which led around to Dakaran's rooms. I spared a passing glance at the inset shelves on the left, where I'd hauled Dakaran's limp frame out from the secret passage just hours before.

The guards opened the prince's door when they saw us coming. Normally, they would have questioned a group of armed men heading for

one of the royal chambers, but after having spent a year living with Dakaran on the garrison, the members of Room Eleven had been back and forth to the palace enough to be generally recognized.

I was glad my roommates had decided to come. I was sure Dakaran would be happy to see them.

"Has he had many visitors?" I asked the guards before heading inside.

The man on the left shook his head. "Only the physickers and Their Majesties."

"Any of them here right now?"

"Physicker Elriss was the last to leave, and that was about an hour ago."

I nodded and headed in, the others following right behind me. The guard who I'd been speaking with stepped in as well and shut the door. Whether we were recognized or not, Dakaran was the crown prince, and if anything were to happen to him, it would be on their heads, so they weren't about to leave him alone, not that they could have stopped any one of us if they had wanted to. Still, I was glad to see they were taking their job seriously, even if Dakaran hated having them there.

Light poured in from the open curtains and filled the sitting room. Most of the time Dakaran kept the curtains closed, as his chambers, unlike those of his parents', looked out over the stables. There was a warm fire crackling in the hearth on the left, and we headed past it on our way to the bedchamber. I stuck my ear to the door on the right to see what I could hear, but after a while I finally gave up and slowly slid the door open.

The room was dim, especially with no outside windows. Only the two sconces on either side of the door were lit, and a couple of candles on the table beside the bed. I couldn't tell if the prince was sleeping. I didn't hear him snoring, and from where we were standing in the doorway, I couldn't see if his eyes were open or not.

I looked at the others and shrugged, then nodded for them to follow me in. We made our way quietly around the right side of the bed where Dakaran was lying. Halfway down, I could see that his eyes were closed. I had a sudden flash of memory to another time I had snuck into someone's bedchambers. In fact, I'd infiltrated two in one night. I remembered the sheer panic in Senator Gerrick's eyes when he woke to find me standing over his bed.

I stopped near the head corner post and looked down at the prince. He seemed to be—

Dakaran's eyes opened, and he screamed when he saw us.

"Well, that was manly," Waylen said, rubbing his ears.

The guards charged into the room, their swords drawn, and I quickly raised my hand. "It's fine. The prince is safe. He was just startled for a moment when he woke to find us standing here."

Dakaran rubbed his eyes and then finally waved the guards out. "I'm fine, but next time wake me before letting any of these oafs in. Bad enough being attacked in the streets like a dog, but to be frightened to death in my own bed . . ." He looked up at us and frowned. "I have half a mind to toss them all in the dungeons for the night."

"If it means not having to look at your ugly mug," Gellar said, "then let's go."

I sighed. I doubted Dakaran had meant it, but it did occur to me that at least in the dungeon I might be able to get some sleep.

The two guards remained long enough to look us over one last time, then finally bowed and exited.

"What are you trying to do, finish me off?" Dakaran asked, attempting, and failing, to sit up. I helped him adjust some of his pillows so he could prop himself against the headboard.

"We just figured we'd come see how you were doing," Waylen said with a smirk, "before heading over to get us some lamb and mint sauce."

Dakaran frowned. "That's not funny."

"So, what exactly happened?" Barthol asked.

Dakaran proceeded to relay the events of the previous night, at least those he could remember. His mind was a bit fuzzy on the details, partly from the shock of it all, and partly from the amount of drink he'd consumed.

"I don't know which hurts worse," Dakaran said, "the hole in my gut or the ache in my head."

"Which just goes to show that you *can* have too much of a good thing," Waylen said.

Dakaran ignored the slight and smiled. "So, you all rode over just to see me?"

"Nah, we were already here," Fipple said. "Another training day for the Black Guild."

Dakaran's smile dropped.

"But," Stumpy quickly added, giving Fipple a cold look, "we stayed after to make sure you were fine."

"Yes," Fipple replied. "What he said."

I chuckled, then looked at Dakaran. "How's the pain?"

The prince pressed on the bandaging around his waist. "Manageable. They gave me a tonic to help with the pain and allow me to sleep." He frowned. "Which is what I should be doing right now."

"Fine," I said, raising my hand. "I think we can take the hint. They just wanted to come see how you were doing and wish you a speedy recovery."

Dakaran grimaced as he tried scooting back down in his bed. "And I appreciate it. Though next time, let me know you're coming, will you?"

I smiled and helped him lower his pillows back under his head. "I'll try to stop by tomorrow."

He nodded and sank the rest of the way under his covers as we headed for the other side of the room. "And shut that door," he said. "It's letting in too much light."

"Sleep well, Your Highness," I said and closed the door behind us.

Waylen patted his stomach. "Well, that was fun. Now let's eat."

The others voiced their agreement as we left the prince to his sleep and headed back down to the main foyer. We were nearly across the atrium's checkered marble tiles when someone called out my name from the second floor.

I turned to find a young boy leaning out over the balcony. He wore a typical runner's uniform of black pants and white tunic, with a blue vest and a fluffy blue hat. He quickly rounded the balcony and headed down the stairs.

I walked out to meet him. "What is it?"

"The king wishes to see you." The little boy was out of breath. No telling how long he'd been looking for me or where all in the palace he'd tried.

"Is he in his study?"

The boy nodded, and I thanked him and sent him on his way. I turned and looked at my friends. "Well, I guess I'm needed elsewhere. Perhaps I'll see you this evening."

Gellar hmphed. "Just don't wake us when you finally do show up."

I grinned sheepishly. "I'll do my best."

Barthol gave me a stern look. "Remember what I said. You've got to take some time for yourself or you're going to burn out."

I knew he wasn't wrong, but unfortunately, I just had too much to do. Too many people needed my help, some more than others. I thought of my friends at Sandstorm. "I'll do my best to get back at a decent hour," I promised, then turned and headed back across the atrium for the stairs.

It felt a little strange walking back down the same hall for the third time today. I stopped outside the king's study. "Is he in?" I asked the two sentries out front. "He's expecting me."

One of the men knocked on the door.

"Enter," the king's voice called out from the inside.

The guard opened it and stuck his head in. "Ayrion's here to see you, Your Majesty."

"Good. Send him in."

The guard took a step back and let me through. As soon as I made it into the room, I bowed. "Your Majesty."

The king rose from his desk and pointed me to the sitting area in front of the large fireplace at the back. "I was starting to wonder if I'd missed you." The sun from the windows on either side of the hearth, overlooking the back of the enclosed courtyard, shone bright through the half-drawn curtains.

"My apologies. After my practice with the guild, my roommates and I went to visit Dakaran." I waited for the king to take his seat before taking mine.

"Ah, and how is my son? I went by earlier, and he seemed to be in considerable pain. The physickers were working on a tonic to help him with it." He shook his head. "Can you believe my son actually refused their help at first and instead tried demanding another cup of wine?"

I frowned. "I'm starting to get a little worried about his overindulgence." Truth be told, I was more than a little worried.

"Yes. I threatened everyone with time in the stocks if I caught a single person trying to sneak him a glass." He looked at me, and I raised my hand.

"He won't get any from me, I assure you."

The king nodded. "So how did you find your men? Still in working order, I hope, after your recent absence?"

"I did, Your Majesty. They have kept up with their training while we were gone." I almost brought up the fact that I'd lost a couple of my men due to transfers but thought better of it. I could handle the issue myself. It wouldn't be fair to Tolin to go over his head. More importantly, I didn't want to put Tolin in a place where the king would seemingly have to correct him. Although there was a time not all that long ago when I would have relished the chance to stick it to the over-captain, those days were long gone.

"Did your meeting with Commander Goring and Overcaptain Tolin go well?"

The king leaned back in his chair. "It did, which is something I wanted to talk to you about."

"Oh?" I twisted in my seat. "How can I help?"

"Goring was going to speak with you about it, but I told him I would prefer to do so myself."

Several possibilities ran through my mind. Did the king want me to kidnap someone? Find him a bargaining chip to force Saryn to the table? Assassinate the overlord if the talks failed?

"As you know, I want to find a peaceful solution to this conflict with Cylmar."

I smiled. "The commander and the overcaptain weren't able to persuade you otherwise?" When the king gave me a curious look, I added, "Overcaptain Tolin didn't seem thrilled with the idea of you meeting with Saryn, especially considering he kidnapped our last emissary and thought to hold him and his wife for ransom."

The king pursed his lips. "True. Saryn has never been the honorable sort, but I think a face-to-face meeting would be preferrable to war. The commander, overcaptain, and I spoke at great lengths about ways we could mitigate the risk. One suggestion was having you and your Black Guild there as a protection unit for myself and those aiding me in the talks. It was actually Tolin's suggestion."

I released a short sigh of relief. I was glad to hear the king wasn't resorting to using my Upakan skills to force a successful talk. "We will do whatever we can to keep you safe, Your Majesty."

However, this did bring up another concern. "I do have a small request to present to Your Majesty regarding the Black Guild, especially if we are to be accompanying you during your upcoming peace talks. I probably should have brought this up with Overcaptain Tolin first, but since we are already here, I might as well go ahead and ask."

The king looked curious. "What sort of request is it?"

"As Your Majesty may be aware, my men have attempted to set themselves apart from the main lancer corps by way of their dress." I cleared my throat. "However, in doing so, they have become a bit of an eyesore and are continually ribbed by the palace guards every time they come and go from practice. They need a designated uniform. It's kind of hard to garner the respect of those around you while wearing a random assortment of hand-me-downs."

The king started to chuckle and raised his hand to his mouth. "Yes, I see your point. I'll look into the matter. Unfortunately, there's nothing that can be done about it at present. Even if I were to hire all the seamstresses in Aramoor, we wouldn't be able to have full uniforms ready to wear by the time we leave, certainly not of any quality I would want my lancers wearing."

"Of course, Your Majesty. I just wanted to present the matter while I had the opportunity."

"For now, perhaps it's best if we keep your men in their official lancer livery. As you say, we don't want to appear lax in our standards during a meeting of this magnitude."

"Yes, Your Majesty. I'll be sure to let them know." I knew they were going to be disappointed in hearing that. Wearing the black—or as close to black as their makeshift outfits could get—was a point of pride for them. Perhaps I could find another way for the men to stand apart.

Thinking about it all, it occurred to me that I didn't know when the king presumed this would happen, and I still had to figure out what to do about Cutter and Avalanche. "Does Your Majesty know when this meeting will likely occur?"

"I hope to set sail as early as next week."

"Next week?" I groaned inwardly. "That is quite soon."

The king's head cocked slightly to the side. "Is there a problem?"

I cleared my throat. "Your Majesty promised me an answer concerning use of the patrollers to weed out the old northeast garrison."

"Yes," the king mused, running a hand down the front of his beard, which had begun to pepper with grey. "I had forgotten about that."

Forgotten? I was a little stunned by the admittance, considering we had just discussed it. I guessed the king had a lot on his mind as well.

"Organizing a raid like that would take some days to prepare for, Your Majesty, and then there's the issue of what to do with those that are captured. I spoke with Her Majesty earlier about various places we could house the street kids in order to keep as many out of the workhouses as possible."

"Good," he said. "Then I will let you and her work out the details."

I grimaced. I doubted the queen was going to be happy hearing that the king had dropped this issue in her lap. I hoped this didn't impact her willingness to deal with the issue of street tribes. Her benevolence and that of certain members of the aristocracy had been one of the main things keeping the Bailey Orphanage afloat.

The king leaned forward. "If I give you a few extra days, how fast do you think you could set sail and meet me at the front? I don't want to postpone arranging a meeting with Cylmar for long. If Saryn gets word that I've arrived at the border, he could try to press for an earlier conflict."

I thought a moment. I was pleasantly surprised he was going to give me any time at all. A war with Cylmar was certainly more important than a battle between two street tribes, but it didn't change the fact that it was my family who was at risk, which made it just as important to me as the tension with Cylmar.

"If you're willing to give me a few extra days," I said, "I will find a way to make it work. Whether we finish or not, I'll be on the next transport out."

The king nodded and then stood, and I quickly followed him up.

"I mentioned earlier that I had something to show you." Without saying more, he started for the door.

I followed him out of the study and into the corridor beyond. What could he be taking me to see? Curiosity had my mind reeling with possibilities as we headed down the hall toward the stairs. Had the king commissioned a new sword for his use? I knew how much the king enjoyed his armament, but if he had such a piece, he would have already been wearing it, making sure everyone saw it.

The sentries outside the door followed us a few steps behind, both still carrying their halberds. I kept beside the king as we began our descent down several flights before reaching the grand staircase leading down to the main floor.

We started across the checkered tiles toward the front. I guessed whatever he wanted to show me was outside.

The guards opened the enormous doors on the other side of the foyer, and we left the palace, heading down the stairs and across the courtyard for the tunnel out into the bailey. From there, we headed left down the cobbled path in the direction of the stables. I was starting to fret that the king had discovered Bozz's role in letting his son out at night. What if Bozz had told him that I had been aware of it as well? A sudden chill ran down my back, and I started to sweat.

The closer we got to the large stone building, the more nervous I became. I spared a passing glance over at the king, but I couldn't read anything from his face. Behind us, the king's patrol had increased from two to six, having picked up a few more of the palace guards on the way.

"Bring him out," the king ordered before we'd even reached the front entrance. He looked at me. "I wanted Dakaran to see this as well, but given the circumstances, I guess that will just have to wait."

I saw some of the stable hands ahead, gathered near the doors, but I didn't see Bozz.

Did they have him somewhere inside? Were they questioning him? My mind raced. None of this made any sense. The king wouldn't have asked me to join him at the front if he planned on punishing me for his son nearly being murdered last night. Of course, he might not have known that I was aware of Dakaran's escapades until now. If Bozz talked, I might not be going anywhere, except perhaps the dungeons.

I scrambled to think of what I could say if he'd outed my involvement. I could tell the king that it was all Dakaran's idea, which it was. I could tell him that he had sworn me to secrecy, which he had . . . sort of. I could say I hadn't been around when it happened, which I hadn't, since I'd just returned from the front.

Who was I kidding? It didn't matter if any of my excuses were true. It wouldn't stop the king from tossing me in the dungeons if he thought I had played some sort of role in the near loss of his lineage.

The loud clap of a horse's hoof echoed down the cobbled floor of the stables, followed by an angry squeal. I looked up to see several men attempting to force an enormous black stallion out of its stall. One of them was Bozz.

I breathed a small sigh of relief, though still unsure what was going on. The only thing I was sure about was that was the biggest horse I'd ever seen. It reared, and two of the men holding its reins were lifted off their feet.

"There he is," the king said with a bright grin plastered on his face as he watched them pull the horse out of the stall and into the center aisle. "What do you think?"

I think I just lost a few years of my life.

The horse suddenly lashed out with its hind legs and smashed the stall door off its hinges, sending it slamming against the back of the stall.

I grimaced. "I think he looks dangerous."

The king laughed. "That horse is worth more than all the horses in the royal stables combined."

I gaped. The horses in the palace stable were highly bred and worth a king's ransom. What was so special about this one? I looked closer.

He had a beautiful sheen to his black coat and tossed his mane proudly as he reared and snorted. He even had long hair on his fetlocks, something not widely seen with most breeds. He reminded me of a pitch-black night, with a single strip of moonlight painted from his forehead down to the top of his nostrils.

"He's beautiful," I said, "but why is he worth more than your other horses?"

"Because he's Rymiran," the king said, like I was supposed to know what that meant. When he saw my confusion, he clarified. "They are a very rare breed of horse that lives on the Rymiran Plains just north of the Sandrethin Mountains. They are said to have been bred using magic, back before the time of the Great Purge."

"Magic?" I turned and looked at the horse.

The king started us forward but stopped a safe distance from the entrance, watching as the men continued to try pulling the massive animal out.

"It's said that these horses are very smart, almost intuitive with those that ride them."

"I'm surprised there are any left, then."

The king chuckled. "They are protected by the crown, and have been for centuries, going back to Torrin himself. They are also extremely difficult to catch, and even more difficult to ride. It's said they choose their own riders."

The stable hands had the enormous stallion almost to the entrance, fighting with everything they had to keep him under control. The tops of most of their heads barely reached his back. None were tall enough to even look over him.

The horse turned and kicked, sending one poor soul cartwheeling backward. I shivered. *You'd have to be crazy to try riding a beast like that.*

"My father owned one, many years back. Sadly, it was killed in battle. Resplendent animal."

"If they're so hard to catch, how did you end up with him?" I asked.

"Quite by accident, I assure you. Apparently, a couple of poachers netted him in one of their wolf traps, and when they realized what he was and were unable to break him, they brought him to Aramoor, hoping to make a sizable profit. The horse injured himself trying to escape, and when he was finally caught, one of the stables in town realized what he was and sent him here to heal. That was a couple of weeks ago." He looked at me. "I'd say he's recovered, wouldn't you?"

"I'd say he doesn't look very happy." I just realized the horse had been saddled. How had they managed that? "You aren't . . . you aren't thinking of riding him, are you?"

The king looked at me and grinned.

AVALANCHE

Chapter 10

"ARE YOU OUT OF YOUR mind, Your Majesty?" I asked, too worried for the king's safety to stop and think about how I was addressing him.

"No one has ridden a Rymiran horse in at least twenty years. I want to be the first."

"The first what? The first one he throws?"

The stallion reared again, sending the stable hands on the right side swinging as they tried to get the enormous horse under control.

I couldn't pull my eyes away from the beast. "This is a very bad idea."

"Hold him steady," the king said, as though they weren't already trying to do just that. Three more ostlers rushed forward to help, and they managed to at least keep the horse on the ground.

The king started toward them, and I stuck to his side, though reluctantly, willing the king to come to his senses before it was too late.

Yesterday I was worried I might have to return the prince's corpse to his parents, now I was worried it would be the opposite. This family was going to be the death of me.

I almost reached out and grabbed the king's arm to stop him, but thought better of it. I certainly didn't want either of us getting any closer, in case those holding the horse's reins lost their grip. I followed cautiously as the king made his way around the right side of the horse.

The horse reared up, and I gasped. This was madness, but it wasn't like I could physically force the king not to do it. *Please let the horse choose him*, I prayed silently, then held my breath as the king stuck his left foot in the stirrup and grabbed hold of the horn. The horse turned its head to see what was happening, and I got a sinking feeling in my gut.

The king steadied himself, then looked at me and smiled.

I gritted my teeth, and my hand slid down my leg. Before I even realized it, I was gripping the hilt of my sword. What was I doing? Embarrassed, I quickly released the weapon.

"Hold him steady," the king said as he swung his leg carefully up and over, taking the reins. As soon as they released the horse, the ostlers moved out of the way—and not a moment too soon.

The black stallion leaped completely off the ground and kicked. My heart stopped as I watched in horror while the king went up with him, holding on for dear life. At any moment, he was going to land on his head on the cobbles. I wanted to throw my hands over my eyes, but I couldn't move, spellbound by the horrific sight.

"Grab the reins!" Bozz shouted, and he and his men tried getting close enough to grab the straps, but the horse wasn't stopping. It continued to jump and kick, jump and kick. There was nothing any of them could do but shout for the king to hold on.

The horse leaped once more, spinning as he did. The king spun as well, but in the opposite direction. He flew out of the saddle, and my breath caught in my throat as he landed hard on the cobbles and rolled. I was thankful he hadn't landed on his head. Quickly, I rushed in alongside the stable hands to pull him out of the way as the horse continued to jump, his hooves coming dangerously close to stomping the king into the ground.

With help from the palace guards, we managed to drag the king out of the way and get him to his feet. The guards checked him over. I couldn't believe he hadn't broken anything. It looked like he'd landed on his arm. His thick velvet robes must have helped cushion the fall.

Behind us, the stallion—who was now free of his captors—stopped jumping and turned to look at the king and the men surrounding him. He lowered his head and snorted, pounding the ground with one of his powerful front hooves. He was angry. Worse, he looked like he was about to—

Sure enough, the stallion released a loud squeal and charged at the entire group.

I drew my sword and leaped in front of the king. "Stop!" I shouted at the horse, as if I actually had a chance of preventing something that enormous from plowing through us all. The weight of its hooves shook the ground under our feet.

The horse skidded to a stop directly in front of me, and my stomach leaped into my throat. He looked at my sword and then at me. Our eyes met, and I felt a strange sensation, like he was looking inside of me, as though he knew me. It was an awkward sensation, like my insides were being scrubbed with sand. My body tingled from head to toe, and a vague feeling of befuddled anger washed over me. But something about it didn't feel right, like it wasn't me. It was like I could suddenly *feel* the horse's thoughts.

It must have surprised him as well, because instead of crushing me to death, he just stood there staring, his big black eyes boring into my own. Finally, he leaned his head forward and sniffed me.

I heard movement behind me, but I didn't dare turn my head to look. Instead, I slowly lifted my hand and waved them back. Soft footsteps from behind told me the men were easing backward, giving me and the giant animal some room. I kept my eyes focused on the horse's and slowly sheathed my blade, trying my best not to look frightened. Somehow, I had the feeling the horse could already sense that I was. I, in turn, thought he seemed more curious than anything.

I held out my hand for him, which he sniffed, then shook his head and blew out his lips. His earlier anger and fear appeared to be abating, and his body relaxed as he continued to look me over, shaking his head and snorting. I guessed I needed to say something, but I wasn't sure what.

"You are a very beautiful animal." It wasn't exactly the grandest of introductions, but it was the best I could do on short notice with a ferocious animal staring down at me.

The horse lifted its head proudly. He was tall enough to actually block the setting sun from my face, casting a long shadow across the cobbles behind me, all the way back to where the king and those surrounding him were standing.

I took a deep breath and dared a small step forward. "I'm not going to hurt you," I said softly. "There's no need to be afraid." I kept my hand held out, sliding my feet forward as I did.

The horse leaned down with its long muscular neck and nuzzled my palm. I smiled, feeling a sudden sense of kinship with the animal. I ran my hand up along the white patch of hair toward his forehead. He nickered, and I relaxed a little more. The horse turned his head to allow me to run my hands down his neck, even going so far as to let me stroke one of his ears.

I looked at the men behind me and smiled. "I think he'll be fine now. He was just scared." I looked up at the giant animal and smiled. "Weren't you, boy?"

He shook his mane.

"It seems the horse has chosen his rider," the king said disappointedly as he and the rest of the men slowly made their way forward.

"He chose me?" I asked, feeling awkward about the whole situation. The king had wanted the horse to choose him, but such a rare and beautiful animal had picked me, a street rat. I looked at the king. "Maybe he can choose again."

"Afraid it doesn't work like that. At least from what I've read. Once chosen, that bond is for life."

"Is that what I'm feeling right now?"

The king looked at me for a moment, then back at the horse. "I don't know. What does it feel like?"

"It's very strange, like someone's watching me. The hair on the back of my neck keeps wanting to stand. I think I can feel what he's feeling."

The king stared at the giant animal, some of the longing he was trying to mask slipping through. "What does he feel right now?"

"Nervous, I think, but also curious. I don't think he knows what's going on any more than I do."

The king pursed his lips, taking a step back and looking at the two of us. He finally nodded. "It's done. We will consider him payment for the life of my son."

I turned. "You're giving him to me?"

"It would seem I have little choice, now that the horse has bonded with you. It would be cruel to simply toss him back out in the plains now that he has chosen a rider."

"I think he will let you ride him now," I said to the king. I looked up at the horse. "Right? You won't throw him again, will you?"

The horse snorted, but I could feel him agree. "Would you like to try again, Your Majesty?"

The king looked at the horse, then back at me. "I think I've had enough riding for one day," he said, rubbing his backside. "I'm going to need to soak in a hot tub for the next couple of days just to survive the last attempt." He looked at the animal and then shook his head. "Pity." He turned to Bozz. "Take good care of him."

The royal ostler bowed. "You have my word, Your Majesty."

"And he will know if you haven't," the king said, pointing at me. "The horse will tell him."

Bozz looked as surprised as me, but quickly nodded that he understood.

The king turned and gave the giant horse one last look. "A king's ransom for a future king's life." He sighed and then headed back to the palace. He stopped after a few yards and glanced over his shoulder at me. "Make sure to name him well."

I bowed. "Yes, Your Majesty."

The king turned and continued on up the cobbled roadway, flanked on three sides by the palace guards.

I patted the horse's neck once more, looking up into his left eye. I had no idea what to name him. "You got any ideas? How about Midnight?"

The horse shook his head and even went so far as to stick out his tongue.

"Guess not."

"That is quite the gift," Bozz said, keeping his distance from the animal, but admiring him all the same. "Worth more than some of these nobles' entire estates."

I looked up at the horse, still having trouble believing he was mine.

I'd never owned anything of real value in my life, apart from my coat and Noph's sword. Granted, I had lived fairly comfortably inside of Sandstorm while I was there, but it wasn't like I could say that I owned it.

The sun was already going down, the evening colors waning in the sky. I couldn't believe how fast the day had gone—the morning spent trying to get Dakaran back to the palace, then lunch with Room Eleven, then the afternoon with the Black Guild, and then checking in on the prince and my meeting with the king, and now being gifted an extremely rare and valuable horse.

I shook my head. "There just aren't enough hours in the day, my friend."

The horse cocked his head at me and gave me a quizzical look.

Behind me, Bozz ushered the rest of the stable hands back to their duties, then leaned against the front of the stables and watched, waiting to see what I was going to do with my newfound gift.

I still had to meet with Tolin about getting my men transferred back, and check in on Master Fentin and Mistress Orilla, not to mention catch a bite to eat. The horse whinnied, and I looked up. "I guess you're hungry as well, huh?" He nodded his head, which left me feeling awkward. I was talking to a horse, and he seemed to understand, at least it seemed to me that he did. Maybe I was just imagining it all, what with the king talking about how rare they were, and how they chose their own riders, and that they had been bred with magic.

The sun had nearly dropped below the Sandrethin peaks behind the palace, its last rays hitting me in the face, forcing me to take a couple steps to the side and use the giant horse to shade my eyes. He was a monstrous animal. Never had I seen a horse so big.

"Well, what do I do with you now?" I didn't know if I should keep the horse here at the palace stables or take him with me back to the garrison and stable him there. I was almost too afraid to ride him. If he was worth as much as the king said, I didn't want to take a chance of him being stolen. But if I didn't ride him, what was the point in having him? Leaving him locked away inside a stall all day every day seemed cruel.

The horse snorted at me, as though agreeing.

Was he able to tell what I was thinking? I shivered. That was eerie. I rubbed my hand down his slick coat. "I think I'd better leave you here for now. You'll get better treatment in the *palace* stables, and certainly better bedding and feed, but I promise I'll come check in on you tomorrow. I promised the prince I'd stop by, so I could do the same to you." I pursed my lips as I looked up into his eyes. I still didn't know what to call him. What was a proper name for such a majestic creature? "How about Your Majesty?"

The horse blew out his lips and eventually shook his head.

"I'll give it some thought this evening," I promised, then led him back to Bozz, who stiffened at the horse's approach. Several stable hands walked over as well in case they would be needed.

"I don't think he'll give you much trouble now," I said, scratching the horse's chin and whiskers. I patted the stallion's neck. "I'll be back tomorrow."

The horse whinnied, and two of the groomsmen cautiously guided him back to his stall, his feet clopping heavily on the stable's cobble floor.

"I wouldn't believe it if I hadn't seen it with my own eyes," Bozz said, shaking his head as he watched the giant stallion being led away without the slightest reluctance. "You are a lucky man."

"Let's hope it holds out."

I left the stables on foot, having decided to walk back to the garrison, and made it through the main gate just before the stars began to appear. I figured my roommates were enjoying a plate of lamb and mint sauce right about now. My stomach was wishing I was doing the same. It had been a long time since lunch, especially after the intense workout with the Black Guild.

I headed into the main building and up the stairs to the second-floor offices. Captain Asa's door was shut, and there was no light underneath as I passed, but I could see a light under the overcaptain's door ahead, so I knocked.

"Enter."

I opened the door and stepped in. "Sorry to disturb you this late, sir. I was hoping to get a minute of your time."

Tolin looked up from his writing. "Yes, I'd like to speak with you as well." He pointed to a couple chairs at the front of his desk. "Have a seat."

I did and waited for him to finish whatever it was he was working on.

Tolin placed the quill down on its tray and reclined in his seat. "Was the king able to reach you after your session with the Black Guild?"

"He was. I'm just now returning from the palace."

Tolin looked surprised. "That lasted longer than I expected."

"Actually, the king had something he wanted me to see afterward. That's why I'm running late."

Tolin smiled. "So, what did you think?"

"Of what? The horse?"

Tolin's brows lowered. "What horse?"

Now I was confused. "What were you just talking about?"

"I wanted to know how your discussion with the king went about using the Black Guild as his personal protection."

"Oh, yes. It went well. I thought it an excellent idea, sir. I told the king we would do our utmost to keep him safe." I figured now was as good a time as any to broach the subject of uniforms. "I also took the liberty to speak with the king while I was there about the possibility of new uniforms for the Black Guild, especially if he is wishing to use us as a protection detail."

Tolin leaned back in his seat. I couldn't read his face, leaving me to assume the worst.

"I would have come to you first, but with the king there discussing the Guild anyway, I thought it best to go ahead and present the possibility."

Tolin nodded. "What was his reaction?"

"He seemed favorable. Although, he did say that for now it would be best if my men would don their normal lancer livery. I don't think he cared much for the idea of them wearing what they have been to a meeting with Overlord Saryn." I shrugged. "Can't say I blame him."

Tolin grinned. "No, I suppose not, though I do believe a uniform for the Black Guild would prove beneficial."

I smiled, glad to hear Tolin agreed. "It would be nice, though, if we had some small way of setting ourselves apart before this meeting. A patch or something."

"What kind of patch?" Tolin asked.

I shrugged once more. "I'm not sure. It doesn't need to be a patch, just something to identify ourselves with."

"What about those bands you and your street people used to wear?"

My head shot up. I hadn't thought of that. Leave it to Tolin to come up with a street tribe solution before me. "We don't have any black ones, though."

"I wouldn't assume that sewing some strips of material for your arm would be too time-consuming. I'll assign the corps tailors to it immediately. I'm sure we can come up with enough bands to fit thirty men."

"Better make it thirty-five."

"Lancer uniforms or not," Tolin said, "I will definitely feel better about the king going to the front knowing he has a protective detail there to watch out for him." Tolin looked at me and lowered his brows. "Now, what's all this about a horse?"

I waved it off. "It's nothing. The king had a new horse in the stables that he wanted me to see."

The overcaptain looked confused. Apparently, the king hadn't mentioned the Rymiran horse to him or the commander during their meeting, which I was surprised by. If anyone would be interested in a horse like that, it would be a lancer.

"So, what was it you came to speak with me about?" Tolin asked.

"While we were away at the front these past few weeks, a couple of my men were transferred." I cleared my throat. "To be blunt, sir, I've sunk a lot of time and energy into training these men. There's not much point in me continuing to do so if they can be snatched up at a moment's notice and dropped somewhere else."

Tolin took a deep breath and slowly released it. "This is the Lancers, which means we have to deal with ever-changing circumstances. However, I do see your point. I wasn't made aware of the transfers, but I'll talk with the commander about it. Do you know the men's names?"

"Elwin and Gilford, sir."

Tolin jotted the two names down. "Both good men."

"Might it be possible to get them reassigned back to this garrison?"

Tolin finished writing their names on a scrap of paper. "I'll see what I can do." He stared at me a moment. "When was the last time you slept?"

"I don't remember. I got some aboard ship. Sort of. Sailing the Rhunarin isn't exactly like riding the Shemoa River. Took me longer than I wanted to find my sea legs."

The overcaptain chuckled at my talk of sea legs. "Anything else I should know about from your discussion with the king?"

I shook my head, thinking back on what was said. "Oh, there is one thing. The king, as I'm sure he already discussed with you, wishes to set sail for the border by this time next week. However, he gave me permission to stay a few extra days to wrap up some business I have here with one of the street tribes."

Tolin's jaw tightened. "Yes, you mentioned your former tribe was having some difficulties."

I nodded. "I'm hoping to eradicate part of the problem by then. The king wants me to work with Her Majesty on solutions for placing the street kids once we take down part of their tribe."

The overcaptain shook his head. "Don't envy you that position."

"It's going to be more difficult than you know. Which reminds me, one of the ideas we had for relocating the older street kids was to place some of the older boys in the Lancers."

Tolin half-coughed, half-choked as he leaned forward. "I hope you're joking."

It was about the reaction I'd expected. "It did wonders for those of us in Room Eleven. I think it can make a difference for them as well. I'm not saying it won't be difficult—"

"That's an understatement. We've got enough on our plates worrying about a possible war with Cylmar. Last thing we need is a bunch of rowdy street thugs being dumped in our laps. To be honest, I'm not exactly happy with this whole situation as it is. We are on the brink of war, and the king is wanting to go to the front to broker peace, which means I need my best men there to help, not running around Aramoor cleaning up the messes of street kids. I thought you had broken from the tribes once and for all."

I was speechless as I sat across the table, staring wide-eyed at the overcaptain. I hadn't realized he still felt this way.

Tolin sighed and sat back in his seat. "I know how important your friends are to you, but with stakes as high as they are, neither of us need more distractions. Your sole focus needs to be here with us. Deal with this as swiftly as you can. The king's life and the future of Elondria could very well depend on it. I know that sounds a bit ominous, but if the king insists on showing up at the front, then we need to make sure he's safe."

I took a deep breath. "I didn't mean to add more to your plate, sir."

Tolin sat back in his seat, still looking flustered by the news of possible street rat recruits. He shook his head. "How do you always end up in the middle of everything?"

I smiled. "Lucky, I guess."

"Not any luck I wish to have," Tolin added. "I hope you are planning on turning in early this evening."

"Planning and doing are two very different things, I'm afraid."

The overcaptain looked down at the papers strewn across the top of his desk. "Don't I know it." He looked up. "Is there anything else?"

"No, sir."

"Thank the Creator," Tolin mumbled to himself.

I tried not to grin as I stood and bowed. "Thank you for seeing me, sir. If there's nothing else you wish from me, I have a few errands to run."

The overcaptain nodded. "Just so long as one of them is crawling under your blankets."

I smiled and nodded, then let myself out. Leaving the main building, I headed over to the stable to collect a horse. The garrison stable hands had one ready within minutes, and soon enough, I was heading out through the gate and back out on the streets. I pulled to a stop at the end of Lancer Ave, watching a few of the wealthier coaches returning to

Bayside after an evening in town.

My stomach growled.

"I hear you," I said, and patted it.

The streetlamps were lit. Their orange glow cast deep shadows across the wide King's Way West while I waited for a couple of pedestrians to pass before starting my horse out the main thoroughfare. I kept the horse to a slow walk as we headed east toward the Merchant District and away from the palace. About halfway, I turned us south on Circle Drive and kept going until nearing the lower tip of the Island. From there I simply followed my nose a couple of streets until I pulled to a stop outside a shop on the left and tied my horse to the hitch out front.

The sign over the shop read: ENDLE'S BAKERY.

It was late enough that they had already closed their stand out front and had taken what remained back inside. The smell of the bread and fruit tarts had me reaching for my coin pouch as I opened the door and stepped inside. There were still a few late shoppers, and it looked like Master Hubert's wife, Storella, was gathering up the leftovers that hadn't sold and wrapping them to sell the next morning at a discount, something those in Cheapside appreciated.

I looked for the tarts and happily found she hadn't stowed them yet.

"Master Ayrion?" a voice called out from the back, and I turned to find Hubert walking across the shop in my direction. "We haven't seen you in here for several weeks. Thought you might have been lured away by one of the other bakeries."

I smiled as I waited for the talkative baker to make it around the shelves and over to where I was standing on the far-right side. "No. I'm afraid I've been away. Just returned from the front early yesterday." It felt strange talking to Master Endle this way. I remembered our first meeting, in which he chased me up the street with a rolling pin, threatening all sorts of violence on me after I'd snitched one of his tarts. I doubted he realized the connection. I had gone out of my way over the years to give him and his wife as much business as I could to make up for it. Not that it was a difficult choice, given the quality of their breads and pastries.

The stout baker patted the front of his apron with his meaty hands and sent a sheen of white powder floating my way.

I sneezed.

"Sorry about that," he said with a warm smile. "Sometimes I forget how much I carry around with me. So, you've been to the front, have you? How bad is it looking? Do you see war in our future?" Hubert shook his head. "I hope not. The wife and I have been discussing it for weeks. Word on the street is that we are heading that way, though." He waved it off. "But you know how word is, unreliable at best, until it's not." He frowned. "I certainly hope it's unreliable now. Don't like the thought of war."

I smiled. "No, don't like the thought much either. I—"

"No, I reckon you don't," he continued. "We serve many of the lancers here, as you know. Good men. They enjoy our tarts especially. Don't they, dearest!" he shouted across the shop, but his wife was too busy with a customer to answer. Didn't seem to deter Hubert much, and he carried right on as if she had. "No, don't like it at all. All those young men going off to fight, many not returning, and those that do, not returning the same." He wiped his hand back through his hair, leaving a white streak of flour along the way. "No, don't like it at all."

Hubert took a breath, and I quickly took the opportunity to get a word in. "I was hoping to catch you before you closed. Had my heart set on one of those sweet cheese-and-honey tarts."

Hubert grinned. "Yes, they are a favorite." He walked over to a table behind me on the right and snatched up four of the better-looking ones from those that remained after the day's pickings and motioned for me to follow him to the back of the shop, where they had their table set for packaging customers' purchases. I hadn't wanted that many, but I refrained from saying so. He wrapped the tarts individually as I fished through my coin pouch. Placing the coins down on the table, I grabbed my tarts.

"You be sure to visit more often while you're here," Master Endle said as he walked me back to the front door. "How long exactly are you here for?"

"At least until next week."

"Not longer?" Hubert frowned. "Be sure to stop by before you go. I'm sure the missus and I can send a few tarts with you for the trip."

"I certainly wouldn't turn that down," I said and quickly took my leave before he started in on another topic of conversation. Master Endle watched from the door as I mounted and headed down the street. It was pretty obvious that the looming war was affecting more than just the palace and the garrison. The price of food was already beginning to rise, Endle's tarts being the latest example.

As soon as I had passed from view of the bakery, I unwrapped a tart and took a big gooey bite. The honey stuck to my beard, but I didn't bother licking it off until I'd finished the entire thing and was starting on the second.

The tarts, though not as soft and warm as they were in the mornings, were as delicious as ever, and I managed to polish all four of them off by the time I'd made it around the southern half of the Island and onto King's Way East. From there, I directed my horse up the east side of Circle Drive and then right on Bailey Street.

I hoped Master Fentin and Mistress Orilla were still awake. I had plenty to tell them.

AVALANCHE

Chapter 11

I SPOTTED A FAINT FLICKER of light coming from the front window of the Bailey Street Orphanage as I guided the horse around to the side and dismounted. I hoped that meant Master Fentin and Mistress Orilla were still up. It wasn't unusual for them to be up reading at this time of evening, though they would have more than likely sent all the children to bed.

I hadn't seen either of them since before I left for the front. Orders had come too quickly for me to do more than send a message that I would be gone. I knew they had been wanting to surprise me with a birthday celebration, but I ended up spending mine aboard ship on our way around the Elondrian coast.

I tied the horse off and took a moment to scan the surrounding homes. The street was well lit from the lamps, leaving the fronts of the three-story residences bathed in its warming glow. Most of the windows,

however, were dark.

"Protector, is that you?"

I turned to find two shadows stepping out from the back of the orphanage and making their way down the side toward me. I didn't even need my Upakan eyesight to recognize the tall lanky boy on the left.

"Collen? What are you doing here?"

"We are on our rounds."

"Rounds?"

Collen and the other boy stopped a few feet away, just inside the light from the streetlamp behind me. "Ever since Avalanche's incursion into our territories, the chiefs ordered a nightly watch on the orphanage. Cutter knows its connection to Sandstorm, and Reevie didn't want to take a chance on the same thing happening to them as Wildfire."

I nodded. "Makes sense. Don't you have other responsibilities at the manor, though?" I thought it strange that the captain of the beaters would be designated to watch duty.

"We all take shifts. I won't have others doing what I would not."

I smiled. Collen would make a fine captain in the lancers. I wondered if he'd ever given the idea of joining any thought. I'd have to mention the possibility to him sometime. "Well, carry on," I said, and even went so far as to offer the two a salute with my fist to my chest.

They both straightened and saluted back.

I left them to their work. Heading up the front steps of the orphanage, I knocked gently on the door, not wanting to wake the children who were already asleep.

I could hear muffled voices coming from inside just before the latch was thrown back and the door opened. Master Fentin held a lamp in one hand and a bludgeon—his cane—in the other.

"Ayrion?" Master Fentin's face brightened, and he called back over his shoulder. "It's Ayrion, dear."

Mistress Orilla's head shot out from behind her husband. As soon as she saw me, she cried, "Get in here and give me a hug."

I obliged.

"You are skin and bones," she said, pinching my cheeks. "Aren't they feeding you in that garrison? You'd think they'd make sure their fighting men weren't starving to death."

"I'm hardly starving, Mistress Orilla," I said with a chuckle.

"Oh, leave the boy alone," Fentin said, shutting the door behind me and ushering us into the family room on the left.

I followed them in. Fentin motioned for me to sit and then took a seat on the sofa beside the fireplace. The curtains in the windows on the left hadn't yet been pulled, and the light from the streetlamps out front cast long shadows across the floor. I took a moment to place a couple of extra pieces of wood on the fire from the stack beside the hearth before sitting. Unhooking the sheath from my back, I hung Noph's old sword on one of the chairs. I left the other at my waist, simply moving it out of the way as I went to sit.

"I'll fetch us some tea, shall I?" Orilla said and disappeared out of the room before I had a chance to tell her she didn't need to bother. Her head suddenly reappeared. "Don't go discussing anything important while I'm gone. I want to hear everything." She vanished again.

Master Fentin smiled and called after her, "We won't."

As soon as we could hear her footsteps shuffling down the hall toward the kitchen, he leaned forward. "She was quite put out when we got word that you and your men were leaving for the border. She had worked quite hard on your birthday party, you know. Even went so far as to force a promise from Reevie and Sapphire that they would be in attendance."

I lowered my head. "Yes. I wasn't very happy about it either. Trust me, I would have much rather been here than on a ship with several dozen lancers, but when the orders came down, we were given less than a day to pack and ship out, barely enough time for me to even send a messenger to let you know."

Fentin removed the spectacles from the bridge of his nose and breathed on them just before polishing the glass with his shirt. He seemed to be killing time until Orilla arrived, not quite knowing what to say that wouldn't be deemed important.

"How has the orphanage been doing?" I asked. "Are you still receiving your monthly stipend from the queen? I was just speaking with her this morning."

"Yes," Fentin said, placing his spectacles back on his nose, "the king and queen have been very good about getting us our funding. Wouldn't still be in operation if not for their generosity."

I was about to mention what the queen and I had discussed, but I thought it best to wait on Orilla for that. I glanced over at the entrance to the family room as I tried to think of something else to talk about that was mundane enough that she wouldn't be upset to miss.

There was one thing. "I stopped by Endle's Bakery this evening for my supper. Can't tell you how much I've missed those tarts of theirs."

Fentin chuckled. "It's been an age since I've had one. We were much closer to the bakery when we lived over on Meadow Way. Orilla and I would sometimes walk over from the book shop and get one of their pies. Strawberry rhubarb was always her favorite."

Before he could continue, we heard footsteps scurrying down the hall and turned to see Orilla shuffling in with a tray of drinks. I hopped up before she tripped over her own feet in her hurry and took the tray, placing it on a small table in front of the sofa.

"I trust you kept your conversation to the weather," she said as she took her seat beside Fentin and began pouring the steaming drink into the provided cups.

The weather. Why hadn't I thought to talk about the weather?

"Of course," Fentin said with a grin as he took his cup.

She handed me mine, and I took a moment to breathe it in. It had the faint hint of orange and cloves, and I blew gently across the top before taking a small sip. It was warm and soothing going down my throat, leaving behind the lingering sweetness of honey.

"So, tell us everything," she said. "Does it look like war?"

"More so every day, I'm afraid." It seemed it was the one topic of conversation on everyone's mind. "However, the king is hoping to find a peaceful solution."

"I pray he can," Fentin said.

Orilla placed her teacup down on the table and studied my face. "You look tired, Ayrion. You need to take better care of yourself."

I smiled. They were like the grandparents I never had. "There's a reason for that, unfortunately." I went on to explain why I hadn't been sleeping and everything that had happened to me since my return to Aramoor, everything from my rescue of Dakaran to meeting with the king and finding myself the proud owner of an actual Rymiran bred horse.

"That is a kingly gift indeed," Fentin said, placing his teacup down to once again rub at his spectacles. It seemed more to give his hands something to do than because they actually needed it. "I've heard tales of those horses since I was a wee lad myself. Never thought I'd know someone who actually owned one."

"And the prince is healing?" Orilla asked.

"He is, thanks to Reevie."

"I hate that it took something like that to get the two of you back in the same room," she added. "Those fences need mending."

"Easier said than done sometimes," I said, thinking about the dismissive way Reevie had treated me while I was there last night and this morning. "But I haven't given up. In fact, I'm working with the queen right now on a way to help keep Sandstorm safe for the time being."

"We've heard that Avalanche has been giving them a hard time," Fentin said. "I remember when those hooligans attacked me in my old shop."

"Actually, those were Rockslide beaters," I said. "Though, strangely enough, the ones that are causing the most damage now are those members from Avalanche that are currently residing in Rockslide's old compound. I've been working with the king and queen on a way to deal with them before they become more of a problem."

Fentin frowned. "I doubt that will set Cutter back for long."

"Yes, I know." I sighed. "But it is all I can manage for now."

"You've always wanted to be rid of the tribes," Orilla said. "It seems that goal might not be too far off. But as far as the Bailey Orphanage goes, I'm not sure we can house another influx of kids at present. We are at capacity. Ever since the fall of Wildfire, our beds have been full. Mind you, we've seen a great number placed in good homes, but we only have so much space, not to mention the extra cost of food. Prices have been steadily rising since news of the possible conflict with Cylmar."

"Yes," Fentin added, "the queen has been very generous, but I'm afraid we already need to ask for a raise in funding from the stipend for us to continue here. I'm not sure how we could take on more."

I frowned. This was a problem. "I guess I'll have to talk with Sapphire about whether Sandstorm can take on any extra kids there." I thought a moment. "I know we've talked about this before, but have you given any further thought about opening a second orphanage?"

The older couple looked at each other, and I could see the hesitancy on their faces.

Orilla smiled. "As much as we would like to help more of the street kids, Fentin and I don't have the strength to keep up with a second orphanage. It's taking everything we have to keep up with this one." She paused, then smiled. "We're getting up there in years, you know. The only way another orphanage could be opened would be additional funding from the crown and some younger hands than ours willing to keep it in operation."

I sat back in my seat and swallowed down the rest of my tea. It was barely lukewarm by the time I finished. "I understand. Honestly, I don't know how you've managed to do as much as you have." I chuckled. "Bet you're wishing you'd stayed in the book business."

Fentin laughed. "There've been times I've wondered." His laughter faded, and his face grew more somber. "Do you have any idea how you plan on weeding out the ruffians inside the old Rockslide compound?"

"Nothing concrete, but I will be discussing it with the queen tomorrow, so I had better get to thinking."

Fentin sat back in his seat and shook his head. "Dangerous business."

"I agree." I placed my teacup down on the table and started to stand. "Well, I will let you get to bed. It's getting late, and I could use some sleep myself."

"Yes, you could," Orilla said, allowing her husband to help her up. "And don't you stay up all night scheming about Avalanche either. You get in bed and get you some rest. You hear me?"

"Yes, ma'am." I started for the entryway, but Orilla stopped me and nudged Fentin.

"Don't forget the . . . you know."

Fentin's eyes widened. "Oh, that's right." He looked at me. "Don't run off just yet. We have something for you."

"For me?"

Fentin walked into the back study through the door to the left of the fireplace. It was dark inside the room, and I could hear things being shuffled about. At one point it sounded like he'd bumped his leg against a chair, or possibly his desk.

"You need some help in there?" Orilla called out, picking up a candle holder and starting for the open door. She'd barely gotten three steps when Fentin reappeared holding something that had been wrapped in a blanket. I couldn't tell what it was from the shape.

"We would have given it to you weeks ago," Orilla said with a smile, "but unfortunately you weren't here."

I joined them at the side of the sofa. "What is it?" I asked, staring at the bundle in Fentin's hands.

Fentin smiled and handed it to me. "Happy Birthday from all of us."

I accepted the package. It wasn't heavy. Whatever was inside felt flexible. What could they have gotten me?

"Well," Orilla asked, "are you going to open it?"

"Just trying to guess what it is first." I quickly unwrapped the blanket and let it hit the floor as I stared at the beautifully designed leather straps and silver buckles.

It can't be.

"How did you . . ." I stared down at the harness and double sheaths, still not quite believing what was in my hands. "I've had my eye on this for some time. How did you know?" I quickly unbuckled the lancer sword from my waist and laid it on the couch, then unhooked the single sheath on my back, the one holding Noph's old sword, and set it down beside the other.

"I don't understand," I said. "How did you afford something like this?"

The older couple smiled. "Sandstorm might have helped," Orilla said.

I was stunned into silence. Reevie and Sapphire had purchased this for me?

Orilla looked at me proudly. "No longer a teenager, but a man."

I grinned back. In truth, I hadn't felt like a teenager in years, especially since joining the Lancers. I quickly undid the straps so I could hook my arms through them. The double sheath made an X across my chest, buckling at the front to a three-sided piece of ornate steel, like a small shield at the center of my chest. My hands shook as I grabbed Noph's sword first. It was by far the better of the two, and I quickly tested my ability to place it in the correct slot. It only took once before my magic memorized the pattern. I did the same for the second, taking a moment to let the weight adjust on my back.

I walked around the room, enjoying the fact that for once I didn't have something bouncing against my leg.

"Well," Fentin asked, "what do you think?"

I turned, my eyes welling with tears. "I think it's one of the best gifts I've ever received. I love it." I snatched the older couple in a deep embrace and held them. When I finally let go, they were both smiling brightly. There may have been tears in Orilla's eyes as well.

"Hopefully it will come in handy in the days ahead," Fentin said, patting my shoulder.

I ran my fingers along the silver plate at the front. "I guarantee it will." I walked over and grabbed the empty sheaths from the sofa.

"Best you get a move on, then," Orilla said, wiping her eyes as she pushed Fentin toward the entryway. "Young man like you needs to get his sleep."

I hugged them both once more, thanking them not just for their generosity, but for having always been there for me and the others over the years. It wasn't until I was out the door and halfway down the front steps that I realized I'd forgotten to ask for one of her mystery meat sandwiches, which was one of the reasons I'd been looking forward to stopping by. And even though I knew if I walked back in and asked for one, Orilla would have obliged, I wasn't about to put them out. Besides, food was almost the last thing on my mind at the moment. I stared down at my new sheath, running my fingers across the metal buckle at the center.

I still couldn't believe it was mine. I knew how costly it was and how much gold Sandstorm must have given. I groaned as I reached my horse and slung the old sheaths around the saddle horn and climbed up. They must have been wondering why I wasn't wearing it last night. I hoped they weren't offended by that, especially with me showing up at their doorstep in the middle of the night needing their help.

I was going to have to make another trip over to thank them and explain why I hadn't been wearing it. I had to inform them of my intentions concerning the former Rockslide compound anyway, so I added stopping by Sandstorm again to my to-do list for tomorrow. Visiting Reevie and Sapphire to thank them for the sword sheath was just one more item to be added to the quickly growing list of things I needed to get done before leaving for the front. How was I ever going to find time to sleep?

Looking around, Collen and the other watcher were nowhere to be seen, possibly on watch behind the house, so I nudged the horse with the heel of my boots, and we started up Bailey Street.

I wondered whether or not I should tell Sandstorm about the possibility of an upcoming raid, since the fewer people that knew about it the better, and also because I didn't want Sapphire and Reevie to think I wanted them to get involved.

Still, there would be advantages to getting their help with the raid. If anyone knew where the Avalanche watchers were set, it would be

Sandstorm. They might also know the typical movements of their beaters and pickers. That information alone might save me several nights of scouting. I spent the entire trip back to the garrison pondering over the best possible way of getting inside the compound and subduing the tribe while causing the least amount of bloodshed.

It wouldn't be an easy task.

Unfortunately, by the time I'd stabled my horse and was heading into Barracks Two, I didn't feel any closer to an answer than when I'd left the orphanage. Passing the station desk, I said goodnight to Lieutenant Huckly, who had kept the same post for four years now. He preferred working the desk, refusing a promotion and the additional responsibility it would bring. I opened Room Eleven's door and found my roommates still up.

They all turned when I stepped in.

Gellar stood. He was dressed for sleep, his red beard hanging down over his dirty white undershirt. "Now I see why we were ditched this evening." He pointed at my new double sheath. "He spent all his gold on that. Just look at that thing."

The others hopped out of their beds and gathered round, circling me as they admired the new gear.

"Someone's getting paid a sight more than the rest of us," Waylen said, twisting his long thin beard around his fingers as he followed the others in a circle around me.

"I'm not getting paid any more than the rest of you," I countered. Of course, I didn't really know if that was the case or not. "It was a birthday gift from friends."

"Those are some really good friends," Barthol said, tapping the metal plate on the front with a thick finger.

"Wish I had friends like that," Fipple added.

"Aye," Stumpy said. "I wouldn't be sharing a room with the five of you if I did."

The others chuckled.

"It's quite the gift," Barthol said as he stopped his stalking and stepped back to admire the sheath as a whole. He pinched his chin. "It suits you."

"What did the king want to speak with you about?" Gellar asked as the men retreated back to their beds, and I began to undress, starting with my sheaths.

"A bit of an interesting story, actually," I said.

"Good," Waylen jumped in. "Nothing like getting tucked into bed with a good story."

I wasn't sure how much of what had happened I should tell them. I was almost afraid to mention the new horse, considering their reaction to my birthday gift. I didn't want them growing jealous of me and resenting me for my recent run of good luck—which I was sure was set to change at any time. Instead, I kept the topic to that of the upcoming raid on Avalanche and my meeting with the queen concerning the orphanage.

"Sounds like your plate is filled to overflowing," Waylen said. "How do you plan on getting all of this done and keeping up with your duties here?"

I looked at him and grinned awkwardly.

His face puckered. "So that's how it's going to be, huh? Drop it in our laps."

"At least the Black Guild practices," I said, feeling a little guilty. "Oh, and I talked with Overcaptain Tolin about our members getting transferred."

"What did Tolin say?" Stumpy asked, crawling into his own bed beside mine.

"He said he'd speak with the commander, but I have a feeling we'll get Elwin and Gilford back."

Gellar hmphed. "I hope we get them back before we leave for the front. Lot of good it will do us if they wait till after."

"And what about their replacements?" Fipple asked. "Tilson and Howell."

"Howell needs discipline," Gellar said.

Waylen rolled over. "And a lot of it."

"Needs humility," Barthol added.

They all grunted at that.

"What he needs is support from us," Stumpy said.

I looked at the one-handed man. "You seemed to have found a rapport with him. You might be our best chance of getting him into some sort of fighting shape before we ship out."

"Fighting isn't exactly his problem," Fipple said. "It's listening to orders and being willing to work with others. One of the reasons the Black Guild is successful is our unit cohesiveness."

I nodded. "I agree. Which is why you need to let me know before we ship out whether you believe they are ready. If not, we cut them loose. We can't afford to put the entire group in jeopardy with a few bad apples."

"Tilson seems eager," Barthol said, "but we'll have to see if his skills improve."

I yawned, unable to stop myself. "We'll discuss it more tomorrow, but right now I've got to get some sleep." I leaned over and blew out my bedstand candle, and before the chorus of snores had begun to emanate around the room, I drifted off.

AVALANCHE

Chapter 12

I WOKE TO SOUNDS OF movement and cracked an eye. The faint grey fingers of dawn crept through the windows, outlining my roommates as they went about their morning routines. They were clearly trying to remain as quiet as possible: moving slowly, tiptoeing as best they could.

With a frustrated yawn, I opened my eyes and tossed back my covers. "I'm awake."

"We were trying to let you sleep," Stumpy said as he strapped on his sword belt. "Heading to breakfast. Want anything?"

I yawned again, my joints stiff and my mind groggy. "I'll meet you there."

The others filed out the door, and I waited for it to shut before crawling out of bed. The days were warm, but it was still early enough in the year for a slight chill to linger in the room at dawn. I was thankful for whoever had gotten up and stoked the fire in the hearth. Grabbing my clothes, I scrambled to the back and placed my pants, shirt, and socks on a rack in front of the fireplace to warm before putting them on—one of the simple pleasures in my life.

After a few minutes in front of the fire, I quickly dressed and strapped on my new sheath, once again testing its weight on my back. It sat higher than my other sheath, which felt a little awkward, but it was sturdy and well made. I adjusted the straps until the sheath rested in the ideal position for me to draw my swords.

Taking a moment to stretch and mentally jot down everything I needed to do for the day, I headed for the cafeteria to meet my room-mates. Breakfast was quickly consumed, and soon enough we were standing out in the main yard discussing the day's activities.

"We should try to catch a meal tonight in town again," Waylen said. He looked at me. "Perhaps this time you'll be able to join us?"

I frowned. "Not sure I can this evening. I'll probably be meeting with Sandstorm about the upcoming raid. I'd planned on taking my evening meal there."

"Maybe we'll see you sometime between now and when we leave for the front," Barthol said, sounding frustrated by the whole situation.

I grimaced and nodded. He wasn't the only one feeling frustrated by it all.

We once again parted ways as my roommates slowly headed for the practice field and I made my way to the stables.

My lancer duties and schedule had grown somewhat flexible over the last couple of years, especially with the added obligation of my continual training with the prince and my work with the Black Guild. Overcaptain Tolin had even granted me leave from my official duties over the next week in order to meet with Her Majesty about my upcoming dealings with Avalanche.

I shook my head as I headed into the stable. How was I going to get everything done and still manage to set sail for the border in time to make sure the king had his protection detail in place?

I released a heavy sigh. Priorities. I had to set them. The problem was that everything seemed equally important.

I mounted and left the garrison, taking the short jaunt to the palace. Several of the items on my list could be marked off with a visit to the royal estate, so that was where I headed first. I only stopped long enough at the bridge to say good morning to Yorig before heading across. He wished me well and hoped that my day was less hectic than it had been yesterday. I hoped it would be as well, but it was still early.

Heading first to the royal stables, I dismounted and handed my horse to Bozz.

"How long will your visit be today?" he asked.

"Better go ahead and take him inside," I said. "I might be here a while."

"Will you be taking the Rymiran out today?" he asked. It sounded more like a strong suggestion than an inquiry.

"That is my intent. How did he do last night?"

Bozz rubbed his dark beard rather vigorously. "He was surprisingly calm. Eerily so, if you ask me."

"That's good, isn't it?"

He shrugged. "I suppose." With a wary eye, he glanced over his shoulder and back inside the stable. "I just don't like the way he looks at me. I get the feeling he's up to no good."

I laughed. "I'm sure it's just your imagination. I'll come by later and take him out."

He nodded. "Good. I'm tired of replacing his stall door. Crazy beast is too big and too strong for his own good."

I didn't know if I liked the sound of that.

Oddly enough, I could feel the horse's curiosity coming from the stables. As soon as I noticed it, I heard a loud stomp. I wasn't sure if he could hear me talking and recognized my voice, or if he could somehow sense that I was there. I suddenly had an unsettling sensation in my stomach and looked at Bozz. "Have you fed him yet today?"

"Not yet. Just making my rounds now. Why?"

"No reason." Was I sensing the horse's hunger?

Shaking it off, I turned and headed for the palace; however, no matter how far I walked, I couldn't shake the feeling that the magic-bred horse was somehow looking over my shoulder. I wished I knew more about how this connection worked between the horse and the rider it chose. I wondered if there were any books on the subject in the library. If anyone would know, I'd bet Her Majesty the Queen would. No one spent as much time rummaging through the stacks as Dakaran's mother.

I groaned audibly. Something else to add to the list.

Inside the palace, I headed up the stairs and back toward the royal wing, following the long corridor past the king's study and then right at the final hall, leading back to Prince Dakaran's rooms. Two guards were waiting outside, and they opened the door when they saw me coming. Both gave my new sheaths appraising looks.

"Have the physickers been by this morning?" I asked.

"No. But they were here last night," the guard on the left said, staring at the two swords rising just above my head.

I nodded as I passed. The guard who'd answered stepped in with me and shut the door.

"Have you heard him stirring yet?" I asked as I walked over to pull open one of the curtains on the side, revealing the sun just breaking over the top of the eastern wall in the distance. I had to squint against the sheer brightness of it. I turned and started across the sitting room. The fire had been stoked on the side, and I could feel its residual heat on the way to Dakaran's bedchamber doors.

"I haven't heard him yet," the guard said. "If he was up, we would have known about it."

I chuckled as I pressed my ear to his door and listened. All was quiet, which could mean he was sleeping peacefully, having found a position that allowed him to breathe without snoring, or he was awake. I rapped softly on the door and got my answer immediately.

"Who is it?" Dakaran called out from the other side.

"It's Ayrion."

"Open the door."

I glanced over my shoulder at the guard on the other side of the room. He hadn't moved from his place in front of the entrance. Opening the right-side door, I stepped inside the bedchamber. It smelled a tinge musty, as though not having been aired out in several days. Dakaran was sitting up in his bed, reading a book by the light of the candles on his nightstand table. The fire in the hearth to the side brightened the room, but not well enough for reading in bed.

"When was the last time you bathed?" I asked. "You stink."

He dropped the book on the bed, not bothering to mark the page. "I don't know. The royal physickers believe me too frail to leave my bed." He pushed back his coverlet and turned, letting his legs drop over the side. He winced as he did, placing his hand over the clean wrapping around his stomach. "I feel better." He held out his arm. "Give me a hand."

I walked over and offered my shoulder, and he stood.

"Should you be getting out of bed so soon?"

"I'm fine. I want to sit in front of the fire."

Apparently, he didn't mean the fire in his bedchamber, as he directed me out the door to the main sitting room.

"What's all this?" he asked, staring at the straps of my new double sheath before tapping the silver plate on my chest.

"It was a birthday gift from some old friends."

"I like it. Makes you look fierce. I want one."

I rolled my eyes. Of course he did. I helped him over to the cushioned chair in front of the grand fireplace and lowered him down gently.

Dakaran looked past me to the guard waiting at the front door. "What's he doing in here?"

"He's making sure you are safe."

"From what? There's no one in here but you." He looked back at the guard. "Call for the attendants to fill my bath. And you can wait outside. I'm perfectly safe here."

"I was just joking about the bathing," I said. "Are you sure you should be getting the wound wet this soon after?"

"It'll be fine. The physickers say they've never seen a wound heal so quickly." He looked back at the guard, and the guard looked at me, then finally bowed.

"As you wish, Your Highness." The guard opened the door and spoke with the other man waiting in the hall. As soon as he finished, the second guard left, and the first stepped out into the hall and shut the door behind him.

"So, how did you sleep last night?" I asked. "Restfully, I hope."

"Better than you, by the look of those circles under your eyes."

"I haven't had much rest in the last couple of nights. No thanks to you."

Dakaran shrugged. "What did I do?"

"What you did was keep me up an entire night worrying about whether you'd pull through or whether I'd be returning a corpse to the palace."

"Oh, that?"

"Yeah, that."

"Wasn't my fault."

"How would you know? You were too drunk to even realize how close to death you actually came."

Dakaran tsked.

The sun rising over the eastern wall quickly filled the room, shining rays through the dust in the air that filtered all the way to Dakaran's chair in front of the fire. "What are your plans for today?" he asked, reclining against the back. "Mine are to do as little as possible." He gently patted his stomach. "Who knew getting stabbed could be so relaxing. Nothing like lying in bed all day with a good book to take the edge off. That and a few sips of Bristonian wine."

I frowned. "That's what got you into this mess in the first place."

He waved the comment away.

I was going to say more about his drinking, especially after his father had threatened the dungeon to anyone giving his son wine, but I was interrupted by a knock at the door.

"Who is it?" Dakaran called out.

"It's the attendants for your bath, Your Highness," the guard in the hall called through.

Dakaran looked up at me, and I sighed.

"Fine." I walked across the room and opened the door. There were at least half a dozen people waiting in the hall in addition to the guards, all of whom were carrying buckets of steaming water. I quickly moved out of their way as they filed through the door and across the room to another set of doors at the back, which led to the prince's bathing chamber. Did they have heated water ready and waiting at all times?

I could hear the water being poured into the bath, and before they had managed to empty their buckets, more were coming in from the hall out front. It was like a well-timed parade. As the new arrivals started across the sitting room, those in the bathing chamber were walking out. Clearly, they were quite familiar with the routine, so I surmised it was one the prince utilized fairly often. He had been forced to live without his luxuries during his time in the Lancers, but he was no doubt making up for that now.

In no time at all, the last of the attendants had left, and the doors were once more shut behind the guards. Dakaran smiled and held out his hand for me to help him up from his seat. I did, and then walked him toward the back, but not before he'd snatched his goblet and glass decanter from the tray beside his chair.

"Your father's not happy with the drinking. You might want to curb it for a while. He's been threatening the staff."

Dakaran grunted. "I know. I had to pay someone to sneak it in."

"Why would you do that? You're going to cost them their job, whoever it is."

He didn't respond.

There was steam slipping out from under the door, and when I opened it, I was met with a billow of thick lavender fog. I had to admit, it was quite nice. Pungent, but nice.

I helped him inside and shut the door. Unlike every wood or porcelain tub I'd ever seen, this one didn't sit on the floor. Instead, it was built inside it, like a pool, large enough for several people to sit.

Dakaran's chamberlain was there to help him take off his clothes and assist in lowering him into his tub. I remained poised at the side in case he slipped on one of the steps heading inside.

Dakaran waved the chamberlain out and then slowly worked his way in and across. He eased his way down into the water and let his arms relax over the sides, taking only enough time to fill his goblet before leaning back and releasing a blissful sigh.

"Feel free to get in," Dakaran said. "The water's perfect. It might even help loosen you up a bit."

"No thanks. I've got a busy schedule. I just wanted to see how you were doing and make sure you were healing properly."

"Well, as you can see, I'm doing just fine." He winced as he turned. "Well, almost fine." He looked up at me through the fog. "You know, this has really opened my eyes."

"Oh?" I took a step forward anxiously. If this experience had managed to put some things into perspective, then perhaps it hadn't all been for nothing.

"You truly are my closest friend. Lying there in that cot at Sandstorm Manor, not knowing whether I was going to live or die, I had plenty of time to think. There I was bleeding out in a dark alley in the middle of the night, and who was it that came for me? You."

I wanted to point out that might have had something to do with the fact that I was one of the only people that knew about it at the time, but who was I to argue with a perfectly good speech about my kindness?

"Ever since I've known you, you've always looked at me and seen *me*, not my father's son, not the heir apparent. You're always there when I need you, all the time spent with me in training."

Of course, that was because his father had demanded it of me.

"Even now, you've taken time to come check on me when I'm sure you have other responsibilities that need accomplishing at the garrison." He smiled. "I just want to thank you for that."

"Your Highness is most welcome."

Dakaran frowned. "Stop with the *Your Highness*. Sounds silly coming from you." He leaned over and grabbed the goblet from the tray beside him and took a sip. "Ooo, that's good."

The prince's sudden outburst of emotion left me feeling a little awkward, and I began to ease my way toward the exit.

"Where you going?"

"As you said, I do have things I need to be taking care of. And I'm glad to see you are doing better." With him drinking the way he was, I was hesitant to leave him there alone. With my luck, he'd slip and hit his head on the side and drown.

"I'm going to have one of the guards wait just outside the bath in case you need anything." I didn't want to tell him I was doing it because I didn't trust him to bathe on his own.

I started for the bathing room's doorway but stopped when I heard the door leading into the hall open and shut and then heavy footsteps start across the sitting room floor. I walked out to see who was coming and then quickly bowed as the king stepped into the bathing chamber.

"Your Majesty."

King Rhydan nodded in my direction, then took one look at his son and the half-empty goblet in his hand and frowned. "Who brought him wine?" He looked at me.

I shook my head. "I assure you, it wasn't me, Your Majesty. It was left by his attendants when they filled his bath."

The king walked over and snatched the goblet from Dakaran's hand and kicked the decanter across the room, where it shattered into a dozen pieces and emptied its contents across the marble tiles. "I will not have a drunkard for a son. Look at Ayrion here. You don't see him wasting his days, lying about, pouring wine down his gullet." He stared down at his son and shook his head sadly. "I had hoped that your year in the Lancers would have weeded out some of these vices, but I think maybe I should have kept you in."

I was glad Dakaran's father was addressing the problem, but I wished

he hadn't invoked my name in the process.

"I am not a drunkard," Dakaran said, his face hardening.

"And not just a drunkard, but a fool," his father added. "It hasn't been two days since they found you writhing in your own blood and sputum outside a Cheapside tavern, and here you are with another drink in your hand." He looked down at his son in disgust. "Have you no self-respect? Take Ayrion," he said, and then walked over and patted me on the back. "A rising leader in the lancer corps, someone that men look up to, and he came from nothing. Less than nothing. A street rat. He wasn't given even the smallest portion of what you've been given, and yet look at all he's managed to accomplish."

As much as it warmed my heart to hear the king praise me in such a manner, I didn't much care for the way Dakaran was suddenly looking at me, as though I were somehow competition. There was both jealousy and rage behind his eyes that I hadn't seen leveled at me before. It hit all the harder, having come on the heels of his confession toward our close friendship. My heart sank.

I turned to the king. "I'm sure the prince's brush with death has more than revealed the dangers of overindulgence, Your Majesty." I was hoping to broker a peace, but instead earned a sharp look from Dakaran that had me wishing I'd kept my mouth shut.

The king looked down at the goblet still resting in his hands and then tossed it to the side. "Apparently not." He shook his head and then left the room.

Dakaran sat there seething. He wouldn't even look in my direction, choosing instead to stare at a blank space on the wall.

"I'll talk to him," I said, and when the prince didn't respond, I quickly slipped out.

I headed after the king, but by the time I reached the main hall, he was nowhere to be seen. As much as I hated the king placing me in the middle of his argument with his son, I could see his point. Dakaran hadn't appeared to have learned much from his near-death experience, other than the fact that if he did get into trouble, he could count on coming to me to help him out.

I decided to head for the royal library. I had promised Dakaran I would talk to his father, but right now was probably not the best time. Perhaps when I found the king in a more favorable mood. Better to let him cool down first.

I figured that while I was here at the palace, I might as well go ahead and see if I could find any information on my new horse. I hoped that one of the librarians could help me discover some reference material on Rymiran stallions. I'd only ever been to the library on two occasions, both times in response to a summons from the queen. She'd been in the study rooms on the second floor.

It took me some time to make my way from the royal chambers down and across to the other side of the palace. The royal chambers were located in the north wing, while the library rested in one of the southern wings. I reached the end of the large hall and stopped outside a set of gold-inlay doors, every bit the size of those at the main entrance. A couple of attendants in their crimson-and-gold uniforms opened them for me.

Inside, I found several of the library staff congregated around the front desk on the left—wearing their white robes with gold etching and red hats—while others were busy moving through the stacks, carrying armloads of books. The library itself took up an entire wing.

"May we help you?" an older gentleman on the left asked as he stepped out from behind the long desk where the others sat organizing stacks of books. His gold hat labeled him chief archivist. "My name is Asarius," he added, noting the swords on my back, but it wasn't until he saw my eyes that he stopped his approach. He was an older man with a white beard that hung all the way to his waist.

"I'm Ayrion." I passed a quick glance up to the study rooms on the second floor. "Is Her Majesty in today?"

The man adjusted his spectacles, glancing up at the second-floor balcony as well. He gave me a suspicious look, and for a moment I wondered if he thought I was there to kill the queen.

"I'm the head of the Black Guild that practices here in the palace each week. We were the ones who saved Ambassador Gorman and his wife from Cylmar a couple years ago."

Asarius's head lifted. "Yes, I did hear something about that. And, yes, there has been talk of an Upakan here in the palace. Though I believed him to be . . . much younger." He glanced back up at the reading rooms on the upper floors. "The queen isn't in at present, I'm afraid." At this point I wasn't sure he'd have told me if she was. "Is there something *we* can do for you? Would you like me to leave her a note?"

I shook my head. "Actually, I was hoping to find some information about . . . that is, you wouldn't know if there are any writings on Rymiran horses, would you?"

The librarian thumbed his chin. "Hmm. You're not the first to ask. His Majesty was in here last week, looking for that exact same material." He turned to some of the other archivists sitting behind the desk. "Have we reshelved those references on Rymiran horses yet?"

"I did," a young woman said. She wasn't much older than me, with thick chestnut hair that hung halfway down her back, though some was draped over one shoulder carelessly. She had delicate features, a very pretty girl actually, but didn't seem to be the type to flaunt it. She looked at me, noting the swords rising behind my head, then back at the chief archivist. "Would you like me to pull them?" Her tone sounded as though she hoped the head librarian would say no.

The older man nodded, then turned to me. "Is this your first time to the royal library, young man?"

"No, sir. Well, not exactly. I've only ever been to the study rooms."

"Ah." Asarius looked at the young woman. "Take him along. He might enjoy seeing the work involved in keeping the stacks running in an organized fashion."

She nodded and stepped away from the desk, motioning for me to follow. She stared at me on her way by, namely my eyes. "I'm Leara," she said, once again giving my swords an uneasy look.

I moved in alongside her. "Ayrion," I said, in case she missed it the first time. I noticed she scooted a couple steps to the side. "I promise I'm not here to hurt anyone."

"Who said you were?" she asked defensively.

"Just saying you don't need to be afraid of me."

"Who said I was afraid?"

I shook my head. "Sorry, you just seem nervous is all."

She straightened her back. "The queen doesn't usually come in this early."

"Oh? I guess I'll have to wait, then."

We didn't have a formal meeting set, but the queen had said she'd wanted to meet with me concerning the upcoming raid. We also needed to discuss the matter of the orphanage and what to do with a possible influx of new children. I wasn't looking forward to asking for more gold.

"What's the Lost City like?" Leara asked suddenly, surprising me to the point of not knowing what to say. She passed me a curious glance as we walked. "You are Upakan, are you not?"

"Yes. But it's been a number of years since I was there."

"Do your people truly live underground? Is the old city still intact? If not, don't you find it rather dangerous to be walking around a place where parts of buildings could come raining down on your head?"

I looked at her. "That's a lot of questions."

She smiled. "Sorry. I'm inquisitive by nature and profession. Acquiring and arranging knowledge are the life goals of a librarian and archivist. I'm sorry if I was offensive."

"Not at all. I'm just not used to people asking. Most of the old city did collapse, forming some very large caverns and tunnel passageways. Many of the buildings are in ruins, especially up top. But there were some sections of the city that simply lowered into the ground whole. My people live in those. There is quite a bit of dilapidation, mostly from age and the lack of upkeep. Upakans aren't exactly known for their work with stone and wood."

Now that I thought about it, my people lived in what most would have considered squalor. Even the homes in Cheapside were better managed than those in the Lost City. I guess you don't really realize how poor you are until you see how others are living.

Leara looked at me and the swords on my back and cocked her brow. "I guess not." We walked a little farther, and she continued to spare passing glances my way, until I finally couldn't take it any longer and stopped.

"What is it?"

"Sorry. It's your eyes," she said, staring up at them intensely. "I've always wondered whether they were a product of prolonged time away from the sun or something else. Do you see differently than the rest of us?" She continued to stare.

"I see better in dark places."

"Do you really? How interesting. Is everything out here too bright for you, then?"

"It was at first. Upakans have to wear shaders whenever they come topside, and I did as well for some time, at least until my eyes grew a little stronger. Now, it doesn't bother me too much. When I first wake in the morning it can be a little jarring if I wake to a brightened room or an early sunrise."

She pursed her lips. "That is very interesting. I'll have to make sure I record that."

I scratched at my beard. I wasn't sure if I wanted her recording that information or not. I guessed it wasn't anything too revealing. I didn't think I'd given away anything detrimental. Besides, she didn't seem overly surprised by my advanced eyesight, even almost expected it in a way. I wasn't sure why or when our Upakan eyes had changed, so there was nothing new to divulge about that.

"Why Rymiran horses?" she asked as we started back through the stacks.

I tried shifting my thoughts back to why I was there. I wasn't sure how much I should say. "The king mentioned them in one of our meetings, and I was curious. Don't know much about them myself. Do you?"

Leara shook her head. "Not really. My area of study is with the histories, Elondrian in particular."

"That sounds . . . interesting."

She smiled in a way that let me know she knew I was trying to be polite. "Most find it rather tedious and dull, but I like looking at how things were and the changes that occurred over the years."

"Good or bad changes?"

"Both," she said. "History is important. Knowing where we came from can better help us determine where we are going."

"Or perhaps don't want to go," I added.

She looked at me curiously. "That is true."

"I guess it would also make a difference who the author of those histories was."

She stopped and looked at me again. "Ever give any thought to donning the white and red?"

I smiled. "Afraid my talents tend to lie elsewhere."

"Pity. I think you have a strong mind for research." She turned and started us up once more.

We stopped about halfway down the center island and looked up. The stacks of shelving rose several floors above us, with walkways intermittently placed in between, allowing those on the upper levels to leave the reading rooms and walk right out into the stacks themselves. Circular stairways led from the floor to the upper levels, and we took one on the left. We climbed two flights and exited onto one of the narrow walkways between.

It was quite an impressive sight.

"How do you keep up with all of these?" I asked. "I can't imagine the filing system used to catalog where everything is at."

"It's an attribute that makes this place one of the great wonders of the world. I believe it was wizards who first designed the original system of book placement. The librarians don't exactly like to talk about it much, but it is our history, and we should recognize it. It has fallen into a bit of a disarray since their time, but we have done our best to keep up with it as much as possible. The books don't see as much use as they once did." She glanced around the closest shelves and then leaned in. "Actually, we don't understand half of it. I think there was an element of magic involved that we sadly no longer have access to."

"Even without the magic, I can't imagine how difficult it must be to keep up with." I gawked over one of the sides as we passed several more shelving units. It almost felt like walking on one of the skybridges over where the Street Guild used to hold its meetings.

"It's a lifetime of work," she said, then started down another aisle. "Over here. We have the Rymiran horses placed under magical creatures since I believe magic played a hand in their creation."

"Do you know what kind of magic?"

Leara shook her head. "Afraid not. I only know that much because I heard the king discussing it with Faulgner."

"Who?"

"He's one of the archivists. His primary study is that of Aldoran animalogy."

"I'm surprised they didn't have *him* escort me to the books. Not that you aren't doing a wonderful job," I quickly added. "But if this is his study, he might be able to give me some better insight."

"I'm sure the chief archivist would have done so, but unfortunately Faulgner is away visiting family, and won't be back for several weeks."

"Oh. So I guess he wasn't around to help the king either?"

She shook her head and then stopped in front of one of the shelving units on the right and pointed to the fifth shelf up. "That's what you're looking for."

The shelf was too high for either of us to reach, so she slid over one of the attached ladders and climbed up. She scanned the spines and grabbed three or four volumes before climbing back down and dropping them in my arms. "That should do it. Those are the same ones we gave His Majesty when he came looking."

"Thank you." I looked around. "Where's a good place for me to read?"

"Try room number three on this level." She turned and started to point back down the aisle we'd just come from and then changed her mind. "Actually, I guess it would be easier if I just showed you." She guided me back through the stacks and across one of the bridges leading over to the right-side balcony, where the reading rooms were located. There were numbers on the doors, and I recognized the one the queen usually frequented. Its door was open, the green interior lit with a warm blaze in the fire.

We passed the room and stopped at the next one down. This one's door was open as well. There was no one inside, so I stepped in. "Can you let me know if the queen arrives? I'm supposed to be meeting with her at some point during the day."

Leara nodded. "I'll leave her a note. Is there anything else you require?"

"Not that I can think of." I looked down at the stack of books in my arms. "What do I do with these when I'm finished?"

"Leave them on one of the tables. We'll reshelve them. Wouldn't want you to try doing that yourself and put them in the wrong place. We'd never find them again."

I smiled. "Thanks for your help."

She smiled as well and then left me to my reading.

I placed the books down on one of the tables, then walked over to the fireplace and stoked the hearth, prodding the coals under the wood with the poker. Once the flames had reignited, I took a few moments to walk the room before taking my seat.

It was similar to the queen's reading room. Same chairs and small sofas in front of the fireplace. Same tables placed sporadically around the outer walls. The only difference was that this room's paint, wallpaper, and decorations had been tinted blue instead of green.

Like the other room, this one had a fair amount of artwork on the walls, which included a couple of beautifully stitched tapestries and several large murals, one of which depicted several half-naked individuals lying about in a forest while reading. There appeared to be a picnic throw and food set out between them. Not really sure why they were in such a state of undress while reading in the middle of a forest, but I guess that was between the artist and whoever had commissioned the piece.

Giving up on understanding the logic of the rather lewd picnic, I fetched a reading lantern from a nearby table and sat down at the table where I had set the books. I rearranged the four books to form a square, so that I could see all the covers at the same time, but before I opened any of them, my stomach began to growl. I wasn't sure if it was because I was hungry or if I was still sensing my new horse. It felt more like me. Besides, Bozz said he had been on his way to feed the stallion, so I doubted he'd be that hungry again so soon. I wondered if the horse could feel my hunger. I shivered. Was there a way to break the bond? Hopefully, one of these books could share some insight.

The title of the first was: *The History of the Rymiran Plains*. That sounded more geographical. I wondered if there was anything in there about the horse breed, or if the librarians had pulled it simply because it had the name *Rymiran* in it. Then again, that particular section was supposed to be tomes on magical animals. Perhaps it had been misshelved. I shook my head. These archivists were too attentive of their filing to have placed the book in the wrong stack.

Before opening it, I looked at the other titles. Perhaps one of them would be a better fit. The one on its right was labeled: *Amberloin's Study of Magical Breeding*. That sounded more like what I was looking for, though it did raise another question: What other types of animals had been bred with magic?

I'd just looked at the next book above it when the door behind me opened. I turned to find a couple of city patrollers—or Blue Capes as we always called them on the streets—standing in the doorway. As soon as I realized who was standing behind them, I quickly stood and bowed.

"Your Majesty."

AVALANCHE

Chapter 13

QUEEN ELLISE STEPPED into the room. "I've been searching all over the palace for you. This is the last place I would have thought to look."

I smiled.

"As luck would have it," she said, "Leara told me there was an anxious young man dressed in black, waiting for me in one of the reading rooms." The queen walked over and glanced down at the table. "Ah, Rhydan mentioned something about giving you a new horse." She smiled. "I don't think he was very happy about the decision."

I frowned. "If I could change things, I would."

She raised her hand. "No need to explain. The horse chooses its rider, not the other way around. And if you ask me," she said with a wink, "I believe it chose correctly, though listening to my husband gripe and complain about his bruised tailbone has not been the joy of my day.

I have a feeling it was more his ego that was bruised than his backside."
She turned and motioned for the two men waiting outside the door to
enter. "Please shut the door behind you."

The taller man on the left turned and shut the door, then followed
the other over. Both wore similar badges on their shoulders and chest—
though the taller man bore a few more than his companion—no doubt
symbolizing advanced rank amongst the patrollers.

I wasn't exactly expecting a formal meeting this quickly, and my
mind raced to determine what all needed to be discussed with them. I
hoped the queen didn't expect me to have a well-laid-out plan ready to
present in less than a day.

The officers slowed as they got a better look at me under the dim
light of the lantern on the table. They both stopped when I turned, and
they saw my eyes. The taller reached for his sword.

"It's fine, Captain. I've known him since he was this tall." She raised
her hand to just below her shoulder. "This is the man I wanted you to
meet. Ayrion is the head of the Lancers' Black Guild and my son's personal trainer."

"Black Guild?" the shorter man on the right looked confused.

The queen nodded. "It is a special unit inside the Elondrian Lancers
who take on challenging missions for the crown. I'm sure you heard of
the rescue of our Cylmaran ambassador a couple of years ago."

The two men nodded.

"Ayrion led that mission."

"But he's . . ." The shorter man looked too embarrassed to continue.

"Upakan?" The queen smiled. "Yes, which I'm sure is why he has
been so successful in training these elite fighters."

The queen seemed to be going to great lengths to emphasize my status as a lancer and my talents as a fighter. I figured it was to keep them

from distrusting my abilities to lead an expedition inside Aramoor. The city proper was considered patroller territory, and I'm sure she didn't want to give them any further reason to resent what they might see as lancer intrusion.

For the most part, lancers and the patrollers tended to stay out of each other's way, but the Blue Capes were always more than willing to arrest rowdy lancers who'd had too much to drink on their nights off. The altercations would generally require a confrontation between one of the garrison's overcaptains and the patroller commandant. I'd even heard tales of a time when the meeting had ended in blows, but that was back when Commander Goring was still an overcaptain.

"Ayrion, this is Commandant Ipsworth," the queen said, pointing to the taller man on the left.

I almost gulped. She had asked the head of the patrollers to be a part of this meeting? Ipsworth had a strong chin and an even stronger mustache that pinched at the ends. His dark, grey-streaked hair was slicked back at the sides.

"And this is Captain Arns," she said, turning to the shorter man on the right. He was stouter than the commandant, with a clean-shaven face and an eye that drifted to the side. "They are here to discuss your ideas for a raid against the old garrison."

I nodded politely to both, though I was cringing on the inside. I wasn't exactly ready for a meeting just yet, especially not one where the patroller commandant was in attendance. "It's nice to meet you," I said. They offered their own polite greetings, and I turned to the queen. "I wasn't expecting a formal meeting so soon. I'm afraid you've caught me off guard."

"I didn't expect we'd discuss strategy at present," she said. "I did, however, want to make sure the three of you were properly introduced. Commandant Ipsworth will be in command of the patroller raid, under your supervision, of course. I wanted to make sure that if I'm not around to facilitate any further discussions, the three of you will be able to continue without me."

I bowed, breathing easier after hearing that. "Thank you, Your Majesty. A very wise precaution."

The other two nodded as well.

"Commandant Ipsworth is head of the central patroller office on the Island," the queen said, "and Captain Arns's office is stationed in the northeast quarter. His territory covers the old garrison where this Avalanche tribe you've told me about has set up their encampment."

I could see why the queen had chosen both of these men. I just hoped they would be easy enough to work with. Having the queen there certainly helped facilitate matters, but whether it was enough to keep our partnership going after she bowed out was a different matter altogether. I wasn't sure either of these men would be willing to take orders from the likes of me.

"Do you have any information concerning the raid that you can give us now?" Ipsworth asked. "A date for the raid, how many you believe are holed up inside, what you plan on doing with them once we finish?"

I liked that the commandant didn't question whether we would be successful or not, but instead simply stated that they would be. I hoped his confidence was born from a knowledge of his troops' experience.

"I do not have a set day for the raid. It will mostly be determined by the tribe's movement, and possibly even the weather. However, I can say that it will need to be soon, as I must sail for the Cylmaran front later next week. And as far as their numbers, I hope to better determine that over the course of the next couple of days as I spend time investigating their movements."

"Can you even speculate?"

"I'd be surprised if there were fewer than a hundred."

The commandant didn't respond, only thumbed the cleft in his chin while nodding slightly.

I was going to need to have another conversation with Sandstorm about what their watchers had seen of Avalanche's beaters, their comings and goings, and how many they estimated might be living there. We were already nearing the end of the week, so time was quickly running out.

"I hope to have answers for you by the end of the week."

Ipsworth glanced at Arns, then back at me. "I would appreciate it if you would include the captain here in your initial investigations. His office will be responsible for coordinating the attack, as they are the most familiar with the terrain." He looked at Arns. "I expect a full briefing afterward. And don't dally. I will not risk my men's lives by organizing a raid on nothing more than a day's notice."

Captain Arns saluted. "Yes, Commandant."

The two men looked at the queen. "Is there anything else you wish from us, Your Majesty?" Ipsworth asked.

She shook her head. "I believe that will suffice, gentlemen. Thank you, Commandant, for your punctual response."

Ipsworth swished his mustache and bowed, then turned to me. "I will expect to hear from you on Eighthday, then?"

"If not sooner," I said with a faint smile, then turned to Arns. "I will stop by your office to schedule our first watch of the compound."

Captain Arns nodded, his left eye not quite looking at me. I found it ironic that I, of all people, should be fixated on another man's eyes. Before Arns could say anything, his commander turned and started for the door, so he quickly followed. The two men stepped outside, but instead of leaving, both turned and waited for Her Majesty.

"I have business to discuss with Master Ayrion," the queen stated.

"You may return to your duties."

The two men bowed and then looked at each other. A single nod from Ipsworth, and Captain Arns shut the door. I wondered if they would wait in the hall for her or take her advice and go back to their duties. The frowns on their faces said they weren't all that comfortable leaving their queen alone with an Upakan. I tried listening for the sound of footsteps outside but could hear nothing but the crackling of the fire in the hearth over my shoulder.

Queen Ellise directed us over to a couple of cushioned chairs near the fireplace, and we sat. "Now, for what happens after this raid takes place," she said. "Rounding up these children is one thing, properly placing them is another. Ultimately, I would prefer to see them somewhere where they can be properly looked after and raised in a manner that will see them become fine, upstanding citizens of Aramoor, but my concern is, what is to stop them from simply leaving and returning to their former tribe?"

"It is certainly a risk, Your Majesty," I said, "one that can at least be mitigated by dividing those in charge from the rest of the tribe."

The queen leaned forward slightly, curiosity on her face. "Go on."

"What I've seen firsthand is that those at the top tend to lead by fear. Remove them, and the rank and file will generally act in a manner that fits their own best interests. Once the leadership is gone, we bring each member in, one by one, so that there is no influence from the others, and give them each a choice between living at Sandstorm or being sent to a workhouse."

"Workhouse? Wouldn't they all choose Sandstorm, then?"

I smiled. "You'll be surprised how many would rather go to a workhouse than betray their tribe. Those that ingrained we wouldn't want at Sandstorm anyway. They are the most likely to run off or cause problems

while they are there. Once we speak with each member individually, we can divide them up."

"And what do you suggest happens to those who refuse Sandstorm?"

"The youngest can be sent to Sandstorm regardless, anyone fifteen or younger. At that age, they can adapt. The older can either go to the lancers or the workhouses. Ultimately, it doesn't matter what you do to some, they will find their way back to Avalanche if they want it badly enough, which means we will have to deal with them at some other time. But that's a problem for another day."

The queen pursed her lips. "You keep mentioning going to Sandstorm. I was under the impression we were taking them to the orphanage as we discussed earlier."

I cleared my throat. "We will, Your Majesty, in a roundabout way."

One look from her, and I could see that I was going to need to explain.

"I stopped by the orphanage last night to visit with Master Fentin and Mistress Orilla and to discuss with them the possibility of an influx of new kids, but they told me they were at capacity, and I don't think they just meant the beds. I talked with them about the possibility of opening another orphanage, but they didn't seem amenable to the suggestion. For one, they don't believe they have it in them to keep up with a second location, which suggests that we would need to find another, much younger couple with the strength to run it. Also, there is the issue of funds."

"Oh, is their stipend not enough?"

"I believe it was, Your Majesty, a few years ago when you started it, but since then we lost two more tribes, which has added quite a few new mouths to feed, and with us discussing adding more, Master Fentin and Mistress Orilla have asked if there is any chance of increasing their stipend. I get the impression they seem to be barely squeaking by as it is."

The queen took a deep breath and slowly released it, sinking back into her chair. "Yes, that is a concern."

"But to get to my final point about the children getting placed in Sandstorm," I said. "Ignoring the orphanage being at capacity at the moment, I would prefer to have the new recruits live under Sandstorm's structure for at least a few months prior to moving them to the orphanage. That will give them a chance to acclimate to their new surroundings and give my friends a chance to work out any aggression. I don't want to send angry or violent kids to the orphanage for poor Master Fentin and Mistress Orilla to deal with. Not at their age."

"A wise decision," the queen said. She stared at the fire a moment in thought. I hoped I hadn't thrown too much on her by suggesting a raise to the stipend. "Would Master Fentin and Mistress Orilla be willing to present their case if I were to arrange some possible benefactors to listen?"

I clenched my fists, trying not to be too overexcited. "I don't see why not. I can be there to help if needed."

"It seems you have enough on your plate at the moment, but if you could offer them your assistance, I'm sure a friendly face in their corner will go a long way."

I smiled. "I wouldn't have it any other way. I'll make sure I'm there to offer any support I can."

"Good." She rose from her seat, and I quickly followed her up. "I want to set up this meeting as soon as possible. I know you have the next few days to prepare for this upcoming raid, but do you think you can spare tomorrow afternoon? I will be meeting with several of those I want you to present to, and it shouldn't be too much of an imposition to request the others meet as well. With the possibility of war, most will come just hoping to obtain some inside information as to what my husband's plans are."

I thought quickly. Today was Sixthday, so that would only give me tonight to scout the old Rockslide compound in hopes of coming up with a plan of action. I wasn't sure that was going to be enough time, but for Master Fentin and Mistress Orilla, it would have to be. Finding some additional benefactors would go a long way to easing their current burdens. I appreciated that the queen had the courtesy to ask. She could have just demanded my presence.

"Seventhday it is," I said. "Where would you like to meet and when? It might take me a little while to get them across town."

"I will send a carriage to pick them up. And I'll have some footmen at the door with instructions on where to bring them. Will you be accompanying them or meeting us here?"

"I'll accompany them," I said as I walked her to the door and opened it.

She looked back inside at the table. "What about your books?"

I looked as well, and sighed. "I guess I'll have to find another day to read them." I left the door open so that Leara, or whoever, would be able to find the books and reshelve them after we left. I hated not getting the chance to read about this horse that I found myself the proud new owner of, but there were more important things that needed doing.

I walked the queen down and then back through the palace, where we parted ways just prior to reaching the main lobby. She stopped to talk with a couple of senators who were gathered outside one of the assembly rooms, and I continued on, exiting the palace via the front courtyard and around to the stables.

My stomach was grumbling loudly by the time I reached the stone buildings, and I could feel a nervous energy in the back of my mind, which I took to be coming from the giant horse. I still hadn't thought of a good name for him, and he clearly hadn't preferred any that I had suggested so far. I shook my head. I had better things to worry about than some animal's name.

I found Bozz helping several men off-load a couple wagons full of grain into the royal stables. "Was he fed?" I asked the head ostler on the way in.

Bozz waved his hand impatiently. "Yes, yes. I told you I would."

I nodded and started down the center aisle, passing one neatly cleaned stall after another. Each had been freshly mucked with a full stock of hay in the rack and clean water in their buckets. The stalls were much roomier here than those in the lancer stable, the horses certainly more pampered. The closer I got, the stronger my sense of the stallion became. I could have probably found his stall with my eyes closed.

The horse stuck his head out the stall door before I arrived and blew out his lips with a welcoming nicker.

"Sorry," I said. "It took me longer than I thought." Actually, it would have taken me even longer had I been given the time to read through those books on Rymiran horses. I looked around for a grooms-man. There were no saddles hanging on the walls nearby for me to use.

"I'll be right back," I told the horse and left to find someone to help me.

I managed to locate a stable hand in the next aisle over and had him come help me find the right saddle. It took both of us to get it on. The giant animal didn't move or even flinch as we cinched down the straps. As long as I was there, he seemed calm, though I could also feel a sense of eagerness, no doubt at the thought of finally getting out of the stable.

An animal that had spent its life growing up wild and free on the plains needed to at least get a chance to move around a little, to step outside and see the sky. It was certainly a pretty day for it.

Unfortunately, our time today would be short. I needed to get lunch. I also needed to talk with Master Fentin and Mistress Orilla about the upcoming meeting with new wealthy benefactors. I knew they weren't going to be happy about that, as neither was much for public speaking. Hopefully, their plight would be enough to loosen the nobles' purse strings.

Along with my stopover at the orphanage, I still had to meet with Sandstorm once again to fill them in on what the queen and I had discussed and to ask them about Avalanche's numbers in the northern quarter, not to mention thanking them for my new sword sheaths.

Where was a pen and paper when you needed it? If I didn't write all of this down, I was going to forget something, and as important as all of this was, I couldn't afford to miss anything.

The giant horse snorted, pulling me from my musings and letting me know he was ready to go.

I turned and looked up at the animal, and he stared down at me. Taking a moment to inspect the saddle, I realized the stirrups had been set too high. I was going to need to get a special saddle made. His back was so wide, I hoped the saddle we were using didn't hurt him.

I grabbed the reins from the stable hand and walked the horse down the aisle toward the front doors where the men were finishing up with the last of the grain sacks. The closer we got, the more elevated the horse's excitement became. His tail swished and his head bobbed. Thankfully, he didn't take off running and drag me along with him. He certainly had the strength to do so.

Instead, the horse stayed by my side and then slowed as we broke through the shadows of the stable and out into the sun, past the empty wagons. The men had finished loading and were climbing back aboard, but not before stopping halfway to stare at the enormous stallion.

"Alright," Bozz said to the wagoners, "get a move on. You act like you ain't never seen a horse before. Can't have you blocking the front of my stables all day."

The men climbed the rest of the way aboard, and pretty soon the wagons were on their way up toward the gatehouse and the palace bridge.

"What do you think, boy?" I asked, patting the horse's strong neck. "Bright enough for you?" I was squinting a little myself in the sun's direct light, my eyes having grown accustomed to the inside of the stable.

The black stallion whinnied once more and then shook out his mane.

"I agree. It's much nicer out here than in that stall." I noticed Bozz and a few of the other groomsmen standing near the entrance watching, no doubt waiting to see if the horse would throw me like he had the king. I tightened my grip on the leather straps. "Now, don't move," I said as I cautiously stuck my foot in the stirrup and aimed for the saddle's horn. "Here goes nothing."

I took a deep breath and pushed up with my leg. I'd half-expected him to leap as soon as my feet left the ground, but he remained poised, and I quickly swung my leg up and over and landed firmly in the saddle. My heart was racing as I clung to the reins. I didn't dare move. So far so good. I looked over at Bozz and the other men and smiled, as though it were nothing at all. I almost released the reins to wave, but I thought that might be tempting fate.

I leaned over and rubbed the horse's neck. "Good boy," I whispered. "Thank you for not making me look like an utter fool." I could feel the horse's desire to move, so I gently nudged him with the heel of my boot, gripping tightly to the reins, unsure what to expect.

The giant stallion started out at a very slow trot down the pebbled drive. I exhaled a giant sigh of relief that he hadn't taken off at a full gallop, which I could sense through our bond he wanted to do.

We took the cobbled road from the stables toward the north end of the palace, and from there onto a wooded trail that led back toward the upper gardens. The gardens were located just outside the practice field that Dakaran and I would occasionally use during the warmer months when he desired to show off his skills in front of an audience. With a day as beautiful as today, there were quite a few people walking the trails and sitting around the small pond and fountain area. Others were reading on benches up under the trees.

Apart from a few of the palace guard, I was the only one riding a horse. Most of those visiting the gardens either lived at the palace or rode in that morning, leaving their mounts in the stables. The giant stallion and I drew quite a bit of attention: curious glances, awestruck gawking. I doubted they were used to seeing a horse of his caliber before, or a rider all in black with two swords rising from his head. I sat as tall as I could, letting them gawk and stare. It felt nice, and the horse seemed to enjoy it as well, as it nickered and snorted every so often, drawing even more attention.

He was a bit of a showman, though I thought perhaps it was more just the enjoyment of being out of the stall than anything. I hated that I would have to return him. The horse snorted as soon as the thought crossed my mind.

Perhaps I didn't have to return him right away. I guess I didn't have to go back to the barracks for lunch, which was one of the places I was wanting to keep the horse away from. Too many lancers there would want to fawn over him or expect me to let them try their hand in the saddle. My roommates were at the top of that list. I didn't want to have to explain where the horse had come from or the kind of horse he was or how he had come to be in my possession. At least not yet.

Thankfully, Overcaptain Tolin was good at showing me a bit more leniency when it came to my attendance at the garrison, especially know-ing my relationship with the prince and the king. I doubted I would be back at the garrison tonight, and I could send word to my roommates of the fact, and they could pass that information on to Tolin. It helped that I was working under the queen's orders, or at least alongside her. Most knew of the queen's soft spot for the street kids, so any mention of the Bailey Street Orphanage would ensure I wouldn't return to some form of punishment. I just hoped my roommates would be willing to take over the Black Guild's training while I was gone. They were the ones I was most concerned with upsetting.

We made two complete circles around the garden area, coming to a stop in some places just to keep from forcing those already there from having to move too quickly out of the way. It also gave the horse a little more time out in the sun. By the time we had finished our amble and made it back to the stables, I had made up my mind to go ahead and ride the horse into town.

We might turn a few heads, but I figured that since I wasn't planning on stopping anywhere too public, it should be fine. There were strict laws governing horse theft, but with a horse like this, I didn't want to take the risk. Stopping to grab a bite to eat at the Rose and Crown might tempt someone to risk getting caught just to have the giant stallion. I thought it best to ride straight through to the orphanage, where I could tie him in the back and out of sight, and from there it was a quick jaunt over to Sandstorm, where Gittrick, the new coachman, was sure to take good care of him.

Bozz was out front smoking his pipe when we trotted off the path and over to meet him. "I'm going to take him into town," I said. "I won't be back until tomorrow."

Bozz pulled the pipe from his mouth. "Do you think that wise?

Would hate to be you if something happened to that horse and the king found out." He grimaced. "Would hate to be me as well. Maybe best you didn't take him. Your lancer mount is still here. We can have him saddled in no time."

I could feel the giant stallion's disapproval at going back in the stables. He wanted to move about, stretch his legs. "I'm sure he'll be fine. Where we're going, they have a private stable where he will not be touched." Bozz didn't look convinced, but I wasn't asking his permission. "I will have him back tomorrow."

Before the head ostler could argue, I tapped the horse with my boot, and we headed up the road toward the bailey and then out across the palace bridge.

I didn't stop on the other side, even though I saw Yorig standing over near the guardhouse. I waved at him on the way by but kept the horse to a steady trot as we passed between the guard towers and started down King's Way West toward the heart of Aramoor.

It was going to be a busy day.

AVALANCHE

Chapter 14

HE SUN WAS HIGH overhead, and my stomach grumbled as we made our way down the main thoroughfare. I could sense the horse's curiosity through our link as we traveled along the crowded streets. I could also sense his excitement. I rested my hand on his neck to calm him and could feel the tension in his muscles. He was trembling. Going from wide-open plains to the bustling center of Aramoor was not something he seemed prepared for.

"You'll be fine, boy," I said. "They aren't going to hurt you. Believe me, I know how you feel." I remembered my first time through the city's wall, seeing all the people. Nothing could have prepared me. The only other city of any size I had visited at that time was Oswell, which had seemed enormous compared to my home in the Lost City, but Aramoor was on a whole different scale. It was the largest city in the known world, a city of commerce and trade, a place where you could find every walk of life in one location. People from as far away as the capital city of Easthaven, which was at the northeast corner of the known map, could be found traversing Aramoor's streets.

I continued to pat the horse's neck and reassure him as I pulled on the reins to turn him off King's Way West before we reached the Island. I intended to take us north along the Tansian River to one of the less-trafficked routes. However, my horse ignored my gentle tugging on the straps and instead started for the main bridge leading over to the Island.

"You don't want to go over there," I said. "It's the most congested place in Aramoor. There's even more people over there than here." The horse didn't seem to care, and his curiosity grew the closer we got. The Tansian split just north of the bridge, dividing into two branches that skirted a large piece of land that had become the city's main shopping district, a place affectionately called the Island. It housed some of the most luxurious shops and eateries in the city.

I rarely came this way, just to avoid the congestion, but it seemed my horse wanted to see it for himself. His head swung back and forth as he stared at all the people, carriages, carts, and palanquins. It was quite the bustling affair, and by the time we'd made it over the bridge, the movement forward had nearly slowed to a halt. The horse didn't seem to mind, which was strange, since all I'd sensed from him up until now was his desire to bolt, to stretch his legs and neck at a full gallop.

"Do you like looking at all the people?"

He nodded, keeping his head held high. Pride filtered back through our link as he strutted down the crowded thoroughfare.

"Quite the social animal, aren't you?" I mused, though I'd be lying if I said I wasn't sitting in my saddle a little higher myself. However, with as many people as the street was holding, my horse was the last thing anyone was stopping to gawk at. In fact, the only people to really notice or care were those trying to cross in front of us. We were the recipients of several angry comments and one brisk fist wave. Though when the older gentleman happened to look up at who he was shaking his fist at, he quickly wilted back into the crowd.

The main street was too congested for my taste, and by the look of it was going to take us a good hour to get across, so I broke from King's Way and took a meandering route past King's Square. The gardens with their trees and water were beautiful, and it seemed a good number of the citizenry agreed, as the pathways through the surrounding fountains were filled.

Realizing we weren't going to get much deeper in than the outskirts of the trees, I guided us down several of the less-frequented streets toward the southern bridge, and finally out onto King's Way East. The shops on both sides were bustling with customers. Not nearly as busy as the Island, but packed enough for us to need to slow our pace in order to keep from trampling anyone.

I remembered my own experience of nearly being flattened by Senator Gerrick's carriage not long after my arrival in the big city. I hadn't thought about it until now, but it occurred to me that I hadn't seen that many carriages racing through the city since. I stopped at the roundabout where Circle Drive met King's Way East and was about to take it north toward Bailey Street when I had a thought. I turned and looked at the East Gate ahead and then patted my horse's neck. I think he could sense what I was feeling, because he suddenly released a loud whinny that frightened a group of women beside us so badly, several dropped their packages.

"Fine," I said, "we can go, but not for long." I didn't even get the chance to tap him with my boots before the horse was already on his way toward the main gate, leaving before I had a chance to apologize to the frightened ladies. I managed an apologetic wave over my shoulder, but it hardly seemed enough.

The city's enormous wall rose in front of us, one of the great wonders of the world. From this far back, I could still see shapes moving along the top: city watchers on duty. The closer we got to the gate, however, the less of the top I could see. I didn't get wall duty that often, but I always enjoyed it when I did. It was an unbelievable sight, staring out over the entire city at once, though I didn't enjoy it all that much during the winter months, especially the overnight watches. The wind that high up was strong, and the cold winter gusts could have you frozen to the bone in minutes.

We passed the eastern lancer garrison on the right and headed through the watchtowers without incident. A couple of the lancers on duty nodded when they saw me. It had been a long time since I'd been through the city's eastern gate. There hadn't been much need of late. I'd been sent on a few patrols over the last couple of years, when highway bandits had been sighted on the main road, but other than that, my time in Aramoor had been spent primarily within the surrounding wall.

Those coming into Aramoor on the left were being stopped and questioned; those with laden wagons were searched. Most were farmers and merchants on their way in to sell their wares, but that didn't stop the lancers from doing their duty. Those of us who were leaving were simply let through, though there was a single-file line that kept us at a slower pace.

"That is quite the animal," a voice in front of me said, and I shifted to the right to see around my horse's head. The speaker was an old man with a long white beard and a faded green robe. His outer cloak had an emblem of a rising sun with three stars overtop. I didn't recognize the crest. I wondered if he was a local nobleman. The garment looked a bit threadbare to be highborn, and he was on foot instead of a carriage, but

I didn't know of anyone who bore a crest that wasn't part of the aristocracy or at the very least on their household staff.

"Thank you," I said.

The man reached up before I could warn him and began rubbing the horse's nose.

"You might want to be careful," I said. "He can be a bit spirited."

The old man didn't seem worried in the least as he continued to rub the white patch. "He is a very special animal. How did you come by him?"

"I, uh . . . he was a gift."

The man pursed his lips and then nodded. "A kingly gift indeed."

I had been so preoccupied with making sure the stallion didn't bite the old man's hand that I almost didn't catch what he said. *Kingly* gift? "Why do you call it kingly?"

The man rested his hand back on the horse's nose, and the horse shivered in response. I could feel something through our link, something I hadn't felt before. It was like a quiet chill running straight through me, somehow leaving me more relaxed. The old man looked up at me and smiled as though he knew a secret. "Yes, you two are a very good match. Treat him well, and he will do the same for you."

I twisted in my saddle, growing a little uncomfortable at that point. "My name is Ayrion. What did you say your name was again?"

"I didn't."

One of the guards behind us shouted to move along, and I turned to see who he was talking to. When I turned back around, the old man was gone. I stood in my stirrups and quickly scanned the line in front of us and behind, even taking a moment to look at those in the opposite line waiting to get into the city, but there was no sign of him.

"Where did he go, boy?" I asked as we started back up once more.

"He couldn't have gotten far." I continued to stare ahead, studying the tops of the heads in front of us, looking for anyone with a white beard or green robe, but there was no one there matching that description, as though the man had never been. "I didn't just imagine him, did I?"

The horse snorted. He felt as bewildered about the situation as I did.

We reached the other side of the wall, and the crowd began to dissipate, making it easier to spot individuals who might be hiding within. I nudged the horse into a trot, and we moved to the side of the road, passing those still meandering along, but there was no sign of the old gentleman. The hair on my arms stood on end.

Finally, I stopped about a quarter mile up the road and turned the horse around. The wall stretched out on either side of us as far as I could see. To the north, the peaks of the Sandrethins rose in the distance. I felt the horse's muscles tensing under me.

"I know, I know." I turned and looked out across the open plain to the south. "Fine. Let's go." I barely had time to tighten my grip on the leather before he took off. When we got a few hundred feet from the road and into the taller grass, he really opened up.

I lowered my head to keep the wind from beating my face as the giant animal raced ahead, his hooves thundering against the ground, flinging up clods of dirt with each powerful step. I'd never moved so fast. I'd run hard on horses before, but nothing like this. This animal had been born to run the open plains. I was afraid he might catch a hole and send us both to the ground, but he never did, apparently quite used to the terrain. From what little I had seen of the Rymiran Plains on my journey from the Shemoa River to Aramoor, it looked very much like the wild fields here outside of the city.

As I clung on for dear life, allowing the eager stallion to get the run out of his system, my mind raced to the beat of his hooves. I tried to recall all the items of importance that needed to be accomplished over the next couple of days. I was starting to feel like I was back in Hurricane, and we were racing against time to finish all our requirements to remain a full-fledged member of the tribal guild. It was those tests, put on us by the other tribes, that had landed me my first introduction to the king. It was amazing to think how my life had changed since then.

A few miles out, the horse finally began to slow. I think it could sense my own hesitancy. Knowing how much I needed to get done, he turned around and started back, keeping his effort to a steady canter instead of an outright sprint. By the time we made it back to the main road, his coat was lathered in sweat, but he seemed more relaxed.

"Enjoyed that, did you?"

The horse snorted.

"I'm glad one of us is having a good time."

Who was I kidding? I had enjoyed that almost as much as him.

We found our place in line and waited our turn back through the wall. The guards on the other side didn't bother stopping us and nodded politely as we passed, though they did pause long enough to stare at the magnificent creature under me.

Ignoring the looks, we headed up King's Way East to the roundabout, and from there north on Circle Drive toward Bailey Street. The horse kept getting sidetracked by those moving up and down the busy roads, curious about everything.

"Come on," I said. "We've got a full day ahead of us, and half of it's already gone."

The stallion seemed to understand, and his pace quickened. By the time we had turned off Circle Drive and onto Bailey Street, most of the foot traffic had been left behind, and we were soon heading through the residential districts. As soon as we reached the orphanage, I pulled around the side. There were several children playing in the drive, all

quickly rushing to get out of the way when they saw us coming.

The kids stood with their backs against the house and gawked, more at my horse than at me.

"That's got to be the biggest horse I've ever seen, Protector," a younger boy said.

I recognized the boy's face but couldn't recall his name. "He's the biggest I've seen as well," I said. I dismounted and walked the stallion back behind the orphanage so he wouldn't be spotted from the road. After tying him to the post of a clothesline, I walked back around. "Don't get too close to him. He's still pretty wild. I wouldn't want to see any of you getting kicked."

"We won't," the same boy said as they all gathered at the corner of the house to stare at the giant animal.

I looked at the horse. "You better be good."

The horse didn't seem to be bothered by the kids, so I left them to their fun and headed around to the front and knocked on the door. A girl of thirteen or fourteen years opened it. I didn't recognize her at all.

"Is Master Fentin or Mistress Orilla in?"

She gulped as she stared up at me, rather wide-eyed, especially at the two swords rising from behind my head.

"I was just here yesterday, and I have some additional information for them." I tried to put her at ease, as she probably thought I was there to do someone harm. "My name is Ayrion."

Her rigid posture relaxed, obviously recognizing the name. "Master Fentin's in his study," she said nervously, "and Mistress Orilla's in the kitchen. Should I fetch them?"

I stepped inside and shut the door. "If you can let Mistress Orilla know that I'm here, that would be helpful." As soon as she started down the hall, I walked into the front room on the left and across to the door at the back, which led to Master Fentin's study. The door was shut, so I knocked.

"This is my bookkeeping time," an annoyed voice called out from the other side. "You know better than to disturb me now. Come back in an hour."

I chuckled. "Well, I certainly wouldn't want to deprive a man of his reading, so I guess I'll just come back at a—"

The door opened. "Ayrion?" The old man pulled his spectacles down to look at me and then smiled. He glanced around the room behind me. Realizing it was empty, he ushered me inside and shut the door. "Don't get much time to ourselves these days, and these old bones need a rest, or they won't be able to keep going. Orilla was just making us a spot of tea. Here . . ." He moved a stack of books from one of the chairs and dusted the seat with his hand. "Sit yourself. Should I fetch Orilla?"

"One of the girls already is," I said and sat down. The curtains at the back and on the side had been opened to let in as much light as possible. The early afternoon sun shone across the papers on Fentin's desk, brightening the shelves of books behind it. There was a small hearth on one side with a crackling fire and two cushioned chairs in front.

"So, what brings you by?"

The door opened before I got a chance to answer, and Orilla stepped in with a tray in her arms. I quickly stood and took it from her and placed it on a small table they had set between their reading chairs. Orilla shut the door, then walked over and gave me a warm hug.

"Didn't expect to see you so soon. I hope it isn't bad news."

I smiled. "Depends on how you look at it, I guess."

"We want to look at it in as positive a way as we can," she said with a skeptical eye.

"Well, it's not exactly bad news." I waited for her to pour three cups and pass them around. As soon as the two had taken their seats, I continued. "I talked with the queen about your situation. Namely, that after this raid, we are going to find ourselves with quite a few additional mouths to feed." I went on to explain about my proposal to keep the extra children at Sandstorm—depending on whether I could talk Sapphire and Reevie into allowing them—for a few months prior to bringing them to the orphanage to be placed.

The two looked concerned as soon as I mentioned the part about bringing them here. "I told the queen of our discussion about starting a new orphanage and also of your need for more funding."

"I bet she didn't take too kindly to that," Fentin commented as he slowly sipped his tea. "The rich don't like parting with their gold."

Orilla hmphed. "Who does?"

Fentin nodded.

"She took it better than I would have thought," I said. "Queen Ellise seems set on trying to establish a second orphanage if needed, so much so that she is planning on meeting with some new wealthy benefactors who she hopes to convince to partner with her to get the ball rolling."

The older couple smiled.

"That sounds like very good news to me," Orilla said. "Not sure how one could look at that any differently."

I cleared my throat. "That's because I haven't finished."

Orilla's smile wilted.

"The queen requests that the two of you present the case to these potential new investors yourselves."

Both of their eyes bulged, and Orilla's mouth dropped open. I was glad she had swallowed her last mouthful of tea beforehand, or she might have choked.

"The queen believes they will respond better to hearing it directly from the source than from just herself. If I had to guess, I think she wants them to not feel as though she is using her influence to force them to give."

"I guess that makes sense," Fentin said, his voice cracking slightly as he licked his lips. "But I don't know if we can stand in front of a group of nobles and tell them to give us their gold."

"I will be there as well," I said, for whatever comfort that was. "And you won't be telling them to give you anything. Your job is just to tell them about the orphanage and all the children you've helped over the last couple of years. Let the queen deal with the financial side. I don't expect you'll find the orphanage all that hard to discuss. No one loves these kids more than the two of you. The queen's right. It's your passion the nobles need to see. I have no doubt you will do the orphanage proud."

"How soon will this meeting be?" Fentin asked.

"She wishes to meet tomorrow afternoon, so I would start preparing what you think you would like to say now. The queen knows I have this raid coming, and she also knows I am set to leave for the front next week, so there isn't much time." I shook my head and took a final sip of my tea. "There never seems to be enough time."

"You're leaving for the front?" Orilla asked. "You just returned."

"It seems things are progressing to the point that my unit might be called into action."

Both Fentin and Orilla shook their heads, their faces concerned.

I leaned forward and placed my teacup down on the table and stood. "I don't have much time to spend, but I wanted to stop by and let you know what is happening and to prepare you. I doubt it takes you long to come up with some moving stories of success you've had with the street kids over your years."

They both smiled. "The problem will be limiting how many stories,"

Orilla said, eyeing her husband.

"The more emotional the better," I said as I headed for the door. The two started to rise, and I waved them back down. "I can see myself out. Besides, you look like you could use a few more quiet moments in front of the fire."

"We aren't the only ones," Orilla pointed out with a raised brow. "You need to get you some rest before you collapse. Your eyes are already reddening, and on an Upakan, it's even more pronounced."

I chuckled. "I promise I'll carve out some time."

The two looked at each other skeptically, and I left them to their tea. Outside, I found my giant horse still standing in back, now surrounded by children. They had flanked him on either side, rubbing him down with their hands. I felt a strong sense of happiness coming from the monstrous beast, and I almost chuckled. As soon as the horse saw me, he stiffened, his glee vanishing as something like embarrassment filtered through him. He had been enjoying the attention, but he was also a very proud animal. I couldn't help but laugh.

"It seems you have taken good care of him," I said as the children all moved back for me to mount. "He appreciates it very much."

"He looked lonely," the boy I'd spoken with earlier said.

"Then I'm glad you were here to comfort him." I turned the horse around, and we slowly headed to the front of the orphanage, with the children following just behind. They watched as we started down the road. I passed one quick glance over my shoulder to find them all standing in front of the orphanage, watching. I guessed they didn't have much else to do. At least they were staying out of trouble.

I nudged the horse, and we picked up our pace.

Next stop, Sandstorm. With two visits to the old manor in just a couple days, it almost felt like old times.

Almost.

AVALANCHE

Chapter 15

THE SUN WAS WARM ON my back as I headed up the lane toward Sandstorm. I passed over a small rise, and the gate became visible just ahead. I could also see movement behind the bars and a few heads popping up over the wall to either side.

"Open the gate," I heard Toots shout before I had even spotted him. The large S adorning the center of the gate split as the left side swung outward, Toots and several others of the Watch waiting to greet me.

"I knew you's couldn't stay away," Toots said, beaming as he wiped his brown hair from his eyes.

I smiled as I pulled the horse to a stop. "With a face like that to greet me, how could I?"

The watchers all gathered round to gawk up at the stallion.

"That there's the biggest animal I've ever seen," one of the girls beside Toots said as she walked over and patted the horse's side. "What's his name?"

"Afraid he doesn't have one yet."

She clicked her tongue. "A horse this pretty needs a name."

The horse snorted. He seemed to agree with the girl's sentiments, though perhaps not the *pretty* part.

"They've already served lunch," Toots said. "Afraid you's a bit late for that. Might be some leftovers, though."

"I'm not here to eat." My stomach growled its disagreement. "Are the chiefs in?"

Toots nodded. "Should be, unless they snuck off the property without me knowing. But that's unlikely, 'cause I got this place locked down good and tight, watchers posted all along the boundary. Couldn't slip a sand flea past without us knowing it. Don't want none of those Avalanche beaters trying to weasel their way in." He patted the hilt of the short sword riding high on his waist. "They'll wish they hadn't if they do."

"I don't doubt it," I said, trying to hide a smile. "I'll leave you to your work." With that, I nudged the horse, and we headed up the drive to the manor house.

The three-story stone building was bustling with activity, kids everywhere—some playing in the trees to the left of the drive, some milling about the courtyard in front, and some tossing around a leather-bound ball on the manicured lawn to the right. The sun was out and the day warmer than most, no doubt leaving the kids anxious to be outdoors. I maneuvered the giant horse around the drive and over to the carriage house on the right. The doors were open, and Gittrick was outside washing the coach.

He looked up at the sound of hooves on the cobbles, and his eyes widened when he saw what I was riding. He dropped his rag on the carriage's front shaft and walked over, looking the horse up and down, though remaining at a respectful distance.

"Back so soon, Master Ayrion?" Gittrick asked.

I swung out of the saddle and handed him the reins. "See that he gets some feed, will you?"

"Yes, sir," Gittrick said nervously. "He's gentle enough to lead, I hope?"

I smiled. "He will be if you treat him right."

Gittrick looked up at the horse and gulped.

I placed my hand on the horse's neck. "Don't give him any trouble, or I'll take you right back to the stables." Of course, I had no intention of riding all the way back to the palace, but I hoped the horse couldn't sense that. I wasn't sure how much he really knew of my thoughts.

The horse blew out his lips, but that was about the extent of his response, so I left Gittrick to his work and headed for the front of the manor.

"Hey, Protector!" Mouse shouted, swinging down from one of the lower branches in a tree on the far side of the courtyard. He ran over, with Squeaks, Petal, and Tubby just behind. They slowed when they caught me about halfway across the courtyard. "Was that your horse? It's a monster. I bet even Tubby could ride it."

I looked up at the giant boy. "Let's not try to find out."

The horse was enormous, but I doubted even he could handle the likes of Tubby.

"Oh, wow, you got you a new sheath." Mouse proceeded to walk behind me to get a better look. "Don't remember seeing that before. Makes you look even more like . . . Death's Shadow."

I cringed. It had been a long time since I'd heard that name.

"It was a gift from the chiefs," I said. "Have you seen them this afternoon?"

"I think Reevie is up in the counting room," Mouse said.

"And Sapphire's in the chiefs' study last I saw," Squeaks added.

Petal cleared her throat. "Bull is out back with Collen training the Guard and beaters."

"And Tubby's right here," Tubby added, clearly wanting to add his own copper's worth to the conversation.

The other three turned and looked up at the giant boy and shook their heads.

I chuckled, then started for the front doors. "I'll see if I can find them."

Mouse and the others watched me go. I was surprised they didn't follow but was glad they didn't, since I had things to discuss with the chiefs. The open gallery inside seemed nearly abandoned, most of the tribe enjoying the outdoors. I headed left toward the west wing but slowed when I heard noises coming from the library.

The door was open, so I peeked inside. Gustory was reciting one of his tales to several of the smaller kids, who seemed completely engrossed in the story, so much so that they never saw me. It didn't appear that either Reevie or Sapphire were in attendance, so I continued down the gallery to the end and then followed the corridor left, where it ended at the chiefs' study. The door was shut, which was a good sign that I would find at least one of them inside.

I knocked and didn't have to wait long before Sapphire's somewhat annoyed voice snapped to open the door. It wasn't like her to be so sharp. She must have been working on something important. I opened the door and stuck my head in.

Sapphire looked up from behind the desk. "Ayrion?" She lowered her quill. "You're the last person I expected to see today, or any day for that matter," she added with a bitter hint of sarcasm. She stayed in her seat, not bothering to get up. She did, however, run her hands down the front of her violet top to smooth the wrinkles, though I doubted she even realized she had done so. Her long braid of blonde hair hung loosely over her right shoulder.

I shut the door and walked over, passing the sitting area in front of the fireplace on the right. The hearth crackled lightly with a few chunks of burning wood. It might have been comfortable outside, but the stone house still remained cool through the day.

Taking a seat in one of the chairs in front of her desk, I leaned back carefully, not wanting to whack my new sheaths against the back of the seat.

She stared at the two swords rising from my back. "I see you finally stopped by to see Master Fentin and Mistress Orilla."

I smiled. "I did. It's partly why I wanted to stop by, to thank you for the generous gift." I smiled. "You should have seen the look on my face when I opened the package."

Sapphire smiled, though she seemed to be attempting to temper it with a strong demeanor. "I knew you had been talking about getting one for some time, and I doubt a lancer salary provides enough for extras, so . . ."

"It was very generous of you." I cocked my head to the side. "How did you talk Reevie into—"

She cleared her throat, looking a little guilty. "He doesn't know. Best we keep it that way."

I nodded in agreement. I hoped to be able to mend the trampled fence between Reevie and me, but judging by the frosty greeting I received from him earlier, it was going to take more than a few conversations. What it would take, I wasn't sure. A grand gesture, probably, but what kind . . . I had no idea.

"I was hoping to speak with the three of you about my meeting with

the king and queen concerning your predicament."

Sapphire placed her quill in its jar. "What predicament?"

"Avalanche."

Her eyes narrowed. "You spoke to the king and queen about our street turf? Why would you go to them? They aren't going to care about whether one group of kids kills another. They'd likely be happy to see us all gone."

"How can you say that, knowing what they've done for the orphanage?"

"There's a big difference in the eyes of the average citizenry between an orphanage and the street tribes. Even you've mentioned on several occasions about wanting to get rid of the tribes altogether."

"True. But that doesn't mean I want them to kill each other off. You know that."

Her demeanor softened. "So, what exactly did you tell them?" She sat back in her chair and began to fiddle with the end of her braid as she always did when deep in thought. "Is that what you meant when you said you had an idea of how to handle Avalanche?"

"In a way. But what I have to say needs to be said to all three of you."

Sapphire stared at me for a moment, and then exhaled loudly. "Fine." She left her desk and headed for the door, glancing at my new sheath on the way by. She stuck her head out and called down the hall. A moment later, a husky girl appeared in the doorway, one I didn't recognize, and after a few words from Sapphire, the girl took off for the next hall down.

Sapphire shut the door and returned to her seat. I could feel her eyes on me as she passed.

"It fits perfectly," I said, shifting forward in my chair so she could get a better look. I reached behind my head and grabbed the hilts of my swords. "Exactly the right size. I love it."

"It certainly goes well with your whole black leather motif," she said.

I smiled. "I thought you liked me in black."

"It definitely emphasizes your Death's Shadow persona."

"You're the second person to mention that today." Perhaps the sheath wasn't such a good look after all. Was being Death's Shadow the aura I wanted to portray? Then again, I was the head of the Black Guild, so I guess it only made sense to look the part. Really, I just enjoyed not having my sword constantly bouncing against my leg.

We chatted idly for a few minutes about the goings-on at Sandstorm, but we were cut short by the arrival of Bull, who knocked first but didn't wait to be announced before opening the door and sticking his head inside.

"Protector, I wasn't sure Misha had gotten it correctly when she told me you were here and wanting to see me. Is that your horse out there? I've never seen anything like it." I barely got the chance to nod it was before he continued. "Where did you find such a beast?"

"Horse?" Sapphire asked. "What horse?"

"You should see it," Bull said and walked over to the window that looked out across the courtyard. We couldn't see the carriage house from there, but the coach that Gittrick had been cleaning was visible. There was no sign of the warhorse. Gittrick must have taken him inside to be fed. Bull shrugged. "It was there a moment ago. You wouldn't believe it if you saw it."

Bull walked back over and shut the door, then started for the empty seat beside mine, but Sapphire stopped him and motioned for us to take our seats over in the sitting area. I noticed her pass a quick glance out the side window once more on her way across the room.

"Two visits in such a short time," Bull said excitedly. "It's starting to feel like old times."

Sapphire grunted as she took the closest hardback to the fireplace on the left. I sat on the right side of the sofa, directly across from her, and Bull joined me, but on the other side, leaving another hardback open next to Sapphire for Reevie if he ever decided to grace us with his presence.

"Did you send for Reevie?" I asked. I wasn't sure, given his earlier attitude, if she thought it a waste of time.

She nodded.

"I probably should have told you not to mention me being here."

"Oh, trust me. I didn't."

I almost smiled.

Bull did.

The door behind us opened without a knock, and a loud groan broke the silence.

"Why is *he* here?" Reevie called out behind me.

I didn't bother standing or attempt to explain my return. In fact, I didn't say anything at all as I waited for Sapphire to do it for me.

"Ayrion said he spoke with the king and queen on our behalf."

"Bleeding pustules! What possessed him to do that?"

I sighed. He was still talking as though I wasn't sitting right there in the room. Reevie reluctantly walked around to the side of the sofa, forcing me to turn my head to see him.

"I'm here for three reasons," I said.

"Hopefully, one of them doesn't involve another stabbing," Reevie shot back, while staring at the back of the empty seat beside Sapphire.

I ignored him. "First, I wanted to thank you for my new sheath . . ." As soon as I said it, I realized I'd stuck my foot in it, having just promised Sapphire I wouldn't mention the sheath to Reevie.

A soft groan came from the seat across from me, and I turned to catch the end of an eye roll as Sapphire shook her head. About that time,

I noticed Bull lowering his.

"What new sheath?" Reevie asked. "Why would he be thanking me for a new sheath?"

I looked over at Sapphire, and her eyes locked on mine and hardened.

"Not *you* in particular," I backtracked, trying to determine how I was going to dig myself out of this one. "As you know, I recently reached my next birthday, and Master Fentin and Mistress Orilla wanted to do something special, so they asked Sapphire what she thought would make a nice gift. A way to thank me for all I've done in arranging their stipend from the crown."

Reevie hmphed.

"Anyway, she was good enough to point them in the direction of this new sheath." I leaned forward for him to see, but Reevie's jaw tightened as he kept his focus on the empty chair.

Bull, however, leaned over and ran a hand along the leather casing. "It definitely suits you."

"Yes, I'm sure it's very nice," Reevie said nonchalantly, this time looking at Sapphire, "but where did those two manage to raise the funds for such a generous gift? Every time I'm over there, things seem to be getting worse."

"They had some coin saved up," Sapphire said.

"And you let them use it on him?"

I ignored Reevie's slight and turned to Sapphire. "I'm surprised you remembered the sheath at all. It's been what, three years since we first looked at them?"

Her cheeks flushed, and she quickly changed the subject. "What was the second thing you wished to discuss with us?"

"Right," I said and reclined in my seat once more. "The last time I was here, I said I might have an idea as to how to help with the Avalanche situation, but I didn't want to say anything until I knew whether it was doable or just a shot in the dark."

"I take it you've gotten your answer?" Bull said.

"I have. As you now know, I spoke with the king and queen about your situation, and they have a lot more sympathy toward the street rats than you seem to believe," I added for Reevie's sake, "especially the queen, which is why they agreed to help fund the orphanage in the first place."

"I still can't believe someone brought the royal family into this," Reevie said offhandedly.

"It shouldn't matter who's involved," Bull said. "The last thing any of us wants to see is a street war."

"Seems to be all but assured at this point," Sapphire said.

I shrugged. "Perhaps. Perhaps not."

"Could you be any more vague?" Reevie grumbled, remaining right where he was on the other end of the sofa, even though there was a perfectly good chair waiting on him beside Sapphire.

I smiled. At least he was addressing me directly. "There could be a street war, but I'm hoping it won't involve any of you."

The three chiefs looked at each other.

"What does that mean?" Sapphire asked.

"When I spoke with the king and queen, I told them of your situation and how the last thing you wanted was a battle with Avalanche. I also explained to them that things were getting more dangerous by the day, and that my goal was to stop Cutter before he could try taking Sandstorm by force."

"And how do you plan on doing that?" Bull asked. "Storm the old Rockslide compound?"

I smiled. "In a manner of speaking."

"Have you lost your flaming mind?" Reevie cut in.

Bull's eyes widened hungrily. "I can have the Guard and beaters assembled and ready in an hour."

I shook my head. "No. I don't want to involve Sandstorm if I can help it."

"Then how exactly are you going to storm their compound?" Bull asked. "You planning on just walking up to the front gate and demanding they surrender?" He chuckled. "Hoping they take one look at your new sheath and run in fear?"

"You're bringing the lancers," Sapphire said, growing suddenly excited. "That's why you went to the king. You needed his permission to use soldiers."

It was my turn to chuckle. "Not hardly. I'm not sending an armed force of lancers to raid a bunch of street urchins. Besides, they have more important things to worry about right now than tribal disputes, trust me on that. Anyway, by law, the crown can't use the military against citizens—even street rats."

The others shrugged.

"Then what are you planning on doing?" Sapphire asked, growing frustrated. Even Reevie cocked his head in my direction.

"I'm sending the Blue Capes."

The room went quiet.

Reevie actually gaped. I knew how much most of the street kids hated the patrollers. Feared them. They spent most of their lives hiding from them, hoping not to get nabbed by one and taken to the workhouses.

Bull was the first to speak. "You plan on leading a force of patrollers against Avalanche?"

I nodded, still unsure how they were taking the news, until Bull leaned back and released a billowing roar of laughter, startling Reevie enough he nearly tripped on his own feet as he hopped back from the sofa.

"Well, isn't that just perfect," Bull said. "The Blue Capes have been wanting to rid Aramoor of the tribes for years, and here you are handing them one on a platter."

Again, I couldn't quite tell if he was angry or thrilled by the prospect. "I'm not here to hand them anything. I'm here to stop bloodshed. The sooner we get rid of Cutter and his ilk, the better it will be for everyone."

"But you aren't getting rid of Cutter," Sapphire pointed out. "You're merely halting his northern pursuits, which is bound to make him even angrier."

"One thing at a time," I said. "At the very least, it will slow him down and give you some much-needed breathing room. It will also cut his force by at least a third."

She nodded slowly, but her eyes were distant, no doubt trying to estimate how bad this could come back to bite them depending on whether I was successful or not. I would have done the same—and had already.

"Do any of you know how many kids are living at the old garrison?"

"At least a hundred, probably more," Bull said. He, like the others, didn't look all that sure.

"And what exactly is going to happen to all these captured kids?" Reevie asked.

"Who cares?" Bull added. "Hopefully they get sent to the work-houses, or better yet, the dungeons." He looked over at me. "Do they send street kids to the dungeons?"

"No, they don't send kids to the dungeons." That was a myth that had been passed down through the ranks ever since I first came to Ara-moor, a way to keep the tribe members frightened enough to not get caught. It had been repeated so many times that most believed it.

I paused in thought.

"I don't like that look on your face," Sapphire said, staring across the way at me. "What haven't you told us?"

I cleared my throat, feeling the hard gazes being leveled in my direction. "Like Reevie, the queen was quite adamant to know what happens to the children after the raid has taken place."

Sapphire groaned. "I'm not going to like where this is going, am I?"

I offered a half grin. "We didn't want to simply toss them all in the workhouses."

"Why not?" Bull said. "I say send them all and good riddance."

Sapphire grunted a slight agreement.

Reevie remained surprisingly stoic.

"Of course," I added, "those who are too belligerent or combative will have to go there, but the goal is to transform as many as we can into productive members of society."

"You sound like one of *them*, talking like that," Bull said. "*Productive members of society.*"

"Sound like one of who?" I asked.

"Like an old person."

"I *feel* like an old person," I said with a lopsided smile. I was twenty, and no longer a teenager. "I suggested we offer the elder boys the choice to join the lancer corps, those that don't want to get stuck in the workhouses."

"Sounds reasonable," Bull said.

"And what about the rest?" Sapphire asked, tugging quite forcefully on her braid.

"The queen would like to rehabilitate as many as we can and send them through the orphanage to find homes, or at the least usable skills and trade."

"Master Fentin and Mistress Orilla can't handle that," Reevie said rather harshly, as if I hadn't considered that already and was purposefully trying to overburden the older couple.

"Yes. I told the queen as much. However, Master Fentin and Mistress Orilla did discuss the possibility of opening a second orphanage."

"And how are they supposed to do that?" Reevie asked, this time actually looking at me. "They can barely take care of the orphanage as it is."

"I know that as well. We would need to find some volunteer workers. A younger couple who could manage it."

Sapphire leaned forward in her seat. "It will also take more gold."

I nodded. "Which is why the queen is organizing a gathering of prominent lords and ladies for Master Fentin and Mistress Orilla to address in hopes of swaying some to become benefactors."

The other three stared at me once more with mouths gaping.

"Did he just say that Master Fentin and Mistress Orilla were going to be addressing the aristocracy?" Reevie asked.

"Not all of them."

"Are you trying to put them in an early grave?" Reevie continued, finally angry enough to address me directly. "Yellow fever! Do you actually think before you act? You'd likely kill them from fright."

My face hardened. "I'll be there to stand with them, as will the queen. She only wants the best for them. She believes the nobility will be more receptive to hearing the street kids' plight directly from their lips."

"She's the queen," Sapphire said. "Can't she just order them to?"

"Not if she wants their support. You can't just order people to spend their money on what you want them to, not unless you want a revolt.

But the queen is smart, she'll know how to manipulate a positive out-come." I thought a moment. "I guess *manipulate* isn't exactly the right word. It sounds a little devious. But you know what I mean."

"Still, that doesn't answer the question as to what is going to happen to all the leftover Avalanche kids," Sapphire said, bringing the conversation swiftly back to the main point.

I took a deep breath, and she seemed to be able to read the answer on my face.

"No." She even went so far as to wag her finger at me. "Don't you even think about bringing them here."

Bull's head shot up. "Here?" He looked at me.

"Then where do you suggest I place the younger ones? Drop them on the orphanage's doorstep?"

"No," Reevie said. "We've already established that Master Fentin and Mistress Orilla can't handle anything more."

"I agree, which is why I suggested that Sandstorm take the younger ones in and begin assimilating them here. Get them ready to be transferred over to the orphanage once their attitudes have changed."

"That won't be easy," Sapphire said. "Just trying to keep them from running away would be a full-time chore."

"I'm hoping they will see how much better it is here than living under Cutter's thumb and fighting each other every day for scraps. I want them to see how living and working together in unity can be so much more rewarding than living in a society where only the strongest survive. And if all else fails," I said with a wily smirk, "have Gustory spin them a tale so frightening it will have them never wanting to run away."

Bull chuckled. "That's actually not a bad idea."

Reevie mumbled something under his breath and shook his head.

"That's a lot of work dropped on our shoulders," Sapphire said.

"But think of the benefits," I added. "You won't have to continue worrying about being flanked by Avalanche from two sides. You could also send your kids out without worrying whether they will return in one piece. If this works, it will at least provide a temporary break."

"Temporary being the key word," she said. "This might postpone Cutter's attempt to take over, but it won't deter it for long, and he will be even more motivated afterward."

All of what she said was true, but I could only handle one thing at a time. Cutter's eventual retaliation would have to be saved for a later time.

"So," Bull asked, when a slight moment of silence presented itself, "what is the third thing you wanted to say? Or was that it?"

I smiled. "That was it." I thought a moment. "Wait. There is one more thing. I've been called back to the front."

Sapphire's brows lowered. "Already? You just got back."

"Things are escalating quickly, and the king wants the Black Guild back at the front as soon as possible."

"War?" Bull asked.

I nodded.

All three sat quietly. Well, Sapphire and Bull sat. Reevie continued to stand.

"How are you planning on doing all of this if you've been recalled?" Sapphire asked.

"I got special permission from the king to stay behind a day or two in order to try to get this taken care of first."

"It's that important to him?"

I grinned. "It's that important to his wife."

"And when do you plan on doing whatever it is you plan on doing?" Bull asked.

"Soon. I hope to scout out the compound tonight. I'm supposed to meet with a Captain Arns this evening. Commandant Ipsworth assigned him to me."

"I don't know anything about Ipsworth," Sapphire said. "Never met him, but Arns is a good man. I've had a couple of meetings with him concerning Sandstorm business. He was Red's contact when Wildfire was still around."

"So you trust him?"

She shrugged. "As much as you can trust any patroller, I guess."

"That's good to know." I glanced out the window behind Sapphire. The shadows cast by the trees were getting longer, which meant I didn't have much time before I needed to make my way to the northeast patrollers' office. "Any chance Cook has something in the kitchen I could eat? I haven't had time to grab anything yet today. Kind of hard to sneak through Avalanche territory with my stomach grumbling."

Sapphire nodded. "I'm sure we can find you something."

AVALANCHE

Chapter 16

ILL WE SEE YOU BEFORE you leave for the front?" Sapphire asked, standing at the front of the courtyard as she and Bull stared admiringly up at my horse. The sun was already dropping below the peaks on the western side of the city, and the deeply colored sky was just showing signs of fading. Most of the kids were inside enjoying one of Gustory's tales before heading off to bed, and those not inside were gathered around the courtyard where the nightly torches were just being lit. Reevie hovered near the front door, watching from a distance.

"I'm not sure. It depends on what is decided about the raid. I'll know more after my meeting with Captain Arns and this evening's scouting."

"Make sure to give us some kind of warning beforehand," Bull said, "so that we can prepare ourselves, in case anything goes wrong. I don't want to face an angry swarm of Avalanche beaters looking for retaliation unprepared."

I smiled with a nod. "Absolutely. I'll make sure you get word before anything is done." Bull had come a long way in the last couple of years since I'd been there. He had really stepped into his role as the third chief. He would have never demanded anything of me before, but now he was looking out for his house.

Bull smiled. "You have been missed." He held out his hand. "If we do not see you again before you go, please be careful."

I shook his hand. "I'll do my best." Releasing him, I tapped the front shield of my new sheath. "This will certainly help with that."

I looked at Sapphire, but before I could say anything, she had her arms wrapped around my neck. She smelled of jasmine and honey, and on her it was a rather intoxicating combination. "Do watch out for yourself," she said before letting go.

"You know me."

"Yes, that's why I mention it."

I turned and looked over at Reevie, who quickly averted his eyes, suddenly interested in something on the doorjamb. "Tell the stubborn oaf I said goodbye, will you? And that I hope to one day earn back his friendship."

Sapphire nodded. "I'll tell him."

"Send those Cylmarans to the Pits," Bull said.

"I'll do my best." I could feel the horse's eagerness to be on our way, so I climbed up onto the giant beast and looked down at my friends. With a brief smile, I turned the horse, and we trotted down the drive toward the front gate.

Toots was there, along with Collen. They had one side already opened and waiting. They waved as I passed.

"Good luck, Protector!" Toots called out.

I waved back and then nudged the horse a little faster once we reached the street out front. We headed down the lane to the next street and slowly worked our way through the city, heading for the largest of the northeast patroller stations. I stopped in front of the towers where the Street Guild used to hold its meetings and looked up at the sky bridges with their glass-sided walkways.

The lanterns inside showed silhouettes of people passing through. I remembered my first time in the towers not long after my arrival to Aramoor, back when Spats was still in charge of Hurricane. It had been quite a thrilling treat to go up. At least, it had been for me. Not so much for Reevie, who nearly fainted when we forced him across, and then he filled one of the decorative vases on the other side with retch.

I couldn't help but chuckle at the memory. I wondered what had ever happened to Gromly, the old bookkeeper in charge of taking roll just outside the guild meeting room. Every time I saw him, he was always wearing his green suit and feathered cap. I never did find out if that was supposed to be a designated uniform or just something he enjoyed wearing. I wondered if he was even still alive. If he was, I wouldn't have been surprised to find him still sitting at his post with quill in hand, waiting for whoever the new owners of the room were. Perhaps, one day, I'd find the time to go up and pay him a visit.

Unfortunately, now wasn't that time.

I went to nudge the giant horse forward, but before I could, he started up the road. The link we shared was strange. Passing under the sky bridges, we made our way around the north side of the tower complex, and from there it wasn't long before we were crossing in front of the old Wildfire compound.

I hadn't seen it since the night of Wildfire's demise, after Kore and Cutter had teamed up to take Red down. Apparently, the new owners of the tall residence had sunk a good deal of gold into having it restored.

The front barely looked the same, what with the new brick and the covered porches and the sculpted statues of large dogs placed about, all looking down toward the street as though keeping watch. I almost didn't recognize it, and in fact had to look at the surrounding buildings more than once just to be sure. I wondered if the new owners had redecorated the interior as well. I remembered Kira's penchant for deeply colorful rooms.

I sighed. So many memories. There was hardly a place in this city that didn't have some attached to it. Most I could probably do without, but there were still plenty that I was happy to recall.

"Let's keep going," I said to myself, or maybe the horse. Either way, I barely had time to turn in my saddle before we were once again heading down the street.

We turned down two more busy thoroughfares before finally pulling to a stop in front of a three-story stone building on the right that had a slow but steady stream of blue-caped men walking in and out of its front doors. Unlike the surrounding buildings, this one seemed built a little more securely, even boasting a couple of square turrets in front and a crenelated roof atop for defending. Not sure what they were supposed to be defending themselves from. I'd never heard of anyone attacking a patroller station before.

It was one of the buildings we street rats had been prone to stay as far away from as possible. I had only been by this particular office once in all my years in Aramoor and had never actually been inside.

Several of the patrollers stopped when they saw my horse, others when they saw me. A man dressed all in black with two swords hanging on his back was sure to catch the eye of anyone whose job was to protect the good citizens of Aramoor. I swung down and tied the horse's reins to an empty spot on one of the hitching rails out front.

"Wish me luck," I whispered to the horse, who released a soft whinny as if to say: *You're on your own.*

No one tried to stop me as I headed for the front door, but those outside watched tensely as I passed. Those close enough to see my eyes moved in behind me and motioned for others to do the same. They probably thought I was there on contract.

They clearly knew little of Upakan business.

If I had been on contract, they wouldn't have seen me coming, and if they had seen me, it would have been too late.

The left door was opened by one of the patrollers who had just stepped out. He fumbled between trying to hold the door open for me and reaching for his sword. I thanked him for his generosity and headed inside.

"Can we help you?" an older lanky man with a grey beard asked, seated just behind the front desk. I passed a quick glance back over my shoulder as I started across the room. The patrollers who followed me in from outside were all standing around the front entrance, keeping a close watch.

I reached the front desk and stopped. "I'm here to see Captain Arns."

More than a few men behind me took a step forward.

I looked at the older man behind the desk. "I have an appointment," I said, speaking loudly enough for the surrounding men to hear. "It was made this morning by the queen and Commandant Ipsworth."

I heard half-drawn swords slide back in their sheaths.

"You're that tutor to the prince, I take it?" the older man said.

"I am."

The stiffness in the man's shoulders loosened slightly. "I'm Sergeant Lowell. I believe the captain's in his office. If you give me a minute, I'll go check for you." He glanced beyond me to the crowd of patrollers standing around. "I'm sure you've got other places to be," he all but shouted. "See that you get there."

There was some momentary grumbling, but by the time I finally decided to attempt a quick peek behind me, half of those who'd been breathing down my neck were filing back out the front doors. There were still plenty inside, enough to make it difficult for me if anything got out of hand, but at least now the lobby had a little more walking room.

It didn't take long for the sergeant to return. Directly behind him was the stout man with the wandering eye that I had met in the library. He was at least fifteen years my senior. The captain walked over and held out his hand.

"I'm sorry, but I don't remember your name."

I took his hand. "It's Ayrion." I wasn't sure if the captain had truly forgotten it or was just wanting to make me feel as little-wanted as possible. Neither he nor his commanding officer had seemed overly excited to be assigned to me, but perhaps I was reading too much into the situation.

Arns released my hand. "Come, we can talk in my office."

I nodded and followed the captain around the front desk, where Sergeant Lowell had already retaken his seat and was waving the next person in line forward. The room was rather quiet as all the patrollers' eyes followed me and their captain down the hall and out of sight. We made our way toward the back of the building and headed into an office on the left. The nameplate on the door read CAPTAIN ARNS. I wondered how long Arns had served as captain of this particular post. Clearly long enough to have garnered a brass inscription on the door.

"Please," he said, pointing to one of a couple of chairs that were seated in front of a small desk near the back of the room.

I walked over but waited to sit until the captain had shut the door and made his way around his desk and sat down. I did my best not to appear to stare at his wandering eye, which was harder to do than I would have thought. When you look at someone, you tend to look at both eyes. I wondered if he ever felt awkward by the way others looked at him, or if, like me, he'd stopped noticing over time.

"I know you aren't exactly teeming with excitement at the prospect of having to work with an Upakan, but I hope we can get past that difference to reach our common goal."

The captain took a deep breath, eyeing me as he did. "That remains to be seen. However, it's no secret I'd rather shovel dung than send my men into harm's way to protect a tribe of street rats." He took another deep breath and then sighed. "But when the queen asks for a favor, you do it."

I wondered if the captain knew of my own involvement with the street tribes or that I, too, had once been labeled a tribal chief. I had a feeling if he had, he might not have spoken so directly. Then again, that might be precisely why he was being so frank.

"I figured the Blue—the patrollers," I corrected quickly, "would have been overjoyed by the prospect of weeding out one of the tribes, especially one as aggressive as Avalanche, and in your own backyard nonetheless."

"I would like to have weeded them all out, but that would prove difficult to do without a full-on armed conflict that left dead children in the streets. Not the kind of image you want the good citizens of Aramoor becoming enraged about." He paused a moment. "Not something any of us really wants to see happen. I must admit, though, that things have grown much quieter over the last couple of years. That orphanage over on Bailey Street has been a big help, I believe. We need more like it if you ask me. These kids don't need to be running the streets, thieving everything in sight and disrupting everyday life." He ran a hand down his clean-shaven face and pinched his chin. "Thankfully, it seems there are only two tribes left. Apparently, the Street Guild's own ambitions brought them to ruin." The captain chuckled. "Strangely enough, I can't help but see the similarities between them and the squabbles here in the Five Kingdoms."

I leaned back in my seat. "Oh? How so?"

"Take Cylmar for example. Here we are on the brink of war, and for what? Because some overlord's desire to have more pushes him to take what isn't his? I guess it doesn't matter how old you are. Humans are going to do what humans have been doing since we first walked this world. Nothing ever seems to change."

Arns was proving to be quite philosophical, not that I could disagree with what he was saying. "Every culture does seem to have its own share of similar problems," I said. "It only seems that the older we get, the higher the stakes. Or perhaps that isn't exactly the correct way to put it. The stakes are just as high for a street kid who gets bludgeoned as it would be for a grown man. Perhaps a better way to phrase it would be that when you are older the scale is much greater. Street tribes inside one city hardly equates to a war between two entire kingdoms."

The captain nodded and stared at me a moment. "So, what's your story, anyway? How does one of the Upaka end up here in Aramoor? I thought your people kept to that wasteland in Keldor. More importantly, how did you earn the ear of the royal family? Did the king request someone from the Lost City to specially train his son?" He stopped and cocked one of his brows. "Ambitious, I grant you."

I smiled. "My arrival in Aramoor is a very long story, and certainly doesn't involve the king. As to my acquaintance with the royal family, it was purely by happenstance."

"Wish I was blessed with such luck."

I laughed. I couldn't stop myself. "Trust me when I say that my luck is not something you want to be blessed with."

Arns sat quietly a moment before leaning forward in his seat. "So, what did you have in mind with this raid? From what I know, those kids are pretty well-guarded inside the old garrison. If the doors are shut, it will be hard to draw them out, or get us in. They can cause a lot of damage from the walls if they have a mind to."

"Trust me. They have a mind to. But as to whether they are prepared, that's a different story, which is why I'm here. My goal is to scout their defenses tonight to see what we might be up against. I don't want a full-on armed conflict if we can help it. The less fighting the better. The only way that will happen is if we can catch them by surprise."

"Agreed," Arns said with a slow but curious nod. "Any thoughts on how we attempt such a surprise?"

"I have a few ideas milling around, but nothing worth mentioning until we see what we are up against. And the only way that will happen is by getting an up close and personal look at Avalanche's compound."

"When do you propose we do this?"

"We?"

"You don't think I plan on sending my men into danger without first seeing said danger myself, do you?"

I sighed inwardly. Of course I didn't fault the captain for wanting to see firsthand what he and his men would be getting into, but I had hoped to go it alone. "I can move through the streets much easier with just myself. I had hoped to scout out the compound tonight and report back with my findings and recommendations in the morning."

"I grew up around these streets," Arns said, his tone letting me know there would be no arguing the point. "If you go, I go. I want to see this place for myself. Two sets of eyes are better than one."

"Can you get around without being seen?"

"I can handle myself." The captain stared at me from across the desk. "So when do you plan on leaving?"

I glanced out the window at the side. The last remnants of the fading sun were clearly gone, its light replaced with that of one of the street-lamps surrounding the office. If Avalanche was anything like Sandstorm, the kids would have eaten their suppers a couple of hours ago and would be crawling into bed about now. "No time like the present."

Captain Arns stood. "Good. I'll saddle my horse."

"No horses," I said, following him up.

"What?"

"We go on foot from here. We won't be able to move within their territory on a horse, not without being seen by their runners, which means we will have to tie our horses up somewhere near their boundary line." I smiled. "I don't know about you, but I don't plan on leaving my horse on a vacant street and hoping no one walks by and steals it. Best we keep them here where they will be safe to leave unattended. It's not that far of a walk."

"The closest crossing will be the bridge over on Silt Street near the wall."

I shook my head. "That's too close to their compound. Avalanche will have their runners all over that bridge. We'd never get across there without being seen. We need to take a more southern crossing. Might even need to go as far as the towers."

"That's a long way around."

"It will give the tribe plenty of time to get in bed and fall asleep."

The captain stepped around his desk and started for the door. "You seem to possess quite a plethora of information on these tribes."

I smiled. "Let's just say I've had my fair share of run-ins with them." The captain started to open the door, and I stopped him. "Do you have

a change of clothes handy?"

"Huh?" Arns turned.

"You can't go traipsing through tribal territory wearing your patroller uniform. With that blue cape, you'll be spotted immediately. We want to blend in."

Arns looked me up and down. "You're one to talk."

"Yes, but my leathers help keep me hidden in the shadows."

"Fine." He looked over at one of his shelves. "I think I have a spare change of clothes around here somewhere. Just give me a moment."

I stepped outside and waited in the hallway to give him some privacy while he changed. When the door finally opened, I almost didn't recognize the man. He was dressed in grey trousers with a brown tunic and dark green cloak with its hood pulled. "Will this work?"

"Much more than the other," I said. I waited for him to lock his door before we started down the hall for the lobby, passing a few other Blue Capes along the way. The lobby wasn't quite as full as earlier, though there were several faces I recognized from passing through the first time. I wondered if they had been permanently stationed there or were waiting to see if their captain would need any help.

"Will you be out long, Captain?"

Arns turned before reaching the front door to look at Sergeant Lowell. "Not sure. We plan on scouting out the old—"

"Probably best not to mention where we're going," I interrupted before he said too much.

He looked at me like I'd lost my mind, so I leaned forward where others couldn't hear. "You'd be surprised how many of your patrollers could be on the tribes' payroll."

"Nonsense." He turned and looked at Lowell. "We're heading over to the old garrison. If I'm not back by dawn, send some men to come look."

I groaned inwardly, suddenly finding myself scanning the faces of those inside, looking for anyone showing too much interest.

"Do you wish me to send some men, sir?"

Arns shook his head. "The fewer the better."

The sergeant nodded reluctantly while keeping a scrutinizing eye on me.

"Let's go," I said, not giving the captain time to continue discussing our plans, and also letting him know that he wasn't the one in charge of this mission. It was fine to let him save face in front of his men, but we needed to be on our way. I left through the front doors and headed down the stairs, not bothering to look and see if the captain had followed.

I walked over and spoke with the giant Rymiran horse. "Looks like I'm going to have to leave you here for now. I reckon you'll be safe enough in front of a patroller office." I patted his neck. "You better behave yourself."

I heard someone whistle behind me and turned.

Captain Arns was standing a couple of steps back, staring up at the horse. "Where did you find an animal like that? He's magnificent."

"A gift from the king," I said, unashamedly using my royal connections to bolster my image, as well as to remind him that I was more than just a mere Upakan. I had a feeling it was going to take a few of these little reminders to keep people in line and to bypass any future headbutting when it came to authority over this mission.

The captain shook his head. "Like I said. I wish I had a little of your luck."

"Be careful what you wish for."

With that, we turned and started down the street.

AVALANCHE

Chapter 17

HE CAPTAIN AND I headed southeast, back along the route I'd just taken, which led us once again past Wildfire's old compound, where we took one of the roads south along the Tansian River until we reached the bridge just below the Tower complex. We crossed over the slow-moving water and circled around the connected buildings. I kept our pace slow, wanting to give Avalanche as much time to get settled as possible.

The streets were mostly vacant, the occasional passerby heading home from one of the local taverns or perhaps a later shift at work. Some of the windows still had the glow of candlelight shining through, those whose curtains had not yet been pulled. Most of the windows were closed.

"So what's your stake in all of this?" Arns asked as we quietly made our way down the side of the wide cobbled lane. I could see Circle Drive just ahead. "Why do you care what happens to these kids? Did the queen volunteer you like us? From what I've heard, she had a hand in establishing the orphanage."

I took a moment to think how best to answer without giving away anything of my association with the tribes. "That's actually why I'm here. The older couple who runs the orphanage are good friends of mine. Sort of the grandparents I never had. They set up the orphanage after their bookstore was vandalized by a street tribe at the behest of a senator." I didn't feel right giving Senator Gerrick's name. After all, he had made good on his mistake and had even been known to give a few pieces of gold here and there toward the orphanage's fund, though probably from a direct request of the queen.

"What would a senator have to do with the tribes?"

I shook my head. Were all patrollers this unaware as to the actual goings-on of their own city, or was it just Arns in particular? Sapphire had mentioned that she had had dealings with Arns for Sandstorm. Did Arns not realize who it was he was speaking with?

"The street tribes have had their hands in many pies," I said. "It's one of the reasons I didn't want you mentioning where we were going. I wasn't lying when I said that there are patrollers, probably within your very station, who are on Avalanche's payroll, and for a certain fee will overlook the tribe's dealings. If the wrong person were to have overheard you tonight, we could be walking into a trap."

The captain's face hardened. "Do you have proof to back up your claims?"

"Not firsthand, but bribing a couple of patrollers is hardly high on the list of improbable connections. I know for a fact that Sandstorm has had several dealings with influential members of the aristocracy, though for anonymity, I can't tell you who. Whether you want to believe me or not, we can't afford to take the chance. For that reason, we need to keep the details of the raid secret. If I have to make that an order, I will." I was uncomfortable talking to the captain so, but he clearly didn't understand what he was dealing with.

Arns refrained from looking my direction, and I thought I caught one of his hands tightening into a fist. "I can't just order my men to follow me on a raid without telling them where we're going or who we are raiding."

"You're their captain, of course you can."

Arns gritted his teeth but didn't argue further.

"It's the way we lancers live. We have to trust that those giving the orders are making the right decisions. We are putting our lives on the line for them, after all. If the men don't trust the ones leading them, the entire corps will fall apart."

"My men trust me."

I looked at Arns, but he kept his eyes focused ahead. "That's good to hear."

We crossed over Circle Drive. It was a little busier than most of the other streets we'd traveled, seeing that it was the main road that passed through every quarter of the city.

Once on the other side, I had us stop. "We've just entered Avalanche territory. Keep your eyes open. They won't have that many watchers out this far, but I don't want to take any kind of chances." With that, I guided us off the main road and over to a smaller side street that paralleled the one we were just on. The smaller street had the added benefit of keeping us locked in shadow as we passed between some of the larger residences.

The farther we went and the closer we got to the old Rockslide compound, the more worried I became about whether the captain's foolish announcement might have preceded us. If Avalanche was to become aware of what we were planning, then this entire mission was for nothing. Even if those inside who had heard Arns's announcement weren't associated with Avalanche, there was a good chance that one or more of them might share that news with someone who was.

I shook off the sense of dread. There was nothing I could do about it now. I needed to keep going and hope for the best.

A noise and then a grunt behind me had me turning around. The captain was down on one knee, pushing himself back to his feet. There was a half-filled sack of ratty material at his feet. "I can't see where I'm going," he hissed in frustration. "How are you able to?"

"My eyes have adjusted faster, I guess. Give it a minute. I'm sure you'll see better. Hold on to my back if you need to, and I'll guide us through."

Arns reluctantly followed my instructions. His hand latched on to my left shoulder, and we started up once more. I took care to skirt any possible obstacles that might trip him up. These side streets weren't the cleanest, and the closer we got to the old garrison, the dirtier they became, most of it leftover refuse from when whoever had been living there had decided to find safer accommodations. Apparently, the city cleaners also didn't care to venture this close to the tribe's den, probably due to run-ins with their beaters a time or two.

I was surprised the patrollers hadn't done something about them before now. The other tribes did their best to stay out of the patrollers' way, as well as to keep the citizens around them happy so they wouldn't get reported. However, Avalanche, and possibly Rockslide before them, weren't exactly the best of neighbors, and didn't seem to care one way or the other.

I wondered if Cutter had some sort of larger connection within the patrollers that left him free to live how he wanted, similar to the connections Noph had set up for Sandstorm back in the day, which Sapphire now maintained.

Much like the last time I had paid a visit to the Rockslide compound, there was a thin layer of fog beginning to form across the cobbles, lending an eerie sort of stillness to the place. One thing about living on the Bay of Torrin: the city tended to gather this mist all year round, its tendrils sweeping through the streets like an extension of the bay itself, reaching out to tug at anyone foolish enough to still be up. It covered the city like a blanket, tucking it in for the night.

Whether that was a good thing or not depended on who you talked to. For those skulking about at night trying to prey on the unexpected, it was clearly a good thing. However, for the unexpected about to have their purse stolen or home broken into, it wasn't such a welcome sight. For Arns and me, who were about to try sneaking through Avalanche's territory, it was hopefully going to prove beneficial.

Arns released my shoulder as soon as we left the alley, and the moonlit street ahead became visible. Doing our best to remain in the shadows at the side of the building, we pressed against a brick wall on the right, staring out at the empty street ahead, studying every alleyway, backstreet, and nook between buildings where some watcher could be lying in wait.

"What are we waiting for?" Arns whispered behind me.

I put my finger to my lips, then turned back to the street. I waited a good ten minutes at least, no doubt driving the captain's patience to the point of breaking. I even picked up a couple of loose pebbles and tossed them up and down the street, waiting to see if anyone would come looking, or for movement of any kind. We would only get one chance at this, so I couldn't risk getting caught now, not before something this unprecedented was about to take place. As luck would have it, the way seemed clear at the moment, so I motioned him forward, and we rushed across the street and ducked into another alleyway on the other side.

This particular lane was a little wider and shorter than the last, affording us at least a modicum of light for the captain to see by. Quickly, we swept from one side to the other, keeping as quiet as possible, skirting a few broken crates. Most of the debris on this street was found piled along the sides of the buildings, possibly indicating a likely route that some of the Avalanche watchers would take. I wanted to get us off this path as quickly as possible.

One downside to the fog was that my eyes couldn't pierce through it like they could the dark, which meant I had no idea what was below my knees at times, and would have to slow so I didn't plow over something.

We stopped at the mouth of the next small passageway and waited, our ears pricked and eyes searching. About the time that I stepped out of the alley to make a break for the next, a piece of metal skittered across the ground from another opening two buildings down. I quickly moved back, and we pressed against the wall as I carefully peeked around the corner, just far enough for one eye to see.

"Stupid blade," I heard an annoyed voice call out, just before a young boy of eleven or twelve stepped out from the opening. A second, taller boy walked out behind him.

"Quit playing with it and you won't keep dropping it, dummy."

I watched as they stood for a moment in the road, both staring at the first child's knife, which he had in his hand. He attempted to flip it in the air and catch it by the handle but put too much spin on it, and it came down blade first. He pulled back just before grabbing it. The knife bounced on the cobbles once again, and I rolled my eyes.

"Told ya," the taller boy said as he watched the shorter one lean down into the fog and feel around for it.

After a minute, the shorter boy popped back up with his knife in hand and waved it proudly at the other one.

"Wonderful. Now hurry up," the taller boy said as he started our way. "I want to get rounds over with so I can get some sleep tonight."

I turned and motioned for the captain to get down. He looked at me like he didn't understand what I was asking, so I quickly pulled him down beside me, and we sank beneath the fog. "Quiet," I whispered. About the time I did, I could hear the footfalls of the two boys drawing near the front of our alley. It was an eerie feeling, not being able to see. Was this what it was like for everyone else at night?

The two boys weren't being cautious with their approach at all. No doubt they didn't feel the need. We were in Avalanche territory after all, and no one would be crazy enough to come in here uninvited, except of course those already living here. There were quite a few vacant homes in this section of the city, and the streets tended to grow more vacant the closer we got to the old garrison.

The footsteps stopped at the foot of our alleyway, and my heart began to race. Were we not down far enough beneath the fog? Could they see us? I wanted to reach up and check to make sure my weapons weren't poking out, but I couldn't afford to move. I held my breath and waited for the steps to start up once more. What were they waiting on?

Metal clanged on the stones a few feet in front of me, and I groaned inwardly. Idiot child. Someone needed to take that knife away from him for good. Hopefully, he'd grab at the blade and cut his fingers badly enough to quit playing with it.

The captain started to fidget beside me, and I tensed. I hoped he wasn't trying to reach for his sword. I started to put my hand on his shoulder to get him to relax when the steps started up again. As soon as they were no longer audible, I released a slow exhale and let myself relax.

Once I felt it safe enough, I tapped him on the arm, and we both rose slowly out of the mist and looked around. If someone had been there, they would have probably died of fright, seeing two floating heads appear out of nowhere.

"Let's go," I whispered, and we raced across the street and down to the next clear opening. From there we cautiously made our way through Avalanche territory, one narrow passage after another, drawing closer to the old garrison. We were close enough to see the city wall rising above the surrounding buildings, like the Sandrethin peaks behind the royal palace. Its ever-watchful gaze kept a close eye on the safety of those inside.

Until now, we had been boxed in so tight that seeing anything but hanging lines of laundry was proving nearly impossible. The garrison was butted against the great wall itself, one of the few places in Aramoor where Wall Street took a detour as it followed the enormous structure around the entire perimeter of the city.

We were getting close. In fact, I was able to see the tops of the Avalanche wall from two streets back, the gate's watch towers rising above some of the buildings in front of us. Unfortunately, the closer we got, the heavier the patrols became, forcing us more than once to seek shelter wherever we could find it. The piles of empty barrels, broken furniture, and discarded waste from those who had moved on proved useful in keeping our approach as hidden as possible.

By the end, we found ourselves on our hands and knees just inside the mouth of the alley. We had one more street to cross. The next passageway ended just outside the garrison wall, to the left of the main gate.

We hunkered down behind a couple of rotten barrels and some empty drawers from an old dresser that was lying a few feet back on the other side of the alley. Quickly, we ducked below the fog as another set of watchers appeared out of the mist, these carrying torches to help guide

their steps.

The narrow passageway I was looking to enter was about two buildings down from where we were hiding. As soon as the watchers passed beyond hearing, Arns tapped me on the arm. "How are we supposed to get a regiment of patrollers in here when we can barely sneak the two of us in?"

"That's why we're here," I whispered back. "To figure that out." I turned around and studied the cobbled street ahead, listening for any sign of footfalls. We'd been sitting there long enough to judge the timing of the patrols and knew we would have a few minutes before the next group came along. Quickly, I motioned him out and, keeping low to the ground, we started across the front of the buildings on our left, making our way up the street to the opening I wanted to reach.

We were about halfway down the front of the first building when I felt something tap my leg. I turned to find Arns pointing behind us. There was a group of beaters headed our way. Whoever they were, they weren't on patrol, and they were carrying torches. What were they doing out here at this time of night?

They were at least three houses back and moving at a determined pace. Frantically, I looked around for somewhere to hide. We were halfway between the alley we'd just come from and the next one up, with not enough time to get to either before they spotted us. Worse, the fog wasn't thick enough here to keep us hidden. *Blazes!* I didn't want to fight these kids, especially not here, where it would alert everyone to our presence.

Without thinking, I reached up and grabbed the handle of the door on my left. It gave. As fast as I dared, I slid it open, hoping that its rusty hinges didn't squeal. Amazingly, they didn't. Behind us, the beaters were now only one house away. I quickly wormed through the doorway with Arns practically crawling over me to get inside. As soon as his feet were past the threshold, I began to slide the door back, but I didn't have enough time and was forced to stop as the first of the beaters reached the building's porch.

Maybe they wouldn't notice the partly open door. I motioned for Arns to move back as the armed boys and girls started past. We crawled behind the door and started to stand. We were only about halfway to our feet when a voice called out on the other side, and we froze.

"Check it out!"

A moment later, a hand reached around the door, and it opened slowly. As fast as we could, we stood the rest of the way and pressed ourselves against the wall right behind the door. The door stopped just before planting into my face.

"What do you see?" someone outside asked.

My heart began to race as a young boy with a dirt-streaked face stuck his head in. I held my breath. *Please don't let Arns do anything foolish.* The boy didn't have a torch, for which I was counting my blessings. If he had, things would have gotten awkward really fast. I readied myself to grab the kid if he turned his head in any further and looked behind the door.

"I don't see nothing," the boy said, then his face disappeared.

"Well, don't just stand there. Shut it back."

The door swung shut with a bang, and we both exhaled softly. Pretty soon, the sound of their footsteps started back up, and the group moved on down the front of the building, their steps eventually fading into the night.

"That was close," Arns said.

"Too close." We waited for the next patrol to pass, then headed back out the door once more, making sure to shut it behind us so as not to attract any more attention. From there, we quietly made our way down the front of the building to the next, then rushed across the street to the narrow passageway on the other side that I had been working us toward. We ducked inside and started through the piles of rubble.

The road running in front of the old Rockslide compound was just ahead, with the garrison wall rising up in back. I could see heads moving along the top of the wall, some taller than others, some high enough to see over, which had me moving even slower.

Working our way through the fog-riddled debris was proving slow going, since we couldn't take the chance of bumping into something that could fall over and alert everyone that we were there. I was doing my best to keep us as close to the side of the alley as possible, but the amount of rubble was making it next to impossible.

A muffled yelp behind me had me nearly tripping over my feet as I reached for my sword. I spun just in time to see the captain pull something out from behind a pile of crates and throw it up against the wall. I barely had time to register that it was a person before I caught a flash of steel. I leapt at the captain and grabbed his arm before he managed to get it up against the boy's throat.

"Protector? Is that you?"

AVALANCHE

Chapter 18

PULLED CAPTAIN ARNS BACK. "I know him. He's with me." I turned and looked at Mouse. "What do you think you're doing?"

"Helping. What's it look like?"

I gritted my teeth. "Like you're trying to get yourself killed and us caught." I glanced over my shoulder toward the other end of the alley to see if anyone had heard Arns's squawk and were coming to investigate. I didn't see any movement, so I backed against the wall, pulling Arns with me.

Arns didn't fight me, so I released him and turned to Mouse. "How did you get in here?"

"Same as I always have. I'm Mouse, remember?"

I started to smile but held it back. There was something infectious about the little rat, even when he was being completely unreasonable, which was most of the time.

"I heard you was going to be scouting out the old compound, so I came to help. I knew you would be here eventually."

"Who is this child?" Arns asked.

"Who's the stiff?" Mouse asked in turn, looking up at the patroller captain with a glare. "He should be glad I didn't slit his throat. I was about to stick him good when you stopped me." Mouse held up his little belt knife, waving it for Arns to see.

"You weren't the one I was stopping," I said.

Mouse's eyes hardened. "I was just getting ready to make my move, is all."

"Should we be having this conversation here?" Arns asked. "Someone might have heard us."

"You mean heard you?" Mouse said with a wry grin. "You sounded like a baby gull squawking for its mother."

Arns's fingers tightened on his blade, and I placed a hand on his arm just in case. I needed to take them somewhere quiet, some place that would allow us to talk without being seen or heard.

"Follow me." I grabbed Mouse by the tuft of his jacket and marched him back through the alleyway in front of me, the captain just behind. At the other end, I glanced both ways, listened, and then moved around to the front of the empty home we were standing beside and tried the handle. It gave freely.

"Where are we going?"

I cupped a hand over Mouse's mouth, and we slipped inside.

The interior was just as dark as the outside and seemingly just as cluttered, as though consecutive groups of homeless had taken up residence over the last few years and left the once-open family room in shambles. It smelled as well: unwashed odor, sweat, and a touch of urine. There was no furniture, but there were several large crates that looked to have been used in its place.

I kept my hand over Mouse's mouth as we made our way across the rickety floorboards to a shallow stairwell at the back. There was enough moonlight coming through the front and side windows that the captain no longer felt it necessary to hold on to my shoulder. The stairwell, however, was a different matter, as it was littered with debris and there was no moonlight to be had, making our ascent precarious. Mouse tripped on a loose board, but I caught him, and we stepped over it and kept going, winding all the way to the top floor.

So far, I hadn't heard any signs of anyone currently living in the place. I hoped the upper rooms weren't occupied by vagrants, though better to run into them than Avalanche kids. Judging by the state of downstairs, it didn't seem as though the place was being used at present.

From the top landing, I made my way over to a rickety door on the right and opened it to find another set of stairs, this one even smaller, and started up once more. I maintained a tight grip on Mouse, and Arns held on to me until we reached the top. Inside was a dust-filled attic I hadn't seen in years: bare walls, open rafters, and the soft cooing of pigeons. It seemed smaller than I remembered.

"Where are we?" Arns asked, attempting to get a look around. He started toward the far side and stopped as soon as his foot caught on an empty chest and nearly sent him toppling over.

"We're in the loft of one of the residences directly across from the garrison's wall." I released Mouse and headed across the room to a shuttered window on the other side that was letting in a modicum of pale light. "I found this place years ago. From this vantage point, you can actually see over the wall."

There was no glass in the window, so I was able to adjust the shutters to get a better view outside and let in a little more light. I waited to move them until it looked like no one from the wall was facing this direction. I couldn't see everyone, so I went slowly. Once they were open, we stepped back far enough to be out of the way of the light shining in just in case someone happened to look up in our direction.

"This is a good spot," the captain said. "I see why you chose it." He took a slight step forward. "I can see most of the garrison from here." His brows lowered curiously. "It's not as big as I'd imagined. Certainly, nowhere near the size of the garrison on Lancer Avenue."

"That is the main building there," I said, pointing to the tallest of the complex structures, which was located straight back from the main gate. "Those on the left are the barracks, where most of the tribe sleeps, or at least it's where the former tribe used to sleep. Not so sure about this one, but I'd imagine it's the same. The dining hall is located behind the main building there, and they have a full set of cells located underneath it."

"Underneath?"

"Yes, the prison cells are underground."

"You can get to it from a hole in the floor inside the kitchens," Mouse said.

"You can also access it from the main building."

"And how do you know all of this?" Arns asked, directing his question at me.

"He's the Protector, that's how."

"Like I said, I've had run-ins with them before." I was afraid that having Mouse there was going to give away my association with the tribes. But after thinking about it, maybe that would at least give the captain a better reason to trust what I was saying, since he would then understand that the streets had been my life.

Mouse turned and looked at Arns. "So, who's this fellow anyhow? Another one of your roommates? I don't recognize him."

I turned to Arns. "This is—"

"My name is Captain Arns," he said before I could stop him. "I'm the head of the northeast patrollers."

Mouse's knife reappeared in his hand. "He's a flaming Blue Coat!" Before I could get a word in, the little picker charged the captain, but I managed to snatch him back by the hood of his cloak.

I spun him around. "What do you think you're doing?"

"Protecting myself," Mouse shot back. He thrust his knife in Arns's direction. "He's one of them."

"And I'm a lancer. I don't see you trying to stick me."

"Yeah, but you're—"

"Captain Arns is here with me," I said. "We are on a mission for the queen to help stop a tribal war. The patrollers are being sent in to raid the Avalanche compound. So in a way, he's here to protect you."

Mouse stared at Arns for a moment, then turned to me and leaned in. "I still don't trust him."

"You don't need to. What you need to do is go home and let us handle it from here."

Mouse stiffened. "I'm not leaving you here with . . . with him." He pointed his knife at Arns. "Everyone knows patrollers are stupid. He'll get you caught for sure." Mouse shook his head. "No. If he stays, I'm staying."

Once Mouse's mind was made up about something, it was next to impossible to get him to budge.

"Fine. But you do what I say. You got it?"

Mouse nodded.

"You're letting him stay?" Arns asked, staring down at Mouse.

I looked at Mouse. "He has a gift for getting in and out of places without getting caught."

Mouse straightened his shoulders and smiled proudly.

The captain stared at the little boy but didn't say anything, then finally turned back to the window and looked out at the Avalanche compound. "Any ideas as to how you plan on getting a regiment of armed patrollers in here without raising suspicion?"

I walked a little closer to the window, keeping my hand on Mouse's shoulder in case he decided to have another go at Arns. "The goal is to catch them unawares, so a direct approach will never work." I studied the surrounding buildings, the wall, the gatehouses, and even the buildings on the other side. It seemed not much had changed since Kore and Rockslide had been in charge of the garrison. Cutter had even kept Kore's two-person patrol on a steady march around the wall.

"There won't be quite as many kids inside as there were when Rockslide was in possession of the garrison," I commented, more to myself than anyone. "Most of Avalanche's members are still in the Temple."

Mouse stiffened. "Hate thinking of what those filthy pigs have been doing to our home. Probably rooted up all of Petal's pretty flowers."

"A problem best left for another day," I said, staring down at the closed gate and the two towers standing guard over it.

"If the gate doors are closed when we get here," Arns said, leaning forward to gaze down at the secured entrance himself, "how are we going to get my men inside?"

"There is another way in. A door, just there," I said, pointing down the wall from the gate on the left, just past the house we were sheltering in.

"I remember it," Mouse said, standing on his tiptoes to see over the higher placed windowsill. "That was Jaden's post." He started to giggle. "Remember how you punched him in the face when he tried telling them who you were?"

"Yes, I remember. Wish it hadn't come to that."

"He still talks about it, you know."

I looked at Mouse. "He does?" That was disheartening. Jaden was one of three Rockslide members we had been forced to bring back with us after Mouse and I had freed the Hurricane pickers Rockslide had captured. If we hadn't brought those three back with us, Kore would have had them punished for letting it happen. All three had acclimated into our tribe years ago. In fact, Jaden was now second in charge of the Sandstorm watchers under Toots.

"Ah, you ain't got to worry. He ain't mad. He just likes to tell some of the new ones how he fought the Protector."

I smiled and then turned my focus back to the predicament ahead. "As I was saying, there's a door just there, in the shadow of the wall."

Arns shrugged. "That's all well and good, but how do we plan on getting through it? I doubt it's being held open for our arrival."

"Thankfully," I said, fishing around in my pants pocket, "I happen to have the key." I pulled out a long metal key I'd gotten from Sapphire at my last visit to Sandstorm. I had taken the key from Jaden when Mouse and I had broken into the compound years ago. We had kept it all this time just in case.

"And how did you come by this key?" Arns asked suspiciously.

I glanced at Mouse and smiled. "That's a bit of a long story, I'm afraid. Needless to say, we have a way in."

"That definitely helps, but even with you holding the key, how do we plan on getting all my men inside a small side door without being seen? We need the main gate open if we plan on getting everyone in at once. We try sneaking in through a single, narrow opening, and me and my men could be left facing a devastating ambush."

"One problem at a time," I said, staring across the street at the old garrison.

"It's a pretty big problem."

I didn't respond. Ideas flooded my mind, but none quite clear at present. I was hoping that in seeing the place, the right plan would take hold, but so far it had just been a smattering of random thoughts, pieces of ideas that I needed to find a way to mesh together into one coherent whole. How were we going to pull this off?

"Even if we managed to get my men through this tribe's territory and all the way here without being spotted, those on the wall would be bound to see a group of men entering the garrison, even from a hidden door."

"Which is why we won't be sending your men through there."

Arns looked at me briefly before turning his attention back to the wall below. "So, you have an idea."

"I have the makings of one. As you say, for this to work, the raid needs to be as swift as possible, catch them before they've had time to prepare. We want them stumbling out of their barracks with sleep in their eyes, wondering what's going on, by the time we overtake them. We don't want them up on the wall or setting up a defensive line below. I don't want a full-on armed conflict if we can help it."

"I don't want that either, but I also won't send my men into harm's way just to make sure we spare a few street thugs. My men will always come first to me."

"As they should. But that doesn't mean we can't take some precautions to avoid as much bloodshed on both sides as possible."

"Agreed. So, if not that door—"

"They need to come in through the widest opening possible, which will be the gate."

"Do they open the gate during the day? Should we try then?"

I shook my head. "We want to wait until they are hard asleep and groggy."

The captain scratched the back of his head. "So what is your plan?"

"The Protector and I are going to sneak in," Mouse said, "like we've done before." He looked up at me with his big brown eyes. "Won't we?"

"I don't know about *we*, but I do plan on sneaking in and opening the gate."

"You won't be able to do that alone," Mouse said. "You'll need me. I distract the guards and you stick 'em."

"I'm not planning on sticking anyone if I can help it."

"Fine, then you bop them on the head."

I sighed. Mouse was right about one thing: he would make a good distraction. It would be better to have two people there than one. Besides, lifting the gate's bracer might prove difficult with only one person, not that Mouse would be much help there. I might need to find someone else to come with me.

Arns scratched the side of his face. "None of this will matter if we can't get my men to the garrison in the first place."

"An obstacle we won't solve by standing around here," I said. "The longer we remain in Avalanche territory, the better our chances of getting caught. Best we make our way back out while we still have the cover of night."

The other two reluctantly nodded, and we headed back down to the main level and the front door. So far, there was no sign of anyone else occupying the place, which I guess wasn't too surprising considering its location. The captain and I waited by the door as Mouse stood by the window, watching for any sign of anyone coming.

"I don't see anyone," Mouse said, and I slid the door open, taking a quick look for myself. The mist hung thicker now than when we had first arrived, covering us all the way to our waistline—and for Mouse, to the center of his chest. It seemed to have a life of its own, moving slowly in patches through the streets.

I motioned them out with a nod, and we headed across the lane and down the front of the next two buildings. I could hear noises further up, so we slowed. I wasn't sure which way the sounds were coming from, but they seemed far enough away that I kept us going regardless. We reached the narrow alley Arns and I had hidden in earlier and started up. It was shorter, and the buildings farther apart, giving us a smidgeon of light to see by.

I tried to keep Mouse behind me, but he didn't like being that close to the patroller captain, so he took the lead. I wasn't much worried about him getting us caught. He was more used to sneaking about than either me or Arns, and he might have even known a better way for getting out than the one we had taken to come in, so I followed his lead.

We were forced to stop twice, as patrols with torches seemed to appear out of the fog from nowhere, ghosts riding on the winds of the ever-moving mist. We were over halfway out when we reached the end of a particular backstreet and found the way ahead blocked, not by rubbish or a dead-end street, but by Avalanche beaters. We hid in the darker recesses near the edge of the building and watched. Several streets on either side had beaters standing guard. Did they know we were there and set a trap to net us? Or was their presence just coincidence?

"What do we do?" Arns whispered just over my shoulder.

"We turn back and try finding another way. But I want to see something first." I attempted to crawl a little closer to the mouth of the alley in hopes I might be able to tell how far down the beaters were set up, that way we'd know how far we needed to go to skirt whatever this was. Unfortunately, the fog was too thin in this spot for me to move out any farther than I was without being spotted. Gritting my teeth, I finally turned to backtrack the way we'd come, motioning for the others to do the same.

As soon as we turned, a clanging noise at the other end of the narrow lane stopped us.

"Stupid knife!" a familiar voice called out, the same boy who'd been practicing flipping his belt knife earlier.

"You're the one that's stupid!" a second, also-familiar voice said.

This was just my luck. If we were caught now, the entire mission could be in jeopardy. This was our one window of opportunity, and it was about to be closed by a foolish child and his ridiculous need to toss a knife.

A hand tightened on my arm. By the size, I knew it was Arns. He was trying to warn me, as though I didn't already know the mess we were about to be in. I motioned for everyone to sink into the fog as best they could, given its patchy nature. My mouth dried. The boys were headed straight for us. If they spotted us, we were going to have a chase on our hands, if not a full-on battle. Of all the alleyways these two imbeciles had to pick to come down, why did they have to choose this one?

With the amount of debris littered across the opening between the two brick buildings, there wasn't much room to move. It wasn't like we could simply crawl to a better spot. We were stuck where we were.

I took a deep breath and slowly released it, doing my best to calm my emotions. I started to reach for one of my swords and stopped. That was the last thing I needed. I felt around beside me. There was a small piece of broken crate on my right. I was half-tempted to throw it as a diversion, but I would have to move to make that happen, and the taller of the two boys was carrying a torch. He would see me for sure.

Blazes! What were we going to do?

I could feel Mouse fidgeting beside me. I hoped he wasn't pulling out his dagger.

By the sound of their steps, the two boys were about halfway down the alley. A few more steps and we were going to be spotted.

I tightened my grip on the broken crate, bracing myself to throw it in case they saw us. Hopefully, it would be enough of a distraction to give us time to get away. If it took the others long enough to realize what was happening, we might even be able to—

A faint thumping sound in the distance had the two boys stopping a few feet back. Those out in the street ahead turned to the left. The sound was growing louder, heavy blows against the cobble. Mouse's head popped up to see what was happening, and I shoved him back down. The boys behind us stopped talking, and the alleyway grew deathly silent. The shorter one even stopped spinning his knife as they both stared out toward the upcoming street ahead.

A trumpeting cry broke the night as my giant black stallion burst through the fog, scaring kids everywhere and sending them scattering. He stopped right in front of our alley, stood on his hind legs, and bellowed. The sound echoed across the surrounding buildings, ricocheting his voice into a chorus of replies. Suddenly, without warning, he dropped back to all fours and took off once more, vanishing into the mist.

"What are you standing there for?" someone shouted out on the street. "He's worth a year's gold! Get him!"

Everyone within earshot took off running. The two boys in the alley behind us shouted: "Wait for us!" They ran right past our hiding place without giving us a second look, then chased after the others.

"Was that your—"

I nodded at Arns before he could finish.

Pretty soon, the street had gone quiet once more, and I crawled to the end of the passageway to spare a quick look. We were completely alone.

"Did you see that?" Mouse asked, his head back above the mist line, eyes bulging. "It was like a . . . like a shade, flying out of the darkness, sent to ferry lost souls to the Pits."

My head lifted. And just like that, I finally knew the horse's name. *Shade!*

I could still feel the stallion's excitement through our link as he ran. He was enjoying the chase. I hoped he could outrun the beaters long enough to get away.

"He's given us our chance," I said. "Best we use it."

Without another word, we left the narrow alley and tore off into the night.

By the time we made it out of Avalanche territory and were back in front of the tower complex with its web of sky bridges, we were all out of breath. The captain seemed to be panting the hardest, going so far as to pull me to a stop. He bent over with his hands on his knees, trying to catch his breath. Apparently, as captain, he'd been spending too much time in his office, instead of out on the streets. I glanced behind us, but all I could see were empty streets and fog. No one was giving chase.

We weren't there a couple of minutes before the heavy clopping of hooves once again broke the silence, and we all turned to see the giant warhorse fly out of the mist behind us. He trotted over to where we were standing and snorted.

"That is quite the horse," Arns said, staring up at the giant animal. The single white stripe down the bridge of the horse's nose shone in the moonlight.

"He is." I walked over and ran my hands along his neck, which was slick with sweat. "Thank you, my friend. We wouldn't have gotten out of there if not for your help." I glanced over at Mouse, who was cautiously keeping his distance, and smiled. "I believe we have found your name," I said, turning back to the horse. "What do you think of Shade?"

"Hey," Mouse exclaimed, "that was my idea!"

The horse pondered the name, or at least I wanted to believe he did. He had a look of deep thought about him, or perhaps his head was twisted to the side because it was sore from the run. I still wasn't exactly sure what all the animal really understood. Clearly, he knew enough to come help us. After a moment, his lips parted, and he offered a brisk nod.

I looked at Mouse. "I think he approves."

Mouse smiled proudly, then dared walking over and placing a hand on the horse's side. "Eww. He's all wet." He patted him a couple of times nonetheless, then stepped back and wiped his hand on his shirt.

I looked up at the sky, where the moon was just reaching its zenith, and yawned.

"My sentiments exactly," the captain said. "I think we've done enough damage for one night. Why don't we meet tomorrow and discuss how we plan on getting my men over to the compound without being seen. But for right now . . ." He yawned himself. "I'm off to bed."

"I'm not sure how much time I'll have tomorrow," I said. "The queen has requested me for a meeting to discuss the future of the orphanage."

I couldn't believe the week was already coming to a close, which meant the king and the lancers would be leaving within the next couple of days. That left me with hardly any time to prepare for this raid, especially since I was also needed to help Master Fentin and Mistress Orilla, which I was more than glad to do. I owed them both a great deal, and they needed all the help they could get.

On top of that, I also was going to have to help deal with the fallout of the raid, providing it was successful, and organize the placement of those we captured. There was so much to do and so little time to do it in. I yawned once more. Before I did anything, I had to get some sleep.

It felt as though I'd been up for a week. Ever since Red—Kira, I corrected myself—and Po had found Dakaran in that alley, I hadn't had two moments to myself.

"If I have the time, and depending on how long the meeting runs, I might be able to stop by afterward, or I could come by on Eighthday."

Arns shook his head. "I won't be in the office. This is my weekend off, and the family is expecting me home." He thought a moment. "What about early morning on Firstday? That will give us a chance to mull things over this weekend and be ready to present ideas first of next week."

"I can't wait too long. I will be setting sail for the front by no later than Fourthday."

The captain frowned. "That's sooner than I'd expected."

"Can't be helped. When the king tells you what he expects, you kindly oblige him."

Arns chuckled. "I would imagine. I've never actually met the king." The sound of a horse and rider passing a few streets down broke my train of thought, and apparently the captain's as well, and we all turned to watch. Arns then shifted his gaze northwest, in the direction of the patroller station. "I better get going. The wife will be worried." He looked at me. "I'll see you Firstday morning, then, correct?"

I nodded.

The captain took one last look at Mouse and Shade, then turned and headed back up the street.

"Where are you sleeping tonight?" Mouse asked.

I pursed my lips. "Not sure." I didn't want to head back to the barracks. If I did, my roommates would probably request my help with the Black Guild's training, or Overcaptain Tolin would require my thoughts on logistics for the upcoming conflict and transportation of the king,

which I would have normally liked to have been involved in, but at present, I didn't have time for any of it.

I looked at Mouse. "I guess I'll be coming back to Sandstorm with you."

Mouse smiled gleefully. "Good choice."

I looked up at the giant horse. "What do you think, Shade? You ready to call it a night?"

The horse snorted.

"Yes, I thought so. You look like you could use a long drink after that run." I wasn't sure if it was the horse's thirst I was feeling or my own. Either way, the sooner we reached the manor, the sooner we both could get our thirsts quenched. With that, I turned us southward, and we headed back to Sandstorm.

AVALANCHE

Chapter 19

I WOKE TO THE PATTER of feet rushing down the hall outside my room. I had decided to sleep on the couch in the chiefs' office upstairs, which had been my old bedchambers, as opposed to waking Bull or Sapphire to see if they had an extra room for me to crash in for the night. The sofa was long enough for me still, and Reevie always kept a spare blanket on it for the times he found himself needing an afternoon nap. With his late work hours at Saban's infirmary in town and his bookkeeping here at the manor, Reevie never knew when he was going to need to catch a few winks. At least, that was the way it used to be, and since the blanket was still there, neatly folded across the back of the couch, I guessed it was still the case. Besides, I didn't exactly want to go messing up the bed at the back just for a single night.

I yawned and opened my eyes. My neck was a little stiff from sleeping on my coat, which I had used for a pillow, so when I rolled over to get a better look at the room, I did so carefully. The room seemed untouched since last night. I'd worried that Reevie would come in, find me, and cause a ruckus.

I was thankful to have been able to catch up on some sleep. The amount of light shining in around the curtains behind the couch said that I had slept well past breakfast. My stomach agreed. I had certainly needed the rest. No telling when I'd get more of the same over the next few days.

Yawning once more, I sat up and slowly began moving my arms and legs to get the blood flowing before standing altogether. My stomach ached from hunger, or was that Shade's stomach? Hopefully the kitchen had some leftovers. One nice thing about Sandstorm Manor was the quality of the food. Even their leftovers were delicious, which was another reason why choosing to bed down here for the night as opposed to the garrison was the wiser choice.

Whatever I did, it would have to be quick. I needed to head over to the orphanage to make sure Master Fentin and Mistress Orilla were prepared for the meeting today. However, I didn't want to leave before I found a chance to speak with Sapphire and Bull about my excursion last night, if Mouse hadn't already told them. I chuckled as I grabbed my swords and headed for the door. Who was I kidding? They probably heard about it as soon as they stepped out of their respective rooms this morning.

I hooked my double sheath on my back and stepped out of the room. "Morning, Protector," two kids called out in unison on their way by. "Good morning."

For a brief moment, it felt as though I'd never left. I closed the door and followed them down the stairs to the bottom floor and across the main gallery, where I left them as they headed out the front door. From there, I continued on through the dining hall, which was still being cleaned after the morning meal. On the other side was a door that led back to the kitchen, where I found Cook busy with two of his staff, washing dishes and beginning preparations for the lunch meal.

After managing to grab a quick plate of leftover eggs and sausage, I sat down at one of the empty tables in the kitchen and ate, not wanting to bother carrying my plate and drink into the dining hall while it was being cleaned. The food was a bit on the colder side, but delicious all the same. It didn't take me long to gobble it down and finish my glass of cider. The cider was tart, but I found it helped clear a little more of the fog from my head. It worked about the same as sticking my face in a cold washbowl before dressing, something my room had sadly been lacking this morning.

I left my dishes in the sink and headed back to the west wing, where I found Sapphire once more sitting at her desk in the study. The door was cracked, so I knocked and opened it.

She looked up and lowered her quill. "I was wondering whether you'd stop by before you left."

I stepped inside but remained by the door. "I gather Mouse already informed you of our outing last night into Avalanche territory."

"He did," she said, leaning back in her chair. "How did it go?"

"About as expected, I guess." I heard footsteps coming down the hall behind me, so I turned to see if it was Bull or Reevie. It wasn't, just another one of the Sandstorm kids on her way to one of the other rooms, so I shut the door before continuing. "I'm not quite sure how we're going to pull this off, though. Raiding the compound, oddly enough, looks to be the easier part. Getting all those patrollers through Avalanche territory without being seen . . ." I sighed and shook my head. "Not sure how I'm going to make that happen."

Sapphire fiddled with the bottom of her braid. "That's definitely a

big problem."

"I don't want an armed conflict if I can help it," I said. "My hope is to get the patrollers in while Avalanche is asleep in their beds. I don't want them up and waiting for us when we get there."

"You won't see us crying over spilt Avalanche blood," she said.

I frowned. "You almost sound like Red."

Sapphire's face hardened a moment, but then softened when she'd had time to think about what she'd said. "Sorry. But if you had watched your kids being beaten nearly to death time and again, you'd be ready to go to war as well. You won't find a lot of sympathy here after what they've put us through over the last year."

"Do I need to worry about bringing the younger kids here? They aren't going to get pummeled in their sleep, are they?"

Sapphire glared at me over the desk. "You should know better than to ask me such a thing."

"Sorry." I tucked my hair back behind my ears with a sigh. "I'm tired, and the queen is breathing down my neck. I want everything to be perfect, but I have too many things on my plate."

Sapphire leaned forward in her chair and rested her arms on the desk. "When have you ever not?" She smiled.

I smiled as well. "You got me there." I paused as my mind wandered once more. "I'm worried about Master Fentin and Mistress Orilla and whether they will be able to continue keeping up with the orphanage, especially now that the queen is wanting to open another."

"Sounds like she's wanting to turn Sandstorm into one, what with you bringing all those kids over here."

I turned and looked out the window at the kids playing in the front courtyard. "Seems you already are."

There was a moment of silence before Sapphire finally scooted her seat back and stood.

"Did you get something to eat?"

"Only just. I was about to head over to the orphanage, but I wanted to stop by first and let you know where we were on the upcoming raid. As of now, I plan on meeting once more with Captain Arns on Firstday, and from there we will determine when and how the raid will take place."

"How soon do you expect?"

"I have to be on a ship no later than Fourthday, heading back to the front, so I expect pretty soon."

"And the queen wants you to do all of this by then?"

I smiled. "Now you see the problem."

She shook her head. "Glad I'm not you. If you need anything from us, let me know."

I offered a sheepish grin. "I wouldn't mind a room for the next couple of nights."

She stared at me a moment, but then finally nodded. "I think we can manage that."

"Thanks." I glanced at her desk and all the papers on it. "I'll let you get back to your work. Be sure to fill Bull and Reevie in."

"Reevie will be in town with Physicker Saban today, but I'll let him know."

"If I don't get back till late, just leave me a note in the stables as to which room I can take."

"Just plan on taking your old room. You were there last night, after all."

"I slept on the couch. Didn't want to mess up the bed in case you had other company. What about Reevie?" The Sandstorm ledgers and its gold were kept in a hidden room next to my old bed. It was where Reevie kept up with the tribe's bookkeeping.

"I'll tell him you're planning on using it for the next few nights. Perhaps he can grab what he needs and work from here." She grunted. "It would be a lot better for all of us if the two of you were locked in that counting room until you made up or killed each other." She cocked a brow. "At this point, I'm not sure which is the more preferable."

I shuddered. "On that note, I guess I'll be on my way." I turned and opened the door. "Not sure how late I'll be tonight." She nodded, and I stepped out. "Want me to close it?"

She shook her head and retook her seat. "You can leave it open."

I headed down the hall toward the open gallery, and from there I left through the front. I only stopped long enough to chat with some of the former Hurricane kids, then made my way over to the stables, where Gittrick had Shade out and saddled.

"I figured you would be needing him this morning," the coachman said.

"You figured correctly. Thank you. Has he been fed?"

Gittrick nodded. "And watered and brushed." He patted Shade's neck. "His hair was a bit clumpy this morning, so I made sure to comb it out."

Shade shook out his mane, and a pleased feeling washed through our link. "So, you like getting brushed, do you?" I asked as I ran my hand along the horse's neck. His skin quivered under my touch. Grabbing the reins, I placed my foot into the stirrup, not an easy task with an animal that large, and then swung myself up.

I looked down at Gittrick. "We'll be back this evening, and probably for the next few days."

He nodded. "I'll make sure to leave the carriage house unlocked. You can bed him down in one of the stalls in back."

"I appreciate it." I went to nudge Shade with the heel of my boot, but before I got the chance, he started into a slow trot down the drive. I was really beginning to like this bond and looked forward to seeing how far it took us.

"Bye, Protector!" Toots shouted when I reached the front gate.

Jaden, the former Rockslide watcher who I had gotten the old garrison's key from, waved from the other side. He had grown several inches since Mouse and I had snuck into the compound and rescued our pickers from the cells beneath. More than once over the years, Jaden had thanked me for taking him with us. Apparently, those living under an authoritarian rule like Kore or Cutter were more than happy to leave their tribe when given the chance.

It was a quick jaunt back to the Bailey Street Orphanage, and the kids out front were thrilled to help me take Shade in back and keep him company. The horse seemed to enjoy the attention as long as they didn't tug on his mane.

I walked around to the front and was greeted by Mistress Orilla, who was standing at the door waiting with a panicked look on her face. "What is it?" I asked, hurrying up the steps when I saw her.

"Where have you been? We were worried you weren't coming. Here we are supposed to meet with Her Majesty the Queen, and we don't even know where to go, or when we are to be there, or what to do when we arrive." She shook her head as she ushered me inside. "Master Fentin is in a frazzled state to be sure. His nerves aren't what they used to be, you know."

"I told you I'd be here to help you."

"Well, you know how he gets."

"We still have plenty of time before the meeting—"

I barely had time to close the front door when she grabbed my arm and practically dragged me into the front room. She quick-stepped us all the way over to Master Fentin's study at the back. "Be sure to tell him all of this." She didn't bother knocking as we barged in. "Look who just showed up. See? I told you, you've got nothing to worry about." The tone of her voice said otherwise.

Master Fentin lifted his head, peering through his spectacles, and his eyes widened. "Ayrion, thank the Creator. We feared the worst. Orilla has been beside herself with worry."

"Me? You've been pacing this room and mumbling to yourself for the last two hours."

"And you've been doing the same in the kitchen."

She huffed and wiped her hands on her apron.

He walked over and patted me on the shoulder. "We are very glad to see you, to say the least. Come, have a seat. We should discuss our plans for how to prepare."

I sat directly across from the two. "I know you are both worried about having to present in front of the queen—"

"Hang the queen," Master Fentin said. "It's those flaming nobles I'm most worried about."

My jaw dropped. That was the most direct I'd ever heard Master Fentin speak. He must have been very scared to be talking this way.

"There's no need to worry about either. All the queen wants you to do is to tell them about the orphanage. You told me you needed more funds to maintain the levels you are at, correct?"

"We certainly do," Mistress Orilla said. "The kitchen, for starters, needs a larger oven. We can't keep cooking for this many children with a single-family oven."

"Perfect," I said, "then that's exactly what you should tell them. They need to see why the extra funds are needed and how they will be put to good use. You can talk about the number of kids per room or per bed. Let them see why the queen's suggestion of opening a second orphanage is necessary. I have no doubt that after seeing the two of you firsthand, they will understand why you need help in running the place."

The two looked at themselves. "Why?" Orilla asked. "Are you trying to say we are old?"

"No, I, uh . . . I just . . ."

Orilla smiled. "Of course we're old. We need help."

I released a small sigh of relief at not having offended them. "Most of these people only know the two of you by name. Meeting you in person will help."

I leaned forward and placed my hand on Master Fentin's knee. "Truly, there's nothing you need to worry about. No one knows this orphanage better than you two. All you will be doing is telling them about it."

"And you will be there with us?" Mistress Orilla asked once again.

I smiled. "Every step of the way."

She looked at her husband, then back at me. "I guess the next question is: When will the meeting take place, so we know how much time we have to prepare?"

"The meeting is set for this afternoon, so we have until then to get ready." I looked at Orilla and grinned. "Plenty of time to get your face on." My comment earned me an exasperated sigh.

"And how will we get there?" Fentin asked. "These legs aren't what they used to be."

"The queen will be sending a carriage, so there's no need to worry about transportation."

The older couple looked at each other, and I could see at least some of the earlier tension ease.

"Truly, you have no need to fear. The worst that could happen is that they decide not to give more."

"That's frightful enough," Fentin said.

"I'm sure the queen's presence will be persuasive enough to loosen some purse strings."

"I hope," Orilla said, though not in a very convincing or optimistic way.

There wasn't much more to be said on how profitable the venture would prove to be, so we spent the rest of the morning making notes about what they might expect to see when they reached the palace and what questions might be presented to them.

Mistress Orilla spent the rest of the morning making herself presentable, while Master Fentin arranged for some of the older kids to keep an eye on the younger ones while they were gone, instructing them that they should be back before the evening meal, but if not, to go ahead without them. Two of the older girls, who helped Mistress Orilla each day in the kitchen, knew what was needed.

Master Fentin had just finished changing into his best suit when some of the children in the yard burst through the front door to let us know that the carriage had arrived. I had thought to ride Shade alongside the carriage but decided that the older couple would probably feel more at ease if I rode with them, so I placed Shade in one of the two stalls in the outbuilding behind the house, making sure he would be comfortable, and instructed a pair of older boys on how to tend to his feeding and watering while I was away. I doubted I would have to worry much on that account. The kids had already been sneaking some of Mistress Orilla's apples out to him while she was preoccupied in her room.

I opened the front door, and we headed out onto the porch, Orilla in her finest dress and Fentin in his wool suit. Orilla gasped when she stepped out the door. The queen hadn't just hired us a carriage, she had sent one of the royal coaches. Even I was shocked by the gesture.

"I guess we'll be riding in style," Master Fentin joked, though the tenor of his voice sounded more like he was trying to talk himself out of running back inside and hiding in his study.

I walked Orilla down the stairs and over to the carriage. Several of the residents were staring out their front windows, those who hadn't come out onto their porches to take a look. The last time one of these carriages had arrived on their street, it had brought the royal family, which had been quite the talk of the neighborhood for some time afterward.

Most of the surrounding residents had been quite vocal in the beginning about having an orphanage next door and hadn't cared for all the children running around as they did, but after the orphanage had received a visit from the king and queen, and they learned that the queen herself had played a part in the orphanage's survival, those same residents were only too eager to help out whenever the need arose.

The coach's footman was waiting for us with the door open and the step box down. He helped the older couple climb on board, but one look at me and my swords and he took a quick step back and let me climb in on my own. Fentin and Orilla looked out the carriage window and waved at their neighbors, who just stood there gawking.

As soon as I was in, the footman closed the door and climbed onto the back of the coach, tapping the top of the carriage to let the driver know that we were ready. A single snap of the reins, and the carriage jolted forward, but we hardly felt it through such plush cushions. The inside of the coach, like the outside, was trimmed in gold. The walls were padded with velvet cushions and soft draperies, and the ceiling was brightened with a beautifully painted floral spray.

Fentin and Orilla spent the whole way to King's Way East admiring the artwork.

"Such lavishness," Orilla said. "I couldn't imagine living with splendor such as this."

I smiled. "You haven't seen anything yet. Wait until we reach the palace."

The two looked at each other, their faces tightening, and I wished I hadn't mentioned it. It seemed to make them even more apprehensive. The rest of the ride was spent in silence as everyone stared out the windows at the passing cityscape. The older couple were enjoying the attention being showered on them by the citizens of Aramoor, who would stop and stare at the passing coach, doing their best to get a look inside, expecting to see the royal family but instead finding us.

The older couple's hands were shaking by the time we passed through the Merchant District and found ourselves on King's Way West with the palace bridge looming in the distance. There was a line of traffic waiting to get across, more than usual. I wondered if the king was holding another one of his open courts today.

Our driver didn't bother stopping to wait his turn, and instead directed us around the stream of people looking to cross and up to the front of the bridge. Those in line quickly moved out of the way when they saw the royal carriage approaching. I opened the door as soon as we stopped and spotted Yorig walking over from one of the guard towers.

"Wasn't expecting to see your head popping out of there," Yorig said as he looked inside, his face growing even more puzzled when he spotted Master Fentin and Mistress Orilla. "What's all this?"

"We've been summoned by the queen. She sent her carriage to pick us up."

Yorig ran his hand back through his ash-blonde hair, tucking it behind his ears. "Some people have all the luck."

I smiled. "Too bad it's not usually good."

He laughed.

I glanced behind us at all the people waiting to get across, feeling a little bad at having just pushed our way to the front. "Why the long line?"

"The archchancellor arrived this morning unexpectedly, along with a delegation from the White Tower. Don't know much more than that. I wasn't on duty when it happened."

"Why would that cause a holdup now?" I didn't know anything about the White Tower, apart from stories my parents had told to keep me from using my gifts.

Yorig shrugged. "Apparently, they are taking extra care with those they are allowing across. More headache for us, if you ask me. Just keep out of their way. They don't seem the friendliest lot."

I smiled, though it was halfhearted. "I'll do my best."

I shut the door, and Yorig waved us on.

Fentin frowned. "That doesn't sound good."

"Nothing to worry about, I'm sure," I said as I glanced out the front window toward the other side of the bridge and the palace walls. At least, I hoped not.

AVALANCHE

Chapter 20

BY THE TIME WE REACHED the halfway point on the bridge, Fentin and Orilla were standing with their faces pressed to the coach window, trying to catch a glimpse of what lay over the top of the crenelated wall. On the right side was the Shemoa River, with its slow-moving currents and steady stream of riverboats, and on the left the Bay of Torrin, which fed into the Rhunarin Ocean. The two finally sat back down and spent the rest of the time staring out the driver's window at the approaching palace and its massive towers and bulwarks.

I watched with excitement as they took it all in, wondering how they were going to react when we stepped inside the grand foyer and saw the true splendor of the royal palace.

I couldn't wait.

The carriage passed between the second set of guard towers without

stopping and headed across the bailey and through the open tunnel leading into the inner palace courtyard, where we circled the large fountain
at the center and stopped at the foot of the stairs leading up to the front
entrance. There were armed men waiting at the bottom. Most wore the
crimson-and-white livery of the palace guards, but there were others in
solid white uniforms that I didn't recognize. Unlike the Elondrian Lancers, whose crest was a sword piercing a gold crown with a rising sun,
these bore a sword alongside a crescent moon. I could only assume they
were part of the White Tower's entourage.

The palace guards watched from the steps while the carriage footman
walked around and opened the door. The footman helped Master Fentin
and Mistress Orilla down and out, but once again stepped aside for me
to exit on my own. A few of the palace guards frowned when they saw
me. Though used to my presence within the palace, the guards still
didn't seem all that keen on having me and the Black Guild around.
They believed the palace to be their domain and weren't happy with the
idea of another group of trained armsmen barging in.

Strangely enough, I wasn't the one bearing the brunt of their curiosity. Their attention was focused on the older couple in common garb
who'd just been given a ride in the king's personal coach. I'm sure the
guards had been made aware of our arrival, though they might have been
expecting something more than the poor owners of a city orphanage.

I turned to escort Fentin and Orilla up the stairs but was slowed
when a group of men in white uniforms started our way. No doubt my
appearance was enough to set them on edge. A couple of the men in
front were carrying open swords, while those behind looked ready to
draw theirs at the first sign of provocation.

The hairs on the back of my neck began to rise. It was one thing to
question a visitor's purpose for being there, it was another to come at

them with blades drawn, especially when you had no authority to do so. What did they think we were going to do, storm the citadel?

I noticed several of the palace guards move in protectively behind Master Fentin and Mistress Orilla, their attention quickly shifting from the older couple to the intruding party of white guards. Knowing how they felt about the Black Guild, I'm sure they were even less thrilled with this new intrusion.

"Surrender your weapons," one of the Tower's guards called out, still several feet away as they slowed their approach. I was so taken back by the ridiculous request, I kept walking without a response, but the steeled look on his face out of the corner of my eye said he wasn't going to take no for an answer, and I stopped.

"And on whose authority do you base such a demand?"

"On the authority of the Tower."

"I don't care if it's a tower, a bulwark, or an entire keep, I'm not about to surrender my weapons to anyone except on the word of my commanding officer or the king, of which you are neither." I looked at the Tower's guards and then at the palace's guards. "I don't see anyone else around here surrendering their weapons."

The man raised his sword and pointed it in my direction. "I said, surrender your weapons." Several of his men drew their swords as well, the looks on their faces telling me they were itching to use them. There were eleven in total, with more at the top of the steps, who were just now turning to see what was going on.

With the way most of these men were looking at me, as though spoiling for a fight, handing over my weapons would probably be a very stupid move on my part. "As I said, I have no intention of giving up my weapons. I'm an Elondrian Lancer and the crown prince's personal trainer. I can't very well train him without my weapons. So unless I hear it directly from the king, then we will be on our way."

I started to usher Fentin and Orilla up the steps, but the men in white started forward, and I stopped again. I kept my hands where they could be seen. The last thing I needed right now was trouble, not with Master Fentin and Mistress Orilla standing beside me. Unfortunately, trouble was staring me in the face, and if there's one thing you learn early on as an Upakan, it's not to turn your back on it, so I held my ground.

I wondered if Room Eleven was inside practicing. I could have really used their help right about now. I didn't want a fight, but I wasn't about to give up my only defense to a group of thugs. If I were to surrender my weapons now, I wouldn't put it past these white guards to try arresting the three of us to take back to their precious Tower. The palace guards would probably be happy to see me go, but they'd be hard-pressed to explain how we were simply handed over without them stepping in.

"We are here by direct request from Queen Ellise," I said again, attempting to deescalate the situation, while making sure the palace guards stepped up and did their duty. "And she won't look kindly on her guests being harassed in such fashion."

The guard sneered. "I don't care if you're here on request from the Creator himself, when the White Tower demands you surrender your weapons, you do it!"

"You don't have the authority to demand anything here," one of the palace guards behind us finally said, a lieutenant, by the patch on his arm. He drew his sword, and the rest of his men did the same. The hairs on my arms joined the ones on my neck. This was getting out of hand quickly, though I was relieved to see the palace guards on my side for once.

I pushed Fentin and Orilla back toward the palace guards. "Whatever happens, stay behind them." They started to argue, but I turned

and gave them a sharp look that had Master Fentin grabbing Orilla's arm and pulling her behind the guards.

The rest of the White Tower's men drew their blades, and out of the corner of my eye, I could see more white uniforms making their way down the stairs. The sound of steel leaving their sheaths echoed across the courtyard. The palace guards at the top of the stairs began making their way down as well. They followed close to their Tower counterparts, making both sides evenly matched, at least here on the steps. Obviously, there were a lot more of the palace guards inside, but by the time they reached us, a conflict like this could already be won or lost.

"Again," I said, this time holding my hands up submissively as I took a small step back, "I'm telling you that we are here by a direct request from the queen." I stared the man down, my face hardening. "We don't want any trouble, but if you attempt to come any further, you are going to get more than you can handle."

"We won't tell you again," the white guard said, his hands tightening on his sword's metal grip. "Give us your weapons."

I raised my hands a little higher. "There's no need for this to turn ugly."

The Tower guards from the top of the stairs moved in beside their counterparts below, bringing their number to over twenty.

"Someone please go get the king or queen," I said, "so we can—"

"Look at his eyes!" one of the Tower guards from the steps shouted. "He's Upakan. He's here to kill the archchancellor!"

The guard I'd been talking with didn't seem to realize what my eyes meant, but he certainly did now, and everyone froze.

There was a single moment of silence, the calm before the storm, a quiet stillness just before everything went toes up.

I barely had time to yank my swords from their sheaths before the Tower's guards rushed in, their blades raised and swinging for our heads.

Apparently, I wouldn't need to travel to the edge of the kingdom to find a war. I could find it right here on the foot of the palace steps.

I deflected the lead guard's sword with my left, still not quite believing this was really happening, and shoved my right through his leg on instinct, as though I were still fighting children in one of our typical street scuffs. Except these weren't children. I kicked the man to the ground and went for the next, dancing between three at once, parrying, blocking, keeping just out of reach of each attack, no one landing a single blow. These men weren't quite as lucky as the first, as my sword slipped in and out of two sides and one upper chest. Still not immediately fatal, but debilitating enough to leave them writhing.

I took down two more before deflecting a third's attempt at my neck. By now, they had managed to push me to the side of the steps and away from the palace guards. The Tower guard was close enough for me to smell his breath. He pulled a dagger and swung, but I blocked and headbutted him in the face. About the time I did, I was hit in the side by something powerful enough to lift me into the air and throw me back against the side of the carriage. I heard bones crack, and searing pain shot through my chest as I fell to the ground, unable to breathe. In my confusion, I looked up to see a black-robed individual walking down the palace steps with additional Tower recruits flanking them on either side.

I couldn't move. I couldn't even gasp for breath. Whatever they'd done to me, I could feel my life slipping away.

Suddenly, I was once again standing in front of the guard I'd just headbutted as my vision returned me to the point just before I'd been hit.

I grabbed the guard and pulled him in front of me and dropped to the ground. The man was suddenly lifted into the air by an invisible force that hit him full-on and threw him backward, just as I had been.

He barely got the chance to scream before he hit the side of the carriage. I didn't bother standing. I knew right where the man in black would be. As fast as I could, I rolled over and threw one of my swords.

It drove straight through the black-robed man's chest. His eyes widened in horror, and he dropped. Before he hit the ground, I was back on my feet and charging straight at those coming down the stairs.

"Stop!" a voice boomed from the entranceway at the top. It was louder than what seemed humanly possible and carried with it a strong sinking sensation that whoever had said it was someone not to be ignored.

The Tower guards—what was left of them—immediately pulled back, forcing me and the palace guards to stop as well. Standing at the top of the steps was a man decked in crimson robes. He wore a crimson mitre atop his head, making him appear even more regal than the king himself, who happened to be standing beside him, looking horrified at the scene below.

The man in red was older, with flowing white hair that curled under, just barely touching his shoulder, and a white beard that had been squared off at the bottom before it reached his chest.

Beside the elegantly dressed man was another man in white robes with crimson etching. He was tall and lanky, with straight raven-black hair and a sharp nose. His eyes looked sunken, making him appear perhaps older than he was. Something about him felt wrong, and it wasn't just the fact that he seemed to be staring straight at me. I got the strange feeling he was looking right through me, like he could make out what my insides were made of. I shivered under his gaze.

The king walked out to the edge of the top landing. "What is the meaning of this?" He turned to the man in red. "Why were your guards attacking my men?"

The man beside him cleared his throat as he looked down on us. "It appears to me that it was the palace guards' fault, led by your assassin in black."

I grimaced.

"I have no assassins," the king said, then turned and looked down at me. "That is my son's personal trainer and an officer in the Elondrian Lancers."

"That's a rather . . . *unique* uniform for a lancer. And an Upakan nonetheless."

"He's the head of the Black Guild," the king said. "Their uniforms differ from the average lancer." He looked back down at me again, his face hard. "I want an explanation."

"Yes, Your Majesty," I said as deferentially as possible, even adding in a small bow. "I was escorting Master Fentin and Mistress Orilla to a meeting with Her Majesty the Queen when these men stopped us and demanded I turn over my weapons in the name of the White Tower. I told them I was an Elondrian Lancer and the prince's personal instructor, and that without a direct order from my commanding officer or from Your Majesty, I wasn't about to turn over my weapons to them. I told them that I didn't want any trouble and that we were here by direct request from the queen herself."

I turned and pointed down to the guard I'd been arguing with earlier, who was now propped up beside one of the wagon wheels, clutching his leg. "That man down there told me he didn't care what the queen said and that when the Tower demands something, you obey."

It wasn't exactly what the guard had said, but close enough.

The king's face darkened as he turned to face the man in red. "Archchancellor Bezaleel, your men seem to be under the impression that the White Tower holds some sort of authority here. I hope this is just the exception and not the rule. As you well know, the Tower is under the purview of the crown. It seems we will need to increase our Inspection Squad visits? I would hate to think that the Tower feels it has outgrown itself."

The archchancellor smiled. "It is most certainly an exception and will be dealt with accordingly." The way he turned and looked down at the wounded man beside the carriage left me rather appreciative that I wasn't him. I had a feeling that whoever the wounded man was, he probably wasn't going to make it back to the Tower—at least not alive.

The man in white robes standing just to the side of the archchancellor watched in silence, his eyes still on me. I could see his fists clenching beneath the folds of his robe. He clearly didn't appreciate the way the king was speaking to his superior.

The king looked down at the dead and dying across the steps, then back at the archchancellor. "It appears our business here is concluded. Kindly remove your men from my home." He then addressed the lieutenant standing beside me. "Please see that Master Fentin and Mistress Orilla are safely escorted to their meeting." He passed one more look at me—one that left me wondering if he was upset with me as well—then turned and headed back inside.

I left the others and walked down to check on Fentin and Orilla, stopping halfway to retrieve my sword from the fallen black-robed individual. I took a moment to clean the blood from each blade on his robes before heading the rest of the way down, where I found the older couple cowering behind a statue on the left.

"Are you hurt?"

They stepped out and looked each other over before finally shaking their heads.

"Then I suggest we head inside."

Fentin looked at me like I was crazy. "Are you sure you don't want to wash up first?"

I looked down at my dark leathers. The bloodstains weren't too noticeable. Besides, I didn't exactly have another change of clothes on hand.

"I'll be fine," I said. "But if we don't go now, we might not get another opportunity for some time." I turned to escort them back to the stairs but stopped when I saw the archchancellor and his men descending. The man in the white robes turned and looked directly at me as they passed. Once again, I got chills from his gaze. It felt as though he were looking inside me.

Soon enough the entire entourage had collected their fallen and were marching toward the exit, where there were carriages waiting.

"Can't say I won't be happy to see their backsides," Fentin said, staring after the white-uniformed armsmen.

Not wanting to sit around and watch, I started them up the stairs, meeting the lieutenant about halfway. He was busy barking orders to have the injured taken inside. He looked from me to Fentin and Orilla. "Are you ready?"

"I can take them," I said. "You have more pressing concerns here."

"What I have is a direct order from the king."

I didn't argue the point, as he was correct, and turned and fell in beside him as we both escorted the older couple inside.

I heard a couple of small gasps behind me as we stepped through the front doors and into the grand foyer, but it seemed the battle had dampened the older couple's earlier excitement; mine as well, which was disappointing. I'd really been looking forward to showing them around.

A man in chamberlain livery with its notable crimson-and-gold colors met us just inside, his shoes clicking on the black-and-white-marble tiles. He stopped when he saw me and paled, then cleared his throat. "I

was sent by the queen to fetch you upon your arrival."

"I hope they are still there," I said. "I'm afraid we're a bit late."

"Yes, I'd say so." This time he didn't look at my face. Were my eyes that disconcerting? Not bothering to expound further, the chamberlain turned and ushered us away from the golden staircase at the center and over to one of several hallways leading off the main room.

Even with the chamberlain being sent to guide us back, the lieutenant never left our side, determined to make sure we arrived at our destination without further incident.

We left the grand foyer and headed down a large hall on the left with windows overlooking the courtyard. Fentin and Orilla did their best to walk a little closer to the windows in order to see out. When they realized the view was simply more of what they had just seen outside, they turned their attention to the long row of gold-framed murals and decorative tables, each topped with a beautifully painted vase filled with an arrangement of seasonal flora.

Moving to the next corridor, we finally stopped in front of a set of double doors with a pair of palace guards standing watch. Both carried ceremonial halberds, both kept a close eye on us. I'd learned from experience that they tended to guard any room occupied by one of the members of the royal family.

The lieutenant stopped as soon as we reached the doors. "I've seen you to your room, and now I must see to my men."

"Thank you, Lieutenant," I said, and without bothering to acknowledge my thanks, he turned and headed back down the hall in the direction we'd come.

The chamberlain looked us over, once again pausing when he came to me. "You sure you want to go in like that?" he said, barely looking higher than my chest.

Again, I looked down at my leathers. The black hid most of it, although I did attempt to wipe the red stains from my hands. When that didn't work, I put my gloves on. "We are sure."

The chamberlain shook his head, mumbling something under his breath about barbarians, but eventually turned and pointed at the two guards and the doors between. "The queen is expecting them."

The two guards stiffened, then shared a glance with each other that said they were unsure whether to let me in. I would have thought that by now most of the palace staff would have at least known about me, so I wasn't sure why they hesitated.

"Are you sure?" the guard on the left asked, looking at the chamberlain instead of me. The chamberlain nodded and pointed once more at the door. The guard shrugged and then finally turned and knocked. He waited for someone inside to acknowledge, then stuck his head in.

"Pardon, Your Majesty, but the party I believe you've been waiting for has arrived."

"I was beginning to wonder," I heard the queen say through the crack. "Please, send them in."

I heard several frustrated comments about having been kept waiting for so long as the guard stepped back. I sighed. This was not the way I had wanted to start this meeting. If they were already growing annoyed by our tardiness, how were they going to feel when we requested they open their purses and give us their gold?

The guard nodded to his comrade, and they opened the doors.

I looked at Master Fentin and Mistress Orilla, or more notably their quivering hands. "I'll go in first. You follow right behind."

They nodded, and I took a deep breath and started for the doorway. "Well, here goes nothing."

AVALANCHE

Chapter 21

S SOON AS I STEPPED through the door, the room turned to chaos.

Men shouted. A few drew their weapons, others scurried back toward the far side of the room. A couple of women shrieked and fainted right there on the floor.

What was happening? I looked at the queen. Her face was pale as she stood there in silence with her mouth gaping.

I recognized one of the men in the front with a drawn weapon. It was Senator Gerrick. My face flushed. Of all people, why did he have to be one of those the queen had chosen to include?

I stopped a few feet into the room.

"My apologies," I said, trying to calm the situation. "There was a bit of a to-do on the front steps earlier. I'm surprised you didn't hear."

"A *to-do*?" Gerrick screeched, looking horrified. "You're covered in blood!"

I looked at the queen, embarrassed. "I'm so sorry, Your Majesty. I didn't have time to wash and change."

She took a moment to gather her wits, then her face suddenly grew very anxious. "Was anyone hurt? Where's the king? Where's Dakaran?"

"They are safe, Your Majesty." I returned to the entranceway to join Master Fentin and Mistress Orilla, who were cowering in front of the doors, which were now shut. If they'd been open, the two might have already made a run for it. "There was a scuffle between the palace guards and those from the White Tower." I thought it best to leave my involvement out of it for now. Last thing I needed was for Senator Gerrick to be armed with anything more to use against me.

"The Black Watch grow more brazen with each new visit," she mumbled to herself.

I wasn't sure who the Black Watch was, but I assumed she was referring to the Tower's guards.

"Why's he got blood on his face, Mommy?" a small blond-haired boy on the right asked. His mother was standing beside him, quite pale faced. The boy couldn't have been much more than eight or nine.

"Quiet, Sedge," a girl behind him said. She was gripping the boy's shoulder firmly, no doubt his older sister, as they shared the same blonde hair and blue eyes. She looked to be around thirteen or fourteen.

I wasn't quite sure how to answer the boy's question without going into details that his mother was sure to not approve of him hearing, so I turned to the queen instead. "His Majesty has ordered the White Tower's representatives away from the palace. Actually . . . from Aramoor itself."

"Well, that's something at least," she said.

"And how did this . . . *scuffle* begin?" Senator Gerrick asked, looking doubtful as to the validity of my story.

"They attempted to stop Master Fentin, Mistress Orilla, and I from entering the palace, demanding that we acknowledge and obey the White Tower's authority."

Gerrick sneered. "Dogs, the lot of them." He looked at the queen. "The Tower's grown too confident to manage. Archchancellor Bezaleel needs to be removed from office."

For once, I found myself agreeing with the senator. Whoever this Bezaleel was, he didn't seem to be on the side of the crown. I wondered if it was the man in red with the tall hat.

The queen remained poised. "And be replaced by whom, Senator? Better the enemy you know."

Gerrick cocked a single brow.

"Before they left," I said, "His Majesty threatened the archchancellor with more Inspection Squads, whatever that is. It seemed to cause some added tension."

Gerrick hmphed. "A lot of good that will do."

The queen looked up from whatever she'd been pondering. "Inspection Squads are sent by the throne to check on the Tower, to make sure they are still working within the purview of their duties. If they are found to be operating outside of their given tasks, then funding can be withdrawn."

"In other words," Gerrick said, "it's in their best interests to keep their noses clean. When force is no longer a viable deterrent, we reach them where it hurts most . . . their purse. And if what you say is true, then I have no doubt His Majesty is already contemplating just that." He looked at me. "At least tell me that the palace guards boxed their ears and sent those white rats scurrying with their tails between their legs."

"They handled themselves valiantly. If His Majesty hadn't arrived and put a stop to it when he did, there might not have been an escort left for the archchancellor's journey back."

Gerrick smiled. "Music to my ears." He suddenly realized he was still holding his sword and sheathed it. Others standing around did the same, and the room slowly began to retake its shape as those who'd originally fled to the far corners made their way back.

The room wasn't one of the larger meeting rooms, but certainly large enough, at least twice the size of Sandstorm's library and with a notably higher ceiling. Like everything else within the confines of the palace, it was beautifully decorated, with gilded trimming and elaborate designs along the white marble walls. Even the furniture had gold embossing. Several large crystal chandeliers hung from the ceiling, and an enormous crimson-and-white rug carpeted most of the room, leaving several feet of marble flooring between the outer edge and the wall. The room smelled of a mixture of strong fragrances—no doubt worn by the nobility—and whatever food had been arranged on the row of tables at the back.

I waited as the group slowly regathered. The girl and her younger brother smiled at me on their way back to their seats. The boy kept trying to run ahead, but she held him back with a death grip on his collar. Their mother, though still pale, at least was willing to cross within several feet of me as she found her chair.

"Again," I said to everyone, though addressing the queen specifically, "I apologize for my state. I promised I would be in attendance, and I had every intention of keeping my word, Tower guards or not."

"There's no need to apologize for doing your duty," the queen said with a kind smile, though I could still see concern in her eyes.

"Aye," Gerrick added. "Any man willing to cut the Tower down to size has certainly got my attention." He looked at the queen. "Let's get this meeting underway, shall we, Your Majesty? I'm quite eager to hear what is being presented."

The queen waited for everyone to retake their seats before she began introductions. "Most of you are already familiar with Ayrion," she said, pointing in my direction. "He is the head of the newly formed Black Guild, as well as the crown prince's personal weapons instructor. However, you might not be as familiar with Master Fentin and his wife Orilla." She motioned for the two to come forward, and I turned and nodded for them to at least step away from the door, where they were still holding a firm position.

They both walked over to where I was standing, several feet to the left of the queen, and bowed, more toward her than the audience.

Queen Ellise smiled and returned her attention to the nobles, of which there were at least two dozen in attendance, not including the young boy and girl on the second row. I would have thought most of the nobles had nursemaids and staff to watch their kids while they were away from home. It was strange to see a mother bringing hers.

"Many of you have been participants in our Orphan Home outreach," the queen said. "I know several of you have donated in support of helping keep the Bailey Street Orphanage open for the last four or five years, and I'm pleased to say that your efforts have been an overwhelming success. In fact, its effectiveness has been such that we are venturing to open a second home as well as increase the stipend of the first, as they have outgrown their ability to maintain the ever-growing numbers."

The queen turned and looked at the front row. "Senator Gerrick, I know you in particular have been vocal in the past about your concerns with the growing number of street kids, and on several occasions have voiced your opinion on trying to resolve that issue."

Gerrick cleared his throat, sparing a brief glance in my direction.

I smiled inwardly. It seemed the good senator recognized me after all.

"I, uh . . ." Gerrick straightened his robes. "Yes, Your Majesty, I have been concerned about the number of homeless children scrounging for scraps. It's a sad state of affairs when a city our size is unable to provide adequate shelter for these little ones."

I bit my tongue to keep from laughing. The queen had nailed him to his seat by using his own past and prejudice against the street rats to force him to open his purse strings and support them. I wondered if the king realized what he had in his wife. Surely he did. Her gift for diplomacy no doubt rivaled his own.

"That is good to hear," the queen said to Gerrick with a knowing smile. "As both a senator and leading member of the royal treasury, I look forward to your donation. I'm sure your generosity will have us all digging a little deeper."

Gerrick tipped his hat in her direction, though the face underneath was quite forlorn. "I shall strive to set an example that will prove worthy of Your Majesty's praise."

The queen smiled cunningly. "I have no doubt." She looked out across the rest of those gathered. "For those of you who have given in the past, I thought it prudent to allow you to hear from the lips of those who have dedicated their lives to helping these children. I wanted you to have the opportunity to meet firsthand this brave couple, who has taken their life savings and put it toward the betterment of Aramoor, and how they have managed to turn these wayward waifs into productive members of society by finding them stable homes and apprenticeships." She smiled at Master Fentin and Mistress Orilla. "They have done our city a great service, and I ask that you acknowledge that with a hand of praise."

The queen began to clap, and the other nobles quickly followed suit. It was a moving sight, watching poor Master Fentin and Mistress Orilla being lauded in front of the nobility in such a fashion. There were tears in the couple's eyes. Of course, that could have just been from the fear of standing in front of such a crowd.

"Is there anything you would like to say?" the queen asked the couple, opening the floor to them.

Mistress Orilla nudged Master Fentin, and he pulled off his hat and straightened his spectacles. "We are very honored, Your Majesty, by you and the esteemed nobles' generosity toward our work. We will strive to make sure your kindness will not be in vain." As soon as he was finished, he placed his cap back on his head.

I chuckled at the brevity of his speech and wondered how long he'd been working on it. Probably ever since I first told them of this meeting. The two stood silently, staring at the crowd, clearly unsure as to what else to say. In fact, the silence grew to the point of feeling awkward enough for me to step in.

"Their Majesties, the king and queen, have already graced the Bailey Street Orphanage with their presence," I told the nobles, "so they can attest to its state of affairs." I looked over at Fentin and Orilla. "I know that Master Fentin and Mistress Orilla are too humble to mention their present needs, so I will mention a few here, and trust me when I say that I do not know half of what they truly need.

"Even as efficiently run as it is, the orphanage is still limited in rooms and beds, which means most of the children are required to double and triple bunk. Food prices have risen to the point that it is now difficult to keep that many mouths fed."

"Don't forget the oven," Mistress Orilla whispered, loud enough for some in the crowd to hear and hide their smiles.

"Yes, they are in need of some basic utilities as well. It is very hard to cook for an entire orphanage with an oven meant for a single family." I glanced out at those watching; most were hesitant to look me in the eyes. I wasn't sure if it was my Upakan heritage or the blood on my face, or both. I worried that my very presence at this point might be more of a hinderance than a help. I hoped I didn't hurt their chances of finding valid funding.

"As Her Majesty has already said," I went on, "the orphanage is beyond capacity, which means a second home will need to be established in order to keep up with the demand. I'm sure that most of you have seen a decrease in patroller activity over the last couple of years, as the number of pickpockets have diminished."

Several of the nobles nodded; a few whispered amongst themselves. I had clearly broached a subject that had some relatable significance.

"With the aid of a second orphanage, along with better upkeep of the first, we will be in a position to house more of these children and see some real change in Aramoor."

I watched the eyes of the crowd, their faces, the expressions of what their hearts were telling them. Most wore their thoughts openly as they nodded or smiled or simply listened intently. Some concealed them with looks of apathy, but those were few and far between.

For the most part, it appeared I was getting through to them. At least I hoped I was and not that I was simply seeing what I wanted to see. Even Senator Gerrick nodded a few times during my spiel, though I had no doubt it was solely for the benefit of the queen.

"I'm sure Her Majesty has more to say on the matter," I said, "but I know Master Fentin and Mistress Orilla will be all too happy to answer any questions you might have . . . and would be willing to open their home for you to visit these children, at your convenience."

A pair of agitated splutters beside me let me know that I might have taken my enthusiasm a bit far, but I wanted the nobles to see firsthand what the orphanage was about, in hopes they would be more willing to give.

"That is a very kind offer," the queen said, then looked at Fentin and Orilla, "but I'm sure the last thing this hardworking couple needs is more people trudging through their home."

Orilla smiled gratefully at the queen, making me feel a little foolish for having mentioned it.

"I want to go see it," the young boy on the second row suddenly called out, earning more than a few chuckles from those sitting closest.

"Hush, Sedge," his sister said, giving the boy a stern jerk.

The queen looked out across those gathered. "Do any of you have any questions for our orphanage workers?"

"Do you have anyone helping you at present?" the mother of the boy and girl asked, color finally returning to her cheeks after her initial shock at seeing me.

"No, my lady," Master Fentin said.

"But," Mistress Orilla added, "the older children help with the younger."

"No paid staff, though," Fentin said, wanting them to realize that they bore the sole brunt of the work.

"Keeping up with these two," the noblewoman said, pointing at her own children, "is difficult enough. You are certainly to be applauded for what you have accomplished, especially considering you have done so on your own . . . and at your age."

I glanced at Orilla, wondering if she had taken offense to the blunt comment. The noblewoman was very straightforward in her opinion, a trait not seen by most of the upper class, as it seemed the wealthier you were, the more guarded your speech became.

Orilla, though, seemed pleased rather than offended that someone else recognized how difficult it must be for them. "Thank you, your ladyship," Orilla said with a nervous smile.

The room went quiet once more as we waited to see if there would be any further questions, but it didn't appear the nobles were all that keen to speak out, or perhaps they didn't really care all that much. It was hard to tell. After a few more uncomfortable moments, the queen finally spoke.

"If there are no other inquiries—"

"How will these donations be collected?" an older gentleman on the third row asked, which I thought was a good question, and one I was surprised hadn't been addressed until now.

"We will collect pledges against the royal treasury," she said, "that way we can be assured the gold makes it into the orphanage's coffers as soon as possible. We will also hold the additional funding for the new orphanage aside in order to begin the process of establishing a new location, which could take some time and planning. We do want to make sure we have the funding necessary to see it through beforehand."

"A wise decision, Your Majesty," the gentleman said, and scooted back in his seat.

"And when will these . . . pledges be taken?" Gerrick asked.

"We can take them today." The queen pointed to two ushers standing on either side of the entry doors, dressed in palace livery, each with a book tucked under his arm. "Speak with either of the treasurer's aides if you are ready to pledge now, but if you find you need more time to assess your potential for giving, then I'd say no later than the end of next week should suffice."

Gerrick nodded but didn't say more.

"Wonderful," the queen said, clapping her hands together. "I want to thank each and every one of you for your willingness to attend. Please help yourself to the food and drink at the back before you leave."

There were several long tables arranged against the wall, directly behind the nobles' chairs, filled with light food and drinks with attendants standing ready to serve.

"Don't feel as though you need to rush off. We'll be around to answer any questions if you so desire."

I could feel Mistress Orilla start to tremble beside me, and I reached down and squeezed her hand. "Nothing to worry about," I whispered. "I doubt they will want to talk much with me standing here. The hardest part is over."

Before I had finished, the aristocracy had already begun to disperse, most heading for the refreshments. A little food and drink went a long way to soften those who felt obligated to be there.

"How do you think it went, Your Majesty?" I asked as she walked over to join the three of us.

"Hard to say. Apart from your rather dramatic entrance, I would have said it went as well as I could have hoped. I knew Senator Gerrick would likely hold the greatest opposition to our plans, but I also wanted him here. If I could convince him to be willing to give, the others would quickly fall into line. He holds a lot of sway with the rest of the noble families."

"It was a daring move, Your Majesty," I said. "Given our history with him, I wouldn't have advised having him here, but I'm glad to have been proven wrong."

"It was very cleverly done, Your Majesty," Fentin said, readjusting his spectacles. "I'm not sure whether he has realized yet that it was his money that helped us open the orphanage in the first place all those years ago, after his hired thugs vandalized our book shop."

She turned and looked at Gerrick, who was helping himself to a few treats from one of the tables on the far side of the room. The others seemed to defer to him as he did. The queen sighed. "I had forgotten

- 306 -

MICHAEL
WISEHART

about that myself. Goodness, if I had remembered, I might have been more hesitant to have requested his presence."

"He didn't seem to recognize us," Orilla pointed out.

"He wouldn't have shown it if he had," the queen said. "He's too much of a politician for that."

"Either way," I cut in, "it seems his involvement has perhaps secured the others."

"Pardon."

We turned to find the mother of the little boy and his sister standing to our left.

"I don't wish to intrude, but I did want to say again how much I admire the work you are doing." She directed her statement to Fentin and Orilla. "I can't imagine keeping up with that many children, and I do realize how important it is to have the older ones watching over the younger." She turned and looked at her own two, who were busy filling their plates at the back. "Mine keep me on my toes daily." She smiled. "Sedgwick mostly, but Amarysia does a wonderful job keeping an eye on him."

Orilla smiled as well. "It's worth every sleepless night, though, isn't it?"

"I wouldn't trade it for anything. They are my heart."

The queen sighed. "I only have one, and sometimes I wonder if perhaps he was too many."

The others laughed. I, however, knew how little she was joking, which almost had me laughing as well.

"I guess we do what we must," the queen said, "and leave the rest in the Creator's hands."

The noblewoman bowed. "If you will excuse me, Your Majesty. I need to see to my children before they clean out all the cakes."

The queen smiled and nodded, and the noblewoman made her way to the back with the others.

"It appears our possible patrons are more interested in the sandwiches than any details concerning the orphanage," the queen said, watching the group at the back hungrily sift through the various trays, "though I don't doubt I will get my fair share of questions from them in the next few days."

"Perhaps that's a good thing," Fentin said without hesitation. "Don't know that the missus here could stand if she were forced to endure any strong inquiries."

"Speak for yourself," Orilla shot back. "Don't think I didn't see your knees trembling through this."

Fentin gave an embarrassed smile.

The queen smiled herself, seemingly understanding their shared fears. "Perhaps we should get our plates as well, before it's all gone."

"I don't wish to offend, Your Majesty," Fentin said, "but I believe it might be best for us to leave these fine gentlemen and ladies to themselves. Perhaps they will feel more at ease discussing pledges with you without us in the room. Besides, after our ordeal with the White Tower, I can think of nowhere I'd rather be right now than at home with my feet up."

The queen smiled once more. "I completely understand. No apology necessary. I will send word as soon as I can concerning any and all pledges received." She untied a small purse from her waist and handed it to Fentin. "I hope this will see you through until we can collect on these pledges."

"Your Majesty is too kind. I'm sure it will do splendidly." He bowed and might have tipped over if I hadn't been quick to lift him back up.

"And make sure to have my coachman carry you home. He was instructed that it would be a round trip." She then pulled me to the side.

"Might I have a quick word?"

"Your Majesty doesn't need to ask," I said and excused myself from the others to join her at the side.

"Have there been any new developments concerning the upcoming raid?"

I nodded. "I had a chance to scout the location last night with Captain Arns. He seems a good man. We are having difficulty, though, determining how to get his men across that part of the city without raising alarm. We want to catch the tribe in their beds if possible."

"Ah, I see. That does pose a problem. Any thoughts on how you intend to accomplish it?"

"Not as of yet. We are scheduled to meet on the first of next week to strategize. I'm hoping to have something ready by that time."

"I know this is a burden on you," she said, "what with the looming war and my husband wishing to sail to the front. I hope you can manage to juggle it all."

I smiled, mostly to hide how badly I wanted to scream. "I will do my best, Your Majesty. I can't promise more than that."

"Yes, well, even the least from you is more than the best from most." She smiled and laid a hand on my arm, then quickly snatched it away when she realized it was coated in blood. She pulled out a kerchief and rubbed at her palm. "Watch out for yourself. Instructors who are willing to put up with my son are few and far between." She winked at me and walked away.

I rejoined Fentin and Orilla, and together we left the queen and her noble guests to their refreshments and made our way back through the palace, this time taking a little more effort to see the lavishness of the decorations. We spent a good deal of time inside the grand foyer as we walked the room.

I had wanted to take them back to meet Room Eleven as they practiced, but I could see the quickly waning enthusiasm on the older couple's face and knew I needed to get them home. I was also aware of all the worried stares I was receiving from those passing through.

"I was planning on taking you to the Rose and Crown for a bit of supper after our meeting," I said as we headed down the front stairs of the palace to the courtyard below, "but not with me looking like this."

Palace cleaners worked to scrub the blood from the front steps of the palace, and we did our best to skirt them as we headed for the royal carriage, which was waiting for us on the far side of the fountain.

"Perhaps another time," Fentin said as we climbed up into the back of the carriage and the footman shut the door. "I believe we've had enough excitement for one day."

"I've had enough excitement for a lifetime," Orilla said. She leaned forward and patted my knee. "But we do appreciate the thought."

The ride home was a somber one as we reflected on the events of the day, no one speaking as we all stared out the windows at the passing scenery. With the stress of the orphanage meeting finally over, my thoughts drifted to the upcoming raid. I only had one good day to come up with a strategy before meeting with Captain Arns.

The carriage rolled to a stop, shaking me out of my deliberations, and by the time I turned away from the side window, the footman had already opened the door and was lending a hand to Mistress Orilla. I was the last to climb down. The footman didn't lend me his arm, but he didn't exactly hop out of the way defensively either as he had before.

We thanked him and the driver and watched as the carriage disappeared down the road before walking back to the front steps. The sun was already changing the sky's colors overhead. I was surprised by how much time had already been lost.

"Would you care to stay for supper?" Orilla asked.

"Thank you, but I think it best I get back to Sandstorm and clean up. I have a feeling if I were to sit down to the table like this, I might put everyone off their meal. Besides, I told Sapphire I'd be there if I could, and since we've opted not to go to the Rose and Crown, I probably better try to oblige."

"Very well," Orilla said. "Then I suppose we will bid you a good night." She turned and headed for the front steps.

Fentin, on the other hand, remained where he was, staring at me intently.

"What is it?" I asked, looking down at my blood-soaked clothes.

"I see now why they call you the Protector. I've never seen anyone fight like that before. Granted, I haven't seen many fights in my time, but I can truly say that the Upaka's reputation is not overstated." With that, he turned and headed up the stairs and back inside.

My heart sank a little. I wished he hadn't been forced to see me like that. I hoped my relationship with them didn't suffer from today's events.

The door shut behind the old man, and I turned and headed around the orphanage for the stable in back, where I could sense Shade's desire to go eat. Before I knew it, we were back on the road and heading for Sandstorm Manor.

AVALANCHE

Chapter 22

FTER A HOT SCRUB in one of the manor's many baths, and a leisurely meal with Sapphire and Bull in the chiefs' dining room, I headed upstairs for an early night. I knew I wasn't going to get much sleep in the coming week, so I figured I'd better get it while I could. It had been Reevie's night to work at the infirmary in town, so we hadn't been bothered with uncomfortable silence during the meal. In fact, it had been quite pleasant catching up with the two chiefs and hearing about all that had taken place over the last year and a half.

It reminded me of how much I had missed the manor, and them.

I plopped down on the bed in my old bedchamber and stared up at the black-and-purple ruffles that ran along the canopy railing. I had taken the actual curtains around the bed down years ago. The last thing I wanted was something blocking my view of the door and windows.

As I lay there, I started to chuckle, which quickly turned into a hearty laugh as I replayed my arrival earlier this evening. My appearance had caused quite the stir downstairs: blood-soaked clothing with face and hands stained red. I'm sure it was a frightening sight to behold. Half the tribe had thought me a faerie specter, come to claim their souls and send them to the underworld. The other half, after realizing it was me, was under the impression that I had up and vanquished Avalanche all on my own, cutting out their hearts and eating them whole.

It had taken the dinner bell to finally encourage the gawkers to leave. That and a sharp word from Sapphire.

I rolled over and stared at the side wall where the hidden entrance to Reevie's counting room and Sandstorm's gold lay. I remembered finding the room during our early explorations, and the look on Reevie's face when we first caught a glimpse of Red's portrait. I'd never had the nerve to ask her how it had come into being.

I finally closed my eyes and did my best to lull myself into sleep. However, my thoughts kept drifting to the upcoming raid. How was I going to get the patrollers through Avalanche's territory?

Looking at it in the simplest of terms, it was clear that the only way we were going to get to the compound was for either no one to be there or for everyone who was there to somehow go blind all at the same time. Since I didn't have any magical ability that could induce blindness, I was going to need to find a way to somehow make all of the Avalanche watchers on patrol disappear at the same time.

I groaned. An entire day lost, and the only solution I could come up with was to make everyone vanish. If I could do that, I wouldn't need to raid the crazy compound in the first place. I did my best to push the thoughts from my head, muddled as they were. I wasn't getting any-where. Best to claim some rest while I was still able. I'm not sure how long I lay there, but eventually exhaustion won out and sleep overtook

me.

I woke to the sound of voices outside my windows and yawned. The rays needling in around the curtains said I had missed breakfast once again, but at this point, food was the last thing on my mind. My head was a little groggy at first, the way it usually was whenever I had slept in beyond what I was used to.

It felt wonderful.

I crawled reluctantly out of bed and started for my clothes, which I had draped over one of the nearby chairs last night, but realized they were no longer there. Someone had been in my room sometime in the night without me knowing. As heavily as I had slept, it probably hadn't been difficult. I walked across the room to the door and opened it just a crack to peek outside. I smiled. My clothes had been laundered. Even my sheath had been cleaned. The leather pants and jacket were hanging from the door, while everything else had been neatly folded and placed on the floor.

Quickly, I opened the door and snatched them up, shutting it again to keep anyone from catching me in my undergarments. I laid the clothes out on my bed. My shirt wasn't fully dry, but the pants and coat were. It seemed they had only wiped down the outside of the coat, leaving the inside pockets and whatever was in them safe from a full dunking. My pants had been stuffed with cloth to help keep their shape while the leather dried.

I didn't want to wait for the shirt to fully dry, so I went ahead and dressed.

After breakfast, I took a few minutes to poke my head into the chiefs' study downstairs to see if Sapphire needed anything from me, then headed outside to saddle Shade. It was my first free day in weeks, and probably the last I'd enjoy for some time to come if the two kingdoms indeed went to war. I didn't want to waste it. If luck were to shine her face on me, perhaps the ride would clear my head enough to conjure a plan before my meeting with Captain Arns tomorrow.

I found Shade in his stall already fed and watered, and by the feeling of contentment I was getting from our link, the giant warhorse's night must have been as pleasant as my own. "You ready to go exploring?" I asked as I reached up to rub his ear. The horse didn't need to snort or whinny or even shake his head. I could sense he was ready to get out of his stall.

Not wanting to wait on Gittrick, I went ahead and saddled him myself, which was a bit more difficult thanks to his size, but I managed. I was cinching the last strap when the coachman came in from his shop around back.

"Sir, you should have gotten me. I would have done that for you."

I smiled. "The day I can't saddle my own horse is the day I need to quit riding."

Gittrick looked around the carriage house. "Is there anything else I can get you?"

"I don't believe so."

"Will you be back this evening?"

"Yes, I should be back later this afternoon. But if I haven't returned before supper, don't wait up. I'll see that he's stabled and fed."

"Very good, sir."

I stuck my foot in the stirrup and swung up into the saddle. With a quick nod to Gittrick, I left the carriage house and headed down the drive for the front gate.

"You's comin' back?" Toots shouted out from the wall on the right as I waited for the watchers to open the gate.

"I'll be here tonight," I answered, and Toots smiled. As soon as they got the doors open, we headed through and up the road. The manor's

drive disappeared behind us as we passed over the ridge.

Instead of heading west to Bailey Street and taking it to Circle Drive as I normally would, I decided to take a less-traveled road south to King's Way East, one I rarely ever took and yet one that had a significant memory attached to it. It had been years since I'd traveled these roads, not having wanted to revisit bad memories, but with my life having changed so dramatically during my time in Aramoor, I found myself wanting to go back to the beginning.

This was a very important spot for my life in Aramoor. It was the first place I had traveled when entering the city all those years ago. It was strange to think about how much of the present had hinged upon that road. Had I not taken it, I might not have become the person I was today.

I slowed when I reached the alleyway where Red and her thugs had left me lying half-naked and bloody. It was also the alley that a certain young crippled boy had found me, and then somehow managed to tote me all the way across town in the rain. I hadn't ever really thought about how great of a feat that had been until now, how much of a distance we had covered from the city's eastern gate all the way around to the old shipyards.

A ragged-looking tabby stepped out of the narrow passageway and looked up at me with sad eyes. I probably looked just as pitiful when Reevie had found me. I nudged Shade, and we continued on. We reached King's Way East, just in front of the city's main gate, and then crossed over and traveled south along the front of the eastern garrison. I'd been there plenty of times to deliver messages but had never been stationed there. It was smaller than the one on the western side, but just as fortified, with its stone walls and towers, and its backside resting against the massive city wall.

I nodded to a few of the lancers on patrol, and they nodded back.

From there I continued south, keeping closer to the wall's perimeter and away from Circle Drive. I wanted to make sure I steered clear of Cutter's territory. Circle Drive ran beside the Temple's southern wall, the one place I didn't want to be, and yet one of the places I most longed to revisit. Instead, I kept to the less-trafficked areas, taking me on a route that ended on Pilneth Lane right in front of the Pit.

I stopped just outside the second entrance and looked in through the open archway. One of the wooden doors was missing. The other lay half off its hinges. The abandoned repository looked exactly as it had seven years ago. The holes dug for the tribes' pit fires were still there, and discarded weapons that wouldn't have been worth reusing still lay spread across the open ground between the gate and the buildings farther in.

"This is where I first made a name for myself amongst the tribes," I said as I patted Shade's neck. It was also the place where Reevie had first given me the name Death's Shadow. Images of that final battle flashed through my mind as I stared through the open doorway. I was almost tempted to ride in to see what had become of the Pit itself, but I still had plenty of places yet to stop.

From Pilneth, we cut onto Mora, which was the one road I knew I would never have to worry about finding Avalanche members on, since it ran the full length of the Warrens boundary.

The Warrens had seven entrances, and I slowed as we passed by the first, looking in to find nothing but abandoned roadways and dilapidated buildings—the leftover remains of the first city of Aramoor, now the claimed territory of the city's underground. I remembered my first time seeing the place, and the hair standing up on my arms as Hurricane marched past each of the seven openings on our way to the Pit.

Two years ago, in this very spot, Sapphire and I had ended our desire for an ongoing relationship. She could see what I could not, how far my life would take me in the direction of the palace, and she didn't want to get hurt any worse than she already had been. I found myself wondering if letting her go had been the right choice.

The ache was still there. I missed her and Reevie both. I nudged Shade, and we kept going, passing several more empty holes in the wall before reaching the one that I had bolted from during our rescue of Red and Po from the underground, a place I hoped never to visit again.

Sadly, it was the place Red had chosen to make her permanent abode. Keeping Shade moving, we crossed over the ground where Spats's older, and much larger, brother, Kerson, had promised to lock blades with me again one day.

The road ahead and behind lay dormant, as it always did during the light of day. It was when the sun set that you wanted to make sure to steer clear.

It didn't take long before Shade and I finally reached the end of Mora and the old city and started northward. We barely made it a couple of streets before I was directing him off the road once more and into another of the city's uninhabited sectors. Stopping just inside the surrounding wall, I dismounted. The worn cobbles under my feet felt almost familiar.

It felt like coming home.

Memories flooded back as I ventured into the old shipyard. I didn't need to hold on to Shade's reins to keep him with me.

"It was my home," I told the horse as we passed through the narrow streets leading toward the back. I turned us down one of the wider passageways and then stopped and stared up at the old stone-and-brick building on the left. The corners of my eyes burned as I read the faded lettering overtop: THE GRANARY.

It was more difficult seeing the old place than I had expected.

"Wait here," I said and started toward the two larger doors at the front, which were closed at present, hopefully meaning that no one had taken up residency since Hurricane had left. Deciding against opening either of them, I walked down to a smaller door on the left. It was un-locked, and I stepped inside.

Everything was still the same, but with a few extra layers of dust. My training course was still sitting in the middle of the room; even the ropes still hung from the rafters. I walked over and gave one a firm tug. Still strong. I couldn't help but laugh as I remembered how much Reevie had hated when I used them.

I walked across the open room to the door on the right and peered in at the old infirmary Reevie had set up for our first batch of refugees, the unwanted injured that the other tribes had kicked out after the battle at the Pit. Bull had been one of those who had come with them. Now he was a chief of Sandstorm.

I pulled open the door leading down into the cellar. More memories emerged as I headed down the rickety steps, not quite believing how small the stairwell was. It hadn't felt this tiny when Reevie and I had taken up residence. I reached the lower level and walked over to one of the old shelves on the right and sparked one of the lanterns that was still sitting undisturbed. The orange glow lit the open room, sending shad-ows dancing across the wood-plank walls.

Like the building above, everything was covered in a thick layer of dust.

The worn cushions I had slept on after my beating from Wildfire were still lying in the corner, tattered and threadbare. The memories washed over me in waves, threatening to drown me in emotion. My eyes began to burn, and I wiped them.

A hint of concern ran through my link and pulled me from my thoughts. *I'm fine, Shade.* The concern lessened.

I blew out the lantern, leaving it on the makeshift table at the center of the room, and started up the stairs. I paused for a brief moment at the step Reevie had used for a trap, the same step Mouse had fallen into. With a smile, I made my way over and up, leaving the Granary altogether. Once outside, I closed my eyes and took a deep breath to calm my nerves. By the time I opened them again, Shade was standing in front of me, giving me a thorough sniff as if to prove to himself that I was okay.

I rubbed the bridge of his nose. "I'm alright. I promise. It just hit me a little harder than I was expecting, that's all." I climbed back in the saddle, and we left the abandoned shipyard the same way we'd come in.

Keeping a northward trajectory, we crossed over the Tansian River where it emptied into the bay. On the other side of the bridge was the city's new shipyard and port. A bell rang, signaling the eleventh hour. I sighed. The morning was moving faster than I wanted it to. It was nearly time for lunch.

Shade's head bobbed cheerfully at the thought of food.

We kept along Bay Street, slowing as we reached the end of the shipyard walls and the beginning of the Bay Street estates. The properties running along the bay were some of the finest in the city, belonging to the wealthiest of Aramoor's citizens. I could just make out Senator Gerrick's home rising over the others.

"Quite a few fun memories there," I said as I directed Shade off Bay Street and east toward the river. If I remained on Bay Street, we would have eventually reached King's Way West, just in front of the palace bridge.

However, I had another destination in mind, so we continued east until we reached Meadow Way, which was only a couple of streets from the edge of the river. I pulled Shade to a stop in front of a small shop on the right with a sign that read: TERRINGER'S DRAPERIES. It was one of the first shops I set foot in after arriving in Aramoor. Of course, back then it hadn't been a shop for household décor.

I swung down and tied Shade off before walking inside. The bell over the door announced my arrival, and I stopped to let my eyes adjust. The inside looked very different. The shelves in front, where Master Fentin's books had been, were gone. However, the shelves around the walls were still there; they'd simply been repurposed to hold bolts of fabric.

"May I help you?" a nervous voice asked from the back of the shop.

"Just looking, thank you."

The man didn't say more, though he did keep a wary eye on me as I walked about the shop. I guess I would have done the same if a man in black leather walked in carrying two swords on his back. As I moved about the place, I made sure not to look the owner directly in the eyes and upset him further.

The door at the back was open, and I could see the stairs leading up to the second floor, where Mistress Orilla would have been busy making some of her famous mystery meat sandwiches. My mouth watered at the thought, and I heard Shade snort out front. I stopped and looked down at the rug covering the center aisle and smiled when I tapped my foot on the hollow trapdoor underneath. My first introduction to Master Fentin and Mistress Orilla had been quite the interesting one.

I thanked the proprietor once more and left him to his work. I thought I heard an audible sigh just before the door shut behind me. I chuckled as I imagined the owner releasing a huge breath of relief. I walked over to Shade and mounted.

"What do you think? Time to eat?"

Shade released a small whinny, causing the horse on the hitching rail next to us to cock its head. With a light tap of my boot, we were back on our way as I followed my nose a few streets over to Master Endle's Bakery. I climbed down and tied Shade to the rail out front, though I doubted I needed to. It was more out of habit than anything, plus others might think I'd forgotten and worry that my horse would wander off.

"I'll be back shortly," I said but stopped. "Oh, I almost forgot. Which do you prefer, fruit or cheese?"

Shade shook his head.

"Ah, good choice. One of each it is." I smiled and then headed inside.

"Master Ayrion," a familiar voice called across the shop. "I didn't think you were to leave until next week?" I looked at him confused and he continued. "You mentioned stopping in to see us before you left."

"Oh, sorry. No, I just happened to be in the neighborhood."

"Very good," Master Endle said as he patted his white apron and sent up another plume of flour to match his cheeks and forehead. He paused for only a moment when he saw my two swords and pursed his lips. "That is quite the getup."

"It was a gift for my birthday."

Hubert's spirits perked. "How wonderful. And are you celebrating today, or just here to satiate your appetite? Either way, you've come to the right place. If you are having guests, I'm sure we can make a special order." He rubbed his hands together greedily.

"The party has already come and gone, I'm afraid. In fact, it came and went without me."

"I beg your pardon?"

"I was at the Cylmaran border when it came. There was no time for celebrating there."

"Ah. Well, better late than never, I always say."

I smiled. "I might be tempted to purchase a few extra tarts, depending on the fruit and how fresh they are."

Hubert clapped me on the back, and I cringed, imagining the large white handprint now adorning my black leathers. "You're in luck, my young friend. We have a fresh batch out just for the afternoon crowd." He guided me to some tables on the right, where his wife generally kept their display of tarts. "The blueberry is good, but the rhubarb is to die for." He snatched up one of the reddish ones with green flecks and held it out to me.

"To die for? Let's hope it doesn't come to that." I sniffed the tart, and it did smell nice, but the sweet cheese was calling my name, and I scooted down the row toward them, passing several other types of fruit, including strawberry, apple, and fig.

Hubert smiled. "I had a feeling you'd reach this side of the table eventually." He crossed his arms. "How many will it be?"

I was feeling generous and did have a few coins to burn. "I'll take two of each and three of the sweet cheese."

Hubert's brows rose in delight. "Sounds like a party after all." He grabbed an empty basket and started snatching up tarts and placing them inside, taking care not to squash any. I followed him to the back counter where his wife, Storella, finished wrapping some fresh loaves for another customer before starting on mine.

"Cheese tarts, I see," she said with a knowing smile. "I make them extra sweet just in case you stop by."

"Much obliged," I said with a grateful smile.

"And extra cheesy," Hubert added, pulling a fresh loaf from the oven with a large peel.

Mistress Storella took my coins and handed me the neatly wrapped package. "I kept a couple out and on top in case you get hungry on the way to wherever it is you're going."

I hefted the package and inhaled the aroma. "You know me too well."

She slid half my coins back across the desk.

I looked down. "What's this?"

"A token of thanks for your service to Elondria," she said with a warm smile.

I thanked her for her generosity, and Master Hubert walked me to the front door. "Make sure you keep yourself safe, lad, you hear? Endle's Bakery will be anxiously awaiting your return."

"Thank you, Master Hubert. I'm sure you'll be one of the first to know when I do."

I shook his hand as well and headed for my horse. I heard the bell on the door ring out as it shut and the sound of Master Hubert greeting newly arrived customers in his typical jovial manner. I pulled out one of the cheese tarts and took another long whiff before stuffing half in my mouth. It was wonderfully sticky, the warm honey sliding down my lips. They must have been freshly baked to still be so soft.

Shade whinnied, letting me know he was still there and displeased for not having been offered one of his own yet. I pulled out one of the rhubarbs and handed it to him as he turned his head to look at me. He gobbled it in one mouthful. A feeling of delight flooded through our link as he swallowed it down.

So far, this had been quite an enjoyable day. I couldn't remember the last time I'd been able to take a stroll through the city like this. I really wished I'd been able to go see the Temple as well. One day, perhaps.

Leaving Southside and the Maze behind, Shade and I headed northeast along the riverfront, passing the Rose and Crown, which had my mouth watering all the more. We weren't that far from Saban's infirmary, and if I wasn't so worried about running into Reevie, I might have even been tempted to stop in. However, with the insistence of my stomach and a little prodding from Shade, I decided to start us back toward Sandstorm. With any luck, we'd reach the manor before they had finished serving lunch.

I needed to check on Dakaran, but I didn't want to take a chance on running into the king, or worse, Overcaptain Tolin, and have one or both decide that they needed my assistance on some upcoming project. This was the first day I'd had to myself in a long time, and I was really enjoying it. So, steering clear of the major thoroughfares, I guided Shade along the backroads around the Island, and then east to Sandstorm Manor.

AVALANCHE

Chapter 23

THE REST OF THE AFTERNOON and evening found me holed up in the library downstairs, drafting scenarios aided by a city map I found rolled up in a collection of charts on one of the upper shelves. There were a couple of detailed printings of the city, some more recent than others. It appeared that not much had changed in this section of Aramoor over the last hundred years or so, apart from the abandoning of the garrison. Houses had come and gone, constantly being torn down and rebuilt, but the streets themselves remained the same, which made planning a little easier.

Reevie had a long night, so he spent most of the day asleep in his own room, leaving me to wander about the place without too much fear of confrontation. Sapphire and Bull had told him of my arrival when he returned, and that I would be around for the next day or two, so I figured he'd probably remain in his room as much as possible.

I didn't exactly want to bother him at the moment, but after my stroll through town and the memories Reevie and I had shared, it made me want to find a way to bury the hatchet once and for all. I just didn't want to pressure him into it. Reevie was never one to be prodded. It was always best to find a subtle approach.

Staring at the maps, I wasn't that much closer to a plan I felt sure would accomplish the task at hand. I had several that would, in the end, weed Avalanche out of the compound and this neck of the city, but most of those scenarios included too much bloodshed, leaving me with the same two choices. Either I could cause a temporary blindness to fall on those outside the compound so they didn't see the approach of the patrollers, or find a way to make them disappear altogether.

Strangely enough, the disappearance seemed easier than the blindness.

Of course, with blindness, I didn't actually mean to snuff out the children's eyes, but instead to trick their perception of what they saw, so that they believed one thing while it turned out to be another.

The second option was to make them disappear altogether. Obviously I didn't possess magic such as that, nor did anyone I had ever heard of, but the goal was still the same: I needed to find a way to make sure the Avalanche watchers and beaters outside the compound were not around when the patrollers crept their way through that section of their territory.

For the blindness, the only logical option I could come up with was to disguise the patrollers and divide them up individually so that they appeared to anyone watching to be nothing more than one of the locals on their way back from work, which would mean spreading them out all across the northeast section of the city so that no more than one was seen at a time. The difficult part to that was to then reassemble them at the right time to be ready to storm the gate, at which time it would be almost a surety that some of the Avalanche watchers would see them.

My other option, making the kids disappear altogether, required me finding a way to clear out a large enough section of Avalanche territory to allow all the patrollers to pass through unseen. The only way I could hope to make that happen was provided to me by Shade when he had managed to draw those beaters away during my scouting expedition with Captain Arns. Unfortunately, I didn't think having Shade run from one street to the next was going to be enough this time. It was going to take a larger distraction.

"What about us?" Bull asked. He had joined me several hours after I began my brainstorming. "Sandstorm could provide a large enough distraction. Collen and I could take our beaters and run them through these streets here." He pointed to some of the larger roads leading toward the front gate of the compound. "That should get their attention."

"I'm sure it would. But therein lies the problem."

"What?"

"We would end up drawing too much attention, and they would put the compound on alert. We want to catch them while they're still sleeping. I don't want an open fight if I can help it. Last thing we need is a bunch of dead kids."

"Would serve them right for what they've done to us," Bull grumbled.

I ignored his sentiments and stared at the map. "You might be onto something, though. Perhaps a small group of beaters might be enough to draw the watchers away from these few streets here, long enough to get the patrollers in. Do you have some beaters capable of running fast enough to keep ahead of Avalanche?"

Bull tucked some fallen strands of blond hair back behind one ear. "I have a few I think can make it."

"If we can make it seem like they're a simple scouting party that unfortunately got themselves spotted, then the Avalanche watchers might be tempted to give chase instead of running back to raise the alarm, especially if they catch you running away from the compound and not toward it."

"Makes sense."

I looked at the map and studied several of the streets leading toward the front, trying to determine which one would provide the best coverage and still get the patrollers close enough to make a run for the gate. Whichever route we chose, I would also need to make sure it wasn't too long of a run for our Sandstorm kids.

"Maybe we could set up a small net for the beaters, so they don't have to run all the way back to the manor." I pointed to a closed alley about four streets southwest of the old garrison. "We could have our kids run for this alley here."

Bull scratched his head. "But wouldn't that block their escape? You'd be leading them into a trap."

"Not if we have some patrollers hiding in the alleyways here and here." I pointed to a couple of narrow passages on either side of the dead-end alley. "As soon as the Avalanche beaters chase our kids in, we close the net by having the patrollers move in behind them and block it off, leaving the Avalanche kids cornered."

Bull pursed his lips as he stared at the map. "Smart."

"But we would need to make sure that your runners are clear on which route to take. If they were to get cornered or lost and started running through these streets randomly, they might draw too much notice. Worse, they might get themselves caught . . ." I paused a moment, another thought suddenly presenting itself. "Then again, maybe that's what we want."

"Huh?" Bull looked up.

I raised my hand. "Hear me out. What if we let them get caught?"

"Who, our runners?"

"Yes."

Bull shook his head. "They would throw them in the dungeons and torture them."

"But what if we don't let it come to that?"

"I don't understand."

"Before they can throw them anywhere, what will they have to do first?"

Bull looked back down at the map. Suddenly, his head shot back up with a smile. "They would have to open the gate."

"Exactly. My plan was to try sneaking into the compound myself and find a way to lift the bracer before being spotted. There would be a bit of a gamble in that, but if we were to let some of our people get captured, they would have to open the gates for us."

"But if they captured us, wouldn't we take a chance of them beating our kids on the way to the compound?"

"Not if our kids are the ones doing the capturing."

Bull sighed in frustration. "You've lost me again."

I smiled. "We stick to the plan: lead their kids away from the compound and capture them inside the alleyway here. But then we swap places with them, dressing them in Sandstorm purple while we don the white bands of Avalanche. We simply gag their mouths so they can't cry out, and then we march them straight up to the gate and knock on the doors. We tell them we've captured some lurkers and plan to take them down to the dungeons for questioning."

Bull's eyes sparkled. "I see. Then once the gate is opened, we make a run for the barracks while the patrollers charge in behind us." He slapped the table. "I can't wait to see the look on their stupid faces when that happens."

"Let's not get too carried away. If there is one thing I know about well-laid plans, it's that they never go the way you hope, and that's when you have plenty of time and resources at hand."

With a strategy that seemed at least remotely plausible—even by my standards—I finally rolled the map up and tucked it back on its shelf. Bull left for his duties, but not before I asked him to talk to Reevie and see how much of his ether he could prepare by the raid. I figured my best chance to prevent a fight would be the use of a strong sleep aid. If I were to break some bottles of the stuff inside their barracks, we could have the kids secured and halfway back to Sandstorm before they woke.

Everything was going to come down to timing. If we couldn't get through the gates before they raised the alarm, then the ether would be rendered useless, and as far as I could tell, it was the best option. Perhaps Captain Arns would think of something better.

I ate my supper with Sapphire and Bull in the chiefs' dining room. Reevie once again didn't show, using the excuse of needing to work on creating more ether in order to meet my ridiculous demands. For once, it was a legitimate excuse.

The food was delicious as always, and the conversation manageable, mostly discussing my plans for the upcoming raid, letting Sapphire voice her opinion on the strategies we'd derived earlier that day. She seemed agreeable to the idea of using Sandstorm's runners as bait.

After the meal, I unwrapped the tarts I'd purchased earlier and handed them out. They weren't nearly as moist as they had been at noon when I bought them, but they still had me licking my lips afterward.

With little left to discuss, we finished our desserts, and I headed upstairs for my room. I was tempted to stop by the infirmary to see how Reevie was coping, but I figured it best to leave him to his work. The less stress on him, the more likely I would get what I needed. Not having much else to do, I decided to make it an early evening and crawled into bed. It might be the last good sleep I would get for some time, and I wanted to take full advantage of it. I doubted I would sleep tomorrow evening. I rarely did before a mission. With thoughts of strategy running through my head, I finally managed to lull myself to sleep, though it was a restless one.

I was up before the crack of dawn, and even had to peek out of the curtains to make sure it wasn't still the middle of the night. I felt rested, but not as rested as I had been the previous morning. Yawning as I finished dressing, I started down the stairs for the kitchens. I hoped Cook was there with something for me to eat before I saddled Shade. I didn't relish going to this meeting on an empty stomach, especially since I had no idea how long my meeting with Captain Arns would last, or when the next chance I'd get to grab a meal would be.

The kitchen staff was generally the first to rise in the mornings, which hopefully meant that I could get some eggs at the very least. I doubted they would have already baked any bread. I could hear the clanging of pots and pans from down the hall and smiled as I made my way through the dining room and into the kitchen.

"Glad to see you're up early," I said to the cook, a man by the name of Solvino. He was short and thin with dark hair and a thick mustache that he liked to curl with his fingers. He had been the cook at Sandstorm since Noph's time as chief. Not sure where Noph had found him or how he'd managed to talk him into cooking for a group of street kids, but Solvino seemed to love his work and didn't have any intention of leaving.

"Where else would I be, Master Ayrion? You've seen the way they eat around here." He clicked his tongue. "It's a wonder I get any sleep at all." He turned and shouted some orders to his three underlings, and they hopped to it. He then turned back to me. "What can I do for you this morning? Up early as usual, I see. Going for a run?" He looked at the weapons strapped to my back, and his face said that he doubted that was the reason for my early waking.

"I have a meeting this morning that I don't want to show up late for."

Solvino laughed. "And by late you mean an hour early." He shook his head. "You haven't changed one bit since you were just a wee thing, running around these halls."

"I was never a wee thing running around these halls."

Solvino paused and twisted the ends of his mustache. "Oh, right. I was thinking of the other one."

By *other one*, he meant Noph, the former head of the manor. He shook his head and sighed. "Sometimes I feel as though I've been stuck in this kitchen my entire life."

I looked around the rather spacious and well-stocked room. "Not a bad place to be stuck in."

Solvino looked around and then smiled. "I suppose not. So, what will it be?"

"Just some eggs and whatever cold meat is left from last night. And some cider if you have it, the stronger the better."

He smiled, then turned and clapped his hands. "You heard him: eggs, meat, cider . . . Let's get a move on."

It wasn't long before I was wiping my face with my napkin and placing my used dishes into the sink. "Thank you," I said to the staff on my way to the door.

Solvino paused working long enough to wave an acknowledgment, and I left.

The sky was grey, and so was everything else when I stepped outside.

The sun was attempting to rise, but it had quite a way to go before it breached the top of the city wall. We were a few streets away from the giant enclosure, but close enough that it took a good part of the morning to make it out of the long reach of its shadow.

Leaving the manor proper, I walked around to the carriage house. The front doors were still shut, but the side was unlocked, and I could see light through the window. I opened it and stepped inside. I heard a hammer on the other side of the carriages and waited for a break in the strikes. "Gittrick, is that you?"

The hammering stopped and a head popped up from behind the far coach. "Master Ayrion?" He walked out, wiping his oil-stained hands on a cloth, which he kept draped over one shoulder. "How can I help? You don't need the coach again, do you?" His face said that he hoped not.

"No. Just came to get Shade." I looked past him to the covered transport. "Something wrong?"

He shook his head. "Just tinkering." He turned and looked at the stalls in the back right, where Shade's head was sticking out of one of the doors. "I can saddle him and bring him out, if you wish."

"Has he been fed?"

"First thing this morning."

I nodded and started for the side door. "I'll wait for you out front." I wanted to see if I could catch Reevie or even Muriel to see how the work with the ether was coming along. I walked around to the front of the manor and headed inside. The infirmary was empty, so I walked down to the library and stuck my head in. It was empty as well. Still too early for most to be out of bed, I guessed.

I started to turn when I heard footsteps coming from the east corridor. Sapphire strolled around the corner and startled when she saw me. "You're up early. Did you go for a run?"

I almost laughed. Was I that predictable? "No, not this morning.

Just wanted to get an early start on the day."

"Have you eaten?"

"Only just. Gittrick is saddling Shade right now. I was hoping to catch someone before I left for my meeting. Any chance you know how Reevie's progress is going with the ether?"

She shook her head. "I'll try to find out from him this morning. When do you plan on being back?"

"Not sure. Depends on how well the meeting goes, I guess."

She nodded, and we stared at each other for a moment before she finally cleared her throat. "Well, I've got work to do, so I better get to it."

"Yes. Me too."

We both stood there waiting for the other to leave first. When we both realized what we were doing, we quickly turned at the same time and walked away.

Shade and Gittrick were waiting for me on the other side of the courtyard. Gittrick wasn't exactly a small man, but Shade standing beside him made him seem it. Gittrick held the reins as I mounted, then handed them up to me.

I thanked him and left the manor, heading northwest for Captain Arns's office. I'd been half-tempted to grab the rolled map I'd been using the day before, but I remembered seeing a couple of maps at the patroller's office, which I was sure would be more up-to-date than the one in Sandstorm's library.

The light was growing stronger overhead, shifting from a dull grey to a soft amber as the clouds began to take on the colors of sunrise. The streets hadn't yet begun to fill, but they were far from empty as the lamplighters went about dousing the streetlamps and those with early shifts or long walks kissed their wives and children goodbye and headed for work.

I reached the station at the same time as the next shift; men in uniform were scurrying in and out of the front doors. Those coming out seemed to be moving a bit quicker than those going in. I found an empty spot on the hitch rail and tied Shade off, noting that not many of the patrollers on duty had brought mounts of their own. They must be provided to them by the office, which had a stable in back of the main building.

I waited until those coming off work had vacated the front of the patroller station before heading inside myself. The station lobby was busy, with most of the newly arrived patrollers all gathered in front of a large board on the side. Getting their assignments, no doubt. We had a similar setup in each of the barracks that let us know which duties we had for the week. I guessed this told which routes they were to patrol and who with. I'd never seen a single patroller on duty alone. They were always in pairs.

I walked up to the counter, listening to the chorus of grunts and moans of those just realizing where they would be stationed today. It was familiar, a sound I'd heard a thousand times before in the barracks, and I smiled on the way by. The desk was being manned by the same sergeant I'd spoken with the last time I was there. Lowell, I believed his name was, but I wasn't certain enough to use it.

"Is the captain in this morning? We have a meeting scheduled."

The sergeant wiped the front of his grey beard. "Scheduled meeting, you say?" He looked down at an open ledger and scanned some of the rows with his finger. "Nope, don't see anything written here. You sure it was today?"

"Very sure."

"There was a light under his door when I got here, so I'd say go knock and find out."

I left the sergeant to his work and started down the hall, which was still a bit in shadow, as the sun had yet to break through any of the windows in the lobby behind me. I could see a soft glow coming from the bottom of the captain's door, just like the sergeant said, so I knocked.

"Is that you, Lowell? Come on in."

I smiled as I opened the door. I'd remembered the sergeant's name correctly after all. "I hope I haven't caught you at a bad time."

Captain Arns looked up from his desk. His eyes were red. "Ah, you're here."

I shut the door behind me. "Please tell me you haven't been sitting here all night."

Arns yawned, and I got my answer.

"I have, but it's nothing to do with the upcoming raid. Commandant Ipsworth is wanting to increase our patroller routes without increasing our ranks. Budgets are tight at present, but with the war looming, he feels we need to be a calming presence in the city, which means he wants us seen everywhere." Arns looked down at his desk and shook his head. "I've been studying the maps, doing my best to figure out rotations that will meet the commandant's demands without killing my men."

I frowned as I looked down as well. It was not an easy task.

"Bad timing to have this happen right when we are planning on executing one of the largest raids we've seen in years. My men are already stretched thin as it is."

"I sympathize, but the queen is breathing down my neck about solving our street rat infestation in the northeast quadrant. And if we were to pit the two charges together, I can tell you whose will come out on top, and it won't be the commandant's. If he's upset, direct him to me, or better yet, the queen."

The captain hmphed. "Not quite as easy as all that."

"No, I guess not. But the sooner we get this raid finished, the sooner you can go back to your regular duties."

The captain looked down at the impossible task awaiting him, then back up at me. "If I were to get enough men together, what do you believe the chances are of us completing this raid a day early?"

"You mean tonight?"

The captain nodded, his eyes nearly glazed over, even the one that had a tendency to wander.

I sighed. "I'm not sure. I wasn't expecting you to have spent the night here in—"

"I'll make it happen," Arns said, leaning back in his chair. "I want this business over and done with. The sooner we get this done, the sooner I can meet the request of my commandant."

"Are you sure? If you have any doubts as to whether it's possible, we can wait another day."

He shook his head. "I don't want to wait." He ran his hand down his face and leaned forward. "We'll make it happen. But first . . ." He stood and walked over to a washbowl under the window and stuck half his head inside. He pulled it back out and grabbed a towel and started drying himself. Wet strands of hair plastered his face, and he wiped them back.

"Much better," he said and walked back to his desk. "So, what do you have in mind?"

AVALANCHE

Chapter 24

APTAIN ARNS AGREED TO my proposal that we use the Sandstorm beaters as bait to clear a route through Avalanche territory, then gain entry into the compound by using the captured watchers. We spent the rest of the morning preparing: working over strategy, mapping out routes, making sure we had the blueprint for the upcoming raid burned into our memories. Once we were out in the streets, we wouldn't have time to stop and pull out our maps and decide what we would need to do next.

The rest would depend on my ability to get into the barracks and deploy Reevie's ether. I hoped he had enough, considering he was about to lose an entire day of preparing it and I had no idea how difficult it was to create or if he even had enough ingredients.

After our meeting, I took an hour to head back to Sandstorm to let them know that the raid had been moved up. As expected, Bull wasn't happy with losing another day to choose his runners and prepare them, and Reevie wasn't happy with losing an entire day to create more of his ether. In the end, Bull promised to be there with as much ether as Reevie could manage.

After a quick lunch at Sandstorm, the afternoon and most of the evening was spent with Arns, assembling our raiding party. Unfortunately, with this being such a last-minute request, the captain was finding it difficult to round up recruits. Most had already been assigned and were patrolling the streets, which meant others would have to be sent out to gather them up, and that would take time and resources that were already stretched thin.

As Arns expected, there was backlash from the other captains, who were angry at losing their men and unwilling to offer more than a basic few. They were under the same scrutinizing eye of the commandant as he was and didn't want a bad report going on their record. However, once Captain Arns had shown them the signed document by the commandant, they were a little more willing, though they still weren't happy about it. All he could do was request the other stations send as many men as possible and hope they showed up.

This did not leave me feeling very confident about our success.

By the time the sun had gone down, we were back at Captain Arns's station, waiting on any stragglers that had yet to make it in. Arns recruited the help of Sergeants Lowell and Wilben, who was a sergeant from another station that he was familiar with and trusted, to help lead the raid. Arns took both men back to his office to lay out our plans for the evening's raid.

"Why now?" Wilben asked. "This all seems hasty. Wouldn't it be better to give us a few more days to prepare, at the least to gather some more men?"

"It would," Arns said, "but unfortunately, with the commandant breathing down our necks, we need to get this over with as soon as possible, and there's nothing sooner than right now."

"Why is the queen involved?" Lowell asked, having only just been made aware of the situation.

"She has a vested interest in the welfare of our street children."

Both Lowell and Wilben looked confused. Wilben looked over at me, where I waited quietly at the side for Arns to answer their questions. "And who is this?"

Arns turned. "This is Ayrion. He's the crown prince's personal instructor. He's also the head of that new group in the lancers we've heard about."

"The black something or other?"

"The Black Guild," I said. "The reason for the haste is that the lancers are shipping out this week, and the queen requests that we see this through as soon as possible. Many aren't aware that it is through her and the king's generosity that the orphanage over on Bailey Street has remained in existence. In fact, I just attended a meeting this past week that she organized with several of the aristocracy to raise funding for a second orphanage. She'd like to see the tribes disbanded and the children funneled through these orphanages and into homes. Keep them off the streets and out of the Warrens."

"A worthy goal," Lowell said. "But how successful that is remains to be seen."

"Why now?" Wilben asked. "The tribes have been here all my life, and probably further back still."

Arns leaned forward in his seat. "It seems there has been word of a possible battle brewing, and we are here to stop it before it happens."

"And why would the prince's personal trainer be involved in all of this?"

"Because I have a close attachment to these streets, having grown up in the tribes myself."

The two sergeants looked surprised, as did Captain Arns. Apparently, the queen hadn't told him of my past prior to our meeting.

"Yes, I was a street rat." With Bull and the Sandstorm beaters now being used to help facilitate this mission, there was no way around keeping my involvement out. One look at me talking with them and it would certainly be obvious I was more than just an acquaintance.

The men looked at each other, and I could see a thousand questions in their stares, but none seemed willing to ask. I wondered if by telling them I had somehow lowered myself in their eyes. When there was no response, I took a step forward and away from the captain's bookshelf. "The goal for this evening isn't simply to round up street kids, but to do so with as little bloodshed as possible. I know the animosity most of the patrollers have toward street rats, but you need to make sure the men under you tonight do not act on it."

The two sergeants looked at each other, and then nodded.

I motioned for Arns to continue, and for the next several minutes, the captain took them through our plans, making sure they didn't have questions and had the routes memorized. The goal was to divide the men into the three groups, making them less likely to be spotted and better prepared to deal with the garrison's three main barracks. One group would be under Captain Arns, and one under each of the two sergeants.

We needed a simultaneous attack on all three. I would never have enough time to run from one building to the next with my jars of ether and hope to catch them all before they had a chance to jump out of their beds and grab their weapons. With three groups, we stood a much better chance of dousing all three buildings before those inside made it out.

Once the plan had been thoroughly laid out, the four of us rejoined those waiting in the lobby. I stood beside the sergeant's desk at the back and out of the way of the patrollers milling about the room. Lots of grumbling could be heard as men continued to trickle in, curious why they had been summoned. The stories ranged from them being called for a special patrol through the Warrens to the king wanting to swell his lancer ranks by recruiting patrollers. The latter had them the most worried.

"Is this everyone?" I asked Arns, who was standing beside me, quietly conversing with Sergeant Lowell. It was getting close to time to be on our way, and sadly the number of patrollers present barely filled half the lobby.

He looked around the room. "Afraid it's all I could get with such short notice. Would you prefer we wait?" I could hear the hesitancy in his voice. The captain wanted this over and done with, and I couldn't blame him. I did too.

I shook my head. "The element of surprise is still on our side."

I counted maybe thirty patrollers. I had been hoping for a much larger number. At least the men had listened to orders and had not come in their uniforms.

"Alright, listen up," Arns said, loud enough for everyone to hear. He waited a moment as the room quieted. "I know most of you are wondering why you've been asked here this evening. First of all, let me alleviate your fears. You are not being called up to the lancers."

Audible sighs of relief filtered across the room, and the men seemed to relax.

"What are we doing here, then, sir?" someone on the left asked.

Arns passed a brief glance my way, and I nodded for him to continue.

"We are going on a raid this evening."

Hands shot up all across the room, and Arns tamped them down by raising his own. "You will be placed into one of three groups. When I call out your name, please move to your designated spot. I will be group one, Sergeant Lowell two, and Sergeant Wilben three. Once you're divided, your leaders will take you to an assigned room and explain what we are planning on doing."

"What are we raiding, Captain?" asked another man on the right.

"We will fill you in when we get there, but for now, listen to your group leaders and follow their orders." He glanced around the room at the frustrated faces. "I will say this: These orders come all the way from the crown, so make sure you handle yourself like Aramoor patrollers. The commandant's reputation rides on our ability to perform our duties this evening."

The grumbling didn't lessen. In fact, if anything, it grew. It appeared the common patroller didn't much care about the commandant's reputation.

I almost laughed.

Arns didn't continue arguing the point and immediately began to divide the men.

It didn't take long for the three groups to meet in their respective rooms, learn of the evening's plans, and assemble back in the lobby.

"Will we be needing mounts, sir?" Sergeant Wilben asked.

Arns shook his head. "No. They would make too much noise and bring too much attention. Best we go on foot."

The men grumbled, not loud enough to point at any specific person, but enough to let us know they weren't happy about the decision. I had a feeling it was going to be a long night.

We left the station and started east until we reached the river, with the outskirts of Avalanche's territory just on the other side. However, instead of taking the much faster northern route over the water, we took the southern one, the same way Arns and I had gone. We followed the river south past the towers and their interconnecting sky bridges, then circled north over the Tansian and came up the other side of the circular white buildings.

The march across the northeast sector was a quiet one for the most part, the men remaining clumped together as we kept to the assigned route. We would have them split once inside Avalanche's territory. The men didn't carry themselves in any sort of formation, but then again, they weren't lancers and hadn't been trained to do so. Walking a beat didn't exactly require the same skill set as that of someone who was military trained. They weren't going to behave in the same fashion.

The streets were mostly vacant, the windows in the buildings dark. The moon had thinned to the point of not being useful, forcing us to depend on the streetlights, which of course grew more sporadic the farther north we went. Pretty soon we were left using a couple of lanterns that were passed down the row, giving off just enough light to keep the men from tripping over each other. The lack of light also meant a better chance of us remaining unseen from a distance, which was important given where we were heading.

The fog was also beginning to set in, clumping around our ankles, keeping our feet from being seen. Hopefully, it would deepen the closer we got to the compound. The more ways we had of hiding ourselves, the better it would be for us.

It had taken us at least an hour to make it down and around the sky bridges and back up toward the outskirts of Avalanche territory. We certainly weren't pressing the men to hurry. We wanted to give those inside the compound plenty of time to crawl in bed and fall asleep.

We crossed over the Circle Drive bridge, and I had the men follow me off the main road and over to a street that ran between a couple of small office buildings that were located on the edge of the residential

districts. A blond head popped out from the side of one of the buildings we were heading for, and I slowed.

"Ayrion?"

I had Arns stop the men, and he walked out with me to meet Bull. "Is everyone here?" I asked, rounding the corner of the three-story building. Arns and I stopped when we saw the lanterns shining out from the narrow passageway ahead.

"We're here," Bull said. "I brought ten. I hope that's enough. Some beaters, mostly runners. You said they weren't going to have to fight, and their best defense would be keeping ahead of Avalanche, so I figured we needed kids who were light on their feet more than anything."

Bull waved the kids out, and they walked to the edge of the cobbled street, toting four lanterns between them. They perked up when they saw me standing there, but then froze when they caught a glimpse of all the hooded figures behind me. I wondered if Bull had told them that the men they would be working with were patrollers. Somehow I doubted it, or they probably wouldn't have come.

There were ten rather nervous faces standing behind Bull. I recognized Stringbean, as he stood above the rest. I also recognized one of the other faces peeking out from behind the others. "Mouse, what are you doing here?"

Bull turned. "Mouse? He's not one of those I chose to be here tonight."

The little picker groaned when I spotted him and stepped out from behind Stringbean. "You didn't think you was going in there without me, did you? If anyone should be going in, it should be me."

"And are you going to be able to outrun their beaters when they see you?"

"I won't have to, I can hide. No one will see me."

Bull rolled his eyes. "We don't want you hiding, idiot. Them finding you is the whole point."

"Huh?"

I shook my head. We didn't have time to try explaining. "He can stay with me. Send the others in like you'd planned." Mouse had originally intended on going in with me to open the gates, but those plans had changed over the weekend. I don't know why I was surprised to see him there. I should have known he would find a way to insert himself.

"Are they ready?" I asked Bull.

"As ready as they'll ever be," he said, glancing back over his shoulder at the awaiting group.

"And the ether?"

Bull blew out his lips, which wasn't a good sign.

"Please tell me you have the ether."

"We have it, but there isn't quite as much as you want." He waved one of the kids forward. The boy unhooked a satchel from his shoulder, and my heart sank when I saw there was only the one, and it didn't appear to be overflowing with canisters. He handed the bag over to Bull, who then handed it to me.

I opened and looked inside.

"Well?" Captain Arns asked, taking a step forward to peer in himself. "Will it be enough?"

I counted maybe six covered jars. I lifted one out and felt the weight, then raised it to my ear and jostled it to see how full the container was. They appeared to be about half filled. I was hoping for at least twice this number of containers, if not more.

I placed the jar back inside and shook my head. "I don't think this is going to be enough to cover three full barracks."

"Reevie said he could have had more if you hadn't pushed the timeline. He said if it wasn't enough to make sure I told you it was *your* fault." Bull grinned. "You know Reevie."

I sighed. "He's not wrong, though. Still, I was hoping he could have made more than this."

"What do you want to do?" Arns asked. "Should we wait?"

I looked at the spindly kids in front of me and the anxious men behind and shook my head. "No, we're here. I don't want to wait another day or two. Given time, as many people that know about this raid, we stand a good chance of word spreading and possibly getting back to Avalanche. Best we go now."

"Do you have enough of your stuff there?" Arns asked, pointing at the satchel.

I stared down at the half-empty bag. "Two canisters per barracks just isn't going to be enough for that much space. It might not be enough to render them unconscious, but maybe it will be enough to disorient. These older barracks are open rooms."

Arns looked at the satchel, then at me. "Like you said, perhaps it will stun them enough for us to get in there and disarm them without too much of a fight."

I took a deep breath and released it. "Let's hope so. I don't see that we have much choice."

Doing this today was looking more and more like a bad idea. But, along with having the increased chance of word getting out, if we waited for another day, it would also mean less time for me to help deal with the aftermath of getting the kids placed before I had to hop on a transport for the front. Time was not on my side.

When was it ever?

"How does this affect the plan going forward?" Arns asked.

"Nothing changes. We go in just as before, which means the first step will be clearing a path to the compound. Once inside, we divide the canisters. Three groups for three barracks."

Bull turned and looked at the kids waiting behind him. "You know what to do. We've gone over it a hundred times."

The kids looked positively frightened, but they were there, which showed their resolve to help Sandstorm.

"If all goes well tonight," I said, "we should be able to keep Avalanche from hurting any more of our members." I wanted to try to motivate them as best I could. "Sandstorm is depending on you to keep them safe. All you need to do is find your assigned street, get Avalanche's attention, and then run." I looked at their arms. "Make sure your purple bands are visible once you get into place. We want them to see who you are."

The kids checked their pockets, some pulling out the purple material to show me that they had them.

Bull turned. "And you still plan on having them run for the blind alley?"

"Yes. We'll draw Avalanche in and close the net behind them."

"Which alley is it?" Arns asked. "Things look different down here at night than on a map." He glanced up the street to the right. "Is that it over there, under that red blanket?"

One of the clotheslines hanging between buildings had a faded red sheet stretched across it. I almost laughed as I nodded. "You couldn't have asked for a better marker than that."

Arns motioned for Sergeant Lowell and Wilben to join us. "That's the alley there," he said, pointing to the red sheet. All the kids looked as well.

"Did you have them hang it there?" Lowell asked.

Arns simply shook his head.

Wilben hmphed. "That was providential."

"Now if only the rest of this mission could be so lucky," I said, more to myself than the others.

Arns pointed at two smaller openings on either side of the homes fronting the alley. "That's where you'll have your men waiting," he told them. "As soon as the last of the kids make it in, you'll close off the alley behind them and subdue."

"Quietly," I added once more. "We start a fight, and we are likely to draw attention." It wasn't exactly the main reason I didn't want them beating these kids into submission, but I figured it was the most logical from their standpoint. It wasn't like I thought every patroller wanted to pound on street urchins, but there were some who wouldn't have minded the opportunity if it presented itself, and I didn't want to give it to them.

I looked at Bull. "And your runners know that they need to meet at the next street up before running back here, correct? We can't have them reaching the alley with their group of Avalanche kids at different times, or the ones who make it in last will be cornered by those already in the alley. If that happens, we're going to have a mess."

Bull nodded. "They know where to meet."

"Good."

Bull wrung his hands. "Are you ready for them to go?"

"I think so. Go ahead and send them out. We'll be ready by the time they make it back."

Bull gathered the kids to him, all but Mouse, who stood beside me and watched the others get ready to head out. "Once you get to your destination," Bull said, "don't forget to put on your purple bands."

"Then what?" one of the kids asked.

"Then draw as much attention to yourself as you can."

"Then what?" another kid asked.

Bull sighed. "Then you run." After a few more words of encouragement, he sent them out.

I hoped they knew what they were doing. Bull had rehearsed it with them enough times, but after that display, I was getting a little worried. I waited until the kids had disappeared into the fog-laden streets ahead before turning to Arns. "Go ahead and divide the men into two groups and have them move into place."

I stood back with Mouse and watched as the captain and his sergeants quietly began to divide the men. I had Arns pull five or six out to place them at the back of the alley in order to protect the Sandstorm kids once they reached the dead end. I made sure they understood that it was the kids with white bands they were to disarm, not the ones wearing purple. Arns made sure he was one of the five in the alley just as a precaution.

Turning, I glanced down the narrow street the Sandstorm kids had taken, but they were nowhere to be seen. Bull had gone with them, but only as far as the next street up. It was the designated spot that the three Sandstorm groups were to return to after they managed to get their batch of Avalanche watchers to chase them.

I could see Bull standing in the distance, holding one of the lanterns. If any of his runners came into trouble, Bull would be there to go after them, though I hoped that wasn't the case. We didn't need to attract every watcher in this section of Avalanche's territory, but we did need to clear as many as we could from here to the front of the compound.

"What about me?" Mouse asked. "What do I do?"

"You keep quiet and out of the way." I didn't want to corner myself by joining those in the alley, in case something unexpected happened and I needed to get out, so I chose a spot along the main roadway that the Sandstorm kids would be running, around halfway between the blind alley and where Bull was waiting to meet them a block farther up.

I found a small cubby to hide in between two houses, one that looked to be collecting quite the stack of throwaway furniture and broken crates. I had to guide Mouse inside, as neither of us was carrying a lantern, and he didn't have the advantage of Upakan eyes.

Then we waited.

I kept my ears perked, listening for any sign of hurried footsteps, hoping not to hear sounds of a fight. The wait drew on, and I began to lose track of time. It felt like we'd been sitting behind these crates for nearly an hour, but I knew it couldn't have been that long. We weren't quite that far from the compound, so the kids might have been taking their time getting into position. They were carrying lanterns to help make sure the Avalanche kids saw them, so I wasn't quite sure why it was taking—

"Where are they?" Mouse whispered, breaking my concentration. "I could have been there and back by now. You should have let me go. I could have gotten those watchers' attention for sure."

I rolled my eyes. "That's what I was afraid of."

A shout pierced the night, and my head shot up. It sounded like it came from several streets away, over near the compound. Then there was another shout, this one a little closer and east of here, then another. The Sandstorm kids had clearly been spotted, and by the echo of the angry cries and calls for chase, they were getting closer.

I crouched behind some broken shelving. This was it.

AVALANCHE

Chapter 25

I POKED MY HEAD OUT of our cubby to see what was out there. The road was paved in darkness and layered in fog. About the time that Mouse had worked his way up beside me, a light burst to life at the end of the road on our left, where the kids were supposed to be meeting. By the height of the lantern, it had to be Bull. He seemed to be casting a marker for the others to run toward.

"What's happening?" Mouse asked. "Who's that? Is it Bull?"

"Quiet. I can't hear."

The shouting was growing louder as the Sandstorm runners drew in their prey. Pretty soon, the first group of Sandstorm kids burst out from one of the streets on the left and stopped in front of Bull. He stood in the middle of the crossroad, directly down the street from where me and Mouse were hiding, but on the opposite end of where they needed to run to.

Suddenly, another group of kids appeared from the right. That made two. Where was the third group? I could hear the angry shouts coming from the Avalanche kids, who were getting closer by the second. *Come on. Where's the third group?* If they didn't show soon, Bull and the others were going to have to make a run for it.

About the time the thought hit me, Bull turned and started running down the street in our direction, bringing the two groups of Sandstorm kids with him. My heart sank. Apparently, the third group hadn't made it in time. I ducked back inside our cubby, pulling Mouse with me, and watched the Sandstorm kids run by. I counted only six. We were missing four, and one of them was Stringbean.

Where was the third group? Had they been too slow to keep up? Had they been captured?

The last of our group had barely made it past when shouts rose behind them, and moments later the Avalanche beaters flew by with bludgeons raised and knives in hand. They looked ready to kill. I waited for the last to make it by before sticking my head out. I hoped Bull and the rest of our kids were able to make it to the alley before the Avalanche beaters caught them.

"Where's Stringbean?" Mouse asked frantically, staring back up the street in the direction the kids had come.

I turned and looked. I didn't see any sign of the missing Sandstorm runners. Cautiously, I moved out, and we started up the side of the road toward the spot where Bull had been waiting on them. We got about halfway before fresh shouts pierced the night, and we froze.

"Run!" someone shouted in the distance.

"That's Stringbean," Mouse said.

They were late, which meant if they headed for the alley now, they were going to run straight into the back of the first Avalanche group.

I spun Mouse around, and we ran back down the street in the direction of the blind alley, passing our hiding spot on the way.

"What's going on?" Mouse called after me, rushing to keep up with my longer strides.

Behind me, Stringbean and our runners were just now reaching the narrow roadway we were in and starting our way. I hit the end of the street and spun to the right, jerking Mouse around the corner beside me.

"What's happening?" Mouse asked.

"Shhh." I cupped his mouth. "Don't leave this spot."

Turning, I looked at the blind alley, which was a couple of houses up from our street, and saw the last of Sergeant Lowell's and Sergeant Wilben's men moving in behind the first group of Avalanche kids. I tried waving for them to wait, but it was too dark, and they'd already gone too far to stop.

There wasn't much I could do about it now, and before I could turn and peek around the corner, Stringbean and our kids burst from the roadway on our left.

"There!" Stringbean shouted, and they ran for the blind alley, not seeing either me or Mouse standing in the shadows of the porch beside them.

Kids with white armbands tore out of the narrow street beside us and raced after the Sandstorm runners.

I unhooked the satchel of ether and handed it to Mouse, then motioned for him to stay, and ran after them. There were at least ten, each armed, each looking ready to put a quick end to those they were chasing. The problem was, they were about to run straight into the backs of the patrollers. I could only hope that in all the confusion, the patrollers didn't turn and think that Stringbean and his kids were attacking from behind.

I raced ahead, reaching the back of the Avalanche ranks just as they headed into the alleyway. They didn't see me. Up ahead, the patrollers had formed a wall of dark cloaks across the alleyway. Some of them turned when they heard the cries of the Avalanche kids giving chase behind them.

Lanterns reflected steel in the patrollers' hands. This was exactly what I was hoping to avoid. There were shouts to surrender from the other side of the patroller line, where they were attempting to subdue and disarm the first two groups that had made it in before them.

Lights from windows of the homes facing the alley brightened as residents began to look out to see what was happening.

"Don't hurt us," I heard some of our kids calling out to the row of caped men ahead. "We're Sandstorm!"

The Avalanche beaters slowed when they saw the cloaked men ahead, no doubt realizing it was a trap. They turned to run only to find me standing between them and their escape.

"It's Death's Shadow!" one of the boys in front squealed, and they all stopped, unsure what to do.

I drew my swords from my back and held them out, hoping to appear as menacing as possible. "Put your weapons down and no harm will come to you."

Behind the beaters, a row of hooded men was slowly working its way up the alley in their direction. If I could keep the fighters occupied, they might be able to get close enough to overpower the beaters.

I pointed my swords at the frightened beaters. "I said put your weapons down. Don't make me come in there!"

Several of those in front quickly threw down their weapons. "We give up!" But there were others in back who held firm.

"What are you doing?" one of the larger boys asked. "Rush him! We need to warn the others!"

I opened my mouth to stop them but didn't get a single word out before four of the boys in back charged me. The others were too confused and too frightened to follow. A couple even dropped to the ground.

I didn't want a confrontation, but it was certainly better to be up against four than all ten.

With no more light than what the Avalanche kids had been carrying, I clearly held the advantage and used it to sweep through the four boys before they knew what hit them, doing my best not to cause any permanent damage, a knee to the gut here, a fist to the face there. Only one managed to make it as far as the opening before I'd kicked his feet out from under him and sent him rolling across the broken cobbles.

He didn't even have time to stop rolling before Mouse was on top of him with his pig sticker, waving it under the boy's nose and threatening all sorts of horrible violence on him if he moved. I tried to hide a smile as I turned to the others, who were already being escorted farther back into the alley by the patrollers. While it wasn't exactly how I'd hoped for this to go down, at least we'd been able to get through the first part of the plan without bloodshed, as far as I could tell. The Avalanche crew were banged up, but none of the injuries I saw looked serious.

"Bring him this way," I told Mouse and grabbed the satchel from him before he got too carried away and accidentally broke any of the canisters. I looked inside to make doubly sure he hadn't, though the lack of dizziness told me the bottles were fine.

I remained behind as Mouse used his pig sticker to encourage the much larger Avalanche beater back into the blind alley where the rest were waiting. I looked out of the alley and listened for any sign that our confrontation had alerted any of the other Avalanche watchers.

After a few minutes of waiting and not hearing anything, I turned to join the patrollers. The lights from the windows overhead had disappeared, the residents not wanting to get mixed up in whatever was taking place below. Shutters had been closed and curtains drawn.

I doubted any of those living here would be getting much sleep this evening. What they didn't understand was that if this went according to plan, they would soon have their neighborhood back to themselves with no more fear of street tribe activity. Perhaps Captain Arns would be able to send patrols through this section of the city in the upcoming weeks and let the residents know. I sighed at the thought, knowing Arns and his patrollers, who were already stretched thin, would not take kindly to being asked to stretch even further.

The patrollers had the Avalanche kids sitting on the ground where the alley butted against the back of a couple of houses. The prisoners were bound, and the patrollers were in the process of getting their gags in place. Most looked frightened out of their minds, some even whimpering as they sat there surrounded by large hooded men. A few of the kids were strong enough to maintain their anger even in the face of what they might have believed was their end. For all they knew, Sandstorm had teamed up with the Warrens and were about to drag them all into the underground.

"What do you want?" one kid managed to ask before his gag was tied into place.

I walked over and looked down at the boy. "We want your help."

"Fat chance! I wouldn't help—"

The material was tied off around his mouth before he could tell me why he wasn't going to help and what he would probably do to me if he were ever freed of his bindings. In the end, it would have been a wasted conversation. The look in his eyes said he wasn't going to sell out his tribe. Besides, if we truly needed information, we could have found out everything we needed to from one of the more frightened children.

"What now?" Sergeant Wilben asked as he, Lowell, and Arns joined me at the back of the alleyway.

"Now we swap places."

"Wouldn't it have been better to use more Sandstorm kids as the prisoners," Lowell asked, "instead of taking these Avalanche kids?"

"Possibly," I said, "but then who would we have gotten to watch all the prisoners? With as few patrollers as we had show up, we can't afford to lose any of them, which would have meant not only bringing a dozen or so new beaters to play prisoner, but another dozen or so to act as guards. That's a lot of kids to be traipsing in here. Also, if things go sideways, our beaters might be able to use the prisoners as leverage if they need to."

"That's under the assumption their tribe even cares about their fellow members," Arns said.

I nodded. "An unfortunate truth. But we can only hope."

Behind us, the patrollers were already untying the Avalanche kids' white armbands and replacing them with the purple. Several of them looked confused; others twisted and turned, trying to keep the hooded men from getting one on their arm. A few well-placed slaps to the back of the head forced them to give in. A couple of the older, larger kids required more force. A few of the patrollers held them down so others could get their bands taken off and the new ones on.

After the prisoners were secured and the Sandstorm kids had their new white bands tied on, I met once more with Arns, Lowell, Wilben, and Bull. We walked halfway up the alley so as not to be heard by any of the Avalanche kids.

"Everyone knows what to do?" I asked, looking for confirmation in their eyes that we were ready for the next step.

"Nothing's changed since this afternoon's meeting, has it?" Bull asked.

I wanted to say no and get on with it, but it was best to make sure everyone was on the same page than to find out later they weren't. "I don't believe so. Our runners will lead the Avalanche prisoners up the main street toward the front of the compound. The patrollers will divide into three groups, taking the back streets and alleys on either side of the main road." I looked at the three patrollers. "Make sure to let the Sandstorm kids keep ahead of you. If there are any lingering Avalanche watchers out there, better they run into them instead of you. Hopefully, Stringbean or one of the others can talk their way out of it if that's the case."

All three nodded.

"By the time the kids reach the gate, you should be in place just across the street from the compound, waiting for the doors to open. As soon as they do, we need you inside as fast as possible. A group of you will need to stay and defend against those coming down from the wall; the rest will need to divide into three groups, one for each of the barracks."

"And we will already be inside?" Bull asked.

"Yes. You, Mouse, and I will sneak in through the side door with the canisters. Once the gate opens, we will each take one of the barracks and unleash the ether." It was a simple enough plan that unfortunately hinged on too many uncontrollable factors, leaving us solely in the hands of providence.

"And what happens if they can't get the gate open?" Wilben asked.

"Then me and the Protector will," Mouse butted in, having sneaked in behind us without me knowing, startling Lowell in the process.

"Let's hope it doesn't come to that," I said. I looked at each of those standing around and by the stalwart expressions on their faces it seemed they knew what was expected. I stopped on Bull, and he simply nodded to let me know he was ready. "Good. Let's hope luck favors us this evening. I'm ready for this to be over."

"As are the rest of us," Arns said, his one eye shifting slightly to the side.

I turned and looked at the barricade of cloaked patrollers behind us and the frightened children sitting in between. I was definitely ready for this to be over.

We gathered up the Avalanche kids, letting the Sandstorm runners do most of the work. I wanted to make sure they could keep the others under control. Stringbean, being the tallest, took the lead, keeping his belt knife pressed against the back of the leader of the Avalanche kids. Every time the larger Avalanche boy tried to wiggle free, Stringbean prodded him with it to remind him he wasn't getting away.

"Give us a good head start," I said to the others. "We need to get inside the garrison before you reach the gate."

Both the captain and the sergeants nodded, as did Stringbean. With an encouraging smile from me, Bull and Mouse followed me as I left the alley and headed for the street Mouse and I had been hiding in earlier, keeping our ears and eyes open. We made our way up the narrow road for the next street up. As soon as we reached the crossroads where Bull had been waiting for the Sandstorm kids earlier, we left the main road and crossed over to a small alleyway a few houses down and headed in.

The passage followed the main road but was narrow enough to ensure that no Avalanche watchers would bother coming down. We walked in single file since we didn't have a lantern and there were no streetlights to brighten our way. The other two held on to me as I guided them through. The lack of light slowed our approach as we followed the backstreets toward the Avalanche compound. I hoped Stringbean and the Sandstorm runners didn't escort their prisoners too quickly and beat us to the gate.

I could see small flickers of light ahead, no doubt those patrolling the compound. We were still at least two streets away from reaching the road that ran along the front of the garrison wall when I stopped us at the end of the alley and peeked around the corner of the home on our right. I didn't see anyone coming, just an empty street with homes that looked to have seen better days and streets in need of repair. It reminded me a bit of the Maze.

"I don't hear anyone," Mouse whispered.

"Shh."

The fog lay heavy across the streets now, leaving the cobbles underneath completely blanketed. More importantly, it was thick enough to have risen above the knees, which was exactly what I was hoping for. Fog this profuse would offer us more ways to keep hidden, especially when it came to crossing the road in front of the garrison.

The alley we were in was wide enough for Bull and Mouse to stand on either side of me, and I reached out and squeezed their arms to let them know it was time. Quietly, we slipped out of the shadows and headed into the open street. We were nearing the other side when Mouse grabbed my arm and stopped me. About the time he did, I heard voices on my left.

Someone was coming around the corner. Quickly, I grabbed both their arms and pulled them down, and we dropped to our bellies below the fog. Just before my head sank through the mist, I spotted light. Whoever was coming had a lantern. I grabbed Bull's and Mouse's shirts and tugged them in the direction of the alley, hoping they got the idea and followed.

Quickly, we crawled on our stomachs toward the other side of the street. I had no idea how far we'd gone. I couldn't see a thing inside the low-hanging cloud. I could, however, hear voices. There was more than one. And they were close. I squeezed Mouse's and Bull's arms once more, and we stopped. I couldn't tell where the voices were.

I spun around so that my body was aimed in the same direction as the street we were on, not wanting to be lying crosswise and giving those coming a greater chance of stepping on me.

I think the others realized what I was doing and began to correct their positions as well.

The voices were now loud enough to hear what was being said, and the fog suddenly brightened as the light approached. Where were they? I held my breath. My heart began to pound when I realized the light was on our side of the street. The flaming idiots were coming right for us.

We couldn't keep lying there. They were about to walk right over us. Quickly, I pushed Bull, who was on my left, and Mouse on my right, and both started to roll in the opposite direction. I had nowhere to go, so I lay as still as possible with my swords digging into my back and a satchel of ether clutched to my chest. I stared up through the haze as the two shadows came right at me. I was about to get stepped on. Frantically, I hugged the bag of canisters tighter and rolled onto my side, just missing the boy on the left and nearly hitting the girl on the right.

The two passed on either side of me without noticing, and I released a long sigh of relief.

Flaming Pits, that was close! I couldn't believe they hadn't seen me through the fog. They must have been too preoccupied with their discussion on why they needed to find another cook. From what little I'd heard, it sounded like if something wasn't done to up the quality of their meals, they were going to cook the cook.

It was a rather disturbing conversation, but at least it had kept their attention elsewhere, because if either had looked down, there was no way they wouldn't have seen me. I thought I was about to have to tackle them both, but was relieved that it hadn't been necessary. Taking prisoners at this point would have made it extremely difficult for the three of us to sneak inside the garrison.

I waited a couple of minutes, just enough to ensure the two had moved on, before slowly raising my head above the fog. Two more heads popped up out of the mist on either side of me, both looking as relieved as I was for not having been caught. I hoped the patrollers were having better luck than we were. Twisting the satchel of ether back around to my side, I nodded toward the alley ahead. We rushed inside, panting as we did, more from the fright of nearly being caught than from the run.

"I can't believe that just happened," Bull said.

Mouse waved it off. "I've seen closer."

Knowing him, it was probably true.

We moved down the alley to the next junction, waiting a little longer at this one before running across the street for the next.

"How close do you think our runners are?" Bull whispered.

I shrugged. I had no idea. I could only hope they weren't already at the gate.

With one last listen, we took off across the street and into the passage beyond, this one rather familiar, as it was about the third time I'd been inside. This particular alley stopped on the other side of the street from the garrison, directly across from the wall and only a couple of houses down from the gate itself. We ducked as a set of torches strolled past. There was enough debris littering the place that we wouldn't have even needed the fog.

Nonetheless, I had us lower to our hands and knees as we reached the far side of the entrance, directly across from the old compound. I studied the top of the wall in front of us but couldn't see any heads sticking over. There were a couple in the gate towers, but they seemed

preoccupied, talking amongst themselves rather than watching the roadway below.

I eased my way forward to get a better look at the gate on our right
and the street leading up to it, the same one I knew Stringbean and the
others would be taking. So far, I hadn't seen anyone, which was a good
sign. I had been afraid that with our unexpected delay back there, we
were late. I turned and looked for the inset where the side door was located, instinctively patting my right pocket where the key was.

"What now?" Mouse whispered after we had scooted back inside
the mouth of the narrow crevice.

"Now we work our way down the front of the homes until we reach
the side door, and then we sneak across the street."

"What if it's being guarded?" Mouse asked.

"Then I will deal with it."

"Do we have some extra cords?" Bull asked. "I didn't think to bring
any with me. Didn't know we'd need it."

"I've got some," I said, patting one of the inner pockets of my coat.
I knew from experience how useful a few extra cords and some gag ma-
terial could be. The last time we came across an unexpected guard,
Mouse and I had been forced to take him with us through the garrison.
I had no intention of repeating that.

"We need to hurry," Mouse said excitedly. "Stringbean and the others could be here at any moment."

"Yes, but we won't do them any good if we get caught, so we wait
for—" I didn't even get my thought completed before I was grabbing
the two of them and pulling them back down as the fog brightened and
another patrol rounded the wall on our left. I could see the glow of their
torch as they passed on the far side of the street. As soon as it faded, we
slowly rose.

I glanced at the two and nodded. "Let's go."

AVALANCHE

Chapter 26

E LEFT THE ALLEY AND crept along the front of the abandoned residences on our left, keeping as low as we could to remain hidden by the fog. We stuck to the deepest shadows, pressing ourselves against the front of the homes, ducking under porches and climbing through and around broken railings, keeping our eyes on the guard towers behind us while we carefully felt our way forward. We stopped at each new opening between buildings to make sure no one was there before crossing on to the next.

The light from another set of watchers on patrol appeared, and we sank beneath the fog. This time we were on the far side of the street and thankfully not close enough to be spotted or stepped on, but that did little to ease my tension. Once again, I held my breath as the fog brightened, then exhaled as the light faded.

It didn't take long to find the spot directly across from the recessed doorway in the wall. The fog was thick enough to keep it mostly hidden, but not thick enough to keep me from seeing that someone was standing in front of it just like before. Lowering beneath the mist, I pulled the others close and unhooked the satchel of ether to place in Bull's hands.

"I need you to carry this across. Wait here until I deal with the guard. In fact, wait until the next patrol passes." I couldn't see if he or Mouse nodded but had to assume they did. Leaving the porch, I crawled out to the roadway and started across the cobbled lane on my hands and knees, staying below the fog.

The thick leather of my pants helped cushion my knees from the rough stone as I worked my way blindly across the street. I didn't have long before the next set of patrollers made it around.

Not knowing exactly where I was, or how close I was to reaching the other side, or where the door and its guard might be had the hair on my arms standing and my heart racing. I worked my way through the ghostly darkness, using my hands as feelers to test the way ahead as I moved across the street. I listened intently for any hint of movement. I hated not knowing. With each new placement of my hands, I was tempted to raise my head and take a look.

Faint voices filtered through the dark and I froze. Looking around frantically, I realized the voices weren't coming from the road, but from somewhere above me, on the wall. Taking another deep breath to steady my nerves, I continued. I'd made it a few more feet when my hand brushed something ahead. It felt like the stone from the lower part of the garrison wall. The problem was, I didn't know where on the wall I was at. I had aimed to cross to the left side of the doorway, but since I hadn't been able to keep my goal in sight, I could have easily wandered off the mark.

Carefully, I slid my hand down the stone to the right, hoping to find an inset where I thought the door might be, but there was nothing but wall. Frustrated, I did the same on the left, but again came back with no hint of which direction I should go. I was about to work my way farther right when voices filtered out of the fog to my left, and these were not coming from overhead. Worse, they were on my side of the street.

My heart started to pound. I didn't have time to waste. Either it had taken me longer to get across than I'd planned or this new patrol was early. Regardless, I was about to be spotted. Staying as quiet as I could, I quickly moved down the wall in the direction I guessed the door was. Thankfully, my hands found an opening after a few feet.

Behind me, the voices grew louder, and the fog was beginning to brighten; they were about to round our section of the wall. It was now or never.

I grabbed my belt knife and shot up out of the fog in front of the door guard. He was so stunned that instead of raising the alarm, he started stammering incomprehensibly. I grabbed his mouth before he could cry out and squeezed in behind him, pressing my blade against the small of his back. As soon as the tip of my knife found its mark, the boy stiffened.

"You so much as blink when they pass," I said, "and I'll feed you your insides, keeping you alive long enough to enjoy them. Do you know who I am?"

The boy nodded with a whimper.

"Good, then you know I keep my word. Not a sound." I kept the knife pressed against his back, lowering myself into the fog as I did.

The patrol started to pass, and I could feel the guard in front of me begin to fidget, so I pressed the blade a little harder, and he stopped.

I hated being below the fog line. I couldn't see what the boy was doing. For all I knew, he was making faces at the patrol to get them to stop. I held my breath and counted the moments until their footsteps disappeared. As soon as they passed, I stood and grabbed the boy's mouth with my free hand. Releasing the knife from his back, I wrapped my arm around his neck and squeezed.

He fought me for a moment, his legs kicking, but I held him tight, pulling him back against the door as I did. Soon, the boy's twitches slowed and then stopped altogether as his body went limp in my arms. I immediately released his neck and lowered him down onto the cobbles, making sure he was still breathing. I slid my knife back in its sheath and pulled out the extra gag and straps from my coat and tied him up.

Next, I pulled out the key and fit it into the lock, praying it still worked. The lever inside snapped. I exhaled a sigh of relief when the handle turned and the door slid open.

A grunt broke the silence behind me, and I spun as Mouse's head popped out of the fog in front of me, Bull almost on top of him.

"I fell on someone," Mouse whispered, looking down at his feet.

"It's the guard," I whispered, fighting back the urge to strangle Mouse. "Help me get him inside."

About that time, a ruckus broke out on top of the wall, and we all froze. Had they heard Mouse's cry? Both Bull and I looked at the little picker, and he shrugged with a sheepish grin. The sound of people running down the wall trailed over our heads as those on watch above headed in the direction of the gatehouse.

"What's going on?" Bull asked.

I stepped out from the doorway and peeked around the corner of the inset. A large group of kids was making their way out from one of the streets and across the road from the gate. I could see Stringbean in front.

"We're out of time."

"They're already here?" Bull peeked around the corner himself.

I turned and grabbed the front of the unconscious boy. "Let's get

him inside."

Bull grabbed the boy's feet, and the two of us hauled him through the door.

"Hurry," Mouse said behind us, watching from the inset. "I hear someone coming."

I pulled Mouse inside as hurried steps approached from the right. I shut the door and locked it, catching only a brief glimpse of three or four kids running by. I had thought to keep it unlocked, but I didn't want those inside trying to escape once we breached the front.

The garrison hadn't changed all that much that I could see, though it was perhaps a bit more cluttered with stacked barrels, broken carts, and empty crates lying in piles near the walls. Some of the piles held old clothing too torn to wear and what smelled like food remains not worth picking through. It seemed Avalanche had set up its own waste dumps inside and then just left them there to rot.

The waist-high fog went from being somewhere to hide to something to be wary of, hiding untold numbers of obstacles for us to step on as we worked our way around the wall. The three barracks in front of us each had torches out front, signaling they were in use. Next to them was the main building and a walkway that led straight to the gate. Behind the main building, I could see the roof to the dining hall, which housed the well Mouse and I had climbed down to rescue our pickers.

"What now?" Bull asked. "We were supposed to be at the barracks, ready to toss in the ether by the time they reached the gate."

"I know. If we hurry, maybe we can still make it in time." I looked at the gate towers on either side of the two wooden doors and saw kids filling each, but so far the doors themselves remained shut.

I took the satchel back from Bull and opened it. "We need to divide these up and get to our places. Mouse, you have the first barracks; Bull, the second." They both nodded, and I handed each of them two of the covered jars. "Whatever you do, don't breathe any of this in."

Clutching the canisters to our chests, we started down the wall toward the first building. I didn't want to cut straight across the entire yard and risk getting spotted from the light cast by the torches on the wall or from the ones lining the open walkway between the front gate and the main building. By the time we reached the first barracks, we were practically jogging.

"Come on, Stringbean," I whispered to myself, "get those doors open." I stopped and looked at the other two when we reached the spot in the wall directly across from the first barracks. "Ready?"

They nodded, and we started around the back of the building. We left Mouse to make his way up to the side entrance as Bull and I headed on to the next.

"Who's there?" someone called out behind us. I turned to find a half-dressed boy walking toward us, looking to be coming from the general direction of the privy. He stopped only a few feet away, as it was too dark to see much of anything except shadow.

I didn't have time to think. Without saying anything, I handed Bull my satchel, turned, and punched the boy in the jaw before he got a chance to realize he was in danger. His eyes rolled back in his head, and he dropped. We didn't have time to stop and tie him up. They could be opening the gates at this very moment. Handing me my satchel, Bull stepped over the boy and made his way to the door on the side of Barracks Two.

I left him and headed around the back of the third barracks, which was about a stone's throw from the main building. From the side, I could see straight to the gate, and so far, the doors were still shut. What was taking them so long? I headed up the side of the building and crouched behind a bush across from the door, hoping no one had spotted me.

I stared at the gate ahead. *Come on, Stringbean.* Why weren't the doors opening? We couldn't very well start tossing in canisters until we could see our people were able to get through. My palms began to sweat as I unhooked the satchel and placed it on the ground in front of me, then pulled out the two remaining canisters. I hoped they would be enough.

All of this would be for nothing if our Sandstorm kids were discovered. If they couldn't get the watchers to open the gate, the Avalanche patrol might realize that they didn't recognize those bringing the prisoners in. On the other hand, who would have ever believed that a bunch of Sandstorm kids would try breaking into the Avalanche compound?

Someone from the gate shouted down to those outside the wall. I couldn't hear what was being said, but at least they were talking.

Come on. Open the door.

A moment later, the same person shouted to those on this side to raise the bracer.

Finally.

I grabbed the two canisters, getting ready to make my move, when the side door of the barracks I was standing beside suddenly swung open. I quickly set the two jars down to free my hands in case I needed to grab whoever was coming out, but they never stepped through. What were they doing? I couldn't see anything from behind the door.

Some noise at the main gate redirected my attention. It sounded like the bracer was beginning to rise, which meant I was out of time. I snatched up the canisters of ether once more and readied myself to rush in when someone on the other side of the door shouted back into the barracks.

"Hey, I think something's happening at the gate!"

My heart sank. *Flaming Pits! They just woke the entire barracks.* I needed to get in there before the kids got out.

I climbed out from behind the bush and grabbed the handle on the back of the door. I was about to jerk it the rest of the way open and release the ether when shouts at the wall had me peeking around the door. The bracer had stopped partway up. There were shouts coming from the other side of the doors, and my heart started to pound. Something was wrong. My mind raced as I tried to decide what to do. I couldn't release the ether now, not if those outside the gate couldn't get in. Yet if I didn't use it, and they did manage to get the gate open, then there was sure to be bloodshed.

The entire plan was collapsing. I needed to do something.

I looked down at the jar. At the very least, I could just pop the lid and toss in what I had and hope for the best. It was better than nothing. Unfortunately, before I could grab the handle, the door flew open and Avalanche kids poured out, all of them running for the gate, some carrying weapons, others still trying to pull on their clothes.

I wanted to scream. We were so close. What happened to the gate?

It was too late for me. My barracks had emptied already, so I rushed back around to the second to check on Bull, only to find him standing at the back panting, still holding his two canisters.

"They almost caught me," he said, pointing back toward the open door where the kids in his barracks were rushing out as well, all heading for the front gate. "What are we going to do?"

At this point, I had no idea. I motioned for him to follow, and we headed for the first barracks, but Mouse wasn't there.

"The door's still shut," Bull said. "You don't think . . . ?"

I started up the side of the first barracks with Bull right behind. If Mouse had already gone inside, he could be stirring a hornets' nest. The closer we got, the more afraid I was that at any moment the door would fly open and Avalanche kids would come rushing out.

But the door never did.

We ducked under a partially opened window on the side, and my eyes began to water. One whiff and I knew exactly where Mouse was. I took a deep gulp of air, then ran for the door and jerked it open. Inside, I found all of the occupants still in their beds or strewn across the floor, unconscious. I'd never smelled a batch of ether this strong. Even without breathing, I was getting a little light-headed. This stuff was way more potent than anything Reevie had made before, making me wish I'd gone ahead and tossed mine in after all.

I found Mouse about two rows in, passed out on the floor. Shards from the two jars lay sprawled across the floor in front of him. I couldn't believe he hadn't made it back out, but then I saw an older, larger boy with his hand locked on Mouse's leg. Whoever he was, he'd managed to keep the little Sandstorm picker in long enough to get caught himself.

I unhooked the unconscious boy's fingers from Mouse's leg, tossed Mouse over my shoulder, and ran out the door, nearly plowing into Bull on the way.

"Is he alive?" Bull asked.

I ran as far down the side of the barracks as I could before gasping for air. I was feeling dizzy and had to lean against the side of Barracks Two just to steady myself. "He's alive. Just unconscious." I carefully laid Mouse down on the ground. "He must have rushed in as soon as he saw them starting to lift the bracer."

"If I'd known how strong this stuff was," Bull said, "I would have tossed mine in anyway."

"Too late to worry about it now." I didn't want to say I was thinking the very same thing. Mouse, as crazy and impulsive as he was, had managed to do what we did not.

Bull kept his eye on the barracks door behind us, one hand resting on his sword. "What about the rest?"

I didn't bother turning to look. "No need to worry about them. No one will be leaving there for some time." I stared at the canisters in Bull's hand. "This is one strong batch of ether."

Bull looked around nervously. "What do we do now?"

"Now we hide Mouse and find a way to get that gate open."

"But what about all the rest of the kids?"

"One thing at a time." I lifted Mouse's limp frame and placed him behind some bushes running along the side of the second barracks. "I doubt anyone will find him here. Come on."

We made our way to the third barracks, where I had been hiding earlier. As soon as we crawled behind the bushes on the side, I opened my satchel, and Bull placed his canisters inside. No reason to be running around with them in our hands now.

"What do we do with them?" he asked.

I handed Bull the satchel. "Hold on to them for now." I wanted my hands free.

We stared at the gates ahead and all the kids waiting just behind. What was happening on the other side? Had Arns and the patrollers come out of hiding? Were they fighting in the streets?

"How do you plan on getting the doors open?" Bull asked.

"I doubt we'll have to wait long. If there is a fight in the streets, I would imagine Avalanche will want to—"

The bracer suddenly started to rise once more as shouts rained down from those on the wall. I still couldn't hear what they were saying, but from the general cries, it didn't leave me with a good feeling in my gut.

"This is exactly what we were hoping to avoid," Bull said.

"I know." I quickly turned and scanned the surrounding yard and buildings. How could I stop this? How could I get them away from the door?

In my desperation, an idea formed, and it was a mad one.

I snatched the satchel from Bull.

"What are you—"

"I'm going to cause a distraction. When I tell you to, I want you to start shouting that Death's Shadow is here."

Bull shook his head. "I don't understand."

"Wait until I'm standing in front of the main building there," I said, pointing directly across from us. "As soon as I get into the torchlight so they can see me, I want you to come out and shout that it's a trap, that Death's Shadow is in the compound. And then say whatever you need to get those at the gate to chase after me."

"Where are you going to go? We're locked inside the compound."

"I'm going to go down."

"What?"

I didn't have time to explain. The bracer was nearly all the way up. I hooked the satchel around my neck and then drew my swords. Leaving Bull at the side, I shot out of the large scrub bush and ran the short distance between the two buildings. By the time I made it into the torchlight at the front of the main building, Bull had already left the bushes.

"Hey!" Bull shouted to those at the wall. He began waving his arms and even started running toward the gate himself. "Look! It's Death's Shadow!"

Those at the gate started to turn.

"It's a trap!" Bull shouted. "Death's Shadow is inside! He's come to kill us all!"

Shouts rose from those on the gate tower, as they, too, had now turned to see what was happening. The gate doors hadn't yet opened, but the bracer was fully removed.

"Get him!" someone on top of the wall shouted, and nearly the entire throng of Avalanche charged at once. Like a stampede of starving kids to the dining hall bell, they came for me, weapons raised and a deadly hunger in their eyes. The ground shook under my feet.

It suddenly occurred to me that this was a very stupid idea.

I waited on the front steps, trying to draw them in a little further. I stared past the horde of angry fighters to the doors, willing them to open so the patrollers could rush in, but the gate remained shut. I could only hope Bull realized it and found a way to get them open himself. Unfortunately, I couldn't stand around and watch. The mass of angry Avalanche kids was nearing the main building, and I was out of time.

Quickly, I turned and ran up the stairs and into the main building's lobby. Shouts for my head rang up the stairs behind me, and I ran for the other side of the room, waiting just long enough for them to see where I had gone before turning and rushing down a back corridor to a door at the end. I had only been this way once before, back when Kore had kidnapped me during a meeting where I was trying to broker a truce. He had hauled me from his office upstairs, through the building, and down this very hallway to the door ahead.

I began to sweat. What if the door was locked? I reached the end of the hall and glanced over my shoulder long enough to see the corridor filling behind me. I grabbed the latch and yanked.

It gave way, and I released a heavy sigh as I snatched open the door and rushed down the stone steps to the bottom, where I found another door waiting. This one was locked.

I banged on the door. "Open up in the name of Cutter. We have prisoners!"

Behind me, the first of the Avalanche kids were just reaching the door at the top of the well. *Come on!* My heart was nearly pounding out of my chest. It was beating so loud I could almost hear it.

"If you don't open, Cutter will cut off your feet and make you dance for your breakfast!"

The lock snapped and the latch was pulled back, but before they could open it, I rammed into the door with my shoulder, knocking the guard on the other side to the floor. Behind me, the kids were nearly halfway down the stairs.

I ran through the doorway only a few feet in front of my pursuers. The garrison cells hadn't changed much. The hole in the wall on the left where Mouse and I had climbed down to rescue our Hurricane pickers was still there, as was the guard table and chairs. I barely caught a glimpse of them as I raced down the corridor of cells.

I was completely blocked in, my only option being to keep running. I raced as fast as my feet would carry me. Angry cries for my death filled the stone tunnels as I ran through them. They had to have known that they had me cornered. The very thought of getting their hands on Death's Shadow was clearly driving them into a frenzy.

The cells began to change the farther back we went, looking less like a stone block structure and more like rooms carved out of rock. I reached the end of the corridor, leaving me only one route, and that was a smaller passageway to the right, so I took it. It led past several more cells, one of which I had spent the night in the last time I was here. Up ahead, the hallway ended at a wall of stone, leaving me with no place to go.

I stopped and turned to face those behind, my swords up and ready. The corridor behind me was quickly filling as the kids cautiously worked their way closer. I needed to hold them back as long as possible. I needed to fill the passage with as many kids as I could manage.

"Big mistake!" one of the larger boys in front said as they made their way down the corridor toward me. They seemed to be taking their time now, knowing I had nowhere to run, as though wanting to savor the moment. He held out his arms for the rest to stop, not wanting to get any closer than he needed to. They were far enough back that I couldn't reach them with my swords. "Cutter is going to be very happy with us when he sees who we've captured." The boy pointed to one of the empty doors on my left. "You might as well crawl in one of the cells now. Unless you prefer we kill you first and then carry your corpse back to the Temple for Cutter to stuff."

By this time, the entire passageway was filled with bodies, all the way back to the main corridor. My only option was to keep them talking as long as possible. I needed to give Bull as much time as I could to get those gates open. If he couldn't, then no matter what I did down here, I wasn't getting out of this alive.

"There is another option," I said, trying to sound serious and in control. I raised my swords and pointed them at the front line of fighters. "*You* could surrender."

The Avalanche beater turned and looked at those behind him and then roared with laughter. Everyone else quickly followed, sending their glee echoing across the surrounding stone. After a while, the laughter died down and the larger boy took a moment to look me over. "They said you were a skilled fighter, not a common jester. Look around you. I don't care how many swords you carry. You aren't getting out of here alive. We have you completely surrounded."

"Actually," I said, raising one of my swords to sheathe it, "I am exactly where I want to be."

The boy smiled. "You want to be cornered down here in the dungeon? Well, congratulations. You got your wish." The kids laughed once more, but not quite as hard.

I needed to think of something to say to stall them, but I was running out of ideas. I slowly unhooked my satchel. "Fine," I said. "If, as you say, I have no way out, then before you do your worst, I offer you these in exchange for my life." I didn't really know what to say, so I went with the first thing that popped into my head, as stupid as it was. Anything to keep them from charging. I'm sure my plea sounded ridiculous, but perhaps it was ridiculous enough to keep them listening.

I slowly opened the satchel and carefully pulled out the first canister, leaving the other three inside. "These are worth a king's ransom," I said, holding the first up for everyone to see, "and I will give them to you if you promise not to kill me."

The boy in front laughed.

As stupid as it had sounded, I wanted to laugh as well.

"And what's to stop us from killing you and just taking them anyway?"

I smiled, frantically trying to think of a good-enough reason. "Because what's inside is extremely fragile and if dropped and broken, it will become completely worthless."

The boy looked at the canister in my hand curiously. "What's in it?"

My smile broadened. "So glad you asked."

It seemed my time had finally run out. Either I opened the canister and let them see or we started fighting. I could only hope and pray that the patrollers had managed to somehow breach the gate.

Taking a deep breath, I opened the first jar and threw its contents across the front line. The liquid struck them chest high, and they all jumped back, inhaling as they did. Eyes began to roll back in their heads and kids started to drop, but not just the ones who'd been touched by the ether—several rows behind as well.

Quickly, I sheathed my sword and opened the next, throwing its contents out over the rows of kids behind. The ether was strong enough to have stopped a zyntar, and with it being unleashed inside an enclosed place like these underground cells, it was permeating everything.

My lungs began to beg for air and my heart pounded, but I forced myself not to breathe. My eyes stung and watered to the point of barely seeing as I opened the last two canisters. I lobbed the first as hard as I could to reach those at the very back before they realized what was happening and ran. The jar shattered against the back wall of the main corridor leading in. With my last canister open, I tossed it about halfway down the rank.

By this time, I was blinded by my own tears. My eyes felt like they were on fire, so I kept them shut as I fought to hold the air in. My heart sank as I realized I wouldn't make it out. I needed air!

Panic set in, and I turned and stumbled into one of the cells to my left and shut the door. I didn't have a key, so I lay in front of the door, hoping my body weight would help keep it shut.

My head was pounding. As soon as I breathed in my first gulp of air, I was going to be as unconscious as the rest of them. I could only hope and pray that Bull was able to get the doors of the compound open or I might not be waking up again, or if I did, it would be in chains.

Not able to hold it back any longer, I lifted my coat over my mouth to perhaps help lessen the blow and sucked in an enormous gulp of air. The room started to spin, and everything went black. The last thought that ran through my mind was that this had to be the stupidest thing I'd ever done.

AVALANCHE

Chapter 27

I COULD HEAR VOICES IN THE FOG as I made my way across the garrison yard. They were muddled and incoherent but definitely coming closer. I slunk back deeper inside the roaming mist, doing my best to remain hidden from those on the wall ahead. The fog was thicker here and gave me a place to hide from whoever was coming. Unfortunately, no matter how far back I crawled, the voices kept getting louder.

There was no way they could have seen me. Cautiously, I lowered myself all the way to my stomach and began to crawl toward the side door. I remembered locking it on the way in, and I quickly fumbled through my pockets until I found the key.

I heard shouts, people calling my name, as the Avalanche patrol hunted me across the garrison. I'd barely managed to escape the cells below. In fact, as groggy as my mind was at the time, I wasn't even sure how I'd managed it. The voices were growing louder. Were they watching me from the top of the wall and signaling my position to those inside?

Frantic, I hopped to my feet to make a run for it, but the fog was everywhere now, and I couldn't see a thing. Behind me, the voices sharpened, building to shouts.

They were almost on top of me. I reached for my swords.

"Ayrion! Ayrion, wake up!"

A splash of something struck my face, forcing me to open my eyes. Everything was a blur. My eyes burned, my nose burned, my chest felt like Tubby had sat on it.

"Wha— What happened?" My throat was raw and dry, and my voice cracked as I tried to speak.

"He's awake," I heard someone say. I couldn't make out who; all I could see were blurry shapes.

"Who's there?" I asked.

"Douse him again," another voice said. I tried to roll over, but two large hands held me down.

"Don't move. We need to wash your eyes."

Before I could ask what he meant, someone pulled open my right eye, and a cold burning sensation flooded my face. Before I could protest, they were on to the other.

I tried sitting up, but whoever was holding me down was stronger than me. "Where am I?"

I reached out with my hands and felt nothing but cold stone.

"Give it a minute. You should be fine."

The burning in my eyes lessened. What had been nothing but blurry shapes before began to coalesce, and faces appeared out of the haze.

"Bull, is that you?"

"It is, and I don't mind saying you gave us quite the scare."

"Stupidest thing I've ever seen," someone behind Bull said.

I blinked several times and wiped tears and water from my eyes. Captain Arns's face came into view. "Quite insane," he said, staring down at me.

I looked at Bull. What were they talking about? My mind was swimming with jumbled memories, none of them clear. "What's going on? Where am I?"

"You don't remember?" Bull asked, suddenly looking concerned. "We are in the Avalanche cells below the garrison."

My memories began to take shape. "I used the ether, didn't I?"

Arns smiled. "I'd say so." He waved a hand in front of his face. "Still kind of strong."

"You got the gate open?"

"I did," Bull said. "Well, we did." He glanced back over his shoulder at Arns. "After your mad dash into the main building, there were only a couple of kids left at the gate, and most of the ones still on the wall. It didn't take me long to dispatch those in front, and I was able to get the doors cracked before those on the wall came down. By then the patrollers had pushed through."

"Dispatch?"

"I didn't kill anyone, if that's what you're asking. Though their heads are going to be pounding for quite some time after they wake."

"Like mine is now." I reached up and pressed a hand against my forehead and found it lathered in sweat.

"When the gate doors hadn't opened," Arns said, "I took a group of men around to the side door you had shown me, but it was locked, so we ended up having to run back to the front. By the time we got there, the gate was just beginning to open."

"Sorry about that," I said. "I didn't want anyone inside escaping."

With some help from Bull and Arns, I was able to make it to a sitting position. Looking around, I realized I was still in the Avalanche cells. The door beside me was open, but I couldn't see anything outside with the two of them blocking my view.

"Did it work? Were you able to round them up without too much fighting?"

Bull chuckled. "Yeah, I'd say it worked." He reached under my arms and lifted me to my feet.

The room was still spinning, but not quite as badly as it had been, so I tried taking a step. My legs gave way, and I would have gone down if not for Bull holding me up. I looked up at him. "I can't seem to feel my legs."

"It'll wear off," Bull said. "At least, it has with the others."

They helped me through the door, and we stopped just on the other side. The corridor was lined all the way back to the first turn with Avalanche kids, all of whom, it seemed, were still unconscious.

"Yes," Arns said, "I would say it worked."

"How long have I been out?"

"A while," Bull said.

Arns shook his head. "Took us hours before we could come down here without getting too dizzy ourselves. We've sent a new person down every hour to test it, but most of them are still lying unconscious between here and the guard station."

"What about Mouse?" I asked Bull.

"He's fine. He came to some time ago. The fresh air helps. Those he doused in the barracks are just now coming around."

"It's going to take a while longer down here," Arns said, careful where he put his feet so as not to step on anyone. "Not a lot of fresh air this far down. We have the doors leading up open, but it's going to take a while to air this place out, I'm sure. Whatever your apothecary put in those jars was potent."

His sentiments left me wondering for a brief moment if Reevie hadn't done it on purpose, hoping to catch me as well, but I waved the notion off, feeling a little ashamed I'd even considered it.

"He probably realized he didn't have enough time to make as much ether as he would have liked," I said, "and instead just made what he could that much stronger."

The two men helped me through the carpet of kids, and we slowly worked our way out of the dungeons and up to where the fresh air awaited our arrival.

Each new breath burned my lungs a little less as we passed a continuous stream of patrollers, carting one child after another up and out of the underground cells. When we reached the lobby of the main building, I was surprised to see the sun shining in through the windows. How long had I been down there? It had been the middle of the night when I'd made my mad dash into the dungeon.

We walked across the porch, and I squinted against the glare of the sun on my face, which I could see had already reached its zenith. The light was blinding, and my eyes were having a difficult time focusing with the amount of water they were still producing.

"Protector! You're alive!" I didn't need to see him to recognize Mouse's voice. I wiped my eyes as he headed up the porch steps, a bright smile on his face. "I did it! I put them all to sleep."

I smiled. "Yes, I know. We found you inside the barracks curled up with one of their beaters."

"Hey, I can't help it if he grabbed my leg. Did you see how big he was?" Mouse grinned. "That'll teach 'em to mess with Sandstorm."

With the steady stream of patrollers heading in and out of the main building with their unconscious charges, I had Bull help me over to the edge of the porch steps and out of their way. I sat down and leaned my shoulder against the railing for support. My head was beginning to clear, but it was still pounding, and I kept needing to dab at my eyes.

"Here," Bull said, handing me a piece of white cloth. "Use this." It looked like one of the Avalanche armbands. I pressed it gently against my eyes, and my vision cleared momentarily. Leaning against the rail, I sucked in several deep gulps of clean air. Well, cleaner than the air down in the dungeon. It smelled a bit of sewage and sweat. When Kore had been in charge of the compound, he hadn't let it get so completely run down. Cutter, on the other hand, clearly had no such proclivities.

I glanced over at the closest barracks and found Sergeant Lowell standing in front with a couple of his patrollers. "What happened to the Avalanche kids that were on the wall?" I asked.

"We have them locked in that building there," Arns said, pointing at Lowell, "along with anyone else who didn't get doused, which isn't all that many, considering you took most of the kids down with you." He shook his head. "What would have happened if we hadn't gotten the doors open?"

I tried to chuckle, but it came out as a hoarse cough. "I guess we wouldn't be having this conversation."

Arns frowned.

"If you hadn't gotten in," I clarified, "whoever found me down there would have probably slit my throat before I woke."

The captain shook his head once more. "Absolutely crazy." A fleeting look of something—respect, perhaps—crossed his face as he said it.

"That's why he's the Protector," Mouse chimed in, bouncing excitedly from one foot to the other. I couldn't tell if he was simply elated to see me or needed to make a run for the privy.

As my mind continued to clear, thoughts of last night began to surface, leaving me with questions. "Why did it take so long to get the doors open in the first place?" I asked, looking up at Arns. "We heard shouting on your side of the wall, but we couldn't hear what was being said."

"Stringbean ran into a bit of trouble," Bull said.

"More than a bit," Mouse added. "He like to have got them all killed."

"Apparently," Bull continued, "he had a difficult time trying to convince the patrol that they were indeed Avalanche. In fact, the discussion got so heated, Stringbean ended up challenging one of the boys to a fight to prove it."

I nearly choked. "He did what?"

Bull laughed. "And before anyone could stop him, they were cudgeling each other in the middle of the street."

"Stringbean?" I glanced around the yard, looking to see if I could spot the tall runner. "Is he alright?"

"Surprisingly enough," Bull said, "he won. The shouting from the wall that we heard was the kids cheering on the fight. It wasn't until Stringbean had laid the other boy out that those on the wall finally decided to open the gates."

"Yeah, but the bracer stopped partway, remember?"

"I'm afraid that was my fault," Arns cut in. "When I saw the Avalanche patrol fighting your boy, I thought they'd been discovered, and I brought my men out of hiding early."

Mouse shook his head and then leaned in to whisper in my ear, "I told you Blue Capes was stupid."

I tried not to grin.

"And you know the rest," Arns said. "By the time your man here"—he looked at Bull—"managed to get the doors open, you and the majority of the kids were already gone."

I glanced around Bull to get a look at the gate. The garrison's front entrance was open. "Did you keep the doors open through the night, like we'd discussed?"

Arns nodded. "And I kept my men out of sight for most of the morning, or at least until any stragglers on night watch made it back. We haven't seen anyone returning to the compound in the last couple of hours."

"Good," I said. "Then hopefully that's all of them."

"I've sent some men out into the surrounding streets to keep watch, but like you said, I think we've got them all."

"So, what now?" Bull asked. "We have a compound full of unconscious kids." He looked over at the barracks. "Well, mostly unconscious." There were muffled voices coming from there, Avalanche members shouting through the door, demanding to be set free.

I looked at Arns. "And your men brought their uniforms?"

The captain nodded.

"Then now's the time to put them on."

"You want the Avalanche kids to see them?" Bull asked.

"It doesn't matter if they see them or not at this point. I'm only worried about those we'll be passing in the streets after we leave here. I want the rest of the city to see this for what it was: a patroller raid. Word will spread quickly enough, and I don't want Cutter seeking retaliation on Sandstorm under the belief they had something to do with it."

"And what about these kids here?" Bull asked, pointing back toward the barracks. "*They* know who's behind this. As soon as you showed yourself last night there was no hiding it."

"Unfortunately, that can't be helped," I said with a short sigh. For a last-minute plan, things could have gone much worse than they had. "As long as we can keep a tight leash on our prisoners and make sure that none escape, we should be able to keep Cutter from finding out who was behind this. That is why it's important that the patrollers be seen." I looked at Arns. "Keeping you in uniform will also give the local residents a sense of security. Seeing the Aramoor patrollers marching these kids out of their community might help people feel safe enough to move back in."

Arns nodded. "I'll have my men change just as soon as we get the rest of the children up from below. I've already sent word back to the station for the wagons." He stared at the line of men walking by with sleeping children in their arms. "I have a feeling it's going to take a couple of trips."

I nodded, and Captain Arns left to attend to his men.

There wasn't much I could do but sit on the porch and hope that the pounding in my head soon faded. By the time the wagons pulled in, I was back on my feet and slowly moving about the yard. The more I walked, the stronger my legs became. Reevie had clearly added something to this particular batch of ether that wasn't in what he usually used. I'd never seen anything he'd used take this much time to recover from.

An overwhelming sense of excitement struck me, followed by a thrilled whinny, and I turned to find that Arns's men had brought Shade back from the station along with the wagons. The big horse seemed mostly unaffected by the events of the previous night, this time having remained where he was instead of coming to look for me. I was surprised he hadn't, considering how nervous I'd been through the entire experience. I wondered if perhaps he hadn't been able to sense my urgency from that far away.

By the time Bull had rounded up the Sandstorm kids and Arns's men were back in full uniform, we had started loading Avalanche onto the back of the wagons, starting with those fifteen or under, the ones we thought young enough to be taken back to Sandstorm first, and they were the vast majority. We gave the older girls the choice of going to Sandstorm as well or being taken to the workhouses, since there wasn't exactly an equivalent to the lancers for them to join. The overwhelming majority chose Sandstorm, many seemingly excited to be out from under the tribe they were in, while others merely chose it as the better of two bad options.

The older boys were given the option of the corps or the workhouses.

Those sixteen and older who'd chosen something other than Sandstorm or the lancers were kept at the garrison for the second load. After we dropped off the first group of kids, the rest would be taken to the patroller station and placed in the cells until I had a chance to move them to their final destinations, which I hoped to see accomplished the next day.

I had Bull place the Sandstorm runners in with the Avalanche kids who were still half asleep and made sure they were wearing their white armbands in case anyone from Cutter's tribe happened to spot our caravan. Most of the Avalanche kids didn't have any bands on, having been woken out of their sleep only to rush to the front gate, and then down into the dungeons after me.

With a little help from Mouse, I changed out of my black leathers and put on a spare patroller uniform that Arns had brought with him for me. One look at me riding alongside the patrollers in my black coat, and every street rat in the city would know who'd been involved in this raid. I moved around in the new uniform, testing my mobility. It wasn't exactly snug, but something felt off. Then I realized what it was. I was missing the swords on my back. Strange how fast I'd grown accustomed to them.

I directed Shade alongside Captain Arns, who was mounted and waiting just in front of the first wagon. With a wave of my arm, the caravan left the garrison and started south through the northeast quarter, making sure its residents got a good look at who we had in custody.

The captain had assigned several patrollers to each wagon to keep an eye on the kids and make sure they didn't try leaping over the sides to make a run for it. It helped that their hands and feet were bound just in case. They had also been gagged. We didn't want them shouting anything about Sandstorm or Death's Shadow.

I adjusted the tie on my blue cape, which tugged uncomfortably on my neck. It felt strange riding through town wearing patroller livery. I thought it bizarre the first time I'd put on a lancer uniform, but this somehow seemed even more awkward. More so when we headed into Sandstorm territory. I spotted some of our watchers rushing back through the streets as they tried to keep ahead of us in order to warn those at the manor. They probably thought we were about to raid Sandstorm, since we had purposefully kept our plans from them.

We finally turned off the main road and started over the hill for the manor. I could see the gate just ahead and all the heads sticking above the walls on either side. They were armed and waiting.

I brought the caravan to a stop halfway down the street. Behind me, Bull hopped off the back of one of the wagons and ran ahead to let our beaters know that they weren't under attack. Seeing all the patrollers behind me, I hoped they would listen. Years of experience had left them extremely cautious when it came to the Blue Capes.

After a few moments of back and forth with Toots, Bull finally turned and waved us forward, and we started moving again. Toots ordered the gates open and then stared at me as I passed; a look of disbelief mixed with a slight hint of disgust cloaked his face as he gawked at my uniform. I kept the wagons moving up the drive, and we stopped at the top between the manor and the carriage house.

Captain Arns pulled his horse a little closer as he took a quick moment to get a look at the place. "Quite the estate for a bunch of street rats. One of these days you're going to have to tell me how you managed it." He twisted in his saddle to survey the wagons behind and the patrollers just now stepping off. "How do you want to do this?"

"We should start by taking them to the carriage house. I've had the coaches pulled out to make room for the kids until we can decide what to do with them. It's the safest place to keep them for now."

I considered asking Arns to leave a few patrollers behind to keep an eye on the Avalanche kids, but he was already under significant pressure from his commandant to ramp up the patrols around the city, so I decided to leave the protection detail up to Collen and his beaters. Besides, I had a feeling Sapphire and Reevie wouldn't be too happy with me if I left a patroller presence here at Sandstorm.

"For now," I said, "let's take one wagon at a time and just sit them inside."

I had already had Gittrick move his family inside the manor for now, at least until we were able to get this all sorted. I had a feeling that with this many kids, it might take a day or two, and I didn't want to put him or his family at any risk by keeping them inside the carriage house with all these Avalanche members just below.

Sapphire and Reevie, along with all of Sandstorm, were gathered out front, watching from the edge of the courtyard. Sapphire left Reevie with the rest and headed down the drive for me. She stopped a few feet back from Shade. "How did it go? We were expecting you here hours ago."

"Afraid that might have been my fault," I said as I swung down from Shade and quickly placed a hand on the horse to steady myself. I was still feeling some of the effects of Reevie's ether. "It's a bit of a long story, and I can explain it later, but your kids are safe, and we managed to

accomplish the mission. So I guess, all in all, it was a success."

She turned and looked at the string of wagons lining the drive. "What am I supposed to do with all these kids?" Even forewarned and having agreed to it, she still looked upset.

"It's probably safest to keep them in the carriage house for now, maybe take the very young and place them in a couple of the upper rooms in the east wing." There were some who were barely old enough to walk and would require a more attentive hand.

"How many of these are going to be staying here?"

"All of them," Bull said on his way by with the first load of kids.

Sapphire gaped. "All of them? But I thought you said you would be separating them out by age."

"We already did that before we left the garrison," I said. "There's another load still there, waiting for us to collect." I watched the kids file by on their way to the carriage house. Most could walk on their own, but some were still too woozy and needed help. "We gave the older girls the choice of coming here to help with the younger ones or going straight to the workhouses. Most decided to come here."

Sapphire groaned as she watched the numbers being unloaded. "I wasn't expecting this many. Will your king and queen be giving me a stipend as well? We're going to need it if we are to feed this many new mouths."

I turned and looked at the manor, an idea forming. "You know, that's not a bad idea."

"Huh?"

"The queen is looking to raise funds for a second orphanage. This would make for an ideal spot."

Sapphire turned on me. "Are you crazy? I'm not running an orphanage!"

"You already are, sort of. You raise most of the kids until they're old enough and tame enough to be placed with Master Fentin and Mistress Orilla. Seems you're halfway there already. If we established Sandstorm Manor as a legitimate orphanage, it would give this place certain protections, and a stable stipend from the crown."

Even though Sapphire's face didn't show anything but her desire to strangle me, her head lowered, signaling that she was at least considering my words.

I shrugged. "Something to think about." It did seem like a good idea, and I hoped she would consider it. I would have to bring it up with the other two as well when I got the chance, but right now wasn't the time. "Do you think you can handle things here?"

"Why, are you about to leave me with them?"

I grinned sheepishly, and her face hardened.

"I told you, we still have another load."

"Just hurry back, will you? Reevie was supposed to be in town tonight, but he's been waiting here in case some of those you brought back needed the infirmary."

"Tell him he can go. We didn't have much of a scuffle, and whatever cuts and bruises there are, I'm sure Muriel can handle well enough."

"It wasn't just that. He also wanted to check them for other diseases to make sure they didn't spread any nasty sicknesses to the rest of us."

"I hadn't thought of that." I looked over at the carriage house and those being escorted inside. "Will you be safe enough?"

Sapphire looked over at the side building as well. "They look more frightened than anything. I'll keep the Guard posted, but I doubt we'll have any trouble. If we do, I'll threaten to send them back to Cutter with a note thanking them for snitching for us."

I shivered. "That would do it."

Sapphire turned and started for the courtyard. Reevie, who was

standing with the rest of Sandstorm, watched the last of the Avalanche kids get carted off to the carriage house.

"Hey," I called after her before she had gotten too far. "Ask him what he put in the ether. That stuff was deadly."

I waited beside my horse as the patrollers finished unloading the last of the wagons. Once everyone was safely stowed inside the carriage house, the patrollers climbed back aboard their wagons, and we circled them around the drive and headed back the way we'd come.

"I should be back by supper," I said to Sapphire and Reevie on the way by. Reevie barely looked up at me as I passed, and Bull was nowhere to be seen, most likely still in the carriage house with Collen, setting up a guard over their new guests.

The Sandstorm kids watched the parade of empty wagons and Blue Capes roll by and down the hill toward the front gate. Toots already had it open, as though eager to see the back of us. I smiled at him on the way by, but he didn't smile back, too preoccupied with keeping an eye on all the patrollers.

"I'm ready to have this over with," Captain Arns said as we left Sandstorm Manor and headed up the road.

I looked at him and nodded. "I couldn't agree more."

AVALANCHE

Chapter 28

HE DRIVE BACK TO THE old garrison was a quiet one. Half the wagons, led by Sergeant Wilben, split off once we reached Circle Drive and made their way back to their respective stations. Our last load was smaller than the previous and wouldn't require as many wagons. We kept four, which would leave us just enough room for the extra patrollers needed to keep the occupants in line.

The Avalanche compound doors were open when we arrived, and Sergeant Lowell and a few of his men greeted us at the first barracks building on the left, directly across from the main office. The shouting and threats from inside that had seen us off earlier seemed to have stopped for the time being.

"Our guests behaving any better than when we left?" Captain Arns asked as he dismounted.

Sergeant Lowell stepped off the barracks' porch with pipe in hand. "Seems they've given up on the shouting and moved on to pouting. I've heard nary a peep from them since after you left. Reckon they've realized there's no escaping now."

I swung down as well, wanting to be there in case those inside decided to try fighting their way out. We had come this far—I wasn't about to take any unnecessary risks.

Arns stepped up onto the porch. "Let's get this over with," he said and waved for the patrollers standing watch at the door to open it.

They did, and five patrollers walked inside just ahead of Arns and Lowell, no doubt to make sure none of the prisoners had gotten loose.

I crossed the porch behind them and peered inside. The light from the windows was enough to see faces clearly. The Avalanche kids were huddled down the center aisle between bunks. Half on the right, half on the left. The boy who'd threatened me in the cells was with those on the left. None of the prisoners had been gagged. The patrollers probably didn't want to take the chance of any of them choking, especially with them having to sit and wait here at the garrison while the first batch was delivered.

"Had to separate them," Lowell said. "This bunch here"—he pointed left—"tried attacking this group here," he said, looking right.

"That's cause they's traitors!" the boy on the left said, glaring over at the other group. Even with his hands and feet bound, he tried to lunge for the other kids, but Lowell and another patroller nabbed him and forced him back down with the others.

Lowell looked up at Arns. "See what I mean?"

The place stunk. When was the last time any of them had bathed? I had a feeling Sandstorm was going to have its work cut out for them. It reminded me of the first time I'd brought Tubby back to the Granary. He hadn't been properly washed in quite some time, and cleaning the giant boy had been a most unpleasant chore.

As soon as I stepped through the doorway, those sitting on the floor turned their angry glares to me. They suddenly didn't seem to care one wit about Arns and his men. I was now the sole focus of their rage. Arns, Lowell, and the rest of the patrollers turned to see what they were looking at.

"Cutter's going to hear about this," the boy who'd threatened me in the cells said with a sneer. "And when he does, he's gonna wipe Sandstorm from the face of Aldor."

I kept my expression blank, not wanting to give him the satisfaction of appearing to get to me. The boy knew his time was up, and he was going out swinging. I couldn't blame him for that.

I stared at him a moment before answering. "If I cared even the slightest bit about anything Cutter could do, I might be worried. But as it stands, he's as insignificant as you are. And after I am done here, I will make sure Avalanche never harms anyone ever again."

The boy's eye started to twitch, but to his credit, he held his glare as I turned and walked away. My threat was hardly real—not that I wouldn't have loved to deal with Cutter once and for all—but Cutter wasn't exactly high on the list of things I could afford to worry about right now. Getting these kids out of the patrollers' hair was the first, and finding a transport to the front was second.

I moved to the side of the porch, my thoughts far away, as the patrollers began to escort some of the kids to the wagons. I watched them getting lifted up into the back. Looking around the empty yard, I couldn't help but wonder if I'd made the right choice. Should I have gone with the king rather than staying behind to deal with Avalanche? Unfortunately, second-guessing myself wasn't a luxury I could afford at the moment.

Cutter was definitely a serious problem, but losing at least a quarter of his tribe was sure to halt his efforts to claim all of Aramoor for himself for a little while. Boxing Sandstorm in had been an important part of his plan. If we could sell that the patrollers were the only force involved, maybe Cutter would leave this section of the city alone.

It was a temporary solution, but a stopgap was my only option at the moment, given the time constraints. Pushing up our raid had been difficult, but if it meant I could set sail a day early, it would have been worth it.

I wondered if the king had already left. Word on the street was that ships had been preparing over the weekend. There was talk of a continuous stream of wagons carrying equipment and provisions from the palace and garrison down to the port. I hadn't yet been to that side of Aramoor to see for myself, though I would tomorrow when I took the older, more-willing Avalanche boys over to the northwest garrison.

The king had said he wanted to leave as soon as possible this week. It sounded like he was making good on his word. I wondered if my roommates were already aboard and whether Tolin had been able to get the black armbands made for my men.

Angry shouts from inside the barracks had me turning as the patrollers marched the last of the prisoners out to the wagons—those who would be heading to the workhouses the next day. The boy who'd threatened me and some of his cohorts fought the entire way out, requiring two or three patrollers per kid, as they had to practically carry them out and force them into the wagons.

While the patrollers loaded the last of the kids on the wagons, gagging each as they did, I made a quick sweep of the office building, looking for anything of value I might want to take back to Sandstorm. The extra mouths needed feeding. What better way to do that than to have Cutter pay for it?

I found a couple pouches of coins stuffed in the back of one of the desks in what used to be Kore's old office. It wasn't exactly a great find, but still enough to help Sandstorm keep the new additions fed for at least the next month.

I stuffed the pouches in my coat and left.

By the time I had made it back outside, Captain Arns and Sergeant Lowell were there and waiting. Shade stood at the bottom of the steps, and I walked him up to the head of the group where Arns sat atop his mount.

"I'll need your help before we go," I said.

"Oh?" The captain looked around the yard.

"We need to close the garrison gate and drop the bracer."

The captain shifted in his saddle to look at the two massive doors ahead. "Then how will we—"

"We'll take the door on the side."

Arns nodded and swung down off his horse, and we tied both behind the last wagon. The captain waved his men on, and Sergeant Lowell started the wagons moving. We followed them across the yard to the gate and waited for all four to make it through before we each grabbed one of the doors and shoved them closed.

The hinges creaked and groaned, but the doors eventually came together, and we lowered the bracer using the rope and pulleys on the side. Once in place, we made our way out through the side door, and I locked it, returning the key to my pants pocket.

"I'll be glad to see the backside of this place," Arns said as we made our way around the wall toward the front. He looked up at the watch towers on either side of the doors. "I'll make sure to keep regular patrols. Hopefully those living here will keep us informed of any unwanted activity."

Untying our horses, we mounted and made our way up the road, watching the walls of the old garrison disappear behind us. This time we took the shorter route over one of the bridges just west of the garrison, and from there southwest to Captain Arns's station. The sun was beginning to set by the time we off-loaded the kids. We placed the more unruly—those we planned on taking to the workhouses—in one cell, and the rest were kept in another.

"How early do you wish to get started in the morning?" Arns asked. I smiled. "Not too early."

"That's good to hear," Lowell said with a yawn. "We didn't exactly get any sleep last night."

Arns also looked relieved at the news. His eyes were red and drooping. The man hadn't slept in two nights, and I was surprised he was still on his feet at all.

A new shift was just coming on duty as the three of us walked down the front steps of the patroller station.

"How long do you think it will take tomorrow?" Arns asked.

"Not long, I would think. If we get started later in the morning, we should be done by midafternoon. Once we drop the first group off at the garrison and get them situated, we will take the second down to the workhouses, and then they'll become their problem."

Arns nodded, then turned to Sergeant Lowell. "I'll try working on the roster schedule for this week before we leave. I should be able to have it finished by tomorrow evening."

"Very good, sir."

The extra patrols requested by the commandant was certainly putting a lot of pressure on the captain and his men, making me feel guilty for pulling them from their regular duties, even if it had been at the behest of the queen.

"I'll see you in the morning, then," Arns said, holding out his hand for me to shake. His grip was strong, despite his exhaustion.

"I appreciate your help, Captain." I shook Lowell's hand as well. "Couldn't have done this without you. I know this was the furthest thing from what you would have wanted to be spending your time doing, but I promise you, you have made a great difference here today. I know the queen will be grateful."

Both men nodded, and we bid farewell and parted ways.

"Well, Shade, what do you think? You ready to go home and get something to eat? I'm sure you're good and tired."

Shade blew out his lips, and I could feel a sense of eagerness as I climbed back in the saddle. I spared one last glance over my shoulder at the patroller office. "Nothing more to see here. Let's go home."

I wasn't sure if it was a slip of the tongue or if I was just falling back into old habits, but calling Sandstorm *home* didn't feel all that strange.

Riding back in, I was surprised by the number of eyes glaring at me from over the wall, weapons still in hand. The sun had already set behind me, and the torches were lit and resting in their brackets along the wall. I stopped in front of the gate. No one was there to open it, so I opened my mouth to shout at Toots, only to glance down and realize what the problem was.

I was still wearing the patroller uniform.

"It's me. Ayrion," I said to whoever was on duty. I was sure Toots had ordered everyone to be in their place, what with the arrival of the patrollers. They were probably worried about a repeat visit.

I didn't see Toots at first, but after a moment or two, his head finally shot up over the wall on the left. Seeing me, he ordered the doors open, and soon enough, three or four kids rushed to accommodate. The gate swung wide, and I rode through, sparing a quick glance to either side of the drive and finding what looked like the entire watch standing armed and ready.

"No one else is coming," I said. "The patrollers are gone." I recognized the irony of the statement with my blue cape swirling behind me. With a soft nudge, Shade headed up the hill toward the manor, and I directed him over to the carriage house first. The coaches were still parked out front, draped in thick tarps. We had no idea how long our guests would be housed inside, and clearly Gittrick didn't want to see the transports sullied from being left in inclement conditions.

One of the kids standing watch outside the carriage house saw me coming and ran around to the side door and stuck his head in. Moments later, Gittrick stepped out and walked around to meet me. The torch-light lining the walkway between the main building and the carriage house covered the side of his face in a warm glow. He had a stern look as he headed toward me, and it wasn't until I had turned into the torch-light myself that his expression softened.

"Oh, it's you, Master Ayrion. The watch boy saw your patroller uniform and thought the worst."

"Understandable," I said with a small chuckle, then glanced at the carriage house. "Do we have a place for Shade tonight? I don't want to risk leaving him in there with the Avalanche kids."

"I can bed him down in the workshop around back. There are a couple additional stalls inside that I've been using for storage. I can clean one of them out."

"Neither of us got much in the way of sleep last night, and we've had nothing to eat today, so make sure to take good care of him."

He looked at me like I'd just insulted his closest family member.

"Sorry, I know you'll take good care of him." I faked a yawn. "Like I said, I'm tired and hungry."

Gittrick waved the matter off and took Shade's reins. "You're handling it better than I would, I assure you."

Somehow I doubted it, but it was kind of him to say. I grabbed my clothes and sheath from the saddlebag before he escorted Shade around back, then walked over to one of the carriage house windows and peered inside. I could see Collen and his beaters moving around the perimeter inside, keeping a close watch on the Avalanche kids, who were bunched together in the middle. They had removed the prisoners' gags, as well as most of their bindings, though there were a few who still had theirs on. I wondered if they had given Collen and the others some trouble.

Realizing there wasn't much for me to do here, and anxious to be out of the patroller blues, I left them to their work and headed for the main house. The courtyard and walkway from the drive to the front doors were lined with torches. Several of the kitchen staff passed me on the way, all carrying baskets filled with food for those in the carriage house. They startled when they saw my uniform but then nodded politely when they caught my face.

I untied the blue cape from my neck and draped it over my arm with my leathers. I didn't like the confounded garment tugging at my neck.

The courtyard was empty. Most were probably inside eating supper, which was where I hoped to be soon enough. Stepping in through the front doors, I stopped, trying to decide whether I should take the time to change first or go ahead and eat.

My stomach let me know what it thought, so I shut the door and followed its advice by heading for the east wing, passing the main dining hall on the way. It was filled with the clicking of dinnerware and the chatter of a dozen conversations, all of which were no doubt centered around the new arrivals.

My stomach growled loudly as I made my way down the hall and around to the chief's dining room, which was kept separate from the main hall, allowing Sapphire, Reevie, and Bull to discuss matters at hand

without prying ears. My mouth watered at the smell of roasted meat permeating the corridor. I tried not to sprint after taking it in.

I succeeded.

Mostly.

The door to the smaller dining room was open, and I found several seats already occupied inside, Reevie's being one of them. All three chiefs were in attendance, along with Gustory and a taller girl I didn't recognize. She was slender, with olive skin and dark hair, almost black, that hung partway down her back. By her frayed clothing, I presumed her to be one of the new Avalanche recruits, though I found her eating with the other chiefs odd.

Bull was the first to see me. "We were betting on whether you'd make it or not."

The new girl turned to look, and as soon as her eyes caught mine, they widened.

Sapphire looked up from her place at the end of the table, where I used to sit, with Bull and Reevie on either side of her. Gustory sat beside Reevie on the left and the new girl beside Bull on the right. I took the seat next to Gustory. I could have said it was because I wanted to keep a closer eye on the new girl, but in reality, I didn't relish the idea of having to stare at Reevie from across the table, or more importantly, him staring at me. I noticed the frightened way the new girl was looking at me and began to regret that decision.

"I was going to change out of these first," I said, looking down at the patroller uniform as I laid my other clothes in the empty chair beside me, "but one whiff of the kitchen's cooking and I changed my mind." I leaned forward and grabbed the closest ladle and began dishing some of the meat and gravy onto my plate. "I haven't eaten since yesterday."

The new girl watched my every move, seemingly enamored with what I was doing. Why my dishing food was all that interesting, I had no idea, but I all but forgot about her once I'd stuffed the first forkful inside my mouth and started to chew. It was as delicious and savory as ever. I figured I'd better enjoy it now, because it would probably be the last I would see of food like this for some time, depending on how this meeting with Overlord Saryn went.

I swallowed and looked up to find the girl still staring. Was it the patroller uniform? I tried my best not to look at her.

"You're him, aren't you?" she said in a guarded whisper, barely audible.

I looked up from my plate, not quite sure how to respond. "I guess that would depend on who *him* is."

"You're . . ." She took a slight gulp. "You're Death's Shadow."

I sighed, then wiped my mouth with my napkin. "Not at the moment."

"You're the one who put everyone in the dungeon to sleep."

"Put himself to sleep too," Bull said with a slight chuckle that turned into a yelp as he received a kick under the table from Sapphire.

I placed my napkin back in my lap. "Yes, that was me."

She continued to stare, and I was suddenly regretting my choice of eating with the chiefs, wishing instead to have taken a plate up to my room.

"I saw you in the Pit," she said, her voice a little bolder. "I was small, but I saw you fight Flesh Eater. They say you're a faerie, that you can't be killed." She stared at my eyes in awe. "You are a faerie, aren't you?"

"No," I said, unsure whether I should be offended by the accusation or flattered. "The closest I've ever been to a faerie is the statue of Egla inside the Temple."

Sapphire growled at the mention of the naked faerie.

I could see the girl wasn't going to be satisfied with a simple answer by the way she continued to stare, so I elaborated. "I am Upakan. My people live in the Lost City up in the northern reaches of Keldor. I assure you, I am not a faerie."

The girl's eyes never wavered, so I did my best to turn the conversation away from me. I looked at Sapphire. "How are . . ." I wasn't sure what to call the Avalanche kids at this point, especially with one of them sitting across the table from me. "How are our *visitors* doing out there? I passed some of the kitchen staff heading out to deliver their supper. Are you planning on keeping them in the carriage house overnight? Might get a little chilly."

Sapphire shook her head as she placed her glass back on the table. "We are going to bring them in and set up blankets in the library." She pointed at the girl sitting across from me. "This is Reina. She's one of the eldest of the lot, and the one the others designated as their spokesperson. We were just discussing the situation before you arrived."

"Always showing up wherever he's not wanted," Reevie groused, which was quickly followed by a high-pitched yelp from him as well.

I tried not to smile.

Sapphire wiped some gravy from her mouth. "Gustory is going to help them sleep with a couple of his stories."

I looked at the bard. "That's a good idea." I hadn't even thought about using Gustory's gifts as a way to ease the transition. My original thought had been to use his gifts to scare some sense into them. However, if anyone could calm a room, it would be him. Reina finally broke her gaze on me and looked at the bard. By the curious look on her face, she clearly didn't understand what the others were talking about or why telling a story would make those outside feel any better.

"I still don't know what we are going to do about feeding so many," Sapphire said, giving me a way to steer the conversation.

I finished chewing what was in my mouth and swallowed. "You really need to give my suggestion of turning Sandstorm into a second orphanage some consideration."

"An orphanage?" Bull looked up from his plate. "What are you talking about?"

Sapphire bit her lower lip, looking agitated at me for bringing it up now. She had probably been hoping I'd forget the matter altogether.

"The queen is interested in opening another orphanage, which is why I took Master Fentin and Mistress Orilla over to the palace last week."

"Yes," Reevie said, "and look how well that turned out."

"You've seen the queen?" Reina's eyes were now bulging.

"Absolutely," Gustory added with a proud smile, one of the first times he'd spoken since I sat down. "She speaks with him regularly, the king as well. In fact, we just had the pleasure of entertaining the crown prince a couple of nights ago."

I thought the girl was going to fall out of her seat; she looked positively faint.

"Ayrion is the prince's personal weapons instructor," Bull said.

Most of those gathered seemed quite proud to admit it, with the possible exception of Reevie.

I wanted to get back to our original conversation. "Our meeting with the nobles was productive. The queen is insistent on a second orphanage, and if Sandstorm were to take on that responsibility, it would afford you protective rights from not only the city of Aramoor, but from the throne itself. And you would also receive a generous stipend each month in exchange for those services."

Bull looked at Sapphire. "Protection from the crown doesn't sound too bad. It would be nice to not have to worry about whether we might get raided."

"Also keeps us from having to pay the patrollers," Reevie said, surprising me in that he almost sounded like he agreed with me. "Plus, we
could use more funding to help with costs around here."

"Yes," she said reluctantly, "and I'm sure it will also come with regulations. People looking over our shoulder at what we do and how we
do it, inspections by city officials, aristocrats trying to tell us how to run
our home."

Bull sat back and pursed his lips. "Didn't think about that."

I wasn't sure what Reevie's expression was since I couldn't see him
from around Gustory, but I had to imagine the thought of inspections
didn't sit well with him either.

"It's not that bad," I said, hoping to alleviate their fears. "Ask Fentin
and Orilla. I've never heard of anyone sticking their noses into their
business."

"Then you clearly don't understand how business works," Sapphire
snapped.

My lips tightened as I fought back the overwhelming urge to counter.

"When wealthy people give you their gold," she continued, "they
don't do it out of the goodness of their hearts and expect nothing in
return. At the very least, they want to know that their generosity isn't
being frivolously spent. They require an accounting of how it's being
used. They might even go so far as to expect a more hands-on approach
and try to take control." Her fist tightened around her fork. "They can
choke on their gold before I let that happen."

Bull nodded silently beside her.

I looked down the table at Sapphire and tried to calm my irritation
at her heated rebuttal of my suggestion in front of the others. She had

clearly developed some business acumen in my absence. I hadn't considered that some of the nobles, or even the queen herself, might have certain demands of Sandstorm if they took the money, or even expect to be involved in the day-to-day operations. The fact that Sapphire had considered this possibility was another testament to how well Noph had trained her. She had clearly spent enough time running the former Sandstorm chief's business dealings to understand how this world worked.

Still, I didn't get the sense that was what the queen had wanted, and most of the aristocracy I'd met didn't seem like they wanted to get more involved with anything that would require additional work. But what did I know? I was just a lowly lancer.

"That is something to consider," I said. "I'll find out more when I get back from the front. I know there was no mention of any stipulations for the gold in the meeting, but that doesn't mean it might not get brought up later. I'll get a more definitive answer from the queen, but at the very least, I hope you'll think about some of the more positive aspects. Like I said, you are practically already running an orphanage now, for all intents and purposes."

I started to lift my fork and then stopped. "Oh, I almost forgot." I reached into my pocket and pulled out the coin purses I'd absconded with after our raid and handed them to Gustory to pass down to Reevie. "These came from the compound. Thought they might help purchase food and clothing for the new kids."

Reina gasped. "You would use that on us?"

I looked across the table, surprised. "What would normally be done with the coins?" Then again, from the unwashed and malnourished appearance of the kids, it didn't look like much had been spent on their living conditions. The smell from the barracks alone said it was barely above squalor.

"That money is to go to Cutter," she said, gazing at the three leather pouches on the table in front of Reevie, "at least most of it. The rest goes to purchase scraps." She stared at the platters of food in front of her. For a moment, I thought she was going to start crying.

"How difficult do you think it will be to assimilate your tribe into this one?" I asked.

She looked up. "What's assim . . . assimoo—"

I smiled. "How hard will it be for your kids to get along with those here? Sandstorm isn't like other tribes. In fact, most of the kids here are from the other tribes, even Avalanche." I nodded to Bull, who was sitting next to her.

Bull shifted in his seat. "I used to be Avalanche as well."

Reina's face returned to the awed look it had held throughout most of our conversation so far.

I was surprised she didn't recognize Bull. She said she had been around when I fought Tubby in the Pit, which meant she would have been there at the same time as Bull. Maybe she had been a newer recruit and hadn't gotten to know everyone.

"I remember what it was like," Bull said. "Fighting for every scrap of food. Avalanche, like most of the other tribes, never looked at each person as anything other than what they could do for the tribe, and by tribe, I mean Cutter. Our value was only based on what we could do for him." Bull looked at me. "You remember what it was like for those of us injured during the battle at the Pit?"

I nodded. "That's why Reevie and I started this tribe. Rejects, all."

"Everyone has value," Reevie said, again surprising me.

"It was why so many flocked to our doors," I said. "Believe me. Those here at Sandstorm have no desire to fight you or Avalanche."

Sapphire cleared her throat. "We just want to be left in peace, but Cutter keeps sending your beaters into our territory and injuring our kids without provocation. Word on the street says that he wants war."

Reina stared down at her plate, embarrassment washing away her earlier fascination.

"The reason for raiding your home last night was to keep that from happening," I said. "We don't want bloodshed. We want peace." I realized I was back to saying *we* again. "Cutter put you and those with you in Rockslide's old compound as a way to flank Sandstorm. We couldn't allow that to happen."

"If your kids are willing to live here peacefully with us," Sapphire said, drawing Reina's attention, "then they are welcome. But let them know that those who won't will be sent to the workhouses. Do I make myself understood?"

Reina nodded. "If you intend to treat them half as well as you do the rest of your tribe and offer them food like this"—she stared at the spread of dishes on the table—"they will do anything you ask. It might take a few days, but I don't think you will find much problem."

Sapphire looked at the others and smiled. "Good."

I scooted forward in my seat and dished up another large helping of the meat and gravy, this time tossing on a couple of boiled potatoes and a roll. Grabbing my plate, I stood. "I will see you all in the morning. I have another long day, and I need some sleep."

"Will you be staying with us tomorrow evening?" Sapphire asked.

"I had planned on it."

There was a groan from Reevie's general direction.

"But it will depend on whether I can find a transport to the Elondrian border. If I can, I might need to stay at the garrison and pack." I shrugged. "We'll see. For now, just plan on me being here." I gathered my clothes and my plate of food and left. I was looking forward to at

least one more night of sleep. Reevie's ether might have left me unconscious, but I hadn't exactly woke feeling rested. All I wanted to do was
eat my food and crawl into bed.

AVALANCHE

Chapter 29

I WOKE FEELING BETTER than I had in a long time. I don't think I turned over once, as I woke in the exact position I fell asleep in. I'm not sure I even dreamed, which was unusual.

The sun shone through the side windows, brightening the room. I had forgotten to pull the curtains last night, but I'd been so tired that the light hadn't disturbed my sleep in the least.

After making the bed, I dressed once again in the spare patroller outfit I'd worn the day before, then gathered what possessions I had, including my black leather clothing, along with my swords and sheath, and made my way downstairs for breakfast. I wasn't looking forward to transporting Avalanche prisoners around town today, but I was eager to have this all over and done with so I could focus on finding a boat to the front. Commander Goring and Overcaptain Tolin were counting on me and my Black Guild to keep the king safe. I couldn't let them down.

I stepped off the final landing and headed down the hall toward the main gallery. It was going to be a long day. Breakfast had already been eaten, and the staff was cleaning the main dining hall as I walked through on my way to the kitchen. They looked up, momentarily startled by my blue cape, but after seeing my face, they went about their work.

"I kept you a plate," Solvino said. He pointed to a covered tray on a table at the back, along with some utensils, a pitcher, and a glass. "There's fresh cream in the pitcher."

"Thank you," I said and made my way across the room, skirting the kitchen staff as they scurried about, cleaning up after the breakfast meal and preparing for the next. I took a seat and devoured the griddlecakes and honey but slowed when I came to the eggs and sausage to keep from giving myself indigestion. I needed to get to the patroller station to meet with Arns, but I had told him it wouldn't be first thing, so I figured I could take a little time to savor the meal.

Once finished, I dropped the dishes in the wash tub, grabbed an apple for Shade, and headed out, thanking Solvino once more on the way. The short man twisted his mustache and smiled, then returned to shouting out orders with ladle in hand, swinging it like a lancer's sword.

I left through the dining hall and took the gallery down to the library. The door was shut, and in front stood a couple of the Sandstorm guards—Toothless and Forehead—both staring rather quizzically at my uniform. The two had become close friends since the collapse of Wildfire. Toothless, who had been one of Kira's personal guards, had apparently decided to stay here when she left for the Warrens.

"Are the Avalanche kids inside?" I asked.

Forehead nodded, still regarding my patroller blues. "Been there all night, except for when they left to eat breakfast this morning."

"Did they eat with Sandstorm?"

"Nope," Toothless said. "They ate after we did."

"Who's in there with them now?"

"Gustory's telling them another tale," Forehead said. "If we're quiet enough, we can hear it out here." He glanced at Toothless, and they both smiled. Gustory's tales were the highlight of the kids' days.

"I'll leave him to it, then," I said, and headed for the front doors.

Outside, I found the courtyard busy with children, some tossing balls, some reading, some stick fighting, all seemingly having a good time. The sun had already broken over the city wall behind them, casting its warm light across the stone pavers. They all turned when they saw me. Those not close enough to see my face took off running around the side of the building at the sight of the patroller uniform.

I waved at Muriel on the way by. She was busy grooming Redwing, who shrieked as I passed. I took the path to the carriage house, noting that the carriages were no longer taking up room in the drive. Gittrick must have moved them back inside after they had relocated the Avalanche kids to the library.

The front doors of the carriage house were open, and I walked around to see about getting Shade saddled. I could feel the horse's delight before I spotted him at the back. His head was outside the stall, looking my way. He whinnied when he saw me.

"What are you going on about?" Gittrick asked, his head popping up from the far side of the carriage to my left. He turned when he heard my boots. "Oh, that's why." He wiped his hands on his grease towel and started toward the back. "I'll have him ready in no time."

"No need to rush. I'm not exactly in a hurry."

"That's a first."

I chuckled. "Has he been—"

"I fed and watered him a couple of hours ago."

I smiled. "I guess there isn't much point in me asking. I'm just not used to owning such a fine animal."

Gittrick waved it off. "I hear you are going to be relocating some of the older Avalanche kids today," Gittrick said as he pulled Shade's saddle from one of the carriers and walked it around to his stall.

"That is the general idea." I joined the coachman at the back and watched as he cinched up the saddle.

"I spent some time here in the carriage house last night while they were here. Most seemed like frightened kids to me."

"Yes, I spoke with one last night," I said. "She seems to think that as long as we are willing to feed and clothe them, the transition will be simple enough."

"Feel sorry for them, really," Gittrick said, walking Shade out through the front.

I followed. "They weren't all so agreeable. We have a group we're taking to the workhouses—some even demanded it."

Gittrick shook his head. "Pride can be a terrible thing sometimes."

"So can hatred." I took the reins from Gittrick and then mounted. "We should be back this evening, but I can't say for certain. If we aren't back by supper, don't bother waiting up. I can stall him if I need to."

"I'm sure I'll hear you if you come in," Gittrick said.

I nodded, and before I got a chance to nudge Shade, we were heading down the drive. I patted the horse's strong neck. "You think you know me, huh?"

Shade blew out his lips, and I couldn't help but laugh.

"Blue Cape!" a couple of the kids on watch at the gate shouted, and several went scurrying into the trees.

"It's just the Protector, you dimwits!" Toots shouted, then ordered the gate opened before turning back to point at my uniform. "Don't like you's wearin' those clothes."

"Can't say I like it much either, but I need to make sure I look like a patroller when I transport the rest of the Avalanche prisoners today.

Don't want Cutter thinking we had any involvement."

Toots nodded sagely. "Quite the excitement we had yesterday. Who'da thunk that we'd have patrollers here at the manor? And who'da believed they would be bringing us a bunch of Avalanche kids?" He shook his head. "Nope. Can't right believe it myself." He looked up. "What do ya think we should do with 'em, now they's here?"

"Treat them like the rest of the tribe, since that's who they'll soon become."

Toots looked shocked at first, then frowned. "They better keep good and clear of my room is all I got to say."

I wanted to roll my eyes, but I guessed it was only natural to be suspicious of anyone who'd been your enemy only two days prior. "I'll see you this evening," I said and then started Shade up the road.

The sun felt good on my back as we headed west toward the northeast patroller station. I hoped Captain Arns was in.

I reached the station and left Shade at the hitch rail and went inside. There were a few patrollers milling about the lobby, though most were behind the front desk, talking with local residents. Sergeant Lowell spotted me and waved me on through with an odd smile. "Captain said to send you on back when you arrived."

"Has he been here long?" I asked on my way by.

Lowell shook his head. "Maybe an hour."

The sergeant was still smiling peculiarly as I made my way down the hall. What was that about? I reached the back and knocked on the captain's door.

"Come."

I opened it and stepped inside. "How are you feeling this morning?"

The captain looked up from his papers and frowned. "Drat!"

"What?"

"I just lost a bet."

I closed the door behind me. "Should I ask?"

"As tired as we were last night, I didn't think we'd see you until after lunch. The sergeant bet me a round of drinks you'd be here before tenth bell."

"Glad to be the cause of such amusement. At least that explains his eerily happy attitude this morning. Wouldn't stop grinning at me."

Arns laughed as he straightened some papers on his desk. "Got to find the enjoyment where I can."

I nodded. We had similar games in the lancers. "How did the prisoners do last night?"

The captain stood. "Those heading for the garrison did fine. Those being sent to the workhouse, not so much. Shouted most of the night, refused to eat, even threatened us with all sorts of bodily harm. Included in that were the death of our families, friends, and I believe there was even mention of beloved pets." He shook his head. "Nothing we haven't heard before, I assure you, and in more colorful ways, though usually those are grown men and not teenage boys." He started across the room for the door. "I hope you're here to take them off our hands."

"I'm here to transport them to their rightful destinations," I said, hoping he wasn't suggesting I move them by myself, "but I can't very well do it alone."

Arns smiled. "No, I suppose not, which is why I've assigned Sergeant Lowell and a few of my patrollers to escort them to wherever you so desire. Unfortunately, as you can see," he said, waving a hand at his desk, "I'm buried in paperwork, or I'd go myself. Commandant Ipsworth sent over additional requests this morning by courier, which is going to require my immediate attention."

"As long as we have enough men to keep the rowdier ones in line, it should be fine."

"And you think you can be finished by midafternoon?"

"I would imagine."

"Good. The sooner I can get Lowell back the better. He's in charge of disbursing schedules—which I should have finished yesterday." Arns took a deep breath and exhaled with an exasperated sigh. He looked like a man drowning with no shore in sight.

"I apologize for the inconvenience, Captain. Again, thank you for your assistance."

"It certainly wasn't something I expected, that's for sure," he said, "but I'm glad we managed it. Those living around the old garrison should be pleased, and it will make patrolling that part of the city easier. And, of course, there was getting to meet the queen." He smiled. "It was worth it just for that honor. To think, a lowly patroller captain sharing a meeting with the high queen herself. I'll be telling my grandkids about that one day."

I smiled and held out my hand. "It was nice working with you, Captain."

He took my hand and shook it. "And I, you. I have a feeling I'll be hearing your name more often."

"Let's hope that's not a bad thing."

Arns turned and headed back for his desk and its stacks of paper, and I left him to it. I closed the door and headed back down the hall for the lobby, where Sergeant Lowell was already waiting for me. His smile was still there, though perhaps not as wide.

"I'll be lifting a tankard on you today," he said, running a hand down his grey beard as he licked his lips. "Well, because of you at least."

"I heard. The captain didn't look too pleased with my prompt arrival."

Lowell patted the coin purse at his waist and grinned. "No, I suppose he didn't." His smirk soon faded. "How soon do you want to load those nasty little ingrates up? I've had to listen to them half the morning, language my momma would have beat out of me with a thick paddle." He shook his head. "I'll be glad to have them out of my cells."

"If you're ready, then so am I."

His face brightened, and he pointed at a couple of patrollers on the left. "Draeus, go hitch up the wagons, and take Milshik with you."

"Yes, Sarge," a patroller to my left said. He and the man standing beside him headed out the front door.

Lowell grabbed a set of keys off a peg behind his desk. "Let's go see how your prisoners are doing, shall we?"

I followed him down an adjacent hall and back to the cells. The only noises were coming from the last two doors, which was where we had placed the rowdiest of the kids. I hung back as the sergeant proceeded to rouse them.

"Rise and shine!" Lowell said. "It's moving day."

"Where's our breakfast?" a familiar voice called out from the cell at the end. It was the boy who'd threatened my life back at the compound. "I demand to speak with the flaming whoreson in charge of this dung-ridden place." The boy hocked up a wad and spat it through the cell bars and onto the floor.

Lowell snatched his bludgeon from his waist and rushed the cell. He slapped the bars with the carry stick, and the mouthy kid inside hopped back. "Try that again, you little whelp, and next time it will be your head." He turned and looked at me. "You see what we've had to put up with?"

I shook my head. The kid was certainly making it worse for himself, apparently too stupid and too stubborn to act any other way.

"Who's out there with you?" the boy asked, pressing his face against the bars to get a better look.

I walked forward to stand beside the sergeant.

The boy's face hardened, but he had enough common sense to take a step back just in case. "Blue suits you, traitor." His face twisted into a sneer. He leaned his head back as if to spit once more, and I lunged forward to grab him between the bars. He stumbled back into a couple of his cellmates, choking on his own saliva.

I looked down at the patroller uniform. "I'm Upakan. I become who I need to be to accomplish my mission. None of this would have been necessary had you kept within the borders of your own territory, but it seems your chief isn't satisfied with what he has and feels it's his right to take what belongs to others."

"The strong rule over the weak," the older boy said with a dark sneer.

"Then what does that make you, holed up in this cage like rats? Lucky for you, that's not how the rest of us choose to live. If it were, you would already be dead. Why allow an enemy to live? Isn't that the Avalanche way? That those deemed too weak and sickly should be tossed back out on the streets like refuse?" I shook my head. "What a sad life." I stared at him a moment before turning to Lowell, who was waiting quietly a few steps back. "Load them up."

I walked away to the sounds of toothless threats as the angry boy, along with a couple of his cellmates, shouted out their hopes for my rather long and painful demise. It was sad to see what their tribe had turned them into. Hatred only spread like poison, leaving those around it ruined. Even with all its faults, I was grateful I had ended up in Hurricane all those years ago.

By the time we reached the end of the hall, nearly a dozen Blue Capes passed us on their way to empty the cells and escort those inside out to the wagons. I waited with Shade as they marched one group after another out of the station and into the back of the prison transports. The first two wagons were loaded easily enough, as those inside were the boys on their way to the garrison to join the lancer corps. The last two required the majority of the patrollers to keep them in line, even after their hands were bound.

I lifted the hood of my cape to hide my face, glad to be riding in front. I could feel the hot glares of the kids in the latter wagons burrowing into the back of my head. The last thing I would have wanted was to bring up the rear and be forced to endure staring at their angry faces the entire way.

Once the prisoners were loaded, the small caravan made its way southwest on Circle Drive, making sure to keep to the busier roadways. By now, word was sure to have reached the Temple about the patroller raid, and I wasn't sure whether Cutter might try to get his kids back. Knowing him, he might think it too much of a risk and cut his losses.

The Avalanche chief had never been one to get his own hands dirty. He preferred to manipulate others to do it for him. In years past, he had used Kore as his bludgeon against the other tribes, but when Cutter saw the right opportunity to be rid of his bludgeon, he'd pounced.

I hadn't seen or spoken with Cutter in nearly two years, but I could only assume he had gotten more dangerous with age.

Needless to say, I kept my eyes open for any signs that we were being followed. The northern business district seemed an unlikely place for an attack. There were far too many pedestrians and too few places to hide, not to mention the proximity to the main garrison. But with Cutter, one never knew.

One thing we had on our side was that Avalanche appeared to have no idea where their people were being taken, which meant I had possibly been wrong in my assumption that Captain Arns had any informants in his station. If there had been, Cutter would have been sure to send the main force of his beaters after us while we were still at the compound, cut off from the rest of the patrollers. But the lack of response said that either there were no informants or the kids the patrollers had direct contact with had already been captured. I hoped it was the former.

Regardless, Cutter would have, at the very least, had someone watching the station last night, which meant it was a safe bet that runners had already been dispatched to the Temple as soon as they saw their kids being loaded onto the prison transports.

Once or twice, I thought I caught movement out of the corner of my eye as we passed a street or side alley, but each time I turned, there was nothing there.

"What do you keep looking at?" Lowell asked.

"Watching for signs of an ambush."

"Ambush. Out here?" The sergeant's head swiveled, and he abruptly began studying each road we passed. "You don't think they'll try anything, do you?" His hand slid to his waist, resting atop the hilt of his sword.

"I hope not." I carried my lancer sword at my waist, underneath my blue cape. The other was still in its sheath, tied to my saddlebag. "Still, I suggest we take the longer route by way of King's Way West. We can cut back toward the garrison once we reach Lancer Avenue. I don't want to ride through the back streets if we can help it."

"That's definitely a long way around. You really think they would try something like that with a patroller escort?"

"Best to be safe. We've made it this far without much injury. I'd like to keep it that way."

The sergeant nodded, though he looked a little skeptical at the thought of an open attack. Still, I noticed that his study of each passing street didn't lessen.

We crossed North Avis and kept straight on around to King's Way

West. The sun was beginning to warm, and I was a little thankful for the cape on my back, which was lighter than my leather coat. I just wished the cape was fastened by clasps or some other means rather than tied at the neck.

We passed a couple of lancers who barely nodded in our direction as we reached the roundabout coming off Circle Drive. With my hood up, they couldn't see my face. I wondered how many lancers had been left behind for city duty, and how deserted the garrison would be when we arrived.

King's Way West wasn't all that busy this time of morning. Most people were either at work or already in town shopping. It was hardly empty, but not up to the capacity one usually saw earlier in the morning. I kept the wagons moving. Thankfully, the prisoners were compliant at present. Along with binding their hands, the patrollers had administered gags to those in the back two wagons. Those in the first two sat quietly without being asked.

A couple of glances over my shoulder made it fairly obvious how nervous the boys in the first two wagons were: eyes shifting back and forth, hands clenched tight, faces taut. They didn't know what to expect, other than knowing their lives were about to change. Like the patrollers, the lancers were something to fear for the common street rat, so being told that their new home would be the north garrison probably had them feeling incredibly distraught.

Better that than the workhouses.

We turned onto Lancer Avenue, passing another group of mounted lancers, who all turned to watch as the patroller escort headed for the front gate. Several wagons of teenage boys wasn't exactly something they saw every day, or ever.

I could see faces peering over the garrison wall ahead, most of them at the two guard towers. They watched with open curiosity as the band of wagons and patrollers headed straight for them. I motioned for the transports to stop just before reaching the main doors and turned to Lowell.

"Stay with them. I'll go explain our presence to the lancers on watch."

"Don't they already know we're coming?"

"I hope. The problem is those in charge who knew of our arrangement are likely all aboard a ship right now on their way to the Cylmaran border."

Lowell's frown deepened. "That doesn't sound reassuring."

I left the sergeant with his men and started Shade toward the gate, where several lancers were already beginning to gather, plainly unsure as to what was going on.

I hoped Tolin had left word with someone here that we were coming. I didn't want to just drop a load of teen boys off without notice. I neared the doors, searching the faces for someone I recognized, and thankfully found one. Lieutenant Huckly stood with the others, holding the in-and-out board.

"Lieutenant, might I have a word?" I said, swinging down from Shade but keeping my head lowered.

The lieutenant walked out cautiously, a curious expression on his face. As soon as he was close enough, I raised my head, and he lowered his board with a short sigh. "Ayrion?"

We were far enough away from the others and the surrounding streets that I needn't worry about my name being overheard, but I preferred not to take chances. "Yes, Lieutenant, but for now, let's keep that between us. I don't want anyone knowing I'm helping the patrollers. Did Overcaptain Tolin inform you of my arrival?"

"He did. But we are short-staffed. I'm not sure what I'm going to do with your . . . your new recruits."

"It doesn't matter what you do with them for now. Assign them cleaning stations for all I care. Just keep them in the garrison. They all know why they're here, and as nervous as they are, I doubt they'll give you much trouble. They just need a firm but fair hand." I looked around. "Who's in charge while everyone is gone?"

"Overcaptain Weller. His leg injury has kept him from the front." Huckly frowned. "None too happy about that, I assure you."

"Who? You or him?"

Huckly chuckled. "Both."

I turned and looked at the caravan of wagons behind me. "Where should we drop them off?"

Huckly pointed left to the barracks closest to the stables. "There are a few rooms recently opened in Barracks Three. We had a small company sent out last week to patrol the roads between Vinten and Fayburn. Seems they've been having an increase in bandit activity down there. They won't be back for another month."

"Are their rooms empty?"

"Their gear has already been placed in storage, so you won't have to worry about the recruits getting into anything they shouldn't."

"Good. We'll follow you in."

The lieutenant nodded and immediately started scribbling on the in-and-out board as he made his way back through the gate. Leaving him to it, I mounted and headed back to where Lowell and the rest were waiting.

"Well? Are we to go in?" Lowell asked.

"We are. They have rooms already assigned and waiting for them."

Lowell rubbed his beard with a smile. "Music to my ears." He turned and waved the wagons forward, and we started through the gate. I shot a quick glance back at a couple of the adjacent streets but didn't see any sign of Avalanche watchers. With lancers on the garrison wall and others patrolling the surrounding streets, it wasn't surprising.

So far, so good.

AVALANCHE

Chapter 30

I COULDN'T BELIEVE HOW empty and how quiet the garrison was: the sound of metal clashing in the practice fields, the rhythmic clopping of horses in a forward march, officers shouting out orders, groups of lancers laughing outside the barracks—all gone. It was eerie.

"It's bigger than I thought," Lowell said, looking around as we made our way past the stables and over to Barracks Three.

"It seems bigger than usual with everyone gone."

Lieutenant Huckly, along with five other lancers, met us in front of the barracks. Huckly counted heads as the wagons pulled to a stop. "I don't think we're going to have enough room. There's more than we expected, and . . ." His count had reached the last wagon. "Are those girls? We don't admit women into the lancers."

I dismounted, signaling the patrollers to go ahead and unload the boys from the first two wagons. "They won't all be getting off."

"Oh?"

The lancers standing with Huckly straightened so they looked down at the new recruits as the boys gathered in front of the building. The lancers scrutinized each recruit carefully, as if judging how long it would take for one or all to make a run for it. It was intimidating.

These boys had probably never lived anywhere but with their tribe, had certainly never dealt with patrollers, let alone Elondrian Lancers—other than to flee from them—and here they were being dropped in the midst of the vipers' nest. Most looked close to tears as Huckly ordered them to line up in single file for inspection. The corners of their mouths quivered as they fought to hold brave faces.

"Sorry lot, this," one of the lancers said as he and a couple of the others walked the line, giving each boy a thorough inspection. "A bit weak in the knees."

I tried not to chuckle. The lancers always had a bit of fun with the new recruits. Supposedly it was their way of toughening them up. My own hazing had come in the form of Tolin assigning me to Room Eleven and had reaped its own rewards many times over.

Even with the ribbing, the lancers were pretty good about taking new recruits under wing, remembering they had been there at one point themselves. And to be perfectly honest, knowing what these same kids had done to Sandstorm, I wasn't exactly brimming with pity.

A particularly gruff-looking lancer whose name escaped me pointed at a boy on the end. "Are you crying?"

The boy shook his head.

"Then what's that dripping from your eyes?" The lancer turned and looked at Huckly and shook his head. "I don't know about these, Lieutenant. Might want to toss them back. Got more growing to do."

"Little late for that now," Huckly said, and the lancers took a few steps back. "We'll see how long they last. Go ahead and take them to their rooms." He looked at the boys. "Lunch will be at twelfth bell. Don't be late."

Lowell walked over as the boys filed away behind the lancers. "I like the way your men work. Discipline is what these boys need."

"And a little encouragement," I added.

Lowell didn't exactly agree with me openly, but he did at least bob his head. After spending part of the night listening to half of these kids threaten his family, I couldn't exactly blame the sergeant for wanting the boys gone, even if these hadn't been part of those causing all the problems.

"If you'll give me a minute," I said to both Lowell and Huckly. "I want to say something to the new recruits. I'll be back shortly."

Lowell grabbed my arm and cleared his throat. "It's getting pretty close to twelfth bell now. Any chance we could catch a meal here before pressing on with the rest of this lot?"

"What do you think?" I asked Huckly. "Room enough at the table for these patrollers?"

The lieutenant looked at Lowell, then back at the rest of his men. "What about them?" he asked, pointing at the last two wagons.

Lowell snorted. "If you try feeding that lot, you'd likely end up wearing it."

The lieutenant gave Lowell a confused look, so the sergeant clarified. "They have a tendency to spit."

"Ah, I see. I guess we could offer them some water, then."

"Again," Lowell said. "Spitting."

Huckly stared at the wagon of older boys and girls and smiled. "You let me deal with that."

Lowell shrugged, then turned to me and smiled. "Sounds like we will be joining your friends for lunch, then."

"Looks that way," I said. "If you'll excuse me." I left them on the covered porchway and headed into the barracks, following the sound of lancers coming from the right. There were two rooms across from each other near the end of the hall. By the time I made it to the rooms, the lancers were bringing in a spare cot. There were thirteen boys altogether, and each room only slept six.

As soon as the lancers were through, I asked them to wait in the lobby by the service desk while I spoke with the boys. The new recruits assembled inside one of the rooms. Most kept as far from me as possible. I might have been wearing patroller blues, but they all knew who I was, and the respect, or more accurately, *fear*, that followed Death's Shadow was still just as prevalent today as it had been two years ago, possibly more so now, given what had just transpired in the old garrison.

"When I was first recruited into the lancers, I was only fifteen, and I was just as . . . well, nervous as I'm sure you are right now. In fact, my first day, I ended up in a knife fight with one of the captains."

The boys gaped at me.

"I don't recommend that approach," I clarified. "Still, I didn't let it deter me. I worked hard, listened to instructions, and eventually earned their respect.

"If you're willing to do the same, you'll soon learn the lancers is a great place to be. You'll find friendships and brotherhood here that will last a lifetime. Some of the closest friends I have in the world are my lancer roommates. If you listen up and apply yourselves to your training, you will learn valuable skills you can take with you for the rest of your life.

"Life in the lancers can be difficult. You're expected to work and follow orders, but as a lancer, you will no longer have to worry about whether you will have a roof over your head or food on the table. I can walk around Aramoor without having to worry about whether there are patrollers nearby. No one looks at me differently. In fact, you'll find that most respect the lancer uniform and appreciate it. Even more importantly, you'll no longer have to fight for scraps. You'll earn your own wages, enough to live your own lives."

I stared at them for a moment, looking to see how much of what I was saying was sinking in. They did appear to be listening, and the intensity in their eyes and occasional head bobs said they might have understood.

"This is the first day of the rest of your lives. I hope you will take my words to heart. You've been given a great opportunity here. Don't waste it."

I turned and started to leave but then stopped. "I will be checking in occasionally to see how you are settling in. Don't make me regret bringing you here." With that, I left and headed back to the lobby where the other lancers were waiting. "I'm through." I thanked them for giving me some time with the boys and then headed outside.

Sergeant Lowell was chatting with Lieutenant Huckly while the rest of the patrollers stood around the final two wagons, keeping a close eye on the prisoners, who kept twisting in their seats to get a better look at the place.

"I believe we're ready, Sergeant," I said.

Lowell finished his conversation with Huckly and started for his horse. "Just point the way."

"We'll be heading to that building over there."

Shade walked to where I was standing in front of the barracks, and we started across the yard together. Behind us, the patrollers were busy climbing back aboard the wagons. Soon enough, the entire entourage was on their way to the mess hall, which was located just to the right of the main building. I tied Shade off in front and watched as the patrollers unloaded the unruly boys and girls from the back.

The prisoners' hands were still bound and their gags firmly in their mouths as they were marched in single file through the front doors. They were led to the first row of tables on the right and told to sit. A few had to be forced down. Outside, twelfth bell rang in the harbor. I looked around. The empty mess hall felt wrong.

"You keep an eye on them," Huckly said to me and Lowell, "and I'll have my men bring out some food."

I nodded, and we took our seats.

The lieutenant and several of his lancers headed to the back and began to dish up the first load of meals. They brought several trays of some sort of meat-and-vegetable dish covered in a strongly peppered sauce. They placed the food down in front of the patrollers, allowing them to eat first while they kept an eye on the kids.

"When you finish," Huckly said, "we'll bring something out for your prisoners."

Sergeant Lowell was the first to dig in, putting spoon to mouth in greedy fashion, finishing off his helping in no time before washing it down with a cup of watered-down ale. He leaned back and patted his waistline. "That hit the spot." His eyes seemed to be watering from the quantity of seasoning in the sauce.

His men weren't far behind, polishing off their bowls fast enough but taking a little more time with the ale.

"Are we ready to give your prisoners a try?" Huckly asked as soon as the patrollers had finished eating.

Lowell looked down the table at the street kids and nodded, so Huckly gave his men the go-ahead, and they rounded up some more trays of food and drink. Apparently, the lieutenant was willing to give the kids the benefit of the doubt and offer them more than a single glass of water.

Several of the kids had sneers permanently painted on their faces as they watched the men in uniform standing around them. They looked like rats in a cage, just waiting for the trap to be set. Clearly, they didn't trust anyone. I was a little hesitant to give them any utensils myself, afraid they might try to use them to fight their way out.

The lancers returned with food and drink but placed it on the opposite side of the table from where the street kids sat.

"What about their gags and bindings?" Huckly asked.

"The bindings stay on," Lowell said, given their hands had been tied in front and not behind, but then motioned for his men to start taking off the gags.

Huckly gestured for his men to join him, and the lancers walked around to the opposite side of the table from where the prisoners were sitting.

"I wouldn't stand there if I were you," Lowell warned.

"We will be fine, Sergeant," Huckly said. "Right now, they are guests of the Elondrian Lancers, and as such will be afforded common courtesy." The lieutenant turned and looked down the row of street kids. "You are being offered food from our very own table," he said. "We are offering hospitality, so I hope you will behave in a manner that reflects that."

The lieutenant took a step toward their table, his face hardening. "Having said that, the first one of you that spits will get the back of my hand, is that understood?"

My brows rose. I'd never seen Huckly this stern before. I liked it. He'd always been somewhat quiet at his post in Barracks Two.

"We are the Lancers," Huckly said. "You act like children here, and we'll treat you as such, which includes bending you over my knee right here in front of everyone."

The boys' and girls' eyes bulged, and the rest of the line of lancers took a step forward as well, causing most of the kids to jerk back in their seats. The lancers leaned over and slid the bowls and cups across the table for the kids to reach and waited for them to gather enough nerve to grab a spoon and start eating. It took a while, but eventually, one by one, they reached for their utensils, hands still bound.

Surprisingly, not one of the kids spat their food. Then again, with a row of armed lancers standing directly over them, even the hardest of the lot had enough common sense not to attempt it.

As soon as their bowls were emptied and their cups drained, we escorted them back to the wagons, passing the other street boys on our way out, being escorted in by a small group of lancers. The boys didn't say anything when they saw us, and instead kept their eyes straight ahead, refusing to look at their former tribe members. I was glad the lancers positioned themselves between the two groups.

"We appreciate the hospitality," Lowell said to Lieutenant Huckly as they stepped outside.

"My pleasure, Sergeant."

Lowell left me and Huckly to talk while he and his men began to load the kids back on the wagons and apply their gags. They wisely frisked each one before lifting them up in back, making sure none had walked out with anything they shouldn't have. They found two spoons and shockingly, one cup, which one of the girls had managed to stuff inside her shirt.

"When are you heading to the front?" Huckly asked.

"As soon as I can." I nodded toward the wagons. "After I drop off this last load, I'll ride straight to the harbor and see if I can find a transport heading in that direction."

"Will you be back to pack up your things?"

"It'll depend on whether I can find a ship. I should be back this evening, but don't hold me to it. If not, you will see me tomorrow."

"I'll let the watch know that you might be coming in tonight," he said as we walked back to the front gate.

Shade strode along beside me without me needing to hold his reins. I felt bad he had missed his lunch, so I pulled the apple from my coat that I had nabbed from the Sandstorm kitchen and handed it to him. "Sorry I don't have more."

Shade snorted but snatched the apple from my hand.

"That has got to be the biggest horse I've ever seen," Huckly said, staring up at Shade as he chewed on his lunch. "And so well-trained. Wherever did you get him?"

"He was a gift."

"Be sure to introduce me to your friends. Clearly, I'm running in the wrong circles."

I laughed, then pulled the hood of my patroller's cloak back over my head before we reached the doors at the front, making sure if there was anyone outside watching, they wouldn't see it was me. I didn't like the way the hood blocked my peripheral sight, but better that than someone recognizing me.

Before mounting, I offered Huckly my hand. "I do appreciate you accommodating these new recruits. Keep an eye on them for me, will you? And please have a little patience. They've lived very different lives than what you're used to, and it will probably take a good deal of time for them to adjust."

"I'll keep my eyes open," Huckly said, shaking my hand.

I mounted and rode back around to the front of the small patroller caravan, where Lowell was waiting. "Ready?"

"As I'll ever be."

I smiled. "I know what you mean."

The sergeant twisted in his saddle and waved at his men, and our small caravan left the garrison and started down Lancer Avenue toward King's Way West. The two now-empty wagons broke from the rest and started back for their station in the east quarter, taking a few of the patrollers with them. I hated losing part of our escort, especially given where we were heading, but there was no sense in toting empty wagons around the city.

The sun was high overhead and warm on our backs as we turned onto the city's main thoroughfare and started east, toward the Island. Reaching the same roundabout that we had come in on, we broke from King's Way West and started south down Circle Drive.

I had never been to one of the workhouses myself, though I'd ridden past them several times while out on patrol. The unfortunate reality was that because of what it was—a place for those too poor to pay their debts or survive on the streets—it was located in Cheapside, in the northern half of the Maze, which meant we would be riding straight through Avalanche territory to get there.

As soon as we crossed the river, I turned us off Circle Drive—not wanting to get any closer to the Temple than I had to—and started north. We followed the river up and around the southern half of the Island, passing the Fishnet on the way. The number of people milling around the tavern's front porch said the lunch crowd was larger than usual, which most likely meant there were ships in port today. The Fishnet was a popular spot amongst sailors on shore leave. This also meant there was a good chance I might find a ship willing to take me to the border.

We passed several smaller roads that would have taken us down and around to where the workhouses were located, but I kept us on a direct route to South Avis, still wanting to stick with the largest roads possible in hopes of dissuading Cutter from any overt attacks. I hated that we had to take these kids straight into their own tribe's territory in order to be rid of them.

The farther we went, the more movement I caught from the corner of my hood as I kept a close watch on the streets and alleys on the right. The left side of the road led to the edge of the river. Slips of shadow in the alleyways on the right kept my eyes moving. I didn't need the rising hair on my arms to tell me we were being stalked. A couple of times, I caught sight of white armbands from a street or two over.

"I think we are being followed," Lowell said, his eyes peeled to each street we passed.

I nodded. "Been trailing us ever since we crossed the Tansian. I'm hoping they are just keeping an eye on us."

"Should we go back?"

"Not when we are this close to the workhouses. It's not like the few extra men Captain Arns can spare would make a big difference."

"The closest station is over near King's Way East."

I shifted in my saddle to get a better look at the next side street and the movement at the other end. "It wouldn't hurt to send someone on ahead to see if they could bring some help. Though by the time they got there and back, we'd—"

Someone shouted behind us, and we both turned. One of the drivers slumped over in his seat, blood on the side of his face. I looked at Lowell. "Run for the workhouses!" I spun Shade around and raced back to the driverless wagon.

The patrollers sitting in the back of the stopped wagon were now pulling the prisoners down into the bed as rocks began to fly out from one of the alleyways beside them. I leapt onto the wagon, pushing the unconscious patroller down into the floorboard, and grabbed the reins.

Loud cracks sounded as several more rocks flew out of the alleyways and struck the sides of the two wagons. I lifted the reins and started to shout at the team when searing pain shocked my right arm, and the straps fell from my hand. The stone landed beside me on the seat. I snatched for the fallen reins, but my arm had gone completely limp.

Frantically, I tried grabbing the reins with my other hand but was soon hit with another rock, this one to the side of my head. Pain racked my entire body, and everything went black for a split second.

Suddenly, I was once again jumping from Shade over to the wagon's seat as my vision pulled me back.

"Go!" I shouted at Shade and then shoved the injured driver down, ducking as I did. The stones flew past, and I was back in my seat, snapping the reins before they could reload.

The wagon jerked, and the horses took off, sending those in the back rolling. Shade was just on my left, keeping pace with the wagon's horses, trumpeting his defiance and snapping at the horses' hindquarters to keep them moving. I shot a glance behind me. At least a dozen Avalanche beaters raced out from the streets behind us, several whirling slings over their heads. The wagon driver behind mine managed to make it out unscathed and was beating his reins as hard as he could to keep up. A couple of patrollers on horseback rode alongside the wagons on the left side, and up ahead, I could just make out Lowell as he rounded the next bend.

"Move it!" I shouted at the horses as we started around the bend ourselves. I went to slap the reins once more, and the breath caught in my throat. Lowell had turned his horse around and was waving his hands, shouting for us to stop. I yanked back on the reins as hard as I could to keep from slamming the horses into some sort of makeshift barricade that had materialized around the curve in the street. Upturned barrels, stacked crates, and broken furniture were strewn across the street, enough to keep a wagon from going through.

The horses squealed as they were forced to turn to keep from hitting the wooden blockade. The wagon started to capsize, briefly coming up on two wheels before slamming back down onto the cobbles, sending the patrolmen and prisoners in back tumbling over each other.

We were stuck, blocked in on the right by a row of houses and the left by the river. We wouldn't be able to move the barricade before those giving chase caught up, and there wasn't room to turn the wagons.

I looked at Lowell. "Get to the patroller station and get help!"

"What about you?"

"Don't worry about us. Go!"

AVALANCHE

Chapter 31

OWELL HAD SCARCELY SKIRTED his horse around the pile of rubble and started into a gallop when Avalanche beaters poured out of a road on the other side of the barricade, just missing the patroller. I breathed a silent prayer that there weren't more waiting farther down that could stop him.

The Avalanche beaters swarmed over their blockade on the far side of the street, where the debris wasn't stacked quite as high. We didn't have time to waste. To keep from slaughtering the oncoming kids, I grabbed two bludgeons from the unconscious patroller at my feet and leaped off the left side of the wagon. Avalanche or not, I didn't want to kill these kids.

"Get the prisoners inside one of those houses!" I barked.

Moving the bound troublemakers was going to be a difficult task, and with their fellow beaters coming to save them, it was going to take

everything we had to hold the others back and give them time to get them safely inside.

A door to one of the houses behind us opened, and a man stepped out. "In here!"

Shouts coming from the street behind us rang out as those with slings rushed up to block off our escape. All we could do was face the attack head on. I couldn't believe Cutter was brazen enough to confront a patroller escort, and in broad daylight.

Hoping that my hood provided enough concealment to keep my eyes hidden, I hit the first group of beaters head on. I used the patroller's clubs in place of my swords to keep from killing the kids, though I wasn't at all adverse to breaking a few bones and bashing a few extra-stubborn heads.

Beside me, several more patrollers appeared, clubs in hand, fighting to hold position as we beat back the attackers coming over the wall. We did everything we could to hold them off, giving the other patrollers the time they needed to get the prisoners out of the wagons and into the house.

I swept through the first wave to make it over. Kids screamed as I broke arms and legs, and crushed wrists and smashed fingers that were gripping weapons meant to kill us.

"Fall back!" I shouted at the others and pushed my way toward the middle as more kids began to make it over. Bodies dropped unconscious in my wake with each precise swing of my bludgeons. I didn't care how old they were or whether they were boys or girls, I simply connected with anyone standing in my way. I had to hold them back long enough for the others to finish their retreat.

More kids swarmed over the wall, blocking us in. We had to pull back before they had us surrounded completely.

We didn't dare turn our backs to run. To do so would be to risk taking a stray bludgeon or rock to the back of the head. One of the patrollers on my right went down, and I jumped in front of him long enough for those beside me to drag him back to his feet. Blood ran down the side of his face.

"Move back!" I shouted, beating kids away as fast as I could. They fought to get at me with clubs and daggers, but I used my visions to prevent them from landing for as long as I could.

There had to be at least thirty or more attacking us by now.

Another patroller dropped with a loud groan, this one with a knife to his gut. The others pulled him up, and we started back through the wagons. I realized the unconscious patroller in the wagon was missing. Hopefully the others had found him and carried him to safety.

The kids with slings rounded the bend to our left, blocking off any escape in that direction. "Keep going!" I shouted at the men, and we stumbled back through the wagons toward the homes on the other side of the street.

We fought like wild men to hold back the tide of children attempting to overrun us. We were just nearing the other side when the kids began to pour out from between the wagons. Those coming up the street on our left rushed to beat us to the houses in hopes of flanking us on all sides. I needed to stop them, but if I broke from where I was at the front of the pack, I was certain our line would collapse.

The patrollers inside the house shouted for us to hurry, but they were too occupied with keeping the prisoners from escaping to give us a hand.

I quickly glanced over my shoulder. We weren't going to make it in time. I started to make a desperate run at those rushing in to outflank us when the sound of pounding hooves had me turning. Shade stormed past those carrying slings, sending them diving out of the way, and then headed straight for the main group, trampling kids as he tore through their ranks. Children screamed and dove back toward the wagons to get out of the way of the monstrous animal. Some weren't quick enough and lay writhing on the street.

"Keep running!" I shouted at Shade, who had opened just enough space between us and Avalanche to make a break for the two-story home behind. Instead of trying to turn and make another pass, Shade did exactly as I said and bolted straight for the barricade. Then, he decided to do the impossible and leaped right over it. I stood there gaping for a split second, and a flash of smug satisfaction filtered to me through our link. The crazy horse was pleased with himself. I shook my head and charged the line of kids running up the street from the side. I had to give the patrollers enough time to reach the house.

I dodged multiple stones, batting several away with my clubs. Most of the beaters rushing to cut us off had swapped their slings for swords or bludgeons. Those who hadn't, I managed to drop rather quickly. I darted through the first group, sweeping legs and cracking ribs.

Behind me, the patrollers shouted for me to hurry. *Good*, I thought, *they must have made it in.*

I sprinted for the door, diving through just before the throng of kids washed over the front of the house. The men inside slammed the door shut as soon as I was clear and dropped a bracer in place.

Rolling to my feet, I turned to find the owners of the house cowering near the back of the room: a man, his wife, and their two children.

I pointed at the two Blue Capes standing closest to me. "Get them up the stairs!" I looked at the prisoners huddled at the center of the room. "Get them all upstairs!"

The frightened family were barely halfway to the staircase when the first rock flew through one of the windows in front, sending a couple of the patrollers diving out of the way to keep from getting hit by stray glass. The leader of the prisoners we'd captured looked up at me, smiling through his gag. He knew we were cornered and there wouldn't be a way out.

"Hurry!" I shouted, snatching several of the kids up and pushing them toward the stairs at the back. "We can't fight them from down here. We need to get to the second floor. Use the staircase to bunch them up and create a choke point." I hoped they didn't simply try setting the building on fire. With kids this crazy, anything was possible.

I turned back to the window and started smacking beaters aside as they fought to get in, doing my best to create a blockade of my own, but there were too many of them at this point. By now, it seemed half of Avalanche's beaters were standing outside. I quickly pulled back, working my way toward the stairs. The few patrollers who'd stayed with me fell back as well. Sounds of struggle coming from the stairwell behind me told me that the last of the prisoners were being hauled up.

By the time I reached the foot of the stairs, kids had wormed their way in through the windows on the far side of the room, some heading for the door to release the bracer. Those in front facing me moved slower than before, cautious, apparently waiting for more of their fighters to make it inside first. I pushed the men behind me back, and we slowly started up the stairs.

"There's nowhere to go!" one of the kids in front called out.

"Surrender now or die!" another said.

"You follow us up these stairs," I said, "and we'll send down your people one corpse at a time."

Muffled whispers spread across the front room below as the beaters slowed even more, giving me and the rest of the patrollers time to get to the landing at the top of the stairs. It opened into a small sitting room at the top that led to a hall behind me with rooms attached, most likely the family's sleeping quarters. Most of the prisoners had been stuffed inside the two closest rooms, guarded by half the patrollers, while the remaining half waited with me in the sitting room.

"Do you really plan on killing these kids?" one of the patrollers asked, looking troubled by the suggestion. In other circumstances, I would have smiled at the expression on his face—clearly patrollers weren't quite the monsters the street kids had always believed them to be.

"Of course not." I kept my voice low enough to not be heard by those below. "But I'm hoping the threat of it will hold them off for now. We need to buy as much time as we can."

The patroller nodded, looking marginally relieved.

"Release your prisoners and we'll leave," another voice called up. It sounded like it came from the kid who had told us we were boxed in.

As I had hoped, the Avalanche beaters didn't immediately storm the stairs, quite possibly because those in front had enough common sense to not want to be the first to get their heads cracked, but hopefully more so because they were taking my threat seriously.

"I don't think you'll do it," the same boy shouted up. "How do you think it will look to have patrollers killing helpless kids?"

"You attacked a city patrol in the process of performing its duties, unprovoked," I fired back. "Then broke into a family's residence and threatened their lives. Word of this is going to spread very quickly. If I were you, I'd leave before this gets any more out of hand. I doubt your chief is going to want your home raided next."

We were met with only silence from below.

I heard moans from the second room on the right. The patroller that had been stabbed didn't sound like he was doing well. We needed to get him to an infirmary. The closest I could think of was probably Saban's, where Reevie worked.

"Let Frog go, and we'll leave!" the boy called up.

Frog? Who's Frog?

"We don't want no fight with the patrollers," the kid said, "but we didn't start this. You were the ones who raided us. You've always stayed out of our business before. Why are you doing this?"

I turned and looked at the patrollers standing beside me and shook my head for them not to respond. I didn't want to take a chance that one of them would say something out of fear for their life and sell Sandstorm out. So far, there'd been no mention of Death's Shadow being involved, which was a good sign.

I turned and whispered to the others, "Any idea which one is Frog?"

Most shrugged or shook their heads.

"Seems we are at an impasse," I called down. "Clearly you want these prisoners returned, yet they are the only thing keeping you from charging up the stairs. We don't want to have to kill anyone, but if it's between you and us, we choose us."

"Give us Frog!"

Who is Frog? I needed to buy us some time. "Give us a minute to talk it over."

I left the stairs and walked into the first room and looked at the first batch of prisoners. "Is Frog in here?" The kids all looked at each other, but none of them seemed willing to say, or perhaps Frog wasn't in this room, so I went to the next, which was the room with the head of this group.

"Which one of you is Frog?" I looked directly at their leader. Cutter valued strength, so this kid was my first guess. Again, no one said anything. Of course, they were gagged, but still, there were no sudden movements from any of them. "The first person to tell me who Frog is will be spared going to the workhouse."

The oldest boy's head suddenly spun on those standing around him, as though threatening anyone who moved with immediate harm.

The patrollers in the room moved to get between the boy and the others, making sure nothing happened.

"This is your last chance," I said. "No one in here will hurt you, I promise. Just tell me who Frog is."

A girl near the wall suddenly ran forward. The older boy tried to get to her, shouting through his gag, but the patrollers held him fast. I untied the cloth from the girl's mouth.

"Do you know who Frog is?"

She turned and pointed to a tall thin boy hiding in the corner. "He's Frog."

The lanky boy's eyes widened.

"That's Frog?" The lanky boy hiding behind the others was the last person I would have expected Cutter to want. I looked at the other prisoners. "I don't know why you're trying to protect him. Seems your fellow Avalanche members below are more than happy to sell you all out so long as we turn Frog over to them."

Several of the prisoners turned to look at the tall boy in the back. Some looked confused, others angry.

"So why do they want him?" I asked the girl.

"He's Chief's family."

"Family?" I looked at the boy, not really seeing a strong resemblance. "Brother?"

She shook her head. "Cousin, I think." She looked over at the tall skinny boy and gulped, then looked at me. "You promise I won't have to go to the workhouse?"

"That's what I said."

She looked at the boy timidly. "He . . . he was the one in charge of the garrison."

The skinny boy shot out of the corner and went straight for the girl, fire in his eyes and a muffled screech on his gagged lips. He raised his bound hands for her neck, but I spun her out of the way before he managed to grab her, and my fist connected to his face. He flew backward onto the floor, blood dripping from his nose.

He writhed and kicked for a moment, trying to fight back at anything close enough to reach. He seemed to have gone completely mad. Two of the patrollers hauled him to his feet as he continued to thrash about.

"So, you're the one who's really in charge? Seems Cutter taught you well, or perhaps conniving cowardice is simply a family trait."

I would have never guessed that this gangly kid was the true leader of the garrison. I was surprised he hadn't asked to be one of those to join the lancers instead of being sent to the workhouses. Or maybe he was hoping his cousin would do just this and try to rescue him. Still, this was a bold move even for Cutter.

I pulled the boy's gag from his mouth. "I doubt Cutter would go to all this hassle just to save his cousin. Cutter wouldn't save his twin brother if he had one. If you want to survive this, I strongly suggest you give me a reason not to turn you over to them."

Frog's eyes widened.

"And when I say 'them,' I mean your fellow prisoners, now that they know they've been sold out for you."

Frog's earlier excitement vanished with a nervous gulp as he glanced back over his shoulder at his fellow prisoners. "I might know where Cutter stashes some of Avalanche's gold."

Well, this just got interesting.

"Bring him," I said, and walked back out the door to the front of the stairs. I made sure my hood was still in place so those below couldn't see my eyes.

"Are you planning on turning him over?" one of the patrollers asked.

"Not if I can help it." These kids were getting desperate and time was running out. If Lowell hadn't made it out safely, then I was going to need all the leverage I could to hold back the tide as long as possible. Sooner or later other patrollers would come to investigate the disturbance. These kids had to know this was their last chance.

I marched Frog back to the landing, blood running down his face. I pulled him close beside me for all those below to see.

"This is your last warning. Take your beaters out of here and be gone, or you'll find yourselves carrying a very dead Frog back to your chief. Somehow, I have a feeling he won't be as forgiving as I am."

The boy at the bottom looked up at Frog, then me. "Cutter also said that if we couldn't get him back, then we were to make sure he died with the rest." He lifted his sword and started for the first step.

Frog panicked and began to flail beside me as he struggled to free himself. Two of the patrollers behind me grabbed him and held him in place.

My heart started to race. This was falling apart fast. "Do you know why Cutter wants him so badly?" I asked, trying to stop the oncoming kids as best I could. "Frog knows where Cutter has been hiding Avalanche's gold."

The mass of armed kids below slowed once more. The older boy who'd been the spokesperson so far was about a quarter of the way up the staircase. The patrollers beside me drew their weapons. This time, it wasn't their beaters.

"That's right. Frog knows where the gold is hidden. If you kill him, you lose your opportunity to find it yourselves." I was taking a big gamble with this one, but it was the only hand I had to play.

There was some mumbling below that finally filtered up to the lead boy. "If Cutter knows that Frog knows, then wouldn't he have already gone and gotten it?"

Frog began flailing all over again, shouting something from under his gag. I turned and pulled it down.

"I'm the only one who knows where it is," he cried out. "It's what keeps me alive."

The boy turned and whispered to some of those behind him before finally turning back around. "I think we'll take our chances with Cutter." He lifted his short sword once more, and they started back up the stairs.

I flung Frog back to those behind and lifted my bludgeons. There wasn't enough room for my swords here, even if I was of a mind to use them.

"I'm warning you, the first one up is the first going back down."

"Get them!" the older boy shouted and lunged up the stairs.

I batted his sword to the side and clubbed him over the head before he reached the landing, sending his unconscious body back down on top of the others. Two more surfaced, and I sent them down on top of the next group.

"Patrollers!" someone shouted below.

The entire mob stopped mid-stairs and turned, everyone listening.

Sure enough, in the distance, the sound of whistles cut through the broken windows below. Soon, hooves joined that of the whistles' shrills, pounding hard enough that I could feel them in the floorboards under my feet.

Suddenly, it was everyone for themselves as children fled down the stairs, fighting each other to get out. I cautiously followed to make sure they were actually leaving and watched the kids race out the front door, some taking the faster route of crawling out the windows, cutting themselves on the glass as they did. I headed across the room and looked out the front.

The kids had all but disappeared down the street by the time Sergeant Lowell and a large company of patrollers rode in from the right.

I breathed a huge sigh of relief, my hands still trembling.

The Blue Capes stopped just on the other side of the barricade, and I could see Shade was with them. I called up to the patrollers on the second floor to let them know it was safe to come down, then walked out to meet Lowell, carefully skirting the injured kids on the ground around the wagons.

Looking around, there were quite a number of injured kids spread across the street from the front of the house all the way to the blockade.

I raised my hand. "We are safe, but we do have injured."

Shade snorted, and I sent him a calm feeling back through our link. *I'm fine, I promise.* The horse stilled but remained poised for action, his eyes on the street to his left, where a large number of the kids had just exited.

"I was worried we wouldn't make it in time," Lowell said as he walked his mount through a small opening the patrollers had just made in the wall. They were busy pulling the rest apart to open the street. "How did you manage to hold them back? From the numbers we saw coming up the street, I didn't figure there'd be much left of you but your bones. They fled like a pack of startled dogs."

"We managed to hole ourselves up on the second floor of that house there," I said, pointing at the home with the broken windows. "We need to make sure we repair the damage caused by the intrusion. Some recognition for the family would go a long way as well. Do the patrollers give out citizen awards? They saved our lives, that's for sure."

The sergeant nodded. "I'll see what can be done." He looked back at the house where the patrollers were just now carrying down the rest of the prisoners. "How many wounded?"

"Mostly shallow cuts and bruises for the patrollers. We did take a couple serious knife wounds and some solid cracks to the head that will need immediate attention, and then there's the kids here on the street. I suggest we load all the injured onto one of the wagons and take them to the infirmary over near the Rose and Crown. The physicker there is one I've had dealings with before and trust."

"What about the prisoners?"

"Have your men take them on to the workhouses. They have thick walls and guards enough to keep Avalanche out, though it wouldn't hurt to maintain a steady patrol of the area for the next several weeks." The workhouses took up a full city block and, like the old garrison, were surrounded by a wall, though it was made of stone rather than wood.

Shade waited until the gap in the road was wide enough before making his way through. He walked over to stand beside me, startling Lowell as he passed. I looked up and patted his neck. "Thank you for your assistance."

"What do you plan on doing?" Lowell asked.

"I'll take the injured with me to the infirmary. If you can spare some of your men for an escort, that would be helpful. The beaters are gone for the moment, but they could be back."

"I'll send half with you," he said, "and take the other half with me. After we deliver these kids to the workhouses, I'll follow."

I nodded. "Probably smartest."

"No!" a girl shouted behind us. "I'm not going to the workhouse! He promised me!"

The patrollers were dragging out the rest of the prisoners, including the girl who'd given Frog up.

"Wait!" I called out, walking over. "She's right. I promised she wouldn't be sent to the workhouse."

Lowell walked over. "Then what are you going to do with her? Just turn her loose?"

"No. Can't risk her going back to Avalanche and outing my involvement." The patrollers had pulled her aside from the rest of the group. "I promised you I wouldn't send you to the workhouse, and I'm a man of my word," I told her, "but I can't just release you either."

"Then what are you going to do to me? I can't go back to Avalanche. If word gets out that I squealed on Frog, Cutter will kill me."

"You're probably right," I said. "Which is why I'm going to send you to Sandstorm with the others. You'll be safe there and will stand a better chance of surviving than out here on the streets on your own. You think you can behave under another tribe? I can tell you, if you don't, they'll gift wrap you and send you right back to Cutter."

She quickly nodded. "I can behave."

I knew Sapphire and the others wouldn't actually send her back to Cutter, but hopefully the threat of it would be enough to keep her in line. She had been one of those to choose the workhouse over Sandstorm, so I didn't know how far her loyalties lay. Perhaps the realization that her chief didn't care if she had remained loyal or not had changed her mind.

I turned to Lowell. "Do you have a patroller or two that can escort her back to the manor?"

The sergeant called a couple of Blue Capes over and gave them orders to take the girl back. I recognized both as two that had helped escort the initial group of prisoners to Sandstorm the previous day.

"Let's load them up," I said to the patrollers who were standing out front. "We'll put the injured in the wagons."

"What about those going to the workhouses?" one patroller asked.

"We'll take them on foot," Sergeant Lowell said. "It's only around the corner, and we should have enough men now not to worry about it."

Once the prisoners were marched over to what remained of the blockade, the rest of the patrollers went about collecting injured kids. A few of the older ones fought back. The rest were unconscious or in too much pain to do anything but accept their circumstances.

By the time the last of the injured were inside the wagons, the patrollers had managed to clear the road. I waved at Lowell, who returned the gesture, and we parted ways. As promised, he took half the mounted patrollers with him and headed east toward South Avis, while I turned the two wagons around with the other half and started back the way we'd come. I rode in front with Shade, making sure to keep a quick pace, as there were men and kids alike who needed immediate attention.

As bad as the incident had been, the only thought wandering through my head was whether Reevie was working today. The wounded definitely stood a greater chance of surviving with him there, but I was probably the last person he wanted to see.

AVALANCHE

Chapter 32

E REACHED CIRCLE DRIVE and once more crossed the Tansian River, making our way north around the Island. From there, we turned onto a street not far from the Rose and Crown and followed it around to Saban's infirmary.

Hopping off Shade, I tied him to the rail and headed inside as the patrollers began off-loading the first wagon. An older gentleman and his wife sitting in the front hall jumped as I barged in.

"Physicker Saban?" I called down the hall.

"How may I help you?" Saban asked, appearing in his office doorway to the left of the entry.

I pulled back my hood. Surprise crossed the physicker's face as he recognized me. "Why are you—"

I cut him off. I didn't have time to explain why I was wearing patroller blues. "I have wounded kids and patrollers outside."

"How far behind?"

"They're coming in right behind me." I spared a quick glance down the hall. "Is Reevie in today?" I'd barely gotten the question out when one of the doors farther down opened and Reevie's head popped out.

"What is he . . ." He realized he couldn't exactly ignore me this time. "What are *you* doing here?"

"I have wounded."

Reevie stepped into the hall. "Sandstorm?"

"No." I didn't get a chance to finish before patrollers poured into the lobby behind me, carrying a couple of their own, along with the first load of Avalanche beaters.

"Those are Avalanche," Reevie said, as though the white armbands had escaped me.

"How many are there?" Saban asked, clearly cataloguing visible injuries as each person was brought in.

"At least twenty," I said.

"Reevie, which rooms are open?"

"Rooms one and two are filled, but three and four are at about half occupancy."

Saban nodded. "See if you can move those in four down to three, and we'll put these in four."

Reevie nodded, and I headed down the hall to help him. He didn't say much to me other than to direct me on who to take where. A couple of the patrollers offered us their assistance, and soon we had at least one completely free room to place the new patients. I helped bring in additional cots, packing them as tight as possible to get all the Avalanche kids into one room. The injured patrollers we put in one of the already-filled rooms, keeping the two groups away from each other.

"What happened?" Saban asked as he started working, gauging each patient's condition to determine who to start with. His wife, Nissa, followed him, taking notes.

"The patrollers were ambushed by one of the street tribes." I didn't want to go into the details.

"Give me some room, please," Saban said and pushed several of the patrollers back from the cots so he could better examine the injured patrollers. He first tended to the patrollers who'd been stabbed while Reevie and I sifted through the injured Avalanche kids, sorting them by severity of their injuries. Some of those who had been trampled by Shade were placed near the front. I recognized a few that I'd gone up against that had made it near the front as well.

"I'm surprised there aren't any that are dead," Reevie said, glancing back at my swords.

"I borrowed a patroller's bludgeons."

Reevie just nodded and went back to work.

Saban and Nissa worked with the most serious injuries while I assisted Reevie in stuffing holes, wrapping cuts, and applying tonics and salves as he instructed. As much as he didn't seem to want me there, he did appear to enjoy bossing me around, which was about how it always had been when it came to working in the infirmary. This was where Reevie shone.

By the time Sergeant Lowell and his men arrived after dropping off the uninjured at the workhouses, we were just beginning to get a handle on the most severe cases. I left Reevie to his work and met Lowell in the room housing the injured patrollers.

"How did it go? Any problems?"

Lowell shook his head. "A few of the kids followed us from a distance to see what was happening, but no further attacks. I don't think they're willing to engage a full company of patrollers." He turned and looked at his injured men. "I still can't believe they went as far as they did. I've never seen a tribe openly attack patrollers in the streets like that."

I filled him in on what we had learned about Frog and the information he had concerning Avalanche's gold.

"Surely they would have considered a possible retaliation of some sort?"

"I'm sure Cutter did, but apparently that gold was enough to risk it. You'll want to question Frog and see if it yields any useful information."

"Is he here with the injured?"

I shook my head. "I think he went with your batch to the workhouses. Your men will know what he looks like if you want to go pick him up." I would love to see Cutter lose a portion of his wealth. I would have preferred to question Frog myself and then give that information to Sandstorm, but I didn't have the time, and better the patrollers end up with the gold than Cutter.

Lowell nodded. "I'll talk with Captain Arns about it this week."

"How are your men?" I'd been working with Reevie on the street kids and hadn't had a chance to check on the Blue Capes yet.

"They'll survive, though they might need to spend a couple days here before going home."

Reevie's head popped in the door. "I need to speak with you."

I almost asked which one of us he was referring to, since he'd been hard-pressed to even acknowledge my existence over the last several days. I excused myself from Lowell and stepped into the hall. The older couple was still sitting in the lobby, looking a little annoyed at having been overlooked by the wave of injured I'd dumped on Saban and Reevie. The rest of the patrollers were nowhere to be seen, most likely outside, where they could avoid being underfoot.

"What is it?" I asked.

Reevie stared at my blue cape for a moment before finally speaking.

"What are we to do with all these kids? And who's going to pay for their treatment?"

I almost laughed. Reevie certainly hadn't changed any, ever the pragmatist. "I don't know. I didn't exactly think that far ahead. I was too busy trying to make sure they didn't die, especially since several of them are here because of me."

"And normally I'd be the first to congratulate you on that accomplishment, but medicines don't come cheap. It's not like I can knock on the Temple door and demand Cutter pay for his kids' treatments."

"No, I suppose not."

"And what are we supposed to do with them once they are treated?"

I stared at him a moment, and then I smiled.

His eyes widened, and he pointed straight at me. "Don't you dare. We've already been saddled with a quarter of this tribe already. We aren't taking any more, you hear me?"

"You know Cutter isn't going to take them back. You know what they do to the wounded and crippled."

Reevie bared his teeth. I wasn't sure if it was for me or Cutter. Probably me.

"Taking the outcast rejects has always been our tribe's way."

"Yeah, thanks to you."

"If it weren't for me being willing to take the rejects and start our own tribe, you'd probably still be living under the Granary floor, begging for scraps. Now, you're a respectable physicker, working out of a notable infirmary while living in one of the biggest manor houses on the east side."

He hmphed. "Sometimes I wonder if it was truly worth all the headaches. I should have left you in that alley all those years ago. If I'd known how big of a pain in my backside you'd become, I would have."

"You wouldn't have left me any more than you'll let these children here suffer because they're poor. You might act tough, but underneath, you're as soft as Solvino's sticky buns."

He grumbled again, but then his face grew serious. "I wasn't joking about the payment. Herbs and tonics and poultices aren't cheap. If we were to start treating people for nothing, we'd be out of business by Eighthday. Then where would everyone on this side of the city go when they're in trouble? Charity is all well and good, but it only goes so far, and then everyone suffers."

"Use the coins I took from the garrison. They should help."

Reevie thought a moment. "I suppose, but we were going to need some of that to feed all these new mouths you keep dumping on us."

"Then talk Sapphire into considering orphanage status for Sandstorm. It will mean permanent funding and protection from the patrollers. Sapphire can continue her side deals if she wants, and it will keep the tribe from going back to picking. It will also be a huge help to Master Fentin and Mistress Orilla."

"Which would be one of the only reasons I might consider it," he said, though I was sure having the extra gold coming in from the crown was sure to add significant weight to his decision. "Sapphire thinks if we take their offer, it will put us in their debt, and they'll use it to regulate us."

"I'll talk with the queen about it when I get back from the front and try to work it out so that you don't end up under anyone's thumb."

Reevie nodded but didn't broach the subject again. "And when exactly is it that you plan on leaving?"

"I'm hoping to be on ship as early as tomorrow. As soon as I leave here, I'm going down to the docks to see if I can find a transport heading toward the front."

Reevie stared off down the hall. "Good. Then I guess we'll finally get some peace and quiet around here."

I smiled. "I'll miss you too."

He spun back around. "Bloody flux! Who said anything about missing you, you big oaf? Go wherever you want. I don't care." He quickly hobbled back down the hall and disappeared inside the first open door.

I chuckled softly and then headed back to the lobby. "I'm sorry you had to wait longer because of us," I said to the older couple on the way by. They smiled at first, then took one look at my eyes and shrank back in their seats, reminding me that I needed to pull my hood back up before I stepped outside.

Most of the patrollers were mingling around the wagons. I didn't see Lowell. The sergeant must have still been inside with his men. I walked over and rubbed the bridge of Shade's nose. A warm, comforting feeling returned to me through our link. In a way, it was almost like I was soothing myself.

The infirmary door opened behind me, and I turned. Sergeant Lowell and two other patrollers walked out. As soon as he saw me, he left them and started my way.

"I probably need to be getting back. I'm sure Captain Arns is wondering where I am."

I held out my hand. "I appreciate your help, Sergeant. I'll be sure to mention your efforts to the queen when next we speak." The sergeant hadn't been there to meet with Her Majesty as Captain Arns had, so I hoped him knowing she would be made aware of his contribution was reward enough.

Lowell straightened as he shook my hand. "Will you really?" He smiled. "I'd appreciate that."

I looked down at my uniform. "Should I have this sent back by messenger?"

He looked at it as well, then shrugged it off. "Keep it. You never know, perhaps one day we will see you in those blues permanently. They look good on you."

I laughed. "Not sure how my commander would feel about that. Or the king."

Lowell grinned, then turned and rounded up his men. He left some behind to keep an eye on the infirmary in case the Avalanche kids decided to try another attack. He also set up a patrol around the area to keep an eye out for any signs of retaliation. I doubted they'd spot anyone. Once we had crossed over the Tansian, there'd been no sign of pursuit.

The patrollers mounted and slowly made their way up the street. I watched as they disappeared around the first bend, then looked up at Shade. "Guess we better get a move on as well."

Glancing back at the infirmary door, I was half-tempted to walk back in, but I figured I'd better leave things as they were for now. Reevie had been forced to talk with me face-to-face, and it seemed the tension between us had lessened. Best to leave it where it was and try again after I returned. Who knew, maybe he'd be so thrilled at having me back safely that I'd be able to pull him from his crusty shell long enough to have a proper sit-down.

Not having any reason to continue hanging around this part of town, I mounted Shade, and we headed southwest for the bay. However, instead of riding into the shipyard and down to the port, I rode a little farther south first. We crossed the Tansian and made our way into the abandoned section of the old shipyards, stopping outside the first building we came to that appeared in one piece.

I swung down and pulled out my leathers and swords from the saddlebag and headed inside. Finding a spot clean enough to change in, I took off the patroller blues and put my black leathers back on. After stowing the patroller uniform in my saddlebag, I mounted, and we headed toward the docks to commission a transport. It felt good being out of the blue cape and back in my regular clothes. I also felt safer having my swords on my back once more, their weight a constant comfort I hadn't realized I relied on so heavily until they were no longer there.

We crossed the river for what felt like the hundredth time today, and I took the first road to the left toward the bay. I could taste the salt in the air. The steady breeze blowing in off the water felt wonderfully cool, the sun resting about halfway to the peaks of the Sandrethin Mountains in front of us.

Our battle with Avalanche and our trip to the infirmary had taken half the afternoon, which meant I needed to get a move on. Third bell had already rung back at the infirmary, so I didn't have much time.

I wanted to find a ship as quickly as possible, so I would have time enough to head back to the garrison to pack before making my way over to Sandstorm for the evening meal, though that was looking highly unlikely. At this point, I was simply hoping to secure passage before the ships' crews headed in for their dinners and nightly entertainment.

I passed several groups of sailors and riverboat men leaving the port as I headed down to the waterfront. The jovial smiles and laughter said they were happy to finally be back on land and looking forward to their one night in town before shipping out in the morning.

The docks ahead were busy, even for midweek, but the piers themselves were barely half-full. I wondered how many ships it had taken to transport the lancers and their supplies. Looking around, I could only assume that was the reason for the many empty berths.

The main office was located about halfway up the boardwalk, which ran between the docks to the left and the warehouses to the right. Dismounting, Shade and I found ourselves keeping close to the right side, allowing those with pushcarts room to move as they loaded and off-loaded cargo from the ships.

"Move along, move along," someone called out behind me, and I directed Shade farther to the right to allow a large cart laden with rope to pass by on our left, hauled by a couple of men in shin-high trousers. They hustled by and continued on up the boardwalk.

I stopped in front of the main building and tied Shade in front of one of the windows so I could keep an eye on him, then walked inside. It certainly wasn't my first time to the port, having been forced to travel back and forth to the Cylmaran border for the last several months. The open lobby and front room weren't quite as busy as the outside. It seemed most of the ships mooring for the evening had been there since that afternoon, their captains already checked in. If not, the office would have been much more crowded. A quick scan of the mostly empty ships said their crews had already come ashore.

There were several people gathered around the shipping board at the side, which listed the upcoming routes for any outbound ships and their available passages. Most ships were more than willing to offer last-minute fares, especially if they were already heading in the same direction. The opportunity to earn additional coin was never turned away, especially when they could charge extra for it.

I waited in line for my turn at the board. Most of the people in front kept a close eye on the board, studying the ships' postings, but there were a couple who turned and, after seeing me, decided they'd check the board later. They either scurried out the door or to the other side of the room, pretending they had something they needed to check on over there until I'd finished.

I smiled politely at each but remained in line until I finally reached the front. I scanned the board. There weren't as many listings as usual, no doubt due to most of the ships having set sail for the front.

"Come on," I muttered. "There has to be someone going my way."

I scanned through the lot and then checked once more. Many were headed back up the Shemoa River, others to the coastal cities along the eastern half of Aldor. There was even one heading as far as Highcrest, up in Sidaran territory, but there wasn't a single ship going in my direction.

Disappointed, I left the line and walked over to the desks at the side, where clerks signed ships in and out, tracked docking fees, and scheduled the loading or off-loading of cargo. An older man with a grey beard sat behind the second desk. He had a pipe in his mouth that puffed rather pungent clouds of white smoke over his head.

"Any ships heading for the borderlands?" I asked.

The clerk pulled the pipe from his mouth and scratched the side of his face with the stem. "Depends on which borderlands you're referring to."

"Cylmaran."

He leaned forward to look at the board. "Everything's already been posted, son. If it ain't there, it ain't goin'."

"I need to reach the front as soon as possible." I would have told him the king was depending on me, but I doubted he'd believe that. "What about as far as Laneer? Or even Terhi?" I figured if they could get me to one of the southern coastal cities on that side of Elondria, I could make my way north from there. It would take me longer, but it would certainly be shorter than traveling around the entire Sandrethin Mountain range. The battle would be over before I got there.

"Sorry, son. Don't know what to tell ya. If you'd been here two days ago, you could have traveled with the king himself. As it is, you're just too late. Maybe something will come in tonight. Check by in the morning if ya want. Can't promise much, but there's always a chance." He popped his pipe back in his mouth and scooted back in his seat as he fiddled with some papers in front of him, clearly not looking to continue our conversation.

I thanked him for his time and headed back outside.

Now what was I going to do? I was tempted to walk the docks and ask each ship personally, though I doubted it would do much good, as those moored would have posted their listings already. All I could do at this point was hope for a ship to sail in this evening, but that was a stretch. The more I thought about it, the more worried I became. What if I couldn't find a transport? Then it struck me. *The queen.* If she were to request passage for me, surely there'd be more than one captain willing to take that commission.

Feeling a renewed sense of hopefulness, I untied Shade, and we started back up the docks in the direction we'd come. Shade and I veered to the right as a couple of large wagons passed, then we stopped altogether for a small train of pushcarts blocking one of the wharfs as they moved crates from a vessel large enough to need three masts over to a warehouse on the left.

"Move yourself . . . and your stupid giant horse!" someone shouted behind me.

I turned. "I can't! They've blocked the—" My breath caught in my throat. "Kettle?"

The short, stout cook from the *Wind Binder*, with his long mustache that hung to his chest, stared up at me. Bones stood beside him. His tall, dark frame still bore the white marks of his people. Both men looked puzzled, clearly trying to determine who I was.

"Ayrion?" A beautiful woman stepped out from behind the others. Hair the color of dark honey fell in thick waves down her back. She was dressed much the same as the last time I'd seen her, though perhaps with curves that were a little more filled out. She still wore her long red coat and captain's hat.

I smiled, still not quite believing my eyes. "Ismara?"

She ran forward and threw her arms around me, causing me to stumble backward. "I can't believe it's you. Every time we come to port, we ask around. But after several years without word, we figured you must have moved on. Then about two years ago, there was talk of a white-eyed man seen about the city, mostly in the company of lancers."

I pulled back to get a better look. "You don't seem to have changed at all, other than to get even more beautiful, if that's possible."

She punched me in the arm. "And you don't look much like a lancer." She stared at my black leathers and double swords. "You look like a proper Upakan."

I chuckled. "Hardly." She clearly had never met any of my people before.

Kettle cleared his throat. "As lovely as this reunion is, my flaming arms are getting tired. Pops ain't light, ya know."

I turned, noticing for the first time that Kettle and Bones were each holding one side of a makeshift litter. Whitey, whose wide-brimmed hat I could see over their heads, was toting the back half. The enormous man smiled when he saw that I had spotted him.

I walked around to find Tressle, who everyone lovingly referred to as Pops, lying on the litter with puckered lips. He looked even older than I remembered: eyes sunken, skin wrinkled and leathery, face gaunt. His hair as white as ever. As soon as he saw me, his eyes brightened.

"It is you, boy! Didn't reckon I'd be laying eyes on you again."

I placed my hand on his shoulder. "What happened?"

"Nothing for you to be worrying over," he said, gently patting his left leg with a wince. "Just a foolish accident."

"Accidents tend to be coming more regular of late," Ismara said with a knowing look.

Pops took a puff on his pipe through clenched teeth. "It'll be fine, as long as these wharf rats don't drop me."

"Where are you taking him?" I asked.

"We were on our way to the port physicker," Ismara said, "but they told us he's out on a call, so now we're going to have to look in town."

I smiled. "I know just the place. In fact, I just dropped off a load of patients there about an hour ago."

"Hope it ain't too far a walk," Kettle said, "cause my arms are givin' out."

"I'll rent us a wagon," I said. "It's too far to go on foot."

"Where's it at?" Kettle asked.

"Just north of the Island."

"The Island? That's a trip up the river to be sure. Ain't got somewhere closer?"

"Not that I trust."

Pops looked up at Shade. "I can sit on your horse if you can manage to lift me high enough. It's just my ankle."

I looked at his leg, which was swelling around the foot. It was either a really bad sprain or broken. "If Whitey can give me a hand," I said, "we can probably get him up on Shade."

"Shade, you say?" Pops looked up at the animal and nodded. "Nice to make your acquaintance, I'm sure."

The horse looked down at him and whickered.

With Whitey's help, we managed to lift Pops high enough to swing his good leg up and over. He yelped when he landed in the saddle, and I tucked his foot in the stirrup to help keep it from bouncing. Thankfully, the row of pushcarts blocking our way earlier had moved on, leaving us with a wide-open walkway.

We'd made it three steps when Pops started groaning. "Take me down, take me down. My foot's bein' ripped off."

The up-and-down movement of riding a horse must have been too much strain on Pops's leg. Bones and Whitey quickly pulled him down and placed him back on the litter while I ran to find a cart. By the time they made it off the docks and around the back of the warehouses, I'd managed to secure a single horse-drawn wagon, one just big enough to fit five of them as long as two rode in the driver's seat.

"Is your father here?" I asked Ismara, wondering if he had retired and left her the captaincy.

"He's dealing with some merchants in town," she said as they began loading Pops into the back of the cart. "We were supposed to meet back at the ship by fifth bell to grab something to eat. It's been a while since we've had shore leave."

Kettle and Whitey both grunted their agreement.

As soon as they finished loading Pops, Ismara climbed up in the driver's seat alongside Kettle and grabbed the reins. She turned to watch as the men climbed in back. "Bones, can you stay behind to let Father know where we've gone? I'm not sure how long it will take. Tell him the crew might have to go on without us."

Kettle groaned beside her, mumbling something about how bad his luck was.

"I can do that," Bones said. He turned and looked at me and smiled, which was always a strange sight with all the white skeletal paint on his face. "It is good to see you again." He patted one of the two kamas strapped to his side. "You make a fine warrior."

"Thank you, Bones. That means a lot coming from you." Bones started to leave, but a thought came to me. "Can you wait just a moment?"

The tall man turned back around as I swung up onto Shade. I turned and looked at Ismara. "How many do you have coming ashore?"

She shrugged. "Perhaps a dozen."

"And how long are you docked for?"

"We planned on being here through the end of the week. Why?"

Sapphire was going to kill me for sure, but this would probably be my only chance to show my old shipmates my life here in Aramoor. More importantly, perhaps I would be able to talk them into taking me to the front. I was sure the queen would be willing to lend some gold to entice the offer. I groaned inwardly. This was all happening at the wrong time. Why did they have to come right when I needed to leave?

"If we can get Pops tended to quickly enough, I might be able to offer you and the crew my hospitality for the evening. At the very least, a place to wash and a solid meal."

"Sounds good to me," she said, nodding at Bones. "Tell Father to wait for us if he can."

The first mate tipped his hat and then turned and headed back down the side of the warehouses.

Ismara looked over at me. "Now, let's get to this infirmary of yours, shall we?"

The harbor bell rang out fourth bell as I tapped Shade with my boot, and we started into town.

AVALANCHE

Chapter 33

E MADE GOOD TIME getting to the infirmary. The sun was nearing the peaks of the Sandrethins as we turned off the street for the front of the building. A few patrollers milled around outside, keeping a close eye on the place. They started toward us as we pulled in but then stopped when they recognized me.

"You need any help?" one asked.

"I believe we've got it." I hopped off Shade, merely tossing his reins over the hitch rail, not worried about him wandering off, and headed for the front door. I'd barely made it onto the porch when it opened and Reevie stepped out. He jumped when he saw me standing there.

"You haven't been sitting out here this whole time, have you?"

"No. I've been down to the docks looking for passage. Come on, I want to introduce you to some friends." I turned and walked out to the wagon, Reevie reluctantly limping along behind me. "You remember me telling you of my time aboard the *Wind Binder*, don't you, back before I arrived in Aramoor?"

Reevie nodded.

"Well, this is some of their crew." I pointed to Ismara, who was just climbing down from the driver's seat. "That's Ismara, and that's Kettle over there, and Whitey, and Pops."

Reevie spotted the litter and pushed me aside. "What's wrong?"

"Took a fall, I'm afraid," Pops said, gritting his teeth. He slapped at Whitey's arm, nearly losing his pipe. "Be careful, you idiot!"

Reevie shooed the others out of the way to get a better look.

"Who's this?" Ismara asked.

"This is Reevie. He's one of the physickers here, and my closest friend."

Reevie paused and glanced back over his shoulder, giving me a surprised look before turning back around and carrying on with his inspection.

"Believe me," I said to Pops, "you're in very good hands."

"Very *young* hands," Kettle added, giving Reevie a good looking-over. "Ain't you got someone older here?"

Reevie sneered but otherwise ignored him. "Looks to be a bad sprain, but we need to get him into better light to be sure. I don't like the amount of swelling. The wound is warm enough that it could be a break, though I don't really feel one." He stepped back. "Take him inside and Saban can have a look."

"Who's Saban?" Ismara asked.

"He owns the infirmary. You said you wanted someone older." Reevie looked at Kettle. "He's older."

I motioned for them to go ahead and carry Pops inside. "I'll be right behind you."

As the door shut behind them, Reevie turned to me. "So, that's your riverboat crew, huh?" He shook his head. "Not impressed." Clearly, he'd found Kettle's ribbing a bit harsh.

"That's only a couple of them, and they're worried about Pops. Don't take it personally. Kettle's just being Kettle. In fact, you kind of remind me of him."

Reevie glared.

"No, really. Both of you have no problem speaking your mind, no matter what."

He hmphed and then started limping away.

"Where're you going?" I asked.

"To find a palanquin back to the manor."

"Can you do me a favor?"

He turned. "The better question is: *will* I?"

"Well, I hope so. I want to introduce my crew to all of you, and this will likely be the only chance I ever get. I haven't seen them in seven years, and I want them to meet my Aramoor family."

"And how does this translate into me doing you a favor?"

I cleared my throat, bracing for his inevitable pushback. "I'd like to bring them to supper this evening."

Reevie's face hardened. "Are you crazy? Don't you think we've had enough of you bringing people to Sandstorm?"

"It will likely be my only chance. I have to leave tomorrow for the front, and who knows if I'll make it back?" I poured on the guilt, thick as sticky-bun icing. "You could be granting a dying man his last wish."

Reevie stared at me for a second, then burst out laughing. "Nice try! I'll give you that."

"Come on, Reevie. I really do want you all to meet. And there really is a likelihood something might happen to me while I'm gone. This could end in war."

Reevie's lips tightened into a thin line. "Fine."

"Here," I said, walking over and unwrapping Shade's reins. "You can take him to Sandstorm. It'll be quicker and save you the cost of a palanquin."

"Won't you need him to get back?"

I grinned. "Not if you send Gittrick with the carriages."

"Carriages?" He growled. "I knew you were up to something!"

"You saw Pops. I can't tote him on that old cart all the way across town. Besides, it will be a great way to show off your status here in Aramoor. I doubt Sandstorm gets the chance to host dinners all that much."

"Are you kidding me? We're hosting a quarter of Avalanche right now because of you!"

I shrugged. "So what's a dozen more?" I was almost tempted to drop to my knees if I thought it would help. "Please, Reevie. I won't ask anything from you ever again."

He rolled his eyes. "Fat chance of that coming true." After chewing on his lower lip for a moment, he looked over at the infirmary. "Fine. I'll see if Sapphire and Bull are willing to send them."

"Have Gittrick meet us at the docks. We should be finished here by then. Oh, and see if Solvino can make a special effort tonight with the meal."

"Anything else, Your Majesty?" Reevie asked as I gave him a leg up onto Shade.

"No. That's pretty much it, I think."

Reevie gritted his teeth as he clutched at the reins, looking more nervous than ever astride the giant horse. "You're sure he's safe to ride?"

"Only one way to find out," I said with a smile, and tapped Shade's flank. The horse took off up the street with Reevie firing off medical curses at me the whole way around the bend. *Take him to Sandstorm*

Manor, I said to Shade through our link. *Keep him safe.*

Turning, I headed inside to find Saban and the others in the second room on the right, where the more seriously injured patrollers were being kept. "How bad is it?" I asked, pushing past Whitey to get a better look.

Saban was sitting beside Pops's cot. He finished applying a thick salve before carefully wrapping the foot and ankle. "Could have been worse," Saban said. "I don't think it's broken, but he'll need to stay off it for the next week or two." He looked at Pops, and the old river boatman smiled.

"Tell them," Pops said, pointing up at Ismara. "They be the ones riding us so hard. Work us somethin' fierce." She crossed her arms and glared down at him, and Pops chuckled. "I'm sure I can manage a week or two."

"Do you have a crutch you can get your hands on?" Saban asked.

"We have one on board," Ismara said.

Saban nodded and then tied off the wrapping. "Good. Then I'll leave you to it. I still have other patients that need tending to."

Ismara paid him while Saban's wife, Nissa, packed up a small container of the salve for Pops to take with him.

"How's it feeling?" I asked, looking at the newly wrapped foot.

The elderly man looked down. "Much better than it did. Whatever he gave me to drink a moment ago is working wonders."

We carried him out and placed him back on the wagon.

Ismara looked around the front of the building before climbing back aboard herself. "Where's your giant horse?"

"I loaned him to Reevie. Faster than renting a palanquin."

"How will you get back? Or do you live nearby?"

"I live at the barracks. It's on the northwest side of the city, over near the palace. But, at the moment, I'm staying with friends in town." I hopped onto the back of the wagon with Whitey. "Hopefully, we'll be able to treat you all to dinner this evening."

Kettle turned around from his seat in front. "Treat us *all* to dinner? Appears the city's been good to you, then."

I smiled. "That's a long story if ever there was one."

Fifth bell sounded in the harbor, and Ismara grabbed the reins. "We can hear about it later, but if we want to get back before the crew leaves, we better go now." She snapped the reins, and the wagon leaped forward, nearly tossing Pops out the back. He shouted something about her trying to kill him off to free up his bunk on the ship.

We managed to make it back down to the port in one piece. We searched the docks, but there was no sign of Captain Treygan or his crew, so we dropped off the wagon and loaded Pops back up on the litter—faster than letting him hop one-legged all the way up the board-walk—and started for the other end ourselves. The boardwalk was still active with ships trying to get their goods off-loaded before the sun went down, but not as busy as it had been earlier.

We were nearing the end of the walk, just passing the third-to-last ship, when I caught my first sight of the *Wind Binder* ahead. Its dark wood and sleek silhouette set it apart from the others. Add in the black sail, and once the sun went down, it almost looked like a marauder, hiding in the shadows like a wraith. It was a beautiful ship, and I was surprised at how much I'd missed seeing her.

She seemed smaller than I remembered, but I had only been thirteen when I was aboard. Apart from the size difference, nothing about her had much changed. *Except for that*, I thought, spotting a large wheel sitting on the quarterdeck. When had they gotten that? When I had sailed with her, the *Wind Binder* had been steered by tiller. It seemed they had given her an upgrade since I'd been gone.

I kept behind the others as we turned and headed down the pier for the gangplank. I wondered if Bones had told them I was coming. No one was there to greet us, so I guessed he hadn't. Bones was the first to see us, blowing a whistle to let the others know Ismara's group had returned. Soon enough, the rivermen were gathered at the side rails, most looking eager to be off ship.

I stood in Whitey's shadow, trying not to draw attention to myself.

There were a lot of new faces aboard. I did, however, spot Bray—Needle, we called him. The ship's navigator was a hefty man who carried a compass with him wherever he went. Behind him, Captain Treygan stepped out wearing his typical long coat and captain's hat. He had more grey in his beard than I remembered, but his face was as strong as ever. I spotted his bone knife strapped to his waist. I had never seen him without it.

"'Bout time you made it back," Treygan said. "My stomach was about to gnaw through my backbone." He started down the plank. "So, what did they say about—" He spotted me behind the others and stopped.

I stepped out from behind Whitey, and Treygan's jaw dropped.

"It can't be." He rushed down the plank, not sparing a second glance at Pops, and threw his arms around me.

He was certainly as strong as ever, and nearly squeezed the breath out of me, but I managed to hug him back. One whiff of that robust all-day-on-the-river scent of his, and the memories of my time spent aboard ship flooded back.

"We've been looking for you for years, lad," he said as he released me and took a step back.

"Ismara said as much."

Treygan turned and looked up the plank. "Bones! Why didn't you tell me you'd found him?"

Bones just stood there with a big goofy grin on his face.

"So, how are you?" he asked, taking another step back to get a better look. "Better than fine from what I can see." He cocked a brow while taking in my leathers and swords. "Mercenary?"

I shook my head. "I'm the head of the Black Guild."

He shook his head, clearly having no idea what I was talking about.

"It's a newly formed unit within the Elondrian Lancers. We were appointed by the king himself. In fact, I'm supposed to be at the Cylmaran border right now with him—"

"With who? The king?"

"Yes, but I had some business here in Aramoor to wrap up first. Unfortunately, I haven't been able to find a ship heading that way to book passage aboard." I studied Treygan's face, trying to read whether he might be willing to take me. "I'd just finished checking the passenger board when I ran into this lot," I said, pointing over at Ismara, Whitey, Kettle, and Pops. "I have a good friend who is a physicker at an infirmary in town, so we took Pops there."

"And what did he say?" Treygan asked, finally walking over to look at the wrapped foot.

"They don't believe it's broken," Ismara said, "but he will need to be off it for the next week or two."

Treygan pursed his lips, then looked up at those on board. "Someone grab a crutch from below."

One of the men I didn't recognize left the rail and disappeared through the door leading into the galley and the stairs belowdecks.

"We were just getting ready to head into town for some food," Treygan said. "Care to join us?"

"Actually, I have other plans."

"Oh?" Treygan frowned. "You can't spare an hour for your old ship-mates?"

"These plans involve inviting you all to join *me* for dinner."

"All of us?"

"As many as want to come."

Treygan glanced back at the ship once more. "Who's on watch to-night?"

Two hands went up. I didn't recognize either one.

"Sorry, men," Treygan said. "Seems you've gotten the short end on this one. We'll try to bring you something back if we can."

The two men nodded reluctantly, disappointment on their faces as they turned and headed back to their duties. The rest made a rush down the plank for the pier. One of those toward the rear of them was holding Pops's crutch. It was short and padded at the top with layers of wrapping to stave off bruising under the arm. Whitey and Kettle, who had seated Pops on the dock as soon as we reached the ship, lifted him back to his feet to see if he could manage the crutch.

"So," Needle said, last to step off the gangplank, "this is the head-strong lad that used to sit up top with me and map out our routes?"

"Not so little now," Whitey countered, though to him, everyone was little.

Needle shook my hand. "Good to see you again, Ayrion. Hope you haven't lost too much of your training, wandering about here on land."

I looked back at the ship and smiled. "I'm sure I can still find my way around a rigging."

"Good man."

"Enough of this prattle," Kettle said, patting his waist. "The man says he wants to treat us to dinner. I say we let him."

"Aye," Pops said, trying to find a comfortable position for his crutch.

"Shouldn't you stay and rest?" Treygan asked.

"Just you try and stop me," Pops threatened, and started down the dock, hobbling until his leg nearly gave out and Kettle was forced to offer his shoulder for support.

Treygan sighed. "Fool of a man doesn't know when to quit." He started for the boardwalk behind Pops and Kettle, and the rest of the crew followed.

"So, tell us everything," Treygan said as I caught up beside him and Ismara.

"That's going to be a long story."

"Then start at the beginning," Ismara said. "Last we saw, you were heading around the Sandrethins with that family from Oswell, the magistrate person we rescued from the slavers."

"Magistrate Sirias."

"That's the one."

I scratched the back of my head. I hadn't thought about them in some time. "Well, after I left the *Wind Binder*, we spent several weeks making our way around the mountains toward Aramoor. As soon as we had cleared the southern peaks, we parted ways, and they continued south to one of the coastal cities . . . Fayburn, I think."

From there, I began the tale of my first encounter with the great city of Aramoor. Treygan kept our pace slow as we strolled down the boardwalk, giving Pops and Kettle time enough to keep up and me time to share my story, though it was going to take a lot more than a simple ramble down the docks. I told them of my first day inside the white walls and of my clash with Red and Wildfire.

"Not exactly the kind of welcome I had expected after such a long journey," I said.

Treygan flipped his bone knife. "Clearly you didn't let that stop you."

I smiled. "You know me, never one to back down from a fight."

"Don't we know it," Ismara mumbled under her breath.

From there, I continued with my story, and by the time we reached the south end of the port, I had just finished the part where Reevie had found me and taken me back to his place to nurse me back to health. "He's the young physicker you met outside the infirmary," I told Ismara.

"How far is it to where we're going?" Treygan asked. "Should we rent some horses?"

Pops groaned at the mention of a horse.

"We are heading for the other side of the city," I said and started up the steps and away from the water. "But we won't have to rent transportation." At least, I hoped not. Sixth bell rang out across the harbor as we made our way around the side of the first row of warehouses. Behind us, the sun was fast sinking toward the mountain peaks, and the sky was just beginning to show its first signs of coloring.

"Please be there," I whispered, holding my breath as we rounded the last warehouse. I breathed a deep sigh of relief when I saw Gittrick and Sandstorm's two coaches waiting for us. I wasn't looking forward to shelling out more coin to rent wagons and horses enough to get the crew across town.

"Transportation has already been provided," I said, gesturing toward the two carriages. Gittrick's oldest boy was atop the open carriage, while Gittrick sat atop the coach.

"And what kind of friends have you been keeping that can afford such luxury as this?" Ismara asked, gawking at our ride. "Are you on staff of one of the noble houses?"

I laughed. "Actually, the estate we will be dining at this evening used to be mine. Well, partly mine."

They both gaped.

Two of Gittrick's younger boys hopped off the back of the coaches and walked around to open the doors. Both Gittrick and his sons were dressed in formal coachmen attire, further raising the impression Sandstorm was already making on the crew. The black-and-purple uniforms looked sharp, and I was grateful they had thought to use them.

"Master Ayrion," Gittrick called down from the top of the coach. "I've been informed to tell you that, uh . . . that we are to make all haste, as dinner will be served promptly at seventh bell."

In other words, Reevie didn't want us dawdling and have to eat a cold meal.

"Thank you, Gittrick, I'm sure we can make it across town by then." I turned to the crew, but before I could say anything, Kettle beat me to it.

"You heard the man. The sooner we get a move on, the sooner we eat. Don't want good food getting cold." He grabbed Pops and practically carried him toward the coach, while Pops glared like he wanted to brain him with his crutch.

The rest of the crew divided itself and climbed aboard their respective rides. I rode in the coach with Treygan, Ismara, Bones, Kettle, and Pops, while Needle and Whitey went with the rest of the crew in the carriage. As tall as Whitey was, the open carriage was the better choice.

Once everyone was in, I tapped the ceiling to let Gittrick know we were ready. I heard a slight slap of reins, and the coach jerked forward. The others sat quietly a moment as they studied the interior. It wasn't exactly trimmed in gold like the royal coach, but its curtains and benches were unfaded and well-kept and its cushions soft. Treygan, Ismara, and Pops sat on one side, while Kettle, Bones, and I sat on the other. Pops kept his leg elevated by resting it in Kettle's lap, who was sitting across from him.

"And you used to own this?" Treygan asked.

"In a manner of speaking."

"I'm all ears," he said, the others staring at me with a hungry look in their eyes that for once didn't involve food.

I continued with my story, starting with my time spent at the Granary and the joining of Hurricane, which led to my first street battle with Avalanche. From there I told them of the Street Guild and its combined resources, affording us meeting rooms at one of the business towers in town.

"One of the big white ones?" Treygan asked.

"One and the same."

"Ain't like any street kids I've ever known," Kettle said.

The others nodded silently as they listened.

"Most of the street kids are exactly like you'd expect," I said, "barely scraping by, resorting to pinching food and cutting purse strings to survive. Those of the tribes living in the wealthier districts obviously did better than those of us living south of the Island."

If I hadn't just battled it out with Avalanche earlier today, I might have been tempted to have Gittrick take the more scenic route past my old stomping grounds, but that wasn't exactly the safest choice at the moment, and Gittrick wisely chose to take Circle Drive up and around the north side of the Island.

"There was one tribe that fared much better than the rest," I said. "Their chief had managed to branch out from mere pickpocketing and had accumulated quite a number of connections within the business community, including some of the nobility. In fact, the estate we are about to dine at this evening was one that his tribe purchased, but I'll speak more on that later."

I went on to tell them about our battle at the Pit and the ousting of Spats, leading to the takeover of Hurricane with Reevie and Sapphire. I told them how we had set our tribe up to be different from the rest. How we were willing to accept anyone.

"I won't lie, those first few years were extremely difficult. Not only was it a battle just to earn enough coin to keep our kids fed, but we were fighting against the other tribes just to exist. Two tribes in particular wanted to see us gone: Rockslide and Avalanche."

I told them of the Guild's challenge for us to earn our place as one of the tribes and how it had led to my first meeting of the royal family. We were just crossing over King's Way West and could see the palace spires rising in the distance when I got to the part about me and Dakaran hiding in the chifforobe in the king's study after I had broken in to steal the royal seal.

Like they had been so many times throughout my retelling, the others sat there with wide-eyed shock on their faces.

"You met the royal family?" Treygan asked.

I grinned. "More than met them. I see them almost every day. I'm the crown prince's personal instructor, and probably his closest friend." I couldn't help but revel a little in my luck of connections. I looked at Ismara. "The black horse you saw me riding earlier was given to me by the king."

Again, nothing but stunned silence.

From there I went on to tell of our takeover of Sandstorm after Noph was forced to escape the city. I told them of Sandstorm's growth and of me eventually joining the Elondrian Lancers, per the king's request. I told them of Room Eleven and our mission into Cylmar to rescue the Elondrian ambassador and his wife from Overlord Saryn, which led to my fortuitous reunion with my father and brother.

I also went on to explain my leaving Sandstorm and a few of the harsh feelings it had brought with it, mainly with Reevie. "I tell you this so you understand why there might be some tension between Reevie and myself during supper."

"He didn't seem all that angry this afternoon," Ismara said.

"Seemed quite pleasant," Pops added. "You don't think he'll have any more of that wonderful tonic the other physicker gave me, do you?"

"I'm sure he'll have something."

"It's a fine sheath," Bones said unexpectedly, catching us all off guard.

I looked over at him and then down at the center buckle of my sheath. "Yes, it is. It was a gift from Sandstorm for my birthday a few weeks ago."

"Quite the generous gift from someone you say doesn't much care for your presence," Treygan said.

"Actually"—I quirked a grin—"Reevie wasn't told about the gift until a few days ago." I waved it off. "Even with the resentment, I still consider him my closest friend."

We turned off Circle Drive and onto Bailey Street. "Up here on the right is the orphanage I told you about." I pointed out the side window, and everyone turned to look. There were a couple of children playing around the front porch. They all looked up as we passed. A couple even waved. Bones waved back with one of his toothy grins, and the kids ran inside.

The sky was awash with color, as the sun was quickly setting, and the lamplighters were already out and moving through the streets. I was glad we were getting here before dark to give the crew a chance to see the place while there was still light. We turned off the last street and headed over the hill. Up ahead, the Sandstorm gate was just beginning to open.

"Here we are," I said, and everyone turned to look.

The carriage holding Needle, Whitey, and the rest of the *Wind Binder* crew was just ahead of us. It didn't stop, and neither did we, as we passed through the gate and started up the drive for the manor house. Toots, Stringbean, and several of the watchers were in formation outside the wall, a strangely formal greeting for so late in the day.

"I still can't wrap my mind around the fact that a bunch of street children live here," Treygan said, "let alone own all of this."

The carriages came to a stop at the top of the drive, just in front of the courtyard. Apparently, the chiefs had called for a full assembly to welcome our guests, because the entire courtyard was filled to the brim. What had Reevie told them? Collen and the Sandstorm Guard were stretched across the front of the courtyard, the beaters in formation just behind, and all in their formal black-and-purple uniforms.

I turned to face the *Wind Binder*'s crew, a sense of pride flooding through me.

"Welcome to Sandstorm."

AVALANCHE

Chapter 34

ONE OF GITTRICK'S BOYS OPENED the door, and I hopped out, stepping to the side to let the rest disembark. In the courtyard, Sapphire, Reevie, and Bull stood quietly at the center of the line of children. Sapphire was wearing one of her formal dark purple dresses with black trim, along with her short swords. I hadn't seen her carry those in some time. By the way everyone was acting, you'd think they were hosting the king and queen.

"Should we get out or cut and run?" Kettle said, looking out apprehensively at the armed kids waiting for them to exit. "Grabbing a stout pint at the Fishnet is looking mighty tempting about now."

"Nothing to worry about," I said, sticking my head back in the coach with my back to Sandstorm. I kept my voice lowered. "This is a formal greeting for respected guests. Though, why they'd be offering it to the likes of you lot, I have no idea."

The crew just stared at me blankly. They didn't seem to get the joke.

I stepped away from the coach, and Treygan was the first out, followed by Ismara.

Sapphire studied both, her face expressionless. She'd heard my stories over the years about the rugged riverboat captain and his beautiful daughter, and how I'd traveled with them down the Shemoa River. I wished I knew what was going on in her head. I couldn't tell how she was going to respond.

Ismara straightened her captain's hat as she turned and got a closer look at their hosts. She moved beside me to make way for Bones. I heard several gasps from the courtyard as the tall, dark-skinned man stepped out, his white body paint gleaming in the light of the lanterns that lined the outer edge of the courtyard. He smiled, then turned to help Kettle with Pops.

More gasps arose, this time from the *Wind Binder* crew, as Tubby stepped out from the front doors of the manor and marched across the courtyard for the carriages. He was wearing his Flesh Eater mask. Those of the crew getting out of the carriage stopped when they saw him.

"What in the flaming Pits of Aran'gal is that?" Kettle asked, trying to climb back into the coach, but Treygan pulled him out.

Tubby stopped just behind the three chiefs and stared at the row of newcomers.

I glared at Sapphire and pointed behind her questioningly.

She turned and sighed. "These are our guests, Tubby. You don't need the mask."

Tubby stared at the rivermen a moment, then finally took it off. Seeing that he wasn't some sort of hideously misshapen monster eased the tension, at least enough for the rest of the crew to join the others in front of the courtyard.

"On behalf of Sandstorm," Sapphire said, "we'd like to welcome the crew of the *Wind Binder* to our home."

Treygan took a step forward. "And what a lovely home it is," he said, loudly enough for all those in the courtyard to hear. "We thank you kindly for your generous hospitality, and may you find favorable winds to fill your days." He proffered a formal bow, hat in hand.

Sapphire bowed her head. "My name is Sapphire, and these are my fellow chiefs: Reevie and Bull. I believe you have already met Reevie."

Treygan put his hat back on. "A few of my crew have, but I have not yet had the pleasure." He looked at Reevie. "We are grateful for your service with our injured crewman."

"I'm afraid I did little but point the way," Reevie said, then looked at Pops. "Though, if you're willing, I'd like to take a look at your foot before you leave. I have a fully stocked infirmary and can offer some little-known salves and tonics to aid in the healing and perhaps lessen the pain."

"Lessen the pain?" Pops's eyes brightened as he steadied himself with his crutch. "I might just have to take you up on that, my lad."

Treygan cleared his throat. "Where are my manners? My name is Captain Treygan, and this is my daughter Captain Ismara." From there, he introduced the rest of the crew down the line, starting with his first mate, Bones, and ending with those of the crew I was unfamiliar with.

Sapphire did the same, introducing her captain of the guard, Collen, and those others who held more active leadership roles within the home, all the way down to Muriel as keeper of the birds and assistant to the physicker. By the time all introductions had been made, the sun had dropped completely, and a few of the brighter stars were beginning to blink into view.

The bell in the harbor rang out the seventh hour, signaling a late dinner. Sandstorm usually ate around fifth bell, but given the circumstances, I'm sure Solvino had been delighted with the additional prep time.

Sapphire, Reevie, and Bull turned, prompting those behind to part, leaving an open walkway across the courtyard from the drive to the front doors. "Supper should be served shortly," Sapphire said. "If you'll follow us." The three chiefs started down the open path, and I motioned for Treygan and the rest of the crew to follow me.

Behind us, Gittrick and his sons drove the carriages over to the carriage house. I could sense Shade nearby and figured Gittrick must have placed him back in his stall. He didn't seem hungry, but it was difficult to tell what he was feeling with my own stomach rumbling.

Most of the crew picked up their pace while passing Tubby. A quick glance back over my shoulder showed a few staring up at him, mouths agape. Guess they had never seen anyone that big before, let alone someone as young as he was. We had determined long ago that he was probably close to my age, though we had no real way of knowing.

We followed the chiefs inside to the open gallery, where they stopped to give the crew a chance to get a look around. Whatever Solvino was working on in the kitchen had my mouth watering as the medley of aromas filtered through the house.

"Welcome to Sandstorm Manor," Gustory said as the last of the crew made it through the door. I hadn't seen the bard out in the courtyard earlier. He must have hung back to offer us his own greeting here.

"We have heard tales of the *Wind Binder* and its crew's exploits for years," Gustory said, tossing a brief wink in my direction. As he spoke, I felt a sense of pride and a thrill of excitement wash over me, no doubt his magic at work. I could see it was influencing the crew as well, as smiles broke out on their faces.

Behind us, the rest of Sandstorm shuffled in through the doors, but instead of continuing to ogle the newcomers, they were ushered down the hall to the main dining room. I guess they hadn't eaten yet either.

Once the last of Sandstorm had made it in and the doors were shut, Gustory continued. "I've even borrowed a story or two of your exploits for my own retellings here for the children, and some I've used to entertain patrons from the most reputable eateries in the city, including Zoralli's."

I blinked in surprise. Zoralli's was well known to be the epitome of fine dining in Aramoor. I had never eaten there myself. It was located on the Main Square, right at the heart of the Island, and certainly cost more than my purse could handle. Only the best of the best were invited to perform there. Of course, when it came to engrossing an audience with tales so wondrous as to arouse the appetite, who better than a magical bard?

Treygan looked at me, confused, and I realized I hadn't made introductions.

"This is Gustory," I said, "a highly sought-after bard here in Aramoor, who has made Sandstorm his permanent place of residence."

"Thanks to you," Gustory added, tapping the side of his nose. "Another exciting tale to be sure."

"And one we can save for later." I turned to Pops and pointed to a door on the other side of the gallery. "That's Reevie's infirmary. Do you need him to look at your foot now or are you fine to wait until after we eat?"

Pops stared at the door a moment, then patted his stomach. "After. Don't want to see my food go cold."

"I apologize that we weren't given more time to prepare," Sapphire said as she directed the crew toward the east wing. "I hope you find our accommodations to your liking."

"To our liking?" Treygan laughed as he followed along. "I hardly think a one of us has ever sullied the floor of such a place as this. I am truly without words. I didn't quite believe our young Ayrion here when he boasted of having been lord of a manor. In fact, it wasn't until we'd passed through the gates and started up the drive that I realized he wasn't pulling my leg, but had understated it by a river mile." He offered Sapphire a warm smile. "We are but humble riverboat men, milady, so I assure you that whatever you provide will far surpass any expectations we might have."

Sapphire smiled at me as we made our way down the hall. "He's not at all what I had pictured."

"Oh?" Treygan chuckled, looking at me. "And what sort of nonsense have you been filling their heads with, lad?"

"Better than you deserve, I'm sure."

Treygan and several of the others laughed.

We reached the chiefs' dining room. The staff had extended the table and arranged it with at least twenty place settings, which was two more than our entire party consisted of, including myself, the three chiefs, and Gustory.

Sapphire walked across the room to her place at the head while Reevie and Bull took theirs on either side, leaving Gustory beside Reevie. All four stood behind their seats until everyone had made it in. I found my place at the opposite end with my back to the door while the *Wind Binder* crew filled in the rest of the empty spots between, with Treygan and Ismara on either side of me. It was a longer table than we were used to, but the room was small enough and lively enough that conversation was easy to catch.

Sapphire was the first to take her seat and motioned for everyone to do the same. There weren't enough staff to have footmen pulling chairs, but there were enough for them to carry in pitchers of drink to begin filling everyone's goblets.

"This is quite the spread," Ismara said, glancing down the table before looking at me. "And you gave this up to sleep in a barracks and eat out of a mess hall?"

"My sentiments exactly," Sapphire chimed in with a playful smirk as she tipped her goblet in my direction.

I took a sip of my spiced cider before answering. "It started as a personal favor to the king. He wished me to be there for his son to help him through his year of service." I went on to explain that every crown prince was expected to undergo a year inside the Elondrian Lancers in order to prepare them for the crown.

"His Royal Highness was a recent guest of ours," Gustory added.

"Yes." Bull chuckled. "I'm sure it was the highlight of his week."

Treygan's questioning look at their comments forced me to briefly describe the recent incident with Dakaran, and Reevie's hand in saving his life.

"You are quite skilled for one so young," Bones said to Reevie from across the table.

Reevie waved the compliment away, but I could see a twinkle in his eyes.

"To answer your question," I continued, turning my attention back to Ismara and her initial inquiry about why I'd chosen to give up Sandstorm. "Yes, living at the garrison isn't exactly a comfort. Not that living here at Sandstorm is always wine and roses. They have their share of difficulties as well—"

"Don't we know it," Reevie grumbled.

"But," I said, "the more time I spent in lancer life, the more I grew accustomed to it, and appreciated it. True, we don't have the luxuries found here at the manor house. I don't enjoy the comfort of my own private room, or the incredibly savory meals, or fancy furnishings, but if given the choice, I would probably choose the same all over again."

I looked at Ismara. "Right now, you share a small ship with a dozen smelly, uncouth rivermen."

"Hey," Kettle said. "I resent that." He tilted his head and took a whiff of his shirt. "Never mind."

I looked at the rest of the crew. "How many of you would be willing to give up the river and the *Wind Binder* for all of this?"

The newer crewmembers looked swayable, but I could see the staunch look in the rest that said they'd rather die than give up their way of life.

Ismara sighed. "Guess you've got a point."

Treygan, who sat directly across from her, smiled proudly at his daughter. He then turned to Gustory. "I'm glad to see our exploits have not gone unnoticed and have proven entertaining to the locals. I hope you have portrayed us well."

"Indeed, sir. I have painted you according to the highest of standards, heroes of the Shemoa, no less."

"You don't say."

"My patrons love hearing of the band of protectors that travel the waterways, seeking those in need, battling Cylmarans and monsters alike to free the oppressed and enslaved. Men . . . and women," he added with a wink toward Ismara, "who risk life and limb for the betterment of all."

"Blimey," Pops said. "Makes us seem right larger than life, it does."

"A little too large, perhaps," Treygan added with an appreciative smile. "And how do we measure up to the image you have been giving us all these years? Not quite as gallant, I assume."

"On the contrary," Gustory said, "apart from the lack of a noted eye patch, you seem the express image of my description."

Treygan cocked a single brow. "Eye patch?"

Gustory shrugged. "I might have taken a few liberties with the characters."

"I'm afraid to ask," Ismara said, though she clearly wanted to know how she stood next to her legendary image as well.

Gustory nodded. "Alas, my depictions of your beauty and grace have fallen short, indeed."

Ismara blushed.

Sapphire, on the other hand, rolled her eyes. She glanced over at the butler standing in a far corner. "Is the food ready to be served?"

Conversation around the table died down immediately as everyone looked across the room for the answer.

"It's on its way even now, milady."

She took a deep breath. "Wonderful. Be sure to tell Solvino we appreciate his and his staff's hard work this evening."

The butler bowed. "It will be my pleasure."

About the time he'd straightened from his bow, several footmen appeared from the hall, bearing trays of food-laden platters, which they promptly began to place strategically around the table. It took a couple of loads for the first course to find its way from the kitchen to the dining room, but the smell alone said it was worth the wait.

After a brief thanks was offered for the food by Bones, everyone reached for the ladles, and the meal commenced.

Solvino had outdone himself. I wasn't sure how he'd managed to prepare a spread such as this in so little time. For starters, there were stuffed apples cooked in a cinnamon glaze and sprinkled with finely aged cheese, and potage with honey and fresh spring fruit adorning the top. For the second course, there was not only wild boar, but venison and pike; and for the main course, stuffed pheasant with sides of buttered potatoes and seasoned vegetables. By the time they brought in the dessert, I barely had room to breathe, and it seemed I wasn't the only one, as utensils moving from dish to mouth began to slow.

I forced myself through the candied fruit and cheese only to find myself staring face-to-face with some sort of blending of sticky bun and fruit tart, with a fruit filling inside the bun. It was the most beautiful thing I'd ever seen—my two favorite sweets in all of Aldor combined into one incredible pastry. It was too good to pass up, and I didn't care if it left me sick. It was going in my mouth.

"I've changed my mind," Needle said, dabbing at his forehead with his napery while scooting back from the table to give his belly room to expand. "I just might be willing to give up the river for meals like this."

The others of the crew nodded in agreement, even Treygan, though I knew better than to believe him.

"We don't exactly feast in such a manner every day," Sapphire said, "but our cook had been preparing a special sendoff meal for Ayrion, which was supposed to be a surprise gift before he headed to the front." About the time she said it, she turned and waved for someone at the door to enter.

I turned to find Solvino standing behind me, his white hat atop his head as he twirled his mustache nervously. He quickly snatched the hat off and looked at me. "I just wanted to say that it has been an honor cooking for you, Master Ayrion, and on behalf of myself and the staff, we wish you and your men . . . and the king, of course, all safety in these upcoming days." He bowed nervously, sparing a glance at the riverboat men.

I wiped frosting from my mouth. "And if this is to be my parting meal, I can think of no one else in Aramoor I'd rather have had prepare it. You have certainly outdone yourself this time, Solvino. Please extend my heartfelt thanks to your staff for their service." I paused a moment, then added, "You have been more than a cook to me and to Sandstorm. You have been a true friend. One can never have too many of those."

Solvino bowed once more, a bright smile on his face. "Thank you, Master Ayrion."

"And if you ever get tired of filling the bellies of those here," Treygan said, "feel free to join me and my men aboard ship. I'm sure you could teach Kettle here a thing or two."

Kettle frowned.

Solvino, on the other hand, gulped as he stared at the captain, clearly not sure whether to take Treygan's offer in jest or in earnest. He simply twirled his mustache once more and forced a smile. "It's a . . . a generous offer, to be sure. But I have a feeling I'll be needed here for many years to come."

He looked at Sapphire, and she nodded that he was excused. With another quick glance around the table at all the satisfied faces, he backed out of the room and quickly left.

Once Solvino had disappeared down the hall, Treygan laughed. "I think he might have taken me seriously."

"*Is* there going to be war?" Whitey asked unexpectedly, staring down at me from a few seats away. He was by far the tallest in the room, and the biggest. He was also generally the least talkative, so for him to speak up in company this size meant it had to have been weighing on his mind.

I took a deep breath and released it slowly. "It's looking more like it every day."

"And you will be going?"

"I should be there already." That wasn't exactly true, as the lancers had only set sail the day prior, but it was close enough to the truth. "But if I can't find a ship willing to take me, I'm not sure what I'm going to do." I didn't look at Treygan or Ismara, not wanting them to feel as though I were expecting them to oblige me, or that I'd wined and dined them as a way to grease the oars, so to speak.

The room quieted, and I purposefully picked at what was left of my last sticky bun, not wanting to look up but growing more and more uncomfortable the longer the silence lasted. Why wasn't anyone talking?

"We were planning on taking leave through the end of the week anyway," I heard Ismara say softly.

I finally looked up to see who she was talking to and found her looking at her father, who was pinching his chin. Treygan looked down the table at the rest of the crew, and one by one they all nodded before he turned and looked at me. "I guess it's decided."

"What's decided?"

"The *Wind Binder* will take you."

"You will? Are you sure? Don't you have business here?"

"Nothing that won't hold until our return. Besides, if war breaks out and the king needs you, I'd rather you be there than here. The last thing we need is Cylmarans overrunning Elondria. Won't be safe for any of us then."

There were more than a few "ayes" heard around the table. They acted as though I alone would be the determining factor for the outcome of this war. I was Upakan, but I wasn't an army unto myself.

"If it helps," I said, "I might be able to get payment from the queen for your time. I was planning on seeing her in the morning to ask her help in securing passage. I figured either she could order someone to take me or provide a purse sizable enough to entice a captain's consent."

Treygan grinned. "Of course, we wouldn't be so crass as to turn down a contribution from Her Majesty, if she desired to offer it."

I smiled. It was the least I could do if they were going to be willing to give up their much-needed shore leave to transport me all the way to the Cylmaran front.

"Shall we retire to the sitting room?" Sapphire said, not really asking, as she stood from her seat and started down the table for the door. "I believe we have drinks ready for your guests."

I followed, the rest of the crew falling in behind me. We left the dining hall to the cleaning staff and walked down a couple of doors to another room of similar size, but one not taken up by a long table down the center. There were chairs aplenty scattered throughout, no doubt gathered from several different locations to accommodate so many. The fireplaces on the sides filled the room with warmth, adding their glow to the already-lit lamps. Tables with drink dotted the room between the different groupings of chairs, all of which were turned inward to face each other.

Reevie and Pops excused themselves for a short time so Reevie could take him down to the infirmary to examine his foot and give him something more for the pain.

In the sitting room, I found a seat next to Treygan and Ismara, with Sapphire, Reevie and Bull not far away.

"Do you still make it as far north as Cretollo?" I asked Treygan, hoping to find out something about Hobb, the ferryman at Oswell.

"Often enough," he said, "when the water permits." The river lowered during the warmer months and was at its highest just after the winter thaw, as the melted snow washed down from the Northern Heights. Treygan pulled out a pipe and joined a few of the others for an evening smoke. "We were there in . . ."

"In Nùwen," Ismara said. "Remember, Tillman was having difficulty with one of his boats."

"That's right. I'd forgotten about that."

Tillman was the captain whose ship Hobb had initially tried to book me passage on, but one look at my eyes and Tillman had claimed his boat too full to take passengers. It had been Treygan who had spoken up during that incident to offer me a place aboard his ship, but at the time, the *Wind Binder* had been thought of as cursed, and Hobb wasn't exactly overjoyed with the idea of me on a cursed ship.

"So, you and Captain Tillman have buried the hatchet, then?" I asked.

Treygan took a puff, letting it snake slowly from his mouth and up over his head. "I wouldn't exactly say we are drinking buddies, but I guess the ice has melted a bit. He still runs the majority of the ships in the northern parts, but when speed is a necessity, the *Wind Binder* is who the customers choose. We are the fastest ship this side of the Rhunarin."

"That's quite the claim," Gustory said, a pad and quill in hand, jotting down anything of note he might use to add to his stories.

"Haven't met a ship that can outrun us yet," Treygan said with a proud smile.

"You haven't seen Hobb in your travels, have you?" I asked, taking a small sip of the wine.

"From Hobb's Crossing?" Treygan asked. He shook his head. "Afraid not. The river's too shallow for a ship our size to make it that far north. Cretollo is about as far as we dare venture without risking ourselves getting shelved in the mud."

I sighed. "That's too bad. I'd love to know how he's doing."

"I was up that way many years ago," Needle said. "Back before joining the *Wind Binder*. I remember the ferryman. Never one to turn a needy traveler away. My horse had gone lame coming out of Oswell, and he put me up for the night and even loaned me another to make it back to Oswell. Don't see that kind of trust in people these days. I could have made off with the horse and there wouldn't have been a thing he could have done about it."

I nodded as I sipped on my drink. "Sounds just like him." I didn't need to go into any detail on my experience with Hobb, as both those from Sandstorm and the *Wind Binder* had heard the tale on more than one occasion.

We spent the next few hours catching up on all the travels the *Wind Binder*'s crew had undertaken since my departure seven years ago. Apparently, they'd made it all the way to Windmeer, and had even taken the East River north all the way to Easthaven, which was quite the feat for a bunch of riverboat men, as most tended to keep away from the open waters of the Rhunarin or the Ozrin. But then, it was the *Wind Binder*, and there wasn't much that ship couldn't do.

After being regaled by tales of Aldor's waterways, the crew prodded me with questions about life as a street rat, so I shared in more detail some of the exploits Reevie, Sapphire, and I had participated in over the years. Bull and Gustory jumped in when we reached the parts of the story they had been involved in. Bull had been with us the longest, so he knew the most. By the time we were finished answering questions from the crew, the bell in the harbor had rung out the first hour.

"Ship's mercy," Ismara said. "Is that the time? We've been talking half the night."

No one seemed all that tired, not with the engaging conversations we were keeping. Gustory had worked his way through an entire pad of paper and had called for another. His poor fingers looked ready to cramp by the time he placed the quill down on the table beside his seat.

"Well," he said with a yawn, "I think I have enough new material to last me for years to come."

Treygan leaned in my direction. "How do we get back to the ship? Is your coachman still waiting?"

"We have accommodations for you here," Sapphire said.

I looked up, surprised by the offer. "Are you sure? What about the

Avalanche kids?"

"They're still being kept in the library for now, but I already cleared out a couple of rooms on the third floor for your guests. We moved some of the kids in to bunk with others tonight, just in case."

That was smart thinking. Leave it to Sapphire to be on top of everything, even with little to no prior notice. She truly had grown into quite the resourceful woman.

I turned to the two captains. "I guess the decision has already been made."

Treygan tapped the remains of his pipe into a catch bowl on the table. "You won't see me turning down hospitality such as this."

"Aye," Pops said, being helped up by Kettle and Whitey. "Be nice to sleep in a proper bed, it would."

Bones walked over to Treygan. "I don't like leaving Ornan and Birg without a replacement."

Treygan waved it off. "It'll be good for them. I remember back in the day when we'd stand watch all night and enjoy the quiet of it."

"Them not enjoying it isn't my concern, Captain. It's whether those two will sink the ship while doing it."

Treygan chuckled and clapped his tall first mate on the back. "I'm sure they'll be fine."

I followed everyone around to the east-wing stairs as we headed up to the third floor. I bid Treygan, Ismara, and the others a good night and left them at the rooms Sapphire had prepared, which were on the opposite end of the hall from mine. After making sure they had everything they needed and telling them when breakfast was generally served, I left them to it and headed to my room. It was going to be a busy day tomorrow, so I needed to make sure I got as much sleep as I could manage.

I stopped outside my door and stared back down the now-empty hall. The *Wind Binder* crew had already made it into their rooms for the night. I almost wanted to pinch myself to believe this was real. Both my families together under one roof. Never in my wildest dreams would I have believed it possible. If only my real family were here as well.

AVALANCHE

Chapter 35

I WOKE TO THE SOUND of someone knocking on my door. I glanced over at the windows and could just barely see the outline of a faint dawn creeping around the edges of the curtains. Three more knocks had me throwing my covers back.

"I'm coming." I hopped out of bed and struggled into my pants as I skipped across the floor, trying to make it to the door before whoever was on the other side knocked it down. The room was blurry, my eyes not quite focusing, so I blinked a couple of times to clear them, then unlocked the door and opened it.

Ismara was waiting in the hall. "You going to sleep all day?" she asked. A smile crept across her face as she took in my state of undress.

"What time is it?" I looked past her down the hall but found it empty. The sconces had yet to be snuffed. "I feel like I just got to sleep."

"It's time to wake those lazy bones and get dressed. We've got a busy day if we want to set sail for the Cylmaran border anytime soon."

I stifled a yawn. "Fine. I'll be down shortly." I'd forgotten the *Wind Binder* crew's sleep habits were early to bed and early to rise. I realized she was fully dressed, long coat and all. "Did you sleep in those?"

"Too warm for that," she said with a wink, then turned and sauntered off down the hall toward the crew's chambers. "You better hurry or there won't be any leftovers."

I chuckled and headed back inside, shutting the door behind me and locking it just in case she returned. My entire body was stiff. Clearly, I'd not gotten enough rest. I wanted nothing more than to go crawl back under my covers, but Ismara was right. We had a lot to do today. I did my best to work the stiffness out of my muscles with some minor exercises and light stretching, then dressed and headed down the hall to look in on my former shipmates. Their rooms were empty, so I followed the smell of sausage down the stairs and around to the chiefs' dining room, where I found the rest of the crew busy stuffing their faces with some of Solvino's finest griddlecakes and honey.

Besides the griddlecakes, there were sausage links, eggs, beans, bacon, bowls of cut fruit, and fresh loaves of steaming bread, along with mugs of watered wine, cider, and thick cream. It was quite the gourmet feast. I wondered if the cook had gone to bed at all. He would have had to be up incredibly early to have a meal like this ready and waiting.

"Thought you were going to sleep the day away," Treygan said when he saw me walk through the door. He cut a sausage with his bone knife, stabbed it, then popped it in his mouth with a look of delight.

"No chance of that happening with Ismara banging on my door at the crack of dawn."

She smirked. "All this time spent on land has made you soft."

Bull choked on a mouthful of griddlecake, honey spraying onto the stubble he called a beard. "If he's soft, then I'd hate to see what you consider strong. Set the Protector loose and he might just take out the entire Cylmaran army single-handedly."

I wiped fruit juice from my mouth after swallowing some not-so-ripe berries. "Let's not get carried away. I barely made it out of Avalanche territory yesterday without the aid of additional patrollers. I don't think I'll be defeating armies anytime soon." I smiled and shook my head. Who did these people think I was?

"Where's Sapphire?" I asked Bull, who was working to finish the last bit of egg on his plate. I wondered how much earlier they had started on the meal before I'd arrived.

"She already ate," he said, taking a swallow from his mug. "Been in her study ever since."

"And Reevie?" I asked, not all that surprised by his lack of appearance. He wasn't exactly a morning person, and I doubted he would make too great an effort just to see me off.

"He left early for the infirmary in town. Said he had a lot of paperwork to catch up on."

I nodded. "Could you have Gittrick ready the carriages after you finish? I'd like to have a word with Sapphire before we leave."

Bull waved his fork at me, the final piece of egg clinging to it. "Already done. The carriages will be ready whenever you are." He stuffed the remainder in his mouth.

"Clearly you've got one up on me this morning."

He smiled. "Happens every now and then."

"I like these cakes," Whitey said, his cheeks stuffed to the brim.

"Yes," Pops agreed. "They are quite fluffy, aren't they?"

"Kettle's are hard," Whitey added.

Kettle sneered. "Feel free to start cookin' for yourselves, you ingrates." He shook his head and looked to the captains. "I knew comin' here was a bad idea."

Treygan and Ismara only smiled.

I finished what was on my plate, washing it down first with a cup of cream, then with a swig or two of the spiced cider, letting the strong herbs clear my head. I looked at Pops. "Did Reevie get a chance to take a look at that foot this morning?"

Pops shook his head. "But he did give me some more of his fancy tonic and salve to carry with me in case it decides to start acting up again. And he said that when we make port, I could come see him for some more. Right nice lad, if you ask me."

I smiled. "One of the best." I wiped my mouth and dropped the linen on the table beside my plate as I turned to Treygan and Ismara. "If you'll excuse me, I'm going to go have a word with Sapphire. I'll meet you out front."

They both nodded, so I left the room and made my way across the manor for the chiefs' study. I knocked, even though the door was part-way open, and waited for her to look up before stepping in.

"I just wanted to say my goodbyes."

She stood from her desk. "Will you be back tonight?"

"I don't think so. Now that I have a ship, I'll pack what I need from the garrison. We might even set sail as early as this evening."

"So, this is it?" She walked around her desk and over to where I was standing just inside the doorway. "We don't see you for over a year, then suddenly you're back here living with us like nothing ever happened. Now you're heading off to war and we might not see you again." Her eyes began to glisten, and she wiped them.

"You aren't crying, are you?"

"Maybe. Is that so wrong?"

"No, but . . . stop it before you have me doing it."

We stared at each other a moment in silence, and then she stepped forward and kissed me. It was one of those kisses she used to give me back before the split, one that had me melting inside. I wrapped my arms around her and held her tight for a long moment before finally releasing her and taking a step back.

"Tell Reevie . . ."

She nodded, wiping her other eye this time. "I'll tell him."

I paused to take a slow look around the room. "I'm going to miss this place."

She punched me in the arm. "Just don't let another year go by before you visit again."

I chuckled. "I promise." I glanced out the window at the side and saw my shipmates making their way across the courtyard. "I guess I better go." I stopped once more and looked her in the eyes. "I love you, you know. All of you."

She sniffed. "I know."

With that, I turned and headed out of the study and back around to the front, where I found Tubby, Mouse, Petal, and Squeaks waiting in the open gallery.

"Didn't think you was going to sneak out of here without seeing us, did you?" Mouse said.

I smiled, feeling a burning at the corner of my eyes. "I'm not much for goodbyes."

They each stepped forward in turn to give me a hug. Tubby simply picked me up and then placed me back down.

"Kill them Cylmarans," Mouse said.

"We'll miss you," Petal added.

Squeaks simply nodded.

I took a moment to look them over, then glanced beyond them and over at the library door, where Gustory and Muriel stood waving. Red-wing sat quietly on Muriel's gloved hand, watching the proceedings with a cautious glare.

I waved back.

"Take care of yourself," Gustory said.

I nodded and then stepped out the door, refusing to look back. Saying goodbye had brought back all those sharp feelings I'd buried the first time I'd had to leave.

My chest ached.

Gittrick had the carriages waiting in the drive. Shade was there as well, looking anxious to be on his way. He seemed well rested; I was glad one of us was.

The crew had already begun to climb aboard by the time I'd made it to the drive. I stopped beside the coach, where one of Gittrick's sons was holding the door as Whitey and Bones attempted to help Pops inside. Above us, an early sunrise was already beginning to color the sky, infusing the clouds with a collage of peach, pale blue, and yellow.

I looked up at Gittrick. "I need to stop by the garrison first to pack before heading to the palace to speak with Her Majesty."

"And I need to see my ship," Treygan said. "We have supplies that need purchasing and a couple of crewmen that need to be relieved." His face suddenly hardened. "Drown me! I promised I'd bring them something when we made it back, and I plum forgot."

"How long will it take you to restock?" I asked. "Think you might have it done by later this afternoon?"

Treygan thought a moment. "If we can reach the shops when they open, we should be shipshape by then."

"If that's the case, you can tell the other two when you get back to the ship that instead of bringing back some day-old food, you'll exchange it for a tour of the palace and a possible meeting with the queen."

Conversation inside the carriage cut off, everyone wearing stunned looks.

"I'll speak with the queen while you stock the ship. Might help my case of asking for some additional funds anyway."

I looked back up at Gittrick. "Take them back to the harbor."

"Where will you be?" Ismara asked.

"I'm going to head over to the garrison and start packing. Then I'll pay the prince a visit and see if I can set up a meeting with Her Majesty while you see to the ship's needs. Afterward, I'll head back to the docks and see how things are proceeding."

"Would you like me to stay in town and wait on you?" Gittrick asked. "That is, if you are planning on taking them to see the queen."

"There's no need for you to sit there all day. I'm sure we can rent some horses to take over to the palace this evening."

"That's a lot of horses," Treygan said.

He had a point. There were over a dozen in the crew. I looked back up at Gittrick. "How about after you drop them off, you return here to Sandstorm so you don't miss lunch, then plan on being back at the port at fifth bell to take us over?"

"Would you be opposed if I were to bring my boys with you to that meeting? I would love the opportunity to see the inside of the palace myself."

I smiled. "I'm sure that can be arranged."

He grinned widely. "Thank you, Master Ayrion. You don't know how much that would mean to me."

I looked back at those in the coach behind us, spotting Whitey's hat sticking above the rest. "I'll see you later this afternoon."

With that, I climbed up onto Shade, and we headed down the drive in front of the carriages. I stopped at the bottom and waited for the gate to open.

"Keep them safe, Toots," I said with a bright smile for the fierce gate-watch leader. Jayden and a few of the others were there with him.

"I always does, Protector. You keeps yourself safe."

"I'll do my best." I saluted the watch with a fist to chest, and they straightened proudly, saluting in return before I rode through the gateway and up the street.

Sandstorm disappeared behind me. I hoped it wasn't the last time I'd get to see it.

I didn't take Circle Drive up and around today, instead opting for some of the smaller roads around the Island, which made the trip a little quicker. I crossed the Tansian just north of the river's split, and from there took King's Way West. The sun was just peeking over the top of the city wall behind me as I made my way toward the garrison's front gate.

The doors were already open, but only a couple of lancers were milling around the watchtowers. It was certainly slim pickings. Most of those chosen to remain behind were either getting a little long in the tooth or were new enough—like the Avalanche boys—to not be battle ready.

I slowed when I reached those on watch. "Is Lieutenant Huckly on duty?"

The older lancer holding the in-and-out board scratched the back of his head as he looked inside the garrison. "He was with the new recruits, last I saw." He shook his head and spat off to the side. "Rough lot, that. Don't reckon they could tell a spear from a lance if you handed it to 'em."

"That's why they're here," I said, a little annoyed. "Who better to train them than the renowned Elondrian Lancers?"

The man wiped his mouth and stood a little straighter. "Right you are, sir."

I wanted to laugh at the ridiculousness of the conversation, considering how un-lancer-like the man was acting. "Can you point me to where the recruits were last seen?"

"I believe they was heading for the armory." He looked at the other two men standing duty on his left, and they both nodded.

"Thank you. As you were," I said, offering a quick salute. The three men came to attention but relaxed as soon as Shade and I left the gate. The armory was on the right side of the garrison, so that's where we went. I remembered my first time to the armory, how nervous and yet excited I had been. Stumpy helped me find my first set of weapons.

I hopped down, tossed Shade's reins over the rail, and walked inside. I found Huckly pairing the boys with new shields. I stood to the side quietly and watched as he made sure the shields fit each boy's frame, waiting as they tested the feel and weight to determine which size was a good fit. Some of the boys were too weak to lift the bulkier ones, but given time, they would grow into them.

One of the boys spotted me by the door and froze. I heard the words "Death's Shadow" faintly escape his lips, and soon all the boys were moving back against the wall. I hated that my presence caused this much of a disturbance, but there wasn't much that could be done about it except to attempt to extend them the courtesy of being treated like any other lancer.

Huckly turned to see what they were looking at. Spotting me, he walked over.

"I see you've got them already choosing their weapons," I said. "How was their first night in the barracks?"

"Quiet, it seems. The guard on duty said he didn't hear a peep from either room."

I smiled. "So, no attempted prison breaks, then?"

He chuckled. "No. They've been surprisingly cooperative through it all." He turned and looked at the boys. "Given time, I think we might make some fine lancers out of them."

"I have no doubt." I walked him back to where the boys were still huddled on the other side, looking at their newly chosen shields. They kept one eye on the shields and one on me. "The streets can toughen you up in ways your average lancer might not have experienced," I said to Huckly. "A good place to start if they are willing to listen."

I looked at the boys. "I'll be heading for the front tomorrow. I hope that when I return, I will hear nothing but glowing reviews from your instructors. Let them see how tough we street rats really are." I smiled, hoping to ease a little of the tension, then headed back to the door, Huckly following just behind.

"I'm going to the barracks to pack my things. I shouldn't be back this way until whatever conflict with Cylmar is put to rest." I held out my hand and we shook. "Look after them for me," I said, glancing over the lieutenant's shoulder at the boys.

Huckly smiled. "I think I can handle that."

I nodded, then left them to their work. Collecting Shade, we headed back across the yard for Barracks Two, and from there I headed to Room Eleven, where I spent the better part of the next hour packing. I wasn't quite sure what all I would need, so I brought everything, which consisted mostly of undergarments and clothing to swap out through the week, or weeks, that I would be at the border. No telling how long this campaign might go for if it got started.

Once I had all of my belongings stowed inside Shade's saddlebags, I headed over to the palace to pay Dakaran a visit, and to see if the queen would be available to see me between fifth and sixth bell.

Yorig greeted me at the bridge, and we talked for a while before I crossed over. I got to tell him about my reunion with my old shipmates and the possibility of bringing them by the palace this evening for a brief tour. Yorig said he wouldn't be on watch at the time, but he wished me luck, knowing I was soon on my way to the front.

I headed over the bridge and left Shade at the stables with Bozz. "Go ahead and stable him for now," I told the head ostler. "I don't know how long I'll be, and I'm sure Shade could use some food and water."

"Shade, huh?" He looked up at the large stallion and pursed his lips. "I can see it." He led the horse inside without so much as a snort from Shade, and I headed around to the palace's front entrance. Inside the foyer, I headed across the checkered floor and up the grand staircase.

"I would have thought you'd leave with the rest of the garrison."

I looked up to find the same lieutenant I had fought alongside against the White Tower's guards walking down the stairs from the second floor. We stopped about halfway.

"I had other responsibilities here that needed seeing to before I left," I said. "But I have a ship getting ready to set sail as we speak."

"I'm sure your men will be happy to see you back."

I nodded, somewhat surprised. It was a rather gracious comment, and from one of the palace guards, no less. I turned and briefly looked back toward the front doors. "How often do we accept visits from the White Tower?"

The lieutenant huffed. "Thankfully, not very often. Their attitude gets worse by the year. They think they're the ones in charge instead of the other way around. I've never had a tussle with them, though. Don't like seeing that happen right here at the palace, and so close to the king."

"Sorry about that, but I wasn't about to hand over my weapons to anyone."

"You were right not to."

"You remember the black-robed person fighting with them?"

"The one you killed?" The lieutenant nodded. "Was he even carrying a sword? I don't remember seeing one."

"I think he might have been carrying something a little more dangerous."

"What do you mean?"

"I think he had magic."

The lieutenant laughed. "I highly doubt that. The Tower hunts wielders; it doesn't hire them."

I shrugged. I couldn't exactly tell him what I'd seen without possibly revealing my own small abilities, so I left it at that.

"If you don't mind me asking," the lieutenant said, "how does an Upakan end up here at the palace, training the king's son? Did His Majesty hire you to come down here? You're the first Upakan I've ever seen, so I'm not exactly sure how that all works."

"Afraid that's a bit of a long story, but I was here in the city quite a while before my first encounter with the king." The lieutenant must not have been posted to the palace until after my confrontation with the palace guards in the king's study. Most of those on staff at the time knew of that situation.

"I've never seen anyone as skilled with the blade. Do you . . ." He paused, clearly trying to decide whether to finish his thought. "Do you train anyone outside the lancers? If so, I wouldn't mind getting a few lessons myself." He held out his hand. "Lieutenant Mattick."

"Ayrion," I said as I shook his hand. "I'm afraid that my commission is solely to the crown prince and the Black Guild, which is strictly a lancer unit." I shrugged. "Perhaps there will come a time when the doors could be open to others, but for now, I don't really have the authority to allow anyone outside the lancers in."

Mattick stared at me a moment and then nodded. "If you do decide to take on some additional trainees, I hope you will consider me."

I smiled. "You'll be the first person I talk to."

"Thank you." Mattick saluted and continued down the stairs.

I watched him make it to the bottom and start across the marble tiles before I continued up the stairs myself. If nothing else came out of our fight with the Black Watch, as Senator Gerrick had called them, at least those of the palace guards who'd fought alongside me now realized the value of what the Black Guild was offering. I hoped word would spread among the guard. Perhaps now we wouldn't see such open condescension in the future.

I left the lobby and continued to climb, making my way up to the royal floor, which held not only the royal chambers but the king's personal study, as well as rooms designated for official meetings and private entertaining. I passed the king's study, his guards faithfully standing before the empty office with halberds in hand. Their eyes followed me down the hall as I headed for the final corridor on the right, just before reaching the king and queen's personal chambers.

I found another set of guards stationed at Dakaran's room. Normally, he demanded they be kept at the end of the hall and not in front of his door, but apparently, either the king or queen, or both, were determined not to give him the chance to sneak out again.

"I'm here to see the prince," I said, not recognizing either of the two men on duty today. "Is he still in bed?" It was only midmorning, so it was safe to assume he was.

"He's in the bath," one of the guards said, then opened the door. Apparently, they knew who I was and didn't feel the need to ask the queen's permission.

I started in, then turned. "Have you seen Her Majesty yet this morning?"

They both shook their heads, so I continued in, and they shut the door behind me. The guards remained outside. I had a feeling Dakaran had ordered them not to enter. I knew how much of a bother it was to him to have them lurking about. I heard some croaking come from the washroom ahead. It sounded like someone attempting to sing, but I couldn't be sure.

I knocked on the door.

"Go away! I told you already, I don't need anyone's help getting in and out of my own bath!"

I chuckled. "It's me."

"Ayrion?"

"You dressed?"

"No. I'm in the tub, you imbecile! Why am I shouting through the door? Get in here."

I opened the door and was met with a face full of steam. I quickly shut the door behind me to keep it from escaping. The room smelled of mint.

"What are you doing here? Why aren't you with my father?"

I could barely make Dakaran out at the center of his inground tub, which was quite full of bubbles.

"I came by to see how you were doing before I left. I had to stay behind a day or two to deal with street-tribe business, remember?" I thought I'd mentioned it to him during one of my earlier visits, but perhaps I hadn't. Or perhaps he'd forgotten. I looked around the side of the bath, happy to see there were no chalices of wine lying about.

"Are you referring to the injured kids they brought in while I was there?"

I nodded. "The other tribe, Avalanche, has been threatening war, and it seems things were escalating, so I dealt with the problem before it got completely out of hand." I didn't go into any specifics. "I've also had a couple of meetings with your mother concerning the orphanage in town. We are raising funds to open a second."

Dakaran yawned. "That's good. Anything else interesting happening out there?"

"And by 'out there,' are you referring to the palace or outside your bedchambers? Have you even left these rooms yet? You need to be up and walking to recover your strength."

Dakaran frowned. "The physickers tried to order me to walk the hall." He shook his head. "Can you imagine that? Ordering me?"

"I'm sure they only want what's best for you. Personally, if I were them, I wouldn't have given you the choice. I'd drag you out of your bed and parade you up and down the corridor in your undergarments if I had to."

He frowned. "You probably would."

"And to answer your question," I said, "yes, there has been a recent development."

"Oh?" The prince looked elated by the news, which I guess is what happens when you spend too much time inside.

I went on to tell him of my meeting with my former shipmates and of their willingness to transport me to the Cylmaran border. "I'm hoping to bring them by later this afternoon and show them the palace, and if your mother allows, to introduce them to her."

Dakaran huffed, splashing the top of the water with his palm. "At least one of us is having some fun."

"Fun? What part of rescuing you in the middle of the night—without sleep, I might add—and saving my former street tribe—again, without sleep—and meeting with the aristocracy to convince them to open a second orphanage, while battling the White Tower's guards, and now preparing to go to war . . . sounds fun?" I shook my head. "Sometimes I really wonder about you."

Dakaran hmphed. "Better than being cooped up in your bedchambers for a week."

I threw my hands in the air. "So get out and walk the grounds. You have the grandest estate in all of Aldor, and you're complaining of being bored? I ought to dunk you until you recant your idiocy."

Dakaran looked up at me and smiled. "I'd like to see you try." He lowered his hands in the water as though getting ready to splash me.

"Maybe later." The last thing I needed was to get wet. "Have you seen your mother this morning?"

Dakaran shook his head. "Have you tried the library?"

"It was going to be my next stop."

"Why do you want to see her?"

"I was hoping to have a word with her before I left for the front, and to perhaps set up a time this evening to introduce her to my former shipmates."

"So, you don't plan on introducing me?"

I crossed my arms. "That would require you leaving your room."

"I thought maybe you could bring them up here."

"Well, you thought wrong."

The prince pouted a moment. "How soon before you leave?"

"Tonight, if we can get the ship ready."

"That soon?" Dakaran sighed. "I guess I'll be sad to see you go."

"Thanks, I think."

"Just don't go getting yourself killed or anything. Who else am I going to have to talk to around here?"

I smiled. "I'll do my best." We stared at each other a moment, but after the silence began to feel uncomfortable, I took a step back. "Well, I better be going. Lots to do before I go. I just wanted to come say goodbye in case I didn't see you before I left."

Dakaran nodded. "Take care of yourself."

"You, too."

With nothing else to say, I left him to his bath and went in search of the queen.

AVALANCHE

Chapter 36

ER MAJESTY'S BEEN IN THERE for the last hour," Leara said as she led me up to the library's second-floor reading rooms. "Asked for tomes on the history of the White Tower. I don't blame her after that incident on the palace steps. Did you hear about it? There was a battle fought right here at the palace between the Black Watch and the palace guards. I heard the palace guards would have killed them all if the king hadn't gotten involved. Heard the guards were led by . . ." She turned and looked at me, face paling. ". . . by a man in black."

"Yes," I said with a half-smile. "I was there."

She stopped before we reached the queen's reading room. A pair of guards stood at the door.

"What was the archchancellor like? I've never actually seen him before. They say he wears a mitre."

"Depends on what a mitre is."

She stuck her hand above her head. "It's a tall hat."

"I see. Then, yes, he has a mitre. But other than that, he looked like any other old man, apart from his rather lavish robes. Clearly, they take their formal wear very seriously at the Tower."

She chuckled, then pointed me toward the queen's door. "Should I announce you?"

"I think I can manage from here."

"I still think you would make a splendid archivist," she said with a wink, then left me to my meeting and headed back down to the front desk.

I nodded to the guards and knocked.

"Yes?"

"It's Ayrion, Your Majesty."

"Come in."

I opened the door and stepped in, then bowed. "I beg your pardon, Your Majesty, but I hoped to ask you for a couple of small favors." I felt almost guilty asking for anything after she'd done so much for Master Fentin and Mistress Orilla.

The queen placed her book down beside her on the sofa and turned. "No need to be so formal, Ayrion. I see you almost as much as I see my own son nowadays. What sort of favor is it you wish?"

Leaving the door open so I wouldn't worry the guards, I walked across the room and stopped in front of her sofa. "I was having a difficult time yesterday, trying to find passage to the border."

She straightened, a concerned look on her face. "We can't have that. I'm sure I can find you a vessel willing to take you, if that is what you need."

"Actually, that's why I'm here. I did find a ship and crew."

"Oh. Well, that's good." She looked confused.

"Strangely enough, the ship I found is the very one I sailed with years ago, shortly after leaving the Lost City to come to Aramoor. The captain and his crew were like a surrogate family to me, and I hadn't seen them since we parted ways seven years ago."

Her face brightened. "That's wonderful news. And you believe they will be willing to take you to the front?"

"They have said they would, even going so far as to cancel their shore leave to take me, but . . . but I was hoping there might be a way to re-imburse them for the added journey and supplies. Is there any chance the crown might be willing to compensate them for their effort? The *Wind Binder* is one of the fastest ships on the water and should be able to get me to the front not too long after the king."

The queen stood. "If it will get you to my husband, then, yes, I will see they are compensated for their time."

I smiled, feeling one burden lifted. "Thank you, Your Majesty. This was completely my idea, not theirs. I have no doubt they would have gladly borne the loss of income just for me."

"They sound like very good friends, indeed."

"Yes." I cleared my throat. "Which brings me to my second request. I was hoping to give them a small tour of the palace later this afternoon around fifth bell, but I would really like for you to meet them if Your Majesty isn't too busy."

She smiled. "It would be my pleasure. Would they care to dine here this evening?"

My breath caught in my throat. "I, uh . . ." I was at a loss for words, certainly not expecting that. "We would be honored, Your Majesty. Are you sure?"

"Unequivocally. I hate dining alone, and with the king gone and my son holed up in his bedchambers, I will be glad of the company."

"I must warn you, they are rivermen, Your Majesty, and don't exactly possess the most proper of table manners." I was imagining Treygan pulling out his bone knife and picking his nails in front of her. The crew eating with the queen could be a very bad idea.

"Wonderful," she said. "It will be nice to dine with some guests who don't have ulterior motives." She sighed. "The nobles can grow quite tiresome."

The queen's forwardness surprised me. "Your Majesty is most kind," I stammered, not knowing what else to say.

She walked over and laid a hand on my shoulder. "Ayrion, what did I just tell you about being so formal?"

"Yes, Your Majesty. I mean, no, Your Majesty."

She laughed. "I'll have some traveling compensation for you this evening when we dine. For now, you'd better leave me to my research. It seems you have quite a bit to get done before you set sail." She walked back to her seat. "Dinner will be at six sharp."

"Yes, Your Majesty." I bowed and quickly left the room, shutting the door behind me. I walked over to the balcony rail and stared out across the stacks for a moment as I let it all sink in. Not only was I going to be able to get Treygan and Ismara some repayment for their generosity, but they were being invited to dine with the queen. Even I had never had that privilege. I couldn't wait to see the look on my shipmates' faces when I told them.

Leaving the palace, I grabbed Shade from the stables and headed for the port to see how things were progressing. I needed to store my belongings, and I had forgotten to tell Treygan I was bringing Shade. I had no intention of leaving the horse behind.

The docks were every bit as busy this morning as they had been yesterday, though it didn't look like there had been all that great of an influx of new ships making berth. I wondered how the two crewmen had handled their overnight watch. Hopefully, despite Bones's sour warning, they hadn't sunk the ship.

I breathed a small sigh of relief when I passed the main office and caught my first sight of the *Wind Binder* ahead. She was still there and in one piece.

"Where's your gear?" someone behind me asked.

I turned to find Ismara walking up the boardwalk in my direction. She must have just come from the office. "I've got it all right here," I said, patting one of Shade's saddlebags beside me as we both stopped for her to catch up.

"Traveling kind of light, aren't you?"

I looked at the two stuffed bags and shrugged. "Everything I own is in there, just about."

"Except the horse," she said, staring up at Shade.

"True." I looked up at the stallion as well and smiled. "Which reminds me. I wanted to talk with you and your father about bringing Shade with me when we go to the front."

"That might prove difficult." She looked from the horse to the ship and pursed her lips. "Not a lot of room on the main deck for a horse his size. I guess we could set up a shade sail as a temporary awning to keep off the sun and the rain."

"A *shade* sail?" I tried not to chuckle.

"Yeah, very funny." She looked up at the horse and then at me. "You know this will mean having to purchase more supplies, right?" She looked down at the pad of paper in her hands and cleared her throat.

"What is it?"

"This is starting to add up. You haven't by chance spoken with the queen yet, have you?"

I smiled. "I don't think you'll need to worry about the extra costs."

"You don't think, or you know?"

"I know."

"Good," she said, the concern lifting from her face. "I'll send one of the men in with a cart to grab what we will need for your horse." She turned, and we continued up the walk toward the ship.

Over half the crew was gone, Pops and Needle being the only two of those I knew still aboard. Needle was busy studying charts in the captains' quarters, while Pops rested his leg in his hammock below deck. I left Shade on the pier and went below to see how the old man was doing. The *Wind Binder* was the only ship docked on our wharf, so I wasn't worried about anyone walking by and snatching the horse, not that Shade would have let them.

Crossing the deck, I stepped into the galley, which was empty. Kettle was likely in town purchasing supplies for the journey. I headed down the stairs into the hold, where I found Pops near the back of the crew's quarters on the left. His eyes were shut, but he wasn't snoring, so I knew he was still awake.

"Asleep on duty, I see."

"Just resting these old bones," he said. His eyes opened as he turned his head to look at me. He tried lifting himself into a sitting position, so I plopped down on the side of the hammock next to his.

"It's been a long time since I've been in one of these," I said. I took a moment to swing back and forth a couple of times, enjoying the motion. I glanced at the surrounding hammocks. "I almost miss it, you know? The gentle sway of the ship as we float down river. Easy to fall asleep. Got a feeling it might be a different story once we hit the open water of the Rhunarin, though."

"Aye, that it will be. We hit a squall, and the ship be rocking for sure. Seen hardened sailors lose their guts during some of those storms."

I grimaced at the thought, remembering what it had been like my first days aboard. "Hopefully we won't have to find out."

He scratched at his white beard and looked up at the rafters. "So, how's it looking up top? Will we be setting sail tonight or on the morning tide?"

"Not sure. I just got here myself. I hope the captain, or *captains*, I guess I should say, will have us shipshape by this evening. I'm planning on taking the crew over to see the palace around fifth bell. Do you think you'll be able to manage that?"

Pops pulled out the bottle from his coat that Reevie had given him from the Sandstorm infirmary. "Just so long as I have some of this swill still left, I'll be right as rain." He smiled. "Don't you worry your young head none over this old cuss. Been through worse, I promise you that."

"I don't doubt it," I said, patting the old man's good leg as I stood. "I'll see if Ismara needs any help up top. The sooner we get stocked, the sooner we can head into town."

Pops nodded, then slunk back down into his hammock and closed his eyes.

I left him to his rest and headed up to the main deck, where I found Ismara directing several of the crew newly back from town. Kettle was one of them, so I figured it must be food stores.

"Need a hand?" I asked, moving to the side of the plank to give those carrying goods plenty of room to make it on board.

"Need five or six," Kettle grumbled, his arms full.

They had wheeled a small wagon down, which was sitting on the boardwalk at the head of the pier. With the help of a few of the crew, we managed to get it unloaded and into the galley for Kettle to begin sorting and storing.

I carried an armload into the galley myself and plopped it down on one of the tables. "How's it going in town?" I asked the gruff cook.

"Finding what you need?"

Kettle grumbled as he sifted through the supplies. "We're finding it, but it ain't easy. Seems the recent sailing of your lancers emptied out most of the shops here at port. The captain's having to look farther in."

I frowned. "I was afraid of that."

Most of the common goods needed aboard ship could be found in the shops surrounding the city's port, but they hadn't exactly been prepared for that many ships setting sail at once, especially ships full of hungry lancers. That was a lot of mouths to feed, and on top of that, the ship would need to carry as much provender as possible to help keep the men fed until further supplies arrived.

"Most of what's left has been bought out and put on hold," Kettle said. "They plan on sending regular shipments to the front."

I smiled. "Got to keep us fighting men from starving."

Kettle stroked his long mustache. "Better you than me."

The rest of the afternoon went about the same, crewmen showing up with wagons and carts and buggies for us to unload. Most of the goods went belowdecks, where they were roped off to keep from tipping and rolling around the hold. Treygan appeared once or twice just to see how things were progressing, but he would just as quickly disappear again. His job was to meet with the merchants and bargain for the best price, then send word to have another cart or buggy brought around to pick up what he'd purchased.

Surprisingly, things went fairly smoothly. It helped to be able to tell the shops that the supplies were heading to the front. The merchants were much more willing to part with the goods when they realized it was in the care of those heading after the king.

"How are we looking?" I asked Ismara, who was just coming up from belowdecks. She had a pad in one hand and stylus in the other as she oversaw the incoming stores, making record of what had been purchased against the checklists of what was still needed. The thick waves of her dark amber hair blew gently in the breeze as she stepped out on the main deck, where I was waiting for something to do.

"I'd say we are looking near ready to sail," she said, holding the pad up to shade her eyes as they readjusted. The sun was beginning to lean toward the peaks behind us, and fourth bell had just echoed across the bay, leaving us less than an hour to finish preparations.

I smiled. "That's good to hear. What's left?" I looked around for Treygan, but it didn't seem he'd returned yet.

She looked down at her list and scanned the sheets, then up at me and frowned. "Gold to pay for it all."

I chuckled. "I'll make sure you get it before we leave."

"Be nice to have gotten it before we had to spend our own reserves. If something happens, it'll set us back."

"One way or the other, I promise you'll get reimbursed. Where's your father?"

"I think he's talking with the harbormaster about our departure. Shouldn't be long. He's been pushing the crew hard to get this done by fifth bell." She smiled. "He seems quite anxious to see the palace. Can't say I'm not curious myself."

We moved across the main deck and out of the way of several of the crew who were busy building Shade's canvas shelter off the port side of the galley cabin. There wasn't exactly a lot of room, but it was enough that Shade would be able to keep the direct sun off his back when he needed it.

"Were they able to find feed?" I asked.

She looked down at her pad for a moment, scanning the last couple pages. "Yes. Brought that on two loads ago."

I didn't remember seeing it, but I didn't want to question her either.

I could always take a stroll belowdecks to double-check for myself. A hungry rumble through my link with Shade said that he wanted me to make sure.

"Looks like we'll be ready by fifth bell," she said, then headed up to the quarterdeck to talk with Needle and Bones, who were standing at the wheel discussing something I couldn't quite make out. I still found it strange seeing the large navigational piece there in place of the tiller, but it seemed to give the ship a more modern appearance.

"I think we're just about ready for that horse of yours," someone behind me said.

I turned to find one of the newer crewmen standing in front of the shade-sail awning they had just finished attaching. They had cut a bale of hay and strewn it underneath for Shade to lie on.

"Should I bring him aboard?"

"Be good for us to see how he fits, see if we need to be making any alterations."

I nodded and walked over to the starboard side of the ship and looked down at Shade, who was standing on the pier below, drinking from his pail. "We're ready."

Shade looked up, water dripping from his lips. I could feel hesitation through our link. He didn't seem all that excited by the prospect of coming aboard.

"You're going to have to do it sometime," I said. "I'll add some grain for your supper tonight."

Shade's ears perked up, and he started for the plankway.

"That's one smart horse," the crewman said as he and the others moved back to give the giant stallion room.

Shade carefully made his way up the plank, seemingly testing its sturdiness with each placement of his hooves. Once on board, I directed him across the deck to the makeshift awning and had him walk underneath. It appeared to be large enough, and he was quick to begin eating his bedding. He snorted at me, and I nodded.

"Fine. I'm a man of my word." I looked at the crewmen standing behind me. "Anyone know where the feed is being stored below?"

One of the men raised his hand. "I can show you."

With that, we headed into the hold and didn't return until I had a pail of grain for Shade to enjoy. Finding the supply of hay and grain below had set my mind at ease about whether we'd be able to keep Shade fed during our journey. I'd even found a bushel or two of apples and brought one up as a treat for him.

By the time I'd made it back to the main deck, Treygan had reappeared. He was standing just in front of the captain's cabin alongside Ismara, both scanning her checklist. He looked up and waved me over.

"And you're sure the queen will be willing to reimburse us for the extra supplies?" Treygan asked.

"That's what she told me this morning, and I've never known her not to keep her word."

He relaxed as he pulled his captain's hat off and wiped his forehead with his sleeve. "Just wanted to hear it from the horse's mouth, so to speak." He looked over at Shade. "No offense."

Shade didn't pay him any mind, too focused on his grain.

"Looks as though we might be ready to sail this evening," Treygan said, scanning the deck of the ship, "if you're of a mind, that is. Can't say I like setting sail at night, but it should get you there faster."

I nodded. "I appreciate it. And to show my appreciation. I have a surprise for everyone this evening."

"Surprise?"

"What kind of surprise?" Ismara asked.

I grinned, unable to hold it back any longer. I couldn't wait to see the look on their faces. "You have been offered something few in Aramoor have ever been given, including some of the nobility."

"Well, sink me," Treygan said eagerly. "Spit it out, lad. What is it?"

My hands were practically shaking with excitement, and a grin split my face. "The queen has invited you to dine with her this evening."

Both Treygan and Ismara froze, their faces nothing more than a blank stare.

I almost laughed. The wait had absolutely been worth it.

Treygan didn't so much as blink an eye before turning around and shouting for the crew to assemble. He waited until everyone was on deck before continuing. "I've just been informed that we've been invited to dine with the queen this evening."

Silence fell across the main deck. A moment later, the entire crew erupted in laughter.

It wasn't exactly the reaction I'd been expecting.

However, when they saw Treygan wasn't laughing, the gaiety died out.

"You're having us on," Kettle said.

"No," Treygan countered as he scanned the men's faces. "And I have no intention of sullying this ship's reputation with the likes of you stinking up the queen's dining hall. Get to the washrooms, the lot of you! And don't come out until you've soaped and scrubbed every inch of yourselves. And make sure you find a set of clothes that won't embarrass me to be seen with you."

No one moved, still unsure as to whether he was joking or not.

"What are you waiting for?" he shouted. "Last ones to make it back will skip going tonight and stand watch instead!"

That did it.

The entire crew sped across deck for the galley door, nearly tearing

its hinges off in the process.

I leaned over to Treygan, trying my best not to laugh. "With a threat like that, they're likely to be jumping in the wash tubs on top of each other." I felt sorry for the attendants at the port washhouse as the stampede of rivermen tore out of the galley cabin, ran across the deck, down the gangplank, and up the dock for the boardwalk. I couldn't hold it back any longer and burst into laughter.

When I didn't get a response, I turned and realized neither Treygan nor Ismara were there. When had they left? I shook my head. This was going to be quite the experience.

I hoped the queen was ready for it.

AVALANCHE

Chapter 37

A DOZEN HALF-NAKED RIVERMEN racing up the board-walk from the washhouse was quite the sight. Water dripped from hair and beards as they fumbled to get into their change of clothes and still keep up with the others.

No one wanted to be last aboard.

Treygan and Ismara were the first back, as the captains' cabin had its own washtub. They laughed as they watched the men clambering down the pier. I thought a couple of them were going to end up in the drink as they raced up the gangway for the ship. Kettle was one of those near the end of the pack, threatening everyone in front of him that if they didn't let him on before them, he'd make them regret it during their next meal.

Pops, because of his injury, had been afforded the opportunity to use the captains' washtub. He still hadn't made it out by the time the crew had assembled, but I had a hard time believing Treygan would force the old riverman to stand watch with his leg.

"Well," Kettle called out, pushing his way to the front. He was completely out of breath as he struggled to pull his shirt over his still wet chest. "Who's stayin' and who's goin'?"

Treygan straightened his hat over his half-dried hair. "None of you, and all of you."

The men exchanged confused looks as they struggled to finish dressing.

Treygan let the confusion simmer for a moment, still trying to compose himself from watching his crew race across the port. "I figured that with us already skipping shore leave, it would be too cruel to force any of you to stay behind for something like this. So, I hired a watch from the port for tonight."

The men cheered, and I leaned toward Treygan. "You'd been planning this all along?"

The captain smiled. "Ever since you invited us to see the palace."

"Then what was all that 'last one back stands watch' stuff about?" I asked, pointing to the men, who were busy chatting excitedly amongst themselves.

He shrugged. "I didn't want to show up late."

Behind us, the captains' cabin door opened, and Pops hobbled out with his crutch. He looked at the men and then at the captains. "What did I miss?"

Everyone laughed.

"Everyone get below and stow your gear," Ismara barked. "And while you're at it, you might want to trim up some of that scrub around your faces and run a hand or two through those mops you call hair. We want to do more than just smell nice when we meet the queen. One look at you lot and she's likely to lose her appetite."

The men nodded and, after being dismissed, rushed down into the hold. When they returned, they looked like a whole new crew: beards trimmed and shaped, mustaches curled, hair brushed, some even neatly tied in back. They looked almost presentable, which for them was saying a lot.

"Now that's a handsome group of men," Ismara said proudly, causing a few to blush.

A single nod from Treygan to the starboard side of the ship and everyone scuttled for the ramp.

I was the last off, taking a moment to walk over and rub Shade's neck. "Be good. You should have enough food and water for now." I had considered riding him over, except his saddle had already been stowed, and I thought it best not to force him over the gangplank more than absolutely necessary. "I'll see you later."

Shade whinnied softly, and I left him to his supper and chased after the rest of the crew, passing a couple of the night watchmen heading toward the ship. Must be from the group Treygan had hired from the harbormaster office.

The fifth bell tolled about the time we rounded the final warehouse and found Gittrick and his boys waiting with the carriages. They were once again dressed in their finest livery, looking more than a little eager to be off, especially considering I'd extended them my offer for a tour of the palace with the rest of the crew.

Everyone loaded up, mostly keeping to the same arrangement we'd used on our way to Sandstorm the previous day. With the addition of Birg and Ornan, a couple of the men in the open carriage had to sit up with the driver.

Before I climbed into the coach, I walked around to speak with Gittrick. "There's been a slight change of plans."

Gittrick's smile faded. "Me and my boys won't be going in?"

"No, you're still going, but after the tour, we have all been invited to dine with the queen."

Gittrick gaped. "I . . . I don't know what to say," he said, tipping his hat. "Thank you, Master Ayrion."

"Let's get a move on, shall we?" I said, climbing into the back. "Don't want to keep the queen waiting."

"No, sir!" Gittrick lifted the reins and shouted, "Giddup there!"

The coach lurched ahead before I'd managed to even get the door shut, and I was thrown forward, almost landing in Ismara's lap.

"This seat's taken," she said with a wink as I stopped my fall only a few inches from her face.

"Sorry." I felt my face flush as I pushed myself back to the other side and sat down directly across from her.

Now that we were actually on our way, it dawned on me how excited I was for everyone to see the palace. I was nervously fidgeting in my seat by the time we crossed onto King's Way West from Bay Street and stopped in front of the palace bridge. A few words to one of the watch and we were heading across.

I had Gittrick stop halfway, and everyone filed out and over to the right wall to have a look at the tail end of the Shemoa River below. Gittrick and his boys joined us.

Needle whistled. "That be quite the fall."

"Looks much higher from up here," Bones said, cautiously staring over from a step or two back.

"It is an incredible view," Treygan said from the other side of the bridge, which looked out over the bay.

The others headed across to the captain's side to see for themselves.

"I wonder how safe this thing is to be walkin' on?" Kettle commented, causing several of the crew to step back from the edge.

"Been here for thousands of years," I said, "so I'm guessing pretty safe."

"Or just very old," Pops added, getting a boost from Whitey to look over the crenelated top.

I walked back to the coach. "We better get a move on if we want to see any of the palace before we dine."

"Aye aye," Treygan said. "Back aboard."

The crew clambered back into the carriages, and we started up once more.

"Where does that go?" Ismara asked as we passed through the watch towers on the other side of the bridge. She was pointing off down the cobbled road to the right.

"That leads to the royal stables, and beyond that to the gardens."

"Gardens? I bet those are something to see."

"You wouldn't be wrong," I said. I directed Gittrick to take us through the tunnel into the front courtyard. We circled the fountain and pulled to a stop at the edge of the steps leading up to the front entrance.

Everyone disembarked and waited at the foot of the stairs. Several of the crew loosed soft whistles as they stared anxiously up at the rising towers.

"I knew it was big," Treygan said, "but it's even bigger than I thought."

"What about us, Master Ayrion?" Gittrick asked nervously from his seat atop the coach.

"Just follow the attendants around to the side," I said, pointing to the right of the fountain. "You can leave the carriages there. They shouldn't be in the way."

He nodded, and then he and his boys directed the two transports over to the right and left them parked. I didn't think we would be gone long enough to require us taking them down to the stables to be completely unhitched.

Once Gittrick and his boys had joined the *Wind Binder* crew, I turned. "This way," I said, and started up the white stone steps leading to the enormous double doors at the top.

I could hear whispered conversations behind me, covering anything from the string of palace guards waiting at the top to the size of the fountain to the massive stone sentinels standing to either side of the front entrance.

I grinned, eagerly anticipating their reaction when the doors opened and they caught their first glimpse of the palace interior.

We reached the top landing and found a chamberlain waiting at attention. He was decked in the usual crimson and gold of his station, and it was clear by the way he was looking at us that he had been sent with a message.

My heart sank. *Please don't let this be what I think it is.* I sighed inwardly. This was just my luck. The queen was probably indisposed with a meeting and had to cancel our dinner. I had really been looking forward to introducing my friends to Her Majesty and showing them my station here in Aramoor, but I had a feeling it was all about to fall flat.

As soon as the last of the crew had reached the top, the chamberlain stepped forward.

"I've been sent by the queen," he said, and my gut turned, "to officially welcome you to the royal palace."

I breathed a small sigh of relief, though he hadn't yet said whether we would still be dining with Her Majesty.

"The queen has asked me to offer you a royal tour before dinner."

Oh, thank goodness. My heart lifted. She wasn't turning us down after all.

The chamberlain turned and clapped his hands, and four of the guards pushed open the great doors.

The sun was setting behind us, and the courtyard was cast in shadow from the palace walls, so when the doors began to split, light from inside spilled out across the entire group.

There were gasps. There were oohs and ahhs. There were even a few colorful words, which had me rolling my eyes in embarrassment as everyone behind me got their first look at the grand foyer. The chamberlain and I started in, but no one behind us moved. I turned to find everyone standing in place, mouths agape. They looked nearly petrified at the thought of going in.

The chamberlain turned when he realized no one was following him.

I cleared my throat. "We didn't just ride all the way over here to look at the front doors. Let's go. We don't want to keep the queen waiting."

The mention of the queen seemed to put a burr under them, and Treygan waved everyone forward through the massive doors and onto the checkered marble tiles. Whitey even pulled off his wide-brimmed hat in reverence, though as soon as he made it over the threshold, he quickly plopped it back on.

"Blimey," I heard Kettle say, and turned. He was staring down at his reflection in the polished floor. "If I'd known it was like this, I might've used a bit more soap."

Several of the others grunted in agreement.

All I could do was shake my head.

It took me a while to coax them in far enough to shut the doors, and when they did finally close, the crew merely stood there in awe, staring at all the gold-inlay décor.

I couldn't help but grin as I watched their expressions broaden the longer they stood there.

"This is the grand foyer," the chamberlain said, then turned and pointed to either side of the doors behind them, "And those are the likenesses of High King Torrin and High Queen Rhoslyn, the first king and queen of the Five Kingdoms."

Well, that's something, I thought. I'd been walking past those portraits for years and never once thought to ask who they were. There were so many portraits throughout the palace that I hadn't bothered.

"The grand foyer here was one of the last portions added to the royal palace nearly four hundred years ago," the chamberlain said. Clearly, the man was well versed in giving palace tours and had his spiel down to an art. "The original palace started as a much smaller construct, back closer to the mountainside, and over the centuries has progressively spread."

After a short circling of the foyer and a more elaborate detailing of the grand staircase, including how many steps in total and how much weight in gold it took to cover the railings alone, the chamberlain took us to the Hall of Kings, where every former king and queen had had their likeness taken and the portraits mounted in continued fashion down the extended corridor. Thankfully, he didn't go to the hassle of naming them all.

He then took us to see a few of the estate rooms, where the formal senate held its meetings, followed by a tour of the kitchens, which had Kettle drooling all over himself. Two of the last big stops were the library—which held everyone quite speechless as they stared at all the floor-to-ceiling shelving lined with books beyond counting—and even a quick look inside the throne room itself.

Every time I saw the grand hall with its green-and-white marble pillars and arched ceiling, I was reminded of my first visit to the palace and getting caught up in the crowd as we were marched in one by one to make our petitions before the king. It was amazing to think of how far I'd come.

I stared across the room to the stairs leading up to the thrones, re-membering how frightened I had been on that first visit. It was my first experience meeting royals, and I'd used it to explain how terrible the kids on the streets had it.

"Dinner will be served shortly," the chamberlain said, drawing me from my reverie and gathering everyone back into the corridor outside the throne room. "We don't want to be late."

We left, and he hurried back across the palace to one of the smaller dining rooms on the kitchen side, which was still large enough to sit twice our number. I could hear soft music coming from inside the room as we approached, reminding me of some of the fancier eateries I'd been to that prided themselves on providing a soothing atmosphere from which to eat.

The chamberlain motioned for the black-uniformed guards waiting outside to open the doors, and the music washed out into the hall. Guards in black uniforms meant only one thing: the queen had already arrived.

Peering inside, I saw that the dining hall stretched out before us, ending on the other side of the room with a twin set of double doors, giving it the appearance of a short but wide corridor. A grand table sat in the center, running nearly the length of the room.

"I was wondering if you were going to show up or not," someone inside called out, and I smiled when I recognized Dakaran's voice.

"My apologies, Your Highness," the chamberlain said as he stepped into the room and bowed toward the left, where Dakaran stood in front of a rather imposing fireplace. "Time got away from us, I'm afraid. We might have taken a little too long with our tour of the library." He bowed once more, and Dakaran waved him out.

As soon as the chamberlain left, I headed in, passing several musicians who were sitting in the corner to the left of the door. Strings and flutes filled the room with a soft, welcoming melody.

Turning, I motioned for the others to follow me in.

Dakaran wasn't exactly the kind of person to make greetings himself, so it was up to me. I offered the prince a small bow, as this was a formal meeting, and those behind me did the same. I then turned to the crew. "I'd like to present His Royal Highness, Dakaran, the Crown Prince of Aldor."

The entire company behind me bowed once more, even more deeply.

"Your Highness, I'd like to introduce you to the crew of the *Wind Binder*." I started with Captains Treygan and Ismara, and then let them introduce the rest of the crew, since I didn't know all their names. Once again, Whitey and the others quickly pulled off their hats, this time leaving them off.

When Treygan had finished, I also introduced our coachman, Gittrick, and let him present his boys, who stood there in quiet shock, much like everyone else.

"It is a pleasure meeting you all," Dakaran said rather formally, and then directed everyone to the table. "Please, if you will join me, I'm sure my mother will be along shortly."

No one moved, so I started forward myself and waved them on. I had thought we would be waiting to take our seats until Her Majesty had arrived, but maybe this meeting wasn't to be that formal, though all the footmen staring at us from around the room said otherwise.

"I'm surprised to see you down here," I said as we walked down the side of the long table to the other end of the room. The table had been fully prepared, but with far too many settings. Our entire group was only enough to cover half, so we kept ourselves to just one end.

"Apparently that soak in the tub this morning did me some good," Dakaran said. "In fact, after you left, I took your advice and even made a couple of strolls around the gardens."

I nodded. "Good to know I'm not just wasting air."

The footmen pulled our chairs out and then pushed them forward as we sat. Several of the crew looked confused and a little startled as the men in black-and-white livery helped them into their seats.

Dakaran and I sat opposite each other near the front, leaving the seat at the head of the table for Her Majesty.

The setting and décor were works of art, and I took a moment to appreciate it. It made Sandstorm's special meal the night before seem almost plain by comparison. Gold-and-white-marble candelabras interspersed with fresh-cut spruce boughs and cinnamon bark ran down the center of the table. The aroma of evergreen and spices already had my mouth watering, even though there wasn't a morsel of food in sight.

Each setting was gold-plated, from the goblets to the most basic of utensils. Even the linens were embroidered with gold and had been exquisitely folded atop each plate. Vases of spring flowers had been placed between the candelabras, and underneath was a deep-blue runner that stretched the full length of the table.

"How's the wound?" I asked Dakaran as the footmen began filling goblets with a richly scented wine and crystal chalices with water. I saw Needle lift his and stare through it at Bones, who smiled and waved from his seat directly across from him.

I shook my head.

"It only hurts when I laugh," Dakaran said.

"Then I guess you've got nothing to worry about."

Treygan, sitting beside me, choked on his wine, which of course caused Dakaran to start laughing.

The prince grabbed his side. "Oh, that hurts." He fought back the urge to continue laughing by reaching for his jewel-encrusted goblet. I groaned as he downed at least a third in one long gulp.

Before I could say anything, the doors on this side of the room opened, and another chamberlain stepped inside to announce the queen's arrival.

Quickly, the footmen helped us scoot our seats back to stand—even Dakaran's—as Queen Ellise made her way into the room. She was the embodiment of elegance. She wore a stunning velvet brocade gown of deep blue and gold with handkerchief sleeves. The entire assembly matched the table's settings. I wondered if it was a coincidence.

I waited along with the rest as the queen glided across the room to the head of the table. As soon as she reached her seat, I bowed. "Your Majesty, may I present the captains and crew of the *Wind Binder*."

Once again, we went through all the formal introductions, including Gittrick and his boys. The queen smiled just as broadly when I presented the coachman and his sons. I was glad she didn't feel I had overstepped my bounds by including them in the invitation.

"Thank you, Ayrion," she said, then looked down the table. "On behalf of myself and the crown prince, we offer you our sincerest felicitations and gladly welcome you to our home. The meal, I promise, will be exquisite. I only hope our conversation can prove as worthy." She smiled. "We royals can be quite the stuffy lot at times."

Treygan was the first to speak, offering a roguish bow, hat in hand. "And if Your Majesty can excuse the humble, and often trying, table manners of myself and my crew, we will do our utmost to keep the conversation as lively as possible and pray we don't embarrass ourselves too greatly in the process."

Say one thing for Treygan, he did have a way with words when he wanted, and could be quite the charmer.

The queen smiled and looked at me. "I like them already." She motioned for the footmen to reseat the group, and as soon as everyone was settled, the head butler clapped his hands, and the doors on this side of the room opened. From the hall, a row of new footmen entered, carrying silver trays with white-and-gold sculptures. Each figure was fashioned into the shape of the royal crown, including even a few colored jewels around the base.

The staff placed the strange pieces on the table between every second seat, giving everyone full access to the artwork. I thought it a strange tradition to have during a meal, but clearly the nobility preferred things differently than the rest of us.

"They are quite stunning, Your Majesty," Treygan said, looking at the carved images. He then looked up. "What exactly are they?"

The queen chuckled. "They are sotiltees."

"Ah." Treygan stared at the piece a little longer before looking back up once more. "And what is that?"

The queen motioned to the footman standing behind her, and he stepped forward and picked up the knife lying on the tray beside the sculpture. Carefully, he cut off one of the crown's tips and handed her the piece, which she promptly stuck in her mouth.

"Sotiltees are sugar sculptures," Dakaran said, looking amused at all the enthralled faces as they began to stare hungrily at the works of art in front of them. "We place them as *warners*." No one seemed to have any idea what he was talking about, so he continued. "They forewarn our guests that the meal is shortly to commence."

"And you can just . . . eat them?" Kettle asked, already reaching for one of the knives.

"Absolutely," the queen said, having finished her piece. "Though, be careful of the spires. They can prove sharp if not chewed properly."

The crew was quick to snatch up the knives on the trays, not waiting for the footmen to do it for them, and began carving the sculptures down to size and stuffing random pieces into their mouths. Pops mostly sucked on his, as he was missing a good deal of his teeth.

The queen didn't bother with any more of the hardened sugar, instead focusing more on conversation as she slowly sipped her wine. "Ayrion tells me you have been sailing the Shemoa for several years," she said to Treygan, who was seated next to Dakaran.

Treygan hooked his hat on the back of his seat, not having any other place but the table to set it. "I've been sailing the rivers since I was a boy, Your Majesty. Traveled from one side of Aldor to the other, seen many a grand sight to be sure, but none so much as the palace here. I've traveled the Ryne River as far north as to catch a glimpse of Mount Ash. I've even sailed the East River all the way to Crystal Lake, and have navigated Virn Run within a day or two's journey of the Angoran Mountains. There's few places the *Wind Binder* hasn't taken me, but I still have a soft spot in my heart for the Shemoa."

The queen nodded. "I hear your ship is said to be one of the fastest on the waters?"

"True enough," he said proudly. "Haven't found the vessel that can beat her yet."

"Before I forget." The queen turned and waved over one of the butlers by the door, who happened to be holding a small tray in one hand with a leather pouch on top. The butler carried it around and held it out to Treygan.

"What's this?" he asked politely, pretending he didn't know.

"It's a small token of my appreciation of your willingness to transport Ayrion to my husband's side. The sooner he is there, the safer I will feel." She leaned forward and patted my hand.

"Thank you, Your Majesty," Treygan said with another bow of his head as he took the pouch from the tray and the butler returned to his place by the doors. "We would have done it without your benevolence, but it is greatly appreciated, nonetheless."

I noticed he didn't look inside the pouch so as not to offend, but judging from the size, it was sure to cover their cost for the upcoming venture.

Ismara, too, nodded her thanks from her seat beside mine. "It is very generous."

Dakaran, for his part, seemed quite preoccupied with the younger captain. The way he stared at her from over his wineglass made me a little uncomfortable.

The queen clapped her hands once more, and the footmen entered, this time carrying off what was left of the sugar statues, to the crew's lament. Needle snapped off one last piece before the footman could haul it away. The sotiltees were quickly replaced with an exquisite selection of foods I couldn't possibly hope to get through. The dishes continued to arrive in timely intervals, and it seemed as soon as one set was placed, the next was arriving.

There were spinach tarts with mushroom sauce and roasted chickpeas with lentils and barley. There were pork and salmon pies, stewed goose, as well as fresh loaves of the finest white bread. They served honey cakes, stewed apples, and ginger-spiced bread. My mouth wouldn't stop watering.

As the footmen brought in the food, they would slowly encircle the table, each with their own separate dishes, allowing those sitting to help themselves. The butlery always started with the royal family and moved left around the table from there, which meant I was always the last to be served, since I was sitting on the opposite side of the queen from Dakaran.

I tried a few dishes I didn't recognize, since I doubted I'd ever get the chance again, and by the time I'd made it about halfway through the selection, the queen was once again clapping for the next course.

I wasn't very fond of the spinach tart and mushroom sauce, but the salmon pie was quite savory. Thankfully, the next course leaned heavily toward meats. There was venison, pork, turkey, and lamb, along with some not-so-common offerings like bear, and even some tastes of the sea like porpoise and whale, along with snails and squid, which I was more than happy to pass on. All in all, it was the most exotic selection of foods I'd ever seen. Even the common meats were flavored above anything I'd had before, including that of the Rose and Crown.

Dakaran took a bite out of a piece of squid and pointed the remainder of the tentacle at me. "I still prefer the lamb and mint sauce at the Fishnet."

The entire *Wind Binder* crew stopped eating and looked up, no doubt stunned that the prince would even know about the Fishnet, let alone eat there. It was located in Southside.

Dakaran looked down the table. "Admit it. That mint sauce is one of a kind."

The crew all nodded, most with food still hanging out of their mouths.

"The sauce is good, I grant you," I said, "perhaps some of the best I've had, but given the choice between it and this." I stared down the table. "Well . . ." I started to chuckle, then lifted another bite of buttered sweet potato to my mouth and stuffed it in greedily.

Treygan smiled. "Aye. I've never seen a spread like this before. Don't even know what half of this is."

This time it was the queen's turn to chuckle.

Dakaran hmphed, glancing at Ismara. "I still prefer the Fishnet."

The queen looked at Ismara as well. "Tell me, my dear, how does it feel to live your life on the water? As beautiful as you are, I would imagine men would be wining and dining you at every port. Do you ever wish to settle down one day, possibly raise a family?"

Ismara blushed and lowered her glass. I noticed Dakaran seemed particularly curious as to her answer, his eyes once again fixated on her.

"I do plan to marry, Your Majesty, one day. I only hope he's a man of the water himself," she said with a slight chuckle, "or we might not be seeing much of each other." She looked over at her father. "I have no intention of leaving the water."

"And I certainly wouldn't want her to," her father said. "She's my good right arm. Couldn't imagine my life without her."

Ismara smiled proudly and continued eating.

"But what if the right offer came along?" Dakaran asked. "Say, from a prince." He smiled over his glass, then suddenly yelped and grabbed his leg, glaring at his mother, who pretended not to notice.

The queen looked at Treygan. "Ayrion mentioned that you have had run-ins with Cylmaran slavers in the past. Have you noticed any such behavior recently?"

"Not in recent years, Your Majesty, thank the Creator. One run-in with them was enough." Treygan took another swallow of his drink and wiped his mouth with his napkin. "I hope I'm not out of place to ask, but with all the talk along the river, and especially here in Aramoor, how certain does this conflict between Elondria and Cylmar look? Will we be seeing war?"

"I'm afraid it is looking rather grave indeed," she said. "I only hope my husband can manage to find a more peaceful solution. No one really wants war, but sadly, sometimes war is inevitable."

The queen ushered in another round of food, and by this time, I was feeling the effects of having gorged a little too much on the last course.

This serving was lighter than the others, consisting of soups and custards. I tried a little of what tasted like some sort of creamy fish chowder, forgoing any of the sweeter dishes. After the soup, we had stuffed pheasant, which was served alongside duck, partridge, and even peacock. Each course was served with a variety of cooked potatoes and vegetables.

I couldn't imagine eating like this every day. I'd never get any work done. I'd be walking around with a constant stomachache.

"What do your markings represent?" the queen asked Bones. "They look similar to those I've seen in my reading on the Blue Isles."

The first mate smiled broadly. "Your Majesty has a keen eye. They are the symbol of my tribe." He began to show her how the way they were placed, and how many, represented various regional tribes and families. He got so excited he started to take his shirt off to show her the rest, but Treygan stopped him before he managed to get it fully unbuttoned.

"It is very fascinating," she said, placing a hand to her mouth to keep from chuckling. Her tone, though, said she actually meant it, which was a credit to her as a leader. She and the king did seem to care about more than themselves.

The conversation once more turned to the *Wind Binder*, and each of the crew chimed in about how they had joined the ship and how proud they were to be serving aboard her. Gittrick and his sons talked about their first coming to Sandstorm and how privileged they were to be in charge of the coach house for such a fine estate. The queen made sure to speak with each of the coachman's boys in turn, so they felt as much a part of the group as the rest.

By the time the meal had ended, no one seemed able to lift themselves from their seats.

"I would offer you lodging here for the night," the queen said, "but I believe you mentioned wanting to set sail this evening."

The crew all looked at the two captains, their faces begging them to reconsider, but Treygan looked at me and finally sighed. "Yes, we really should be going." He turned to the queen. "As you said, the sooner we can get Ayrion to the front, the safer Your Majesty will feel."

The queen smiled. "You are a good man, Captain Treygan." She then looked at Ismara. "And you have a fine daughter; cherish the time you have together."

The queen stood, and the footmen pulled out our chairs so we could follow her up.

"It has been my honor, "she said to the captains, "to get to know you and your wonderful crew, as well as Master Gittrick and his sons. I hope this is not the last we see of you."

Treygan and the crew bowed.

The queen turned to me and took a step closer, placing a hand on my arm. "Keep my husband safe."

I bowed as much as I could while she held my arm. "I'll protect him with my life, Your Majesty."

She smiled and then headed out the door.

Dakaran walked around to my side of the table and held out his hand. "Keep yourself safe, you hear?"

I shook it. "You do the same. When I get back, I want you fully healed and ready for our next lessons."

He smiled, then looked past me to the rest of the crew. "It has been a pleasure sharing our table with you this evening." He stopped and held Ismara's gaze a moment, then finally turned and followed his mother out.

"What now?" Pops asked, hobbling over with his crutch.

Treygan turned. "Now, we get back to the ship and make ready to sail."

AVALANCHE

Chapter 38

ITHIN AN HOUR OF RETURNING to the port, the *Wind Binder* was underway. The trip around the southern coast was almost pleasant, at least for me. Shade, on the other hand, took sick before we'd even left the harbor, which to my regret also meant that I shared in those feelings. This was certainly a drawback to our magical bond.

The weather was fair, apart from one day of squalls while heading around the Copper Islands. The storm left everyone drenched and miserable, but thankfully wasn't bad enough to fear any permanent damage to the ship. Treygan spent a good deal of time in his cabin, studying charts to plot the fastest route to get me safely to the front, while the crew handled the daily duties of the ship.

Not being a member of the crew myself, my duties were to do my best to keep out of the way, though I did jump in periodically when needed, especially in the rougher seas. I was surprised how much I remembered from my time aboard the *Wind Binder*. Most of my days, however, were spent running drills and keeping my body and mind sharp as I prepared for whatever might be awaiting me when I arrived.

What would have taken several weeks of travel by horse, we managed to cover in just a few days, and before the week was out, we were sailing up the Pyruvian River on our way to Belbridge.

The bridge near Belbridge was one of the largest and most traveled routes between the two kingdoms. It was a bridge that I remembered all too well on my one and only trip into Cylmar. I had been forced to fight my way back across that bridge during my rescue of the Elondrian ambassador and his wife.

Earlier this morning, we'd left the coastal city of Laneer, which was located at the mouth of the Pyruvian, just before it fed into the Rhunarin Ocean. We learned while we were there that the king and the main Elondrian fleet were only a day's journey ahead, which meant we had somehow made up almost two days' travel. The *Wind Binder* was fast, but it wasn't that fast. Commander Goring must have moored their ships during the storm as a precaution.

I wondered whether Cylmar would send ships of their own. Over-captain Tolin had argued that they would instead send their forces by foot from someplace like Dorwall south to the border, the same trek my roommates and I had taken to rescue the ambassador. The swamplands south of Dorwall made travel down the Ryne River precarious at best, and probably wouldn't be the safest route to transport their army. According to the lancer outpost at Laneer, the only ships to have passed within recent weeks looked to have been fishing vessels.

Thankfully we were reaching the final leg of our journey. The distance from Laneer to Belbridge was about two days by boat, but with the *Wind Binder*, I was hoping to make up some of that time.

"I'd say that by tomorrow afternoon, we should be looking for a place to dock," Treygan said, standing to the right of the helm. Needle guided the wheel as Treygan studied his chart, both listening for Whitey on the forward deck to shout back soundings.

I had climbed up to the quarterdeck to get a better view, but so far there wasn't much more to see than grasslands on either side of the river—a sight I was very familiar with, having traveled this route several times over the last year. We passed a couple of small fishing villages outside Laneer, though these weren't much more than a few ramshackle buildings and a couple of docks. There were several such communities spread up and down the river, though more on the Elondrian side than on Cylmar's. There were even a couple of larger townships, most running ferries back and forth across the water.

The communities out here on the border didn't seem bothered by the hostilities between their kingdoms and, in fact, from what I'd seen and heard from those we'd talked with, they had kept up trade between themselves. If only Cylmar's leadership would follow their example. For as long as I had been aware of the world outside the Lost City, it seemed Overlord Saryn had not been satisfied with what he had and always wanted more. His eyes were fixated on the Black Hills and their lucrative ore mines.

The situation reminded me of Cutter and the conflict between Sandstorm and Avalanche. It was shocking to see how the greed of one individual could have such devastating ramifications. The king had the right idea in wanting to broker a peace. The last thing I wanted was to be involved with another war, but sometimes the only way to have peace was to remove the obstacle standing in its way.

"Aye," Treygan said, pulling me from my musings, "I'd say we need to find a place to dock by tomorrow at the latest. We take the ship any farther upriver than that, and we risk running into whatever's happening up there. I wouldn't want to get cornered by Cylmaran ships and have to fight our way out. We might be fast, but we aren't exactly prepared for battle."

I nodded. "I don't want to put you or the crew in any kind of danger. I'm sure Shade and I can make it to the main encampment from wherever you drop us off."

The day was cooler, but the clouds coming off the ocean to the south looked a little ominous, bringing with them a slowly building wind, which helped us move up the river in a timely manner. Traveling by river always took longer than out on the open water, especially since we were heading north against the current.

"Looks like we'll be getting wet," Ismara said, climbing the stairs to join us on the quarterdeck. She stared out at the darkening horizon behind us.

Treygan turned and pursed his lips. "We might be able to keep ahead of it for a while, but if the winds don't shift, it may be best to lay anchor till it passes."

"Do you think we might reach Ranool before it hits?" I asked. "We could dock there and wait it out."

Ranool was one of the oldest cities found along the Pyruvian, smack-dab between Laneer and Belbridge. It was most notable for running the largest ferry between the two kingdoms and had at one time been a major crossroads between Cylmar and Elondria, back before the Belbridge bridge had been built. Now, it wasn't much more than a large fishing town. From what I'd been able to surmise on my previous visits, the local farmers on the Elondrian side of the river were the cause for most of the traffic, as those living in Cylmar would often come to Ranool for the food those farmers supplied.

"I don't know," Treygan said. "It's still a half-day's journey, but if the wind holds steady, there's a fair chance." He looked up. The afternoon sun was already dipping. "If we do make it, it won't be until after dark."

"If we could reach Ranool, you could let me and Shade off there."

"You wouldn't want to try getting closer?" Ismara asked. "Belbridge is at least a good two days' ride from Ranool."

I shook my head. "Most of the lancer transports are being sent through Ranool. It's safer for the ships to have us meet them there than travel any farther north and risk coming too close to the lines of skirmish. I wouldn't be surprised if the ships ahead of us are docked there already. It's the safer route, and with them escorting the king, I've a feeling they'll be taking as many precautions as possible."

"If that's the case," Ismara said, "I'm surprised we haven't run into any of their ships heading back to Aramoor."

Treygan folded his chart and tucked it into his belt. "I'm sure it'll take them a while to off-load that many vessels, let alone secure transport from Ranool to Belbridge. From what Ayrion has said, it sounds like they were carrying at least a quarter of the Elondrian army."

"Close to it," I said. "They've been slowly moving lancers to the front for the last couple of months. "As far as securing transport from Ranool to Belbridge, I'm sure Commander Goring would have already made preparations for the wagons and horses from camp to be waiting on their arrival."

"Sounds like war's all but guaranteed," Needle said, his eyes focused ahead as he continued to make small adjustments to the wheel.

I sighed. "More so by the day."

Whitey shouted back another depth finding, and Needle turned the wheel to compensate, taking us into deeper water. Below, the crew gathered around the side rail to get a look at another small Cylmaran fishing community off the port side. We passed several two- and three-man boats along the waterfront; most looked to be packing in their fishing for the day as they hauled in their nets and started for shore.

"Looks like they don't want to be out on the water either," Needle said as we passed.

"They see what's coming," Ismara said.

I watched the small village until it had disappeared behind us. "I'm surprised we haven't seen more of the larger fishing trawlers."

"What do you mean?" Treygan asked as he stepped away from the port-side rail, where he, too, had been watching the Cylmaran village disappear into the distance.

"The lancer post at Laneer said the only ships to enter the Pyruvian were fishing vessels. I expected to have passed a few more than we have by now."

"I don't think they meant today, specifically," Treygan said. "Got the feeling they were referring to travel in general." He cocked one of his brows. "Why? You think they're going to sneak the Cylmaran army up-river on a couple of net draggers?"

I smiled. "I suppose not."

The supper bell rang below as Kettle called the crew to come get it while it was hot. By then, the sky overhead was clouding to the point that the sun could no longer be seen, and the darkening horizon behind us continued to gain ground. Treygan and Ismara were right—it looked like we were in for a rough one.

I headed down with the first group, stopping by the makeshift overhang to see how Shade was doing. He slowly nibbled on the hay, quenching his thirst from the now-half-empty bucket. I patted his neck and rubbed behind his ears. A warm, comfortable sensation fed back through our bond.

"How's your stomach doing, my friend? It doesn't feel quite as bad as it did when we first left." The calmer water on the river had lessened the sickness. I looked up. "It looks like we will be getting wet again, I'm afraid. We're hoping to dock at Ranool this evening." I smiled. "I'm sure you'll be glad to finally be off this boat."

Shade snorted and then nudged my coat with his face.

"Sorry, no apples. But I'll see if I can snatch one from below after I eat, okay?"

"You coming?" Ismara asked, almost having to shout to be heard over the growing wind. She was holding the door to the galley open for me.

I rubbed the bridge of Shade's nose and then headed inside with her.

Half the crew was sitting at the tables, their food already served. I joined Ismara in grabbing a plate and dishing out whatever Kettle had warming in one of the pots on the stove. It looked to be fish stew, probably left over from the previous night, with a few extra ingredients tossed in for good measure. There was also some hard bread for dipping and some pea pudding on the side. If Treygan had gotten the extra gold from the queen—or if I had been willing to wait another day before sailing—they might have splurged a bit more on the food. But since neither of us had, they kept the supplies to a minimum in case the queen didn't come through.

"How's he doing?" Ismara asked, taking her seat beside her father as she pointed back toward the galley door. I figured she was referring to Shade.

"Better than before," I said, blowing on my first mouthful. "Being off the open water has helped." I ate the first bite and immediately grabbed the salt box and sprinkled some on. The fish had a strong taste, but there was a definite lack of seasoning to go with it. Either that or I'd been far too pampered by the meals we'd taken recently at Sandstorm and the palace.

"It's been a long time since I've sailed these waters," Treygan said.

"Why'd you quit?" I asked, continuing to work my way through the stew, scooping most of it with my bread instead of my spoon. It wasn't very good, but I was hungry and, more importantly, needed to keep up my energy.

"Not enough business along this stretch," Treygan answered. "You've seen the villages out there. Couldn't drum up enough work to keep a ship like ours afloat. And with the tensions between these two kingdoms over the years, growth out here's been slower than a snail in a tar pit."

"Makes sense," I said, chewing my next bite.

Treygan shrugged. "The Shemoa has its problems too, as you've well seen, but at least there is potential for growth, and we've been known to take the odd trip or two up the Taloos."

"We've even been to Rhowynn," Ismara added. "Not exactly Aramoor, but for Keldor, certainly worth a visit."

"Any place you haven't been?" I asked.

They both thought a moment before Treygan finally spoke. "I've been up the Bull-Isra River, but only so far as Rhyndir, just before the river splits into the Bull and the Isra." He pinched his chin. "Never liked the thought of going any farther north than that. Too close to the White Tower for my taste." He shivered. "Something about that part of the Razor Spine always got my skin a-crawling."

"I had my first run-in with the White Tower this past week," I said.

"You don't say." Treygan's bone dagger began to spin in his hand. I didn't remember him even pulling it out of its sheath. "I've had the unfortunate luck of running into them a time or two over the years. Never a pleasant experience, I assure you. Best advice I can give is: if you ever

see those white uniforms, find somewhere else to be."

I nodded. "Found that out for myself the hard way."

"Oh?" Treygan looked up from his plate. "You actually talked with some? Thankfully, I've never had that pleasure."

"Not sure *talking* would be the best way to describe it, unless of course you consider killing half a dozen of them and leaving the rest bleeding across the steps of the palace meaningful conversation."

Treygan's knife stopped, and both he and Ismara stared at me with a look that could only be described as horror, amazement, and disbelief all rolled into one. Some of the other crew sitting at the next table over, who'd been listening in, stopped eating and turned.

"You did what?" Treygan asked.

I went on to explain in detail the events leading up to and including the battle with the Black Watch and its eventual ending.

"You actually saw the archchancellor?" Ismara asked.

"I did. Not sure what all the fuss is about, though. He's just an old man with a really big hat."

"As big as mine?" Whitey asked from the table behind me.

"It was taller," I said, holding my hand up over my head in approximation.

Treygan pulled out his pipe and stuffed the bowl. "You have lived quite the exciting life, my young friend."

"To say the least," Ismara added. "Though I'm not surprised. Even back then, we could see the river wasn't for you."

"What do you mean?" I asked, feeling a little hurt.

"It's not that we wouldn't have loved having you stay," she said, "but it just wasn't in your blood. Either you have it or you don't . . . and you didn't."

I was surprised. "I thought I fit in with the crew rather well during my trip down the river. Are you saying I didn't?"

"No, you would have made a fine riverman, but anyone could see your heart wasn't in it. It's just something you're born with." She pointed at me with her spoon. "But now look at you: dining with the royal family, personal friends with the crown prince, living in grand estates, leading lancers into battle . . ." She shook her head. "Clearly, you were meant for other things. Still, to me, you'll always just be Ayrion, the strange boy with the pretty eyes."

I smiled, blushing a little under her gaze. I wanted to tell them I wasn't exactly the one who'd be leading the lancers into battle, but then I figured there was no point. It wasn't like they would be around to know the difference.

The door to the galley opened, and Bones stuck his head in. "The wind's picking up out here, Captains." Behind him, I could see the sky was darkening as well, and not just from the sun's passing.

Treygan, Ismara, and the rest of the crew, who'd taken first seat at supper, stood and headed back to their duties.

"Has anyone taken a plate down to Pops yet?" I asked, dropping my tin plate and utensils off in the wash bucket.

"Was going to after y'all finished stuffin' your gobs," Kettle said.

I grabbed a fresh plate and began dishing up another helping. "I'll do it." I wanted to get back out on deck to see how close the storm was, but I hadn't been down to see Pops since earlier that morning, and he was due a visit. I carried the plate and mug down the stairs and found the old man resting in his hammock. This morning, he'd been up and moving around the hold, doing his best to stretch his legs. Now, he looked to be enjoying the extra sway of his bed.

"I was wondering if they'd forgotten me," Pops said when he saw me coming. "There seems to be an extra pitch to the boat. What's happening up top?"

"Storm coming in from the south, and we're trying to outrun it to Ranool." I placed his food and drink on a barrel at the end of his hammock to help him up into a sitting position, then handed him the food, which he began devouring rather quickly.

He made a face after his second mouthful. "Needs salt."

I groaned. "Sorry about that. I forgot to sprinkle some on before coming down. You want me to go get it?"

He waved it off with a half-filled spoon. "Had worse." He continued to eat.

"How's the leg? Any better?"

Pops shrugged. "Could be. Pain's more dull than sharp."

"Do you still have some of Reevie's tonic left?"

He nodded and tapped his pocket.

"What about the salve? You need me to help put some more on?"

He shook his head as he swallowed another pull from his mug of watered ale. "I'll be fine till we anchor."

I glanced back over my shoulder toward the stairs. I heard Pops sigh, and I turned.

"Get on with ya," Pops said. "I'm sure they be needin' your help up top. No need lollygagging down here on my account."

I smiled. "Just wanted to make sure you got some supper."

"Right happy you did," he said. "Before you go, though, could you light a couple more of the lanterns?"

"I can do that." I quickly lit a couple of the closest ones hanging on the posts around his bed, and even one or two over by the stairs. After wishing him well, I grabbed a couple apples from the barrel and headed up to see if the captains needed any help. I passed the second half of the crew on my way out as they quickly dished up their food and began stuffing it in their faces. Not a lot of time to sit and talk with the coming storm.

MICHAEL
WISEHART

The wind nearly jerked the galley door out of my hand when I opened it. Above me, the black sail strained away from the mast, pushing the *Wind Binder* ever faster as she cut through the water ahead. Whitey and a couple of the crew continued to call out depths from the forward bow as Needle adjusted course to match, everyone trying their best to keep ahead of the storm.

I stopped to see how Shade was doing before climbing up to the quarterdeck. The stallion seemed agitated as he moved about under his shade sail, his head shifting back and forth as he watched the crew scramble about the deck. I gave him the apples, which he took gratefully. They seemed to calm him momentarily.

"How much farther to Ranool, you reckon?" I asked Treygan as soon as I made it up to the top deck. The sun had already set to the west, making it difficult to see how close the storm was on our tail. By the way the wind was whipping through my hair, I had to imagine not far.

Treygan shrugged. "It's been many a year since I've sailed this stretch of water. Don't recognize a lot of it. And now that we've lost the sun, it's any man's guess." He turned and looked out at the darkness behind the ship. "But if this wind keeps up, we'll be reaching it sooner than expected. Keep your eyes open. Hate to pass it in this weather. Easy to do once the rain starts."

The storm seemed to be bringing with it a warmer front. The air, instead of cooling as the sun fell, grew uncomfortably sticky.

We sailed by another small Elondrian village off the starboard side; the only way of knowing were the lamps in the windows of the homes closest to the water.

The stars would have filled the sky by now if it weren't already filled with thick clouds. I caught the first drops of rain on my cheek. Behind us, the sky and river lit up as a bright flash filled the horizon, followed by a thunderous clap that set my knees to shaking. It almost felt as though I'd been hit by the lightning myself.

Several of the men on deck jumped when the thunder struck.

A sharp twinge of fear shot through me, and it took me a moment to realize it wasn't me, but Shade. The unexpected boom had clearly shaken him.

"This is a bad one," Needle said loudly over the wind as he kept his eyes on the forward deck, where Whitey and the others were. "Dangerous time to be traveling unfamiliar waters. We could easily ground the ship or tear open the hull."

Treygan nodded. "Just keep a steady course. We can't be that far from Ranool."

The rain began to harden, moving almost sideways in the wind. It struck my neck and the back of my head, soaking my hair, so I tied off the wet strands with the black headband Sapphire had given me for my birthday three years ago.

This storm was shaping up to be worse than the one we'd faced out on the ocean, except, thankfully, we didn't have to worry about the ship sinking from waves.

"All hands on deck!" Treygan shouted, which was echoed by Bones down below. The galley door opened, and those of the crew still eating came rushing out, including Kettle, his apron still tied on.

More flashes lit the sky, these much closer than before.

"Should we lower the sail?" I called over to Treygan, who was watching his men below from the quarterdeck railing.

"No! We'll run with her!" The captain had one hand on the railing to steady his feet and the other on his hat. The corners of his mouth quirked upward as he turned to look at me. "Don't worry!" he said, tapping the railing. "She can handle it!"

I wondered if Commander Goring and Overcaptain Tolin had decided to wait the storm out at Ranool, or if they had already off-loaded and were setting up camp somewhere along the road. I guessed it would depend on how long it took them to transport the food and supplies onto the wagons. Either way, with this wind, we were certainly catching up.

Ismara reached the top step of the quarterdeck, and I grabbed her arm as a gust of wind hit her full on. She took hold of the railing and moved down to where her father stood beside the helm. "We might need to anchor and wait it out. Whitey's having a difficult time keeping up with the depths. We're moving too fast through the water, and the rain's making visibility next to useless!"

Treygan took a deep breath and released it as he looked up at the black sail overhead. He finally nodded. "Very well. We can—"

"Fire!" someone shouted, and we all looked down at the main deck. My first thought was that somehow one of the lanterns I'd lit for Pops had fallen and ignited, but looking around, I didn't see anything other than the lanterns lining the edge of the ship. I didn't see or smell any smoke either.

Then I noticed Bones waving his arms from the foredeck.

"There!" I shouted to the others and pointed up at the first mate.

"What's he going on about?" Treygan said. "I don't see any fire."

"Fire off the bow!" Bones shouted again, pointing behind him toward the river ahead.

This time we looked out beyond the ship and into the darkness ahead. Sure enough, there was a glimmer of light flickering in and out of the storm farther north. It was barely discernible, but it was there. We raced for the stairs and down, then made our way up to the foredeck.

"We've got fire ahead, Captains!" Bones said, running with us to the bow, where several of the crew were already gathered and looking. They moved aside when they saw us coming.

I reached the rail and looked out at the water ahead. From the side, I heard Whitey continuing to call out depths. The rain was thickening, making it almost impossible to see what was happening. I might have had Upakan sight, but that didn't help me see through the storm any more than it had through the fog-covered streets back in Aramoor.

I wiped rain from my eyes as it continued to drain down the front of my face and stared into the darkness ahead. The flashes of light grew, no longer coming in bursts and flickers, but now holding steady like a small torch in the distance. The lightning and thunder pounded around us as the wind forced us closer with each new gust.

"Is it Ranool?" Kettle asked. "You think one of the buildings caught fire?"

The closer we got, the larger the blaze became.

"That's more than just one building," Ismara said. "That looks like the whole flaming town is on fire."

"No!" I shouted, finally close enough for my eyes to see. "It's not the town. It's coming from the river." The breath caught in my throat when I realized what I was looking at. "It's the ships! The Elondrian fleet is on fire!"

AVALANCHE

Chapter 39

REYGAN LIFTED THE OCULAR to his eye to get a closer look. "I see movement. There's still people aboard."

Treygan handed me the spyglass, and I quickly stuck it to my eye. My fingers tightened around the metal casing when the scene came into focus. "They're under attack!" Shimmers of metal reflected in the fire's light.

"Are you sure?" Treygan asked, leaning out over the railing as if that was somehow going to help him see better.

"I see Elondrian colors," Ismara said beside me, looking through her own ocular.

I looked closer and could just make out uniforms of red and black battling against our Elondrian crimson and gold. "Cylmarans! How did they get aboard?" It looked like the majority of the fleet was anchored a few hundred feet off the Elondrian side of the river, but from this distance, I couldn't tell much more than that. I handed Treygan back his spyglass.

"The ferries," Treygan said, staring through the spyglass. "They must be using them to reach the convoy." He turned to Needle. "Bring us starboard. I don't want to be out in the middle and risk being spotted."

Needle turned the wheel, and the *Wind Binder* slowly angled toward the Elondrian shore.

Another bolt of lightning streaked the sky, lighting the grim scene ahead as the storm pushed us closer. Pretty soon, we didn't need the spyglasses to see that the Cylmaran side of the river was filled with red-and-black uniforms, all clambering aboard flatboats and rowboats and anything else they could find that would carry soldiers from shore out to the ships.

Volleys of arrows flew in both directions. Those coming from the shore were lit, striking the sides of the lancer ships, some holding their flame long enough to ignite whatever mark they found.

The fires we saw, however, were coming from several ships just downriver of the main fleet. They were completely engulfed, but none bore the Elondrian flag. In fact, they looked too small to even be part of the convoy. They looked more like—

My eyes widened. "The fishing trawlers!"

"I see them!" Treygan said.

They weren't using the net draggers to transport soldiers after all. The trawlers had been scuttled to form a blazing blockade across the river. It was a safe bet they had done the same upriver to keep the convoy from making a run for it.

I looked up at the storm. It seemed even the weather was on their side. "You couldn't have asked for better weather to run a maneuver like this. Visibility this low and you could practically move an entire army without anyone the wiser."

"Where's the king?" Ismara asked, still studying the ships ahead.

I looked through the fire to the ships beyond, searching for some sign of the king's vessel, but didn't see the royal crest flying from a mast. They may have left the king's vessel unmarked for his protection.

"He's probably in one of those there," I said, pointing to three ships on the right that were separated from the rest of the convoy. They were anchored about a ship's length away from the others. Those on the left were positioned in such a way as to form a line of defense against the Cylmaran side of the river. However, I doubted they had ever expected to actually need it.

"Commander Goring must have decided to wait out the storm aboard ship," I said. "You see there?" I pointed to a couple of vessels docked along the city's port. "Those are probably supply ships getting ready to off-load in the morning."

The others turned their attention back to the fleet out on the river, where the battle was taking place. Fires could be seen around each of the protecting vessels on the left, where stray arrows had found purchase, igniting wood and canvas, even through the rain. They must have been using some sort of pitch as an accelerant. Men in red-and-black uniforms were climbing up over the sides, fighting their way aboard, working from one ship to the next.

Had Saryn moved part of his army south? Were those at the bridge just a diversion, or had this all been a spur-of-the-moment decision? I racked my brain, trying to figure out how this had happened. Either way, it looked like nearly a third of Cylmar's army was out there fighting to reach the convoy.

I squeezed the ship's rail, my knuckles whitening. I felt completely helpless, knowing there was nothing I could do but watch as the battle raged ahead. The lancers were water-locked, and there certainly weren't enough rowboats to carry their men from one ship to the next.

I balled my fists as I tried to think of a way to get to the king. What was I going to do, swim? Maybe I could take one of the *Wind Binder*'s boats and row over. But even if I somehow made it against the storm's current, their archers would probably just mistake me for one of the Cylmarans and shoot me down before I'd climbed halfway up the side.

This was ridiculous!

I tried to see if I could spot any of the Black Guild aboard. Even though we were now close enough to smell the smoke from the wreckage ahead, we weren't close enough for me to make out faces. I was sure they were there, but I had no idea which ship. It was impossible to tell one lancer from the next.

I used the ocular to get a better look. Lancers lined the outer rails, but none of them were wearing black material on their arms. Perhaps Tolin hadn't been able to secure the armbands before he left. Maybe he forgot. It likely wasn't high on his list of important tasks that needed accomplishing before leaving for a mission that was looking to end in war.

I handed Treygan his spyglass and wiped water from my face. The storm seemed to be building, the wind and rain beating hard enough to make it difficult to be heard.

"What should we do?" Ismara shouted.

"I don't think they've spotted us yet," I said. "We're still in the shadows." The dark wood and black sail were helping to mask our approach.

"Won't be hiding here for long if this lightning keeps up," Treygan said, about the time another roll of thunder rumbled.

The tension in my bond with Shade was growing. He wanted off the ship.

"I still don't see how you plan on getting to the king," Ismara said.

I studied the river ahead, then pointed to the port. "Maybe we can skirt the battle on the right and make a run for the docks." I honestly had no idea what I was going to do from there. "Maybe I could find a small boat to row out to the ships."

"In this storm? Are you crazy?"

I threw my hands up. "I don't know what else to do. I don't want to put all of your lives at risk. Your job was to get me here, not join the war. You've done your part. Now it's up to me."

"We've got a problem," Treygan said, pointing to the rest of the convoy ships on the left, currently under attack. He handed me the ocular, and I quickly held it up to my eye. "There," he said, "just coming around the first ship."

Several flatboats had pulled away from engaging the first line of ships, and instead were now working their way around to the three behind. They had rows of shields along the edges of the boats, and more held overhead, protecting the occupants from the arrows being fired at them from the convoy. However, it seemed the Elondrian archers' releases were growing fewer by the moment as the fighting aboard their ships increased, drawing their attention inward.

The last thing we needed was for the Cylmarans to make it to the king's ship. I wondered if the others had spotted the coming boats yet. In the pitch of night, under rain this heavy, they might not have.

With the lancers stuck aboard the various floating vessels, it made it impossible for them to fight as a unit. They were trained and equipped for the ground. Worse, three quarters of Elondria's army weren't even here. They were still waiting for us at Belbridge. If the Cylmarans made it to the king, there was no way for Commander Goring to form a mounted retreat. They were stuck in the middle of a river surrounded by blazing ships.

I clenched my teeth. I had to give it to Saryn. Whoever his military tacticians were, they had done a fantastic job of setting this up. Knowing how much Rhydan was hoping to keep the kingdoms from engaging in an all-out war, the meeting was the perfect opportunity for sabotage, which was undoubtedly why neither the commander nor the overcaptain had been happy with the king's decision to attempt it.

I watched helplessly as the smaller boats worked their way farther around the front. The fleet's sails had long been furled, and they didn't have the momentum to try getting away, not to mention the fiery blockade that awaited them if they tried.

"They need to get the king off those ships and into Ranool," I said. "They're blocked in on three sides."

"Aye!" Treygan said. "And they better get a move on if they plan to. Those boats aren't stopping. And if the Cylmarans take control of even one of your convoy ships over there," he said, pointing left, "they could cut anchor and turn the ship far enough starboard to probably reach those three beside them."

I grimaced as a chill cut through me. I hadn't thought of that. I was thinking too much like a lancer when I needed to be thinking like a riverman. Right now, all I knew was that I had to find a way to stop them.

But how?

I was torn between my duty to the king and wanting to keep my friends safe. However, as much as I wanted to make sure nothing happened to the *Wind Binder*, protecting the king was my ultimate responsibility.

I turned to Treygan, but before I could say anything, he grabbed Whitey, who was still sounding depths in the middle of the chaos, and pushed him toward the foredeck steps.

"Tell Needle hard to port! We're gonna sail straight through that blockade and right over those flaming whoresons!" Before I had a chance to respond, he spun to the rest of the crew. "Arm yourselves! The *Wind Binder's* going to war!"

The crew stood there a moment, as though waiting for him to say that he was just kidding. When he didn't, they scattered, racing down to the galley door and from there into the hold to gather their weapons.

"Are you sure about this?" I asked, relief washing over me. "This isn't your fight."

Saying the words eased a little of the guilt I was feeling for inadvertently dragging them into this. I had been hoping he'd be willing to help, though I hadn't thought he'd put the *Wind Binder* in the very middle of the war.

Treygan turned to the forward railing and stared out through his spyglass, wiping hair from his face. "If Saryn kills the king and manages to thwart a quarter of the Elondrian army, ain't none of us going to be safe."

The ship suddenly pulled to the left. I grabbed the railing as the bow angled away from shore and out toward the middle of the river and the row of flaming trawlers blocking us from the convoy. My heart was pounding. I reached up on instinct and grabbed the hilt of my two blades. I didn't draw them, only reassured myself that they were there.

The fiery blaze leveled across the river ahead drew steadily closer. Thankfully, the *Wind Binder* was a smaller ship with a much sleeker design than what the blockade had been intended for, which gave us quite a bit more maneuverability when it came to squeezing through tight spaces. Though I doubted the ship's designers had planned for her maneuverability to navigate through ship-size bonfires.

The flaming row of net draggers in front of us weren't exactly holding line, as the wind and water had begun to pull them apart enough to allow some space between. There was only so much a couple of anchors could do when trying to hold a ship against a current. The openings might not have been wide enough for one of the larger vessels, but perhaps it would be enough for us. Treygan seemed to think so.

The crew was back on deck in no time, armed and waiting. Most carried swords and daggers, some had long pikes. There were even a few bows and quivers slung across some backs. Along with the weapons, they had also brought up several stacks of shields, which they kept aboard in case of archers. Bones ordered a couple of the larger ones taken up to the quarterdeck to protect Needle, who couldn't leave his post.

Turning back to the battle, I pointed to the three ships behind the others. "How close do you think we can get? If you can get us close enough, I might be able to leap aboard as we pass."

Treygan studied the vessels, judging the distance between them and the row of convoy ships beside them on the left. "I don't think you're gonna have to worry none about us getting close. Got a feeling we'll be scraping hulls just to get by."

A loud whinny broke through the storm behind me, Shade's anxiety growing. He could tell I wanted to leave. I left Treygan and Ismara and headed down to the main deck. Shade was still under his awning, watching the crew running about, getting ready for battle. The stallion knew something was wrong; he could sense my own fear through the link.

"I'm sorry, boy," I said, rubbing the bridge of his nose to calm him down. "I've got to go, and I don't have any way to bring you with me. And even if I did, there's nothing you could do out here in the middle of the river. Besides, I don't have any armor for you to wear. You'd be a sitting target." I shook my head. "You need to stay here where it's safe."

Shade snorted, but he didn't have much of a choice. The convoy vessels were larger than ours, and the only way I was going to be able to get aboard one of theirs was if I jumped from one of the upper decks. There was no way Shade was getting up there to follow.

"I promise I'll be back," I said, rubbing one of his ears. "Don't worry about me." I grabbed one of the crew on their way by. "Make sure to get some shields here to protect him." The man looked at the horse, then nodded and ran to get some help. I patted Shade's neck one last time. "Wish me luck."

Shade whinnied as I turned to head back up top. About the time I did, Pops stuck his head out the galley door.

"Get back in the hold!" I shouted over the wind. "We're about to go to battle."

"I can fight," he said, trying to juggle a sword and his crutch at the same time.

"You can't even stand, you crazy fool. Are you trying to get yourself killed? Get below deck."

Kettle saw him and quickly pulled the old riverman back inside.

I shook my head and climbed up to the quarterdeck, where Treygan was giving Needle instructions. The hefty navigator kept shaking his head as he stared out at the closing row of fire ahead.

"Are you mad?" Needle shouted. "You'll sink us for sure."

"We can make it!" Treygan said, his wet hair whipping about his face. "If you can thread the Black Hills, you can cut through that barricade."

"I wasn't doing it in the middle of the night, and during the mother of all storms!"

"You're the best navigator on the water," Treygan said.

Needle looked like he wanted to retch. These were riverboat men, not trained lancers. They'd proven on more than one occasion to be able to handle themselves in a fight, but this was a battle between kingdoms. However, the water was their domain, and no one was better on it than they were.

Ismara and Whitey shouted instructions from the foredeck. The light from the flames ahead was enough to see by, and we were close enough to feel their heat. Hopefully the rain would cut down on some of it as we punched our way through. I prayed the wind held to keep our momentum going. The faster we were able to get through the wreckage, the less likely it was for any of the fire to latch on to the *Wind Binder*.

Treygan ordered everyone into the galley as we neared the blockade. I grabbed a wet tarp and, with Bones's help, covered the side of Shade's overhang, holding it up to help block some of the heat. Treygan did the same for Needle as the two remained at the helm.

The fire roared as it devoured the fishing vessels, consuming everything it touched. The rain wasn't going to make a dent against an inferno of that magnitude. The heat was intense, and my skin felt like it was sizzling, bringing back memories of the day I'd been branded as one of the rejects. I could almost feel the heat of the branding iron on my flesh once again. I was thankful for the meager protection the soaked canvas offered.

My heart pounded in my ears as the *Wind Binder* came within a few feet of the blazing ship on the left. The fire seemed to be alive. If I listened hard enough, it almost seemed to be talking as the wood crackled and split.

Sparks and bits of flame, wood, and ash spat out across the upper and lower decks. I wanted to stick my head out to make sure that none of the floating debris had found its way into the mainsail, but the heat held me back. I hoped the water-soaked sail was enough to withstand anything it might come in contact with. At least it wasn't being showered with flaming arrows like the fleet ahead.

Smoke burned my eyes, and the heat nearly stole my breath. I quickly started rubbing some of Shade's water from his bucket on his face and then lifted the bucket to let him drink. "Calm down, boy. It's going to be alright." The sight of the fire had him wanting to run, and I had to use our link to keep him in place, continuing to talk to him, sending him a sense of control.

Pretty soon, the flames were behind us, and I was breathing once again. I dropped my side of the canvas and stepped out to join Bones in searching the ship for damage, starting with a thorough inspection of the sails. From what I could see, they didn't look to have taken any damage, but there were a few large pieces of burning debris that had made it on board, which we kicked over the sides.

Ismara was the first to stick her head out of the galley, and seeing we'd passed the fiery blockade, headed back out on deck. The rest of the crew were quick to follow and began to find their places along the edge of the ship, some climbing up to the foredeck to get a better look at the oncoming battle, which was now only a few hundred feet off the bow.

The last time I'd been in a skirmish with the *Wind Binder*, we'd fought against Captain Owen. Except, in that situation, we had a hold full of newly rescued slaves who'd covered their bodies in white paste and filled their mouths with a blood-red jam. They'd come screaming up from belowdecks like an apparitional horde, scaring the attacking sailors so bad they dove over the sides. Too bad we didn't have something similar now.

The wind and rain continued to beat down on the ship, cutting visibility and drowning us in its wrath. Just another misery in a long line of terrible circumstances.

I joined Treygan and Needle on the quarterdeck, the convoy looming just ahead. I could hear screams of the injured and dying as the clanging of steel and wood echoed off the water between rolls of thunder. The river below was filled with blood and bodies, many being sucked under us as we pushed steadily closer.

"What's that?" Ismara shouted from the other side of the helm, her spyglass up as she stared off toward Ranool's port. "Something's happening at the docks!"

I turned to look, and the breath caught in my throat. "It can't be." I grabbed Treygan's ocular before he got the chance to lift it. The docks were covered in red-and-black uniforms. Like ants across a dead carcass, they flooded out of the city and up onto the supply ships, killing those in charge of guarding the food. I stared in bewilderment. "I don't understand. I was here less than two weeks ago. There were no Cylmaran soldiers on this side of the river." Had they attacked Ranool while we were gone?

Treygan took his ocular back and looked for himself. "If they get those ships out of dock, the king is going to be completely surrounded."

I started to panic as the Cylmarans began tossing bodies over the sides of the ship. They were completely overrun. "I'm sure Goring and Tolin were relying on Ranool as an escape route." I turned and looked at the three ships out in the middle of the water. "Waylaying those flatboats isn't going to do much good if the Cylmarans get those supply ships out in the river. They could use the current alone to push them close enough to board."

"A few well-placed boat hooks would do it," Bones said behind us as he stared out at this new predicament. "Some grapple and rope, and they could secure the supply ships long enough to get over."

"Grapple and rope?" Treygan lowered his spyglass and turned. He had a strange look on his face. "I have an idea!"

AVALANCHE

Chapter 40

HIS IS MADNESS, CAPTAIN!" Needle shouted over another roll of thunder.

"You said the last one was madness too," Treygan fired back.

"Well, this one's truly insane!"

"Just hold her steady! I want you to thread that eye! And when I tell you, cut her hard to starboard."

"You're going to rip us in half!"

"She'll hold! She has to."

We were now within a stone's throw of the battle, and the Cylmaran flatboats were nearly to the sides of the first ship. From this distance, we could see that all three of the lancer ships had been lashed together and had gangplanks set up for traversing between them.

The archers aboard the outermost vessel fired at the oncoming boats. The Cylmaran's shields held off the majority of the volleys, but there were the occasional arrows that made it through, their passage announced with a deathly shrill. The flatboats were packed to the edges, as were the rowboats following in their wake. There had to be at least a hundred men making up the boarding party.

Most of the *Wind Binder*'s crew waited belowdecks to keep the Elondrian vessels from mistaking us for a Cylmaran warship. Captain Treygan remained at the helm alongside Needle, while Ismara was belowdecks with the crew waiting for her father's signal. I took my place alone up on the forward deck. I wanted to be the first person the lancers saw, in hopes someone recognized me and ordered their men not to shoot. Either Commander Goring or Overcaptain Tolin had to be aboard, and as close as we were, they were bound to have been informed of a strange black ship that seemed to be crewed by only three people suddenly appearing off their stern.

My hands shook as I held on to the bow's railing, watching as the front of our ship cut through the water, heading for the narrow opening between the three warships on the right and the rest of the fleet on the left. Ahead, the Cylmaran boats caught sight of us, helped by a bright streak of lightning. The men screamed for their oarsmen to turn around, but it was too late. I stared over the bow, torn between horror and a crazed anger as they dove into the water, but there was nowhere for them to go.

Someone on the lancer ships to my right was shouting orders. The bellowing sounded like Goring's tenor. My shield rested against my leg, ready just in case those orders were for their archers to cut us down. To my relief, no arrows were discharged, even though the entire side of their ship was lined with Elondrian crimson-and-gold uniforms, many holding bows that were pointed in our direction. Treygan and Needle stood behind a couple of wooden barriers the crew had erected on the quarterdeck to protect the helmsman.

By the time our ship had made it halfway up the side of the first vessel, I caught my first glimpse of Goring, standing on the foredeck of the ship we were passing, Overcaptain Tolin at his side. As completely ridiculous as I'm sure I looked—appearing out of the night on the bow of a ghost ship—I almost felt like throwing them a wave just to let them know it was me and not a specter.

The two men stood with mouths gaping as they watched us pass. I didn't see any sign of Room Eleven or the Black Guild, but I didn't have time to continue looking, as my attention quickly shifted down to the Cylmaran boats and the soldiers we were about to sail overtop of.

Screams and cries for help, along with the sickening thud of so many bodies striking the lower hull, sent my stomach reeling. I'd been in a number of battles in my life and had killed more than I cared to remember, but never on a scale like this before. Even our last fight with the Cylmaran slavers in the Black Hills hadn't seen half the deaths I had just witnessed in that moment. Even though I'd been training with the lancers for battles such as this for the last several years, I had a feeling the reality was going to be far worse.

I was no longer on the streets fighting with children.

I jumped back just before an arrow dug into the wood in front of me. I turned to the main convoy off the port side, but I didn't see who'd fired it. Probably just a stray. The battle was raging on those ships, both sides struggling to take control.

Turning away from the battle aboard the fleet's ships, I quickly shifted my attention to the task ahead, the same task that one of the best navigators on the water had called complete and utter insanity. The *Wind Binder* cut between the ships with barely room enough to fit a single skiff. No one but Needle could have made such a narrow passage at that speed, and in the middle of a raging storm.

But that was the easy part.

Up ahead, the northern blockade waited, its fire lighting up the entire river and part of the port. I could already feel its heat from the front of the ship. The trawlers and net draggers seemed to be drifting slowly toward the convoy, their anchors not enough to hold them in place against the swell of the river. With the wind forcing us toward them, even if we were able to cut sail and swing the boat, the inertia alone would still carry us straight into the flames.

I looked back at the helm. Whatever the captain was planning, he'd better hurry. From where I was standing at the bow, I could just make out the docks coming into view off the starboard side as we pulled past the other ships. The Elondrian supply vessels were doing their best to push out into the river, even resorting to using the oars to get enough leverage as they left berth. Normally there were towing vessels for such things, but with these ships having been commandeered, they were on their own.

"Hurry!" I shouted back to Treygan and Needle. "They're leaving the docks!"

Ahead, the flames were drawing closer, the heat building. If Treygan didn't do something soon, we were going to ram right into the trawler inferno.

The wind and rain continued to course down on top of us, hindering visibility and making the task of holding the ship steady nearly impossible. I didn't know how Needle had managed to keep us from slamming into one or both of the other ships.

Now that my job was done—namely, keeping the Elondrian troops from raking us with their archers—there wasn't much need for me to remain up front. I had intended on trying to leap over to the lancer vessel, but after hearing part of Treygan's insane plan, I'd decided to wait and save it for our second passing, if there was one. Having seen Goring and Tolin standing there, I almost wished I'd gone ahead and jumped.

Quickly, I raced back to the foredeck stairs, staying as close to the railing as possible to keep my footing. The heat from the barricade pelted my back.

"To your stations!" Treygan shouted as I headed down the port-side stairs. Ismara and Bones were the first out of the galley as the crew raced back up onto the main deck, where they took up their positions along the sides. Fear and intense focus plastered their faces as they crouched next to the rigging, their ears perked as they listened for their captain's voice. Everyone seemed to be in their place but me.

I rushed across the deck, passing Shade on the way. He whinnied for my attention, but I didn't have time to stop as I made my way up to the quarterdeck. I reached the top and joined Treygan and Needle at the helm. Behind them, Whitey crouched beside the capstan, holding a carpentry saw.

"Looks like your plan worked!" Treygan shouted. just as another boom of thunder shook the ship. "We're still alive."

I nodded. "At least they know we aren't the enemy."

The stern of the *Wind Binder* had fully cleared the three lashed warships off our starboard side, and we were beginning to pull away, leaving only a ship's length between us and the fiery barricade of fishing vessels ahead.

"What are we waiting for?" I asked nervously, watching the flames getting closer with each passing breath.

"We've only got one chance at this," Treygan said. "Too soon and we'll plow into the other ships. Too late and . . ." He looked out at the flames, his meaning clear. He took a moment to study the inferno ahead, as well as the ships off the starboard quarter, then swept his gaze across the *Wind Binder*, where the crew readied the mainsail for rotation. The captain studied everything.

The tension was about to eat me alive. *Come on!* How much longer was he going to—

"Mainsail haul!" Treygan finally shouted. "Bring her about! Hard to starboard!"

The crew grabbed the rigging and began to turn the mainsail and shift the boat—a difficult maneuver on a good day. In high winds like this, it was foolhardy at best and risked snapping the mast.

"Helm!" Treygan called to Needle, who grabbed the uppermost handles of the wheel and yanked down, spinning the barrel as fast as he could. The bow of the ship began to turn even more, and I grabbed the railing to keep from going down. The sail swung outward against the wind, and the entire ship tilted, coming partway out of the water as we fought to change direction. I clung to the railing to keep from sliding across the deck.

"Hold her steady!" Treygan shouted, clamped tight to the rail himself.

The ship turned into the wind, using the current as she fought to come about. I stared out at the looming wreckage just off the port bow and realized with a sinking feeling that it wasn't going to be enough. Treygan had waited too long. We were about to spin broadside into the flames.

Treygan shouted. "Drop anchor!"

I glanced back over my shoulder as Whitey released the capstan ropes and kicked the locking mechanism. The enormous pin spun, and the anchor dropped from the ship and hit the water.

My heart pounded as I braced for the inevitable jolt when the anchor buried itself into the river's bed, but nothing happened. The ship swept straight for the flames. Why wasn't the anchor catching? How deep was this water? The *Wind Binder* was now only a dozen or more feet from the trawlers, and if something didn't happen, we were all about to be cooked alive.

I could feel Shade panicking below.

Beside me, Needle and Treygan held the wheel to keep her turning.

"We're not going to make it," I said to no one in particular, raising one hand to shield my face against the heat as the other clung to the rail.

"We'll make it," Treygan countered.

Suddenly the chain and rope behind us snapped tight, and I was flung forward. I would have gone over the rail if I hadn't already been bracing for the heave. We lurched hard to starboard and away from the barricade, the anchor swinging us around like a taut pendulum.

The ship groaned, and I watched the mast with bated breath, fearing it would snap under the strain and drop to the deck, killing both Shade and the crew. The longer I watched, the more certain I was, but just when I thought the ship would flip completely, Treygan shouted out another order, and the crew began pulling back on the lines. The black sail rotated once more, and the *Wind Binder* slowly tilted back into place without losing either the mainsail or the mast.

I took several deep, calming breaths, before I finally managed to speak. "That was a close one."

"Too close!" Treygan and Needle shouted back in unison.

Using the anchor as a fulcrum, the *Wind Binder* pulled away from the fiery wreckage and cut across the bow of the three lashed Elondrian ships. A quick glance showed many of the lancers aboard were frozen in place, unable to believe their eyes as we spun the *Wind Binder* around the front of their convoy.

Ahead, the supply ships—now laden with Cylmaran soldiers—were moving away from the docks and making their way out into the river. Red-and-black uniforms lined the front and side, anxiously waiting to come within reach of the Elondrian ships.

"They're heading straight for the king," I said.

Treygan didn't even bother looking. "One thing at a time." He turned and looked at Whitey. "Cut anchor!"

Whitey immediately started hacking the thick rope around the capstan with his saw, its teeth chewing through as fast as his massive arm could move it.

"Don't we need that?" I asked.

"Not as much as we need to keep from hitting them," Treygan said, pointing at the three lashed ships off the starboard bow.

As relieved as I had been at not being roasted alive, I hadn't considered the fact that turning away from the wreckage meant turning into the three much-larger warships. Now my heart was racing all over again, and I bit my lower lip as the *Wind Binder* continued its turn. He was right. If we didn't get the anchor cut in time, the line was going to swing us straight into the bow of the third ship. A collision with any one of them would surely punch a hole in the bow.

"Done!" Whitey shouted as he tore past me down to the main deck. The rope that had been holding the anchor in place was now gone, but the momentum of the pendulum swing was still carrying us in.

"Captain?" Needle was beginning to pale as we drew down on the warship ahead.

"She'll make it," Treygan repeated. I wasn't sure if he was trying to convince us or himself.

The front of the Elondrian ship was lined with lancers, all staring at the *Wind Binder* in trepidation as she sailed straight for them.

"Ease the sheets!" Treygan shouted, and the crew lessened the lines, cutting the oncoming force of the wind.

"We're slowing!" I said.

"Not enough," Needle countered, holding the wheel steady.

He was right. We were beginning to shift, but it wasn't going to be enough. We might escape ramming the other ship head on, but we were certainly going to be scraping hulls, which could still mean a puncture and our ship going down.

The captain started counting down from ten.

What is he doing?

As soon as he reached *one*, he shouted down to the deck. "Mainsail haul! Hard to starboard!"

The crew immediately grabbed the lines and began to rotate the mainsail. The yard shifted to the port. I grabbed the rail once more as the wind filled the sheet and pushed us sideways in the water and away from the Elondrian vessel.

I exhaled sharply, feeling almost light-headed from holding my breath. "I can't believe that worked!"

Treygan laughed. "Neither can I! But that might have been the easy part." He pointed off the port side. To our left, the commandeered supply ships were heading straight for us.

This was crazy. I'd barely caught my breath from the last near-death experience, and now we were jumping headlong into another. As fast as the supply ships were moving toward the three Elondrian warships, it looked as though we were going to get squashed between them.

I looked up at the sail, but before I could tell Treygan that it was slowing us down, he shouted down to the crew.

"Raise the sail!"

His order was quickly echoed by Ismara, and the crew grabbed the halyard lines and started to pull. Slowly, the black sheet began to rise, cutting the wind's hold over us as we used the river's current to keep us moving. We needed as much speed as we could get if we had any hope of making it through without getting rammed by the supply ships.

Again, I found myself holding my breath as we started between the warship on our right and the commandeered supply ships coming in on our left. At this point, the current was our only momentum.

"Hooks to stern!" Treygan shouted, and the crew raced up the stairs to the quarterdeck, carrying shields in one hand and boat hooks in the other.

The crew lined up at the stern railing, knotting their hooks with rope that had been staged at the stern for this purpose, and then fastened those ends to whatever they could find, whether it was the railing or even the empty capstan. They waited anxiously at the back as the *Wind Binder* started between the two groups of ships.

The first of the commandeered ships was moving in fast, utilizing oars to build momentum. I held on to the rail at the helm and waited as they maneuvered their stolen ship to rake us along the port side, which would lock the ships together and allow them to board us. We couldn't let that happen. A boarding party that size would sweep across our ship in no time.

I grabbed the railing and squeezed. *Come on!* If there was ever a time for the *Wind Binder* to earn her name, it was now.

Rain pelted my face, and a streak of lightning momentarily blinded me.

"Ready hooks!" Treygan shouted as we reached the halfway mark.

The crew began to spin their grapples, waiting for the order.

The ship shuddered slightly, and I could hear wood scraping as we ran alongside the hull of the Elondrian ship, trying to get through before we were hit by the Cylmaran vessel.

"Hold her steady!" Treygan said.

Needle rubbed his face on his shoulder, trying to wipe water from his eyes without releasing the wheel.

A volley of arrows flew from the Elondrian ship and over to the Cylmarans, several striking and sticking into our mast on their way across. I was surprised there were no archers on the Cylmaran ship firing back, but perhaps they were too busy holding up shields to protect against the incoming volley.

The Cylmaran ship was only a couple feet from us now and moving in fast.

We weren't going to make it.

As we passed the main deck of the Elondrian ship on our right, I could see a very nervous helmsman on board, staring over his starboard side at us in bewilderment.

"Brace yourselves!" Treygan shouted.

I grabbed the railing just before the bow of the supply ship hit our port quarter. The railing shattered as the bow of the supply ship struck us and veered off.

"Release!" Treygan shouted, and the crew launched their grapples just as we began to pull away from the Cylmaran ship.

The hooks found their marks along the front rail of the supply ship, some digging into the backs of soldiers standing at the bow. Men screamed as the ropes went taut and the current started to pull us and the Cylmaran vessel downriver and away from the Elondrian ships.

The initial jerk pulled the Cylmaran ship back toward ours, forcing our crew to quickly tension the ropes to keep the other ship from freeing itself. The bow of their ship hit us once again. This time the soldiers were waiting, and several managed to leap aboard before we separated once again.

Half the soldiers attacked those holding the hooks, the other half focused on cutting the ropes free. I drew my blades and raced across the deck.

Whitey leaped in front of a crewman and took the flat of a Cylmaran blade across his back. The enormous riverman shouted, then spun around and slammed his giant fist into the soldier's jaw, sending the soldier and his teeth flying across the deck.

The next in line swung for Whitey's head, but Whitey dove backward, and Bones caught the sword with the hook of his kama. Before the Cylmaran could pull back, Bones buried the other kama in the man's chest.

"Save the hooks!" I shouted to Bones and tore into the soldiers coming for the crew. I hit them from the side. I didn't think they even saw me until I was on top of them. My blades found their marks, and three men lay dead at my feet in the blink of an eye. As Bones and Ismara fought to hold off those chopping at the ropes, I turned to face the remaining five.

The first three lifted their swords and rushed me as one. I danced between their blades, using the darkness to my benefit, slipping between their strikes as I slid my weapons in and out of their chests. All three dropped, rain washing their blood across the deck.

That left only two.

As I kept them occupied, Treygan moved up behind them and plunged his sword and bone dagger into their backs. The men's faces seized and their eyes rolled up in their heads, both dead before they hit the deck.

"That'll teach you for boarding my ship uninvited!" Treygan spat. He left the corpses and ran back to the helm.

I joined Bones and Ismara. Between the three of us, we made sure all the men who'd made it aboard were dead and left their bodies to bleed across the deck. We'd lost at least three of the hooks, but the rest seemed to be holding. By the time the soldiers on the other ship had managed to cut them away, it was too late. We had pulled them beyond the Elondrian warships, and they were now following us headlong down-river toward the fiery blockade.

Unfortunately, there were still three more commandeered ships behind it.

"Lower the sail!" Treygan shouted, and the crew rushed by on their way back down to the main deck.

The south barricade was quickly coming up ahead, its fires still burning bright. I didn't see an opening on the side we were headed for, which meant if we didn't get the ship turned, we were going to hit it straight on. Frantic, I ran down the quarterdeck stairs and joined the crew on the port side as we fought to lower the mainsail. It was the only thing that could keep us from being set ablaze.

Shade cried out when he saw me, but I didn't have time to look. I did attempt to send a small amount of reassurance to him through our bond, but I doubted he believed it, since I was sure he could sense my true feelings.

Treygan called for Needle to bring us hard to starboard. Once again, the wheel spun and the *Wind Binder* tilted port side, sending me and the crew sliding into the port railing as the starboard side of the ship lifted out of the water. A quick glance over my right shoulder told me that the Cylmaran supply ship was trying to do the same, but it was far too bulky and didn't possess the maneuverability of the *Wind Binder*. They passed us as we fought to bring ourselves around. Sweat ran down my back at the heat coming off the wreckage.

We loosed the sheets, and the black mainsail finally unfurled and dropped into place. It snapped tight against the ropes, and the wind filled it, hurling us the rest of the way around and away from the encroaching fire.

I exhaled sharply and started back up the stairs to the quarterdeck.

We were now headed right back into the battle. I glanced over my shoulder at the sound of shouting—the supply ship was headed directly into the flaming wreckage. Men jumped overboard on all sides as they hit the inferno.

"I can't believe that worked!" I said to Treygan.

He looked at me, his face pale. "Neither can I!"

"What now?"

"Now, we'll see what we can do about the northern barricade. If we don't get it moved, it's going to float right into your convoy."

I didn't like them taking so many risks, but it didn't change the fact that Treygan was right. If we couldn't stop those flaming trawlers and net draggers from floating any farther downriver, they were going to set our own ships ablaze.

"I'm afraid I'll have to leave you to it," I said. "I've got to get to the king before the rest of those supply vessels manage to board. I'm not doing any of you much good here."

"What do you call that?" he said, glancing back at the dead Cylmarans. "Good to see your Upakan training hasn't gone to waste." He turned his attention back to the narrow passageway between the ships ahead as we made our way back around for the same gap in the convoy we'd taken earlier.

Up ahead, the fiery barricade was beginning to split apart. I couldn't tell if the ships had burned down to the water line or if the river's current was pushing them apart. I just hoped there was enough room between them for Treygan to take the *Wind Binder* safely through.

"Take care of my horse," I said to Treygan as I offered him my hand.

He shook it with a nod. "We'll keep an eye on him. Good luck to you."

"And to you." I nodded at Needle, then turned and quickly made my way down to the main deck. I stopped by Shade's awning before heading to the foredeck.

"It seems we've survived so far," I said, rubbing behind his ear. "I'm sorry I'm going to have to leave you now, but you'll be much safer here." I looked at the looming battle ahead. "At least I hope so." I was really wishing I had left him back in Aramoor. I looked up at the helm. "Don't give the captain a hard time, you hear me?"

Shade snorted and nudged my chest.

I rested my head against his. "Take care of yourself." With that, I turned and scurried past the crew, who were busy angling the mainsail once again. I glanced back toward the galley door, wondering how Pops was doing below. Hopefully he didn't try coming back up on deck.

"Be careful out there," Ismara said as I started up the stairs.

I turned to find her and Bones tying off one of the sheets over at the side. I smiled. "You as well."

I didn't have time to say more, so I quickly headed up to the foredeck and positioned myself at the starboard bow railing. I hoped Needle could get me close enough to make the jump.

The fires on the convoy ships off the port side looked to be getting worse. Thankfully, the archers had stopped loosing volleys from shore since they were now just as likely to hit their own as they were the lancers. Studying the passageway ahead, it looked like the distance between the convoy ships on the left and the king's vessels on the right had shrunk. I hoped the *Wind Binder* could still make it through.

"Hold her steady!" I heard Treygan shouting behind me over the thunder and rain.

I gripped the rail, judging the distance between me and the lancer ship to my right. It was coming up quickly as the storm filled the black sail and sent us racing toward the fight. The lancers that had been lining the side of the Elondrian ships on the right were no longer there. A few lookouts stood along the rail, but the rest had evacuated, probably repositioned on the third ship on the far side where the Cylmarans were looking to board, which would make my leaping over a bit easier. I didn't have to worry about being skewered atop some lancer's spear when I tried to clear the railing.

I hoped I wasn't too late. I had no idea how many Cylmarans had been in Ranool or how many we had just sent into their own fiery blockade, but having been chased by them before in Ecrin, I knew they weren't the sort to just give up. Doubtless Commander Goring and Overcaptain Tolin were doing everything they could to hold them off. Hopefully my men were there with the king.

The bow of the *Wind Binder* came alongside the stern of the Elondrian ship. Even from the upper deck, I was barely high enough to reach the other ship's main deck, which was just ahead.

I couldn't decide if I wanted to climb up on the rail and jump over or attempt a running start across the deck. After moving away from the rail to get a better look, I decided it was too high to attempt to jump up on and then over. Best to do it with one sturdy leap instead of taking the chance of tripping on the *Wind Binder*'s railing and plunging into the river, only to be squashed between hulls.

My heart was pounding as I climbed up onto the railing, the wind doing its best to blow me off balance. Another flash of lightning lit the sky, and I grabbed part of the rigging to keep from falling. The wind was so much stronger when I was standing on the railing than when my feet were planted firmly on deck. We passed the other ship's quarterdeck, which was too high for me to reach, and the stairs leading down to the main deck.

I held my breath as I waited for my opening. *Closer . . . come on, just a little closer . . .*

Now! With a silent prayer in case anyone was listening, I jumped.

AVALANCHE

Chapter 41

I GRABBED THE ELONDRIAN ship's railing and swung my-self over. My heart was still pounding when my feet reached the other side. I was immediately met by a couple of lancers on watch who had spotted my jump and rushed over. I turned and waved to Trey-gan as the *Wind Binder* continued past, letting him know I'd made it.

"You're as crazy as they say," one of the lancers behind me said.

I wiped water from my face. "Where's the king?"

"He's in the hold of the second ship."

"He's belowdecks?" That didn't sound like the smartest place to be. I could see Goring wanting to keep the king as far from the fight as possible, but if the Cylmarans broke through the line, the king would be left with no place to retreat. "And the Black Guild?"

"They're down there with him."

"Where's Overcaptain Tolin?"

"He and Commander Goring are on the far ship where the Cylma-rans are trying to board." He looked at the other two lancers standing with him. "We've been ordered to stand watch in case more of those Cylmaran boats try working their way around again." He looked off the bow and over at the *Wind Binder*. "I don't know where you found that ship, but I've never seen anyone run maneuvers like that before."

"And you probably never will again," I said, pride seeping through the fear I'd been feeling since Treygan had put his crazy plan into action. I spared one final glance at the black ship as it sailed straight for the fires ahead, then started across the deck for the planks that connected the two ships. I hoped the *Wind Binder* made it. I was halfway across when one of the soldiers behind me shouted.

I turned to see him pointing to something off the port side. All three lancers were now staring over the rail, so I ran back to see if more of the Cylmaran flatboats had been sent around. "What's going on?"

I didn't see anything in the water.

"There," the man I'd spoken with earlier said, pointing at the first of the convoy ships, which was about half a ship's length ahead of ours.

"What?" I asked. "I don't see anything."

"The anchor!" he said. "It's gone. They've cut it."

"They what?" I looked up at the bow. He was right. The closest ship was already beginning to turn in the current—*toward* us. The fighting on board was still raging, but somehow the Cylmarans had managed to take over the ship's helm.

"It's heading right for us!" one of the other lancers said.

I grabbed the man and pushed him toward the other ships. "Run! Get help! Let the commander know we are about to be boarded."

I turned to watch the oncoming vessel as it veered in our direction, trying to judge where the ship would hit. If they made it on board, the king was going to be surrounded. There was no stopping it now that the current had it. I doubted the damage would be great considering how slow it was moving, but I could already see Cylmaran soldiers working their way up to the forward deck, getting ready to leap aboard. They were met by a small force of remaining lancers who were trying to hold their position.

The majority of the fighting looked to be centered on the main deck and spilling up onto the quarterdeck, around the helm. The lancers were trying to regain control, but the Cylmarans appeared to be winning.

The Cylmarans reached the top deck and were immediately met by the Elondrian lancers, but they weren't likely to hold long against such overwhelming numbers.

The lancer beside me blew his whistle. Within moments, lancers from all decks ran to the sound.

"Ready your pikes and follow me!" I shouted, then raced up to the foredeck to meet the approaching ship and lend aid to those already fighting. Steel clanged and shouts of battle rose from both the oncoming ship and the outermost ship in our lashed convoy behind us. Apparently, the Cylmarans coming in from the city port had begun to make it aboard on the far side.

No one had even suspected the Cylmarans might attempt an attack like this mid-voyage. Three quarters of our army were still in Belbridge with no idea of what was happening, and no way for us to inform them, not that it would have mattered. By the time anyone reached the camp, the battle would be over.

"Brace yourselves!" I shouted, as the two ships were about to collide. We jumped back from the rail just as the other ship rammed into it. The shock sent me to my knees, and I spun to the side in time to dodge a large chunk of wood that cracked off in the strike. The lancers around me had fallen as well but were quickly getting back to their feet.

"Pikes up!" I shouted as I ran back to the rail, swords drawn, to meet the oncoming rush. Instead of us making it aboard their vessel to help the few lancers still remaining, those lancers retreated onto ours, many injured, as others tried dragging them from the fight.

"Fall back!" an officer from the other ship shouted. I recognized Captain Asa's booming voice. The lancers quickly retreated, dragging as many of the injured from the fight as they could. Asa was the last across, and I managed to pull him back just as a dozen hooks flew across the rail.

"Good of you to join us!" he shouted when he saw me.

Everyone moved back from the side to keep from getting caught by the hooks as the Cylmarans pulled the bows of the two ships together.

To my right, the fiery wreckage continued to burn, providing just enough light to see by. Its warm orange glow punched through the downfall, reflecting off the steel of our swords.

"Cut those lines!" Asa shouted, raising his battle-axe as he ran to cut the lines free.

I grabbed him and pulled him back. "No point, sir! The current alone will hold them in place. We need to hold the breach!"

The Cylmarans broke through, and I cut down the first two, tripping several others as they were pushed forward by those behind.

"You heard the man!" Asa shouted. "Get the injured out! The rest of you, to me!"

Asa stood at the center with me as we braced for the first wave, his axe ready to swing. A chunk of railing had been torn apart on both ships, leaving a small opening wide enough for one or two men to make it across at a time. The rest were already beginning to climb the rail, swinging over from the rigging to leap aboard.

The warmth of my magic built in my chest as the front wave of Cylmarans tried to breach the guardrail. The first across were met with pikes. Men screamed as the lancers' weapons plunged through them, some impaling more than one boarder. Blood sprayed. The sickening taste filled my mouth, and I fought to slow my breathing.

Most of the lancers focused their efforts on those trying to leap over the railing, catching many in the air and sending them screaming down to the river below to drown or be smashed between hulls. Some made it across and immediately engaged the lancer watch. I remained with Asa at the breach, dropping soldiers as fast as they came across.

My swords never stopped, each new swing bringing the promise of death. Body after body piled at my feet, each fresh kill numbing me inside until I felt nothing but desperation.

I *had* to keep the king safe.

We held for as long as possible, but there simply wasn't enough of us to counter the numbers coming over the side. It wasn't long before we were forced to give ground.

I lost count of how many Cylmarans I'd cut down, focusing solely on keeping my blades moving as I ducked and dodged and deflected the steel coming at me. My visions filled my eyes as my magic sang, a blazing torch that raged through all my senses. I had only ever relied on my visions to this extent twice before: once when the tribes had battled outside the Pit, and the second when I held the bridge against the Cylmarans during my rescue of the Elondrian ambassador.

This was so much worse.

I spun left, dodging a thrust to my chest. I ducked under a second and slit the soldier's throat, then drove a sword out the back of the first. They both dropped, and I swatted at the next. My visions were coming so fast I wasn't sure I could keep up with them. My body seemed to move of its own accord. Bodies were piled high enough to block the breach in the railing, halting those trying to board.

But not for long.

Lancers began to drop. Several men to my left fell, and Asa roared in pain. Before I could turn to help, another wave struck, and I plunged my sword through the first soldier, kicked him backward, then sent two more after him for good measure.

Using the brief respite, I rushed to Asa. He'd stumbled back, hand clutching his face. Blood ran freely down his cheek, but it didn't stop him from burying his axe in the neck of the next Cylmaran and spitting on the corpse as it fell.

The captain clenched his teeth against the pain, blood soaking into his ducktail beard. I pushed him back into the arms of a pair of lancers.

"Get him out of here!" I spun back around, getting my sword up just in time to keep my head on my shoulders as I deflected a blade on my right. I could hear the ornery captain doing his best to order the men to release him, insisting he was fine.

A new surge of Cylmarans forced their way farther across the deck, and I had to pull back. A quick glance over my shoulder showed we'd lost at least half of our fighters. We gave up more ground.

Where was our help?

Those few who were left had dropped their pikes and switched to their swords. They gathered to me, and we formed a small wall that was being pushed farther back by the moment. I kept my swords moving, no longer worried about clean strikes, lashing out at anything that came close enough to hit, whether it was hands, arms, or legs.

My gut roiled with horror at the mutilation and anguished cries, but I forced it down. Fear and adrenaline overpowered my urge to retch, and I kept fighting.

Two more lancers went down beside me, one taking a sword across the shoulder and neck, which nearly decapitated him.

"Pull back!" I shouted, and we retreated down the stairs to the main deck, then ran for the gangway. There was no way we could fight that many in the open.

I stood at the bridge and raised my swords as the dozen remaining lancers moved in behind me. "Stand your ground!"

Red-and-black uniforms flooded the deck. The Cylmarans didn't seem to have any specific command structure—no one leading the way, no one shouting orders. Almost as though it was every man for himself, with the only objective being to get to the king and kill as many Elondrian soldiers as possible along the way.

The first wave of men hit. Water and blood were flung from my face as I moved between enemy strikes, delivering my own deadly blitzes in return. Eyes bulged, mouths gaped, and death rattles sounded as I stabbed and sliced and cut apart anyone foolish enough to come at me. My magic was a fire in my chest. It almost felt like a living thing. The heavy rainfall did little to cool the blaze as it grew inside me. My magic wanted to take over.

The Cylmarans continued to pour across the deck of the first ship. Beside me, the lancers were dropping one by one, overwhelmed by much greater numbers. I could hear the battle on the third ship raging somewhere behind me as I struggled to keep my swords moving. Bodies were everywhere, and I fought to keep my feet under me as I continued to send even more down to join them.

By now we'd been pushed across the gangway, nearly onto the second ship, where they had the king in hiding. My arms were tiring, and my visions battered me, my body reacting before my tired brain even realized what it had seen. My magic was nearly out of control. It wanted to be freed. What would happen if I did let it take control? Fear flooded through me at the thought.

I became aware of Shade nudging me through our bond, and I

leaned on his presence to fight the magic back down.

My swords were taking a beating, and I knew they were going to have to be swapped out. Noph's sword had served me well. I didn't want to lose it, but I needed blades sharp enough to cut flesh.

I kept my arms moving, using the least amount of effort possible to get the task done, trying to conserve what strength I had as I sent one man after another to the great beyond. We'd lost half of those who held the gangplank. Where was our help? Was the battle on the third ship so great that none could make it here?

"We need help!" I shouted over my shoulder, hoping someone behind could hear me. My heart sank as my cry was met with silence. A lancer to my left took a sword to the chest and dropped. I started to shout once more, but before I got a chance, a wave of crimson-and-gold uniforms raced onto the gangplank from behind and slammed into the Cylmaran soldiers, forcing them back across.

"So you finally decided to show up," Overcaptain Tolin said, thrusting his sword through the neck of a Cylmaran.

First Asa, now him. Where did they think I'd been?

"Better late than not at all!" I shouted back. A streak of lightning left me momentarily blinded. Strangely enough, my visions still worked even with my eyes shut, and I cut my way through three more men as I waited for the blinding light to fade.

"Did you just kill those three with your eyes closed?" Tolin asked.

I wasn't sure how to answer. He'd clearly caught me. Best to change the subject. "Where's Commander Goring?"

"On the third ship, holding back those coming in from the stolen supply ships. Where's Asa?"

"He was injured. I had men take him below."

"I'm sure he didn't appreciate that."

"Cursed like a Bristonian sailor the whole way," I said, parrying another blow and sending the sword's wielder to the deck.

Tolin's swordsmanship was excellent, on par with my own in my current state of exhaustion. The enemy rushed forward, heedless of the death awaiting them, trying to force us back across to the second ship. They must have figured the king was somewhere aboard.

"We can't hold like this much longer," I said, cutting down one of the Cylmarans trying to reach Tolin. "If they break through, the king's going to be like a fish in a barrel."

"Safer than up here at the moment," Tolin said, blocking an oncoming sword with his shield, sweeping the man's guard wide and finishing him off with a swift thrust. His sword and shield moved as extensions of his arms as he held his ground, hacking his way through the horde of bodies ahead.

"It won't be safe for long!" I said, nodding toward the port side. The next ship in the convoy looked to have been overtaken as well, and they were attempting to turn the ship enough to reach the one that hit us.

The Cylmarans were about to get reinforcements.

The rest of the fleet looked to still be under lancer control, but I had no idea how long that would last, considering the Cylmarans looked to outnumber us nearly two to one.

With Tolin's lancers at our side, my small team managed to push the soldiers back far enough to make it onto the first ship's deck once again. Presently, we had the advantage with better-trained troops, but that would be nullified when those additional Cylmaran soldiers flooded onto the deck.

There had to be a way to stop them.

"We need to rotate," I said. My sides ached, my arms screamed, and it was hard to get enough air to keep going.

"What?" Tolin continued swinging and blocking, never missing stride. He was over ten years my senior but had the stamina of someone far younger.

"We need a plan," I said, panting. "And I need to rest before my arms fall off." I cut the legs out from under a man on my right, stabbing him on his way down, then parried two more on my left, both swinging for my head. I found myself wishing for a shield.

"Rotate!" Tolin shouted, and the lancers at the rear pushed forward, replacing those of us in front, allowing us to move away from the fighting to rest.

I made it to the back, my swords held loosely at my sides, my arms cramping under the strain. "We need to figure out how we're going to stop this new wave. It's only a matter of time before we're overrun."

Tolin doubled over, trying to catch his breath. "I'm open to suggestions."

I looked out at the ships off the port bow, then back at the burning wreckage behind us, a hint of an idea forming. "We let them come."

Tolin straightened. "What? You don't want us to stop them?"

"No, I do, but not in the way you think. Let them board the first ship—as many as we can get—and then we cut the ship free and send it into the flaming barricade. Depending on how many Cylmarans we trap aboard, we might be able to rid ourselves of a significant enough number to turn the tide in our favor. Even if they jump overboard before they hit the barricade, the distance to shore will probably kill most of them."

The overcaptain took a moment to study the battle ahead as it raged across the main deck. Our men were gaining some ground, pushing the Cylmarans back toward the other side. His eyes narrowed. "It could work. But we would need to evacuate those belowdecks first."

I nodded. The Elondrian military employed more than just lancers. Civilians were contracted to aid in the war effort: craftsmen and cooks, wagoners for transports and ostlers for the horses, along with a host of other laborers that took care of the soldiers' daily needs. Many of those had traveled over by land already, but those who had not were sheltering belowdecks.

The second ship in the convoy off the port side was already shifting in the water. It wouldn't take them long to reach the first and then send its men across and over to our three.

Tolin looked at me and nodded. "I hate losing one of our ships, but let's do it." He stared at me a moment. "You realize that we'll not only need to cut the bindings here, but someone will have to make it all the way to the bow of that ship and cut the anchor? The same bow that is about to come under siege by Cylmaran soldiers."

We both looked at where the two ships had collided and the open passage between.

"Any ideas on how we manage that?" he asked.

"Without being seen," I said.

He cocked one of his brows. "Sounds like something an Upakan would be good at."

I smiled. "If you can evacuate those below, cut the lashing, and pull the gangplank, I'll find a way to get to the anchor."

He nodded, and I turned and started for the galley door behind us.

"Where are you going?" Tolin called after me.

"To report to the king."

Tolin waved me on, and I grabbed the handle of the galley door. I barely got it open before I was leaping to the side and swatting away two swords aimed for my gut. "What in the flaming tongues are you trying to do?" I shouted.

Barthol and Fipple jerked back in shock.

"We-we thought you were one of them," Barthol said. "We were

told to kill anything that came through that door not wearing crimson and gold."

"Is that Ayrion up there?" I heard Gellar shout from below.

"Yes," Barthol shouted down to him.

"How'd he get aboard?"

"I don't know."

"Oh, for pity's sake." I pushed past my roommates and quickly headed down the stairs.

The underbelly of the ship was much larger than the *Wind Binder*, and from the looks of it, had at least two or three decks. The first held the galley, filled with tables and benches, where the crew no doubt ate their meals. I could hear the groans of men dying. They must have set up the infirmary below.

The Black Guild quickly assembled as I reached the landing. The men were wearing black bands on their arms. Tolin must have been able to get them after all. I spotted Elwin and Gilford as I scanned the group. Apparently the overcaptain was able to transfer them back in time. Tolin had really come through for us. I even spotted Howell and Tilson. I hoped the two new recruits were up to the task.

"Tilson. Head below and see if you can find me a carpentry saw." I pulled my swords from their sheaths. "Gilford, find a smithy and have him put a new edge on these."

The two men ran to carry out their assignments, and I turned to the group. There seemed to be one very important person missing.

"Where's the king?"

"I'm here," a voice called out from behind my men.

The Black Guild parted, and the king stepped forward, decked in his royal armor. He looked ready for war. More than ready, in fact. His jaw was set, and his hand gripped the hilt of his sheathed sword. His ornate armor, though quite fetching, clearly stood out and was going to draw unwanted attention. That was a problem.

"We need to get you out of that armor, Your Majesty. Every Cylma-ran up there will be drawn straight to it. Perhaps you will allow one of my men to wear it as a decoy."

"Not on your life," the king said. "I will not cower while another man takes my place."

"Your protection is our primary duty, Your Majesty. I made a prom-ise to the queen that I would keep you safe."

"And you will," he said. "But I have no intention of sneaking around like a common gutter thief."

"But, Your Majesty—"

Rhydan raised his hand. "I'll hear no more of it."

I bit my tongue but relinquished my argument with a bow. "As Your Majesty wishes."

Waylen cleared his throat and tried to change the subject. "How'd you get here so fast? Fly?"

I smiled. "No. Some friends brought me." I quickly filled them in on what had been happening. "They're trying to keep the barricade up-river from reaching our convoy."

"Those are quite the friends," Fipple said.

Stumpy patted me on the back. "It's good to see you."

The king growled, staring up at the deck above us. "I should be up there fighting with my men. Not cowering belowdecks."

"You should be keeping your head as low as possible, Your Majesty," I said, "since it's the one they're after. We have a plan."

"Commander Goring? What does he have in mind?"

I shook my head. "Overcaptain Tolin and myself." I sketched the outline of the strategy, what little there was.

"And how exactly are you going to get to the anchor," Gellar asked, "with their army standing between you and it?"

"By keeping as far away from them as I can."

Everyone looked at me, confused.

"I don't have time to explain. Post a guard outside the door. If this doesn't work and we get overrun, the last thing we need is His Majesty getting stuck down here in the one place there is no escaping from."

"My thoughts exactly," the king said with an eager smile as he patted his sword. "Let me fight."

I shook my head. "The commander is correct, Your Majesty. This is the safest place for you. But that could change rather quickly, so be ready."

Rhydan frowned. "I've been ready since we saw the first hail of flaming arrows hit the fleet's sails."

Fipple straightened his topknot, then pulled up his hood. "I'll stand watch. Those are my countrymen out there, and I want to be at the front if anything happens."

"I'll join him," Gellar added, unhooking his battle-axe.

"Anyone spot Saryn yet?" Fipple asked. "I have a piece of steel that needs bleeding on."

"That coward wouldn't be caught within riding distance of here," the king said. He looked at me. "If you see the overcaptain or commander up there, be sure to tell them I said they were right. They'll know what I mean."

I knew what he meant as well. Neither of them had wanted the king to put himself in such a precarious position.

Tilson was the first back, carrying a saw. It wasn't quite as big as the one I'd seen Whitey use, but it would work.

"What's it for?" Tilson asked.

"Sending a bunch of Cylmarans to the bottom of the river." I smiled at his confused look as I tied the saw to my belt with some twine.

Gilford wasn't far behind Tilson, his head popping up from the steps below. "Best he could do in so little time," he said, climbing the rest of the way up and handing me the blades.

I felt the edges. "Better than what I had." I sheathed both and headed up the stairs and back out onto the main deck of the second ship. Gellar and Fipple stood guard on either side of the door as I passed.

I didn't see Tolin anywhere, but there was a line of people rushing across the gangway from the first ship to this one. None of them were wearing uniforms, which meant Tolin's men must have already begun evacuating those below. The overcaptain certainly wasn't wasting time. To my left off the starboard side, those under Commander Goring's leadership were battling across the deck of the third ship. Both sides seemed evenly matched for the moment.

Now for the difficult part: getting over to the bow of the first ship and cutting the anchor without being seen. It would have been an easy thing to simply climb up on the foredeck of this ship and hop over, except I'd be hopping straight into the middle of the Cylmaran ranks. There was no way I could get to the anchor's rope from there, which left me with only one other option.

I looked up.

AVALANCHE

Chapter 42

HE RAIN CONTINUED TO FALL, the deck planking slick as I made my way across the second ship toward the quarterdeck steps on the port side. I scaled the stairs and headed to the stern of the ship, passing several lancers standing ready along the sides with pikes in case any Cylmarans thought themselves clever enough to try sneaking aboard without us knowing.

I waited, watching to make sure there were no other Cylmarans trying to get over before climbing up onto the rail and using the rigging to leap over onto the rail of the first ship. I grabbed hold of the shrouds to keep from slipping off.

The battle raged across the main deck below, slowly moving toward the far side of the ship as Tolin and his men gained ground, forcing the Cylmarans back up the stairs toward the bow.

From my height up on the quarterdeck rail, I could see the additional troops from the second convoy ship now piling onto the first. It wouldn't be long before they were boarding this ship and pushing Tolin and his men back.

My time was running out.

I looked up. The only way for me to get to the anchor unseen was to climb over their heads.

Quickly, I began to climb the rope ladders up to the top of the mizzenmast. The rope was slick from the water, but my gloved hands held firm. Thankfully the sails were furled, so my way was clear as I carefully inched out across the spar and grabbed a line that ran up to the bottom of the crow's nest on the main mast.

Below me, the fresh Cylmarans tore through the breach between the first convoy vessel and the first of the lashed ships that Tolin and his men were fighting to hold. The momentum that Tolin had gained stopped instantly. In short order, he and his men were losing ground. I had to reach the bow before the lancers were pushed all the way back to the ramp. Tolin was trying to buy me time, but if the Cylmarans managed to make it aboard the second ship, the king's life was going to be in immediate danger.

I could see our lancers on the starboard side already beginning to cut through the lines mooring the first and second ship together. I had to hurry. If I couldn't get the anchor cut, this was going to all be for nothing, and with the new Cylmaran soldiers, Tolin had no chance of holding them back.

Pulling my attention away from the fighting below, I looked up and out across the open nothingness I was about to have to cross to get to the central mast. It was a good thing heights didn't frighten me, because I was about to be hanging a hundred feet over the deck.

The wind seemed a thousand times stronger up here than below.

Rain lashed at my face, and the rope was nearly pulled from my grasp, but I managed to wrap my legs around it and shimmy out. The howling of the wind tearing across the lines filled my ears, drowning out most of the battle below, causing the rigging to creak and the folds of my coat to snap.

I looked down to check my progress just as a flash of lightning ripped across the sky, blinding me.

My hand slipped, but I clung to the rope until my sight returned and my heart stopped pounding. Taking a deep breath, I started forward. I inched across the rope like a loop worm, my hands trembling, the rain making it hard to find purchase on the slick rigging.

Soon enough, I reached the undercarriage of the crow's nest on the main deck and worked my way around to the other side of the mast. This cross line stretched to the foremast at the bow. It was going to be the longest of the climbs, and the most precarious, as I would be crawling straight over the battle below. If someone were to look up at the right moment, I'd be a sitting duck to anyone with a bow.

Shaking my hands to get the blood circulating once more after the first climb, I grabbed hold of the next rope and swung myself out. This time, instead of focusing on the rope, I looked down at the fighting below, watching for any sign of being spotted. Keeping my head tilted so I could see the battle had me dizzy, and it slowed my progress.

This might have been worse than my climb up Howling Gorge during the Tri'Nephrin. One slip and it would be the end of me. Worse, if I did fall, I'd probably end up taking out several lancers in the process. Another flash of lightning struck, and I clung to the rope as I closed my eyes, hoping no one saw me while I was distracted. I quickly opened them again and scanned the fighting on deck. It didn't seem like anyone had noticed me, so I continued on, my heart pounding as loudly in my ears as the rolls of thunder.

The rain pelted my body, doing its best to fling me from the rope. Water ran up my face as I hung upside down, some going in my nose. I had to keep lifting my head and blowing my nostrils clear to keep from drowning.

About halfway across, an ear-piercing crack of thunder struck without warning, and my hands slipped. I fell backward, dangling from the rope by only my feet. My stomach leaped into my throat as the ship below began to spin.

As fast as I could, I scrambled for the rope, managing to grab hold with one hand and pulling myself up enough to get the other around as well. I didn't move for some time, panting uncontrollably as I worked up the courage to keep going.

I carefully scooted the rest of the way across. Once I reached the foremast, I wrapped my arms around the shroud, giving myself a moment to catch my breath. Below, Tolin and his men had been pushed back to the main deck and were losing further ground by the minute, being forced toward the king's ship. I could see the overcaptain near the front, repeatedly looking toward the bow, no doubt wondering where I was and when the anchor would be cut.

Most of the ropes lashing the two ships together had already been severed. The only pieces left were at the gangway.

From my vantage point, I could see that at least half of the new reinforcements hadn't yet made it aboard. They were getting tangled up in the narrow opening between ships, helped by the slower retreat by our lancers. It didn't look like we'd get the rest on until Tolin and his men were all the way back aboard the king's ship. Tolin had wanted me to wait to cut the anchor free until we had as many Cylmarans on board as possible to send into the flames, but at this point, just getting it cut seemed the more prudent choice.

The capstan at the center of the forward deck was overrun by Cylmarans. No way I could cut the ropes from there like I'd seen Whitey do back on the *Wind Binder*. That left me with one other choice.

I worked my way around to the front of the foremast. If I couldn't cut the rope on the deck, I was going to have to do it from outside the ship. So, instead of taking the shroud rigging down—which would have dropped me onto the bow railing, the very place I didn't want to be seen—I grabbed one of the lines that ran out to the bowsprit mast, hanging just off the front of the ship. Once there, I should be able to shimmy back to the front rail and climb down to where the anchor's rope passed through the hull.

Quickly, I started working my way down the rope, passing the end of the bow and out over the rushing water below. I watched the water drawing closer as I neared the end of the line. One slip and the current would drag me under. I reached the end of the rope at the tip of the bowsprit mast and grabbed the rigging underneath the furled sail. From there I climbed down to the hull at the bow.

By the time I reached it, I realized the hole where the anchor rope fed through was too far down and to the right for me to reach from where I was. I took a moment to wipe the water from my face as I tried to think what to do.

How close were the Cylmarans to the king's ship? I needed to move faster.

I scanned the mast, panic starting to bleed through what little control I still maintained over my composure as I frantically tugged on all the lines one by one to see how stable they were and where they were connected. My arms screamed from the climb, and my hands were raw despite the gloves, but if I rushed and cut the wrong one, I'd send myself into the river.

I found what I thought was a single line that might hang low enough for me to swing over to the anchor if cut. Hooking my legs around the different rope for leverage, I pulled out my saw and began to cut. The teeth dug in, and the rope I needed eventually snapped, dropping down to the bow. Tucking the saw between my teeth to free my hands, I grabbed hold of the rope and started down, wrapping my legs around it for balance. I was low enough now that I had to contend with the river spray in addition to the rain as I attempted to lower myself far enough to swing over to the anchor.

Once in place, I began to rock the line.

The wind fought against me as I tried to gain enough momentum to swing over. My teeth bit into the saw's handle, the taste of wood oil a grateful reprieve from that of blood.

Unfortunately, I wasn't close enough.

I swung out and back once more, reaching out with one hand to grab hold of the thick cable.

But I missed.

I still wasn't far enough.

Grinding my teeth against the saw, I swung out and back once more. This time my fingertips raked the edge. Just a little more. I put everything I had into this pass, swinging as far back as I dared, but something shifted, and my rope started to lower.

I reached the outermost peak of the swing and started back, but my rope suddenly lost tension. I looked back and gasped. The rope was pulling free from the mast overhead.

I wasn't going to make it.

Clinging as tight as I could, I stretched out my arm, far enough I thought I might tear something free, but the rope gave way altogether, and I plummeted toward the river. I shouted as I went down, just managing to grab hold of the thick anchor line as I hit the water.

The fall jarred the saw from my mouth, and it dropped into the river.

No! I scrambled to grab it before it was sucked under, but I was too late. The panic that had been only seeping through before burst open like a dam as my only hope of cutting the anchor free disappeared from view.

I was mad enough to chew through the cord with my own teeth. I wanted to scream, but little good that would do other than to alert the Cylmarans to my presence. What now? The rope was gone, the saw was gone, and I was hanging from the very thing I needed to cut.

Desperately, I drew my sword and climbed up the rope as far as I could, then hacked at the rope below me. The water was freezing, and my hands began to tingle. I had to hurry. I had no idea what was happening above me. For all I knew, the Cylmarans had already pushed their way onto the king's ship. With heavy swings, I beat at the thick binding.

It was slow work. The saw would have cut through this in no time, and even with a newly sharpened edge, my sword just wasn't making a very big dent. Still, I continued to chop, swinging as fast as I could and with all the might I could muster.

"Come on, you wretched piece of string. Cut!" I slashed and chopped, and even tried using the blade as a saw, which only seemed to waste my time and sap what little strength I had left after my climb across the ship. My hands were going numb, and I was hardly a third of the way through, but I couldn't stop. My men were depending on me. Tolin was depending on me.

The king's life was in my hands.

Gritting my teeth, I continued to swing. I was barely halfway through when the entire ship shifted in the water.

I stopped hacking and grabbed the rope, holding on as the current started to turn us. What now? I couldn't take any more surprises. The rope loosened for just a moment and then snapped tight. Tolin must have ordered the rest of the lashing cut. The ship was drifting on its own. Blazes! I wasn't ready. I lifted my sword to swing again, and the ship lurched even harder. My numb fingers dropped the blade, and I wasn't quick enough to grab it before the current had it and pulled it down.

This was a nightmare! Thankfully, I hadn't been using Noph's sword to cut with.

The rope under me suddenly jerked tight once again, and I was nearly flung off. This time it was followed by a loud snap as the heavy line split right where I'd been cutting. I almost screamed for joy. I'd done it. Then it hit me.

I was still clinging to the rope with nowhere to go and no way to climb up.

This was just my luck. I was going to end up riding this thing all the way back into the flames. Above, I could see soldiers leaping over to the king's ship from the one I was still clinging to, desperate to get off before the two completely separated.

If they could do it, so could I. I swung what was left of the anchor's cord, each new pass getting me a little closer to one of the rope ladders hanging over the side of the main deck. I had to be careful. One wrong push from the river and the two ships could collide, and I'd be smashed between the hulls.

About the time we started to pass the first of the ladders, men began to fall past me into the water as those on board the second ship piked any trying to get over. A Cylmaran in the water grabbed for my rope, but a swift kick to the face sent him down.

Swinging back one last time, I pushed with everything I had and swung outward. Releasing the rope, I hit the side of the ship right between two of the ladders, missing both. I snagged the bottom of the one on the right just before hitting the water and held on for dear life.

Fear driving me on, I scrambled up the side of the hull to the main deck rail, only to find it lined with Cylmarans. How had so many gotten aboard?

I looked over my left shoulder at the first ship. It was now too far away for anyone else to cross, and as the river pulled it away, it dragged the convoy ships with it. The decks of the first ship were filled with soldiers, watching helplessly as the current pulled them southward. My plan had worked, at least partway. Unfortunately, there was still a large number of soldiers that had been able to make it aboard before I'd cut the anchor.

Grabbing ahold of the railing, I dangled against the hull as I slowly worked my way up to the bow, my fingers all but numb. I had to get to the king, but the battle on deck was in my way. Climbing up, I managed to swing myself over the rail.

I landed on my backside and didn't move for several minutes as I tried to catch my breath and let the blood reach my extremities. The fighting was relegated to the main deck below, giving me a moment to rest while I pulled off my boots and emptied them of water. I didn't have time to try to squeeze my socks, so I pulled my boots back on and stood. My legs were a little wobbly, but at least I could feel them once again.

I reached for my sword and scanned the fighting below. I didn't see the Black Guild or the king anywhere on deck, even though I'd told them to bring him up if the Cylmarans managed to get aboard.

On my left, the battle was still raging, with Commander Goring on the third ship as he and the majority of the lancers fought to keep those coming in from Ranool's port away from this one.

Not wanting to continue hiding on the foredeck, I headed down the port-side stairs—the starboard side was brimming with Cylmarans nearly all the way to the galley door—and pushed my way through the Elondrian Lancer unit along the galley wall. I had to get to the king.

The two sides seemed evenly matched at the moment.

I reached the door and ducked. A Cylmaran's blade struck the wood where my head had been, and I grabbed the man's arm and pulled him forward hard enough to deliver a head-butt to his face and a knee to the groin. I then used him as a shield to shove those behind him back far enough to get the door open.

"It's me, Ayrion!" I shouted to those inside, not having time to try thwarting what was sure to be several more swords from my men.

Sure enough, Barthol, Gellar, and Fipple were standing there waiting to cut down whoever came through. It looked like they already had a small pile of bodies stacked behind them in the kitchen. I kicked the Cylmaran I was holding back into his own soldiers and shut the door behind me. I looked for a lock, but apparently it had been ripped off.

I didn't stop to talk and headed down the stairs.

"I'm ready," the king said, his sword up. "What are we waiting for?"

"I'm surprised to still find you here at all," I said, still half out of breath.

"Tolin ordered us to stay," Barthol called down. "With the other ship severed, he thought he could handle the rest." He scratched at his beard. "I don't think he was expecting so many to get on board before the lines were cut."

"From what I saw, he could be right," I said. "For now, we wait here. If we hadn't managed to cut the ships free, it would be a different story." I looked up at Barthol, Gellar, and Fipple at the top of the stairs. "I'll send more men up to help you. The rest of you I want here with the king."

I chose five men, and we made our way up the stairs into the galley. I was thankful for the short reprieve and used it to gather my strength as well as hunt through the dead Cylmarans for another blade. I hated that

Tolin and his men weren't getting such an opportunity, and if it wasn't for the king, I would have already ordered my men back out to help the lancers, but we had a job to do.

The galley door opened, and Gellar planted his axe in the Cylmaran coming through. Fipple plunged his sword into the one behind him. Barthol kicked the dead men out and the door shut once more.

"Those men out there need our help," Gellar said. "I don't like sitting in here on my hands while they're out there dying."

"Neither do I," I said, "but our first priority is the safety of His Majesty."

"Don't worry about me," Rhydan called up from below. "I can look after myself."

I walked over to the top landing and looked down. "Our sole job is to worry about you, Your Majesty."

The door opened once more, and Barthol started to swing but stopped when he realized it was a lancer. The frantic man rushed inside, his face covered in blood. Barthol shut the door behind him.

"Commander Goring's down!"

It took me a moment to process what he'd said. "What about his men?" I asked.

"The line's breaking."

I heard what I thought was Tolin's voice shouting something out on deck, but another roll of thunder kept me from making out the words. It wasn't like the overcaptain could simply stop fighting here and take what remained of his men to the third ship. The king's safety *was* my first priority, but the lancers being overrun would put him in even worse danger.

"What are you waiting for?" the king asked, already climbing the stairs, clearly knowing I only had one choice. "Can't wait in here any longer."

"Draw swords!" I shouted as the rest of my men charged up the stairs, forming a wall around the king. There were about thirty wearing the black armbands. I couldn't help but smile when I saw that the king was wearing one as well. I'm sure it bolstered the men's spirits.

"I want Room Eleven surrounding the king at all times." I turned and looked at the rest of my men as they began to file into the kitchen. "Work as a unit. Do not get separated. This is what we've been training for. We are the Black Guild. Let's show them what that means."

The men shouted their readiness, and I felt a surge of warmth in my chest. It wasn't just my magic. My men were getting their chance to prove themselves. My blood pumped as I turned to the door, waiting for Barthol and the rest of Room Eleven to take up their spots around the king. Rhydan wore a nervous grin. He nodded at me when our eyes met.

"Stay on me!" I shouted and then turned to the door and raised my swords.

If only my family could see me now.

AVALANCHE

Chapter 43

HE DOOR BURST OPEN, and the Black Guild flooded onto the deck.

"On me!" I shouted, and we rushed back through the Elondrian ranks for the starboard gangplank. As much as I wanted to help Tolin quell what remained of those aboard, we needed to get to the more pressing battle on the third ship. With Goring down and the Cylmarans pressing, the lancer line was falling apart.

We reached the gangway as a pair of lancers rushed by, carrying the commander. His face was covered in blood, and he looked to have taken several stab wounds to the chest. One look and I could tell the man wasn't going to make it. The king pushed his way through to the commander's side.

"Goring, can you hear me?"

The commander's eyes opened partway.

Rhydan grabbed his hand. "Stay with us, Commander. You hear me? That's an order."

Goring tried to open his mouth, but nothing came out. His eyes went blank, and he exhaled his last breath.

The men holding him looked at the king as though not sure what to do. They turned to continue their way to the galley, but Rhydan stopped them. "Put him against the rail and get back to your men."

The lancers carefully laid their dead commander against the rail and rushed back to the third ship. The Black Guild followed.

By the time we climbed aboard, the lancer line had collapsed altogether, and a growing knot of Cylmarans were making a run for the gangplank. The lancers who'd been toting the commander were cut down in front of us and their bodies trampled under the stampede.

"Brace yourselves!" I said, glancing over my shoulder to make sure the king had returned to his spot between Room Eleven. He had. I immediately turned to face the horde of red-and-black uniforms heading our way. Like the swell of a river flood about to wash away an unsuspecting village, the soldiers came for us with death in their eyes.

My chest burned as my magic flooded through me. I took two steps away from the men behind me to give myself room, then cut through the first of the Cylmarans to come within reach.

I focused my visions, moving between the soldiers' swords while planting my own in every bit of flesh they came in contact with. Bodies dropped to the deck, spraying blood and gore enough that even the wind and rain couldn't immediately wash away. Another streak of lightning had me closing my eyes once more and letting my visions guide my steps while I picked off the next in line.

No matter how many we killed, more seemed to pile in behind. How many men had Saryn hidden within Ranool? Beside me, I could hear the cold clash of steel as my men fought to hold the line, cutting down the Cylmaran waves as fast as they came.

Slowly, we began to push the enemy back. The lancers that had been under Commander Goring fell in beside us as we fought our way across the deck toward the starboard side of the ship. The Cylmarans weren't prepared to face an elite group of fighters like the Black Guild, and they fell at our feet, men screaming in pain, begging for mercy but dying all the same.

My arms were tired, every muscle burning. I didn't know how much longer I could keep going, but our need to stop the flow of enemy soldiers had me fighting through the pain. My swords worked through the enemy with deadly accuracy, painting the deck with the remains of those that came too close. I dove and ducked, spinning around each thrust as I chopped and hacked my way forward. I ignored the metallic tang of blood in my mouth, focusing on the task ahead and the push of my magic.

My body seemed to be moving almost on its own, and not just because it was nearly numb from the swim in the river and the continuous strain of keeping my swords moving as I danced between the Cylmarans' attempts at my life. It was more than that.

Something deep inside me flared, a heat that kept my movements honed and my blades deadly. I struggled to keep it at bay.

I felt like I was fighting a battle on two fronts. I didn't know what my magic was doing or what would happen if I gave myself over to it fully. I was afraid to find out. The thought of losing control was terrifying, considering I was in the middle of a battle with all of our lives on the line. What if I gave in and then couldn't stop it?

The Black Guild, along with what remained of the lancers, continue to forge ahead, fighting alongside each other as a single block, like a smithy's hammer striking against the Cylmaran line and pushing it back toward the far side of the ship.

Water sprayed from my face with every turn and spin and swing. Pieces of men flew around me as my swords met flesh. Cries and screams were drowned out by the storm, the cacophony of noises only honing my focus to a razor's edge.

We were nearing the starboard side when the ship suddenly tilted.

The movement wasn't extremely noticeable, hardly enough to slow the fighting, but enough for me to have felt the shift. My first thought was that perhaps our anchor had been cut. But why would . . . and then it struck me. They might be attempting to do the same thing we had, sending us floating straight into the burning wreckage downriver.

I pulled back from the immediate fight, letting those behind move to the front. I needed to see what was happening.

"What are you doing?" Gellar shouted, amputating parts like an inexperienced physicker with every swing of his battle-axe.

"I need to see something," I shouted, then looked for someone I could get to help me. Howell was just behind the king and didn't appear to be engaging anyone directly at the time. I called for him, and he pushed his way forward. "Lift me up," I said. "I want to see what's happening."

The larger man lowered his hands and boosted me up high enough to see over the fighting in front of us. One look at the port and the city beyond and my fears were confirmed. We were moving in the water. The ships were no longer anchored. I glanced behind me toward the second ship, where Tolin and his men were still fighting. It appeared their anchor had been severed as well, as both our ships were moving away from the rest of the fleet.

Tolin's lancers had not only managed to hold their own, but it looked like they had cut down the majority of the soldiers that had made it on board before the ships were separated. Some were already trying to abandon ship, having seen they were fighting a losing battle, or perhaps because they knew where our ships were now heading.

"Down," I said to Howell, and he lowered me back to the deck.

"What did you see?" the king asked, trying his best to peer out between the fighters around him.

"Our anchors have been cut. We're drifting downriver toward the fires."

"How do we stop it?" the king asked.

"I don't know that we can. The supply ships are still holding on, which is weighing us down even further. We need to cut them loose, if for no other reason than to stop the flow of soldiers coming aboard."

"But that still doesn't stop us from floating back into that flaming pile of wreckage behind us," the king said.

I looked up. "If we can lower the mainsail, that should help. The wind might hold us in place, or at least slow our descent."

"I can lower them," Howell said. "I worked on a shipper out of Duport for ten years before joining the lancers."

"I can go as well," Tilson said. Like Howell, he'd been kept near the center of the group, not seeing as much action as those who had been training for the last few years.

"We'll need a helmsman," Howell said, "to hold her in the wind."

"That's not going to make much difference with three ships attached to us," I said. "We need to cut the others free if we have any hope of keeping out of the flames."

"What's happening?" a familiar voice called out from behind.

Tolin pushed his way through my men. He stumbled forward, blood-soaked and looking half-dead himself. I guessed he and his men had dealt with those on the other ship. I didn't know how many lancers he still had with him, but we were going to need every able body.

"The anchors have been cut," I said.

"Yes, I know. They cut ours just before jumping overboard."

"The other ship's free of soldiers?"

He nodded. "Cut down to the last man, those that didn't dive over."

"Good. Then we'll use that ship to make our escape."

"What?"

"Can you hold the other ship long enough for Howell and Tilson to get the sails down?"

"If you can keep those here at bay, we can. I can assign some of my men to help."

I nodded. "Once the sail is down, we'll cut the lashing and separate like we did the first ship. If there's anyone belowdecks here, we need to get them out and over to the second ship."

Tolin nodded. "You and your men focus on holding the Cylmarans back, and we'll evacuate the lower decks."

"Fine. Take the king with you. It'll be safer on the other ship than here." I looked at Waylen and Stumpy. "Go with the king."

"I want to fight!" the king said.

"Not as much as we want you to keep your head," Tolin interjected, and then turned His Majesty about face and marched him back through the group. I was glad Tolin felt comfortable enough to handle the king in such a way. If Rhydan had demanded to fight, I doubted I'd have been able to stop him.

With the king's safety now under Tolin's command, I pushed my way back to the front of the battle, alongside Barthol, Fipple, and Gellar, who looked to be tiring, their swings not quite as fast or as sharp as earlier. Unfortunately, with Tolin pulling most of what was left of Goring's lancers to evacuate and secure the ship behind us, we were beginning to lose ground once again as more of the Cylmarans forced their way on board from the supply ships.

From what I could see ahead, they still had at least a ship's worth of men left, while our numbers were waning under the oncoming assault.

"How many of these flaming cutthroats do they have?" Gellar shouted, his battle-axe lodging in the side of one soldier on his right. He jerked the head out and swung for the next.

"Too many," Barthol said, his own swords whipping through the air as he blocked and parried, fighting to cut through the wall of men in front of us.

My own swords continued their dance with death as the heat of my magic churned inside of me, yearning to be set free. I tore into the Cylmarans, dropping bodies, hoping to drive those following back.

Inch by inch, the Black Guild fought their way forward, their dedication and training showing through. Most lancer units crumbled under such an outnumbering force. I had no idea how long we had been fighting, or how many we had lost. We might have only been thirty strong, but we fought like three hundred, holding back the horde of soldiers trying to reach the king.

My arms were heavy, my swords even more so, but I kept going, blocking left, ducking right, sliding the blades in and out of one chest or neck or gut after another. The rain was a blessing, as it was the only thing washing my face and mouth from the refuse of bodies I'd hacked my way through.

"Retreat!" I heard someone shout behind us. It sounded like Over-captain Tolin.

Had they already gotten the sail down? How long had we been fighting?

"Retreat!" I shouted as well, and my men immediately disengaged from the Cylmarans, grabbing our wounded as we went. We couldn't exactly turn and run, but those of us at the front could give those behind time enough to get the wounded and dying back across.

Room Eleven stood at the vanguard, fighting with every last bit of strength to hold back the tide that was quickly pushing us across the deck. My foot caught one of the dead, and I went down. I cut the legs out of three Cylmarans while I scrambled to get back up. A large hand grabbed my coat's collar and dragged me back.

"Can't afford to lose you now," Barthol said, his breath coming in ragged gasps. Beside him, Fipple raged as he cut and slashed and stabbed at one Cylmaran after another, his hatred for Saryn clearly having taken over. Gellar's axe swung all over the place, more in an attempt to keep the soldiers back than to go head-to-head with them.

Fipple cried out as he took a sword to his right shoulder. I blocked the next swing, and he quickly switched stances, using his other hand. His injured arm hung limp, but he continued to fight as we worked our way back toward the other ship.

We were nearing the gangplank on the port side when I caught sight of an unexpected wave of red-and-black uniforms rushing across the foredeck above us. They were making their way around to the port stairs to try heading us off. If they managed to get in behind us, we'd be completely surrounded.

"Hold here!" I shouted to the three of them and ran for the stairs and the oncoming soldiers. There was no way I could hold them back for long, but it just needed to be long enough to allow my friends time to get back across the gangway. As soon as I left my place, the front of our line began to crumble, but there was nothing I could do about it. I had to stop the Cylmarans from cutting off our retreat.

I made it halfway up the stairs before I hit the first wave of soldiers, cutting down those in front and sending them tumbling down the stairs behind me. I fought my way to the top, desperation driving me. I was

exhausted. Every part of my body ached, begging me to stop.

"We're coming!" I heard Stumpy shout behind me, and I managed a quick glance over my shoulder to see him and Waylen rushing back across the gangplank to help the others. Why weren't they protecting the king? I gritted my teeth and pushed forward, fighting to give my friends every last moment I could afford to help them make it to the other ship.

Spinning under a swift lob for my head, I threw another quick look down the stairs, only to find His Majesty and Tolin charging into the fray along with what remained of the Elondrian lancers. Our numbers had been severely diminished, but at least they were nearing the bridge between ships. Rhydan's face was set in grim satisfaction as he handled his sword and shield like a trained lancer.

My magic continued to burn as I fought to cut through the growing number of soldiers, who were no longer interested in trying to reach my friends below. Now their goal seemed to be focused solely on cutting me off, or better yet, cutting my head off.

My swords sliced through the air, sending one corpse after another down to the deck. How much longer did I need to keep going? Surely they'd gotten everyone off by now. I needed to find a way to retreat myself, but by the time it occurred to me, I was completely blocked off from the stairs. With my back pressed against the ship's railing, I struggled to keep going.

"Get off the ship!" I heard someone shouting behind me. It sounded like Barthol, but I wasn't sure. I couldn't turn my head to see. One falter, one single miss of a blade, and I'd be dead. My visions were beginning to take over, and I was starting to lose sight of what was real and what was magic. From the corner of my eye, it looked like the other ship was moving. I panicked. Had they already cut the lines?

I opened the throat of a man on my left and buried my sword in the chest of the one beside him, then kicked the next back into the rest. I glanced behind me only to find I was right. The ships were parting, and I had no way to reach them. If I tried climbing up on the rail to jump over, they'd cut me down before I'd made it halfway up. Soldiers were leaping over the side to get at the other ship, others to escape the flaming wreckage behind us.

My swords kept going as I worked my way down the side rail, fighting all the way to the bow, hoping to find an open spot along the side where I could leap from, but by the time I'd reached the bow I realized I had nowhere left to go. A third of the forward deck was flooded with Cylmarans, all wanting my blood. Couldn't they see we were all about to be burned alive? You'd think they would have at least tried to save themselves. Perhaps they didn't realize how close to the flames we were.

I dodged a thrust to my chest, only to take a slice to my right arm. There were too many weapons coming at me to keep up with. My coat was helping to guard against some, but not all. Each new cut left me bleeding a little more, drawing me closer to the point of not being able to continue. My visions helped me to avoid the most deadly, but they couldn't stop them all.

My arms burned and my chest ached. I was hardly able to draw breath, and when I did, it felt like drinking fire, which only added to the desperation of my magic as it tried to claw its way out. I was too weak to stop it. I was also too weak to keep going. I had no idea what the magic might do to me if I did let go, but I was about to die.

Letting it take control was my last option.

So I did.

All of my walls came crumbling down at once as I gave myself over to it. My body felt as though it was moving on its own, as if I was a spectator, simply watching as something else worked through me, something dark and deadly. I seemed to find a renewed sense of strength. It wasn't mine, but it was there. My swords tore through men as they sought to relieve me of my life. I danced and weaved and parried my way through the throng of red and black, more red now than black, as I soaked their garments in blood.

Death was all around me. It felt as though I had become death itself—Death's Shadow. I fought with a rage and strength I didn't know I possessed. It was thrilling and terrifying. Bodies began to pile up around me as those in front struggled to retreat, fighting each other to keep away from Death. My entire body was the weapon. How it was still able to keep going, I didn't know. It defied all logic.

By the time my swords had stopped and I looked up, the enemy was gone, either from the work of my blades or from diving over the sides. I collapsed to the deck, unable to do anything but lie there amongst the dead and struggle for my next breath. The fire in my chest cooled as my magic receded, leaving me all but helpless as the rain washed over me. I could hear what sounded like my name being called beneath another roll of thunder. Otherworldly voices riding on the wind.

Was I dying? Was I already dead?

The pain wracking my body let me know in no uncertain terms that I was still very much alive, though I wasn't sure for how long. I could almost feel the icy fingers of death creeping across the deck for me.

Lifting my head, I saw fires raging just off the stern. As the heat washed over me, I raised myself with quivering arms to stare out through the spindles in the forward rail. The king's ship was still holding in the river in front of me, one sail unfurled as it fought to keep its place, unwilling to allow the river to pull it any farther south. My ship, on the other hand, had no such inclination and was letting the current pull it into the flames.

I crawled to my knees. My men were standing at the stern of the ship, watching, shouting my name. Tolin was there, as was the king. Their encouragement was enough to force me up to my feet, and I stumbled to the railing and clung to the wood to keep from dropping back to the deck. It looked like they were trying to let down one of their boats, little good it was going to do in a storm like this.

The heat was building behind me as the stern of my ship neared the inferno. Even if I managed to follow the rest of the soldiers overboard, I didn't have the strength to paddle myself out of a dry creek bed, let alone fight the undercurrent of a swelling river.

Still, after thinking about it, drowning would be preferable to burning alive, so I sheathed my swords and crawled over the railing. My legs were barely strong enough to hold my weight, and I clung to the wood to hold me in place. The water below looked inviting. It would be an easy thing to simply let go, but I was too stubborn for that. I'd gone through too much getting to this point just to throw it all away.

I tightened my grip on the rail, the edge digging into my palms. This couldn't be my end. I had so much left that I wanted to achieve. Foremost was to grow the Black Guild, to see it gain a name amongst the lancers. I wondered how many of my men we'd lost, how many had given everything to their duty. All I knew at that moment was that I didn't want to be one of them.

Shouts rang out from the other ship as they yelled for me to jump in. Boy, were they going to be surprised when I hit the water and sank like a rock. The rowboat was just now reaching the water, and I couldn't tell who was aboard, but I waved and shouted them off. Anyone stupid enough to try rowing in a storm like this under a current this strong was just going to end up dying with me.

My mind drifted at the thought of my pending death.

Instead of looking to the past at life's possible regrets, I looked to the future. I wondered what would happen to Sandstorm and all my family there if I didn't return. I hoped they would at least take my advice and claim orphanage status. It was the only permanent solution I could think of to gain them protection from Cutter.

I was glad I had gotten the chance to see them all once again, to live there amongst them, even for a few days. And even though all wasn't forgiven, I had managed to bring Reevie out of his shell long enough to have a couple of meaningful conversations. I regretted not being able to make things right with him. He was my oldest and dearest friend. I hoped Sapphire and Bull kept an eye on him.

Another wave of heat struck me from behind, and I turned to see the back of my ship was now engulfed in flames. There was little for me to do now but jump. If I died, at least I could say I'd taken as many of the enemy with me as I could and fulfilled my duty to the king. I'd promised the queen to keep her husband alive, and so far, I'd kept that promise.

Straightening, I took a deep breath and prepared to jump. The water was cold, and it wouldn't take long for my limbs to numb, so I needed to focus on keeping them moving for as long as I could. I took one last look at the fiery trawlers behind me and stood, holding on to the top of the rail behind me for balance.

"I want to live," I said and slowly let go of the rail.

Before I could jump, I caught sight of something out of the corner of my left eye. I grabbed the wood and pulled myself back just before I tumbled overboard.

I turned, and my heart skipped when I saw the *Wind Binder*'s black sails moving out from behind the far side of the king's ship. I heard Treygan shouting orders from the helm as the bow began to swing in my direction. The sails were down as they used the current to sweep around behind the larger Elondrian vessel.

My men shouted from the king's ship to those aboard, pointing in my direction. A sense of dumb luck tore through me as the smallest bit of hope surfaced, reviving what little spirit I was still clinging to.

Behind me, half the ship was now engulfed. I didn't have time to wait. If I didn't jump now, I was going to be sucked in with the rest of the wreckage. Standing once again, I looked out at the *Wind Binder* and took a deep breath.

Please let them catch me before I go under. With what little strength I had left, I bent my knees and dove off the front of the ship and into the freezing water below.

AVALANCHE

Chapter 44

HE AIR WAS RIPPED FROM my chest as I hit the water. I don't know how far I sank beneath the surface before my limbs began to move, but when they finally did, it felt like thousands of tiny needles stabbing at the same time. I kicked as hard as I could, using the brightness of the flames to know which way was up.

The current was strong, its arms wrapping around me as it pulled me down into its embrace. But my will to live proved stronger. I thrashed my way upward. My head broke the surface, and I sucked in a life-sustaining breath, inhaling both air and water with a desperate yearning to survive.

I took a brief moment to get my bearings, choking and coughing as I continued to fight for each new breath. The ship behind me had stopped, apparently caught on the wreckage, where it continued to burn. Fires reached up the mast and into the sails above. I hoped Tolin had gotten everyone out from below.

Turning, I began to swim against the current as hard as my feeble arms and legs would allow. After several long moments of struggle, I realized I wasn't actually going anywhere, and in fact was losing ground. Searing heat washed over me in waves, and the flames rained chunks of wood and ash down on me as I fought to keep ahead of the barricade. To my left, the *Wind Binder* was making her turn, but she just wasn't close enough to reach me.

Someone swung a rope and weight over the side—it looked like Bones—but the rope wasn't long enough, and he began pulling it back in. Dread set in when I realized my hope for rescue was swiftly fading. Treygan was shouting, and the black mainsail began to lower as they tried to use the wind to steer them a little closer, but they could only go so far without risking the ship.

There just wasn't much they could do. I felt Shade through our bond and did my best to comfort him. He seemed almost crazed. I could hear him screaming aboard the ship. *It's all right. You'll be fine. Don't worry about—*

The giant stallion leapt over the side of the ship.

"No!" I screamed, as if that was somehow going to magically fly him safely back aboard. He hit the water with a colossal splash, and as soon as he broke the surface, he started straight for me. The crazy, foolish animal was going to get himself killed along with me.

Then I noticed he was dragging something behind him.

A rope.

I swung my limp arms as hard as I could and kicked my numb legs, fighting to reach him. My body was completely drained. I didn't know how I was still moving. Visions of my drowning struck, one after another, sucking away all hope of life and rescue as I was forced to watch each prediction of how it would end. Pretty soon, I realized the visions had stopped, and I actually was drowning. My arms had given out, and I was sinking below the surface. I had nothing left to give.

Shade screamed. The sound filled my ears, but the emotion behind it somehow gave me just enough will to force out a couple more kicks. It wasn't much, but it was just enough to reach the top of the water. Something latched on to the neck of my coat, and I looked up to see that Shade had me in his mouth. He struggled to turn, but the current was too strong.

"Hold on!" Kettle shouted over the side as the *Wind Binder*'s crew fought to turn the ship back north again. We were too close to the wreckage for them to reach us as they started to pass. Without warning, the rope snapped taut, and Shade and I were jerked forward through the water. I hooked my left arm around the rope and pulled myself onto Shade's back. I was too weak to even raise my head, so I slumped over the giant stallion and watched the shoreline move as we were slowly pulled away from the fires.

The heat eased. Soon enough, the shouts from aboard the *Wind Binder* became more recognizable, and by the time I managed to get my head turned to look, Shade and I were floating just beside the ship as the crew hauled in the rope.

"We're coming," Bones called down. The tall first mate climbed down the side and lowered himself into the water. He pulled me to the side, tying another rope under my arms.

"No!" I said, half-delusional, trying to push him away. "Not without Shade."

"He's next," Bones said, pushing me up toward the ladder, but once again I tried to resist. The rope under my arms snatched me into the air as the crew above hauled me up. I flopped onto the deck, limp as a rag, then rolled to my side, retching some of the water I'd swallowed earlier.

"Shade," I croaked. "Help him."

"We are," Ismara said, dragging me away from the railing.

They lowered a large net typically used for loading heavy crates. I watched as Bones and another member of the crew worked the net under Shade, careful not to get his legs caught in it. When finished, Bones waved for those aboard to begin lifting. Pulleys connected to the boom arm groaned as the crew lifted the net up and over the rail, lowering Shade back aboard.

With Whitey's help, I managed to get back to my feet, but I collapsed into the big riverman's arms with the first step. He took it in stride, scooped me up, and carried me over to Shade. I placed my hand up under Shade's jaw and lifted his head up to mine. Water ran from his long black mane down the white bridge of his nose. A deep sense of loyalty hit me through the bond, the intensity of the emotion a blazing heat that radiated from the stallion. We were bound to each other. He was never going to just stand by and let me die. In that moment, I knew I would be just as willing to do the same for him.

"Thank you, my friend. I owe you my life."

Whitey sat me down beneath Shade's overhang, and I looked up at him curiously. I couldn't believe he was up and moving about after having taken such a nasty cut from a Cylmaran's blade. "Shouldn't you be below having someone tend to your back?"

Whitey tilted his wide-brimmed hat up and snorted. "No Cylmaran sword is gonna put me down. I don't even feel it."

The man was clearly delusional. As soon as he stood and turned, I saw that he was bleeding through the hastily applied dressing, soaking the back of his shirt in blood.

"Hooks to stern!" Treygan shouted above us, and the crew raced up to the quarterdeck.

I grabbed Whitey's arm before he could get away. "What's going on?" The words burned in my mouth. My throat was raw from my lungs continually expelling water. I felt like I'd swallowed half the river.

"We're going to tow the king's ship. The current is pulling them downriver toward the wreckage." With that, he took off after the others.

Pops's head emerged from the galley door on the other side of the deck. Seeing me, he hobbled over to where I was propped against the cabin wall. "Worried sick about you, boy!" he said. "What was you tryin' to do, take on the whole flaming army all by your lonesome?" He plopped down beside me on the now-soaked bale of hay.

"If that's what it took," I said with a sad smile.

He ruffled my hair. "You're plum lucky to be alive."

"Don't I know it," I said, reaching up to pat Shade, who was helping himself to some of my seat.

The old riverman looked me over. "Looks like you needs to be seen to yourself. Counting nearly a dozen cuts."

I looked down at my somewhat ripped coat and groaned. Cuts covered my arms, chest, and no doubt my back. "As soon as I catch my breath, I'll be sure to get them tended to."

"Quite the mess you've dragged us into," Pops said.

"Not what I wanted, that's for sure."

He scratched the top of his head. "Well, I reckon it was due. We dragged you into the last one. Guess it was our turn." Pops smiled as he leaned back against the wall.

"Release!" Treygan shouted.

"How's the rest of the fleet?" I asked.

"Seem to be holding their own," Pops said, glancing off the port side. "At least what little I could see when we passed earlier. Kettle keeps telling me to get below like some tottering old fool."

I smiled, understanding his frustration now that I was unable to do much more than sit and breathe. The ship jerked, and I would have fallen off my seat if Pops hadn't grabbed me. The crew must have managed to get the hooks over.

"Looks like we're towing the king's ship."

I looked to the right, off the starboard bow, and caught my first glimpse of Ranool just ahead. I was surprised how far we'd drifted downriver. I also wondered how many, if any, Cylmarans were still in the city, and what they might have done to the people living there.

"Were you able to remove the blockade north of the convoy?" I asked.

"Aye. Just finished pullin' the last toward shore before finding you. We was headin' down to see what could be done about those on the south end of town when the lancers on that ship behind us began shoutin' you needed help."

"Lucky for me."

Pops pursed his lips. "Someone up there's lookin' out for ya." He patted his injured leg. "Just wish that same someone would drop some of that luck my way every once in a while."

I smiled, then leaned back against the wall of the captains' cabin and watched the lightning flash in the distance. The storm had finally moved far enough away that the thunder it produced was little more than a low rumble, more felt than heard. The rain had lessened, signaling the end of the storm. I focused on my breathing, trying to regain what little strength I could manage in case I was needed. Thinking back, I wasn't sure if the storm had helped or hindered our side. A bit of both, probably. It had given the *Wind Binder* the necessary speed to reach the battle in time but had made conditions during the fight precarious at best. Regardless, I was thankful to be alive. So many of my lancer brethren had not been as lucky.

How many of my own men had fallen? How many would yet succumb to their injuries? I needed to get back aboard the other ship and find out, but just the thought of standing had me coughing once again. Instead, I turned my focus back to seeing what I could of the battle at hand, and as if in answer, I heard someone on the deck above shout.

"They're in retreat!"

My head shot up, and I looked at Pops. "Who? The Cylmarans or us?"

Pops shrugged. "How would I know? I'm sittin' here with you."

I held out my arm. "Can you help me up?"

Pops stood and, bracing himself with this crutch, hooked my arm over his shoulder and lifted me to my feet. My legs were even more wobbly than his, but somehow the two of us managed to cross the deck to the port-side rail and look out. We were just passing the last of the convoy ships standing guard between us and the Cylmaran shoreline when I spotted the boats.

Pops pointed excitedly.

"I see them." I released a heavy sigh as I watched dozens of rowboats and flatboats pull away from the convoy, heading back to shore. Whoever was left aboard the ships appeared to be letting them go.

"We've got 'em on the run!" Pops said with a hoarse laugh that turned into an even hoarser round of coughing.

"That we do," a voice behind us said. I turned to find Treygan stepping off the port stairs on my left and back on deck. He walked over to stand beside us at the rail. "It's good to see you alive, my brash young friend. You seem to have more lives than a river cat."

I smiled. "How's the king's ship?"

"Still afloat, for now." He turned and stared at the city's port. "I wonder if we should attempt docking. You think there's any more of them hiding in the city?"

I turned and looked at the empty piers. "I don't know. My guess is probably not. I would imagine they used every able body in the attack, but I can't promise it." I looked back at what remained of the fleet. The ships were still on the water, but there were fires yet to be put out, and many were missing more than half their sails. It was going to be quite the task getting them ready to make the trip back to Aramoor.

"Best we wait for the lancers to do a sweep first," I said. "For now, as long as we have winds coming up from the south, we should be able to ferry the king's vessel far enough north to anchor and wait for the lancers to see if it's safe. Commander Gor . . ." I lowered my head. I had forgotten the commander was no longer with us. I took a deep breath and tried again. "I'm sure Overcaptain Tolin will send riders ahead to Belbridge for reinforcements."

"Do you think this might stop the war or hasten it?"

I chuckled as I stared out at the wreckage around us. "I think we just fought it."

"Huh. I was expecting something much bigger."

"My guess, Saryn is already on his way back to Ecrin. I could be wrong, but I'd be hard-pressed to see him trying anything after a defeat here. Knowing him, this was all just a ruse to get Rhydan out of Aramoor. Now that his plan failed, I don't see him wanting to continue."

Treygan nodded. "If what you say is true, that would be good news indeed."

We watched the Cylmarans retreat as we hauled the king's ship farther up the river, eventually anchoring just north of Ranool. The *Wind Binder* only had a single anchor left, but it seemed enough to keep us in place. Treygan kept the two ships as close to the middle of the waterway as possible, at least until the rest of the fleet could send boats over to the city's port for a look.

By the time the remaining lancers had reached the city's port, the storm had long passed, and the sky was beginning to color as a new dawn rose to greet us. As soon as I had managed to get my numerous wounds tended to and get some breakfast in me, several rowboats arrived bearing summons for me and the crew of the *Wind Binder*.

I was the first up the ladder of the king's ship, my head popping over the side to find the king, Overcaptain Tolin, and what remained of the lancers on board, including the Black Guild, standing at attention as they awaited the arrival of the *Wind Binder*'s crew.

One of the crewmen helped me on board, my legs still struggling to hold their own. I'd barely made it onto the deck when Rhydan walked over and wrapped me in a bear hug. I froze, stunned by the king's emotional welcome.

"It's good to see you alive, son. You have done your people proud this day." He released me and stepped back beside Tolin, who was smiling proudly as well.

I wasn't sure if by "my people," Rhydan was referring to Elondria or the Upaka. Perhaps both?

Beside Tolin stood Barthol and the rest of the Black Guild, the black bands on their arms proudly on display. Cold fingers squeezed my chest as I looked over my men.

Nearly a third were missing.

I hoped their absence was due to injury and not death. Room Eleven had made it out alive, for which I was grateful. None of them appeared to have been seriously injured, though Fipple's arm was in a sling. He should have been resting in his bunk, not moving about the ship, but I laughed at the thought of a physicker telling the stubborn Southern Watcher to sit on the sidelines.

I stood to the side and waited for the rest of the *Wind Binder*'s crew to make it up. Bones was last, following after Pops to make sure the old man didn't slip and fall. As soon as they were aboard, Tolin called to the lancers, and they saluted fist to chest—an acknowledgment of the highest respect. Tears burned my eyes at the sight of these warriors paying homage to a crew of simple rivermen.

Rhydan stepped forward. "You have the undying gratitude of an entire kingdom, and the respect of its king."

I glanced at the crew. Every member of the crew to a man was smiling proudly, some even had tears in their eyes as they took in the grateful men before them.

I stepped forward on wobbly legs. "Your Majesty, may I present to you the crew of the *Wind Binder* and their captains: Captain Treygan and his daughter Captain Ismara."

Treygan and Ismara quickly removed their hats and bowed deeply, then at the king's insistence, proceeded to introduce the rest of the crew.

"It is an honor to meet you," Rhydan said once the introductions were complete. "As long as we have gallant men and women such as yourselves watching our waterways, I know our kingdom is in good hands."

Treygan bowed once more. "The right place at the right time, Your Majesty."

The king harumphed. "Nonsense. From what I've seen and heard, you have one extraordinary ship and crew. I don't believe I've ever seen a ship move on the water quite like that before. Remarkable."

Treygan beamed. "She's a fine ship to be sure, Your Majesty. Gotten us out of more scrapes than I care to admit."

"Is this the same crew that brought you to Aramoor?" Rhydan asked me. "The one you said rescued some of our citizens from slavers?"

I nodded. "They are, Your Majesty."

"I take it that was just being in the right place at the right time as well?"

Treygan smiled.

"Well," the king continued, "it seems we owe you for more than your timely rescue here. I aim to see that debt repaid as soon as we return to Aramoor."

"Not necessary, Your Majesty. Knowing that we were able to have offered assistance is payment enough."

Rhydan smiled and looked at me. "I can see why you like them so much." He then turned to Treygan. "But I won't let it be said that the high king doesn't pay his debts."

I could see the wheels in Treygan's head turning as he tried to guess what sort of repayment the king had in mind. I wanted to laugh, but I was simply thrilled by the fact that the *Wind Binder* and crew were finally getting the recognition they deserved.

Rhydan looked out toward Ranool and what remained of his fleet. "Given the present circumstances, I believe my usefulness here has come to an end." He turned to Treygan. "And since your fine ship seems to be one of the few to have come out of this unscathed, I hope you will consider providing me passage back to Aramoor?"

Both Treygan's and Ismara's eyes widened, and Treygan bowed once more, hat in hand. "It would be our honor and privilege, Your Majesty. Though, I feel I should warn Your Majesty that we are a humble ship and cannot offer the sort of . . ." He cleared his throat. ". . . accommodations, Your Majesty might be accustomed to."

Rhydan laughed. "Wonderful. Last thing I want is to feel pampered. Nothing like eating with the men to keep me from getting soft."

Kettle's face turned white as he realized he would be responsible for feeding the high king. I almost felt sorry for him, especially after seeing the sort of luxuries the king was used to dining on at the palace.

"Then, if Your Majesty has no objections to roughing it with a bunch of rivermen," Treygan said, "we would be happy to escort you back to Aramoor."

The king nodded. "Excellent. I'll have my things sent over this afternoon. How soon will you be ready for the return trip? Will you need a day to re-equip your vessel?"

"Aye," Treygan said, glancing over at Ismara and Bones, and lastly at Kettle. Ismara and Bones both nodded. Kettle, on the other hand, stood there with his mouth partway open, like a fish out of water trying to suck air. Treygan finally turned to the king. "We can be ready to leave on the morrow, if Your Majesty so wishes."

The king spared a passing glance at Overcaptain Tolin, then nodded. "I believe I can handle my business here by this afternoon and be over there no later than . . . let's say sixth bell? Will that give you time enough?"

"Ample, Your Majesty."

"Excellent. Then I'll let you get to your preparations." He looked the *Wind Binder* crew over once more. "You have served Elondria well. Wherever stories of this battle are told, your contribution will not go overlooked."

The entire crew bowed once more, then turned to disembark.

"Ayrion. A word, if you don't mind." The king motioned me over, and I joined him at the side. "I want you and your men to escort me back to Aramoor. Do you think there will be enough room aboard the ship for them?"

"It will be a tight fit," I said, picturing the *Wind Binder*'s hold, "but I think we can manage it."

Rhydan nodded. "I'll cover any provisions you think your friends will need. I'm sure we still have plenty of food stores available."

I smiled. "That will be helpful." Kettle would be overjoyed to hear

that bit of news.

"And I'd like to see you and Overcaptain Tolin in my cabin as soon as you get the chance."

"I can come now."

"No." The king laid his hand on my shoulder. "See to your men first."

I nodded, then bowed slightly before walking back over to the starboard railing. Most of the *Wind Binder*'s crew had already made it down the ship by the time Tolin dismissed his men. Bones and Pops were the last to go, but I had them wait as I leaned over the side to call down to those in the boat.

"The king has just informed me that we will have the run of the food stored aboard ship and any other provisions you think necessary for the journey back." I looked at Kettle. "You might want to stay and go through the supplies to see what you need."

Kettle nodded. "The least they could do," he grumbled, grabbing the ladder and starting back up.

"His Majesty has also requested the Black Guild to escort him. Will we be able to find enough room for bedding?"

"Forget the bedding," Kettle said, halfway up. "How many more mouths is that to feed? Do I look like a garrison cook?"

"Plan on at least twenty-five additions, including me and the king." I wasn't exactly sure how many of my men had made it through the battle, but I was hopeful.

Kettle muttered under his breath as he climbed the rest of the way, accepting a hand from Bones at the top.

"We don't have enough bedding aboard for that many," Treygan said. "They'll need to bring their own."

Ismara stood. "I'll stay as well. While Kettle digs through the food stores, I'll see to the rest."

I nodded. "I'll see if Overcaptain Tolin can assign some men to help you."

"Do you wish me to stay?" Bones asked as he helped Ismara on deck before lowering Pops down over the side.

Ismara shook her head. "Kettle and I can handle it."

"I'm glad you think me so capable," Kettle groused, clearly still upset with the thought of cooking for all the newcomers, let alone the king.

Ismara rolled her eyes. "We'll be fine."

Bones nodded and then climbed down with Pops. Treygan waited for them to settle into their seats before pushing off. I watched the boat start back through the water, then turned to Ismara and Kettle.

"I'll find someone to escort you down."

I left them at the side and spoke with Tolin, who grabbed a nearby lancer to escort them below. Soon enough, the three were heading across the deck for the galley door. They passed my men, who were huddled in a group on the far side of the deck, clearly waiting to speak with me.

"How are you?" Tolin asked. There was concern on the overcaptain's face as he looked at my wobbly legs and the cuts festooning my coat. "We feared the worst when you didn't make it back aboard with your men. I don't know how you held the Cylmarans off like you did, but if that is the kind of training we can expect from your Black Guild, I might need to take a few lessons myself." He smiled and then gave me a curious look. "There is something special about you. I don't know what it is, but it's there."

I almost got the feeling he was referring to my magic, though I'd been very careful to never mention it. Still, the overcaptain was intuitive, and I doubted he would chalk my survival up to luck alone.

"Pops says I have someone up there looking out for me."

Tolin cocked a brow. "You've got something, that's for sure. I've never seen anyone fight like that before." He stared at me a moment, then shook his head. "Quite remarkable."

I nodded, not wanting to say more, already uncomfortable with the direction the conversation was taking. Best to change the subject. "How's Captain Asa?"

"Alive, but I'm afraid he's lost the use of his eye."

"Can't say I'm surprised. It looked pretty bad." I glanced over my shoulder at the group by the galley door. "The king ordered me to see to my men before our meeting."

Tolin nodded and clapped me on the shoulder. "Whatever the reason, I'm glad to see you're still with us." He then turned and headed up to the quarterdeck, while I walked over to talk with the Black Guild.

I barely made it halfway across the deck before they were rushing to greet me. Barthol was the first to reach me, lifting me off my feet as he squeezed me into his barrel chest. I sucked in a deep breath as pain lanced across my chest and back as he no doubt ripped open some of the wounds.

"Thought we'd seen the last of you when our ships parted. I should have known better than to bet against you."

He placed me back on deck, and the other members of Room Eleven got their hugs and shoulder claps in as well. I resorted to handshakes and nods with the rest.

"How many did we lose?" I asked, looking around the faces, trying to see who might be missing.

"Eight," Gellar said. He took a step back, and only then did I notice he was limping.

"Five more belowdecks," Waylen added. "They're being seen to by the lancer physickers."

Stumpy shook his head. "Two aren't expected to make it."

I looked out across my men more closely, studying each face. How-ell, the gruff recruit Stumpy had taken underwing, wasn't there. The last I'd seen of him had been when he and Tilson volunteered to lower the sails.

"Howell?"

Stumpy shook his head once more. "He didn't make it. Ran back aboard to help with the retreat."

My heart sank. The man had been so eager to join the Guild and had lost his life because of it. I felt like I'd failed him. Like I'd failed them all somehow.

Gellar and a few of the others listed off the names, each a heavy weight placed directly on my shoulders, and by the time they'd finished, I felt about as low as one could get. These were all men under my com-mand, men I had worked with every day, shared meals with, laughed with. Faces I would never see again.

"I'm going to see to those below," I said, my eyes burning as I fought back the tears. "When I get back, I have a meeting with the king. His Majesty has requested we escort him back to Aramoor aboard the *Wind Binder*."

"Will there be enough room?" Waylen asked.

"It will be close quarters, but we can make it work. We've slept in worse."

"That's for sure," Gellar said. "Dorwall comes to mind."

I shivered, remembering the harrowing experience we had lived through in that town, and the invisible lunatics who had terrorized it. I still had nightmares of what we'd found in the magistrate's basement and often wondered what the people had done with the remaining twin.

"The *Wind Binder* won't be as spacious as one of the ships of the fleet," I said, "but she and her crew will be very welcoming." I turned to

Fipple. "Why aren't you resting? It's not going to heal properly if you keep moving it about. You need to be in bed."

"I'll crawl into bed once we reach Aramoor," he said stubbornly.

There was no point in arguing with him; I could see the determination on his face.

I left them and headed down into the ship's hold to see the rest of my men. I visited for a while with all five of the injured, spending some extra time with the two who were clinging to life, reassuring them that their families would be looked after.

I spent a few minutes with those who'd died, thanking them for their service. I hoped their souls could hear me and rest easily knowing we would provide for their loved ones. Their bodies had been wrapped and placed with the rest of the fallen lancers. A couple were missing, unable to have been collected during the battle, Howell being one of them. They'd been aboard that final ship, their bodies consumed by the fiery wreckage.

I barely made it out of the ship's infirmary before I broke down. I didn't want to cry in front of my men, so I crawled into a corner behind a stack of barrels and sobbed.

It must have been building for some time, for when the dam finally broke, there was no holding them back. I don't know how long I had sat there, but by the time I'd managed to climb my way back above deck, I didn't feel like I had any tears left. I felt numb—a welcome sensation after my grief. I tried my best not to think about those we had lost as I crossed the deck, heading for the captain's cabin. I wanted to go into this meeting with a positive attitude.

I wondered what the king wished to discuss—plans for his departure? It felt a little strange, meeting with him and Overcaptain Tolin like this. Debriefings were for the officers, and I was not one. Still, I was curious to see what they wanted.

Two of Room Eleven stood guard outside the king's door. Barthol being one, Stumpy the other. Stumpy saw my red eyes and patted my arm as I waited for Barthol to knock.

The king's voice called in answer, and Barthol opened the door. I thanked him with a smile, then took a deep breath and headed in.

AVALANCHE

Chapter 45

OVERCAPTAIN TOLIN WAS already present, both men sitting at a table in the center of the room, which was large enough to fit a dozen people. Lanterns hung along every arched beam, including the ones over the table. Most were unlit, as the sun filled the room with ample light from the windows along the sides.

The captain's cabin was exquisite. A large bed was fastened to the stern wall underneath a grand set of bay windows that looked out over the river behind. Shelves of books were built into the walls on either side of the bed, along with an assortment of chifforobes and chests for clothing. There were two doors just inside the main entrance. One built into the port-side wall, the other into the starboard. The door on the starboard side was open, revealing a washtub. The other was closed, no doubt hiding the latrine.

Waist-high cabinets were built into the port-side wall, running just underneath the windows, displaying an assortment of food and drink, along with oddities the ship's captain must have collected over the years, plus tools used for charting maps. The cabin was constructed of a rich red wood I didn't think I'd seen before, and the windowsills were set with gold inlay. Everything in the cabin was tidy and had been polished until you could see your reflection.

I feared the king was going to be sadly disappointed with the accommodations he would find aboard the *Wind Binder* after staying in luxury such as this. The riverboat's cabin wasn't half the size of this one and certainly didn't possess any of the lavish amenities.

"Come, take a seat," the king said. Charts and drawings of strategic movements littered the table. Most appeared to have been created with the terrain at Belbridge in mind.

"Will we be pulling our troops back from the bridge?" I asked, taking a seat.

"We were just discussing it," Tolin said. "I believe we need to wait and see what response, if any, the Cylmarans will have before planning a withdrawal. I've already sent scouts across the river."

I nodded. "I still can't believe Overlord Saryn managed to pull this off. How did he take Ranool?"

The king leaned back in his seat, stroking his silvery beard. "The reports we've heard from the city say that the Cylmarans ferried their soldiers across the river in fishing boats about a half-day's journey north and south of town."

"The same boats they used to set up their blockade after we arrived," Tolin added.

The king nodded. "Once they had enough men, they stormed the city from behind. They killed the lancers stationed there, blocked off the roads, and held the city hostage until we arrived."

"How is Ranool faring?" I asked, not having heard anything official yet from those who'd gone ashore.

"Better than us, that's for sure," Tolin said.

"It seems the Cylmarans kept the townsfolk locked in their homes. As long as they didn't give the soldiers any trouble, they weren't bothered."

"The storm was a lucky break for them," Tolin said, referring to the Cylmaran army. "They were able to move their boats into place and their troops just offshore without us spotting them until it was too late. By the time the barricades had been lit, the ships on the far side were already taking fire."

It still seemed strange. "I was just here a couple of weeks ago. There was no sign of any of this. How would they have known when to prepare?"

"Our coming wasn't exactly secret," the king said. "The meeting has been set for weeks. It was just a matter of sitting and waiting. Our fleet wasn't something we could hide from the public, nor the caravans of wagons as we loaded. It wouldn't have been difficult for someone to grab passage to the border prior to us leaving. I'm sure Saryn has his spies in Aramoor, just like we do in Ecrin."

"The commander and I were sure he would try something," Tolin said, his jaw tightening at the very mention of his former commander. "But we thought it would be at the bridge where the meeting was to take place. We weren't expecting a battle on the water."

"We still managed to send the Cylmarans packing even though we were down nearly three-quarters of our full strength. That's something to be extremely proud of. You and the commander have trained them well." I looked at the king. "Thank you for the recognition of the *Wind Binder* and her crew."

The king smiled. "More than deserved. How are your men?"

"As well as can be expected, under the circumstances."

"It's never easy losing men," Tolin said, offering me a sympathetic look.

I nodded, trying my best not to dredge those earlier feelings back up.

"I will say this," Rhydan said, shifting in his seat to look at me, "after seeing the way your men handled themselves out there, I want to reassign them to my personal guard, and increase their ranks."

Increase? I was glad to have gotten the king's approval, but the thought of adding more to my plate by growing the Black Guild was daunting.

"I'm not sure how much further I can spread myself, Your Majesty. Between my duties to the Guild and my duties at the garrison, I'm not sure I'll have the time to add in the extra training sessions a larger unit would require. And that doesn't include my time spent with the prince's lessons."

The king smiled. "You misunderstand. I want you and your men to *become* my personal guard. Your military contracts will be transferred from the lancers into this new division."

I spared a passing glance at Tolin, who didn't seem that surprised by any of this. "So, we will no longer be lancers?"

Rhydan nodded. "That is correct. The overcaptain and I have been discussing it for some time."

I looked at Tolin once more, and this time he nodded. "Then who do we report to?"

"Your men will report directly to you," Rhydan said, "and you will report to me."

"But doesn't Your Majesty already have a royal guard? The black uniforms I see around the palace?"

"Yes. They will be folded in under your command. I would feel much safer knowing the men responsible for the safety of my family have undergone the type of training your Black Guild receives." The king pursed his lips. "Though, I don't much care for the name Black Guild. Sounds a little ominous. Perhaps we can find something more suited to guarding the king. I'll give it some thought."

"How will this work?" I asked. "Would we keep our place at the garrison?"

"No. You will be permanently stationed at the palace. If you are to see to the protection of the royal family, I want you within shouting distance. I will see that you and your men are assigned rooms in the palace, and suitable office space. You will, of course, take your meals in the palace kitchens like the rest of the staff."

My mind was suddenly reeling with possibilities, just imagining what it was going to be like to live at the palace. The one downside was Dakaran. I shuddered at the thought of him requesting my presence every time he got bored. Still, a few well-placed words to Their Majesties might keep him in check. I had so many questions, but I needed to make sure my men would be taken care of.

"What about those men with families?"

The king thought a moment. "As long as you maintain guard postings in the palace day and night, I'll leave rotations up to you. That should allow those with families to come and go."

The more I thought about it, the more my initial excitement began to wane. This was going to be a lot of work. There were untold numbers of things I hadn't yet thought of that were going to be needed.

"So?" the king asked. "How does this sound to you?"

I looked at Tolin, feeling a bit overwhelmed, but the overcaptain's face was expressionless, not giving me even the first clue as to whether he thought this was a good idea or not. I guess it wasn't exactly like I was being given a choice. When the king says he wants you to lead his protective detail, you say—

"It sounds like a worthy challenge, Your Majesty. I'm honored that you would even consider me for such a position."

"You've more than earned it, Ayrion. I can't think of anyone I would want standing by my side more, other than perhaps Overcaptain Tolin, of course," he said with a polite nod in the overcaptain's direction, "but he will be far too busy moving into his role as the new commander of the Elondrian Lancers."

Tolin sat up, his face showing the first hint of emotion as his eyes brightened.

"That's right," the king said with a smile. "I will be making your promotion official as soon as we get our men back to Aramoor. With the loss of Commander Goring, I can't think of anyone more capable of filling his shoes."

I was pleased for Tolin. He would make a fine leader of the lancers. I was also thrilled to get to see an official promotion ceremony. I'd never seen one of this rank before, but I'd heard that there was quite a bit of pomp. From what I was told, Commander Goring's ceremony had taken place inside the throne room, with the entire aristocracy in attendance.

I wondered if my men would be there as well, whether we would already have taken on the role of the king's personal guard. If so, I imagined us standing there with cheap black material tied to our arms. Not liking the image that conjured, nor the grumbling I was sure to hear from my men if that were the case, I turned to the king and cleared my throat. "Your Majesty, might I make a request?"

He motioned me to continue.

"If my men and I are to be reassigned, would we be required to keep their uniforms, or would it be possible to have new ones made? If Your

Majesty doesn't have any objection, I have always admired the black uniforms worn by your personal guards. The black would suit us well."

The king reclined in his seat. "Obviously, you won't be able to continue wearing your lancer uniforms, and I do like the way the black uniforms set them apart from the palace guard." He nodded. "Yes, I will have the royal tailors get to work on them as soon as we get back. Perhaps we will have them ready in time for the overcaptain's ceremony."

I nodded, trying not to smile too broadly, as I was eager to relay this news to my men.

The king looked at Tolin, then back at me. "Unless you have anything else pressing, I will bid you a good morning. I have a few more matters to discuss with the overcaptain before my departure. Please do not speak of his upcoming promotion to anyone. We want to keep that under hat for the time being, at least until after we have laid Commander Goring's body to rest."

"I understand, Your Majesty. May I be allowed to tell my men of our reassignment?"

Rhydan thought a moment, then nodded. "Yes. It should help keep their minds off their fallen comrades."

I stood and bowed, then left the two men to their conversation. Once back out on deck, I stopped and took a deep breath, letting the newly risen sun wash over my face as I closed my eyes and drank in its warmth.

"Anything interesting discussed?" Barthol asked.

I turned back to the cabin door, where he and Stumpy stood watching with eager smiles. "You could say that."

We stared at each other a moment before Stumpy finally asked, "Well, are you going to tell us what it is or just stand there grinning like a fool? I take it it's good news?"

"It is, but you'll have to wait for the rest of the Guild to hear it. This evening, probably, once we are all aboard the *Wind Binder*."

Barthol frowned. "That's a long time to have to wait. Can you give us a hint?"

I thought a moment. "Sure. We're getting new uniforms." With that, I turned and left the men to ponder over the possibilities as I headed below to see how Ismara and Kettle were finding things.

Even though Kettle tried masking his true feelings with a frown and a constant barrage of complaints, he did appear more upbeat about his prospects of cooking for such a large number once he got a look at the food stores aboard the king's ship. By the time he was done directing the ship's crew as to what he wanted transferred over to the *Wind Binder*, I was worried whether there would be enough left for Tolin and his men. I was sure each ship had their own supplies, but we'd lost at least three in the battle, not to mention the supply ships.

I finally decided that if Kettle had requisitioned too much, the ship's quartermaster would let me know.

Ismara managed to find the extra bedding needed for the additional crew and organized transfer of the Guild's gear over to the *Wind Binder*. By the time we had finished making trips between the two vessels, the afternoon was spent.

Although I had feared the king's belongings would end up taking several additional trips, to my surprise, Rhydan left most of it behind, keeping only a single change of clothes, along with some personal items for grooming. Apparently, when he said he didn't wish to feel pampered, he meant it.

Perhaps he didn't want to make the *Wind Binder*'s crew feel uncomfortable. The lancers were used to transporting the king from one location to another, but these were simple hardworking men of the river, and Rhydan seemed to want to fit in. Even the two outfits he had chosen for the voyage were plain in comparison to what I was used to seeing him wear. He'd look more a lesser lord than the high king.

As promised, Rhydan made his final departure from his warship over to the *Wind Binder* by sixth bell. I had rowed ahead with the Black Guild to make sure things were settled before he arrived. We stood along the railing with Treygan as the rest of the crew lined the deck, awaiting His Majesty's rowboat.

His boat pulled alongside the ship's dark outer hull, and Rhydan lost no time clambering up the ship's ladder. Barthol and I offered him a hand, and as soon as he stepped onto the deck, everyone aboard promptly bowed.

The king took a moment to look around before speaking. "You have a lovely ship, Captain. My compliments. If you wouldn't mind, I'd appreciate a quick tour. Any vessel capable of what I saw out there has more than earned my respect."

Treygan bowed, his captain's hat in hand. "It would be my honor, Your Majesty." He stepped forward and gestured toward the captains' cabin. "Should we start with your quarters?"

Rhydan smiled. "Excellent." He turned and looked at the Black Guild. "At ease, gentlemen."

My men relaxed, and I turned to Barthol. "Keep them out of the crew's way. I'll join the king on his tour."

Barthol nodded, and the Guild slowly dispersed. Ismara turned and dismissed the *Wind Binder*'s crew as well. "Back to your duties. We sail at dawn."

I followed Treygan and the king over to the cabin door, but before they went in, Rhydan walked over to Shade's awning. Treygan and I joined him.

"I see you survived after all, you magnificent creature." Rhydan carefully held out his hand, watching Shade's reaction. Shade nudged his hand, clearly fine with being petted, so the king proceeded to stroke the stallion's neck. "You chose your rider well."

"I owe him my life," I said.

Shade whinnied softly and even went so far as to nuzzle the king's hand.

Rhydan patted the horse's nose. "Have you named him yet?"

"I have, Your Majesty. His name is Shade."

The king stepped back and pursed his lips as he looked the horse over. "Yes, I can see it." With a final nod, he turned and headed back to the cabin.

I followed him and Treygan over but waited just outside the open door. I figured the fewer people inside, the roomier it might look.

Ismara had clearly spent a good deal of time in there today, as the place looked about as clean and welcoming as one could get on a riverboat. The pillows had been fluffed and arranged neatly on the bed. There were several extra lanterns set about the room. The red velvet curtains at the back were open, revealing three small windows that looked out over the warship behind. There was a small table at the center of the room with additional lanterns hanging overtop.

"This will do nicely," the king said and then smiled as he pointed to the small closet where his clothes were hanging. "I see you have already seen to my things. Thank you."

"We have a private washtub here," Treygan said, pulling back a makeshift privacy curtain on the right. "And the latrine is just in there," he said, pointing to a closed door on the left.

The king nodded. "Very good."

We left the cabin and headed across deck for the galley. I heard pots and pans and curses being flung about inside before we'd ever even opened the door. I looked at Treygan, and we both braced ourselves for an embarrassment.

"I apologize in advance for my cook," Treygan said to the king. "He can get a might touchy in stressful situations." Treygan paused a moment. "Who am I kidding? He's always touchy."

The king chuckled. "I'll be hanged if I've met one that isn't."

Treygan opened the door, and the king stepped inside. We followed him in, letting our eyes adjust to the dimmer light as we scanned the room for Kettle, who was nowhere to be seen. That was odd, considering all the ruckus we'd just heard.

"This here is the ship's galley," Treygan said, still looking for where Kettle might have vanished to. "Not much to look at. Most of the crew eats their meals here. Not enough space to fit everyone at once, so we generally go in turns. But considering the new additions, we might try setting up some more seating areas below."

Rhydan nodded. "Weather stays beautiful like today, I'd be happy to take my meals on deck."

"Where are those flaming onions?" a voice shouted from somewhere down in the hold. Several thuds could be heard, sounding like crates being tossed about. "What was that flaming boy thinking, inviting all these people aboard for us to ferry all the way back to Aramoor? Do I look like a garrison cook? And what was the flaming captain thinking allowing it? Who ever heard of a riverboat cook serving the flaming king? He takes one bite of this swill, and I'll be clamped in irons!" There was a pause before he started up again. "What good are you, sittin' over there? Get over here and help me find where they put those flaming onions!"

Treygan's face paled, and I'm sure mine wasn't far off. I couldn't imagine what the king was thinking.

Suddenly Rhydan burst out laughing. He laughed so hard it was impossible not to join him. Pretty soon we were all three laughing hard enough to attract the attention of Kettle, who stormed up the steps, face red as a turnip. "What in the flaming Pits are you laughing—"

Kettle went white as a sheet when he saw who he was yelling at, and he quickly bowed, his legs wobbling like a man who'd tried to bury his troubles at the bottom of a bottle. "Your Majesty. I, uh, I didn't know it was you."

I heard Pops snickering somewhere below, and Kettle's fists balled up.

The king smiled. "I'm sure whatever you whip up will hit the spot, onions or not."

Kettle looked as though he wanted to throw himself in the river.

"I know how troubling it can be to keep a boat of men fed," Rhydan said, "so please don't let me stop you."

"Thank you, Your Majesty." Kettle bowed and quickly vanished back down into the hold, no doubt to find a quiet place to crawl into and die.

As soon as he disappeared, the king headed down, with us right behind him. "It's quite shallow," he remarked, admiring the shape of the *Wind Binder*'s underbelly.

"Yes, Your Majesty," Treygan said. "Makes it easier when traveling the riverways."

"And this is the men's sleeping quarters?" the king asked as he walked over to where the hammocks hung between posts.

"Aye, and we've set up bedding here along the front for your men." He was talking to the king, but Treygan looked at me when he said it.

I nodded.

Pops hopped out of his hammock, using his crutch to keep himself upright. He bowed. "Your Majesty."

"My apologies," the king said. "I didn't mean to disturb your sleep."

"How can a man sleep with all the racket going on down here?" he said loudly, looking over at the stacks of food where Kettle was no doubt hiding. Pops smiled at the king. "The name is Tressle, Your Majesty, but my friends call me Pops."

"Well, Pops, you look like a man with stories to tell."

"These old eyes have seen many a sight over the years, that's for sure, but standin' face-to-face with the high king was never one I would have hoped to achieve. I have been truly blessed. First, we dine at the palace with the queen and crown prince, and now we break bread with the king himself, and aboard the *Wind Binder*, no less." He shook his head. "Yes, siree, blessed indeed."

The king smiled, and even went so far as to pat Pops on the shoulder. He took a quick look around the hold, then headed back upstairs. As soon as we reached the galley up top, he turned and looked at me. "Dinner with the queen?"

"I can explain." I told him about my meeting with Her Majesty in hopes of introducing her to my friends, and of her invitation for us to dine with her and Dakaran.

The king listened intently, nodded occasionally, and then went quiet for a moment after I finished. "Surprised you managed to get my son out of his room," he said. With that, he headed back out onto the deck.

From there, Treygan spent the next hour showing him around the rest of the ship. They spent a large portion of that time at the helm with Needle as Treygan attempted to explain the maneuvers we had pulled off during the battle.

"Thankfully," Treygan said, pointing back to the capstan, "Ranool had a spare anchor and line for us to install, or we might not have been going anywhere. We have a second up on the foredeck, but I prefer to have two available, especially when crossing open water like the Rhunarin."

"Understandable," Rhydan said.

By the time the tour was over and Rhydan had been introduced once again to the members of the crew—of which he took time to talk with each—the sun had begun to set, and Kettle was ringing the dinner bell.

The crew had managed to set up a couple of seating areas down below using barrels with wood planks stretched overtop. The meal wasn't exactly up to palace standards, but it was one of the finer spreads Kettle had whipped together, earning him a strong "compliment to the chef" from the king, praise from the Black Guild, and several complaints from the *Wind Binder*'s crew as to why he hadn't been serving this sort of quality before now.

Kettle had recruited one of the newer crew members to help in the kitchen, and I had assigned him two of my own men. There wasn't much to do aboard ship, so I made sure they were put to use where possible. All in all, the meal turned out just fine, giving Kettle the confidence to carry on.

The night watch had been assigned evenly between the *Wind Binder*'s crew and the Black Guild to give the crew a chance to get more sleep, as they bore the majority of the workload during the day.

After dinner, I told my men about our reassignment. The men were stunned by the news. No one spoke for several minutes, at least until Gellar asked about whether this transition would be coming with a raise in pay. I groaned inwardly but promised I'd ask. Waylen was ecstatic, knowing he would be taking his meals at the palace and no longer having to suffer through the garrison's mess hall.

The rest kept asking what their rooms would be like. My answer that I didn't know was followed by wild speculation. It wasn't like I had lived there myself. The new uniforms seemed to be the least important to them, though they did like the idea of keeping them black. I told them that the king didn't much care for the name Black Guild and would be looking for something better to replace it with, something more befitting the protection of the high king. No one really seemed to care what we were called; living in the palace seemed to overshadow everything else.

We ate an early breakfast, the king having risen before most of the crew, and by the time the sun was beginning to poke its head above the eastern horizon, we were weighing anchor. Most of the wreckage had been pulled to the side of the river and left to burn, leaving us a clear passage south.

The citizens of Ranool were going to have their work cut out for them, fishing bodies out of the water for some time to come. The banks were lined with the dead on both sides for miles as we continued down-river. We even spotted a few just north of Laneer. Tolin said that he would assign a couple of regiments from the main camp to come help with the retrieval and burials.

Not being in a rush, we anchored in port for the night and waited for the new dawn before heading out into the open water.

The trip back saw nothing but clear skies and fair winds. It was a sailor's delight. But as nice as it was, everyone was lined up anxiously along the starboard rail as we made our way into the Bay of Torrin, all waiting to catch our first glimpse of the white walls of Aramoor.

"There she is!" Whitey called out from the front, pointing ahead off the starboard bow as we rounded the bend into the back of the bay.

I breathed a small sigh of relief at seeing the city ahead. It was good to be home.

AVALANCHE

Chapter 46

I WOBBLED AS I STEPPED off the ship behind the king. After almost a week of the constant rocking of the deck beneath my feet, I had to relearn how to walk again on solid ground. Thankfully, I'd made several trips to the border in the past few months, so each time relearning to walk on land was a shorter process. I scanned the docks for any signs of danger as I followed behind Rhydan, waiting for the dizziness to pass. Shade followed me up the pier, weaving a little drunkenly himself.

My men and I had remained aboard ship while waiting for a port messenger to send for the king's carriage and several teams of horses for the Black Guild. Rhydan had insisted my men take leave once we reached Aramoor, saying they had earned it and that it would give his staff time to make the necessary arrangements for the Guild's transfer to the palace. The men were quite eager for the time off, most having family and friends to visit. However, knowing they were to become the king's new guard, they wanted to be sure the king was escorted safely home, even though the king's carriage arrived with its own protection detail.

Once the king was safely back at the palace, my men left, riding back across the bailey toward the bridge. I left Shade with one of the palace guards and followed the king up the stairs. Queen Ellise waited at the top, her hands folded and head erect, looking the perfect image of sovereignty, but there was an eagerness in her eyes and a bright smile on her face that said she was overjoyed to see her husband safely returned.

Rhydan, for his part, snatched her up and swung her around, then held her close and kissed her. I almost felt like I needed to turn away. It was the most improper thing I'd seen them do in public. They had always been pillars of strength and resoluteness, staunch in their demeanor, but here they were swinging each other about like a couple of newly bonded lovers. You would have thought they hadn't seen each other in months, instead of the week and a half that he'd been gone.

"Is it over?" she asked, peering up at Rhydan.

"It's over," he said.

"The meeting was successful, then?"

"Oh, there was no meeting." He looked at the guards and chamberlain standing just behind her and lowered his voice. "We'll talk of it inside."

The queen nodded, then walked over to where I was waiting quietly on the top step. She hugged me before I could even bow. "Thank you for keeping your promise."

I smiled. "Of course, Your Majesty."

She released me and returned to her husband's arm, and the two headed inside. The king's guards, in their black uniforms with falcon crests, were quick to cut me off as they fell into place behind the royal family. I smiled, picturing their reactions when they learned that I was about to become their new leader.

I followed the small entourage to the royal wing and down the long hall past the king's study, figuring since I was here, I might as well check in to see how Dakaran was doing. I didn't want to hear him complain to me the next time I visited about how I had refused to come see him. The king and queen continued to their private chambers, and I cut down the corridor on the right, which led to Dakaran's rooms.

The guards outside the door knocked, and to my surprise, the prince himself answered the door. He grabbed my arm and pulled me into the room. "Tell me everything!"

I spent the next couple of hours talking with him about the battle, but I didn't tell him about my pending transfer to the palace or the Black Guild being reassigned as his family's new guards. The longer I could hold off telling him, the better for me. He would find out eventually, and I had a feeling that when he did, my already-slim free time would become nonexistent. I'd worry about dealing with the aftermath later.

Dakaran looked much better than when I had last seen him. He moved freely about the room—no wincing or gritting of the teeth, no gentle pressing around the wound every time he turned in his seat. He even had most of his color back.

"I take it you took my advice and left your room while I was gone. You're looking a lot stronger."

He nodded. "Walking helps."

"So, your physickers knew what they were talking about?" I prodded.

He grumbled and left it at that. A minute later, he lifted his head and smiled. "Want to get some lamb and mint sauce tonight?"

"Are you mad?" I couldn't tell if he was joking, so I glanced around the room to see if he'd been drinking. "Have you been into the wine again? After what happened the last time, why in Aldor would you want to set foot in there again?"

He shrugged. "As long as I've got you there to protect me, I doubt I'm likely to end up in the alley again."

I released a frustrated sigh. "I think we better stay away from the Fishnet for a while. Besides, I wouldn't put it past your mother to have posted lookouts around the place just in case you tried sneaking out again."

Dakaran grimaced. "You're probably right."

I stood from my seat near the fireplace. "And I have other people I need to visit."

"Oh? Who would want to see you?"

"I'm going to Sandstorm."

"The street kids? You'd rather hang out with them than the crown prince?"

"Yes," I said with a ready smirk.

Dakaran pouted. "And what am I to do with no one here to keep me entertained?"

"Try giving the library a visit."

He grimaced. "I hate reading."

"Then have one of the archivists blindfold you and carry you into the stacks to see whether you can find your way back out."

He looked at me like I was crazy, but then pursed his lips. "Actually, that doesn't sound too bad."

I shook my head. There was no hope for him. "I'll be off, then." I headed for the door. "Don't bother getting up."

Dakaran grinned. "I won't."

I left the prince to his chair and made my way out of the palace. I looked around the courtyard, but Shade was nowhere to be seen, so I walked around to the stables and spotted him standing outside. Thankfully, he was still saddled. Bozz was somewhere in the back, but I didn't feel like waiting around to speak with him, so I mounted and headed into town.

The dizziness from my time on the water had all but gone, the last remnants fading as I sucked in deep breaths of fresh air. My stomach began to grumble as the sun made its quick descent behind me toward the Sandrethin cliffs, which for me meant it was getting close to supper.

I stopped at the orphanage first to let Master Fentin and Mistress Orilla know I was back. Some of the children were playing toss in the street, while others read on the porch, occasionally looking up to watch those playing with their ball. I pulled to a stop next to the house and dismounted. Kids were already shouting through the front door that I was there.

I barely got Shade tied before both Master Fentin and Mistress Orilla shuffled around the side of the house.

"Come give me a hug," Orilla said, grabbing me before I had a chance to move.

I hugged her tight. She smelled like apples and pepper, a strange combination. The odd scent tickled my nose, and I breathed shallowly to keep from sneezing on her. I hugged Fentin as well, his spectacles falling halfway down his nose in the process. He'd forgotten they were there, again.

"It's good to see you, my boy," he said with a bright smile. "We feared the worst."

"Been fretting since the day you left," Orilla said, taking my arm and directing me around to the front porch.

"When did you get back?" Fentin asked. "There's been no word of the fleet's return."

"We only just arrived."

One of the children held the front door open, and we walked in and found our seats in the family room. The older couple took the couch, and I chose a chair in front of the windows.

"Not to sound like we wanted you to be gone longer," Fentin said, pulling out his pipe and packing it, "but why are you back so soon? Did something happen? Did Saryn surrender?"

I chuckled. "No, he most definitely didn't do that." I went on to explain the entire incident, leaving out only the parts I'd been sworn to keep secret. When I finished, they were both speechless, Fentin dabbing at his forehead with his pocket hanky.

"That is quite a story," Orilla said briskly. "Would you care for a sandwich?" Before I could say no, she was up and out the door.

I didn't stop her. It had been a while since I'd had one of her mystery meat sandwiches, and I couldn't think of anything I wanted more. There had been many times over the years I'd thought to ask what she put in them, and a few years back I'd even gotten up the courage to ask. The only answer I got was that the not knowing was part of what made them taste so good. I never asked again.

I felt Shade's hunger through our link, and I told him I'd see if they had any apples on hand before we left.

It was a pleasant visit, but I couldn't stay long if I wanted to get to Sandstorm before their evening meal. It was the best chance I had of catching everyone at the same time and hopefully preventing having to relay the same story over and over again.

After devouring my sandwich like a starving beggar and inquiring after an apple for Shade, I parted ways with the older couple and headed back outside, taking a moment to let Shade enjoy his apple as promised. He'd gobbled it down before we even made it out of the drive.

The sky was a pasty grey overhead as we headed down Bailey Street. Thankfully, Sandstorm Manor wasn't that far of a ride, and by the time I caught sight of the gate, the sky was beginning to darken.

"Protector!"

Toots's voice was unmistakable. The head of the Watch rushed down off the wall and to the gate. In all his excitement, he forgot to have someone open it, so after removing the bar himself, he immediately began yanking on the left side.

"What's all you good-for-nothins gawking at?" he shouted to the others who were standing around watching him sweat. "Get over here and help me!"

As soon as they got the gate open, he rushed out and ran over, but then took one look at Shade and decided to keep a step or two back. "We thought you left a week ago. Why's you back? You decide not to go? You decide to stay here with us?"

I smiled and dismounted. "No, I went. But I've returned."

Toots scratched the back of his head. "That was fast."

"I'm just glad it's over. Anything new here? How are the Avalanche kids fitting in?"

Toots frowned. "Fair, I suppose. Still don't like thems taking up so much room."

I wondered if Cutter had given Sandstorm any trouble. Sapphire was probably the person to ask. "Are the chiefs in?"

"They's about to eat."

I smiled. "Perfect timing, then." I walked Shade through the gate and up the drive to the carriage house. The windows were dark, so I peeked inside. A single lantern hung in back near the stalls, but there was no sign of Gittrick or his family.

"Master Ayrion? Is that you?" I turned to find the coachman walking around the side of the building from one of the workhouses in back. "I thought I heard a horse."

"Yes, I'm back." I handed Gittrick Shade's reins. "See that he gets some extra feed tonight, and throw in some oats and carrots. He deserves it, believe me."

Gittrick stood there with Shade a moment, looking like he wanted to say something. I had a feeling it was about my trip, so I gave him a quick sketch of the last few days, promising to tell him more later, but that I wanted to get inside before the meal was over.

"I'm glad to hear that it's over, and that you're back safe." He started to turn. "Oh, thank you once again for allowing me and my sons to join you during your meal with the queen. I can't thank you enough. It's something we'll never forget."

"Least I could do for your help toting all of us all over Aramoor."

Gittrick smiled and walked Shade around to the front of the carriage house while I made my way across the manor courtyard for the front doors.

The gallery inside was empty, but from the sounds coming from the east wing, it seemed everyone was still in the dining hall. Doing my best not to be seen, I headed toward the chiefs' private dining room. The door was open, and they were all there, including Gustory, who was in his usual spot next to Reevie.

The butler standing in the hall turned when he saw me, but I raised a finger to my lips and walked over to the doorway. I wanted to see how long it took for them to notice me.

"The maids are getting tired of cleaning sheets," Bull said to Sapphire as I listened in.

Sapphire frowned. "Same kids?"

Bull nodded. "The bed-wetting, though, is the least of our problems. Several of the rooms are complaining about Avalanche kids waking in the middle of the night screaming, scaring everyone else in the room."

"It's to be expected," Reevie said. "Their lives have been upended. The younger ones are having a difficult time adjusting."

"How long can we expect it to go on?" Bull asked.

Reevie shrugged. "Until they feel safe."

"I can try working with them," Gustory said. "Perhaps a special bed-time story for them before they turn in for the night could help."

Sapphire sighed. "We knew it would be difficult at first, but—" She looked up and, seeing me in the doorway, gasped, causing the others to turn and look.

"Protector! You're back." Bull was the first out of his seat and across the room to greet me, forgoing all decorum as he lifted me off the floor with his embrace.

The others hurried over as well. Gustory offered me a strong shake of the hand and a pat on the back. Reevie presented a half-smile and nod. Sapphire was last, with a firm hug and a gentle kiss to the cheek.

"Did you even leave?" she asked. "You couldn't have possibly made it all the way to Cylmar, had your meeting, and returned."

Bull looked skeptical as well. "There's been no word from the docks about the fleet. Trust me, we'd know. We've had someone there every day since you left."

"You weren't supposed to tell him that," Reevie groused. "Now he's going to think we care."

Gustory raised his hands to quiet the others. "Why don't we give him a chance to explain."

The chiefs nodded, and we all returned to the table, but not before I stepped into the hall and asked the butler to bring an extra setting for me. Orilla's sandwich had hit the spot, but I had a lot more spots left to hit, considering I hadn't eaten since breakfast that morning.

I was surprised that they had someone watching the docks and yet hadn't noticed me, but they might have been watching from a distance, looking for a fleet of ships to arrive and not paying attention to the single vessels coming and going.

"So, what happened?" Bull asked, barely back in his seat as he scooted to the edge, anxious to hear the tale of my adventure. And what a tale it was going to be. I'd had three other stabs at getting it perfected before coming here, so I was certainly ready to deliver.

By the time I was done, there wasn't a closed mouth in the room—and not just because the roast and potatoes were especially tasty this evening, which they were.

Gustory spent my entire retelling scrawling in his journal, his fingers flying to keep up with me. "This is some top-shelf storytelling here," he said, not looking up from his pad. "I'll be booked for months, and in the finest establishments. High demand, that's what I'll be in. The only bard to have spoken with someone who was actually there. The only one who knows what truly happened."

"At least until the fleet returns and word spreads like shingle fire," Reevie pointed out.

"True, but if, as Ayrion says, the fleet is long in returning, I'll be the most sought-after bard in Elondria." His hands quivered as he continued to scribble. I wasn't sure if it was from the excitement of entertaining the masses with my harrowing near-death experience or from the thought of the gold and accolades he was sure to acquire.

Sapphire took a sip from her mug and gently placed it back on the table. "And the king is really going to move you out of the lancers and have you live with the royal family at the palace?"

"It's not like we will be sharing a room or anything," I said. "I'm sure they'll find some remote place in the back where we won't be in anyone's way. Probably won't be much different than what we have at the garrison."

"You're going to be eating at the palace," Reevie said with a grunt. "Of course it's going to be different."

Bull pointed at me with his spoon. "I think it's a smart move on the king's part. Who better to have protecting his rump than you and your men?" His eyes narrowed. "So does that mean that if we were to pay you a visit, we would be able to get a tour of the royal house?"

"When have you ever paid me a visit?"

Bull shrugged. "Who wants to see the inside of a garrison?"

I chuckled. "I suppose I could get you a tour, but I'd wait until I've had a chance to settle in first."

Bull nodded. "Good. Gittrick won't shut up about it. I'm sick of hearing how incredible it was dining with the royal family, and getting to see the throne room, and the royal library, and the kitchens." He jabbed his spoon at me again. "I'm telling you, if I have to hear it one more time, I'm going to toss him in one of his horse troughs."

The others chuckled.

"And you don't believe there will be any further escalations with Cylmar?" Sapphire asked.

I shook my head. "I don't think so. As many men as they lost, even Saryn wouldn't be so stupid as to confront us head on now. I think the whole thing was an attempt to eliminate Rhydan. I don't think he ever had any real intention of going to war, especially not where he would be at a disadvantage. He might be cowardly and despicable, but he's not stupid."

"Remind you of anyone else?" Reevie asked offhandedly.

Bull nodded. "Cutter."'

I looked at the others. "Has there been any word on how Cutter is handling losing the old garrison? Does anyone know if our ruse worked?"

"The Temple's been rather quiet of late," Sapphire said. "I don't know that I like it."

"Calm before the storm," Gustory added dramatically.

My gut roiled. I wasn't sure if it was his magic or the fact that I should have stopped after a second helping.

"For now, no news is good news," I said. "Can't spend every day worrying about what hasn't happened."

"She can try," Reevie added.

I was thankful his verbal jab wasn't being directed at me for once.

The room quieted for a moment, and I thought it a good time to bring up another point of interest. "Have you given any more thought to the orphanage suggestion?"

I could hear Sapphire rolling her eyes in the length of her sigh. "We have spoken with Master Fentin and Mistress Orilla, and they don't believe taking such a status will necessarily entail being under direct control of the crown. So far, they've never been given any prerequisites for receiving their funding, but that doesn't mean it won't happen. And until we have something more official in hand, like a signed agreement stipulating precisely what would be expected of us, I don't believe it's in our best interest to move forward."

"So, you are against it, then?"

"No. In theory, we are in agreement on the benefits it could bring Sandstorm, but we would like some guarantee from the queen that we won't be subjected to overhanded authority. An annual accounting to the crown of finances and the like is fine, so long as we can run Sandstorm as we see fit without aristocratic oversight."

"You're doing it again," Bull said, frowning at Sapphire. "You know I don't understand half of what you're saying when you start talking all businesslike."

Sapphire pressed her thumbs to the side of her head. "In other words, we ain't signing anything until we know the queen, or any of those other high-nosed good-for-nothings, aren't going to try telling us how to run our business." She looked at Bull. "How's that?"

He smiled.

I nodded reluctantly, understanding. "Better safe than stuck in a relationship you can't get out of. Now that I'm back, I can speak with Her Majesty and let her know your reservations. I think she'll be willing to cooperate, especially considering this is an already-established home for orphans. We won't need to go to all the work of building something from scratch. And I would love to see Sandstorm put under the protection of not only the patrollers, but the crown itself. If that were to become known, I don't think you'd need to worry about Cutter again."

"I don't know why you don't just round up all the patrollers in the city and attack the Temple right now," Bull said. "Get rid of him for good."

"Because," Reevie cut in, "as wonderful as it would be to get rid of Avalanche once and for all, not even patrollers are going to have the stomach to go in and slaughter a bunch of kids."

"They don't have to kill them all," Bull said, "just the ones who try stopping them."

"Which is probably going to be most," Sapphire added. "Cutter can be very persuasive. Scared kids can be easily led, especially by someone with a tongue slicker than an otter's back."

Bull pointed across the table. "What about Gustory?"

The bard looked up from his scribbling. "Don't bring me into this."

"What about him?" Reevie asked.

"You wanted a slick tongue," Bull said. "His is as slick as they come."

Gustory grunted. "Thanks a lot."

"You know what I mean. You talked Kore's fighters down when they attacked Sandstorm. Couldn't you do something like that with Avalanche?"

I looked at the bard. It wasn't that bad an idea. I hadn't considered using Gustory's magic as a way to possibly get us into the Temple and deescalate things long enough for the patrollers to round the kids up.

"I'm good, but I'm not that good," Gustory said. "My stories don't always work. If they are already enraged, it's almost impossible to get them to listen. They have to be calm enough to think in order for my words to get through. Telling them a bedtime story in the middle of a battle probably isn't the best idea."

My excitement waned as I remembered what happened during the fight at the Rose and Crown. Gustory had gotten everyone in the crowd worked up, but once the actual fighting had started, he'd been unable to talk them down. Still, it was something to consider.

"Then why did it work with Kore's fighters?" Bull pushed.

Gustory shrugged. "Luck. Perhaps they weren't as committed, or something gave them pause. I don't know. I'm not saying it wouldn't work here, I'm just saying that I wouldn't hang all our hopes on it."

"It seems the best option for now is to get the crown's protection," I said. "That is, once we determine whether it will come with any unwanted provisions," I added for Sapphire's benefit.

"Where will you be staying now that you are being transferred out of the garrison?" Sapphire asked, no doubt in a ploy to change the subject. "You said the king still has to find and set up rooms. Will you just remain at the garrison until then or . . . somewhere else?"

I couldn't tell if she was hinting that she wanted me to stay here, or just needed to know if she was going to have to make a room ready for me. I hoped it was because she wanted me around. I would sleep more comfortably here than on my cot in the barracks. "Until we are officially transferred out," I said. "I assume we'll keep our place in the garrison, but the king has given me and my men a few days off to recover, so I was hoping you wouldn't object to me staying here for a couple more days."

A smile played at the corners of her mouth, almost too small to be noticeable if I wasn't looking for it. She turned to the other chiefs.

"Absolutely," Bull said, no hesitation.

Reevie's answer was slower in coming. "Fine. As long as he stays out of my way and doesn't send any more people to my infirmary."

Sapphire looked at me. "I guess we are in agreement. We've kept your room as it was since you left."

"That was only a week and a half ago," Reevie pointed out.

I almost wanted to laugh. Good to see things hadn't changed all that much. One of these days I was going to find a way to clean the slate with him for good. It didn't seem like talking would be enough. Perhaps a little more of my presence here at Sandstorm would do the trick. My best chance was now, because once I took on my role among the king's guard, my free time was probably going to disappear.

I thanked them for their generosity and promptly retired to my room. I wanted to get an early start in the morning. My first task was a conversation with the queen, though I wondered how available she would be, given her husband had just returned and the pair had acted like he'd been gone for ages. I guessed there was only one way to find out. The sooner I could get a definitive answer from her about the orphanage situation, the sooner we could get some sort of protection set up for Sandstorm.

AVALANCHE

Chapter 47

I WOKE FEELING BETTER than I had in a very long time. The nightmares of what had taken place aboard ship, of the men who'd died, of my part in many of their deaths, had haunted my sleep. Each night got a little better as time slowly healed those unwanted memories. All the stress that had been hovering over my head for the last several weeks was gone as well, and I had some very exciting times ahead to look forward to.

My service in the lancers was coming to an end. It had been a wonderful experience, and I wouldn't have traded it for anything, but I was looking forward to this next chapter in my life as leader of the king's protectors.

Somehow, it felt as though things were finally slowing down.

It was the end of one season and the beginning of another. I hoped this one would be a calmer, more serene time. Since my arrival in Aramoor, I had been running at full speed with barely time enough to catch my breath, and now, for the first time, things were coming together. Once I found a way to keep Sandstorm safe, all the stress I'd endured from my years within the street tribes would finally come to an end.

I doubted we'd see another battle like this one, not after the defeat Saryn had seen and the exposure of this treacherous plot for truce. The other kingdoms weren't going to look kindly on such actions. Cylmar would be reeling from the economic toll of this act for years.

The only thing I would have to worry about from now on would be training the king's guards and assigning the occasional escort when the royal family felt the need to leave the palace. It was going to be tough at first, as my men and the existing king's guard were melded into one unit, but once that blending had taken place and I had a working duty roster set, I was looking forward to a simpler life. One that consisted of nothing more strenuous than following the royal family as they moved about the palace. My most disconcerting worry would be how many evening shifts a month I might feel obligated to take. I chuckled. I couldn't wait.

I found fresh undergarments laid out in front of my door, another thoughtful gift from Sapphire. She didn't miss much. After dressing, I headed down to grab a quick breakfast in the kitchen, taking a few minutes to chat with Solvino about the battle. Once finished with my meal, I walked over to the carriage house and chatted with Gittrick while he saddled Shade, filling in some details about our excursion to the Cylmaran border and my new position at the palace, which I'd skipped in my rush to make it to dinner the previous night.

By the time Shade and I had left the manor and were heading up the street, the morning sun was just beginning to take hold. I inhaled a deep breath of cool air, filling my lungs and clearing my head, the perfect greeting to the perfect day. I stopped by the garrison first to see if any of my men had returned. None had. I was glad they had taken the king up on his offer of leave.

I found Overcaptain Weller and Lieutenant Huckly in Weller's office and briefed them on the events at Ranool, starting with my departure from Aramoor and ending with my arrival the previous night.

"I would have expected you here as soon as you returned," Overcaptain Weller groused. "Your assignment here hasn't been revoked yet, so I expect you to behave in the manner of a true lancer."

I stood at attention. "Yes, sir."

Lieutenant Huckly rolled his eyes, but as he was standing a little behind the overcaptain, Weller didn't see.

"But considering the fine work it sounds like you and your men have done, I guess we can overlook it this time."

"I appreciate your patience, sir. The king granted me and my men leave to recoup from the journey before assuming our new responsibilities. If you don't have any objections, I'm on my way to the palace now to meet with Her Majesty."

Weller cleared his throat. "Well, I, uh . . . yes, I guess that will be fine. Dismissed."

I saluted and left his office. Huckly followed me out.

"Don't worry about him," Huckly said. "Weller's been like this ever since the regiments left. He didn't care much for getting left behind."

"Once I'm gone," I said, "I doubt I'll be back for a while. If the king is able to arrange lodging, I have a feeling he's going to want us stepping into our new roles as soon as possible."

"You won't be sleeping here, then?"

I shook my head. "I already cleaned my stuff out of my room before heading to the border. So, other than being here for the official transfer of my position, I doubt I'll have need to be back, and I'd rather not get caught underfoot with the overcaptain."

Huckly smiled, and I clapped the lieutenant on the shoulder. "You're a better man than me to put up with him."

Huckly grunted. "He'd be lost without me."

I had no doubt it was Huckly keeping the day-to-day duties running, not Weller. The overcaptain wasn't the most organized. We left the building and stepped out onto the front steps. "How are the new recruits behaving?"

"See for yourself."

Huckly walked me over to the practice fields, where the former Avalanche boys were working with some of the older lancers on the basics of weaponry. We stood under a nearby awning to keep from being seen as they ran through sword routines. I watched as they paired off, one attacking, the other defending, then nodded. "It seems they're doing just fine. Have they given you any trouble?"

"No. Been quiet for the most part; mostly keep to themselves."

"It'll take some time to draw them out."

Huckly nodded. "If the war truly is over, time is something we will have plenty of."

We turned and started back for the main building. "If you need me," I said, "just send word to the palace. Nine times out of ten, I'll be there, at least during the day."

We shook hands, and Huckly headed back inside. I climbed onto Shade and headed for the palace. Ninth bell rang in the harbor as I stopped to chat with Yorig at the bridge towers, briefly sharing the highlights of the river battle at Ranool. I didn't want to take too much time, as the line of those wanting to get across the bridge was beginning to grow, and Yorig needed to get back to work.

I waved and told him we'd talk more later. There was going to be plenty of opportunity since my travels across this bridge were looking to increase exponentially. I left Shade with Bozz, who demanded I give him the details of our trip upriver as well. He'd heard rumors but wanted to know for himself which were true and which were scullery maid gossip.

I was getting worried that with as many people as I was having to tell about our recent conflict that by the time poor Gustory began making his rounds to the inns and eateries, the news would have already spread. Still, I doubted it could match hearing it from a bard of his caliber, and with the addition of his magic, he was sure to enthrall any audience. Leaving Shade in Bozz's capable hands, I headed inside to see if I could find the queen.

I'd barely made it in the front doors when a young runner hopped up from a cushioned bench and rushed over with a missive from the prince. I thanked him, and he ran off, looking relieved I had shown up as early as I had. I wondered if he'd been instructed to sit in the lobby all day waiting for me to arrive. I took a minute to read the note, which basically asked me to come see him when I arrived. I groaned as I stuffed it in my pocket and headed across the grand lobby and up the stairs.

What did Dakaran want this time? I hoped to cross paths with the queen on my way, but as my luck generally held, there was no sign of her by the time I reached Dakaran's hall, so I went to see what His Royal Annoyance wanted.

The guards knocked when they saw me coming.

"Unless you're Ayrion," Dakaran called through the door, "go away!"

I grinned at the men. "Good thing I'm Ayrion."

Neither one cracked a smile.

Folding them into my command might prove more challenging than I had hoped. They opened the door, and I walked in.

"I heard you were looking for me," I said as I walked across the room.

"Yes," Dakaran said, standing from his chair by the fire. He waited until I was in front of him and then crossed his arms. "So I hear you're going to be living here at the palace."

I froze. "How'd you find out?"

"Father told us last night over dinner. Needless to say, I was shocked that my best friend hadn't bothered to tell me himself."

"I . . . I just didn't want to mention anything too soon. Nothing's official. We're still waiting to see if they'll have room." It was a little lie, of course, but it was better than him realizing I hadn't wanted him to find out, at least for a while, even though I knew that was impossible.

Dakaran's frown suddenly twisted into a goofy grin. "Not to worry. I told Father I'd take care of it myself."

"What do you mean, *yourself*?"

"I'll make sure you have the best accommodations we can find. I know of some great rooms that aren't being used on the floor just below this one. You can come and go at will, and you'll be close enough for us to sneak out as often as we wish."

"I can't be sneaking off like that anymore. I have work to do here, and men I'll be responsible for leading. How do you think your father's going to feel, after handing me this responsibility, if I up and shirk my duties to go running into town with you?"

Dakaran waved it off. "You're responsible for the royal family, are you not?"

"Of course," I said, not liking where he was going with this.

"And I'm one of the royal family, correct?"

I nodded again.

"And since I imagine that seeing to my safety will require you being near me at all times . . ." He left the thought unsaid, but I definitely understood.

I smiled. "Ah, I see. You seem to believe that your father has assigned *me* as your personal protection, when in fact he has given me an entire regiment for that purpose."

Dakaran's grin slipped. "What?"

"I'm going to be so busy working out schedules and keeping up with training sessions, I'll barely have time to sleep at night, let alone go gallivanting around town. Not saying we can't still find the occasional evening to get away," I added, wanting to give him at least some hope.

"I guess we'll have to wait and see." Dakaran's smile returned. "But I have a feeling you'll come around soon enough."

There was no point in arguing. Best to let it be and hope that once the new position started, he'd realize I wouldn't be able to keep sneaking out with him. In fact, with me being the one in charge of his safety, and given the fact I knew his secret way in and out of the palace, it would prove even harder for him to get away with it. I wondered if he'd thought about that yet or not.

I hoped I could find some common ground that would keep everyone happy. I didn't want my living here to end up causing more problems down the road.

One way to start was to make sure he felt included. Letting him help pick out our accommodations was an excellent way to do just that. By the end of the day, we'd managed to scour more than half the palace, coming away with some very good possibilities. The rooms weren't as grand as the royal estate rooms, but they were far better than anything I'd ever lived in before now, including Sandstorm. The room he chose for me was a full suite similar to his own, with a main sitting room, a private washroom, and a separate sleeping room with the largest bed I'd ever slept in.

I didn't let myself get my hopes up, especially after seeing it, since I had a feeling the king and queen probably wouldn't want me staying in something that nice. It looked more suited to visiting dignitaries. But after Dakaran made a well-meaning plea on my behalf, it seemed his parents were so thrilled by his involvement in royal affairs that they agreed to give me the room.

I was so delighted by the gift, I figured I'd have to find a way to schedule some in-town outings for the two of us after all, just to pay him back. Which meant I was going to have to assign some overnight watch duties for myself. After seeing the room and listening to him talk about the joys of having the staff fill me a personal bath every evening, I figured it would be worth it.

We then spent time searching the palace for lodging for the new guards and found some very nice rooms set up near the back, near our indoor training room. With the king wanting me to increase the guards' ranks, I was probably going to need different rooms for their lessons. The sleeping rooms were away from the beaten path, which I had a feeling most of my men would appreciate, as they always felt self-conscious walking through the palace. They were also far grander than anything we had ever stayed in at the garrison.

The rooms came in different sizes, some small enough to sleep three, others large enough to accommodate six quite easily. I was sure Room Eleven would prefer to remain together, so I kept my eye on one of the larger ones for them. We also found a sizable room nearby, which Dakaran thought we could convert into a dining hall for the men. There were a couple of rooms he thought would work for bathing, and one for recreation. The recreational room came with a small library already set up with groups of seating, along with small tables for food and drink. There were even some old instruments along the back wall for entertainment, in case any of the men could play.

There was room enough for not only the Black Guild but the palace guards and whatever new recruits we were able to assemble in the future.

I wanted to tell him this was all too much, but the more excited he became, the more it rubbed off on me. I hoped the king and queen would approve Dakaran's suggestions. If they did, my men were going to love me forever. Last on the list, Dakaran found me an office on the first floor, right off the main foyer. It was probably twice the size of Overcaptain Tolin's at the garrison, and much better furnished. It came with an entire wall of built-in shelving for books and knickknacks, expensive furnishings, including a full desk and small sitting area that would have made Sapphire envious. I almost felt guilty about it. Almost.

By the time we were finished and I was getting ready to leave, I'd all but forgotten the whole reason I had come to the palace in the first place. Dakaran and I had just left my hopefully new office and were heading down the corridor to the main lobby when it dawned on me that I still needed to speak with the queen.

"Is your mother around?"

Dakaran shrugged. "How should I know? I've been with you all day."

"I need to see if she has a few minutes to speak with me. Do you know if she had any meetings today?" Looking out through some of the windows in the foyer, I could see by the longer shadows in the courtyard out front that the sun was already beginning to drop. I couldn't believe how long it had taken us to search the palace for accommodations. The place was truly enormous.

"We can find out," he said, and I followed him back up the stairs to the floor holding the royal wing. Up ahead, the king stepped out of his study on the left, and we stopped.

"Is Mother in her chambers?" Dakaran asked.

"I believe she's in the garden," Rhydan answered. "Something about wanting to get in a walk before dinner." He looked at me. "Will you be joining us this evening?"

"I, uh . . ." I hadn't exactly planned on taking my meal at the palace. I figured Sapphire and the others would probably be expecting me, but turning down an offer from the king without a good reason wouldn't be a wise decision. "If Your Majesty hasn't had enough of me already, I'd be delighted."

He smiled. "Excellent. We'll see you there." He turned and headed down the hall for his chambers.

I looked at Dakaran. "If you want to get washed up, I'll see if I can catch your mother in the gardens." I was hoping he'd let me speak with her alone.

Dakaran thought a moment. "I guess after all the walking I've done today, a soak might be in order."

"Fine," I said, inching my way backward down the hall, "I'll see you later. Wait, which dining room?"

"The one we ate in with your riverboat people."

I nodded and headed back down the hall. Leaving the palace, I made my way around past the stables. I heard Shade whinny from inside. Clearly, he could sense my presence and thought I was coming to get him. *Not yet*, I said. *We'll leave after I eat.* That seemed to appease him for the moment, so I continued down the path and into the trees, which led back to the upper gardens.

It was the same gardens and fountain area that Dakaran and I used for our training on beautiful days like today. There were others walking along the path, mostly members of the nobility who tended to frequent the lush and vibrant grounds. I also passed several of the palace staff, no doubt opting to get some fresh air on one of their breaks.

I found the queen near the back. She wasn't that hard to spot with her royal guard walling her off from the rest of the garden's occupants.

They seemed to be there more to keep those in the garden from pestering her while she read than for any dire need of protection. Seeing me coming, they stiffened.

"Her Majesty doesn't wish to be disturbed," one of them said as I stopped in front of the two.

"Would you mind asking her if I may have a quick word?" I was looking forward to my new position. No more begging permission to speak with a member of the royal family.

The man on the left shook his head. "She made it clear that we are not to—"

"Let him pass," Queen Ellise said behind them, and the man turned, then bowed when he saw that she was looking at him. The queen was sitting on a bench under a white oak with a book in her hand and several more stacked beside her on the seat.

I bowed. "Thank you, Your Majesty." I stepped between the two guards, stopped in front of her, and bowed once more.

She moved some of her books aside and motioned for me to sit. "Were you and Dakaran able to find some suitable arrangements for your men today?"

"We were, Your Majesty, thank you, provided Your Majesties approve. They are certainly better than we deserve."

She looked me over. "I take it lodging isn't why you've sought me out."

"No, Your Majesty. I wish to speak on the matter of the new orphanage."

She closed her book, using her finger to mark her place, and placed it in her lap. "You'll be pleased to hear that we have raised quite a tidy sum," she said with a warm smile, "and there are still a few more on the fence. But I'm certain I can bring them around."

"That's wonderful, Your Majesty."

She chuckled. "I think your rather surprising entrance might have convinced a few as to the urgency of the need. I know Senator Gerrick was impressed, though more with your killing White Tower guards than anything, I suspect. Still, after you and Master Fentin and Mistress Orilla left, he pledged a very lucrative amount, encouraging many of the others to do the same."

"I'm relieved to hear it, Your Majesty. However, the funds aren't exactly why I'm here."

"Oh?"

"I believe I have a solution to our problem with finding a location for a second orphan house."

"Intriguing. Go on."

"Even with the money, finding an optimal location will probably prove difficult, and then there's the building and furnishing, and locating attendants who will be suitable to the task."

"Yes, I suspect it will take some time," the queen said.

"Or perhaps not," I added.

Her eyes narrowed. "You have a solution in mind?"

"I do, Your Majesty. I've spoken several times of my former tribe."

"Hailstorm, isn't it?"

"Sandstorm, Your Majesty. Slightly more annoying than a hailstorm, what with sand getting in your eyes and ears, and nose . . ." I flashed her a grin. "Anyway, Sandstorm owns a manor estate in the far northeast quarter, which I believe would make a wonderful orphan house. In a way, it's been acting as one for the last several years. They have good rapport with their neighbors, and there is plenty of space for the children to run about without becoming a nuisance. In fact, it's not that far from the Bailey Street Orphanage. For the last several years, we've been running street kids through Sandstorm before slowly moving good candidates over to the orphan house for Master Fentin and Mistress Orilla to begin the process of finding them homes. I believe it will make the perfect location for a second orphanage."

The queen thought a moment. "And who is in charge of this manor?"

"My former co-chiefs: Reevie, Sapphire, and Bull. Sapphire is the glue that holds it all together, the one with the business sense and organizational skills to make sure every child under their care is looked after. Reevie, who you already know, is the physicker who helped save Dakaran a couple weeks back. And then there's Bull. I chose him as my replacement. He's newer to the position, but he's strong, loyal, and would give his life for anyone there."

The queen listened until I was done. "It's clear you've put a lot of thought into this. Is there any other reason why you prefer this choice to building something new?"

I wasn't sure whether she was saying that she would rather start from scratch or just assessing why I was volunteering my friends. "I think Sandstorm would make the best choice because it's been tested. They have years of experience dealing with very large groups of children."

"And yet, I still feel there's more to it."

I smiled. "Your Majesty is perceptive. Yes, there is another reason for using that location and their services. Apart from the help it would be to have a stipend coming in to support the children, if they were an official orphan house, it would give them a legitimate station within the community, which I assume would allow them to fall under the protection of the city patrollers. That would be beneficial for them when it comes to Avalanche."

"That's the other tribe you mentioned that was looking to cause your friends harm?"

I nodded. "It is. But if it is known that they have patroller protection,

I believe that will keep the other tribe off their backs."

The queen nodded. I wasn't sure if that meant she agreed or simply wished for me to continue. Now for the difficult part. "However, the main reason I've come, besides presenting this offer, is that after talking with my former chiefs, they are hesitant to agree to this transition. They are afraid that any help from the crown would come with burdensome regulations and oversight that would make their jobs too difficult to execute properly."

I tried to be as polite about Sapphire's concerns as possible, attempting to find the best way to say that they didn't want the crown, or any of the aristocracy, breathing down their necks.

"Sapphire is worried about what stipulations might come with an orphanage stipend. In her experience, nobles don't give gold away without having a hand in how it's spent."

The queen smiled. "She seems like a very smart girl. I would like to meet her. I would like to meet all of them. We'll have to arrange a trip in the near future so we can better assess the situation. I might not be as persnickety with my giving as experience may have taught her, but I must do my due diligence. Like your Master Fentin and Mistress Orilla, you vouching for them holds a lot of weight, but I want to meet who I plan on doing business with face-to-face to see how they measure up."

"Understandable, Your Majesty. I would do the same."

"I can promise that there will be no overbearing rules or regulations attached to the stipend," she said, "but I would like a quarterly update on progress. I don't want another situation to happen like what has befallen the Bailey Street Orphanage, in that the numbers have grown to such an extent to cause undue hardship on those involved. This way, I can satisfy the nobles with progress and perhaps even use it as a way to entice them to continue giving."

I nodded. "That sounds reasonable. I'll be sure to pass it along this evening."

The queen looked up at the fast-coloring sky. "You better get a move on if you plan on getting across town before supper."

"Actually, His Majesty asked me to join you this evening for dinner, if that is agreeable with you."

She reached over and patted my hand. "Of course. You are always welcome here, Ayrion." She stood, and I followed her up, then leaned over and grabbed a stack of books. "No need," she said. "My men will take them." She looked over at the two guards with their backs to us and lowered her voice. "I guess they will be your men soon enough."

With the guards' help, we collected the books and started back up the crushed rock path for the palace. The sky was thick with deep purples and golds as the setting sun began to ebb in the sky. We passed to the right of the stables and were just starting into the tunnel for the inner courtyard when someone shouted my name.

I turned to find one of the bridge guards heading our way at a run, wearing an expression somewhere between exasperation and surprise.

As soon as he was close enough to spot the queen behind me, he stopped and bowed.

"Your Majesty! My apologies. I didn't see you there."

"It's quite alright," she said. "What is it?"

"There is someone at the gate who wishes to speak with Master Ayrion. He said it was urgent and that he would not leave until he'd seen him." The guard looked at me. "I told him I wasn't even sure you were here, but he insisted."

"Did this person give his name?"

"It was kind of a funny name, sir, which is why I was hesitant to let him across, I believe he said his name was Bull. Do you know him?"

"Yes. Did he say what he wanted?"

"He didn't, but from the way he demanded we look for you, I'd say it was serious."

I turned to Her Majesty. "I'm afraid I might not be able to join you this evening for dinner after all. Please give the king my apologies."

"Of course. I do hope it is nothing untoward. If there's anything we can do, don't hesitate to ask."

I bowed. "Thank you, Your Majesty." Then I turned and ran after the watchman.

What could be so important that Bull would show up here? If he'd gotten us all worked up just to have me give him a tour of the palace, I was going to toss him off the bridge.

I chased after the watchman all the way back to the other side of the bridge. I could see Bull's sandy-blond hair on the right just in front of the guard tower. As soon as he saw me, he ran out to meet me. The look on his face said he wasn't here for a tour.

"What's going on?" I asked, a little out of breath. "I was just on my way to a meal with the royal family."

"It's Reevie."

"What about him? Is he hurt? Did something happen?"

"The infirmary was attacked."

"What? At Sandstorm? Was it the new Avalanche kids?"

"No. Not Sandstorm. Saban's infirmary in town."

"What happened?"

Bull took a deep breath. "It was Cutter."

AVALANCHE

Chapter 48

UTTER?" I WAS SPEECHLESS. "How do you know?"

"Saban's son showed up at Sandstorm about an hour ago and told us that his father's infirmary had been attacked. He said they were wearing white armbands."

"Wasn't there a patrol on the place?"

"The patrollers pulled most of their men off the infirmary about two days ago. Guess they figured if nothing had happened so far, it probably wasn't going to. They had some men inside. I'm not sure how many. We did find bodies. They must have put up a fight."

"And Reevie was there?"

"Yes."

"He's not . . ."

Bull shook his head. "No, at least, I don't think so. But both he and Saban were taken, along with a number of injured patrollers."

My mind raced. Was this a deliberate attack because Cutter knew Reevie was there, or was this just a retaliation against the patrollers and he got lucky by nabbing Reevie as well? It didn't matter. At this point, all I could think about were the horrible things the demented Avalanche chief might be doing to Reevie. For all I knew, Reevie was already dead.

No. Cutter wasn't that stupid. He would use Reevie somehow to get at Sandstorm. At least, I hoped that was the case. It was the only thing most likely keeping him alive.

"Have you assembled Sandstorm's Guard and the beaters?"

Bull nodded. "Collen's getting them armed as we speak. Sapphire sent me to find you immediately."

"They haven't already left Sandstorm, have they?"

"No. We were waiting to see if I could find you first. If not, they have orders to start heading south as soon as the sun goes down."

This was worse than a direct attack on Sandstorm. Cutter was forcing us to leave the protection of our manor and come to him. Then again, he might not even have known Reevie was working there. Still, it didn't change the fact that Cutter had him. We didn't have a choice.

"Why do you think he's doing this?" Bull asked. "Seems a stupid move to kidnap wounded patrollers. Does he want an all-out war?"

I looked past Bull out at the city, pondering that very question. The answer hit me like a brick-laden sack. "The gold."

Bull cocked his head. "What?"

"I bet you anything Captain Arns managed to get Frog to talk. If the patrollers have Cutter's gold, then they've backed him into a corner." I balled my fists. "Why did they have to do this now? They're putting all of our lives at risk." I looked at Bull. "Do you have a horse?"

He nodded and pointed to the far side of the guard station where several horses were tied.

"Good. I'm going back into the palace stables to get Shade. Ride back to Sandstorm and make sure they don't leave, at least not yet."

"What are you going to do?"

"I'm going to get us some help."

"Where?"

"The patrollers."

"But they're the ones who got us into this mess."

"And they're also the ones who kept you safe by weeding out the old compound."

"But this is the Temple, Ayrion. We aren't going to get through those gates. Not even if the patrollers had a battering ram."

"We won't have to."

Bull looked at me like I'd lost my mind, then his eyes widened. "The tunnel. We can sneak in without them knowing."

I grinned. "Exactly."

I collected Shade and galloped northeast for Captain Arns's patroller station. Men in blue capes were already gathering. A line of them stretched up the front steps and into the brick building. They looked like they were getting ready for another raid.

Leaving Shade at the rails, I pushed my way up the stairs and into the front lobby, doing my best to try to see over the men inside. Unlike the first time I was there, those who saw me moved out of the way as best they could, considering the crowd inside. Several who caught my eye nodded as I passed. Apparently, my time spent fighting alongside them had made an impression.

I could hear what sounded like Arns's voice on the other side of the room near the front desk, so I skirted the perimeter of the crowd and pushed my way over to the desk. Sergeant Lowell was there. As soon as he saw me, he held up his hand to have me wait, and then leaned over and whispered into Arns's ear.

Arns excused himself for a moment and waved me back into the corridor.

"What's going on?" I asked, following him toward the back. "I just found out that Saban's infirmary was attacked. Is that correct?"

"Word travels fast," he said somberly as he directed me into his office.

I stepped inside. "What are you planning on doing?"

He walked in behind me and shut the door. "Better question is, what are you planning? I doubt you'd be here without something in mind. I've already sent word to the other patroller offices of the attack and have asked for reinforcements. One way or another, we are going to get our men back."

There was no sense in beating around the bush now. "You found the gold, didn't you?"

Arns looked surprised, his lazy eye sliding to the right. "How did you know—"

"I put two and two together. There's only one reason Cutter would do something this brash, and that's if he didn't believe he had any other choice." I stared at him a moment, waiting to see if he'd admit to it or not.

He finally nodded. "Yes, we managed to get Frog talking, and surprisingly it didn't take much convincing. Got the feeling he didn't harbor much love for his cousin. A few well-placed threats, and he led us right to the gold." He looked at me a moment. "I'm sorry we didn't give you forewarning. I didn't like leaving Cutter's cousin in the workhouses for long and risk them coming under attack as well. With the knowledge Frog had, it wouldn't have taken Cutter long."

I sighed. "You've put us all in a bad spot. Did you not think there would be repercussions? The gold is what kept that entire tribe running and Cutter in power. Without it, they'd probably eat him alive."

"We had no idea they would attack an infirmary. There'd been no activity anywhere near there for over a week. Had we known, we would have been better prepared." He lowered his head. "That's on me."

At least he was a big enough man to admit his failure. "I know the Temple. You won't get inside those walls easily. By the time you manage to come close, they'll have already killed the prisoners."

Arns released a frustrated sigh, then marched over to his desk and stared down at the papers on top. "Do you have a suggestion?"

"If I were Cutter, I'd attempt to trade the prisoners for the gold."

Arns's jaw tightened as he looked over at me. "And if we don't?"

"Be prepared to watch him execute your men publicly and drop their corpses over the wall."

Arns hit the top of his desk. "Then how do we stop him? If we capitulate and give him the gold back, it will send the message that all he needs to do to get what he wants is kidnap people and ransom them back. This situation will only grow worse."

"I agree."

"So, I ask again, how do we stop him?"

"By getting inside without him knowing."

Arns turned. "How do we do that? You know a way in?"

I took a deep breath, not really wanting to spill too much, but I didn't have much choice. "Yes, but for this to work, we need as many of your men waiting outside the gate and ready to breach the walls as we can get. Sandstorm is arming up now and getting ready to march that way."

"Why are *they* going?"

"Because Avalanche kidnapped one of their chiefs. I've sent word to hold them off for the moment, but as soon as the sun goes down, they're heading south, with or without me."

"Then what do you want to do?"

"I want to get my hands on Cutter and squeeze the life out of him."

Arns crushed a wad of paper on his desk. "Get in line."

"But I also don't want to turn this into a bloodbath with hundreds of dead children. As good as it will be to get rid of this tribe, that would leave a permanent stain on all of us."

"Agreed. So, how do we get in and put a stop to this with as little killing as possible?" His head lifted. "Got any more of that ether stuff?"

"Afraid not. Even if we did, these kids know we're coming and are already waiting. The only reason it worked before was I was able to lure them all into one place. Don't see that happening here, not with them waiting on the wall while Sandstorm and the patrollers march against it."

"Then what are we going to do? You mentioned another way in. Where is it?"

I hesitated again. I didn't like giving away such secrets, but if I stood any chance at all of rescuing Reevie, I was going to need the patrollers' help. It wasn't like we were ever going to be taking up residence in the Temple again. "There is a secret tunnel that leads under the wall from the forest on the southeast corner."

"And Cutter doesn't know about it?"

I shook my head. "Cutter didn't take over the Temple until after we left. In fact, the tunnel was how we made it out without him finding us."

Arns nodded but didn't say anything.

"I will lead a small team in to capture Cutter. We get him, and this whole thing ends."

"Why a small team? Why not send everyone in that way?"

"The more people we send in, the greater the risk of being seen. We need to get to Cutter before he can order the prisoners killed, and then

we use him to force the tribe to stand down. Without Cutter, none of this is going to work."

"How many do you think we'll need? I can get four or five of my best—"

I shook my head. "No patrollers."

"What? Why?"

I stiffened, growing impatient at his constant questions. My friend was probably being tortured, and I was being forced to waste precious time explaining every little thing. "Because I need people who know the layout. Once inside, we'll have to separate to check the compound, and your men can't do that. Besides that, they look like . . . well, men. We need scouts that can blend in."

The captain didn't look very happy about being left out, but there wasn't much I could do about it. Going in with his men was a sure way for us to get pinched. "I need you and your men outside the gate with Sandstorm, ready to charge those doors if something happens."

"And what if something happens?"

"Then you do whatever it takes to get in."

"But you just said that you thought the gate was impenetrable."

I balled my fists. "Do you have ladders?"

"A few."

"Bring them, and as many shields as you can carry. They might have archers." I glanced out the side window. The light of dusk was nearly gone, which meant my time was running out. "We need to go. And don't worry about trying to keep your approach hidden. They'll have watchers on all the roads, and if I know Cutter, they'll already be waiting for you when you get there."

"So you want us to just sit outside the gate and do nothing?" The captain was looking more agitated by the moment. I had to remind myself that it was his men who had been killed. I wouldn't be any less upset at not being able to play a more direct role if our places had been switched.

"Try talking to them, see if you can somehow convince them to let the prisoners go."

"You said that wasn't going to work with this Cutter fellow."

"It won't."

Arns's nostrils flared. "Then why would you tell me to do that?"

"Because we need them talking as long as possible. We need their attention on you and not on us sneaking in behind them."

He stared at me a moment, determination in his eyes. "Do you have some sort of signal to let us know when to attack or if we even need to?"

"I'm sure you'll know it when it happens. If they capture us inside, you'll find out just as soon as they start tossing our bodies over the wall. However, if we manage to get our hands on Cutter, then you'll see the gates opening."

Arns huffed, not looking very happy with the situation. "Not much to go on."

"It's the best we've got."

We both left the office and headed out to the lobby, where he began giving his men their orders. I pushed through the throng of anxious patrollers and made it out front, climbed on Shade, and we raced southeast for Sandstorm. I hoped I was able to get there before they left. The sun was already down, and the first of the stars were just beginning to wink into existence.

We tore through the mostly empty streets, the wind cooling my face and calming the turmoil roiling inside me. I slowed my breathing and tried to concentrate on what lay ahead. I'd barely gotten back from one battle only to step straight into another. This was absurd. The wounds I'd acquired from the last conflict had just begun to heal, and I had yet

to find a good tailor to mend the damage to my coat. Not the best time to be taking either back into battle.

I reached Sandstorm in good time and pulled to a stop in front of the gate.

"Protector?" Toots's head popped up over the wall on the right. "Why's you here? Thought you was goin' to the Temple."

I looked through the gate and up the drive to see if I could spot our beaters. "Have they already left?"

"Yep. Not's long ago."

"Did they say which way they were heading?"

He shrugged. "Don't knows about that."

"Did Collen leave any beaters here to guard the manor?"

"Yes, they's up at the house."

I nodded. "If things don't go well, tell them to be ready to get our people out."

"And go where?"

I thought a moment. "Take them to the docks if you can. Find Captain Treygan of the *Wind Binder*. You met him when his crew came to visit a couple of weeks back. Tell him what's happened." It occurred to me that I needed to stop by the Bailey Street Orphanage to let them know to do the same. "And make sure you take Master Fentin and Mistress Orilla and the kids there with you. Is Gittrick still here?"

"Yes."

"Tell him what I've told you." At least they'd have a couple of adults there to help if they needed to make a run for it. "I've got to go." I turned Shade around, and we galloped back up the road and around until we reached Bailey Street. The lane was mostly empty, though the sound of pounding hooves had a few of the residents peeking out their windows. I pulled up in front of the orphanage and hopped off.

The house was dark, but I could see some light around the edges of the curtains on the front windows, which meant the older couple was probably in the family room reading before bed. I knocked on the door, trying not to wake the rest of the house. It took a moment for Master Fentin to answer the door.

"Ayrion? Is everything alright?"

"No." I stepped in, and we headed into the front room, where Orilla was sitting on the sofa with a book in her lap. She looked up when I walked in.

"This is a late visit. Should I get some tea?"

I shook my head. "Not a visit. I needed to tell you what's happening in case . . . well, in case the worst happens."

"Worst . . ." She stood, Master Fentin moving into the room to stand beside her.

"The patrollers found Cutter's gold, so Cutter attacked Saban's infirmary."

"Oh no!" Orilla covered her mouth. "Reevie?"

"He was taken, along with Physicker Saban and the rest of the injured patrollers. It sounds as though Avalanche killed some of the guards inside. The patrollers are on their way to the Temple right now, and so is Sandstorm. I'm riding down to meet them. If something goes wrong and we are . . ."

"Don't even think such a thing," Orilla said, her hands trembling.

"If Cutter wins, I wouldn't put it past him to come for what's left of Sandstorm and even the orphanage, just out of spite. I've already told those at Sandstorm that if the worst should happen, get everyone out and find the captains of the *Wind Binder*: Captain Treygan and his daughter Captain Ismara. They will be able to help."

"How will they help? Are they supposed to sail us somewhere?"

"No, but they just saved the king's life and ferried him all the way back to Aramoor. If anyone can get you into the palace for help, it will be them."

"How will we know if something goes wrong?"

"One way or another, I'll send word. I'll leave some of our people on the outskirts, and if they see things aren't going in our favor, they will come." I was leaving a lot of this up to chance, but it was the best I could do given the circumstances.

"We'll be praying that doesn't happen," Fentin said. He walked forward and laid his hand on my shoulder. "Keep them safe, you hear? And do me a favor: put an end to that flaming tribal chief once and for all."

It was strange to hear calm, soft-spoken Fentin speak this way, but after all the years of Cutter's treacherous behavior, it was definitely warranted. I nodded and then headed for the door. "Make sure to keep a watch tonight. You might even want to have your kids dress and pack, just in case. Better ready than not."

"We'll be ready," Fentin said. "Good luck to you, son."

I smiled and left. Jumping up on Shade, we flew down the street for Circle Drive and from there south toward King's Way East. I hoped I wasn't too late. Stopping by the orphanage had taken time, but I didn't want to trust sending one of Toots's watchers over, hoping they gave the right message. If something happened to us, I needed the orphanage ready to evacuate.

I reached the roundabout and started across King's Way East. About halfway, I spotted a couple of kids in black hoods and purple armbands crossing a few streets east of me. I quickly circled back and headed for the street I'd seen them go down.

I pulled to a stop and found the narrow lane filled with Sandstorm beaters, all staring out at me like a bunch of rats trapped in the hull of a ship. I breathed a small sigh of relief.

"Protector?" Collen pushed his way to the front.

I looked across King's Way East to the small street they had come from. There were nearly as many on that side as this one.

"We weren't sure you were coming," Collen said.

"I asked you to wait." I stared down King's Way East toward the city's main gate. There wasn't much activity, so I turned and waved the rest on. It would take all night if we waited for them to cross two at a time. If the lancers came to inspect, I could say they were with me.

The rest of the Sandstorm beaters and guards rushed across the road. The stream of kids stretched the entire length of King's Way East. Thankfully, we managed to get them over with no one coming to inspect. Bull brought up the rear.

"Sorry we didn't wait," Bull said, "but Sapphire wanted us to go. She said it was going to take a while to get us down there, and that we might as well make the best of the time. We don't know what Cutter might be doing to Reevie. We figured it best to wait for you there."

I twisted in my saddle, scanning the faces gathered. "Where's Sapphire?"

Bull pointed ahead. "She's at the front."

I hopped off Shade and walked him into the narrow street. "Let's find her. I want to talk with the three of you," I said, indicating to Collen he was one of those three.

I left Shade with some of the kids and headed down to the next road crossing with Bull and Collen. By the time we got there, I spotted Sapphire coming our way. Behind her loomed the giant shadow of Tubby, complete with his Flesh Eater mask, curtain cape, and hood. He had to be at least nine feet tall now.

No one really knew anything about Tubby, his origins, or where he'd come from. Rumors were that Avalanche had found him wandering around the old docks as a child, as though he'd washed ashore from some unknown fishing vessel. Other than his slow-moving mind and his incredible growth, not much about the boy was known. To most, he was something to be feared, but to us, he was just Tubby, the fun-loving child everyone at Sandstorm enjoyed playing with.

"Protector? You made it!" Mouse rushed out from around Tubby's legs.

I should have known the little scamp would be somewhere about, which I was glad of, because he was one of those I wanted to take with me into the tunnel. He knew the Temple inside and out and could easily move about without being seen.

"I'm glad Bull found you," Sapphire said. She had both her swords strapped at her waist.

"Captain Arns and his men are on their way to the Temple as we speak, might even be ahead of us. Take Sandstorm to join him at the front. Keep back in the trees for now. We don't want you easy targets if they have archers."

"What about you?" she asked.

"I'm going to take a team down into the tunnel."

She nodded. "Bull said you were planning on using it."

"My hope is to get my hands on Cutter and stop this before we end up filling the compound with dead children."

"Or before he does anything to Reevie," she said, her jaw tightening. "If he hurts him, there won't be enough of Cutter left to identify."

"I'll come with you into the tunnel," Bull said, but I shook my head.

"I want you here with Collen to lead our people in if things don't go according to plan. The patrollers are going to need as much support as they can get. We might have captured the north garrison, but that was only about a quarter of Avalanche."

"Did you find out whether or not the patrollers found Cutter's gold?" Sapphire asked. "I'd love to know why this is happening now."

"They did. Arns told me himself. Cutter's got nothing left to lose, and my bet is he tries trading the injured patrollers for it."

"What about Reevie?" Bull asked.

"I don't see him trading Reevie with them. If I were Cutter, I'd use him to barter for Sandstorm Manor. Two birds with one stone."

"I hadn't even thought of that," Bull said.

"Whatever happens," I said, "you need to keep Avalanche's eyes on the gate so we can sneak in without them knowing."

"Do you think the wall is where Cutter will be?" Sapphire asked.

"I would imagine so. He loves the sound of his own voice, so I think he'll enjoy seeing all of us squirming. To him, he holds the upper hand—"

"He does," Sapphire said.

"Regardless, we need to keep him talking for as long as possible."

"Who's going inside?" Bull asked.

"I'm going," Mouse said, his pig sticker already in hand. "I know right where to plant this. Between his stinking ribs."

"I want you with me," I said, "but not to kill Cutter. We need him alive to call off his tribe. You know the Temple and are small enough to blend in with the rest of the kids. I need three more like you, all who know the place well enough to get around without being noticed."

"No problem." With that, Mouse raced off into the throng of beaters and guards before we could stop him. A few minutes later, he was back with two beaters and one guard, each of which had been with us when Hurricane had been living at the Temple all those years ago. The two beaters were Kiff and Linny, twin brothers who'd been abandoned at birth and forced into the workhouses until they were old enough to escape. They were lucky Hurricane had found them before Avalanche had. The guard was Ellie. She'd arrived at the Granary along with Bull and the rest of the rejects after the battle at the Pit. She was a tough little scrapper and had quickly worked her way up through the beaters to be one of the few girls to join the Guard.

Surprisingly, even after six years, all three still looked young enough to blend in with the rest.

I was the only one who stood out. I looked at Bull. "Let me have your cloak." He handed it to me, and I put it on over my coat and raised the hood up over my swords. It wasn't perfect, but better than nothing. Thankfully, we were doing this in the middle of the night. I wasn't about to let these kids go in by themselves.

I turned to Sapphire, Bull, and Collen. "I'll tell you the same as I told Captain Arns: don't worry about trying to sneak your way in through the Maze. Cutter already knows we're coming. Get there as quickly as you can. By the time you reach the patrollers, we should be heading into the tunnel."

I started to turn but stopped. "Oh, and leave a few watchers on the road. If things don't go the way we hope, I want them running back to warn Sandstorm and the orphanage. I've given both instructions to flee to the port and find the *Wind Binder* crew if things go badly."

"Smart," Sapphire said. "I should have thought to do the same."

We all finally nodded and parted ways. I didn't get back on Shade, since the other four kids were running with me, so the giant horse trotted along beside us as we made our way back to Circle Drive and started south at a brisk pace. It didn't take us long to reach the back southeast corner of the Temple's property, which was hedged by a stand of trees thick enough to mask us from the Temple's wall ahead.

I left Shade just inside the first row of trees and told him to stay hidden until we returned, hoping he understood what I was saying. The rest of us headed into the thicket. We had to stay close, single file, to keep from losing each other in the dark. The trees were thick and tightly bunched together, and it took a while to work our way through the underbrush quietly.

I looked for some sign of where the grate covering the entrance to the tunnel was located, but it had been years since I'd been here, and my memory was a little fuzzy. We couldn't use lanterns or torches for fear of signaling our approach, and the kids behind me kept bumping into each other as they tried to keep up. This was going to be more difficult than I thought. The undergrowth had expanded. Nothing looked the same.

"Over here," a voice called out softly somewhere ahead of us.

We all froze.

"Who was that?" Mouse whispered behind me, and I put my hand over his mouth.

"Quiet. I don't know." I scanned the trees, but I didn't see anyone. Suddenly Sapphire's head popped up from a cluster of vines farther up. I gritted my teeth. Why was she here? I grabbed Mouse. "Come on. It's Sapphire." How had she gotten here so quickly? She must have run the entire way. Apparently, my orders held little sway when it came to some of the Sandstorm chiefs.

We worked our way around the thickest of the vines to reach her.

"I thought I heard you coming," she said.

"What are you doing here?" I whispered, trying not to sound too angry, just enough to let her know I was.

"Going with you inside. The Temple was my home long before any of you came along. And if anyone is going to get their hands on Cutter, it's me."

"What about our fighters?"

"They're in good hands. Bull and Collen can manage well enough without me."

It was too late to try to stop her now, not that I could have. "How'd you find it?"

"Accident. I got turned around, tripped, and landed right on top of it."

"Lucky for us." I waved her back and reached down and grabbed the top and pulled. It held fast. "Help me."

Everyone moved around the grate and felt along the ground until they had found an edge to grab.

"All together," I said. "One, two, three, pull."

We heaved, and the grate gave way. I nearly tumbled backward but caught myself and then slid the lid to the side.

"What now?" Ellie asked, looking down into the blackness with the rest. She carried a pair of long bludgeons at her sides.

"There should be a set of metal handholds attached to the side to climb down with."

"I don't see anything," Kiff said.

"Me either," Linny added.

"Just wait here." I grabbed the first rung and started down. I spotted the old lantern in the same spot down below that I'd left on our first trip through the secret entrance. I smiled. Cutter hadn't found the place. Up until now, I had been acting as if that was the case, but now I knew. I reached the bottom and grabbed a striker from my coat. Using it and a piece of dried brush I'd found above, I managed to get the lantern lit.

I lifted the light out toward the tunnel ahead, and as expected, it was empty. Above me, I heard footsteps and looked up to see Mouse, Kiff, Linny, and Ellie heading down. Sapphire gave them a head start before climbing in herself. The cover was too heavy to try moving back into place on her own, so she left it, though she did pull some of the low-hanging vines overtop to hide the entrance.

She reached the bottom, and we all gathered around as I raised the lantern for them to get a better look.

"Not very big, is it?" Kiff said.

"Nope, not that big at all," his brother was quick to echo.

"And dusty," Mouse added, his face puckering as he started to sneeze.

"Stop him," I said, and Sapphire covered his mouth just before he released it.

I breathed a small sigh of relief. I doubted the noise could have made it all the way back down the tunnel and through two different walls to reach Reevie's old infirmary, but I wasn't taking any chances. I gave the little picker a stern look, and he shrugged at me with a mousy smile.

"We've got to be as quiet as possible," I said, then turned toward the tunnel opening and waved them forward.

I led and Sapphire brought up the rear, with Ellie between Mouse and the twins.

We were about halfway down when Sapphire stopped us. "Do you hear that?"

I turned. There were some shuffling noises back near the entrance. Had Bull decided to come down as well? *Idiots.* Did no one listen? I'd just started back through the group to find out what was going on when something large fell from the top, hit the bottom of the tunnel, and burst open.

"What was that?" Mouse asked.

I looked down to see a blackish liquid slithering across the stone around my feet. I leaned down and stuck my finger in it and sniffed. My breath caught in my throat.

"Run!" I grabbed those in back and shoved them toward the other side of the tunnel.

"What is it?" Sapphire called back as we tore down the narrow rock

walls of the passageway.

"It's black briar!"

We barely made it five steps before another cask flew down to the bottom and shattered, this time accompanied by a torch.

AVALANCHE

Chapter 49

THE STRONG BRISTONIAN DRINK ignited before the torch even hit the ground.

"Run!" I pushed my terrified crew toward the steps that led up to the secret room behind the infirmary, praying the door wasn't locked. Black liquid raced down the stone floor toward us, and the flash of its ignition blinded me for a brief moment. I stumbled but continued racing ahead.

We fled up the stairs toward the door. Mouse was the first up, and I held my breath as he grabbed the handle. It opened, and I sighed in relief. At least we wouldn't be cooked to death. I was the last through the door and quickly shut it behind me to block the oncoming heat. If the fire made it all the way to this side of the tunnel, it could follow the stairs up. One thing was certainly clear: there was no getting back out. We were trapped inside.

"There's someone over here!" Ellie hissed, and I turned with the lantern. As soon as the light found her, she gasped and quickly shuffled back and away from a patroller on the floor. He was dead, his throat slashed.

"They're all dead," Sapphire said, and I spun the light around, frantically searching the bodies. The small antechamber was filled with them.

"Reevie?" Sapphire immediately started combing through the pile. We all did.

By the time we reached the last corpse, we were out of breath, our hearts pounding and our hands covered in blood.

"He's not here," she said, breathing a heavy sigh of relief. The bodies were all patrollers. It was obviously a relief not finding Reevie, but these were men I'd worked with. I even recognized a few faces as those I'd fought alongside during the Avalanche attack near the workhouses.

I handed Mouse the lantern and drew my swords. I could still hear the fire burning in the tunnel behind us. Smoke was beginning to work its way under the door.

"How did they know we were here?" Sapphire asked as she and the other four huddled near the back of the room. It was the only place without a corpse.

I shook my head, staring down at the bodies. "I don't know. The only way we knew about this place was because Reevie found it by accident years ago after spilling some herbs on the floor."

I looked at the hidden door leading out into the infirmary. Reevie's basket, where he kept his apples, lay quietly in the dust beside it, still untouched. This didn't make any sense.

"Maybe someone saw us from the road and followed us here," Ellie said nervously, gripping her bludgeons.

"I didn't see anyone," Kiff said.

"Neither did I," Linny echoed.

I heard voices in the next room and held up my hand. "They know we're here."

There was no time to hide now, so I braced myself just behind the door. The best chance we had was a swift attack in hope of catching them off guard. I motioned for the others to gather up beside me and whispered, "There's still a chance they believe we were caught in the fire. When I open the door, we rush in. Whatever happens, try not to kill Cutter if you can help it." I added the last with a knowing look at Sapphire.

She sneered. "Can't promise anything."

Tightening my grip, I counted down. As soon as I hit one, I yanked open the door, and we ran headlong into a barricade of metal bars. The room had been turned into a cell.

We were trapped inside.

Laughter spilled from somewhere on the other side of the room. A moment later, Cutter, wearing his wide-brimmed hat, stepped into view. Beside him were a few of his Guard, each holding a prisoner in front of them as they moved into place.

"It's Reevie," Mouse said, and I held up my hand for him to keep quiet.

Reevie, Physicker Saban, and at least one of the patrollers were paraded out, each with a knife to their throat. All three looked like they'd been given a savage beating. Their faces were cut and bruised, the cuts old enough that the blood had dried. A thought flashed through my mind.

I could end this.

I could throw my knife and kill him right here. But I only had the one, and there were three prisoners. Also, we needed Cutter alive.

"Well, well, well," Cutter said, keeping his distance, "look who we have here. Throw out your weapons."

When no one moved, Cutter pointed at the older boy holding Reevie, and the boy tightened his knife at Reevie's throat. Reevie squealed, and blood welled just beneath the blade and slid slowly down his neck. I bit my tongue to keep from grabbing the knife behind my back.

"I'm going to peel the skin off you like a snake!" Sapphire said, her teeth clenched.

Cutter grinned. He waited a moment, and then his eyes hardened. "Don't make me say it again."

I looked at the others and nodded, and we tossed our weapons through the bars.

Cutter waited until the last of them came through. "Now raise your coats and spin so I can see you aren't hiding more." We did, which had a couple of us tossing a few more knives out as well, hidden behind our backs.

Cutter smiled. "I've been waiting for this for a long time, but never in my wildest would I have hoped to have netted the great Ayrion himself." He looked a little perplexed. "Last I heard, you were out fighting some war with Cylmar."

I didn't respond, my mind racing to think of a way out as I scanned the nearby shelves inside Reevie's old infirmary, looking for anything that might be of use. The place looked like a storage room now, nothing that resembled a place for healing. I did spot a set of keys resting from a hook on the right wall beside a small table and chair, but nothing we could hope to reach.

"This is truly an honor," Cutter said with a deep-seated grin. "And Sapphire, you are looking as radiant as ever. It's almost a shame to have to spoil such beauty."

"Come over here and try," she said.

I placed a hand on her arm. "It was a stupid move on your part,

Cutter, to kill your leverage like this." I looked back at the dead men in the cell with us. "Now there's nothing to stop those patrollers out there from coming in and killing the lot of you. And with your only escape route set ablaze, it looks like you're as caged in here as the rest of us."

Cutter chuckled. "Always a step behind." He looked in at the dead. "I don't need all of them to bargain with. I only need enough to persuade. As long as the Blue Capes think I have their men, they'll behave. Just like Sandstorm." He looked over at Reevie. "Rather a twist of luck to find the cripple working there. What are the odds? Been this close to me all this time and I didn't even know it." He laughed. "I honestly had no intention of dragging Sandstorm into this fight . . . yet. My grievance was with the patrollers." His smile vanished. "That is, until a couple of loose lips told me that it wasn't the patrollers who were really behind this. Was it?"

The hair stood on my arms. He knew.

His grin reappeared. "You'll be surprised how fast people will talk when you start cutting on them. Very clever using the patrollers the way you did. And I thought I was manipulative. Credit where credit is due."

I wanted to cut the smug grin off his face.

"Things haven't looked this good since I stuck my blade in Kore and claimed Rockslide as my own." Cutter's smile deepened. "You should have seen the look on his face."

"Your ambition is what's going to kill you in the end," Sapphire said. "And I'm going to be there when it happens. My eyes are going to be the last thing you ever see."

Cutter laughed. "By the time this night is over, I'm going to be rid of Sandstorm once and for all, much like I took care of Red and Wildfire. Either I will own the streets or none of us will. Your time as chiefs has come to an end."

Reevie and the other two started trembling at Cutter's talk of everything coming to an end, but they did their best not to move, as the blades were still pressed against their necks.

I wanted to tell Reevie I was sorry I had left him for the lancers, but the last thing I needed to do was to say something that sounded like goodbye. They needed to be strong, not feel like I'd given up and we were all about to die.

"It seems you have been planning this for some time," I said, earning a proud look from the Avalanche chief. "I'm curious, though. How did you know about the tunnel?"

Cutter grinned. "Oh, I thought you'd never ask." He turned and motioned for someone in the hall to step in. A hooded figure with their head lowered walked across the room and joined Cutter at the front.

My mind raced. Who had betrayed us?

"I told you it would work," Cutter said to the cloaked individual, "but even I didn't know it would work this well. I believe you have something you'd like to say?"

My chest tightened as I tried making out the face beneath the cowl. It would have had to be someone inside of Sandstorm, but who would have sold us out, and why?

The robed individual chuckled. "I say you cuts their feet."

The breath caught in my throat as the speaker pulled back his hood, and I found myself staring into a set of eyes I hadn't seen in over six years.

Spats!

"It can't be," Sapphire murmured.

The former chief of Hurricane took a step forward. "Bet you never thought to see me again," he spat, aiming most of his anger in my direction.

"I'd always wondered what really happened to Spats," Cutter said.

"I figured the lot of you had killed him and dumped his body in the bay. Imagine my surprise when he showed up here at my doorstep expecting to see you and found me instead." Cutter looked at me and clicked his tongue. "Wouldn't think I'd have to tell an Upakan this, but when you get rid of someone, make sure they can't come back." He chuckled. "Finding out about the secret tunnel was certainly the advantage I needed. Granted, I hadn't planned on using it quite so soon, but when I realized we had accidentally captured one of Sandstorm's chiefs in our raid, well . . ."

I stared at Spats. He'd grown, and was a little more filled out, but he still had that same bright red hair and weaselly face. His high-pitched whiny voice was unmistakable, and his glee at plotting our downfall showed he hadn't changed much during his absence.

"I've been waiting for this for years," Spats said to me, but then included Sapphire in his statement with a quick glance in her direction. "I couldn't have dreamed of it happening in such a glorious way, though. And now, here I am, back in my city after all these years, with nothing to stop us. Cutter has promised me the Temple for my help, and as soon as we take Sandstorm, my return and revenge will be complete." He looked at Cutter. "I want you to make Ayrion die slowly."

Cutter looked at me, then shrugged. "As long as he's dealt with permanently, I don't care one way or the other."

Spats looked at me and Sapphire, a wicked grin spreading across his face. "Hurricane will be mine again." His grin suddenly vanished, and his eyes bulged.

He released a bloodcurdling scream and started to convulse as blood bubbled from his mouth. Before he could say a single word, he pitched over face-first onto the floor and went still.

Behind him, Cutter held a bloody knife. He looked down at Spats's body and shook his head. "Just as stupid as he ever was. Fool actually thought I was going to give him his tribe back." He laughed. "Like I was going to share my power with him." He knelt down and wiped his blade on Spats's coat, then tucked it neatly back in its sheath and stood.

I fought to hold my own rage at bay. The man's bloodlust had Master Fentin's words replaying in my head. *Put an end to him once and for all.*

Cutter clearly had no qualms with killing anyone who got in his way, which meant we needed to be extra careful since he had Reevie, Saban, and the last wounded patroller still within reach.

We were truly stuck.

"What do you plan on doing with them?" I asked, motioning to Reevie and the other two. "Trade them for your life?" I didn't want to mention the gold, since Sandstorm wasn't supposed to know anything about the patroller raid.

"I've got a lot more to trade for than that," he said, not mentioning the gold either. He turned and looked at the guards and then pointed to the door. "It's time we were off."

His guards dragged Reevie, Saban, and the patroller toward the door.

"Just do what they tell you," I said to them. "It'll be alright."

Cutter chuckled. "Oh, I very much doubt that."

"Where are you taking them?" I asked, unable to think of what else to say to keep them there.

"We have business at the wall, but don't worry. I haven't forgotten about you. We'll have plenty of time to get reacquainted after I deal with the Blue Capes out front. One way or another, everything changes tonight."

Cutter and his guards pulled the prisoners out of the room and shut the door behind them. Sapphire immediately pulled on the bars. I did the same, but they weren't budging.

Why had Cutter left us alone? Then again, where were we going to
go?

"He has no intention of leaving any of them alive," Sapphire said,
then turned and looked down at me. "What are you doing?"

"Looking for weapons," I said, moving between the dead patrollers.
I came away empty.

"Did anyone else get the feeling that Cutter was almost hoping for a
fight?" Sapphire asked.

"Seems a foolish move on his part," I said. "Cutter's not the type to
risk his own life. It's the only thing he truly values."

"And his gold," Mouse said. The little picker tried to squeeze
through the bars, but they were set too close for his head to fit.

I wondered if Captain Arns was willing to trade the gold back for his
men. If he did, what was Cutter's next move? The more I thought about
it, the more I didn't like where it ended.

Sapphire turned to me. "Even if Cutter manages to threaten the patrollers enough to get them to turn over his gold, how would he do it?
One way or the other, he would have to open the gate, wouldn't he?"

"None of it matters," I said, staring at the dead men behind us, finally coming to a very terrible conclusion. "He's already lost his
bargaining chips. As soon as he killed these men, he put a mark on his
head that he'll never get rid of. When the patrollers find out that their
men have been executed, there's nowhere in Aramoor Cutter will be able
to hide."

Sapphire's head lifted, her face going pale. She finally realized what
Cutter's end goal was. "He's pulling a Noph."

I nodded. "He wants a battle."

"Why would he want that?" Ellie asked, looking as confused as the
other three.

"A distraction," I said, growing more terrified by the moment. "If he manages to persuade the patrollers to give him his gold, what better way to escape than to start a full-scale war?"

"But he set his tunnel on fire," Kiff said.

"Yeah," Linny echoed. "Can't go through there."

"Trust me. He'll have a way."

"Which means . . ." Sapphire gulped, then looked at me. I could see in her eyes she realized what Cutter was going to do. "He's going to kill Reevie."

"He's going to kill all of them." I ran back to the bars and began to kick at the door. "We've got to get out of here." I continued to kick, but they were too strong to move and too thick to bend. I roared in frustration, loud enough to scare the twin brothers, then moved back from the gate. If we didn't get out of here, Reevie and the rest were going to be used to ignite the battle. Tossing their corpses over the wall was all it would take.

I snatched open the door leading down into the tunnel, and the heat nearly took the breath from my lungs. I slammed it shut, but not before I'd filled half our cell with smoke. My eyes began to burn, and we all started to cough.

"What are we going to do?" Mouse asked. He rushed back to the bars again and tried to squeeze through once more. "Someone push me!" he shouted.

Both Linny and Kiff ran to help. One tried pulling on the bars while the other tried pushing on the back of Mouse's head. Mouse squealed until tears were flowing down his cheeks, until finally they had to stop, and he stepped back. He held the sides of his head where the bars had scraped his scalp so badly he had ripped some of his hair away.

"I can't do it," he said, whimpering. "I'm not Mouse anymore."

I tried kicking at the door once more, even attempting to run and throw myself at it, hoping the weight would jar it free, but nothing worked. This time it was Sapphire's turn to scream in frustration, startling me and the others.

"What are we going to do?" she said. "He's going to kill Reevie." There were tears in her eyes as well, but that might have just been the smoke.

"Hey," Kiff said. "Look."

"Yeah, look," Linny said.

"What is it?" Ellie asked as the rest of us headed back to the bars.

The twins pointed at Spats. "He's moving."

Sure enough, the former Hurricane chief twitched. He wasn't dead after all, at least not yet. Spats lifted his head, blood dripping from his mouth. He looked up at us, then slowly over at the door.

"Get us out of here and we can help you," I said, though I doubted there was anything anyone could do to save him.

Spats's breaths were labored and wet. He turned and looked back at the door once more, then slowly spun himself around and began to pull himself across the floor in the opposite direction. What was he doing?

Blood trailed behind him as he tried forcing himself on.

"The keys," Sapphire said. "He's going for the keys. Hurry," she urged him. "You can do it. Get us the keys and we can help you."

Spats slid his way over to the side wall and looked up. I didn't think he had the strength left to get to them, but suddenly, his trembling arms pushed up, and he was on his knees. Each strained gasp of breath sounded like his last. He wasn't going to make it. He looked up once more, and with everything he had, he grabbed hold of the table beside him and pulled himself up just high enough so that his wavering hand could flick the key ring off its hook.

He dropped back to the floor and collapsed on top of the keys. He

didn't move for some time.

"Is he dead?" Mouse asked, all of us pressing our faces to the bars to get a better look.

"I don't know," I said. His chest didn't seem to be moving.

"Spats! Get up!" Sapphire shouted, spurring the rest of us to start shouting as well.

Spats jerked, his head lifting once more. We continued to call his name, encouraging him to keep going, that he was almost there, just a little further. Spats fumbled around for the keys and turned. Slowly, he inched his way back across the room, sliding through a trail of his own blood.

"You can do it," Sapphire said. "Get us the keys so we can save you."

Spats slid like a snake across the wooden planks, but every minute he took was another closer to Reevie's death. He slowed when he reached our weapons, and he exhaled sharply. It sounded like a death rattle. He didn't have any time left.

"Throw them!" Sapphire shouted.

Spats looked up at the two of us, blood pooling onto the floor. "Cut . . . his . . . feet," he said and half-threw, half-slid the ring of keys the rest of the way to the door. He released a final garbled breath, and his head slumped back to the floor.

I snatched up the keys and tested each one until the lock snapped open. Mouse was the first out. I grabbed my weapons and then went to check on Spats.

"Well?" Sapphire said.

I looked up and shook my head. "He's gone."

What a sad end to such a sad life. If only he'd stayed away.

"We've got to go." I sheathed one of my blades to keep one free hand, and then we raced across the room and threw open the door. I barely took the time to look and see if there was anyone outside before rushing into the dimly lit corridor beyond. Time was something we didn't have. Cutter could already be on the wall making his deal.

"This way," I said, and we sprinted down the hallway. Memories of better times flooded my mind as we passed between rooms. The carved images on each door reminded me of the beauty the place had once held. Now, it was only a shell of its former self.

Three years under Cutter and Avalanche's control, and the Temple's face had been heavily marred. There were holes in the walls, stinking piles of rubbish along the floors, and cracked doors—some missing altogether. It was a sad sight to see, and the last thing I needed to be focused on, so I turned my attention back to the task ahead.

Please, let Reevie still be alive.

The halls were empty, everyone no doubt at the wall. We reached the archway leading out and ran into a pair of beaters on their way in. I grabbed the first and jerked him inside. The second barely had time to squeal when I yanked him in as well and clobbered him over the head with butt of my sword until he went limp.

I turned to find Sapphire's arm wrapped around the first boy's neck. His legs eventually quit jerking, and his eyes rolled up in his head. I grabbed her to keep her from strangling him to death, and we left their bodies lying in the corner. I stopped at the archway to see if anyone else was coming and then lifted my hood. We still had to cross the front gardens if we wanted to get to the wall.

"Come on." I led them out of the main building and down the steps to the path leading through the gardens to the Temple's gate. Torchlight from the buildings behind us guided our steps until we were farther in, where the torches were replaced by the occasional lamp along the pathway. The shrubs and flowers and trees looked unkempt and overgrown.

"Look what they've done to this place," Sapphire whispered angrily beside me.

I shot a quick glance off to the right, down one of the paths leading over to Egla's fountain. It seemed the naked faerie was still standing, looking out over her sad wilderness of a garden. We passed a few other Avalanche members, but no one bothered stopping us or even gave us a second look. Most didn't even make eye contact, keeping their heads lowered as they scurried to wherever it was they were going.

There was a voice coming from the wall ahead. I couldn't tell whose it was or what they were saying, but I had to assume it was Cutter calling down to Captain Arns, no doubt still making his trade. We broke through the last of the overgrown shrubs and slowed when we caught our first glimpse of the gate ahead.

Moonlight spilled across everything. Dozens of torches lined the top of the wall where we had built platforms to stand on to defend against anyone coming to invade. The irony wasn't lost on me. Straight ahead, the double doors of the gate were braced with a very large beam, and on either side was a guard tower filled with beaters.

The open yard between the gardens and the gate were filled with fighters, and so was the top of the scaffolding just behind the wall, all armed, all looking ready for battle. Just how many kids did Cutter have?

"How do we get it open?" Mouse asked, peeking out from between me and Sapphire as he stared at the enormous chunk of wood bracing the back of the gate.

"I'm not sure opening it is the best option," I said. "Once those doors part, there'll be no stopping what comes next." I could see Cutter's hat at the top of the scaffolding on the right, his head looking over the wall. His guards were beside him, gripping the legs of three individuals who had been lifted up in order to stand on the wall itself.

"Which one's Reevie?" Linny asked.

"Yeah, which one?" Kiff echoed.

The blue cape was easy enough to spot, but from the back, at this distance, and at night, it was anyone's guess as to which was Saban and which was Reevie.

"I can find out," Mouse said, and before either me or Sapphire could grab him, he shot out between us and disappeared into the Avalanche ranks.

"Idiot," Sapphire said.

"Let him go." I pointed over to the right side of the wall. "Let's see if we can get closer. We need to hear what they're saying." The Avalanche ranks thinned the farther from the gate we got, but we were still some distance away from the steps leading up to the guard tower where Cutter had Reevie and the others.

I wasn't sure what to do. If we tried pushing through, we'd attract attention. Last thing I wanted was to risk Cutter seeing us and killing the prisoners. I hoped Mouse was smart enough not to let that happen, as most of the time he didn't stop to think, he simply responded.

"What now?" Sapphire asked as we came to a huddle at the side. "We need to get closer to those steps."

I took a moment to sheathe my sword, pulling the cloak's hood up to help hide them. "Let's spread out. We might be able to work our way closer if we aren't bunched together." I pointed to the wooden tower and steps beside it leading up the platform at the top of the scaffold. "That's our goal. But whatever you do, don't attract attention."

The others nodded and broke off, spreading out along the back of the ranks as we slowly started in. This was not how I had planned on this going. I only hoped we weren't too late.

AVALANCHE

Chapter 50

HE REAR AVALANCHE FIGHTERS were packed tight but not as crammed together as those up near the gate. I kept as close to the scaffolding as possible as I slid slowly through the crowd, trying to hunch down to keep from standing out. I was grateful it was dark. The moon was out, but its pale light only did so much. Torches were spread through the gathered army, but even their light cast shadows and tricked the eyes as the flames danced in the evening breeze.

Someone above me called down to those outside. I had a difficult time catching what was said, but I thought I heard *gold*, *prisoners*, and *basket*. What did a basket have to do with any of this? Maybe he planned to lower a basket over the wall to collect the gold? I needed to hurry. If Arns agreed to this, Cutter wasn't going to need Reevie any longer and would probably use the prisoners to spark the fighting.

I moved faster, pushing my way through the gathering as I worked to get as close to the steps as I could before the kids were simply pressed too tightly together for me to continue. There was no way I was getting any closer to the stairs, and apart from scaling the side of the scaffolding, I had no way of getting up to the top.

"Hey, quit pushing," someone on the steps above me said.

I looked up. Even from where I was at the bottom, I could just make out Mouse's disheveled head working its way through the throng of beaters on the stairs above as he headed for the upper platform. Crazy picker was going to get himself and everyone else killed for sure. Still, perhaps he could get close enough to save Reevie.

I, on the other hand, was trapped. I couldn't move forward without causing a scene, and if I moved any closer, I was going to lose sight of Reevie. From here, I could see that he was the one on the left end, closest to Cutter and the guard tower. Saban was beside him, and the patroller on the right.

The three were holding on to each other to keep from falling. The top of the wall wasn't all that thick, and walking around on it would have been precarious during the day, let alone in the middle of the night while fearing for your life. One wrong move and they could slip over the side. At twenty feet, it might not be high enough to kill them if they did, unless they landed wrong, but it would certainly leave them crippled. I wished I could hear more of what was being said, or knew what had been said already. I turned and poked the boy next to me.

"I just got here, is he telling those patrollers where to go throw themselves?"

The boy nodded. "Yeah. Gonna kill those three up there and toss them over if they don't give us what they took and leave us alone."

"What'd they take?" I asked.

The boy shrugged. "Beats me, but if they know what's good for 'em, they'll give it back."

"What's the basket for?" I asked.

The boy looked at me like I was an imbecile or something. "To get what they took, of course. We ain't lettin' 'em in here, that's for sure."

I looked up at the top of the scaffolding platform in front of us, trying to decide what to do. Someone pushed up behind me, and I turned to find Ellie.

"Seen anyone else?" I asked.

She pointed straight ahead, and I scanned the crowd until I caught what I thought was Sapphire's blonde hair about halfway between me and the stairs leading up the scaffolding. One of the two heads beside her turned far enough for me to see it was one of the twins.

I heard a raised voice coming from the other side of the wall. Probably Captain Arns. I hoped Arns hadn't brought the gold with him. If Cutter was going to kill the prisoners anyway, I didn't want him leaving with his pockets lined. Staring over those in front of me, I couldn't tell if there was a basket there or not.

"Have they lowered the basket yet?" I asked the boy beside me.

"Don't know. I think, maybe. Can't tell from here."

I kept my eyes glued to Cutter's hat, which was the most of him I could see from this vantage. I watched his movements for any sign of lowering or raising a basket, then realized that was stupid. He wouldn't do it himself, so I switched to those standing on either side of him, including the members of his Guard, though they seemed to have their hands full making sure the prisoners didn't tumble over the side.

Something was happening up there, but I couldn't see what. Suddenly Cutter's hat turned, and he walked over to the edge of the platform to look down at us. He raised a basket over his head and shouted. "We won!"

I couldn't believe it. Arns had turned the gold over after all. Was he trying to buy us more time? Or perhaps he thought we'd been captured or killed.

"The Blue Cape cowards have bowed before us," Cutter shouted, "and given back what they took!"

The kids around me cheered, though they had no idea what they were cheering for. This wasn't looking good. I scanned the distance between me and the stairs and shook my head. Sapphire and the twins were already pushing their way forward, but they weren't going to make it either. I looked over at the scaffolding. It was my best option.

"They attacked our compound in the north and took our people hostage," Cutter continued to shout down to his tribe. "Stuck them in the workhouses, and if that wasn't enough, they rode, bold as brass, straight into the Maze and killed some more. Are we going to stand for this?"

"No!" the kids shouted all around me, raising their weapons. I had to duck to keep from getting hit by someone's homemade short spear behind me.

"So I ask you, what should we do with these prisoners? I say we send their bodies over the wall!"

"Kill them!" the crowd shouted.

Our time was up. I turned and punched a boy on my right in the side of his head, sending him plowing into two more, then beat my way through the bloodthirsty mob, knocking kids left and right until I reached the edge of the scaffolding's braces.

Cutter waved his arms once more. "I say we send their patroller down to them first!"

I started up the side of the scaffolding's frame, board by board. Halfway up, I heard someone up top cry out, and then everyone below me shouted. The fire in my chest began to rage once more. As angry as I

was, I couldn't even begin to imagine what Arns was feeling. I shouldn't have waited so long. *Hold on, Reevie, I'm coming.*

"The Blue Capes have teamed up with Sandstorm!" Cutter shouted down. "And we have their chief!"

"Kill him! Kill him!" the mob cried out.

"No!" Sapphire screamed as she tore up the stairs, stabbing and bludgeoning anyone who tried to stop her, throwing their bodies off the side as she and the twins fought their way up.

The crowds stopped their shouting momentarily, unsure what was happening.

Cutter's head appeared over the edge as he looked down to see who was screaming. I leaped up another rung, and his eyes caught mine.

He gulped. "It can't be. Kill them!" he shouted to everyone below, just before he disappeared back over the top of the platform.

I grabbed and kicked and pulled my way up the side of the scaffold until I reached the top rail, then leaped to the side as a sword sank into the rail where my hands had been. My magic heated, but I forced it back down and grabbed the arm of the guard who'd tried to decapitate me and pulled him over the side.

Saban and Reevie were the last on the wall, about twenty feet down from where I'd come up. Cutter's guards hadn't killed them yet, but they were trying to. With one of their group already thrown over, Reevie and Saban had realized they had nothing left to lose, so they fought with everything they had to keep from joining the patroller.

I leaped over the rail and onto the platform, but before I could get to them, a wave of beaters rushed up the stairs between us, and I drew my swords.

"Reevie, I'm coming!" I tore into the pack, cutting through them as fast as I could, trying my best not to kill the kids as I did. I kicked several back down on top the others to give myself enough time to get by, then cut the legs out from under the guard trying to kill Saban on my way to Reevie.

I shouted at the guard to stop, but he was too quick, and I watched as he lifted Reevie over his head and threw him over the side.

I screamed.

Something inside me tore free. Magic flooded through me unchecked, and I plunged my sword into the guard's chest before he even had a chance to turn around. I watched as he fell over the side, dead.

I tried to breathe, but nothing would come. I felt completely numb. Visions swept over me, and I rolled away from the wall as half a dozen more beaters lunged for me. I cut them down two at a time before I managed to catch my first breath and force my magic back down. The dead kids behind me should have ripped my insides apart, but they had indirectly helped kill Reevie, and I felt nothing for them at all.

The next wave poured out behind them, but they were met by Sapphire, Ellie, Kiff, and Linny as the small group swept through the beaters from behind, finally managing to reach the platform.

Leaving them to take up the fight, I ran to the wall and looked down, bracing myself for what I knew I would find—Reevie's broken, limp body.

He wasn't there.

Where was he? I scanned the crowd of patrollers pounding on the gates to the left with their shields up. There were ladders on the way behind them. Below me, just beside the wall, was a group from Sandstorm, including Tubby.

My heart skipped a beat when I looked closer. *Reevie?*

"I caught him!" Tubby shouted proudly. Farther down, I saw the body of the patroller lying to the side. He hadn't been so lucky.

My mind was racing nearly as fast as my heart, but I needed to think.

We'd saved as many of the prisoners as possible, but we still had to stop this war, and if we didn't get those gates open, the Avalanche fighters were going to kill those of us trapped on the inside. Tubby. I needed him.

I looked back over the side, spotting Collen. Bull was over at the gate with Captain Arns and Sergeant Lowell, leading the main bulk of Sandstorm's fighters.

"Tubby! I need you up here!" I looked at Collen. "Get him a ladder."

Saban was now back down on the platform with Kiff and Linny, who had disposed of the guard I'd cut the legs out from under earlier.

"Where's Reevie?" Sapphire shouted, her swords hacking away at the mob of Avalanche fighters trying to reach the top.

"Safe! Tubby caught him."

She breathed a sigh of relief and kept fighting.

"Where's Cutter?" I asked. I looked down the platform, but there was no one there.

"I don't know!" Sapphire said. "Mouse?"

I'd forgotten all about the little picker. I scanned the scaffolding and even over the side at those trying to come up, but I saw no sign of him. I yanked off Bull's cape. I didn't need to hide now.

Kids started screaming that Death's Shadow had come for them. Those who had moments ago been fighting to reach the top of the platform fled back down the stairs.

That name, Death's Shadow, had me turning to look at the bodies behind me, kids I had just had a hand in killing. My gut twisted. For the first time, I hated the magic inside me. I couldn't let it take control again.

Someone roared behind me, and I turned to see Tubby's hands gripping the top of the wall. He pulled himself up and over, still wearing his Flesh Eater mask.

"Tubby, we need to get the gate open. Can you lift the bracer?" Before I could say anything more, the giant boy ran down the wall past the tower and grabbed the pulley rope attached to the bracer. When we lived at the Temple, it had taken Toots's entire team to lift the heavy beam, but one leap over the side from Tubby, and the bracer swung upward.

Kids below screamed in fear and ran when they saw Flesh Eater flying over them. With a strong heave of his shoulder, Tubby forced one of the doors open, and I heard Captain Arns and Bull both shout out a charge.

I ran back to the stairs, but by the time I got there, they were nearly empty, so I darted down behind Sapphire and the others. I followed them all the way to the bottom, mentally preparing myself for a full-scale battle with Avalanche.

It took me a second once I reached the bottom to realize that no one was there. The kids were fleeing back toward the compound now that the gates had been opened and their fearless leader had vanished. Without Cutter's overpowering presence, it seemed most of the kids had no desire to fight.

"We've got to find Cutter!" I said to Sapphire.

"Why?" Ellie asked. "We were supposed to get him to stop the war, but it looks like we might not have to."

"Yeah," Kiff added, pointing back at all the retreating kids. "Looks like Avalanche doesn't want to fight any more than we do."

"No," Sapphire said. "If Cutter manages to get away, we'll be looking over our shoulders the rest of our lives, wondering if, or when, he might be waiting in a dark corner with a knife in his hand."

"And just because they are retreating now," I said, "doesn't mean they won't regroup later."

I grabbed Ellie, Kiff, and Linny and pulled them to the side. "You three look for Mouse. Check each body if you have to."

I raced toward the main building, following the flow of white armbands as kids fled through the garden walkways, trying to escape the oncoming patrollers. I hoped the few who hadn't fled came to their senses quickly. Better to surrender than to fight and die.

Sapphire kept pace beside me, knocking kids aside, sending them flying into the mud, into the bushes, into each other. I don't think she had yet gotten over the fear of thinking Reevie was dead, her mind set on Cutter.

I needed to get my hands on him. The snake was going to answer for everything he had done. I knew better than to look for him anywhere near the fighting. He was too smart and too skilled a manipulator to be out here risking his own life. Knowing him, he would have had a way out.

If only I knew what it was.

"Where are we going?" Sapphire asked, sending two Avalanche kids face-first into a giant shrub.

"Back to the infirmary. Cutter had to have a plan for getting out of here, and that's the only way I know besides the front gate."

She nodded, and we raced up the stairs of the main building. We fought our way down the corridor toward the infirmary. Kids were packed into the hall like fish in a barrel, if the fish were all trying to swim in the same direction. Most didn't really know we were there. Those close enough to see my eyes or my black leathers squealed and either tried running faster to get ahead of us or turned to face the onslaught of those coming behind.

We reached the infirmary and found several clusters of kids hiding around the shelves and under the table. One look at us, and they ran out the door.

"He's got to be here," I said, hopping over Spats to check the cell with the dead patrollers. There was still smoke coming through the door. I reached for the handle, and my visions stopped me, but not before it treated me to feeling the skin melting from my palm. I grimaced, trying to erase the memory of the pain, and grabbed one of the patrollers' capes. I wadded the material up and used it to turn the handle, the smell of scorched wool filling my nostrils. The door opened, and a thick cloud of smoke billowed out and enveloped us.

I shut the door immediately and began coughing. "There's no way he got through there."

"Then where did he go?"

"You lived here longer than me," I said. "Do you know of some other way out?"

"No."

We left the cell and headed back out into the main room to catch our breath. The door opened, and several more kids with white armbands ran in. They got one look at us and ran back out.

Sapphire looked down at Spats's bloody body and shook her head. "After all these years, he shows up thinking he's going to get his tribe back and ends up like this. Part of me actually feels sorry for him." She turned with a quizzical look on her face. "How did you make Spats disappear all those years ago?"

We both looked at each other and had the same realization. "I'm so stupid," I said. "It can't be that simple." We ran out of the infirmary, pushing our way through the crowd toward the back of the main building. From there, we headed out onto the covered walkways that ran from the main building to several smaller ones behind, mostly used for sleeping quarters.

We hopped off the porch and sped across the open patch of ground behind it where I used to spend my days teaching the Hurricane Guard.

I remembered the time I'd brought Room Eleven here after our battle inside the Warrens, and how Sapphire had fought Stumpy in that very spot. So many memories were tied to this place, but this was not the way I had wanted to revisit them.

"Where do you think he would have it?" she asked.

"As far from the fighting as possible." I took her hand, since the only light we had in this half of the compound was what moonlight filtered through the clouds and trees. I stopped just behind the last building and scanned the wall ahead. "There," I said, and we continued forward, all the way back to where Muriel used to keep her pigeon coops.

The ladder was propped against the back wall, and we climbed to the top. It was a bit heavy to try dragging over the wall ourselves, so I decided to knock it back down to keep any more of the kids from getting out. I doubted anyone would see it hidden behind the bushes at night. We both rolled over and hung down from the top of the wall as far as we could and then dropped and rolled.

"Which way?" she whispered, drawing her swords once again. I could see there was only one thing on her mind.

I scanned the ground until I found a trail of trampled grass and torn underbrush and pointed left, which led northeast and away from the secret tunnel. It was also the route that would take him the farthest from everything. We followed his trail, which seemed to stumble all about the place and even circle around once or twice. Either Cutter was constructing some sort of elaborate ruse to mask his trail or he wasn't carrying a lantern and had no idea where he was.

We were nearing the street behind the compound when the first sound of something ahead caught our attention.

Voices.

We picked up our pace. Who was Cutter talking to? Did he have someone waiting with a ride out of here?

A high-pitched cry shot through the trees, and Sapphire grabbed my arm. We both recognized the voice.

Mouse!

AVALANCHE

Chapter 51

E RACED AHEAD, more concerned with speed than silence now as we listened for the voices again. We were just reaching the outer edge of the trees when I caught movement ahead. I drew one of my blades and kept going.

"What did you think?" I heard Cutter say. "A little rat like you was going to catch me off guard? Going to take down the chief of Avalanche?"

Up ahead, I saw Cutter's wide-brimmed hat as it headed toward the outer edge of the tree line. There were about half a dozen of his Guard waiting, along with several horses. One of the larger boys had Mouse in his arms.

"Hold him steady," Cutter said, starting for Mouse with his dagger drawn.

"Cutter!" Sapphire shouted, and we tore out of the brush and straight for the Avalanche chief.

Cutter flinched, not expecting the two of us to come flying out of the woods. I grabbed my belt knife and threw it at the boy holding Mouse, the dagger lodging in the guard's shoulder. The boy screamed and stumbled back, releasing Mouse. Mouse turned to run, but Cutter snatched him and spun him around, his knife to Mouse's throat, using him as a shield. "Don't come any closer!"

I grabbed Sapphire's arm and pulled her to a stop a few feet away from where Cutter stood just inside the edge of the trees.

"You've got nowhere to run, Cutter," I said. "Just turn him over."

"And what, you'll let me go?" He laughed. "Do you think me a fool? No, I think I'll keep your young friend here nice and close. Maybe once I leave, I'll let him go."

I knew that wasn't going to happen.

Cutter glanced behind him and back to where his guards were holding the horses. He was still about fifteen feet from them. "How'd you know I'd be here?" he said, slowly scooting backward.

"Those dead patrollers," I said. "I knew you'd run. The only thing keeping you here was your gold."

"Which begs me to ask: How did you escape the cell?"

"Like you said, when you get rid of someone, make sure they can't come back."

Cutter cocked his head quizzically, clearly not understanding.

"Spats was still alive."

Cutter sneered. "Pathetic weasel's harder to get rid of than the pox." He continued to move Mouse back toward the horses.

Sapphire and I moved with him.

"I said stay back."

This wasn't working. If he got to the horses—

I reached out with my bond. *I need your help.* I looked at Cutter's guards. "You know he's just going to leave you as soon as he gets the chance, or worse, kill you."

"Don't listen to him," Cutter said. "He's just trying to keep us from leaving."

"Leaving is exactly what I suggest you do," I said. "Get as far away from Cutter as you can. Do you think he's going to share his gold with you?" I laughed. "He just betrayed your entire tribe. How far do you think you'll get before he does the same to you?"

The guards looked at me, then at Cutter, the large bag of gold conveniently gripped between the fingers of his free hand.

"Shut your mouth," Cutter said, "or I'll kill him right here." He pressed the blade to Mouse's throat even tighter and Mouse squealed.

"You kill him," Sapphire said, "and there won't be enough of you left for them to identify after I get my hands on you."

I looked at the guards once more. "If I were you, I'd run for it. You're outside the walls. The patrollers don't know you're here, at least not yet. But when they track Cutter down and find you, you'll never see the light of day again."

The older boys looked at each other, then back at Cutter. They were considering it.

Cutter could see it as well. "Don't even think about it!"

"He's right," one of the boys said. "They're after you, not us." The guard looked at the others and nodded, and they started for their mounts.

"No! Wait! You can't leave me. I've got the gold."

The boys stopped. A couple of them looked at each other and then back at Cutter, and I could see they were thinking the same thing—if they killed Cutter, they could simply take the gold for themselves. But if they tried that, Mouse was going to get caught in the middle.

I took a step forward, raising my swords. "You try it, and you'll answer to me." I still wasn't sure if I needed Cutter to get Avalanche to stand down, but better to have him than not.

The guards backed away, deciding that escaping was their only good option. Leaving Cutter to fend for himself, they continued for their mounts but stopped at the sound of hooves galloping up the road.

Shade charged out of the darkness, screaming in challenge. He reared up and released another thundering cry that had all the other horses whinnying in response. The warhorse wheeled and bolted up the road, and to my surprise, the other horses followed swiftly, echoing his call. Just as quickly as he had appeared, Shade and his small herd vanished into the night.

The guards shouted and chased after them, leaving Cutter standing there by himself. His horse was the only one that hadn't run off, and only because it was tied to a tree. The horse shrieked its outrage at being left behind, dancing in place, trying to free its head.

"Fools, the lot of them!" Cutter spat. He looked at me and Sapphire, then tightened his arm around Mouse, his blade hand shaking nervously.

Mouse tried not to move.

We took another step forward.

"Stay back! I'm warning you. You take another step and I'll slit his throat." Cutter dragged Mouse back toward his horse. If he managed to get to it, I'd have no way of catching him, and knowing Cutter, he'd kill Mouse before he left just to slow us down.

I had to do something, but what? If I charged him, he'd slit Mouse's throat before I could get three steps, but I was out of options. I raised my sword and prepared to run when something detached itself from the trunk behind Cutter and slipped a blade under his chin.

The Avalanche chief froze.

"I've been waiting for this day for two and a half years," Kira purred.

Cutter's eyes bulged when he heard her voice. "Red? What are you doing here? Last I heard, you was selling yourself out to the Warren Underground."

"I just happened to be in the right place at the right time," she said, the same excuse she had given me after finding Dakaran. She seemed to be in a lot of places at the right time. "Word reached me that there was a battle taking place between tribes with the patrollers in the middle of it . . . Well, I just had to come see for myself."

"Doesn't explain you here with a sword to my neck," he spat.

"Oh, I'm getting to that. I decided to come take a look-see for myself, and sure enough, for once, the rumors were true. Well, I said to myself, what would a good-for-nothing coward like Cutter do if he was caught in the middle of a fight?" She pulled her sword closer, and he straightened to keep it from cutting him. "The same thing all cowards do. They run. But where, I asked myself. So I did a quick sweep of the Temple's tree line and happened upon a small group of Avalanche Guard hiding a bunch of horses out here as far from the fighting as possible." She shook her head. "I said to myself, that couldn't possibly be his plan, now could it? To just up and leave his entire tribe to fend for themselves? He isn't that heartless, is he?" She laughed. "Well, of course you are. So, I stole my way through the trees and simply bided my time till you arrived."

"I've got gold," Cutter said, holding up the bag and jingling it for her to hear. "I'll give you half if you hold them off long enough for me to get away."

Kira looked over at me and Sapphire and hesitated. For a split moment, I thought she was actually considering it, but then I saw her eyes darken.

I quickly raised my hands. "Kira, wait! We need him alive. We might need to use him to force Avalanche to surrender."

She looked at Cutter. "Oh dear, my hand is feeling a little shaky." She moved it slightly, and Cutter winced and stiffened even further, blood trickling down his neck. "Oops. You see? When I get all excited, sometimes I can't control myself. If I were you, I'd let the little one go before my blade slips any further."

I held my breath, waiting to see what Cutter would do. His arms suddenly dropped, and Mouse ran for me and Sapphire. Sapphire shoved him behind us.

"Fine, you've got me. Now—" Cutter's eyes widened, and his mouth opened in a gasp, but no words came out, not even a scream. He wore the same look of shock and panic I'd seen in Spats's eyes. I looked down. The tip of Kira's sword was sticking through the front of his chest.

"Kira! I told you we need him!"

Kira didn't even acknowledge me as she leaned over to whisper in Cutter's ear. "This is for my tribe." She yanked the blade out and watched as Cutter's legs gave way, and he dropped onto the dirt.

It was too late. I hoped Captain Arns and Bull were able to talk Avalanche down, because we'd just lost our best opportunity.

Sapphire didn't hesitate and headed straight for Cutter. She dropped down on her knees beside him and looked him in the eyes.

"I promised you my face would be the last thing you'd see in this life."

Cutter spat blood, then sneered up at her as he tried to close his eyes, but Sapphire grabbed them and held them open herself. I'd never seen this side of her before. I knew she'd hardened over the years, but this was something I would have expected out of Red.

Red, for her part, stood beside the tree and watched. The look on her face said she was just as surprised as I was.

It didn't take long before Cutter was still, his eyes as lifeless as all those patrollers he'd had murdered in his cell. Sapphire grabbed the bag of gold and stood.

"What are you going to do with that?" Kira asked, staring at the large sack.

"We are going to speak with Captain Arns about divvying it out between Sandstorm and the patrollers," I said, walking over with Mouse in tow. "Sandstorm has a lot of new mouths to feed, and Cutter just murdered a number of their men. They have families that should be seen to."

"Too bad," Kira said. "I could have done a lot with that."

Sapphire reached into the bag and pulled out a couple of pieces, which she tossed to Kira.

"Mighty kind," Kira said. She smiled and tucked them into her pocket.

"Where's Po?" I asked, sheathing my sword.

"I left him in the woods around front to keep out of the way."

Mouse tugged on the sleeve of my coat. "I was brave, wasn't I, Protector?"

"You was stupid," Kira said.

Sapphire walked over and hugged the little picker. "Yes, Mouse, you were brave." She then slapped him softly on the back of the head. "Next time, listen when we tell you something and don't run off. You scared me near to death." She put an arm around his shoulders and held him close as we all started for the road.

We'd barely made it onto the cobbles when we heard a horse come galloping up behind us. I turned and looked up.

"Thank you, my friend," I said to the giant stallion. Shade nickered, and I sensed that he was pleased with himself. "Couldn't have done that without you," I agreed.

"Where'd you get a horse like that?" Kira said, gawking at the monstrous animal.

"A gift from the king."

She gaped even further.

"It's Shade!" Mouse said. He looked up at Sapphire. "I named him, you know."

She rolled her eyes. "We all know. You've told us half a dozen times at least."

"We have to get back inside," I said. "They could still be fighting, and we need to find a way to force Avalanche to back down, since someone just killed our best opportunity to make that happen," I added with a sharp look at Kira.

She shrugged. "He deserved what he got."

"Perhaps, but you could have waited until after we saw whether we still needed him."

"Who are you kidding? Once he was in patroller custody, there's no way I could have gotten to him."

"I don't have time to argue," I said and climbed up into the saddle. I looked down at the three of them. "I can't carry all of you."

"I'm not sitting on either of their laps," Kira said. "I still have *my* dignity. I'll find Po and we'll be off."

I leaned over and helped Sapphire and Mouse up onto Shade, then looked at Kira. "Keep out of trouble."

She smiled up at me, winked, and then vanished back into the trees.

"Hold on," I said to the others, and Shade took off down the road.

We hit Circle Drive at as close to a gallop as I felt safe to push Shade. From there we turned onto the Temple's drive, racing up the brick path for the wall ahead. Suddenly I felt my magic wither inside me, which meant Po must be nearby. Kira said she had left him in the woods, but

I didn't have time to look.

I kept us heading straight for the gate. I couldn't tell if there was a battle still going inside or not. The front yard between the gate and the gardens looked empty of fighting, but there were bodies. Thankfully, there were nowhere near as many as there would have been in a full-on assault. Most of those on the ground appeared to be moving.

"Reevie! Saban!" I shouted, hopping off Shade. Some Blue Capes standing guard out front turned when they saw us coming. The torches along the wall were enough to light the front of the entrance and keep us from tripping over our own feet.

"The physickers are tending to the wounded," one of the men said as we approached the front.

"It's over?" Sapphire asked.

He nodded. "We've got them cornered inside. They're hiding in the main building."

"Captain Arns hasn't gone in, has he?" I asked.

"Not since last we heard."

I handed Shade's reins to Mouse. "Keep him here."

The little picker nodded, and Sapphire and I ran inside. I spotted Reevie and Saban on our left, and we made our way over. There were a couple of patrollers around them holding lanterns to give them enough light to work from.

"How are you?" I asked.

"Alive, thanks to you two," Saban said, looking up from where he was bandaging one of the Avalanche kids.

"Busy," Reevie added, "and flaming thankful for whoever taught Tubby how to play catch." He looked up at me and Sapphire. "Thank you for coming after us." He glanced back toward the gate. "Where's Cutter? Did you find him?"

"We did," Sapphire said.

I frowned. "Let's just say he won't be hurting anyone else ever again."

"Good." Reevie motioned with his head back toward the main building. "You might want to try giving the patrollers a hand. Not sure what it's going to take to smoke those kids out of there. I think Gustory is with them now, but I'm not sure even he can get them to come out."

"Do either of you need anything?" I asked.

"Your Captain Arns sent some men to the infirmary," Saban said, "to let my wife and son know that I'm safe and to have them come with supplies to treat the wounded."

It sounded like they had everything in hand, so Sapphire and I left the two physickers to their work and headed for the gardens. We slowed when we found Captain Arns and the rest of the patrollers spread out around the building, sticking mostly to the left side. I spotted Sergeant Lowell with a group of men over by the dining hall. Bull and Sandstorm appeared to be guarding the right side of the complex. Tubby waited quietly just behind Bull, while Captain Arns looked to be keeping his distance, passing furtive glances up over his shoulder at the giant boy.

Sapphire and I joined them near the front as they stared at the door leading into the main building, and at Gustory, who was standing at the bottom of the stairs.

"What's happening?" I asked.

"Cornered some rats," Arns said, then looked at me. "Sorry, poor choice of words." He looked back at the building. Faces peered out from the door and windows. "I think the fighting's over, what little there was, but I'm not sure what it's going to take to convince them of that and bring them out. The bard there seems to think he might be able to talk them out, but right now, it doesn't seem to be working."

Gustory turned and walked back to us. "He's right. It's just not having an effect. Those kids are simply too afraid. Their fear is overwhelming anything I'm capable of saying to them."

"What about Reina?" Sapphire said.

"Reina?" Bull looked confused.

"Who's Reina?" Arns asked.

"She's the spokesperson for the new kids you dropped off on our doorstep," she said, a not-so-subtle accusation in her tone. "The others looked up to her," she said, "so she might be able to talk these here into surrendering peacefully."

Arns looked at me, then back at the building full of angry and frightened children. "Worth a try. Is she here with you?"

Sapphire shook her head. "I'll have to send someone back to get her."

"We also need to send someone over to Master Fentin and Mistress Orilla's," I said, "and let them know that all is well and not to worry."

Sapphire nodded. "I'll have Gittrick and his family bring the coaches for our people."

"Good idea," Bull said. "Not sure how many of them can walk back."

Since it looked like I would be of little use getting the kids to come out, I went to help Reevie and Saban however I could.

It took an hour or two, but once Reina arrived, she and Gustory were finally able to persuade the Avalanche kids out of their compound long enough to talk them into surrendering. They told them of Cutter's betrayal, and how their chief had planned on using their deaths to escape, along with all of their gold. Needless to say, by the time Gustory finished, Cutter should have been very glad he was already dead, because if they had ever gotten their hands on him, it would have been a much more painful way to go.

While Reina and Gustory worked their magic, Gittrick and his sons carried one load after another back to the manor house. Word reached the orphanage of our success. When our messenger returned, she said that all the kids had been down in the main rooms with their belongings, ready to leave at the first sign of trouble. They were very appreciative of us letting them know.

We spent the rest of the night treating those caught in the battle on both sides, and by the time we were done, sleep was the only thing on our minds as we loaded the last of our members on the final coach, heading back to Sandstorm.

Captain Arns and Sergeant Lowell remained with the Avalanche street kids, setting up rotations to keep watch over them until it was decided about what to do with them. Arns agreed to split Cutter's gold evenly, allowing Sandstorm to take what they needed to help with the new recruits while the patrollers used a good portion of what was left to aid the families of the fallen.

It was strange to think that the time of the street tribes was coming to an end, and it had only been accomplished by the union of two very unlikely bedfellows: street rats and patrollers.

Sandstorm was now free to live their lives unencumbered by the fact that at any moment, they could come under attack. Speaking of things to worry about, I hadn't yet spoken with the chiefs concerning my meeting with the queen. Considering how the night had gone, that could be saved until after we had managed at least one good night's rest.

I wasn't all that worried. One meeting with the king and queen, and I had no doubt an agreeable solution could be found. It was in the interest of all parties concerned, and both the queen and Sapphire—though strong willed—were level headed. I wouldn't be all that surprised if they hit it off. I could see a lot of each in the other.

Crawling into my bed after seeing to our wounded, I stared up at

the ceiling and took a few minutes to simply breathe, allowing myself to shed all the worry and stress I'd been holding on to for the last several weeks.

It felt as though my life was finally coming into focus, my purpose defined. For the first time, I felt I was able to let go of my past and reach out for what was to come—a simpler life.

AVALANCHE

Chapter 52

IT TOOK SEVERAL DAYS, but with the help of the patrollers, we were able to remove the remaining Avalanche kids from the Temple. The problem was what to do with them. Sapphire and the other chiefs were against taking any but the very youngest back to Sandstorm. They simply didn't have enough room for that many kids.

In the end, as much as I would have liked to offer the rest of Avalanche the same choice given those living at the old garrison, it simply wasn't possible.

"I don't like sending so many of them to the workhouses," I said. I had dropped by Sandstorm for a visit after a hectic week at the palace preparing for Overcaptain Tolin's upcoming ceremony. I was enjoying a rare quiet evening in front of the fire in Sapphire's study with the chiefs.

"Couldn't be helped," Sapphire said. "You saw the same thing I did.

If the patrollers hadn't been there, those kids would have been unmanageable. We can't have people like that living here at Sandstorm. We have a difficult enough time keeping up with those who actually want to be here."

"Most of them lived too long under Cutter," Bull said. "They've adopted his way of thinking."

Reevie nodded. "We can't have bullies like that living here. We have too many children under our protection that could wind up hurt. Half the kids we are taking in are coming with previous scars. No telling what they endured to survive in a place like that."

I couldn't argue. Those kids had eagerly called for the death of Reevie, Saban, and the patroller. It was sad what they had been turned into, but the chiefs were correct—they had the safety of their own to think about first.

"How's Mouse doing?" I asked. I hadn't seen much of the picker since our ordeal at the Temple. My new duties, and getting my men situated at the palace, had kept me too busy to visit Sandstorm much over the last month.

"He's alive, thanks to Kira," Sapphire said, which couldn't have been easy for her to admit.

"I'd say he's nearly back to his old self," Reevie added.

Bull chuckled. "If by *old self* you mean pestering everyone to no end, then yes, he'll be fine. Tubby, Petal, and Squeaks were certainly glad to have him back. The small group of misfits wouldn't have been the same without their leader."

"And you've recovered from their visit?" I didn't need to specify whose visit I was referring to. The royal family showing up at your house for dinner was not an evening you forget. The visit had been my first official outing in my new position. I'd assigned a small contingent of my men to accompany us, mainly Room Eleven, since they had some prior acquaintance with the tribe. "I'm sure Solvino and his staff were beside themselves."

"They were out of sorts the entire week leading up to the meal," Sapphire said with a slight grin.

"That's a nice way to put it," Reevie added. "I've never seen Solvino so hysterical. He was serving lunch for breakfast, breakfast for dinner, and forgetting some meals entirely the whole week. Man didn't know which way was up or down."

"And yet, he still managed to pull it off," Bull said.

"It was one of his best meals I've had here," I added. "And that's saying a lot. I know both of Their Majesties enjoyed it. Even Dakaran, though he wouldn't admit it." Dakaran had been more interested in showing his mother and father the infirmary, where Reevie had managed to snatch him back from the icy fingers of the underworld.

The meal had been very well received, and the discussions lively but productive. In the end, as I had expected, an agreement was reached for Sandstorm Manor to take on the official title of an Aramoor orphan house, and as long as Sandstorm could provide the crown with adequate quarterly reports on the orphanage's status, the queen promised no further outside interference.

"Will it be that much more work preparing reports for Her Majesty?" I asked, mainly addressing Reevie, since he was the one who kept up with the books for most everything.

Reevie shook his head. "It will just be a matter of making a copy. I was expecting her to request more records than she did."

I leaned back in my seat and smiled. "I think the queen enjoys having a connection to something outside the palace and the aristocracy. Getting those reports is her way of maintaining that tie."

"She also said that she would be visiting throughout the year," Bull said, seeming happy at the prospect of further contact with the queen.

"But not without prior warning," Sapphire added firmly.

We sat in silence a moment, using the opportunity to work through several more sticky buns and the accompanying pitchers of cream. There weren't many evenings like this, where I got to sit and talk. It was nice to finally be able to carry on a discussion with Reevie without it feeling awkward. The events over the last couple of months had gone a long way toward mending some of our broken fences. There had been no formal conversation where we had expressed wanting to repair our friendship— that wasn't our style—however, the renewed dialogue and time spent together said we were well on our way.

"How are preparations coming up at the palace?" Bull asked. "I'm sure Tolin's big ceremony is causing quite the to-do."

"They are coming slowly," I said, licking glaze from my fingers. "It's been difficult getting my men adapted to the new routines."

It had taken nearly a month, but Overcaptain Tolin had finally brought our lancers home for good, the threat of war having all but dissipated after our battle on the Pyruvian River. Once they were back, the Black Guild—which the king had renamed the High Guard, since, as he stated, we were the high king's guard—was officially transferred from the lancers to the palace.

"I like the new uniforms," Sapphire said, having seen them during the royal family's visit. "Seems to keep with your former Black Guild."

I smiled and nodded. The black uniforms were the same as those of the king's original guard. They were beautiful, sleek, and deadly, much like the falcon on the crest they bore.

"Why aren't you wearing one?" Reevie asked. "The king doesn't mind you wearing your leather coat instead?"

"It was actually as much the king's idea as mine," I said. "In fact, he insisted on it. With all the new black uniforms moving about the palace, he prefers being able to pick me out of a crowd." As much as I loved the way the new uniforms looked on my men, it was a relief to be able to keep wearing my familiar black leathers and double sheaths.

"How are you liking the new accommodations?" Bull asked. "One of these days you're going to have to give us a tour." The others nodded.

"They're very comfortable," I said. I hadn't told them about the grand rooms Dakaran had chosen for me. "My men were thrilled with their new quarters, and even those with families in town usually stay a night or two a week, depending on duty rotations."

"Was there any difficulty with the transition?" Sapphire asked. "How are the old guards handling working under you? I'm guessing there've been some . . . adjustments." Being the head of a large street tribe turned orphan house, she knew all too well the kind of adjustments it took to get newcomers settled.

"I won't lie, it has taken some time for them to be willing to accept my command. There might have been a few examples made, but nobody's pride was wounded enough that a little time won't eventually heal."

Sapphire smiled knowingly.

Some of the old guards, mostly those who had fought with me against the White Tower's forces, had been eager to learn what I'd been teaching the Black Guild. For the holdouts, it took just a few training sessions to get their noses out of the air. Being humbled by even the lowest of our trainees was enough to see them come around.

Lieutenant Mattick, who I had fought alongside against the White Tower's guards, was one of the first to volunteer for a placement in the new High Guard as soon as I offered enrollment. I had promised him that he would be the first to know if I was ever in the position to open my teaching to more than the Black Guild.

Word of the High Guard and its Upakan captain had spread throughout the kingdom, in no small part due to a certain bard with a magical tongue. Everywhere we went, citizens smiled and waved, some even saluting. It was a good feeling to be able to ride around town with my head held high, no longer worrying about people seeing my eyes.

"I'm just glad to see things finally calming down around here," Reevie said. "Captain Arns was good enough to use some of Avalanche's gold to repair the damage done to the infirmary."

I smiled. "Strange to think of a street tribe working hand in hand with patrollers."

Bull grunted. "Not something I would have ever thought to see in a hundred lifetimes."

"And not just patrollers, but lancers as well," Sapphire said, no doubt referring to the time Hurricane had sheltered Room Eleven after our battle inside the Warrens.

A lot had changed over the years, prior prejudices being among them.

"Does Tolin seem anxious about the new position?" Reevie asked.

I shrugged. "Not sure. He's already taken on most of the duties of commander, unofficially. He certainly has some big shoes to fill."

Once back from the front, Tolin had begun recruiting heavily to regrow the ranks after the losses taken on the Pyruvian. Captain Asa, who now wore a permanent eye patch, which he said gave him quite the in with the ladies, had been promoted to the rank of overcaptain. He had taken on much of Tolin's old duties as Tolin got ready to assume those of the former commander Goring.

"How much longer will the *Wind Binder* be in port?" Reevie asked. He knew I'd been spending as much time with my former shipmates as I could manage while they were still here. The extra gold the queen had provided for conveying me to the front had been enough to allow them some much-needed time off, not to mention the promised reward from the king for their service during the battle. They weren't about to leave without collecting. The crew had taken several meals a week up at the manor house, and even one or two at the palace, where they recounted to the queen and Dakaran their part in what had taken place at Ranool.

"I think they are planning on setting sail this week, though I'm not sure when."

"I know you'll be sad to see them go."

I nodded. "I will. But we plan on keeping in touch. Now that they know where I'll be, sending word whenever they make port shouldn't be difficult."

"How is Fipple's shoulder?" Reevie asked.

"Much better," I said. "He's out of his sling altogether. Pops is walking without his crutch, and Gellar is no longer limping. You ever get to selling those salves and tonics of yours, you'll make a fortune."

Reevie smiled, and we all stared quietly at the fire for a moment, listening to the soft, comforting crackle of the flames as they ate their way through the wood.

Eventually, I bid them all a good night and rode Shade back to the palace. I hadn't meant to stay as long as I had, but I didn't know when I'd get another chance like this for all of us to just sit and talk. Tolin's promotion was tomorrow, which promised to be a very busy and stressful day for me, so I wanted to be sure I got plenty of sleep. The formalities were to take place in the afternoon, but there was much I had to do before then.

Sadly, sleep was not so cooperative. I only managed a few hours before I was up and running. I ran through one last ceremony practice with my men, then spent the rest of the morning holed up in my office, worrying about all the many ways I might bungle everything up. This was to be the High Guard's first formal appearance. I wanted to make sure it went off without a hitch, but my imagination kept inviting new and inventive ways for it to all go wrong.

I checked my appearance in my new chambers' standing mirror and admired the tidy needlework that had gone into the mending of my long black leather coat. I didn't know what they had used as treatment, but the leather was as soft as ever. I straightened my coat and checked my double sheath, making sure the chest plate shone and that I hadn't missed any spots while cleaning the leather. Even through two battles, I'd managed not to lose Noph's old sword. I had traded my lancer sword in for a nicer one I'd found in town. It wasn't as fancy as Noph's, but it was just as well balanced, making it a good match.

I took a deep breath and slowly exhaled. My stomach was starting to knot. I couldn't tell if it was nerves or if Shade was hungry again. I hoped Bozz checked on him soon. I didn't want to go through the ceremony worrying about my stomach growling. I left my rooms and forced myself to stroll down the hall to the grand staircase when what I really wanted to do was dash up to the royal wing. A stream of nobles was making their way through the palace entry below.

I could see the torches out front had been lit, and a long row of carriages waited to be cleared as the king and queen's guests arrived. I made my way up a couple more flights and back toward the royal wing, passing a pair of the High Guard standing watch at the king's study, which had a permanent guard now that our ranks had filled to the point that we could maintain a steady posting on rooms that were most often frequented.

I headed down the hall leading back to Dakaran's chambers, nodding at two more of my men standing watch at his door. I stepped between them and knocked. "It's time, Your Highness," I called. I took a few steps back and waited. Soon enough, the door opened, and Dakaran stepped out, arrayed in his formal robes.

"Well, let's get this over with," he said with a sigh. "At least there should be some very good wine served."

"It's Tolin," I said as we walked together up the hall. "I would have thought you would be at least a little more supportive."

"Oh, I am. I like the commander and all, but these ceremonies can be quite tedious. Trust me, after a few dozen of them, you're going to feel the same way."

Dakaran waited at his corridor's junction while I walked over and knocked on his parents' chamber door. I nodded at the two men standing watch out front. All of the men chosen for room watches this evening were newer recruits. I wanted to make sure that those who had taken part in the recent battle were assigned to the ceremony, especially Room Eleven. I glanced over my shoulder, relieved to see my former roommates waiting to escort Their Majesties. That meant one less thing that could go wrong today, so of course my brain supplied a dozen other unlikely things to take its place.

The king and queen's door opened, and Rhydan was the first out. I stepped to the side and bowed. "Your Majesty." He smiled as he passed. Along with his royal robes, he wore his crown, something he didn't don except on special occasions. He said it gave him a headache. Behind him, the queen glided out in a rich gown of crimson and gold that matched her husband's robes. I bowed once more. "Your Majesty." She, too, smiled and found her place alongside her husband.

"Your escort awaits," I said, pointing back down the hall.

Dakaran moved in behind his parents, and with a nod from the king, I took my place in front, and we started up the hall. Room Eleven, along with a few others who'd been with me since the beginning, quickly separated and moved into a protective but formal formation around the royal family. Instead of taking the stairs down to the grand foyer, we continued straight to the far side of the palace, where we took the back stairs down to a small sitting chamber just off the throne room's front lobby. I could hear people still being ushered past and into the main hall.

A flight of stairs farther down would have taken us to a second sitting area on the other side of the main hall just behind the thrones, but with this being an official ceremony, we were to escort the royal family in from the front entrance and down the central aisle all the way to the dais. The master of ceremonies had said something about it being a more regal entry that showed additional respect to the proceedings.

Several more of my men waited in the antechamber, and the rest had already taken positions inside the throne room itself, along the outer walls and down the aisle. We'd drilled these maneuvers for a week to make sure everyone knew their place. I hadn't realized how taxing it was to hold a single ceremony. My belief that I would find my duties a little more relaxing seemed a bit hasty now.

My back was sweating more now than it had been facing down the trawler fires on the Pyruvian. I didn't know why I was so nervous. All I knew was I couldn't wait for this to be over. I was looking forward to a hot bath this evening. Dakaran had been right—I now took one every chance I got.

Why was I thinking about bathing at a time like this?

Steering clear of my bathing habits, I focused on how full the throne room would be for an occasion such as this. I'd never been to an official ceremony before, but I figured with it being a military promotion, not all that many of the nobles would attend. Much like Dakaran, I assumed most would find this sort of thing dull. Although, if there was a formal banquet afterward, attendance would probably be up, and from what I'd seen of the kitchen's cooking over the last several days, the food was certain to be worth attending for.

I wondered if anyone besides the aristocracy had been invited. Surely they would have allowed for Tolin's family and friends to be there to celebrate with him.

We waited and waited, until I didn't think I was going to be able to wait any longer. I was about to leave my place in line to ask one of the ushers what the holdup was when the door finally opened and the master of ceremonies stepped in, wearing his official feathered hat.

He bowed. "I apologize for the wait, Your Majesties. It is time."

I nodded to my men, and we headed out into the lobby, which stood just in front of the double doors leading into the throne room. We waited as the doors parted and the master of ceremonies walked through and onto the green-and-white marble tiles to make the official announcement. He stopped at the back of the center aisle and struck his staff three times, its echoes filling the vast chamber.

"Their Royal Majesties King Rhydan and Queen Ellise. And His Royal Highness Prince Dakaran."

I heard fabric rustling as the people inside came to their feet, followed by a short trumpet fanfare. I made an effort to keep my hands from shaking as I checked my men one last time. Barthol and Gellar stood behind me on either side of the king and queen, while Fipple, Stumpy, and Waylen took up position behind them, surrounding Dakaran. Three more brought up the rear.

I sucked in a deep breath, and we headed through the doors, walking in an agonizingly slow procession down the center aisle. I was stunned by the size of the crowd.

I kept my head forward, but my eyes scanned those on either side of the aisle. It looked like the entirety of the highborn class was present, which would have filled half the room, but I didn't see an empty seat.

Who were all the other people? The rows were filled with aristocracy and commoners alike, all dressed in their finest, all looking excited to take part. It was strange to see both sharing the same room, let alone the same seats.

We continued on, and I kept my head held high as we neared the front. Suddenly my eyes lighted across some faces I recognized: Captain Treygan and Captain Ismara, both in their best coats, with hats off in respect. Beside them stood the rest of the *Wind Binder*'s crew, filling an entire aisle by themselves. How wonderful for the king to have invited them. It seemed fitting since it was in part their efforts that had allowed this ceremony to even take place.

I smiled at them when I passed, but then my breath caught in my throat when I spotted, just in front of them, Master Fentin and Mistress Orilla. They both waved as I walked by. Why had they been invited? They didn't know Tolin.

I was just recovering from that shock when I saw the occupants of the seats directly in front of them. My chest tightened when my eyes locked on Sapphire and Reevie. I couldn't believe it. I had to look twice.

Bull was there as well, standing beside Camilla, the tall raven-haired messenger he'd had a crush on since before I'd even left for the garrison. Next to them was Gustory and at least two dozen more from Sandstorm, including Tubby, who, though seated, still towered over those around him; Mouse, who waved as hard as he could; Petal and Squeaks; Collen, who had his arm around Muriel; Toots, who looked about as nervous as one could get; and Jaden, the former Rockslide guard who Mouse and I had captured and brought back to Hurricane during our first raid of the Rockslide cells.

The row in front of them was filled with Forehead, Toothless, Stringbean, and Gittrick and his whole family, along with Solvino and most of the kitchen staff. And to my very great surprise, sitting on the end of the aisle just in front of Sapphire and Reevie were Kira and Po. Kira winked at me as soon as our eyes met. My head spun with both delight at seeing my street rat family there and fear they would do something crazy and embarrass me to death in front of the entire aristocracy.

The front four rows were filled with lancers. Overcaptain Asa and Tolin were sitting on the end. I even spotted Sergeant Huckly in the group.

By the time we had made it to the steps leading up to the platform, my heart was racing like it'd just climbed Howling Gorge or jumped in the Shemoa to rescue Hobb.

I was finding it hard to breathe.

Stepping aside to allow the royal family to pass, I watched as they made their way up the stairs for the thrones at the top of the dais. Both the king and queen gave me reassuring smiles, leaving me curious. They knew how nervous I'd been about ensuring the newly formed High Guard made a good first impression.

The royal escort and I separated and moved to our positions on either side of the steps. I scanned the room, checking on the rest of my men. Everyone was where they were supposed to be. Most of the hard work was done. Getting the royal family in and up to their seats was the trickiest part; now all I had to do was stand here for however long and try to keep from looking too nervous. I continued to scan the crowd, my eyes continually wandering back to the right side where it seemed most everyone I knew was standing.

The master of ceremonies waited for the royal family to take their seats before striking his staff three more times to begin the official ceremony. I wondered how long it would take. I had asked Tolin what he thought, and he told me Commander Goring's had lasted at least an hour. I settled in to wait.

The king stood and began the proceedings by giving a moving speech about the order of the Lancers and the important role they played in the protection and structure of Elondria. He spent several long minutes discussing Tolin's stellar career. Some of the details were new to me, as they had taken place long before my arrival in the lancers. Several other members of the court spoke as well, along with a number of Tolin's officers and men, all testifying to his outstanding leadership and years of service.

Those from the court didn't seem to sway Tolin that profoundly, his face remaining as stoic as ever. However, as soon as his fellow lancers began to give their testimonies, I saw Tolin's outer shell begin to crack, the emotions peeking through, if only slightly, as he would smile at the jokes and tighten his jaw during the more emotional spiels. The biggest reaction came from newly promoted Overcaptain Asa. As soon as Asa began his rather long-winded speech highlighting Tolin's bravery and loyalty and friendship, Tolin's eyes began to water.

The parade of speakers didn't seem to have an end, and I got the feeling that perhaps Dakaran had it right when he talked about the tediousness of it all.

As soon as the last person had spoken, Tolin himself was called to the front. The king rose from his seat and walked down to stand in front of the overcaptain.

After saying a few ceremonial words, he stepped over to a table stationed between the first row on the left and the steps up to the thrones. The table was arrayed with various items I hadn't taken time to inspect on the way by. The king took two badges from the end and attached them to Tolin's uniform, followed by a sash, to which he pinned two medallions. Finally, the king presented him with a new sword before turning to those in attendance.

"I wish to present to you, your new commander of the Elondrian Lancers, Commander Tolin."

The entire room stood and erupted in applause and cheers. Tolin couldn't hold back a smile any longer as he stood there basking in the very well-deserved glow of praise.

The king dismissed Tolin to his seat, then returned to his throne and sat, signaling for the crowd to do the same.

"I know there have been many a rumor and story swirling around Aramoor about the recent battle with Cylmar," Rhydan said. "Many of you are here because I promised you a true telling of those events."

I groaned inwardly, imagining how long this was going to take.

"I want to start," Rhydan said, "by saying that I have never seen braver men than those who fought and died to protect their kingdom in the face of overwhelming odds. Their sacrifices will live on in our memories forever. The city will be opening its coffers to see to the families of those who did not return."

The crowd gave its hearty approval to this statement. My mind went straight to Howell and the other men I'd lost during that conflict. My chest tightened all over again, and I fought to keep from tearing up.

"Along with those that gave their lives," Rhydan said, "were those who gave their health. Many came back not as they had gone, a shade of what they once had been, and they deserve all the recognition and help Elondria can give. Likewise, we will provide for these brave men and their families in proportion to what they lost."

The king paused for another round of applause, this one more solemn. I couldn't help but look at Overcaptain Asa and his patch.

"Along with those who gave their lives and those who gave their limbs in the call of their duties, I would also like to recognize those who put themselves at risk when no call had been given."

My heart started to pound. Was he about to recognize the *Wind Binder*?

"I would like to acknowledge some in this room who, with no thought for their own lives, risked everything to come to our aid in the most dire of times. These individuals are seated here with us this afternoon. They had no prior knowledge of my intentions to publicly recognize their bravery, but I would ask that Captain Treygan, Captain Ismara, and the crew of the *Wind Binder* please stand."

My eyes immediately began to burn. I couldn't help it as I watched my river family rise from their seats.

"These outstanding rivermen and women sailed their ship straight into the heart of enemy waters and not only defeated an entire Cylmaran ship by themselves, but saved our fleet from a fiery blockade and pulled us to safety." He looked down and motioned them to the front.

The crew looked at each other nervously, then stepped away from their seats to meet him at the foot of the stairs, where he presented each by name with a pendant from the table that he placed around their necks. He then turned to the crowd.

"These pendants represent the highest honor of service, and wherever seen will be a testament to their bravery. Ladies and gentlemen, noble and common, I give you the crew of the *Wind Binder*."

The room erupted once more in applause, everyone standing.

I bit my tongue, bit my lip, even pinched the life out of my leg to keep from weeping like a baby in front of the entire gathering.

The crew stood in awe as they received the unexpected adulation of a grateful people before finally returning to their seats.

"I would also like to recognize another very special group," Rhydan said, "one of whom recently saved the life of my son."

Murmurs spread through the audience, and I watched Reevie's and Sapphire's faces pale as they and the rest of Sandstorm suddenly realized what was about to happen. Apparently, they'd been just as in the dark as the crew of the *Wind Binder*.

My heart was beating hard enough to hear at this point.

"We have a very gifted healer in the room with us this afternoon, and if it wasn't for his expertise and his companions' hospitality, the kingdom might very well be without its heir." He pointed toward Sandstorm's two rows. "Physicker Reevie, if you'll please stand."

I couldn't hold it back any longer. Tears flowed as I watched my best friend slowly stand from his seat.

"This young man managed to pull my son back from the grip of death and give him back to me. I will forever be in his debt."

I saw Kira whispering to Po, no doubt telling him that if it wasn't for them finding Dakaran in the first place, no one would have been rescuing anyone.

The king motioned for Reevie to join him at the front, and I watched as he nervously limped his way down the aisle. "I believe someone else wishes to present this award," the king said after shaking Reevie's hand.

Dakaran stood from his seat and walked down the steps. Taking a medallion from the table. He turned and placed it over Reevie's head, and then after shaking his hand, turned to the crowd. "I would like to present Physicker Reevie."

The room once again broke out into applause. Reevie's cheeks were wet. Sapphire was crying as well as she watched.

"I would also like to present two additional honors," Dakaran said, "to two individuals who also played an important role in the rescuing of my life. Mistress Kira and Master Po."

Both Kira's and Po's eyes nearly popped out of their skulls as they stood and walked down to stand beside Reevie. Kira grinned playfully at Dakaran, while Po looked ready to lose his lunch. Dakaran placed their medals around their necks, and the people clapped once more. As soon as the applause ended, the three retook their seats, and Dakaran headed back up to his.

This was turning out to be the greatest day of my life. Seeing so many of my friends publicly recognized. I felt nearly faint and prayed I didn't embarrass myself and my men by going all wobbly-kneed right in front of everyone.

The king, who had moved to the side for his son to present the awards, retook his place at the center of the aisle. "There are young men and women here this afternoon who have recently joined Her Majesty the Queen in taking on the challenge of opening a new orphan house here in Aramoor. My family has dined at their home, and I look forward to our ongoing partnership in the aid of those less fortunate. I would like to present to you the heads of Sandstorm Manor: Mistress Sapphire, Physicker Reevie, and Master Bull."

All three stood from their seats, and the room showered them in praise.

The king raised his hands. "Will all those associated with Sandstorm Manor please rise."

Everyone on the two rows stood from their seats, except for Tubby, who'd clearly been instructed to remain seated to keep from scaring too many people. They must have gotten there before the rest of the crowd had begun showing up.

It was incredibly heartwarming to see the looks of glee on the street rats' faces as they were, for the first times in their lives, being looked up to and not down on.

The ovation eventually began to die down, and they sat.

The king, however, did not return to his seat. "I have one final presentation I wish to make this evening, and this one is of special importance to me. This is a person I have come to know and respect, someone who I first met right here in this very room when he was barely chest high. He has since grown into one of the finest young men I've ever had the privilege of knowing."

My knees were now trembling uncontrollably. *Please don't pass out, please don't pass out.*

"His skill with weaponry is unsurpassed, as is his determination to protect those who need defending. He led a special team into the heart of Cylmar and rescued our Ambassador Gorman, along with his lovely wife, Neina." The two waved from their second-row seats on the left. Beside them, I spotted Leara, the library archivist who'd helped me locate books on Rymiran horses, and next to her was Chief Archivist Asarius. Leara smiled at me when she saw me looking. "He has since formed a special unit inside the lancers with the sole purpose of guarding the king during battle, and it was in part because of his efforts and those of his men that we managed to thwart the Cylmarans' cowardly ambush and send them fleeing back to Ecrin."

I couldn't believe he was saying all of this right here in front of the entire nobility. I spared a passing glance up the steps behind me to the other two seats at the top. Both the queen and Dakaran were smiling in my direction.

"This young man," the king continued, "and his unit recently relinquished their lancer positions to form what I have deemed the High Guard. Their duty will be to the full-time protection of the royal family, both here and abroad. I have spent weeks trying to find a special title that I could offer this young man, but sadly, I must admit I came away empty. However, the queen, having scoured through some of the ancient texts from the time of High King Torrin, found reference to a king's champion. I would like to revive that honor here today."

My mouth was as dry as a bone, and I pressed my hands to my legs to keep them from shaking.

"Ayrion." The king turned and motioned for me to join him. I felt the eyes of the room follow me across the marble tiles as I focused on keeping one foot in front of the other. I couldn't believe this was happening.

The king waited until I was standing beside him before continuing. "Ayrion is Upakan." The king paused as hushed whispers filtered through the crowd. I didn't need to guess what sort of sentiments they relayed. My people were despised by pretty much every kingdom alike. Apparently, the king wanted them to know. At the very least, it would make first introductions easier if my eyes weren't a constant surprise. Also, I wondered—or perhaps hoped—that this would somehow raise my people's image in the eyes of Elondrians.

The king took something off the table and held it up. "This ring symbolizes not only your place as the head of the new High Guard, but your new title as well." He took a moment to look me in the eyes. "Do you accept this honor and responsibility here before the Creator and the people of Elondria?"

I hoped my voice didn't crack. "I do."

Rhydan smiled proudly and took my hand and placed the ring on it. The ring was a silver band holding a black stone. On the stone was the falcon crest of the High Guard.

Once the ring was on my finger, the king leaned in and hugged me, right in front of everyone. He then turned and took a step back to address the crowd.

"I present to you Ayrion, Guardian Protector to the Realm."

The great hall filled with applause as I looked down at my two rings: the High Guard on the left, and my father's on the right, each a part of who I was. One, a tie to my past. The other, my future. I wouldn't be who I was today without both.

I looked out across the crowd, scanning the faces of my Aramoor family and friends as they clapped and cheered. This was the start of something new. I didn't know what life had in store for me, or for any of us, but as long as I had these people at my side, I had no doubt we could face it together.

The End of AVALANCHE

Book Six of

The Street Rats of Aramoor

Dear Reader,

I HOPE YOU enjoyed this sixth book in the Street Rats of Aramoor series. If you found the story entertaining and would like to see more, then please consider helping me reach that goal by leaving a quick review on Amazon.

Reviews are very important. They help encourage other readers to try the books.

Thank you in advance!

Want to be notified when the next book comes out? If so, go to this address: *www.michaelwisehart.com/join-the-wielder-council*

>> LOVE FANTASY MUSIC? Stop by Aramoor Market and take a listen. Over 30 minutes of original fantasy score, written for The Aldoran Chronicles by award-winning film composer Will Musser. You can also grab the digital hi-resolution images for each of the maps, as well as the character art.

« *https://www.michaelwisehart.com/aramoormarket* »

<< Keep reading for a FREE offer >>

Find Me Here

For the Latest News

« www.michaelwisehart.com »
« facebook.com/MichaelWisehart.author »

STREET RATS OF ARAMOOR

(20 years prior to the Aldoran Chronicles)
Book 1 | *Banished*
Book 2 | *Hurricane*
Book 3 | *Rockslide*
Book 4 | *Sandstorm*
Book 5 | *Wildfire*
Book 6 | *Avalanche*

THE ALDORAN CHRONICLES

Prequel | *Shackled*
Book 1 | *The White Tower*
Book 2 | *Plague of Shadows*
Book 3 | *The Four-Part Key*
Book 4 | *The Tunnels Beneath*

<< Keep reading for a FREE offer >>

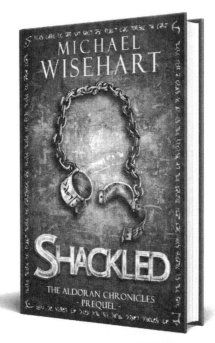

Acknowledgements

I THANK GOD for the doors and windows He's allowed to open in order for me to reach this point.

I want to thank my parents *Mickey and Julie Wisehart* for their unending loyalty, encouragement, and support over the years. None of this would be possible without you—love you both.

I want to thank my Author Team, whose endless talent, time, and dedication have made this project possible:

AUTHOR TEAM

I want to thank my cover illustrator, who took a written description, along with some reference photos, and brought the Battle of Ranool to life in a very breathtaking way—*Dongjun Lu "Russell"*

I want to thank my interior illustrator for her creativity in designing our first look at The Temple—*Elwira Pawlikowska*

I want to thank my content editor, whose red pen never seems to run out of ink—*Nathan Hall*

I want to thank my line editor, who always finds the most appropriate word choice—*Danae Smith*

I want to thank my copy editor, who keeps my scripts clean and my readers happy—*Crystal Watanabe*

ICHAEL WISEHART graduated with a bachelor's degree in business before going back to school for film and starting his own production company. As much as he enjoyed film work, the call of writing a novel got the better of him, and on April 14, 2014, he started typing the first words of what would become two epic fantasy series: The Aldoran Chronicles and the Street Rats of Aramoor.

He currently lives and writes in North Georgia.

Glossary of Terms

Street Tribes of Aramoor

Avalanche [*a-vuh-lanch*] Tribe color is white. Chief is Cutter.

Hurricane [*her-ĭ-cane*] Tribe color is blue. Chief is Spats.

Rockslide [*rock*-slide] Tribe color is green. Chief is Kore.

Sandstorm [*sand-storm*] Tribe color is purple. Chief is Noph.

Wildfire [*wild-fire*] Tribe color is red. Chief is Red/Kira.

Months of the Year

Aèl [*ay*-el] First month of the year.

Sòl [*soul*] Second month of the year.

Nùwen [*noo-win*] Third month of the year.

Manù [*mah-noo*] Fourth month of the year.

Toff [*toff*] Fifth month of the year.

Kwàn [*quon*] Sixth month of the year.

Nor [*nor*] Seventh month of the year.

Èldwin [*el-dwin*] Eighth month of the year.

Kùma [*koo-muh*] Ninth month of the year.

Akòsi [*uh-kah-see*] Tenth month of the year.

Èshan [*ee-shon*] Eleventh month of the year.

Zùl [*zool*] Twelfth month of the year.

New Character Glossary

(Introductory characters not mentioned in prior books)

Asarius (Uh-sar-ee-us) Chief archivist of the royal library. Older man with a grey beard and spectacles.

Arns (Arnz) A captain in the Aramoor Patrollers, whose office is located in the northeast quadrant. He is a stout man with a clean-shaven face and an eye that doesn't seem to stay in one place, having a tendency to drift from side to side.

Birg (Berg) One of the new crewmen on board the *Wind Binder*. Stands watch overnight while the rest head to Sandstorm.

Bulsby (Bullz-bee) A one-year veteran of the Black Guild. An inch or two taller than average with a barrel chest. Similar in height and weight to Howell and has a round face with thick brows that shelve a set of bright green eyes.

Draeus (Dray-uss) One of the patrollers in the northeast patrol station under Captain Arns.

Ellie (Ell-ee) One of the Sandstorm Guard who goes with Ayrion down into the secret tunnel. She arrived at Sandstorm along with Bull and the rest of the rejects after the battle at the Pit. She is a tough little scrapper and quickly works her way up through the beaters to be one of the few girls to join the Guard.

Elriss (El-riss) Senior physicker at the palace.

Elwin (El-win) One of the Black Guild to be transferred to another garrison.

Faulgner (Falg-ner) One of the royal library attendants. An archivist. His primary study is that of Aldoran animalogy.

Gilford (Gil-ford) One of the Black Guild to be transferred to another garrison.

Gittrick (Git-trik) New coachman for Sandstorm.

Howell (*How-ul*) New recruit in the Black Guild. He is an inch or two taller than Ayrion, and quite thick in the chest and arms. He looks to be in his thirties with brown hair that hangs to his shoulders, though tied back with a single cord. He also wears a dark scowl with teeth gritted hard enough to crack nuts.

Ipsworth (*Ips-worth*) Commandant of the Aramoor patrollers. Taller man with a thick mustache, a strong chin, and grey-streaked hair slicked back at the sides. He is the head of the central patroller office located on the Island.

Jostlin (*Jahs-lin*) One of the Sandstorm watchers injured by Avalanche beaters.

Kiff (*Kiff*) One of the Sandstorm beaters who goes into the secret tunnel with Ayrion. Twin brother to Linny. Abandoned at birth and forced into the workhouses until they were old enough to escape.

Leara (*Lee-air-uh*) One of the royal library attendants. An archivist. Focuses her study on the Elondrian histories. Not much older than Ayrion, with thick chestnut hair.

Linny (*Lin-ee*) One of the Sandstorm beaters who goes into the secret tunnel with Ayrion. Twin brother to Kiff. Abandoned at birth and forced into the workhouses until they were old enough to escape.

Lowell (*Low-ul*) Desk sergeant for the northeast quarter patroller office. Older lanky man with a grey beard.

Mattick (*Mă-tic*) Lieutenant in the palace guards who fights alongside Ayrion against the White Tower forces. Joins the High Guard as soon as Ayrion opens enrollment.

Melon (*Mell-un*) One of the Sandstorm watchers injured by Avalanche beaters.

Milshik (*Mill-shick*) One of the patrollers in the northeast patrol station under Captain Arns.

Misha (*Mee-shuh*) One of the cleaners at Sandstorm.

Nemeth (*Neh-meth*) Young lancer in barracks number three. Holds Tolin's horse.

Norell (*Nor-ell*) Former coachman to Sandstorm. Kept up the carriage house and carriages.

Ornan (*Or-nun*) One of the new crewmen on board the *Wind Binder*. Stands watch overnight while the rest head to Sandstorm.

Reina (Ree-in-uh) Spokesperson for Avalanche prisoners. Caught during city raid and taken to Sandstorm. She is tall and slender with olive skin and dark hair that hangs halfway down her back.

Rhoslyn (*Rawz-linn*) High King Torrin's wife. First queen of the Five Kingdoms.

Shelmik (*Shell-mick*) A two-year veteran of the Black Guild. Average height, a little skinnier than most, but quite agile with his blade. He has a long face with a hooked nose and dark brown eyes.

Solvino (*Sol-vee-no*) Head cook at Sandstorm. Midforties. Short, thin man with dark hair and a thick mustache that he likes to curl upward. Been around since Noph was chief.

Tilson (*Till-son*) New recruit in the Black Guild. About average height, perhaps late twenties with dark brown hair. He has a strong chin and eyes that look ready to learn.

Triss (*Triss*) One of the Sandstorm watchers injured by Avalanche beaters.

Tudwell (*Tudd-well*) Stable hand at the main garrison in Aramoor.

Weller (*Well-er*) Injured overcaptain in charge of garrison after everyone leaves for war.

Wilben (*Will-ben*) Patroller sergeant from one of the northeast quadrant stations. Chosen to help lead the raid against Avalanche.

Stop by and visit:
www.michaelwisehart.com